INTO THE
WONDER
DARK

INTO THE
WONDER
DARK

LILIAN T. JAMES

Crystal Pages Publishing
is an imprint of Aleron Books LLC

First printing edition 2023

Cover Design : The Book Brander
Title Illustration : Etheric Tales & Edits
Chapter Header/Part Spread Designs : Eternal Geekery
Map Design : Chaim Holtjer

Regular Edition Paperback ISBN-13 : 978-1-958763-14-8
Limited Edition Paperback ISBN-13 : 978-1-958763-15-5
eBook ISBN-13 : 978-1-958763-11-7

To those of you who are as patient as the trees, waiting for your enemies to fall so you can strengthen your roots with their corpses.

ositive, upbeat set of ideas for our future. This book will inform all of
committed to a great future for our children."

—**R. Edward Freeman,** author of *The Power of And:
Responsible Business without Trade-Offs*

sser offers the reader a wide-ranging blueprint for a better future rooted
ation, which is different from sustainability as practiced in today's
boardrooms. Combining prospective storytelling with hard data on
cial and global challenges, as well as practical guidance on how to take
is prophetic masterpiece brings a thriving future into the present."

—**Chris Laszlo,** PhD, author of
Quantum Leadership and *Flourishing Enterprise*

is the new sustainability. To better understand why, go no further, and
book."

—**Jonas Haertle,** Chief of the Office of the Executive Director,
UN Institute for Training and Research

ead for everyone ignited by regeneration! Wayne's clear style, underpinned
pening data on global challenges, addresses a wide audience, fostering
ent and integrated thinking in all who want to take action and thrive."

—**Jacques Vandermeiren,** CEO of the Port of Antwerp

Visser's book is just about as timely as any book published today could
be. It is a must-read—NOW!"

—**Ervin Laszlo,** author of *The Upshift: Meeting the Challenge*

g is a wonderful orientation to the thinking and practices required for our
to address the many shortcomings and great possibilities before us today. "

—**Jed Emerson,** author of *The Purpose of Capital:
Elements of Impact, Financial Flows, and Natural Being*

"When you look at planet Earth from a living-systems perspective, you realize that sustainability is not a goal in itself; it is the by-product of the biological process of regeneration. . . . In his newest book, *Thriving*, Wayne Visser makes a solid case for regeneration. He offers not only points for action but many beautiful, heart-stirring poems drenched in wisdom that will stay with you."

—Leen Gorissen, innovation biologist and author of *Building the Future of Innovation on Millions of Years of Natural Intelligence*

"Positivity is the main takeaway of *Thriving*. Visser demonstrates how people, the planet, and business can prosper sustainably in the future. This commitment to regenerative solutions is also why Randstad is a proud supporter of the world's first academic chair in sustainable transformation at Antwerp Management School, resulting in the development of the Future Resilience Index and the Good Work Goals. Along with Visser, we strongly believe that putting people first is essential for the health of our economy, society, and nature. That is the only way to cocreate a world for us all to thrive in."

—Jacques van den Broek, CEO of Randstad Group

"Consistent with our J&J credo, Professor Wayne Visser shows that caring deeply about people and the environment, and using science and innovation to create scalable solutions, is the best way to ensure a future in which nature, society, and the economy can all thrive together. The book's inspiring examples, underlying science, and pragmatic advice make it an essential guide for leaders who want to make a positive impact and leave the world better than they found it."

—Kris Sterkens, Company Group Chairman of Janssen Pharmaceutical Companies, Johnson & Johnson, EMEA

THRIVING

The

BREAKTHROUGH MOVEMENT *to* REGENERATE NATURE, SOCIETY, *and the* ECONOMY

WAYNE VISSER

FAST
COMPANY
Press

Fast Company Press
New York, New York
www.fastcompanypress.com

This work is being published under the Fast Company Press imprint by an exclusive arrangement with Fast Company. Fast Company and the Fast Company logo are registered trademarks of Mansueto Ventures, LLC. The Fast Company Press logo is a wholly owned trademark of Mansueto Ventures, LLC.

Distributed by Greenleaf Book Group

For ordering information or special discounts for bulk purchases, please contact Greenleaf Book Group at PO Box 91869, Austin, TX 78709, 512.891.6100.

Design and composition by Greenleaf Book Group
Cover design by Greenleaf Book Group
Cover images: komkrit Preechachanwate; Ekkamon Thiansimuang; Chansom Pantip, used under license from Shutterstock.com
Interior images designed using resources from Flaticon.com and TheNounProject.com

Publisher's Cataloging-in-Publication data is available.

Print ISBN: 978-1-63908-007-6

eBook ISBN: 978-1-63908-008-3

Part of the Tree Neutral® program, which offsets the number of trees consumed in the production and printing of this book by taking proactive steps, such as planting trees in direct proportion to the number of trees used: www.treeneutral.com

TreeNeutral®

Printed in the United States of America on acid-free paper

22 23 24 25 26 27 28 29   10 9 8 7 6 5 4 3 2 1

First Edition

For all who inspire hope through action,
who refuse to give up on people and the planet,
and who are helping regenerate nature, society, and the economy

To Indira,
who embodies the spirit of thriving

To Andi, Dorian, and Veneta,
who will inherit the world we regenerate

To Mom, Dad, Juanita, and Jordan,
who remind me that there are many ways to thrive

THRIVING

Our life is so much more than a duty or a chore
Of merely getting by without a why or what for
The law of tooth and claw, the struggle to exist
To rally and resist against life's slow decay
The way of entropy, of living just to see
Another day, to stay, to endure and survive
No, life is meant to thrive

In nature all things grow, from seed to tree, we know
The cycle of living through giving, of reap and sow
The flow, things come and go, the cycles of grooming
From sprouting to blooming, of stretching for the light
The bright palette of hope, the diverse ways to cope
To cherish and flourish, bursting forth and alive
For nature means to thrive

Society lives too, a melting pot we brew
From cultures and crises, with spices for flavor
And kindness to savor, ideas for conceiving
And goals for achieving that stretch us and bind us
That find us, together in all kinds of weather
Wanting what's fair, to care, longing to love and strive
For society to thrive

The markets live and breathe in complex webs we weave
The synapses of trade have made the things we need
Each deed a chance to lead, while tech is getting smart
Yet still, it needs a heart, a compass as a guide
To tide us through the storm and find a better norm
A breakthrough to renew, an innovation drive
Yes, markets too can thrive

All life is meant to rise, to reach up to the skies
To move beyond the edge, to fledge with hopeful cries
Life tries until it flies, it shakes and spreads its wings
And trills each note it sings, while given time and space
The race of life is run, full powered by the sun
On land, in seas, like bees' sweet nectar from the hive
All life is made to thrive.

Contents

Foreword

Having once nearly drowned off the coast of South Africa, Wayne Visser knows what it is like to be frightened for one's own life—and he also knows what it is like to be terrified that our very civilization is heading for the abyss. But there is an immense gulf between those who respond by marching up and down the high street with placards and those who work into the system to effect real, and increasingly radical, change.

An effective educator, Wayne is also a poet—and it shows. The words, the language, in this book are chosen and honed to build a sense that even this existential crisis of ours can be successfully overcome. This stubborn optimism, as Christiana Figueres describes it,[1] is critical if we are to make the transition to societies and economies that help create and sustain the conditions for more life, of all species.

A central theme in *Thriving* is that "all organisms, including humans, live and breathe and continue to exist because they regenerate. The same is true for other living systems, such as ecosystems, societies, and economies. Without regeneration, there would be no spring flowers; no seasonal return of birds, bees, and butterflies; no babies being born; no infants turning into children, teenagers, and adults; no start-up enterprises; no corporations; no technology innovations; no political parties or governments; no development of countries; no rise of civilizations; no forests and oceans alive with species; no living earth."

At the same time, Wayne stresses, we also see many forms of *degeneration*—processes of decline, decay, and death. Worse, he notes, scientists "say that there is an inherent tendency in the universe toward disorder or chaos, called *entropy*. The world tends toward disorganization, they say, and we see the signs all around us. We are born, but we also die. Beyond the human life cycle, whole species emerge and go extinct. Companies are formed and file for bankruptcy. Stock markets have bull runs and crashes. Economies boom and go bust. Civilizations rise and they fall. Ecosystems thrive but can also collapse."

Still, as he assures us, "life constantly triumphs over death; it tends toward *synergy*, where parts join to form a greater whole. Living systems create structure in the midst of randomness; they allow order to emerge from chaos. This is thriving, and it is a life-affirming process that does not happen by chance. It takes energy and resources and time. It requires the forging of complex relationships."

Around the world, people are now finally waking up to the fact that regeneration has to be central to everything we do. No longer is it enough to try to slow down the processes of degeneration. Thriving applies "equally to nature, society, and the economy, encompassing our health, organizations, infrastructure, technologies, resources, and ecosystems. To use a medical metaphor, . . . thriving is not a drug cure for a particular disease but rather the necessary shift to a healthy lifestyle."

Ask Wayne what he intends his book to be, what he wants us to take away from it, and this is how he puts it: *Thriving* is *not*:

- A denial of the scale and severity of the problems now facing the world

- An exercise in blind optimism in technology or other miracle-cure solutions

- A self-help book or a collection of "happily ever after" prescription

Instead, he explains, *Thriving is*:

- An attempt to make systems thinking more accessible and applicable

- An offer of pragmatic hope linked to purpose-driven creativity and innovation
- A "possibilist" book rooted in the power of transformational movements

That last point is the essence of his story. He is, above all else, a "possibilist." And this is a state of mind, a state of being, that I recognize from all the great changemakers I have been privileged to meet and, in many cases, work with over the decades.

My own conclusion is that we are at one of those great civilizational inflection points that comes perhaps once in a lifetime. But this time, instead of world wars waged against other societies, we have been waging an unwitting war against our own planet—and, tragically, we have been winning.

The "black swan" trajectories that now have the power to send our economies spiraling off into the abyss press in with increasing urgency, among them the climate and biodiversity emergencies that are increasingly obvious to ordinary citizens in the form of once-in-a-lifetime floods, droughts, and conflagrations.

Happily, we also see growing numbers of "green swan" trends, driving us toward breakthrough forms of progress. It is time for us all to step up—or get out of the way. Wayne Visser has stepped up in *Thriving*—and invites us all to do likewise.

John Elkington
Cofounder of SustainAbility and Volans
Author of *The Green Consumer Guide* and
Green Swans: The Coming Boom in Regenerative Capitalism

PROLOGUE

Hope

In the face of an absolutely unprecedented emergency, society has no choice but to take dramatic action to avert a collapse of civilization. Either we will change our ways and build an entirely new kind of global society, or they will be changed for us.

—Gro Harlem Brundtland and colleagues, "Environment and Development Challenges: The Imperative to Act"

Be Aware but Not Afraid

I will never forget the day I nearly drowned. My wife and I were enjoying a beach vacation at Sodwana Bay along the South African coast of KwaZulu-Natal. My parents were there too, and it happened to be their wedding anniversary. When we arrived at the beach, we paid scant attention to a sign warning of dangers. Beware of hippos, sharks, crocodiles, and the strong current, it said. I was born and grew up in Africa, and signs like this are not unusual or cause for any great panic. They simply mean keep your eyes peeled and your wits about you; be aware but not afraid.

Of the four risks, the least obvious one turned out to be the deadliest. When my wife and I went for a swim in the ocean, the waves were big and the tide was strong, but this only made it more fun. Neither of us is a stranger to swimming in the ocean, and we had no fear. However, at a certain moment, we noticed that we were no longer able to touch the seabed. A riptide, which is a strong undertow current, was dragging us farther and farther out to sea. When we tried to swim back to the shore, it was futile; the current was too strong.

In the end, by swimming diagonally across the current, we made it back to the beach. But there were a few frightening minutes, as we became fatigued, when we didn't think we would make it. We nearly drowned. When you come face-to-face with death like that, it gets you thinking deeply about life. Life is fragile and precious, and we have so little time on this earth. My relief was quickly followed by gratitude for being alive—for being given a second chance—and then reinforced by a strong resolve to make a positive difference in the world with whatever time I had left.

I see this personal story as a powerful metaphor for the state of the world. The fact is that we face many serious risks as a global society—climate change, pandemics, growing inequality, species extinction, extremism, cyberattacks, toxic pollution, and many others. And like the sign on the beach, they are all dangers that we have been warned about but have chosen to ignore or downplay.

I understand why we do this. Responding to the global challenges we face interferes with our plans. They are, as Al Gore put it, inconvenient truths.[1] The outcomes may be too scary to contemplate, and the solutions may be too expensive. No wonder ignorance is bliss. There are none so blind as those who do not want to see. But closing our eyes does not make the problems magically disappear. On the other hand, if we can face up to the dangers and turn them into opportunities, our lives can be even better than before. If we can weather the storm, we will be more alive than ever.

I learned some interesting lessons that day—and maybe we can apply them to our global challenges as well. I realized that it was not the riptide that would have killed us. Rather, it was the fact that we panicked and nearly lost hope. We almost gave up the fight. This book is about *not* giving up. Its main theme is *thriving*, which is not unlike what I experienced in the wake of my encounter with death. I felt alive, invigorated, rejuvenated, and filled with renewed purpose.

In the same way, right now, we are navigating extraordinary global crises that could result in either the collapse or the thriving of nature, society, and the economy. It is a time of great transformation in the world, when rapid changes are bringing innovative solutions to counter the great dangers we face. In the pages that follow, I share stories of the hundreds of ways in which we are choosing life over death and possibility over despair. My message is simple: Don't panic! There is hope. We will survive. We will even thrive. I know this because it is already happening all around us.

Thriving as a Force for Life

Thriving is possible for life on earth because of regeneration. All organisms, including humans, live and breathe and continue to exist because they regenerate. The same is true for other living systems, such as ecosystems, societies, and economies. Without regeneration, there would be no spring flowers; no seasonal return of birds, bees, and butterflies; no babies being born; no infants turning into children, teenagers, and adults; no start-up enterprises; no corporations; no technology innovations; no political parties or governments; no development of countries; no rise of civilizations; no forests and oceans alive with species; no living earth.

Thriving is a natural process. But it is not the only process of life. We also see degeneration—processes of decline, decay, and death. Scientists go further to say that there is an inherent tendency in the universe toward disorder or chaos, called *entropy*. The world tends toward disorganization, they say, and we see the signs all around us. We are born, but we also die. Beyond the human life cycle, whole species emerge and go extinct. Companies are formed and file for bankruptcy. Stock markets have bull runs and crashes. Economies boom and go bust. Civilizations rise and they fall. Ecosystems thrive but can also collapse.

Yet it is this very somber reality of degeneration that makes life all the more incredible, since living organisms—and living systems more generally—regularly and continuously defy those processes of destruction and death. Life constantly triumphs over death; it tends toward *synergy*, where parts join to form a greater whole. Living systems create structure in the midst of randomness; they allow order to emerge from chaos. This is thriving, and it is a life-affirming process that does not happen by chance. It takes energy and resources and time. It requires the forging of complex relationships.

To be sure, life does not always thrive. But as humans we can consciously choose to create or destroy, to build up or break down. We do not always choose wisely. We sometimes choose short-term gain over long-term survival. We choose selfish actions over sharing with others. We choose personal comfort and convenience over fairness in society or balance in nature. But we also often make positive choices—choices of solidarity and conservation, choices that will benefit our children and their children, choices that respect the dignity of others and the right of all life to exist. These are choices in support of thriving.

Our choices matter now more than ever. The decisions we make and the actions we take in the next 10 years will determine whether nature, society, and the economy break down or break through. I am confident we will choose to thrive—as many have done before us. Regeneration as a path to thriving can be traced throughout history, as seen through the eyes and actions of philosophers and scientists, governments and religions, merchants and artists. What is new, however, is our deeper understanding of the science of thriving and how it can be practically applied in areas such as agriculture and architecture or business and leadership.

Each discipline has been quick to claim a version of the concept for itself—especially the regenerative agriculture movement—and in the pages that follow, I celebrate many of these practices. But I also hope to show that, to thrive, we must apply regenerative thinking equally to nature, society, and the economy, encompassing our health, organizations, infrastructure, technologies, resources, and ecosystems. To use a medical metaphor, the movement toward thriving is not a drug cure for a particular disease but rather the necessary shift to a healthy lifestyle. The metaphor is especially apt, because our world *is* sick; in some instances, it is even dying. In the fateful tango between life and death, degeneration has claimed the upper hand in many areas. But we still have the chance to tip the odds back in our favor, toward life and thriving.

What Happened to Our Common Future?

As a global society, we began paying attention to thriving a little more than 30 years ago—and I have been fortunate enough to have been along for the ride. In August 1990 I embarked on one of the most exciting journeys of my life, flying from Cape Town, South Africa, where I was still an undergraduate taking a degree in business science, to Tokyo, Japan. There, I was joining 200 other young people from 50 countries at a global conference on sustainable development, organized by the Association of International Students in Economics and Commerce (AIESEC).

At that time we represented the next generation, and by all accounts our future was not looking so bright. In 1987 the United Nations had issued its investigative report called "Our Common Future," in which the term *sustainable development* was coined and defined for the first time, as "development that meets the needs of the present without compromising the ability of future generations to meet their own needs."[2] The report painted a disturbing picture of the world, with looming crises in population, food security, species loss, ecosystem collapse, energy, climate change, and urbanization.

We had all gathered in Tokyo, bursting with enthusiasm and bright-eyed naïveté, to discuss those problems and to give our input—as the voice of the next generation—to the upcoming World Conference on Environment and Development in Rio de Janeiro in 1992, more commonly known as the Rio Earth Summit. Strange to say, but as we grappled with those weighty issues, we all felt a sense of overwhelming optimism.

These were solvable problems, we believed, and the world's political leaders were finally taking notice.

Fast-forward to the present, and I find myself taking stock. How far have we come? Did anyone pay attention to our young voices of concern and hope? The answer, it seems, is a paradox. Many of the problems are much worse today, while many of the solutions are further advanced. Social and environmental issues were peripheral in 1990, especially for business, which tended to respond with social responsibility and charity initiatives. Today sustainability is high on policy-making and boardroom agendas, often even baked into their manifestos and strategies.

Of course, saying sustainable development is important is one thing, but changing how we do things is an entirely different challenge. So have we made any actual progress? On some issues, absolutely. Spectacular progress, in fact. Literally hundreds of millions of people have been lifted out of poverty and given access to food, education, health care, and economic opportunities. We know, because that's what the world set out to do in 2000—under the aegis of the UN Millennium Development Goals—and we tracked those remarkable achievements until 2015. We have real cause for celebration.

At the same time, on other issues, we have made far less progress. In truth, that's just me putting it politely. When we look at the trends for challenges such as income inequality, biodiversity loss, climate change, chemical pollution, and gender inequality, the world has been going backward, not forward. It's as if we are speeding toward a cliff at 100 miles an hour, and instead of hitting the brakes and making a U-turn, we are stepping on the accelerator with no apparent intention of deviating from our suicidal course.

The Choice to Hope

Why would we behave in such an irrational way? Over the years, I've come to realize that investing in thriving is a lot like going to the dentist. Most of us really don't want to do it, even though we know it's good for our health. We rationalize that it may not be necessary. And, besides, it's inconvenient, expensive, and probably painful too. So we ignore our better judgment and delay taking action. And, of course, the longer we wait, the worse the problems become and the more painful and expensive the treatment will be when we finally take remedial action.

The good news is that the various forms of decay we see in nature, society, and our economies are serving as triggers for six societal shifts or great transformations, which we explore in this book. That is part of the reason why, despite the challenges, I am hopeful about our common future. But you should not confuse my hope with blind optimism. Let's be honest: If thriving were easy, I would not be writing about it. Rather, hope is an action verb—a way of seeing and being and having an impact in the world. Hope is a choice. I choose to be hopeful because hope is grounded in the possibility for change. Hope knows that people are resilient and resourceful. It taps into work on solutions. Hope understands tipping points. It is fueled by progressive social movements. Hope lights a candle in the darkness. It is infectious. Hope inspires. If you want to understand hope as an active force for change, I highly recommend Rebecca Solnit's book *Hope in the Dark*.[3]

Being hopeful, in turn, allows me to be positive, which is another choice. Austrian psychiatrist Viktor Frankl observed that even in the Nazi concentration camps (of which he survived four), people could choose their attitude.[4] And having a positive attitude often means being *for* rather than *against*, being *pro* rather than *anti*. This is also the spirit embraced by Hans Rosling, author of the fabulous book *Factfulness*, who encourages us to all be possibilitists.[5] A better world is always possible, for three compelling reasons: (1) We have seen improvements in the past; (2) we have a hand in creating the future; and (3) being positive is a more effective and satisfying way to be in the world.

Having said that, if our hope and optimism is to be grounded in reality, we also need to be more radical. Maybe you already are and don't know it yet. *Radical*, from the Latin *radicalis*, simply means "forming the root." It is common knowledge that we need to get to the root of problems if we want to solve them. In the same way, if we want to change an organization or our society, we have to change its underlying roots—its values and culture, its rules and beliefs, its embedded power and incentive structures. To be radical, therefore, is to work at the level of systems change.

This book tells the stories of many who are working tirelessly to create a radically better tomorrow. The hundreds of examples I share are all testimony to the fact that each of us can be a constructive force for thriving—and, more importantly, that there are many who are rising to the challenge and taking bold action. At a time when we are asked on a daily basis to stand up for our values, this is a book about why we have every reason to be positive about the future. But to succeed, it will take everything that we are as humans—our capable hands and our compassionate hearts, our brilliant minds and our creative imaginations. Therefore, I invite you to join me on this journey. And I trust that by the end, you, too, will hope and believe that a better world—*a world regenerated*—is not only possible but already being born, that you will, as expressed in my poem to conclude this prologue, be an optimist.

BE AN OPTIMIST

Be an optimist
Not because the future is bright
But because bright people are working
To make the future better
Be an optimist
Not because the news is good
But because good people are showing
That change is always possible
Be an optimist
Not because the world is fair
But because fair people are fighting
For justice wherever it is needed

When ordinary people do extraordinary things
Let your heart beat a little faster
Knowing that you too are ordinary
When inspiring leaders rise to our biggest challenges
Let your sights be set a little higher
Knowing that you too can inspire
When young voices join in the call to action
Let your efforts go a little further
Knowing that you too can always do more

Be an optimist
Not because the night is over
But because we carry the light of values
And remember the promise of dawn
Be an optimist
Not because victory is certain
But because we have the opportunity
To still make a positive difference
Be an optimist
Not because the earth is a haven
But because we have a growing desire
To be guardians for all life

When the clouds of gloom are gathering
Let your knowledge of the sun and skies above
Be a vision that brings perspective
When the drums of war are beating
Let your refusal to cast others as villains
Be a declaration of our common humanity
When the tides of bigotry are rising
Let your belief that we all have equal worth
Be a boat that will never capsize

Be an optimist
Not because you ignore the facts
But because the wider landscape of facts
Tell a story of remarkable progress
Be an optimist
Not because the glass is half full
But because we always have the chance
To tap a greater source of power
Be an optimist
Not because you are blind and deaf and dumb
But because you see and hear and speak
More clearly what is possible.

SECTION I

THE GREAT RESET

To achieve a better outcome, the world must act jointly and swiftly to revamp all aspects of our societies and economies, from education to social contracts and working conditions. Every country, from the United States to China, must participate, and every industry, from oil and gas to tech, must be transformed. In short, we need a 'Great Reset' of capitalism.

—**Klaus Schwab**, "It's Time for a 'Great Reset' of Capitalism"

Klaus Schwab captured a unique moment in history in the midst of the COVID-19 pandemic when he called for a *Great Reset*. A crisis is the perfect moment to bring about fundamental change, and the bigger the crisis, the bigger the opportunity. The coming decade will be a time of rebuilding, similar to the periods after the 20th-century world wars. This is our chance to *build back better*, to use another political slogan—to reshape the world and its economy to be fairer and more inclusive, while reversing the catastrophic breakdown of the climate and natural systems on which we depend.

These are noble intentions, but for them to be anything more than political rhetoric, we will need a clear lodestar to guide us on our journey. And we will need a way to test our progress and hold our leaders accountable. In Chapter 1, I present thriving as that guiding light and show how the science of living systems gives us a set of criteria against which to measure success. Then, in Chapter 2, I look at what's not working today, where our global systems are breaking down, and how these can serve as triggers for societal transformation.

CHAPTER 1

Thriving

When we try to pick out anything by itself, we find it hitched to everything else in the universe. One fancies a heart like our own must be beating in every crystal and cell.

—**John Muir,** *My First Summer in the Sierra*

A Dream Come True

As I looked out of the window of the small nine-seater, twin-propeller plane, what I saw filled me with an indescribable sense of joy. Stretching from horizon to horizon, for as far as my eyes could see, were vast swaths of uninterrupted tropical rain forest. This was a dream come true. I was flying over the Amazon region of Ecuador from the town of Macas to Tzapapentza, a community of 300 indigenous Achuar people, living in a remote part of the jungle near the border with Peru. We were visiting the area in 2014 as part of a sustainable development program organized by my friend and colleague, Roberto Salazar. Our day trip to Tzapapentza was

on of the Achuar president, Jaime Vargas, who was
ted as president of the Confederation of Indigenous
dor.

wn on a rudimentary landing strip, we found the com-
embled under a large open-air pergola. Without delay,
President   nd the leader of the community took their seats on chairs
opposite each other in the middle of the assembled group. Both looked
impressive in their regalia of face paint and brightly colored feathered head-
dresses. The community leader also had a symbolic rifle lying across his
lap, a symbol of his role as protector. They entered into a melodic call-and-
response greeting, passing on news and asking and granting permission to
enter the community, all while drinking *chicha*, a sour fermented brew,
from patterned bowls made from clay. In a gesture of hospitality, bowls of
chicha were also passed around to each of us guests.

This is a community that understands thriving. They are living in harmony with nature and its cycles, surrounded by the forest and living almost
entirely from what it produces for their shelter, food, and well-being. At
the time, they were also engaged in a protracted battle to protect the forest
from mining interests. For them, digging for metals or drilling for oil is
sacrilegious, because the forest is a living being, a physical manifestation of
the spirit Arutam.

I do not want to romanticize the situation. As idyllic as this sounds, the
Achuar are not stuck in time or disconnected from the wider world. Our
visit was not a performance for tourists or a public relations exercise. The
president was there to listen to the needs of his people.

Their most immediate request was to have a road built, which would
allow them to get forest produce, such as the delicious star apple fruit, to
the national and international market. It still takes as many as 12 days
by foot and boat to reach the nearest road. The Achuar live in traditional
housing made from timber and have some basic facilities already, including
electricity from solar panels and a small information center, which connects
them to the internet. They wear Western clothes and have a school and

dusty sports field, where they play football and Ecuavoley, a national variant of volleyball. But they want to continue developing.

I tell this story of the Achuar people of Tzapapentza because it is a microcosm of the struggle for thriving. The Achuar are fighting to preserve the regenerative capacity of nature, knowing that they depend on the environment for their physical and spiritual well-being. They remain unimpressed by the rags-to-riches promises of extractive companies, but at the same time, the community is income poor and lacks access to basic health services. There are no clinics or medical professionals in their village, and any emergency cases have to call on the flying doctor. We can learn a great deal from the Achuar about natural thriving and social thriving practices, such as inclusion and equality. But they still need economic regeneration and are missing some elements of social regeneration, such as community health. The challenge is to pursue these without sacrificing nature and eroding the solidarity that is at the heart of their beautiful culture.

Seeing the Forest for the Trees

Choosing life and living over death and decay is the essence of thriving. Thriving is about working with, rather than against, the complex living systems of which we are a part. Thriving means taking the time and making the effort to understand the many interconnections between the parts, and always asking who—or what part of the system—is benefiting or suffering as a result of our actions. Thriving is allowing nature, society, and the economy to all flourish together, rather than trading one off against the other. And ultimately, thriving is about making sure that life on earth, in all its glorious diversity, not only survives but also fulfills its vast potential.

In some ways, thriving is the new sustainability. Sustainable development will not disappear, not least because the Sustainable Development Goals run until 2030. But sustainability as an idea—just surviving and enduring—has always been rather uninspiring. Besides, it is frequently misused by business and government. (*Sustainable economic growth* is a favorite mantra.) In contrast, thriving is a much more exciting idea. And it's not new. Thought leaders such as Paul Hawken, Michael Braungart, Bill McDonough, and John Elkington, among others, have been vocal advocates of thriving for years. Hawken also has a new book called *Regeneration* that I highly recommend.[1] The difference now is that we're starting to see science-based applications emerging, such as regenerative agriculture and restorative design.

To understand thriving, we need only look to nature. Take forests, for example. Without trees, there are no forests. Yet forests are so much more than trees. Forests are complex living systems, but they also serve as a good metaphor for systems thinking. When we say we "can't see the forest for the trees," what we mean is that we are too zoomed-in and focused on the parts (the individual trees) to appreciate the larger whole (the forest). In fact, as humans, we are often spectacularly bad at seeing or understanding the bigger picture. We lack the necessary perspective, which requires zooming out and noticing how everything is connected to everything else, not only in space but also in time. The forest is not just a collection of trees; it is a web of relationships between trees and countless other organisms and natural forces.

Even when we look at the whole forest, we are missing much of what makes it work as a living system. For instance, when you dig into the world of mycorrhizae—fine, hairlike filaments of fungus that attach themselves to the roots of plants and trees—a whole other world exists. These mushroom fibers reach out hundreds or thousands of times the length of each tree root, sourcing water and essential nutrients for the plant. They also form a vast underground communications network—which has been called the Wood Wide Web—that allows trees to alert one another to threats and provide intensive care to ailing trees or vulnerable offspring, much like an intravenous drip supplying nutrients.

Everything That Surrounds and Connects Us

When we think in systems, our perspective changes. Imagine a tree in an orchard. How do we ensure a bountiful crop of sumptuous fruits? The secret is to create an environment that enables the tree to flourish: fertile soil, regular water, protection from diseases, shelter from the elements, and enough sunshine. Similarly, when it comes to nature, society, and the economy, thinking in systems encourages us to create enabling environments for all life to flourish.

Key Concept: Environment

The environment is literally everything that encircles us. The word is derived from early 17th-century Old French: *en* and *viron* (circle). When it was introduced into the English language in 1828 by Thomas Carlyle, he elaborated the concept to mean "the aggregate of the conditions in which a person or thing lives."[2]

The environment comprises nested living systems, including people and all other organisms, as well as their complex and dynamic relationships: the incredible web of life. The notion of living systems being *nested* is a bit like a Russian doll, where inside each doll is another smaller doll. Similarly, each system exists within another system. In fact, all of life is characterized by nested webs: Cells join together to form organs and other biological systems, which make up our human bodies; we group together into social systems, such as families, communities, organizations, cities, countries, and societies; and we are all part of the earth's dynamic, self-regulating ecological systems.

At a macro level, we can see that the economy is nested within society, which itself exists within and is entirely dependent on nature. Seeing the whole system means recognizing the earth itself as a living, self-regulating organism, which is what NASA scientist James Lovelock proposed in 1979, calling it the Gaia hypothesis, after the Greek goddess of the earth. At first glance, this is an audacious idea. But the science of complex living systems has continued to develop, and the evidence is increasingly compelling. In the same way that microorganisms contribute to our body's health—and sometimes its demise—we, too, must decide whether we are a species that is good for the earth's health or more like a deadly parasite or an infectious virus.

Understanding thriving, rooted in systems thinking, is deceptively easy and fiendishly difficult at the same time. When I first encountered systems science, it wasn't called that, and I didn't yet know how it could be applied in practice, but I knew I had discovered something potentially world changing. It came to me by way of Jan Smuts, a South African statesman and naturalist philosopher, who wrote a book in 1926 called *Holism and Evolution*, in which he claimed to have found nothing less than "the ultimate synthetic, ordering, organising, regulative activity in the universe, which accounts for all the structural groupings and syntheses in it."[3]

Smuts began by critiquing the prevailing view of science, the legacy of Isaac Newton's clockwork universe, which held that a system can be understood by reducing it to its component parts. Smuts saw this reductionistic view of reality, which he called *mechanism*, as a fixed dogma in which "there could be no more in the effect than there was in the cause; hence creativity and real progress became impossible."[4] By reducing nature to an aggregation of dead parts, science was missing the living wholes that make up the complex web of life.

A Theory of Living Systems

Smuts's theory of holism suggests that every organism, every plant or animal, is a whole, with a certain internal organization and measure of self-direction and an individual specific character of its own. This is true of the lowest microorganism no less than the most highly developed and complex human personality or society. Smuts also saw holism as the driving force behind evolution, which creatively enables the development of ever more complex and significant wholes.[5]

Key Concept: Holism

Holism—a term that Jan Smuts coined and derived from the Greek *holos*—proposes that wholes are "the real units of Nature . . . a unity of parts which is so close and intense as to become more than the sum of its parts."[6]

As an aside, Smuts was involved in drafting the original charter of the League of Nations, which later became the United Nations. He also crossed political swords a number of times with Mahatma Gandhi, when Gandhi was a young lawyer in South Africa advocating for the rights of Indians. Before leaving South Africa in 1914, Gandhi sent Smuts a pair of sandals as a gift, which Smuts returned on Gandhi's 70th birthday, remarking that "I have worn these sandals for many a summer . . . even though I may feel that I am not worthy to stand in the shoes of so great a man. It was my fate to be the antagonist of a man for whom even then I had the highest respect."[7]

Smuts was not the first systems scientist. That title probably belongs to the genius Leonardo da Vinci, whose studies of nature and society showed a remarkable appreciation for their dynamic processes, whether it was the swirling vortices of water and air currents that he drew or his metabolic designs for cities as living organisms, where people, goods, food, water, and waste need to flow unimpeded. As modern-day systems scientist Fritjof

Capra noted, reflecting on the theme of his book *The Science of Leonardo*, "His science was radically different from the mechanistic science that would emerge 200 years later. It was a science of organic forms, of qualities, of processes of transformation."[8]

Capra, an Austrian-born American physicist, has done more than most to help articulate, synthesize, and popularize systems science, recounting its fascinating history and teasing out its fundamental principles in his book *The Systems View of Life: A Unifying Vision*, coauthored with Italian chemist Pier Luigi Luisi.[9] Besides paying tribute to Leonardo da Vinci, Capra traces the roots of systems thinking to various pioneers, movements, and concepts, such as organismic biology, cybernetics, tektology, general systems theory, synergetics, complexity theory, chaos theory, fractal geometry, autopoiesis, and social systems theory.

Key Concept: Systems Thinking

Fritjof Capra describes systems thinking as "thinking in terms of connectedness, relationships, patterns, and context."[10] This is consistent with the root meaning of the word *system*, from the Greek "to place together."

In the pages that follow, I weave in many of the ideas behind these rich bodies of work. Together they add layers of understanding to what living systems are and how they function. Systems may be living or nonliving, but I focus on the living systems that make up nature, society, and the economy. This provides a solid scientific foundation for thriving. To make this clearer, I have distilled these fundamentals into characteristics against which to test our thinking and practices. The six keys to thriving are complexity, circularity, creativity, coherence, convergence, and continuity (Figure 1.1).

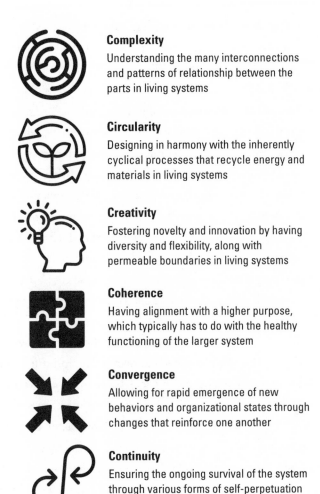

Complexity
Understanding the many interconnections and patterns of relationship between the parts in living systems

Circularity
Designing in harmony with the inherently cyclical processes that recycle energy and materials in living systems

Creativity
Fostering novelty and innovation by having diversity and flexibility, along with permeable boundaries in living systems

Coherence
Having alignment with a higher purpose, which typically has to do with the healthy functioning of the larger system

Convergence
Allowing for rapid emergence of new behaviors and organizational states through changes that reinforce one another

Continuity
Ensuring the ongoing survival of the system through various forms of self-perpetuation or reproduction

Figure 1.1: *The six keys to thriving*

The Key of Complexity

We live in a world of mind-boggling complexity. And speaking of the mind, let's start there, since it gives us a good idea of just how complex living organisms and systems are. According to the latest estimate, we are born with around 86 billion neurons in our brain, and this stays roughly the same throughout our lives. Neurons are tiny nerve cells that transmit information using electrical and chemical signals in the brain. The pathways or conduits of those electrochemical signals are called *synapses*. By comparison, a fruit fly has 100,000 neurons, a cat has 250 million, a chimpanzee 7 billion, and an elephant 257 billion.

Synapses in the brain are a great example of complexity, which in scientific terms means relationships or connections between parts in a system. At birth, each neuron has about 2,500 synapses, and by age three, when toddlers' learning is accelerating, there are about 15,000 synapses per neuron. The youngsters are literally making new connections and detecting meaningful patterns about the world around them, which is reflected in the brain's activity. Over time, this settles back to about 1,000 synapses per neuron, meaning that there are trillions of synapse connections in the average human brain. And each synapse can be firing anything between 1 and 200 times per second.

If that's all a bit mind-blowing, that's exactly the point. Leaving aside our brains (which some of us have been known to do from time to time), there are countless other biological and social systems in the world, each with unimaginable numbers of connections. So if life sometimes feels overwhelmingly complex, that's because it really is. Now factor in nonliving, technological systems, which have been growing exponentially ever since Charles Babbage invented his 1822 "difference engine"—named for its capacity to perform mathematical computations and hence widely regarded as the first computer. The complexity has only compounded.

Complexity in Focus: The Enigma Code

The key of complexity is powerfully demonstrated by what went on at Bletchley Park, the World War II British intelligence site, which is famous for cracking Germany's Enigma code under the leadership of the mathematical genius Alan Turing. What made the cryptic codes so hard to decipher was their complexity; the number of possible combinations was 15 billion trillion (that's 15 with 18 zeros). What's more, the code was changed every 24 hours. That is a lot like life. Every day we face new possibilities, fresh surprises, novel connections, and unexpected events. Our lives may seem routine, but order on the surface hides a complex cipher of continuous, dynamic interactions. Our lives are a puzzling, fascinating Enigma code.

Everywhere we look, if we pay enough attention, we will see complexity, often manifesting in unexpected ways. There's a Netflix series called *Connected*, presented by science journalist Latif Nasser, that beautifully illustrates this point. One whole episode is dedicated to dust, for example, which reveals surprising connections between fossilized fish, sand in the Sahara Desert, Atlantic hurricanes, oxygen-generating phytoplankton, and soil fertility in the Amazon rain forest. Another episode explores hidden mathematical codes that recur in nature and society, connecting everything from volcanoes and astronomy to political elections and social media. Not only does this put the joy of discovery back into science; it also introduces a mainstream audience to the science of complex living systems, without ever calling it that.

This still leaves us with the question of how we can navigate through complexity. In today's world, it is not only the problems that are complex but also the solutions—and the tide of (often contradictory) information adds to our bewilderment. There are two mantras that I use like oars to help steer me through complexity. First, the *how* is as important as the *what*; for example, we should always ask: Is the proposed solution fair and inclusive? And second, the *context* is as important as the action; hence, we should always reflect on who or what benefits or suffers as a result.

One person who has long been at the forefront of studying complex systems, and applying that knowledge to business, is MIT faculty member Peter Senge. I invited him to speak on systems thinking at an event linked to my chair in sustainable transformation at Antwerp Management School. His three takeaways on making systems thinking work in practice are (1) make it visible (most of us don't know where our food, clothing, gadgets, or energy comes from); (2) make it human (put names and faces to the next generations that will benefit or be harmed by our actions today); and (3) make it collaborative (no system is ever changed without long-term, multi-stakeholder partnerships).

Sage advice. From the perspective of thriving, the important point is to remember that, no matter how bewildering it may seem to us, complexity is a good thing. Complexity increases the functionality of a living system and strengthens the likelihood that thriving will occur and that the system will survive and flourish.

The Key of Circularity

The second key to thriving is circularity. Nature and society, as with all living systems, are characterized by flows. It's no accident that enforced self-isolation and restricted movement during COVID-19 times made us anxious, frustrated, bored, and stressed. Complex living systems are not designed to be static. Energy, materials, and organisms all flow and interact through the system, keeping it alive. Living systems need borders as well (membranes, in biological terms), but these are porous by design, allowing exchange with the surrounding environment. Similarly, our social systems, from families to countries, and our natural systems, from gardens to biomes, should be designed for dynamic flows.

Unfortunately, we are not that good at understanding and keeping track of flows in our economies, societies, and ecosystems. If I use the analogy of a bathtub, in society we are often focused on the level of the water, which systems scientists call *stocks*, rather than the water coming in from the tap or leaving through the drain, which are the *flows*. For example, we look at how much freshwater we have today rather than the rate at which it is being depleted or replenished, or we focus on how many women are in the workforce rather than whether the gender pay gap is increasing or decreasing.

The most obvious example of "bathtub thinking" is that we must decrease the use of nonrenewable resources—such as fossil fuels, minerals, and groundwater—and switch to mainly consuming renewable resources. That's because, in nature, everything is recycled. Paul Hawken articulated this rather elegantly in his classic book, *The Ecology of Commerce*, when he noted three ecological principles: (1) Waste equals food; (2) all growth is driven by solar energy; and (3) the overall well-being of the system depends on diversity and thrives on difference.[11]

Circularity in Focus: Spaceship Earth

The key of circularity was already foreseen in the 1960s by Kenneth Boulding, Barbara Ward, and Buckminster Fuller, who wrote about Spaceship Earth—a closed system where a problem for one is a problem for all and where resources are finite and must be continually recycled. Interestingly, Boulding, an economist, contrasted the *spaceship economy*—which exists "without unlimited reservoirs of anything, either for extraction or for pollution, and in which, therefore, man must find his place in a cyclical ecological system"—with the *cowboy economy*, where the cowboy is symbolic of the illimitable plains and associated with reckless, exploitative, and violent behavior.[12]

Without the ecological principle of circularity, the earth would collapse under its own weight. To illustrate, imagine if the 10,000 acorns and 200,000 leaves that a mature oak tree produces every year were not biodegradable. Very few acorns become new oak trees, so within a decade, we would be wading knee-deep in leaves and acorns. Now let's scale that idea up. The earth's total living biomass (the sum of all living materials) has been estimated at 1.1 trillion tons. Think of what would happen if all of that material simply accumulated year after year rather than being broken down and recycled back into food for nature's processes and organisms.

As it happens, we do not need to imagine this scenario. In recent times, human-made materials, which scientists have called *anthropogenic mass*, have been doubling roughly every 20 years. This is because, on average, each person produces anthropogenic mass equal to more than his or her body weight every week. In 2020, for the first time, the total anthropogenic mass surpassed all global living biomass.[13] The problem is that much of what we are producing is not biodegradable. Rather than being food for nature's cycles, our manufactured plastics, chemicals, and heavy metals are toxic for life.

Another key element of circularity in systems is the existence of feedback loops, which are processes that cycle back on themselves to either reinforce or diminish the original effect. Unless we identify, understand, and respond to these feedback loops, we can find ourselves with exponential growth and system collapses. More than 10 years ago, climate scientists identified numerous climate-change tipping points.[14] Each of these, of which there are now 16, creates a self-reinforcing feedback loop in the climate system that perpetuates global warming.

To illustrate further, the fires blazing that have devastated the Amazon, Australia, Turkey, Europe, and California in recent years are a worrying sign of a climate-change tipping point. In the case of the Amazon, climate change dries out the rain forest, which results in more fires, which release carbon into the atmosphere and also reduce carbon absorption by the forest, resulting in more climate warming. It's a dangerous, vicious cycle. There was a time when such economic, social, and environmental crises were *over there*—someone else's problem. Now, breakdowns in one part of the world can rapidly spread to every other part, as we have learned all too well from the COVID-19 pandemic. There is no *away* anymore.

In contrast to feedback loops that reinforce and amplify growth effects, thriving systems use balancing or canceling feedback loops. Biodegradability or recyclability of materials is an example of a balancing feedback effect that allows the system to continually use materials without their accumulating and overwhelming or poisoning the system they are designed to serve.

The Key of Creativity

There's something your parents never told you: Messiness is okay; in fact, it may even be good. As children, we are schooled in the virtues of being neat and tidy, ordering and classifying everything, and generally cleaning up. But nature is messy. Think of random trees, fallen leaves, skewed branches, tangled roots, unruly brambles, unsanctioned mushrooms. Yet there is order in the chaos. Natural systems have design principles and recurring patterns, but there is a lot of flexibility for experimentation, adaptation, and diversity. We can apply the same lesson and let a bit of messiness back into our lives.

It is true that we see order and structure everywhere in nature, but it is more emergent than deterministic. This means that nature allows for creativity and change. It does not prescribe every outcome but rather creates the conditions for innovation. A failure to understand the emergent nature of life is one of the reasons why the centrally planned economies of communism failed and why many top-down hierarchical companies fail. Newton's image of a clockwork universe needs to be reimagined as an organic cosmos, since complexity theory shows that the patterns of life are not rigidly determined or hierarchically controlled. Rather, simple rules applied to complex, apparently chaotic systems allow order to emerge. The interactions themselves cocreate the patterns.

Where those interactions occur is also important. In living systems, most creativity happens on edges and boundaries. If you sometimes feel as if you're on the fringe, fear not, for fringes are fabulous places. Roadside fringes are where poppies bloom, and hedge fringes are where birds nest. It is on the fringes that change is catalyzed. In his theory of holism, Jan Smuts highlighted this principle by talking about *fields*, which are the "natural shading-off continuities" of wholes, as opposed to something that encloses things or people in hard, artificial boundaries.[15]

Metaphorically, the mainstream is like a neatly tended grass lawn, where everything and everyone unorthodox are regarded as invasive weeds. Yet even manicured gardens have their fringes where biodiversity thrives. So, too, in society, where activists, entrepreneurs, and changemakers breathe new life into dysfunctional habits and outdated ideas. If we want to transform our ecological, social, and economic systems to be more innovative, creative, and healthy, we need more people who will operate on the fringe and be proud to do so.

Creativity in Focus: Weedy Entrepreneurs

The key of creativity is demonstrated by entrepreneurs who are like weeds—and I mean that in a positive way. First, like weeds, entrepreneurs are tough and tenacious; they never give up and often grow despite inhospitable conditions. Second, entrepreneurs are often scruffy and wild. They don't conform to the tidy, manicured, and mowed business "lawnscape"; they live on the fringes of convention. Third, entrepreneurs bring color and new life; in the same way that wildflowers are good for biodiversity and attract insects and birds, entrepreneurs are good for socioeconomic life. So let's celebrate our wonderful, weedy entrepreneurs.

Like weeds, creative disruptors are seldom welcomed by the entrenched establishment. Our systems often lack creativity because we get stuck in the prison of convention. Another word for this prison is our dominant *paradigm*, from the Greek word for "pattern." When Nicolaus Copernicus proposed his heliocentric hypothesis—that the earth revolves around the sun—it helped to catalyze the scientific revolution. That's a great example of a paradigm shift: Nothing changed physically, but our worldview was profoundly altered forever. This is the deepest and most difficult kind of change—to achieve a collective mind shift. And those in power, such as the Church in Copernicus's time and corporate and political elites now, will always resist.

We see this with one of the most important shifts happening today as we challenge the prevailing economic paradigm. Over the past 50 years, we conducted a global economic experiment by embracing an approach called *neoliberalism* or *free-market fundamentalism*. Now the results are in, and the conclusion is this: It failed. Don't take my word for it. Whether it's Klaus Schwab, founder of the World Economic Forum, or Pope Francis in his latest encyclical, more and more opinion makers are recognizing that an unregulated market has been good for the rich and powerful but hardly anybody else. Conversely, stakeholder capitalism still embraces the market but welcomes government regulation and civil society advocacy to ensure more fair, inclusive, and sustainable outcomes.

Such forces of creative destruction are essential for living systems to evolve and thrive, whether they are economies, societies, organizations, people, or ecosystems. Thriving happens when we catalyze creativity by having permeable boundaries, allowing time and space for exploration and overlap, and encouraging cross-disciplinary thinking and cross-functional collaboration.

The Key of Coherence

While living systems need creativity to evolve and adapt, they also need coherence to function as a whole. In nature, DNA is often what gives coherence to systems. Our biological programming allows our cells to multiply, specialize, and then work in unison as a whole body. It also gives us instincts, such as the fight-or-flight response in the face of danger. But even in biological systems, coherence is much more impressive than mechanistic preprogramming. Instead, we see a level of self-organization that almost defies belief. In his wonderful book *Emergence*, Steven Johnson gives examples of this, from slime mold and termite colonies to city neighborhoods and artificial intelligence systems. As he puts it, "When enough individual elements interact and organize themselves, the result is collective intelligence—even though no one is in charge."[16]

Take slime mold, for example. For much of its life, the mold exists as thousands of distinct single-celled units that are classified as a type of amoeba. But under the right conditions—when the weather is cool and there is a large food supply—those myriad cells coalesce into a larger unified organism that slowly crawls across the garden floor, consuming rotting leaves and wood as it moves. Coherence emerges. Perhaps you are more familiar with corals, which are actually colonies made up of hundreds of thousands of individual coral polyps, the animals primarily responsible for building coral reefs.

In a similar way, lichen—which covers around 6 percent of the earth's surface—is a symbiotic composite organism. It emerges from algae or cyanobacteria living among the filaments of fungi. Both organisms benefit, exchanging protection, moisture, and nutrients for carbohydrates produced by photosynthesis. The cooperating organisms can live separately but in a different form. However, when they collaborate as lichen, they are neither plant nor fungus. Lichen is remarkable in other ways too: It can survive the vacuum of space and long periods of drought. It also shows one of nature's most beautiful color palettes.

Coherence in Focus: The Flocking Phenomenon

The key of coherence is beautifully demonstrated in the spontaneous self-organization we witness when birds flock or fish move in schools. What's more, this holds a key to how we can change complex systems such as divided societies, unsustainable economies, or toxic politics. When we apply the natural phenomenon of murmuration (flocks of birds moving together) to social systems, we find that a purpose-aligned minority (anything from 5 to 25 percent) can move a random crowd toward a common goal, even without coordination.[17] When you join a flock and add your voice—or more powerfully, your actions—you amplify a movement. And movements, representing shifting social norms, are what ultimately change complex systems.

One of my favorite examples of coherence are ant colonies. Ants, much like bees, display incredibly sophisticated social structures. The colony self-organizes to forage for food, defend the nest against intruders, cultivate farms of mushrooms underground, feed the queen and her offspring, take out the trash (literally, there is a special area for disposing of waste), and lay their deceased to rest in an ant cemetery. And all of this takes place without a leader. Don't be fooled into thinking that the queen is directing her minions; she is just laying eggs. How is this possible for individual ants with brains a million times smaller than those of humans?

This emergent coherence is one of the seemingly miraculous characteristics of complex living systems. Ant biologist Deborah Gordon has spent much of her academic career studying this phenomenon. Based on her scientific observations, she has derived five principles necessary for self-organization to occur:

1. *Grow your group.* There has to be a critical mass of individuals for the system to self-organize—that is, there is a minimum threshold of complexity needed for the system to function effectively as a collective.

2. *See ignorance as useful.* Although living systems may be complex, the operating principles or guiding instructions need to be simple. In the case of ants, their language consists of around 10 distinctive pheromone signals.

3. *Encourage random encounters.* High levels of individual freedom give each individual a chance to experience different parts of the whole system, while also increasing the likelihood of discovering new risks or opportunities.

4. *Look for patterns in the signs.* Organization in a system depends not only on lots of interaction among individuals but also on the ability to detect how frequently different kinds of encounters occur.

5. *Pay attention to your neighbors.* No individual needs to have a big-picture overview of the system; it is enough to exchange local information with lots of individuals that you meet along the way.[18]

The key to thriving is to ensure that there is coherence in the system, which is ultimately about collaboration. In social systems, having leaders who can articulate a shared goal will certainly help, but it is worth remembering that people—much like slime mold, ants, or birds—can and do self-organize to create coherent action.

The Key of Convergence

Another important key to thriving is convergence, which is the process that causes complex living systems to sometimes change very rapidly. Systems scientists call these *bifurcation points* or, more popularly, *tipping points*. They are when we get a perfect storm of different elements coming together and reinforcing one another. At a high level, we could say that socioecological breakdowns, technological breakthroughs, and rising social movements create conditions for convergence and a resulting "systems flip" toward thriving.

Convergence in Focus: Carriages to Cars

One of the great proponents of technological convergence is Tony Seba, a Silicon Valley entrepreneur and author of *Clean Disruption of Energy and Transportation*.[19] In one of his presentations, he shows a photograph of Fifth Avenue, in New York City, in 1900. The street is full of pedestrians and horse-drawn carriages, with a single motorized car in the picture. Then he shows a photograph of the same street in 1913, and it's all cars, with just one horse-drawn carriage. In 13 years the transportation system of a major city flipped, and it was because of convergence: Oil production made fuel cheap, coal tar brought street paving, and Henry Ford's assembly lines made cars affordable.

We are spectacularly bad at predicting these disruptions; instead, we constantly underestimate the power of convergence. For example, in the early 1980s, AT&T asked consulting firm McKinsey to estimate how many cellular phones would be in use in the world at the turn of the century.[20] They predicted 900,000. And what really happened? By 2000 there were 109 million mobile-phone users. The "experts" were off by a factor of 120. In Africa it took just six years for mobile phones to go from zero to overtaking the number of fixed-line telephones.

History is littered with examples like this, and today, we see history repeating itself, with the so-called experts underestimating the powerful convergence of changing economic models, societal norms, environmental conditions, technology advancements, and human capacities, which are going to flip our global system toward ubiquitous sustainable technology within 10 years.

The switch to renewable energy and fully autonomous electric vehicles is a classic case in point. Unsubsidized solar and onshore wind are the cheapest source of new power generation for nearly half the world, according to Bloomberg in June 2021.[21] It's happening. The only question is who the winners and losers will be. On that score, Los Angeles plans to be a winner. The city struck a 25-year deal in 2019 for solar and battery power at a price that, according to *Forbes*, "crushes fossil fuels, buries nuclear."[22] At 1.997c/kwh (cents per kilowatt hour) for solar and 1.3c/kwh for batteries, it's half the cost of power from a new natural gas plant.

You've probably heard of Moore's law for computing. The Los Angeles deal demonstrates something similar, which is Swanson's law for solar energy, named after the founder of SunPower Corporation, who observed that the price of solar drops 20 percent for every doubling of cumulative shipped volume. Since 2010, the cost of utility-scale solar power has dropped by 82 percent, and that of onshore wind by 39 percent. Currently, costs go down 75 percent every 10 years.

Something similar is happening with battery technology, and when it comes to low-carbon futures, batteries are the game changer. Without effective energy storage at scale, renewables will remain peripheral. But the revolution is already happening. Lithium-ion batteries cost 89 percent less in 2020 than in 2010, and prices will almost halve again by 2030.[23] Installation is expected to grow 122-fold by 2040, according to Bloomberg New Energy Finance, creating investment opportunities of $622 billion.[24] Most of this growth will be in utility-scale storage, like Tesla's Megapack and GE's Reservoir battery farms, but linking domestic batteries to the grid is also happening, as we see with the Social Energy network in the UK.

Simultaneous rapid advances in artificial intelligence, batteries, electric vehicles, and renewables are showing convergence in real time. All these, as well as other solutions that will allow us to thrive, are going to be adopted much more quickly than the incumbent leaders of business and government expect, not because the technologies are new but because they are converging.

The Key of Continuity

The ultimate goal of living systems is continuity: the ability to survive as long as possible and then to renew or reproduce. In nature, organisms engage in a plethora of strategies and tactics to ensure that they can stay alive. But evolution has also made sure to prioritize reproduction, which is genetically hardwired as a fundamental driver of behavior: Find a mate and procreate. Hence, we have a multilevel dynamic: First, ensure individual continuity; then ensure genetic continuity and thereby also ensure collective continuity. It is the same with families, organizations, cultures, and whole civilizations.

Despite continuity being such a fundamental driver in nature, as humans we seem rather inept at ensuring our own long-term survival. Jared Diamond, in his book *Collapse: How Societies Choose to Fail or Survive*, gives many examples of communities and civilizations that have collapsed.[25] The five underlying causes are climate change, hostile neighbors, the loss of essential trading partners, environmental degradation, and how the society responds to those four factors. If we are to learn from history, global climate damage and ecological breakdown are huge red flags that we should not be ignoring.

Continuity in Focus: Cathedral Thinking

The key of continuity is evident in what has become known as *cathedral thinking*. In 2019 the Sagrada Família cathedral finally got its building permit—137 years late—and it's still not expected to be completed until 2028. That's not an unusual time line. Notre Dame in Paris took 182 years to build and was more than 850 years old when the fire of 2019 did so much damage. It will be restored and may last another 850 years. In medieval Europe multigenerational planning was inspired by the glory of God and the ego of kings (and occasionally queens). What about today? How often do we take actions that even our great-grandchildren will benefit from? Is belief in a flourishing earth and thriving society enough? What is our modern-day equivalent of the Native American Iroquois sustainable development philosophy of thinking seven generations ahead? Roman Krznaric calls this being "the good ancestor" in his book of the same name.[26]

We seem to be trapped in a world of myopic short-termism, driven by a capitalist system that is obsessed with quarterly returns for absent shareholders. According to McKinsey research, this does not even make economic sense. Their 15-year analysis of short-term- versus long-term-oriented companies found the long-term firms showed 47 percent more revenue growth and 36 percent more earnings, had $7 billion more market capitalization growth and a higher total return to shareholders, and led to the creation of 12,000 more jobs. One distinguishing feature is that long-term companies invest almost 50 percent more in research and development, including during financial crises. It is time companies challenged quarterly capitalism and focused on long-term value creation.[27]

According to the former managing director of McKinsey, Dominic Barton, such capitalism for the long term requires three shifts. First, business and finance must change their incentives and structures to fight what Barton calls "the tyranny of short-termism." Second, stakeholder value needs to be embraced, with a clear message that this is not at odds with optimizing overall corporate (including financial) value. And third, boards need to govern like owners rather than play second fiddle to dispersed and disengaged shareholders. Writing in 2011 in the wake of the global financial crisis, Barton concluded with this warning: "If capitalism emerges from the crisis vibrant and renewed, future generations will thank us. But if we merely paper over the cracks and return to our precrisis views, we will not want to read what the historians of the future will write."[28]

Getting humanity to change our collective time horizon is the mission of the Long Now Foundation, which is building a clock that will keep accurate time for 10,000 years. This is the brainchild of computer scientist Danny Hillis as a way to challenge our short-term thinking—and it's actually happening. Deep inside a mountain in West Texas, surrounded by 5,000-year-old pines, its marine-grade stainless steel, titanium, and dry-running ceramic parts are being assembled. In our hurried, harried lives where we are brainwashed into thinking that time is money, let us pause and remember that time is also continuity; time is the only future we will ever have.

Besides changing our perspective on time, another way to bolster continuity and ensure thriving is to build resilience, a theme we return to later in the book. Living systems regularly survive crises because they have design features that allow them to absorb shocks and bounce back from disruption. In particular, what allows living systems to continue after a disaster is that they have defense mechanisms and high levels of diversity that allow them to adapt creatively. They are also often decentralized and have spare capacity or slack in the system, so shocks to one part do not automatically debilitate all the other parts.

In COVID-19 times, we have certainly learned a thing or two about resilience and what it takes to ensure continuity for individuals, organizations, economies, and societies. Now we need to apply those lessons to all types of living systems, including nature, business, government, and civil society.

Making a Dent in the Universe

With the foundations laid for understanding thriving, the next chapter reflects on the forces of breakdown, or degeneration, that we face. In doing this, I am taking the advice of Admiral James Stockdale, who survived seven years as a prisoner of war in Vietnam. He advocates embracing the Stockdale Paradox: You must confront the most brutal facts of your current reality yet always keep faith that you will prevail in the end.

Thriving is a reason to keep faith. It is a positive answer to the question: What will you leave behind, for your children and the world? Steve Jobs, cofounder of Apple, is famous for having said that we should all strive to "make a dent in the universe." That is the hope and promise of thriving: to leave a good legacy for our children and grandchildren, to leave the world in better shape than we found it, and to create living space for the myriad other organisms that share and shape our beautiful planet earth. And because we remain far from that goal, thriving requires a revolution, in both thinking and action.

REVOLUTION

There's talk of revolution
In the markets and the streets
There's talk of love and hatred
In the rhyme of hip-hop beats

They say a change is coming
To the corridors of power
They say the day of judgment
Draws nearer by the hour

There's news of revolution
In the papers and the wires
There's news of greed and hunger
And it's spreading like wild fires

They say the planet's burning
From our love affair with stuff
They say we're suicidal
For not knowing what's enough

Let's start the revolution
For the migrants and the slaves
Let's start regeneration
With the sun and wind and waves

They say the world awakens
As the networks spark and grow
They say the future brightens
As we share the things we know

Let's join the revolution
At the factories and the farms
Let's join the call to action
Syncing hearts and linking arms

They see a new age dawning
As the prophecies unwind
For the biggest revolution
Is a metamorphic mind

So be the revolution
For the ninety-nine percent
Be the change you want to see
And make your chosen dent.

CHAPTER 2

Paradox

It was the best of times, it was the worst of times, it was the age of wisdom, it was the age of foolishness, it was the epoch of belief, it was the epoch of incredulity, it was the season of light, it was the season of darkness, it was the spring of hope, it was the winter of despair.

—**Charles Dickens,** *A Tale of Two Cities*

The Worst and Best of Humanity

I know what the worst of times and the best of times look like, because I have lived through both. I was born in Zimbabwe and grew up in South Africa at a time when these countries were still ruled by colonial white minorities that systematically oppressed their Black and Brown majority populations. Both nations practiced institutionalized racism with the backing of the law and the enforcement might of a police state. I did not actively advocate for these despicable policies; nevertheless, I was complicit in upholding the evil system known as *apartheid*. In Cape Town, South Africa, I went to a whites-only school, enjoyed visits to whites-only beaches, and used whites-only public toilets.

By the time I went to university in 1988, thankfully, the edifice of apartheid was crumbling, and by 1990, President F. W. de Klerk was enacting numerous reforms: undoing the ban on Nelson Mandela's party, the African National Congress; placing a moratorium on the death penalty; ending the state of emergency; and starting the release of political prisoners. At the same time, I was belatedly being educated about the injustices of apartheid—largely thanks to my professor of labor economics at the University of Cape Town, Francis Wilson, and the enlightened programs of AIESEC. I am living proof that it is possible for values to change.

On May 10, 1994, I celebrated with millions in South Africa and around the world when President Nelson Mandela was inaugurated as the first democratic leader of the country. We were euphoric about the political miracle that had happened, and I felt deep solidarity and pride in our reborn nation. The hard tasks of reconciliation, building national unity, and ensuring economic development still lay ahead, but we were in the process of regeneration, and there is nothing more life affirming and inspiring than having such a positive collective purpose. Even today, more than 25 years later, the process of South Africa's regeneration is not complete—some might argue that there have even been lapses into degeneration—but no one ever said thriving is easy.

Looking back at South Africa and the world, then and now, perhaps we should not be surprised at the lack of progress on many issues. Societal transformation is a generational undertaking, and we are still midtransition. That battle for equality and dignity in South Africa took nearly 50 years of relentless activism against the minority-ruled nationalist government that took power in 1948. It was an ugly war, and many lives were lost in the process. But in the end, history will judge that it was worth it. Thriving triumphed. South Africa showed the world what is possible—the worst and the best of what humans are capable of.

In retrospect, I can see clearly that apartheid was a system based on three destructive values. It was *exclusive* (benefiting the minority in power), *exploitative* (abusing labor and human rights), and *extractive* ("cashing in" natural resources). Value was being created but only for the few, at the expense of the many and the environment. That degenerative system was dismantled by Mandela's government, but it seems to me that we still live within a system of global apartheid, which is exclusive, exploitative, and extractive. The only difference is that South Africa's apartheid was a political system fueled by misguided nationalistic ideals, and our global apartheid is an economic system fueled by misguided neoliberal capitalist ideals.

A Moment of Dangerous Opportunity

It is this conviction—that we may have won the battle against apartheid in South Africa, but we still need to win the war against global apartheid—that has driven me in my own work to advance sustainable development during the past 30 years. But now it seems to me that we are at an inflection point. In the same way that South Africa could have descended into civil war and economic chaos but instead chose the road to an inclusive, empowering, and restorative future, so, too, we have a choice as a global society between degeneration and regeneration, between falling apart and coming together, between fragmentation and integration, between decline and thriving.

This crisis is a civilization-wide challenge to which we can and must rise. But will it be enough to trigger the Great Reset that the World Economic Forum is calling for? Naomi Klein, who has made a career out of studying crises and capitalism, says a shocking event such as a financial crisis or a pandemic is necessary but not sufficient.[1] The other two vital ingredients, she says, are a utopian imagination (meaning a compelling vision of what *better* looks like) and movement muscle (namely, an organized mobilization of people behind powerful causes). We also need to go beyond *no* (what we don't want) to *yes* (what we do want).

Most likely, therefore, those who are expecting society or the economy to transform post-COVID will be disappointed—but they will not be wrong. The calls for a Great Reset or for green bailouts will find traction in some places but not in others. Most governments, companies, and citizens will try to get back to normal, to restore business as usual. But do not mistake the lack of widespread visible changes for a lack of underlying, more fundamental change. The system has already shifted irrevocably—and some of the most profound and impactful transformations will be from small changes in mindset and actions that even now are rippling and accumulating across our interconnected global society.

We face many important questions as we enter this reset era. One could be: Should we kill off sustainability at the same time? Will it help or hinder our great transformation? Already John Elkington, who coined the *triple bottom line* of sustainability in 1994—by which he meant a company's social, environmental, and economic impact—retracted it 25 years later as a failed management concept, in the same way a corporation might recall a faulty car.[2] One problem with the sustainability agenda—including the 17 UN Sustainable Development Goals—is that rather than being transformational, as Elkington hoped, it has been a story of compromise.

There is a danger that we continue to advocate for sustainable development while failing to change the underlying system that is the root of our unsustainability. There is also the danger that, whatever progress we may be making on sustainability, the forces of breakdown will overtake and overwhelm us. It will be a case of too little too late. That's why the paradigm shift I am most excited about—and the one that has unprecedented potential for resetting our relationship with nature, society, and the economy—is thriving, the subject of this book. But before we begin to explore the six shifts powering that compelling vision of the future, we must begin at the time and place in which we find ourselves.

A Tangle of Knotty Problems

Many of you may, like me, be feeling discombobulated. That's a strange word. But then, these are strange times. The word means confused or disconcerted, which surely captures the prevailing zeitgeist. We are caught between conflicting yet simultaneous realities: of suffering and tragedy happening all around us to millions of people, and, for some, of healing, rejuvenation, and reconnection to family and nature. Some are going through the fire of crisis, stress, and overwork, while others are in the quiet eye of the storm, a place of eerie stillness, isolation, and inactivity. The years 2020 and 2021 have been nothing if not strange. It has been a time of paradox, when apparent contradictions are the new normal.

And yet, as I describe shortly, COVID-19 is only one of many crises the world faces right now. We need to step back and consider all the other ways in which these are discombobulated times. After all, we may have walked through the inferno of a pandemic, but we will emerge on the other side to find that there are other fires blazing. Some have been raging for years and have not gone away during our moment of distraction, such as income inequality and climate change. Others are newer but spreading with worrying speed, such as recent waves of divisive populism and the digital divide.

Fresh Insight: Wicked Problems

Large global challenges are often talked about as being *wicked problems*. The term was first coined by Berkeley design professor Horst Rittel in 1967[3] and then elaborated in 1973 as having special characteristics.[4] Originally, they were thought of as dilemmas facing the planning profession; however, they have gained universal significance and have some interesting properties. For example, every wicked problem is a symptom of another problem; hence, wicked problems never have easy solutions. In fact, they are almost by definition unsolvable. Nevertheless, in our efforts to tackle them, we can produce better or worse outcomes.[5]

My own preference is that we should think of our global challenges as *entangled*, rather than wicked, since the latter implies something evil and tempts us to look for villains. Instead, these problems—for example, poverty, climate change, and species loss—are more like an entangled ball of twine. How knotty the problem is depends on whether it is loosely or tightly entangled and whether there is alignment or divergence between those tugging at the strings. Simply pulling harder on one string will probably only make it worse. The way to untangle these problems is to work patiently, locally, carefully, and collaboratively at loosening and unraveling.

So let us briefly grapple with six tangles of knotty problems, which I call the forces of fragmentation. Together they form a web of breakdown, including degradation, depletion, disparity, disease, disconnection, and disruption.

Degradation: The Crime of Ecocide

When I look at the Norfolk countryside of England around where I live, what I see is a degraded landscape: vast agricultural fields devoid of life, except for the single crops they grow; huge dust-and-mud pens where livestock are factory farmed; and a patchwork of trees that have been left in strips or small groves. What I am witnessing, and what is even more evident in cities, is the degradation of ecosystems. Nature's communities of life—which would normally flourish through symbiotic relationships in forests, grasslands, wetlands, lakes, oceans, and other habitats—have been eroded and, in some cases, even eliminated.

This degradation of our ecosystems has been underway for hundreds—perhaps even thousands—of years. Historian Yuval Noah Harari, in his book *Sapiens: A Brief History of Humankind*, points out that humans are responsible for the extinction of megafauna (large animals) on virtually every continent on which they have set foot, from Australia and Europe to North and South America.[6] Species such as saber-toothed cats, mammoths, giant ground sloths, lions, rodents, koalas, kangaroos, emus, and native American horses and camels, all of which had flourished for tens of millions of years, disappeared shortly after humans migrated to their habitats.

Sometimes this environmental destruction contributed to the demise of human societies as well. According to Jared Diamond, the civilizations of the Greenland Norse, Easter Island, the Polynesians of Pitcairn Island, the

Anasazi of southwestern North America, and the Maya of Central America all collapsed at least in part because of environmental exploitation.[7] This included deforestation and habitat destruction, soil depletion, water mismanagement, overhunting, overfishing, the effects of introduced species on native species, overpopulation, and the increased impact of each person. Other growing risks, such as human-caused climate change and the buildup of toxins in the environment, are more recent and may yet contribute to the collapse of civilization.

These historical examples notwithstanding, we are without a doubt in a new phase of ecological destruction, both in terms of scale and speed. There is even a proposal to name a new geological epoch: the Anthropocene—an age where the geophysical and chemical conditions of the earth are being changed by humans. The atmospheric chemist Paul Crutzen and biologist Eugene Stoermer, who proposed the change, suggest the late 1700s as the start of the Anthropocene, pegging it to the beginning of the Industrial Revolution with James Watt's invention of the steam engine in 1784; it is also when glacial ice cores show an increase in the concentration of several greenhouse gases, in particular carbon dioxide (CO_2) and methane (CH_4).

Degradation in Focus

There is compelling evidence for the degradation of ecosystems by humans. For example, the 2019 *Global Assessment Report* from the Intergovernmental Science-Policy Platform on Biodiversity and Ecosystem Services finds that natural ecosystems have declined by 47 percent on average, relative to their earliest estimated states; approximately 25 percent of species are already threatened with extinction in most animal and plant groups studied; biotic integrity—the abundance of naturally present species—has declined by 23 percent on average in terrestrial communities; and the global biomass of wild mammals has fallen by 82 percent since prehistory.[8]

The Living Planet Index, first launched in 1998 by the World Wide Fund for Nature (WWF) and now managed by the Zoological Society of London, tracks more than 20,000 populations representing more than 4,000 species of mammals, birds, fish, reptiles, and amphibians from around the world. Their most recent findings show a 68 percent decline in these populations since 1970. We are literally committing ecocide. I used to think that word—*ecocide*—derived from *suicide*. After all, destroying the web of life will ultimately lead to our own demise. But now I think it's more accurate to link ecocide to *homicide* and *genocide*—killing on a mass scale. The worst part is, like the psychopath or genocidal maniac, we seem to lack empathy for our victims.

To make sense of these and other statistics, the Stockholm Resilience Centre has provided a visual and data-based representation of our ecosystem risks by identifying nine planetary boundaries: quantitative thresholds beyond which the risk of ecosystem breakdown increases dramatically. For two boundaries—biosphere integrity (including genetic diversity) and biogeochemical flows (notably of phosphorus and nitrogen)—we are already in the high-risk zone. For an additional two—climate change and land-system change—we face increasing risk. Ocean acidification is nearing the danger threshold, while stratospheric ozone depletion remains in the safe zone. For chemical pollution and atmospheric aerosol loading, we do not yet have the necessary data to assess the risk.

Depletion: The Limits to Growth

I grew up in the beautiful city of Cape Town, South Africa, which is nestled under the shadow of Table Mountain, fringed by white sandy beaches, and surrounded by kaleidoscopic vineyards. Here it is easy to feel that you have discovered paradise on earth. Imagine the shock when, in 2018, Cape Town announced that it was three months away from Day Zero—the day when the city's water taps would run dry. Fortunately, drastic measures were taken, citizens' behavior changed, and the crisis was averted, for now. This is a stark example of the depletion of natural resources, and it is happening all around the world. We are using up nonrenewable resources such as groundwater, minerals, and fossil fuels and consuming renewable resources such as freshwater, clean air, fertile soils, and timber faster than nature can replace them.

This is no great revelation. We have known about the depletion of natural resources for decades. World Environment Day was first celebrated in 1972, a special year: The UN also convened its landmark Conference on the Human Environment in Stockholm, and the Club of Rome published its controversial *Limits to Growth* report. Together these sounded the first of many severe warnings by scientists that the world is on a dangerous path and needs to change course. Yet it seems that, rather than the accumulated wisdom of hindsight, we have nearly 50 years of willful inaction. Can we turn a blind eye much longer?

Depletion in Focus

The trend of depletion of natural resources is most evident in the Great Acceleration, a set of socioeconomic and ecological exponential growth charts. The 24 indicators of this planetary dashboard were first introduced by the International Geosphere-Biosphere Programme in collaboration with the Stockholm Resilience Centre in 2004 and updated in 2015. They plot data such as economic growth, population, foreign direct investment, energy consumption, telecommunications, transportation, water use, the carbon cycle, the nitrogen cycle, and biodiversity. All reveal the same exponential growth pattern since 1950, slow at first but then rapidly rising. These are sometimes referred to as hockey-stick curves because of their shape.

Our addiction to growth and consumption has a double impact: We deplete resources and we increase waste and pollution. Since many of these resources are nonrenewable, sooner or later they will run out or become too expensive to access. Technology goes a long way toward extending the life of these finite stocks—as we have seen with oil extraction from deep ocean beds and tar sands, or natural gas fracking—but these all have their own negative economic, social, and environmental consequences. The same applies to the depletion of our healthy soils, natural forests, fish populations, minerals, and water.

Water is a good illustration of the trend. Astronomer Carl Sagan's description of the earth as a "pale blue dot"[9] and Sir David Attenborough's reference to our "blue planet"[10] allow us to conjure up images of a beautiful watery home. But the impression that water is abundant on earth is misleading. If all the world's water were gathered into a sphere, it would be 11 percent the size of the earth; freshwater would be 2 percent—and since 1900, freshwater withdrawals have increased sixfold. Already, the World Resources Institute estimates a quarter of the world's population faces extremely high levels of water stress, and MIT research predicts this may rise to 50 percent by 2050.

The more resources we use, the more waste and pollution we produce. When we think of waste, we often think of "trash," especially litter—and we tut-tut about the developing countries where communities and rivers are choked by plastic. At the same time, we conveniently hide or ignore the high-consumption, throwaway lifestyles of middle- and high-income consumers, which have far bigger impacts that are much more perilous for the planet. We must shine a light (or turn a mirror) on our own mountains of waste food, packaging, and products, which are conveniently out of sight, away from our clean streets, tidy offices, and serviced cities.

In 2021, July 29 was Earth Overshoot Day—the day when our resource consumption exceeded the earth's capacity to regenerate those resources in that year. This means that every year, we go into ecological debt. To use a banking analogy, we start eating into our natural capital stocks rather than living off renewable interest. But then the metaphor breaks down. Financial debt comes with a price: punitive interest rates. These act as an incentive to avoid debt or to get out of debt quickly. With ecological debt, we lack that pain point. There are consequences, but we don't feel them directly or immediately. Until we do. And then our worst imagined futures start to come true.

Disparity: Please Mind the Gap

When I was a teenager, I volunteered for a work camp to help build a community center in a rural town in Namaqualand. This is a dry region along South Africa's northwest coast that bursts into spectacular carpets of colorful daisies every spring. Most people in the town were unemployed, although some managed to find work in the copper and diamond mines. There I made a friend, Johnny Beukes: a smart, hardworking, positive, proactive, and caring young man—someone I would have trusted with my life. He gave me a glimpse into how tough life could be in a poor rural town in South Africa as a person of color. The world of difference between Johnny and me had nothing to do with differences in our abilities and everything to do with differences in the opportunities we had each been given in life.

That is the essence of disparity—the fact that inequalities exist for billions of people, not because they deserve less but because they are discriminated against, economically marginalized, or not lucky enough to be born into privileged circumstances. Amartya Sen, in his book *Development as Freedom*, changed the debate on poverty when he pointed out that inequality of capabilities is even more important than income disparity.[11] By capabilities, Sen meant a person's freedom to choose what to be and do. For example, unequal access to education, health, technology, and power is a fundamental driver of perceived and actual inequality in society. Hence, unequal access to opportunities lies at the heart of disparity as a force for breakdown in society.

Despite progress made by the Millennium Development Goals between 2000 and 2015 and by the Sustainable Development Goals since 2015, there is still growing inequality in the world. But you may be asking: Why should we care about inequality? Part of the answer is that inequality is simply unfair. But disparity also imposes costs on society. In Richard G. Wilkinson and Kate Pickett's book *The Spirit Level*, they highlight 11 health and social problems that are associated with higher levels of inequality, citing data on physical and mental health, drug abuse, education, imprisonment, obesity, social mobility, trust, community life, violence, teenage pregnancies, and children's well-being.[12]

The UN similarly finds that high levels of income inequality are associated with lower productivity, less durable economic growth, lower trust and social cohesion, social anxiety and class conflict, more homicides and criminal violence, lower diffusion of sustainable technology, and less support for low-carbon policies.[13] Income inequality is also linked with low income mobility—meaning individuals' ability to improve their socioeconomic status—and can be exacerbated by technological innovation, climate change, urbanization, and international migration.[14]

Disparity in Focus

We face a paradox: Despite hundreds of millions of people having been lifted out of poverty, income inequality has grown over the past 40 years. "The World Inequality Report, 2018" notes that, between 1980 and 2016, the bottom 50 percent of the world's population captured 12 percent of real income growth, while the top 1 percent captured 27 percent.[15] In other words, the rich are getting richer faster than the poor are getting richer. Consequently, the gap between the rich and the poor is widening. Look at the extremes, and the disparity is even more stark: Incomes of the top 0.001 percent (think billionaire elites) grew at 240 percent compared with around 70 percent growth for the bottom 10 percent.

Of course, inequality is not only about income. Any unfair exclusion or unequal treatment of a particular group in society or the economy is a form of disparity. We see this most obviously in discrimination, where people of different ethnic backgrounds, physical and mental abilities, and sexual preferences are treated differently and excluded from opportunities. Even on gender equality, where we expect progress is being made, the trends are worrying. The World Economic Forum's *Global Gender Gap Report, 2020* tracks gender parity in 156 countries across four dimensions: economic participation and opportunity, educational attainment, health and survival, and political empowerment.

According to their findings, based on current trends, it will take another 135 years to close the overall gender gap, which is ludicrous and totally unacceptable. Good progress has been made on educational equality, where 95 percent of the gap has been closed, and similarly in health and survival, where 96 percent equality exists. But in political representation, only 26 percent of parliamentary seats and 23 percent of ministerial positions are held by women.[16]

Worst of all is the situation on gender equality in economic participation and opportunity, where the world is actually going backward. In 2020, November 4 was Equal Pay Day in Europe, which is the day that women symbolically start to work for free for the remainder of the year because of the gender pay gap. Globally, there's still a 42 percent overall gap between men and women in economic participation and opportunity.[17] If nothing changes, it will take 267 years to close the gender pay gap and 145 years to close the political gender divide.

Disease: An Ill Wind That Blows

I have a special relationship with Venice. It is where, on a gondola, I proposed to my lovely wife by reading her a poem titled "Say I Do." I can see you rolling your eyes; it doesn't get more clichéd than that, I know. Venice is also the city where I bought a Venetian mask (yes, another cliché). More to the point, I discovered that the popular masks shaped like the beak of a bird used to be worn by doctors during the Black Death plague in the mid-1300s. The purpose of the long nose, which would sometimes be stuffed with herbs and flowers, was to keep away bad smells, known as miasma, which were thought to be the principal cause of the disease.

We've come a long way in 800 years, yet we are still vulnerable to various forms of ill health. That is the underlying meaning of *disease*: the absence of physical and mental well-being, resulting in poor health. We should be rightly proud that the world has made remarkable progress on improving health. After all, billions of people are living longer and healthier lives compared to previous generations. Significant inroads have also been made into preventing and treating infectious diseases. Despite all this progress, however, we need to keep an eye on areas of ongoing or rising concern.

Disease in Focus

Today, more than 70 percent of deaths are due to noncommunicable diseases (NCDs), most notably cardiovascular disease, cancer, chronic respiratory disease, and diabetes. There are strong correlations between these NCDs and lifestyle choices, such as tobacco use, air pollution, unhealthy diets, physical inactivity, and harmful use of alcohol.[18] In addition to these physical diseases, there are mental illnesses. Depression and anxiety affect 10 percent of people, cost the economy $1 trillion a year, and have doubled over the past 25 years.[19] Sometimes, these conditions are called lifestyle diseases or diseases of the rich, and around 40 percent of annual deaths from them are regarded as preventable.[20]

The role of diet in health is getting more attention lately as the data becomes clearer. For example, 2018 Oxford research found that eating predominantly plant-based diets could reduce premature deaths from chronic diseases by more than 20 percent, besides cutting greenhouse gas emissions by 54–87 percent, fertilizer application by 18–25 percent, and cropland and freshwater use by 2–11 percent.[21] In support of these findings, the UK Health Alliance on Climate Change has called for a tax on meat to improve health and reduce carbon emissions. Their survey of British health professionals found that two-thirds agree with this double-benefit approach.[22]

Health is not only about physical fitness, diet, or tackling diseases but also about mental well-being. Mental health issues account for 20 percent of those living with disabilities, and people living with mental health conditions are more likely to face other physical health problems (such as HIV, TB, substance abuse, and noncommunicable diseases), taking 10–20 years off their life on average. More than 80 percent of people experiencing mental health problems are without any form of quality, affordable mental health care. Yet for every dollar put into scaled-up treatment for common mental disorders, there is a return of four dollars in improved health and productivity.[23]

While there are many kinds of mental health disorders, one that is especially relevant for business is burnout, which the World Health Organization included in 2019 for the first time in its International Statistical Classification of Diseases and Related Health Problems. Globally 264 million people suffer from depression and symptoms of anxiety, which cost the global economy $1 trillion each year in lost productivity. Burnout symptoms range from feelings of anxiety, low mood, and detachment from day-to-day life to not being able to cope at all with work or life and being hospitalized as a result of mental breakdown.

Despite the looming crisis of deteriorating mental well-being in the workplace, governments spend only 3 percent of health budgets on mental health. Meanwhile businesses see rising long-term sick leave, spiraling staff costs, and a never-ending recruitment treadmill. According to a Gallup survey of more than 12,650 employees, the leading causes of burnout are unfair treatment at work, unmanageable workload, unclear communication from managers, lack of manager support, and unreasonable time pressure.[24]

Disconnection: The Ones Technology Left Behind

I grew up on the cusp between the industrial and information ages. My high school class was the first to be allowed pocket calculators during math exams, and when I went to university, email was still brand new. It was two years after I graduated that the World Wide Web was made public. By then mobile phones were taking off too, and the rest, as they say, is history.

More than 145 years have passed since Alexander Graham Bell spoke his famous words into the telephone: "Mr. Watson, come here, I want you." Since then, the world has grown more connected than Bell could ever have imagined. The Information Revolution really has changed the world—and for the most part, it is for the better. The benefits of digital connectivity are rather obvious. Computers, mobile phones, and the internet provide access to knowledge, market data, and economic opportunities. But for all its wonders, technology has never been equally distributed. This is why the so-called digital divide is such a concern as a force of fragmentation and breakdown. It acts as an amplifier of inequalities.

Still, you may be wondering if there really is a problem; surely the whole world is connected by now? Today, around 2 billion people still do not have internet access, while a rich minority of the world's population charges ahead with the latest advances from the digital revolution. This is the meaning of disconnection: It's about the gap between those who have access to technology and those who don't, and at the other end of the spectrum, it is about technology replacing humans.

Disconnection in Focus

Despite all our progress in getting the world online, there is still a big gap between developed, developing, and least-developed countries (LDCs), which the *Digital Economy Report* of the UN Conference on Trade and Development makes clear. In 2018, for the first time, more than half of the world's population got online (51.2 percent), but only one out of five people in LDCs have internet access, compared with four out of five for developed countries. Affordable internet access exists in only 40 percent of low- and middle-income countries, leaving 2.3 billion people unable to enjoy 1G mobile broadband plans (let alone the dream of 5G).[25] And remember, while these populations try to catch up, others are already rapidly adopting technologies such as artificial intelligence and virtual reality. And so the gap grows.

There is also a gender digital divide. In two-thirds of all countries, the proportion of women using the internet is lower than men. And as with many products and services, there is also a poverty premium, where the poor pay more. According to the Alliance for Affordable Internet's Affordability Drivers Index for 61 countries, 7 out of the lowest-scoring 10 countries are low-income countries, and 7 are African countries. Across Africa, the average cost for 1G of data is 7 percent of the average monthly salary (and in some countries, it is as much as 20 percent).[26]

While low-income countries are struggling to catch up with access to basic information and communications technology infrastructure, they are rapidly falling behind the next wave, which will be enabled by 5G wireless technology processing around 1,000 times what today's systems are capable of. The United States and China are emerging as digital giants that may dwarf our current divide. For example, together they account for 75 percent of patents for blockchain (a secure way of digitally recording transactions), 50 percent of global spending on connected devices (the so-called Internet of Things), 75 percent of the world market for public cloud computing, and 90 percent of the market capitalization value of the world's 70 largest digital platforms.[27]

Besides gaps in access to technology, there is also the problem of human replacement by machines, which began with the original Industrial Revolution and will now spread wider and cut deeper in economies around the world. Analysis by the Brookings Institute for the United States, covering trends from 1980 to 2030, concludes that 25 percent of jobs face a high risk of being automated in the coming decades, while an additional 36 percent face a medium risk.[28]

Disconnection is therefore also about our ambiguous relationship with technology. It's about admitting that every breakthrough in technology has its dark side. Thomas Midgley invented leaded fuel and chlorofluorocarbons, which brought improvements in fuel efficiency and refrigeration but ended up causing lead poisoning and the ozone hole. Biofuels offer a source of low-carbon energy but can compete for land with agriculture. Renewables and batteries promise an end to climate-warming fossil fuels but can be linked to minerals that exacerbate conflict and violence. Social media gives us a voice but is used to spread fake news and undermine democracy. That doesn't mean we should reject these technologies, but we must remain vigilant about unintended consequences—and work hard to address them.

Disruption: It's Going to Be a Bumpy Ride

Disruption is a fact of life, but some shocks are bigger than others, and they affect everyone differently. Those that made a big impression on me in some way include the first Gulf War, 9/11, the 2008 financial crisis, and, of course, the COVID-19 pandemic. My work has also made me aware of numerous disasters, from industrial accidents like the *Exxon Valdez* and Deepwater Horizon oil spills to corporate scandals like Enron, Lehman Brothers, Teflon, and Volkswagen's Dieselgate. Often disruption is a local affair, such as when I was on a world lecture tour in 2010 and was left stranded in Mexico following the unexpected bankruptcy of the national airline, Mexicana. But some crises have also acquired global status, while others may start in one place and ripple through our interconnected world to make themselves felt near and far.

When it comes to global crises, sadly we are spoiled for choice. We have all lived through the catastrophic impact of the COVID-19 pandemic, which infected around 192 million people and caused more than 4 million deaths by the middle of 2021.[29] By comparison, the 1918 Spanish flu infected 500 million people and killed 50 million; the 2002–2004 SARS outbreak infected around 8,100 people in China and Hong Kong, with 774 fatalities; and the 2012–2015 Ebola outbreak in West Africa killed around 11,300 people.

Disruption in Focus

Besides pandemics, natural disasters wreak havoc with our lives. In 2020 wildfires, storms, floods, and earthquakes claimed some 8,200 lives, with global losses of $210 billion, of which only $82 billion (60 percent) was insured.[30] In 2020 California recorded a total of 9,600 wildfires in the state, with 10,500 structures damaged or destroyed. And in Oregon about 4,000 homes were damaged or destroyed by wildfires. In the previous year Australia's wildfires burned 18 million hectares, destroying more than 5,900 buildings, including 2,800-plus homes. A billion animals, not including many more bats and insects, were estimated to have died during the fire and afterward as a result of lost habitat and food sources.

Disruption is one of the six forces of fragmentation or breakdown in society because it undermines the integrity of our global socioeconomic and ecological system. These shocks to the system—in the form of not only natural disasters and health pandemics but also political conflicts, market crises, and industrial accidents—threaten the stability of our institutions and the overall functioning of our societies. The good news is that, compared with major catastrophes of the past, fewer people are dying from disruption. In fact, in the past 100 years, the number of deaths from natural disasters has more than halved.[31]

But crises can still turn our lives upside down. The 2008–2012 global financial crisis showed us how market failure can be hugely disruptive. According to Better Markets, the United States alone lost more than $24 trillion in economic value, while 46.2 million people were pushed into poverty and more than 30 million people into unemployment. The COVID-related global recession of 2020–2021 has in many ways been worse. Similarly, for industrial accidents, the disruption can be catastrophic. The 2010 Deepwater Horizon explosion and related oil spill caused BP to lose 50 percent of its market value in 50 days and has, to date, cost the company $65 billion.

Unfortunately, disruptions like climate change will get worse before they get better. One industry that knows this all too well is the insurance industry. And it seems that rising climate risks—such as more frequent and intense storms, floods, droughts, and fires—are becoming uninsurable. What does that mean? It means that if insurance companies tried to cover all these risks (for businesses, citizens, or cities), they would go bankrupt.

This is the reality we face. And yet, despite being in the middle of a climate emergency, (almost) no one is panicking. Why? This is human nature. I remember being at the gym when a fire alarm went off. No one panicked. No one even moved. Each individual assessed the situation. Can I see fire, smell smoke, see others taking action? No. Am I being told to leave? No. Is it inconvenient? Yes. Eventually we were evacuated, and it turned out to be a false alarm. It's the same with climate change. Many still hope it's a false alarm. It isn't. But until we personally see or feel the danger, we tend not to panic or change our behavior.

Chaos Points and Decision Windows

When I deliver lectures or programs, I often introduce the key concept of *decision windows*. In complex living systems, big disturbances lead to either breakdown or breakthrough. In social systems, there is always a decision window when our actions make a big difference in determining the outcome. This is one of the findings of chaos theory, the so-called butterfly effect, which was inadvertently discovered in the 1960s by the meteorologist Edward Lorenz.

After building a simple weather forecasting model with three coupled nonlinear equations, he found that the final outcomes were highly sensitive to initial conditions. Tiny variations at the start would produce vastly different weather patterns at the end. Despite the complex mathematics that have developed as a result of his experiment, chaos theory has been distilled into a simple meme: the metaphor of a butterfly flapping its wings and causing a hurricane on the other side of the world.

That's why decision windows matter—and they do not last forever. Eventually, a disturbed system will reach what system scientist Ervin László calls a *chaos point*, when nothing we do will affect the outcome anymore.[32] Why is that? I know it sounds very fatalistic, but this is a science-based conclusion. It is what happens with reinforcing feedback loops, which turn into vicious cycles of exponential growth.

To illustrate the effect, consider the melting of permafrost, which is frozen soil in northern countries. As the global temperature goes up and the permafrost melts, vegetation trapped in the soil begins to decay and emits methane, a powerful greenhouse gas, which in turn results in more global warming. This is why we need to act now, because many of the decision windows are closing.

The Parable of the Woman with a Leaky Bucket

It's time to take a deep breath, relax, and reflect a little. Let me tell you a story. Every day a woman fetches water from a river in two buckets, each suspended on the end of a wooden pole across her shoulders. One day, she overhears the buckets talking. "I'm old and leaky," says one. "I fear I will be replaced."

So the woman asks the rickety bucket, "What do you see on our daily journey?"

continued →

"When I'm empty on the way there," the bucket replies, "I see only barren ground."

"And on the way back, when you're full?" she asks.

"Then I see beautiful wildflowers."

She nods and smiles: "Your leaking drops of water made that beauty possible."

The moral of the story is that even when things seem bad, when everything is going wrong, some good can still come of it.

All this talk of breakdown and closing decision windows can be rather dispiriting. Fear not: Even though we face multiple forces of breakdown, we can still take something positive from our global situation. In fact, they may be just what we need to kickstart our revolution toward thriving.

The Six Shifts

The six forces of breakdown are, in fact, triggers for transformation, leading directly to the six counterforces of breakthrough—restoration, renewal, responsibility, revitalization, rewiring, and resilience. These are summarized as six shifts in Figure 2.1 and form the heart of the book. We will be looking at the progress and innovations happening in each transformation area, before reflecting on how thriving can be integrated into organizations and what kind of leadership is required to make the changes happen.

The six shifts are how we put systems thinking into practice. They are the way that we divert the breakdown of complex living systems onto pathways for thriving. But we do not embark on this journey empty-handed. We bring a wealth of experience in turning crises of breakdown into opportunities for breakthrough, not least because that has been the story of the past two years. COVID-19 has affected all our lives in one way or another. Collectively, the world has been through the fire and, like tempered steel, emerged stronger as a result.

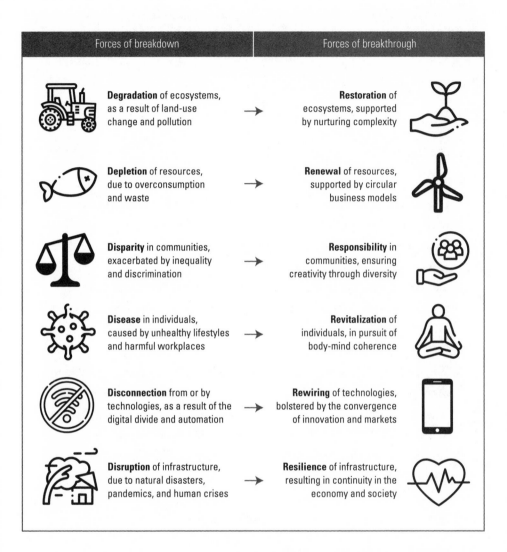

Forces of breakdown	Forces of breakthrough
Degradation of ecosystems, as a result of land-use change and pollution →	**Restoration** of ecosystems, supported by nurturing complexity
Depletion of resources, due to overconsumption and waste →	**Renewal** of resources, supported by circular business models
Disparity in communities, exacerbated by inequality and discrimination →	**Responsibility** in communities, ensuring creativity through diversity
Disease in individuals, caused by unhealthy lifestyles and harmful workplaces →	**Revitalization** of individuals, in pursuit of body-mind coherence
Disconnection from or by technologies, as a result of the digital divide and automation →	**Rewiring** of technologies, bolstered by the convergence of innovation and markets
Disruption of infrastructure, due to natural disasters, pandemics, and human crises →	**Resilience** of infrastructure, resulting in continuity in the economy and society

Figure 2.1: *The six shifts from breakdown to breakthrough*

As the saying goes: We should never let a good crisis go to waste. This ubiquitous proverb—variously ascribed to Winston Churchill, Rahm Emanuel, and others—could never be more apt than today. So before we dive into the refreshing waters of regenerative solutions, let us pause and ask ourselves: What can we learn from the global pandemic? Are there lessons in systems thinking that we can take with us into our exploration of the transformation pathways? I have identified 10 COVID-19 lessons, although I'm sure you can think of more.

Lessons in Systems Thinking from COVID-19

LESSON 1: DON'T PANIC!

These are the words on the cover of Douglas Adams's sci-fi book *The Hitchhiker's Guide to the Galaxy*. It's advice we should all heed when a crisis wreaks havoc with our lives. Put another way: Keep Calm and Carry On. That meme comes from a 1939 British government poster during the lead-up to World War II. During any crisis, we are fighting an emotional war, and the ensuing weeks and months require level heads but also open hearts. Panic inevitably leads to bad choices. So whatever the crisis, let's not panic.

LESSON 2: GET LOCAL

When the world *out there* seems to be swirling out of control, it helps to zone in on your own world *right here*. How is your home, your family, your garden? How are your friends? Notice the simple things: the spring flowers or the fall leaves, the reliable postman or the chatty shopkeeper, the tail-wagging dog or the curled-up cat. When you focus on what's right in front of you or immediately around you, you gain perspective. It becomes clearer what needs doing. You take back power. Anxiety goes down. You are grateful for simple pleasures and small blessings.

LESSON 3: LISTEN TO THE SCIENCE

COVID-19 made it more important than ever to ask for evidence, to follow the data. But we must also be wary of how science is being used by politicians and corporations. We saw vastly different political strategies to tackle COVID-19—all claiming to be following expert scientific advice. This is nothing new. When Rachel Carson built her scientific case against the harmful use of herbicides and pesticides in agriculture, eloquently captured in her book *Silent Spring*, the agrochemical industry wheeled out their scientific counterexperts.[33] Big Tobacco and Big Oil have done the same. So, yes, in a crisis, we should support science-based decisions but also remain vigilant about vested interests.

LESSON 4: PIVOT TO LIVE IT

As the pandemic started to turn our lives upside down, adaptation became the new mantra. Pivoting means rapidly changing tactics, heading in a different direction, or adopting new strategies—and it goes as much for individuals and companies as for governments and social movements. Typically, Millennials and Gen Z are more adept at such swift adaptation, as we saw with the Fridays for the Future climate protests that pivoted to #DigitalStrike and #ClimateStrikeOnline, urged on by their über-resilient leader Greta Thunberg. In Asia, they began rapidly redirecting their energies to filing lawsuits. Whatever the crisis, adaptation is the key to survival.

LESSON 5: MAKE MORAL CHOICES

The pandemic called for moral duty to triumph over political expedience or commercial interests. In 1807 when the British Parliament abolished slavery throughout its empire, it was a decision based on morality, not economic benefits or national populism. We faced a similar watershed moment with COVID-19, and we continue to face moral choices with the climate emergency and other crises. Will our politicians put the health of their citizens and the planet ahead of economic risks and political gains? Will our business leaders prioritize employee welfare and ecological integrity over profits? Will our scientists and professionals embrace open collaboration across boundaries? Will each of us make personal sacrifices for the common good? Morality is always a choice. We need to choose what's right.

LESSON 6: IMAGINE MULTIPLE FUTURES

How will the COVID-19 pandemic play out—or the next global shock, for that matter? For a long time, we couldn't be sure. Crises are extremely complex, and the situation can change day by day. That's perfect territory for scenarios. I was reminded of this by scenario strategist and coauthor of my first book, Clem Sunter. During the first months of the pandemic, he sent me his scenarios for the epidemic: Much Ado About Nothing (everyone is overreacting); the Camel's Straw (triggers a global recession); Spain Again (a repeat of the Spanish flu pandemic of 1918); and Tightrope (the delicate balancing act between preserving lives and livelihoods). Scenarios, unlike forecasts, allow us to imagine, simulate, and prepare for different outcomes, adjusting as the future unfolds.

LESSON 7: UNDERSTAND EXPONENTIAL GROWTH

COVID-19 is finally teaching us the nature of exponential growth. It's a painful lesson but a necessary one. In essence, it's about how exponential change—such as the number of new COVID-19 cases or deaths from the pandemic—seems slow at first and then accelerates. The ecological impacts of economic growth over the past 50 years have the same devastating viral curves. Viewed from the earth's perspective, humans are the out-of-control virus. Exponential growth in a finite system is unsustainable. Period. But remember: Solutions—for the pandemic and the sustainability crisis—can also spread virally.

LESSON 8: WATCH FOR TIPPING POINTS

The COVID-19 crisis started to push us toward several positive tipping points. One is the reclamation of space in cities for pedestrians and cyclists. Many cities in Europe, from Milan to Brussels, used the pandemic to accelerate plans to get more cars off the roads, while New York began phasing in 100 miles of car-free streets. Delivery robots and drones are another trend that will likely advance much more quickly because of the virus. And virtual meetings, conferences, and classrooms have been pressure tested as never before, forcing technology improvements and behavior changes that nudge us toward more climate-wise choices, postpandemic.

LESSON 9: KNOW THAT EXTREME CHANGE IS POSSIBLE

Humans are nothing if not adaptable. In fact, sociocultural adaptation is probably our evolutionary edge as a species. During COVID-19 we saw adaptation in action every day: individuals and families adapting to lockdown with modified social behavior; companies and industries adapting to shuttered workplaces and disrupted value chains with creativity and solidarity, including many reinventing their production lines to provide vital health-care goods; and governments adapting with herculean efforts to support health services and launch economic rescue packages. Postpandemic, we emerge with the powerful new knowledge that extreme adaptation is possible.

LESSON 10: TRANSFORMATION IS ALWAYS MULTILEVEL

The COVID-19 pandemic taught us what transformation looks like during a crisis. Here are six signposts, which you will spot throughout this book: (1) Be resilient—do what it takes to survive; pivot, adapt, bounce back. (2) Be inclusive—help the most vulnerable; volunteer, donate, pool resources. (3) Be frugal—find ways to do more with less; reuse, recycle, go circular. (4) Be connected—use technology to increase communication; work remotely, check in, share solutions. (5) Be healthy—put people's well-being first; exercise, destress, allow recovery. (6) Be systemic—remember the bigger picture; embrace complexity, tackle root causes, invest for the long term.

Moving through the Tangled Maze

With these 10 lessons in systems thinking safely stashed in our backpacks, along with the six keys to thriving that we picked up in the last chapter, we are ready to begin our climb from the dark valleys of breakdown to the heady heights of thriving. Let's think of them as our vital kit of water bottles, energy bars, warm clothes, fire starters, and first-aid essentials. They will not flatten the steep slopes that lie ahead or relieve us of the considerable effort of our great ascent, but they will ensure that we are ready to take on the elements, that our strenuous hike will be more doable, and that the summit will seem less distant. Knowing that we are all in this together, connected and determined to succeed, we are ready to embrace the complexity of what lies ahead.

COMPLEXITY

We're moving through the tangled maze
Connecting and reflecting
We're weaving on our loom of days
Creating and remaking

The map is never true or clear
The path is never straight
And yet a pattern will appear
For we who watch and wait

We're surfing on the waves of change
Trusting and adjusting
We're dancing through the halls of strange
Twirling and unfurling

The music beat can always shift
The tides will ebb and flow
And yet a movement will emerge
To take us where we need to go.

SECTION II

REGENERATING NATURE

Today we are faced with a challenge that calls for a shift in our thinking, so that humanity stops threatening its life-support system. We are called to assist the Earth to heal her wounds and, in the process, heal our own—indeed to embrace the whole of creation in all its diversity, beauty and wonder.

—**Wangari Maathai,** Nobel Lecture, 2004

The first shift to thriving leads to the restoration of ecosystems. We've already touched on how the complex web of life, made up of myriad organisms living in community, has been degraded by humans changing the land and oceans. These ecosystems are incredibly resilient, but they are not immune to collapse. Fortunately, they bounce back with remarkable vigor when we give nature space and time to thrive. In Chapter 3, we see how this is starting to happen as more and more governments, businesses, and nonprofit organizations embrace the ecoservices economy, which values nature's services such as water purification, food pollination, and climate regulation.

For the second shift to thriving, instead of extracting precious materials from the earth, we choose the renewal of resources. Our strategy for reversing the great acceleration of economic growth and its concomitant spike in consumption is to redesign our economy to mimic nature, where everything moves in cycles. Hence, one organism's waste is another's food; energy is transferred but never lost. In Chapter 4, we look at how the linear economy of take-make-use-lose is being transformed into a circular economy of borrow-make-use-return, in which materials are seen as nutrients for nature and production.

CHAPTER 3

Restoration

We forget, in a world completely transformed by man, that what we're looking at is not necessarily the environment wildlife prefer, but the depleted remnant that wildlife is having to cope with: what it has is not necessarily what it wants.

—**Isabella Tree**, *Wilding: The Return of Nature to a British Farm*

Where I Feel Most Alive

I often say that natural forests are my "soul place," by which I mean that they are the environment where I feel most alive. Over the past 30 years, I have been fortunate enough to visit many incredible forests around the world. You already read about my special experience with the Achuar people in the Amazon rain forest. I have also been mesmerized by hummingbirds in the cloud forests of the Andes and enchanted by the Mayan temples hidden in the forests of Tikal in Guatemala. I have looked back in time in the 130-million-year-old Taman Negara forest in Malaysia and had magical encounters with wild lemurs in the forests of Madagascar.

In Australia I have gazed down from the giddy heights of a 47-meter spiral tower in the tree canopy of the Otway forest, while in Sequoia National Park in California, in the United States, I have caressed the fibrous bark of giant redwoods. In Zimbabwe I have returned often to the misty forests of Victoria Falls, which is known locally as Mosi-oa-Tunya, meaning "the smoke that thunders." In South Africa I have wandered the trails of the Knysna forest, where a few shy elephants still eke out their clandestine lives, and in Kosovo I have hiked up to the beautiful Lake Leqinat in the alpine forests of the Accursed Mountains.

When I am in these forest ecosystems, it feels sacred. I am connecting to life at its most bountiful, in a place where there is still a complex dance of symbiosis: organisms practicing mutual reciprocity, benefiting one another and the living system that they help keep alive. In these wilderness zones, I wax lyrical about trees, seeing them as members of a sacred council, guardians of time, keepers of ancient wisdom, and the elders of our earthly tribe. I wonder what they would teach us if we had the humility to sit at their feet and listen. What secret knowledge about surviving and thriving and growing old gracefully? What patient lessons about thinking big, starting small, and aiming high?

I am recalling these excursions and sharing how I feel because it highlights what is at stake when we destroy ecosystems and, conversely, what priceless treasures we are saving when these vital habitats are protected and restored. When I went trekking in the Khao Yai forest in Thailand, which is a UNESCO World Heritage Site, within a few hours, I saw white-handed gibbons, elephants, great hornbills, macaque monkeys, black giant squirrels, monitor lizards, tree snakes, flying geckos, scorpions, and porcupines. The forest creates an enabling environment for life to flourish. This is why planting trees is not enough; we need to protect and expand forest ecosystems.

The same is true of all ecosystems. The earth is a living system made up of eight biomes—temperate forests, tropical rain forests, deserts, grasslands, the taiga (also known as the boreal forests of the north), the tundra, the chaparral (or Mediterranean forests), and the ocean. Each is a self-regulating natural system that maintains a dynamic balance and creates the conditions necessary for life in that ecosystem. As such, they demonstrate all the keys to thriving: They are complex, circular, creative, coherent, converging, and continuous. They are not "nice to have"; they are vital for our survival on this blue-green orb we call earth. It follows naturally that we must value our ecosystems.

Valuing Nature's Services

In order to turn degradation around, we need to understand that nature is not just a larder of resources to plunder for our economies; it also provides vital *ecosystem services*, which are all the ways in which nature contributes to human well-being.[1] In 1997 ecological economist Robert Costanza led the first attempt to value these services of nature and concluded that the economic contribution is in the range of $16–54 trillion per year, with an average of $33 trillion per year. And because of the nature of the uncertainties, this was considered a *minimum* estimate.[2] A 2014 update by Costanza and his colleagues, with more and better data, estimated total global ecosystem services in 2011 at $125–145 trillion per year. They also estimated the loss of ecoservices from 1997 to 2011 due to land-use change at $4.3–20.2 trillion per year.[3] The precise number is less important than the general message, which is that ecoservices contribute more than twice as much to human well-being as the measured global economy.

Key Concept: The Ecoservices Economy

The counterforce to degradation is creating restoration through the ecoservices economy and allowing biodiversity to flourish. The ecoservices economy is about finding solutions that help us to ensure services such as pollination, climate regulation, and

continued →

water purification, while adopting practices such as conservation, reforestation, rewilding, and regenerative agriculture to reverse the damage done to nature by unsustainable economic activities.

There are at least four types of ecosystem services:

1. *Provisioning services*, including food, timber, fiber, or other provisioning benefits.

2. *Regulating services*, including flood control, storm protection, water regulation, human-disease regulation, water purification, air-quality maintenance, pollination, pest control, and climate control.

3. *Cultural resources*, including recreation, aesthetics, scientific resources, cultural identity, a sense of place, and other cultural benefits.

4. *Supportive processes*, including basic ecosystem processes such as soil formation, primary productivity, biogeochemistry, nutrient cycling, and provisioning of habitat.[4]

The ecoservices economy includes any goods and services that protect, preserve, and, most importantly, enhance the ecosystems on which society and the economy depend, thereby restoring habitats that allow biodiversity to flourish. In the past 10 years, this fledgling economy has got off to a rather feeble start. When in 2020 the UN's *Global Biodiversity Outlook 5* reviewed the 20 biodiversity goals set by the world in 2010 in Aichi, Japan, not a single goal had been met, and only six were partially met.[5] Lamentably, instead of investing in ecosystem services as a way to "build back better," we have seen $151 billion in bailouts for the fossil-fuel industry during the COVID-19 pandemic.

Over half of global gross domestic product, or GDP (a measure of economic activity, including all goods and services produced and traded)—$44 trillion—is threatened by nature loss. Three sectors account for 80 percent of threatened or near-threatened species: food, land, and ocean use (72 percent); infrastructure and the built environment (29 percent); and energy and extractives (18 percent). These are the findings of the "Future of Nature and Business" report by the World Economic Forum. It also notes that 15 transitions in these three socioeconomic systems could deliver $10.1 trillion of annual business opportunities and 395 million jobs by 2030. Among these opportunities are making $2.7 trillion in green investments, giving a 370 percent return; retrofitting cities for eco-efficiency (with $825 billion in benefits); and better management of wild fish (a $172 billion opportunity).[6]

There are major economic beneficiaries for all ecosystem services, especially in the areas of food and health. Humans consume 7,000 plant species as food and use almost 20 percent of plant species for their health benefits. Whether it's aloe vera from Mexico, chamomile from Croatia, or murumuru from Brazil, nature is big business. A report called "The Big Shift," from the Union for Ethical BioTrade, distills lessons from 50 major players in the cosmetics, health, and food industries, such as Natura and Weleda. They conclude that biodiversity is core to these multinationals' business success, that it is inherently linked to people, and that it needs engagement and partnership to be sustainable. They all agree: Biodiversity regeneration is the next crucial step.[7]

The Battle to Save Nature

Despite these opportunities, so far we are losing the fight for biodiversity protection and restoration—but at least we are shaping a global plan. Some of these ideas have filtered through into the UN's Post-2020 Global Biodiversity Framework. The final text was still being negotiated at the time of writing, but the aspirations are good. These include, for example, no net loss of ecosystems by 2030 and increases of at least 20 percent by 2050;

cutting pollution by 50 percent; and protecting biodiverse areas, covering 30 percent of land and sea areas, by 2030. We currently protect around 15 percent. We need to get behind this initiative. All life on earth depends on it.

The idea of protecting places of outstanding natural beauty is not new. The conservationist John Muir was one of America's most eloquent and successful advocates for the preservation of wilderness areas, such as Yosemite and Sequoia National Parks, both established in 1890. We should treasure not only these wild spaces but also the wisdom that Muir gleaned from spending so much time in nature. He understood nature's therapeutic power, reflecting that "going out . . . was really going in."[8]

Today, the United States has 63 national parks covering an area of 211,000 square kilometers. But that is by no means the record holder. Australia has the greatest number of national parks (685), followed by Thailand (147) and India (116), while Canada, Australia, and Brazil top the tables for the most land under conservation. The countries with the highest percentage of their land protected are Zambia (32 percent), Israel (30 percent), and Costa Rica (25 percent).

In terms of area, the Northeast Greenland National Park protects 972,000 square kilometers, which would make it the 31st-largest country in the world if it were a nation state. The Kavango-Zambezi Transfrontier Conservation Area, incorporating parts of Zambia, Botswana, Namibia, Zimbabwe, and Angola, comes in second and is 16 times larger than Belgium. It is followed by the Great Limpopo Transfrontier Park, joining South Africa, Mozambique, and Zimbabwe.

But, of course, biodiversity is not evenly spread across the world. Whenever I am back in Cape Town, I go walking on Table Mountain, which has 2,200 species of flowering plants. Compare this to the UK, where I now live, which has 1,500 species in total. Some locations are richly endowed by nature, and some are not. And some governments have protected nature better than others.

Today, you will not be surprised to know that the most biodiverse country in the world is Brazil, with the most plant and amphibian species, second most mammals, and third most birds, reptiles, and fish. Columbia,

Indonesia, China, and Mexico also make the top five. These are among the 17 megadiverse countries that have at least 5,000 species of endemic plants and border marine ecosystems. On the other hand, measured in terms of species per unit of area, smaller countries rise to the top, including Brunei, Gambia, Belize, Jamaica, and El Salvador.

Protecting biodiversity in the oceans is just as important. The world's largest marine reserve is Hawaii's Papahānaumokuākea Marine National Monument, which covers an area of 1.51 million square kilometers. Other major ocean reserves include the Phoenix Islands Protected Area surrounding the Republic of Kiribati (408,250 square kilometers), the Great Barrier Reef Marine Park off the coast of Australia (344,400 square kilometers), and Galapagos Marine Reserve of Ecuador (133,000 square kilometers). At present, there are more than 17,000 marine protected areas, but these account for less than 7 percent of the ocean, and in many of these reserves, fishing is still permitted.

Hot Trend: 30 by 30 Conservation Goal

Protecting 30 percent of land and national waters by 2030 is a target being set by major international environmental organizations. A McKinsey report called "Valuing Nature Conservation" quantifies the costs, benefits, and best potential locations for achieving this ambitious goal. The authors conclude that it could cost $20–40 billion a year, but the economic benefits from ecotourism and sustainable fishing alone could be at least three times greater while creating 30 million new jobs. Other benefits include cutting CO_2 by 0.9–2.6 gigatons annually, increasing GDP by $300–500 billion, and lowering the risk of new zoonotic diseases (like COVID-19) by up to 80 percent.[9]

It seems we have done something good, but not enough. And I worry that these nature reserves have lulled us into a false sense of security. After all, we need to be bringing nature back into our cities and onto our farms rather than designating a few "green lungs" or "blue zones" as our escapes from the concrete jungle. On the other hand, having been fortunate enough to experience vast areas of wilderness where all of life can flourish—such as the Ecuadorian Amazon rain forest, Kruger National Park in South Africa, and the Galapagos Marine Reserve—I am convinced that nature reserves are essential. To give other species a chance to survive and thrive, we desperately need these sanctuaries for life, protected from humans.

Where the Wild Things Are

The answer to the question "How can we stop 1 million species from going extinct?" is *space*. One species (*Homo sapiens*) has crowded out 8.7 million species. We have to create more space for nature. To make this possible, we will need to set science-based targets for biodiversity. The plant-based food and drinks company Alpro is pioneering this approach, working with the International Union for Conservation of Nature and WWF to set 50 percent natural vegetation as a planetary boundary and a global goal. As mentioned in Chapter 2, planetary boundaries are quantitative thresholds beyond which the risk of ecosystem breakdown increases dramatically.

We know that nature is on the ropes, bruised and battered by dumb agriculture and dumber economics. But another thing we know is that, given half a chance, nature bounces back. Ecosystems are resilient and designed to flourish. The most powerful and effective action we can take is to step back and give nature space and time to recover. We saw this during the COVID-19 lockdown. Nature made a comeback. NASA released satellite images showing nitrogen dioxide pollution over China all but disappearing, while fish were spotted in the clear waters of Venice's canals, and moose and deer were seen roaming towns.

We have seen similar instances of nature regenerating in the wake of industrial disasters, such as the nuclear reactor meltdown in Chernobyl in 1986. But health crises, global recessions, and catastrophic accidents are not a sustainable solution to ecological decline. We don't need (or want) a repeat of pandemic lockdowns, stalled travel and tourism, or poisoned zones where human habitation is no longer deemed safe. Rather, we want to take smart actions to give nature the time and space it needs to recover.

Consider, for example, a case from Mongolia. In the 1950s China constructed a railway—along with a fence—across the Gobi Desert. The Mongolian gazelles and wild asses called khulan soon disappeared, their natural range cut off. Now, 65 years later, the Wildlife Conservation Society removed a short 2,300-foot section of fencing. And surprise, surprise, the gazelles and khulan are back. Take down more fences, and wildlife will return. This is an example of restoring wildlife corridors. It's something that the Nature Recovery Network is trying to do in England, by finding ways to add 500,000 hectares of new wildlife-rich habitat that will link together existing areas of nature.

Rewilding is another exciting new approach. The basic idea is to protect an area from overcropping, overgrazing, overplanting, and overfishing, thus allowing nature to return in abundance. At one end of the spectrum, rewilding is a hands-off approach to managing land; at the other end, it includes the reintroduction of species such as bison, wild pigs, or top predators, such as wolves.

Case Spotlight: Rewilding in Yellowstone

The reintroduction of wolves into Yellowstone National Park in 1995 has become a rewilding classic. The story is artfully told by George Monbiot in his book *Feral*, as well as in a TED Talk he delivered called "For More Wonder, Rewild the World." Monbiot describes how, to the park management's surprise, the wolves changed the whole ecosystem. By creating what are called *trophic cascades*, they recovered the biodiversity that had been lost. It began with the deer. Since they were now potential prey, the deer moved more frequently and avoided valleys, gorges, and river edges where they might get trapped. As a

continued →

result, the trees had a chance to grow, which in turn attracted birds and beavers. The beaver dams created habitats for otters, muskrats, ducks, fish, reptiles, and amphibians. The rivers even changed shape, as erosion decreased. The wolves also hunted coyotes, which led to the recovery of rabbit and mice populations. The rabbits and mice, in turn, attracted hawks, weasels, foxes, and badgers. The carrion left by the wolves provided food for ravens, bald eagles, and even bears, which were also attracted by more berries on the regenerated trees. An entire ecosystem was brought back to life through rewilding.[10]

Beavers, like the wolves, are known as a *keystone species*, since they have such a catalytic effect on the ecosystem. In Europe the reintroduction of beavers is showing that nature is infinitely better at managing itself than humans are. Beaver dams—and the changing river habitats they create—increase flood control, purify agriculturally polluted water, raise water levels, and create highly effective nitrogen and carbon sinks. The biodiversity dividends are also substantial, since beaver ponds increase plant, bird, and wildlife variety; improve water quality; and raise salmon and trout populations. This one species supports thousands of species.[11] In Europe reintroductions have boosted beaver numbers from 1,200 in 1900 to more than a million today.[12] Rewilding is a win-win solution.

Rewilding is one approach to restoring nature, but it is not the only approach. Another is illustrated by an inspiring project in Africa called the Great Green Wall, launched in 2007. The vision is to grow a greenbelt of trees 15 kilometers wide, stretching 8,000 kilometers across the continent and spanning more than 20 countries, from Senegal in the west to Djibouti in the east. The Great Green Wall is regenerating life in every way: creating jobs, reversing desertification, increasing biodiversity, healing soils, and making the Sahel region fertile again. Finally, here's a wall we can all celebrate and support!

Companies are realizing that regeneration of nature provides a relatively inexpensive natural climate solution. Hence, we see Apple partnering with Conservation International to protect and restore the 27,000-acre mangrove forest in Cispatá Bay, Colombia, which is expected to sequester 1 million metric tons of CO_2 over its lifetime. We see Unilever creating a $1 billion Climate and Nature Fund to support landscape restoration, reforestation, carbon sequestration, wildlife protection, and water preservation.

Hard as it may be for some to believe, even Walmart is committing to become a regenerative company—"one that works to restore, renew and replenish in addition to preserving our planet; and encourages others to do the same."[13] At a much smaller scale, Scottish craft beer company BrewDog, which already runs on wind power and gas made from malted barley, now plans to restore 1,500 acres of native forest (replacing livestock grazing land) and 550 acres of peat lands to reach carbon neutrality.

The Trillion-Tree Challenge

Did you know that some trees practice social distancing? And they do it for more or less the same reason that we do. Margaret Lowman, a forest-canopy specialist, theorizes that these gaps between treetop foliage—called *crown shyness*—are a way to prevent insect "pests" and diseases from spreading. It's a tree version of self-isolation. The social distancing also minimizes storm damage from the branches of adjacent trees knocking or falling against one another. Dendrologists have observed the phenomenon in forests around the world: in lodgepole pines in British Columbia, Australian eucalyptus, Malaysia's Borneo camphor, Sitka spruce, and Japanese larch.

The more we learn, the more we realize how incredible trees are. Some even have superpowers. In South America, Brazil nut trees grow 14 stories high and are the Amazon's rainmakers, each pumping 3.5 bathtubs of water into the atmosphere every day. In Asia, Indonesia's 7.1 million acres of stilt mangrove trees, covering an area the size of Belgium, can store 5 to 10 times as much carbon per acre as a rain forest. And in Africa, the Congo's

Afrormosia teak trees have fire-resistant bark and support an entire ecosystem of plants and animals. This trio of arboreal superheroes is doing its best to save the earth. But we need a lot more like them to regenerate our forests.

Wales is taking a lead by growing a forest that will span the length and breadth of the country, joining existing protected woodlands with large-scale tree-planting projects. The endeavor forms part of the country's low-carbon delivery plan and is aiming to plant 10,000 acres per year. Forests are a one-stop shop of ecological, social, and economic benefits. They simultaneously tackle climate change, create biodiversity habitats, provide recreational space, protect water sources, purify the air, and prevent soil erosion. Between 1990 and 2015, the top planted forest growers were China (79 billion hectares), the United States (26 billion hectares), and Russia (20 billion hectares).

This is a great start, but we will need much more ambition across the world to restore our forests. Pakistan is proving that you don't have to be a rich, developed country to show leadership. In the midst of the COVID-19 crisis, the country demonstrated a new triple bottom line: responsibility, resilience, and regeneration. Day laborers who had become unemployed during the pandemic were given the option to become "jungle workers," planting saplings as part of the country's 10 Billion Tree Tsunami program. Although 500 rupees ($3) per day for planting trees is only half of a typical precrisis wage, it is nevertheless an act of responsibility to give people a financial lifeline and the dignity of a job. It is also helping the society and the economy to be more resilient, while regenerating the ecosystem.

When we hear numbers like these—a million, a billion, or a trillion—we struggle to get our heads around what it means. So here's a quick thought experiment: Imagine standing under your favorite tree, surrounded by nine trees. Can you visualize what that might look like? Now if you have 10 clusters of trees like this, it would create a small woodland of a hundred trees. Join together 10 small woodlands, and you have a small forest of a thousand trees. A thousand small forests mean a really big forest with 1 million trees. Now imagine a million big forests. That's a trillion trees: 1,000,000,000,000, one-sixth of the trees that used to cover the earth. Imagine all those trees absorbing carbon and creating habitats for biodiversity to flourish. That's the vision of 1t.org, a platform launched at the World Economic Forum in Davos in 2020 for planting a trillion new trees by 2030. It is a powerful movement that anyone can and should join.

Key Concept: Natural Climate Solutions

Planting trees—or better still, restoring forests—is a natural climate solution. As George Monbiot put it in the video he copresented with climate activist Greta Thunberg, "There is a magic machine that sucks carbon out of the air, costs very little and builds itself. It's called a tree. A tree is an example of a natural climate solution. Mangroves, peat bogs, jungles, marshes, seabeds, kelp forests, swamps, coral reefs—they take carbon out of the air and lock it away. Nature is a tool we can use to repair our broken climate. These natural climate solutions could make a massive difference."[14] What's a massive difference? Well, consider that just the peat lands in the Congo Basin store the equivalent of three years of global fossil-fuel emissions.

Investment in natural climate solutions, such as restoring forests, drove a 264 percent increase in the volume of *offsets* generated through forestry and land-use activities between 2016 and 2018. An offset is where carbon emissions in one place are canceled out by carbon absorption or emission reductions in another place. This is really good news, since protecting and restoring forests, wetlands, mangroves, and other habitats that act as carbon sinks have multiple other benefits, such as biodiversity enhancement, erosion prevention, and flood protection. I hear lots of criticism of carbon offsetting, mostly because people don't like companies paying for offsets while continuing to pollute. But nature doesn't care where or how carbon is absorbed. We need both: less emissions and more sinks.

Rhapsody in Blue

Restoration of ecosystems needs to happen not just on the land but in the oceans. The recovery of whale populations is a great example of ocean rewilding. It's what happens when we give nature time and space to thrive. In this case, the 1986 moratorium on commercial whaling was key. In the Azores, for example, around 25 species of cetaceans (whales and dolphins) can now be spotted. Some whales remain on the endangered list, but there are positive signs. Humpback whales were hunted almost to extinction, with just a few hundred remaining in the 1950s. A recent study by the Royal Society estimates that there are now 25,000, which is 93 percent of their pre-exploitation population.[15] Japan's resumption of whaling since 2019 could reverse all these gains.

Restoring our oceans is good not only for whales and dolphins but also for the fish that supply the primary protein source for 3 billion people. It takes five times the effort to catch the same number of fish today as it did in 1950. That's what scarce supply means. One sustainable solution could be precision fishing. Similar to precision agriculture, this means using smart technologies, big data, and advanced analytics to target fish more precisely rather than scooping up unwanted species and destroying coastal ecosystems in the process. This could help address the devastating levels of by-catch that were highlighted in the *Seaspiracy* documentary on Netflix. McKinsey estimates precision fishing could cut the annual operating costs of fisheries by $11 billion, increase profits by $53 billion by 2050, and simultaneously double the total fish biomass.[16] These are high-tech solutions for high-stakes problems.

Another approach is aquaponics. No doubt you're familiar with aquaculture and probably hydroponics too. Aquaponics combines the best of both. Upward Farms recently raised $15 million for scaling its symbiotic agricultural model, in which the nitrogen-rich wastewater from fish tanks is used to fertilize leafy greens. This is a way to mimic what nature does, turning waste from one process into food for another. The jury is still out on whether this can be scaled in a sustainable way. Any intensive agriculture creates unintended and often unwanted impacts. But there are definitely community and environmental benefits from local circular-economy-inspired food production.

Innovation will be essential if we are to protect and restore our oceans. An invitation to speak at the Ocean Race Summit in Genoa gave me a great opportunity to talk about corals. Around 500 million people earn their livelihoods from the fishing and tourism opportunities that coral reefs provide. Coral reefs account for less than 1 percent of the ocean and yet manage to provide food and shelter to more than one-quarter of all marine species in the ocean. But scientists predict that, over the next 20 years, 70 to 90 percent of all coral reefs will disappear because of warming ocean waters, ocean acidity, dragnet fishing, indiscriminate tourism, and pollution.[17] Since 1995 the Great Barrier Reef has already lost half of its corals through a process called bleaching, where the coral polyps die. However, a newly discovered coral fragmentation method reduces coral reef regeneration time from 75 years to just 3.

Key Concept: Blue Carbon

To avoid catastrophic climate change, *blue carbon* in the oceans will be key. Since 1955 the oceans have absorbed more than 90 percent of the excess heat trapped by greenhouse gases and up to half of the excess carbon. Their inherent capacity as a carbon sink is reaching its limits, but the oceans also hold our best hope. Ocean biomes such as kelp (seaweed), seagrass, mangroves, and corals can fix carbon quicker and in greater volumes than terrestrial sinks such as forests. We need nothing short of a blue carbon revolution.

Scientists in Wales are pioneering seagrass restoration as a natural climate solution. Seagrass covers just 0.2 percent of the ocean but provides 10 percent of its carbon storage. This remarkable plant stores carbon at

35 times the rate of tropical rain forests and creates habitats for 40 times as much marine life as seabeds without grass. But pollution and shipping are destroying seagrass at an alarming rate. (The UK has already lost 90 percent.) Now in Dale Bay, in Wales, the Seagrass Ocean Rescue project is placing miles of rope with little burlap bags and a million seagrass seeds on the seabed. Regeneration is happening.

There is another solution that can capture and store carbon cheaply and naturally for 1,000 years: kelp farming. Coastal ecosystems typically absorb up to 20 times more carbon per acre than land forests. Specifically, around 200 million tons of carbon dioxide are being sequestered by kelp and other forms of macroalgae every year. That's equivalent to the annual emissions of the state of New York. Aquaculture company Running Tide plans to add to nature's efforts and turn kelp cultivation into a scalable natural climate solution. By attaching these kelp forests to biodegradable buoys, in time they will sink to the bottom of the ocean.

We might also need to think of the ocean not only as a carbon sink or a source of fish but also as a zone of production. Today we have offshore platforms primarily for deep-sea oil and gas extraction and wind farms. In the near future we will most likely move to multipurpose offshore platforms that combine wind-, solar-, and wave-energy generation; aquaculture farming; hydrogen production; ship servicing; and even maritime tourism. Sustainable designs will be key to avoid simply transferring existing terrestrial impacts to the oceans.

The Secrets of Soil

Every year the social and environmental cost of mainstream agriculture in the United States is $85 billion. The decades-long drive for efficiency has optimized food output instead of food quality, soil health, carbon absorption, animal welfare, biodiversity protection, and smallholder farmer livelihoods. A major culprit has been the widespread application of chemical fertilizers since World War II.

In my Norfolk village in England, along the river, there's an old bone mill, which used to crush bones (including from humans) for agricultural fertilizer. The plant-growth benefits of bonemeal and nitrogen were discovered by German chemist Justus von Liebig. In 1841 British industrialist John Bennet Lawes turned this knowledge into the world's first artificial fertilizer factory at Rothamsted. Liebig tested organic and chemical concoctions on 24 strips of land and found that fields treated with chemical fertilizers retained 2 or 3 wild plant species, while untreated fields supported 50 species. So we knew from the start: Artificial fertilizer wipes out biodiversity.

Key Concept: Regenerative Agriculture

Regenerative agriculture is a way to farm in harmony with nature while reversing the negative impacts of the mainstream agricultural industry. One of the main goals of regenerative agriculture is restoring the living health of the soils. There are various techniques used—planting perennial crops and cover crops, using organic compost as natural fertilizer, increasing crop diversity and crop rotation, introducing animals on the land in ways that mimic nature, practicing minimum tilling, and turning agricultural waste into biochar that is reintroduced into the soil. If regenerative organic agriculture were applied to all farmland, we could lock away 15 billion tons of carbon, thereby reducing atmospheric carbon to preindustrial levels within 20 years.

Some still question whether regenerative farming is more sustainable than mainstream agriculture. For instance, several studies have suggested that lower yields from organic farming increase land use and therefore impact. However, this is a false conclusion for three reasons. First, organic farming takes more land precisely because it is less intensive and allows space for nature to flourish. Second, organic yields improve over time—and start off low because previous agro-industrial methods have stripped the soil of nutrients. Third, there is no shortage of arable land if we reduce meat consumption. (Beef production uses 60 percent of the land to supply 2 percent of the calories.)

As already mentioned, besides using organic fertilizers, a key technique of regenerative agriculture is crop and livestock rotation. When my grandparents were farming in Africa, this was standard practice. It was only when intensive agro-industrial farming took over that we began to ignore nature's need for diversity and regeneration. Now science is finding that not only is crop rotation environmentally and economically beneficial, but more is better. An experiment in Iowa, in the United States, with multiyear combinations among corn, soybean, oat, and alfalfa crops concluded that four-year rotations can reduce fossil energy by 60 percent and freshwater toxicity by 93 percent, while improving soil quality, increasing corn and soybean yields, and significantly improving overall economic returns.[18]

Another regenerative technique is to convert organic agricultural waste into biochar, which is easily created by heating agricultural waste in the absence of oxygen, a simple technique called pyrolysis. Years ago, James Lovelock, the originator of the Gaia theory, which hypothesizes that the earth behaves like a living organism, said that the only way to reach the required scale of carbon sequestration is to work with nature. His proposed solution was biochar.[19]

Biochar is a carbon sink that could, given the global scale of agriculture, sequester billions of tons of carbon. It also increases agricultural yields, decreases erosion and chemical pollution, and improves water retention by almost 40 percent. A company called Husk in Cambodia creates biochar from some of the 150 million tons of rice husks worldwide that are either burned or left to rot. By plowing nutrient-rich biochar into the soils of smallholder farmers, Husk has increased yields by 40 to 100 percent in a single year. And for every ton of biochar that they create, Husk sequesters 1.33 tons of carbon.

Many regenerative farming practices are ancient. For example, the disruption of supply chains during the COVID-19 pandemic is bringing back the thousand-year-old farming practice of floating gardens, called *chinampas*, in Mexico. These gardens were built by the Aztecs and are one of the most productive agricultural methods, with up to seven harvests per year. The farmers grow greens, herbs, flowers, fruits, corn, beans, and squash in the lake region of Xochimilco in the south of Mexico City. The land was largely abandoned after the devastating 1985 earthquake, but now it's making a comeback as a trusted local source of organic, healthy food with a cultural heritage.

Another example of ancient wisdom is the technique of fog catching, to reduce water use in agriculture. In recent years fog-catching nets in Peru, Bolivia, Colombia, Mexico, and elsewhere have been successful in harvesting 200–400 liters of freshwater every day. Yet in Pantelleria, an Italian island off the shores of Tunisia, their circular stone-walled gardens (*giardini panteschi*) have been capturing fog for hundreds (perhaps even thousands) of years. Just when we think we've invented something new, history reveals that humans have been smart and sustainable for a long time. It's almost as if we're living in an Age of Amnesia, in which we've thrown out centuries of collective wisdom in favor of quick-fix science and get-rich industry.

The Paradox of Modern Agriculture

There is a great paradox in modern agriculture. The agro-industrial sector is feeding people and starving the planet. In 1962 one farmer fed 25.8 persons; today it is 155. But our mechanistic, chemical-intensive methods are turning biologically rich soil into sterile dirt. As a result, nutrients in our foods have declined as much as 80 percent since 1940. You have to eat eight oranges today to get the same amount of vitamin A as our grandparents got from eating one. Moreover, if we change the approach to regenerative, organic, and biodynamic farming, agricultural land could absorb more than our annual carbon emissions each year. It's time to save our soil.

More often than not, intensive farming has wiped out nature-friendly, small-scale agriculture. This was the case in Sri Lanka. During British colonial occupation, rice cultivation and native jackfruit trees went into decline, replaced by lucrative export crops such as tea, rubber, and cinnamon. Then, in 1915, Arthur V. Dias, a fighter for Sri Lankan independence, realized that the country faced starvation if World War I dragged on, so he started a campaign to plant a million jackfruit trees. Jackfruit is the world's largest tree-borne fruit and known locally as the *bath gasa* ("rice tree"). Dias's regenerative foresight ensured food security during two world wars, a 26-year civil war, and, most recently, the COVID-19 lockdown.

That same level of foresight is now needed among the food giants. Only 10 companies—Nestlé, PepsiCo, Coca-Cola, Unilever, Danone, General Mills, Kellogg's, Mars, Associated British Foods, and Mondelez—control almost every large food and beverage brand in the world. What if these companies woke up to regenerative agriculture? The good news is that many of them are doing just that. Nestlé, Unilever, Danone, and Mars are among the 21 companies that have joined the World Business Council for Sustainable Development's One Planet Business for Biodiversity (OP2B) initiative, which is focused around scaling up regenerative agricultural practices, boosting cultivated biodiversity, eliminating deforestation, and restoring natural ecosystems.

More specifically, Nestlé will spend more than $1 billion to pay a premium to more than 500,000 farmers and 150,000 other ingredient suppliers who adopt or support regenerative farming practices that improve soil health and reduce dependence on synthetic fertilizer. Danone's support for regenerative agriculture focuses on protecting soil, empowering a new generation of farmers, and promoting animal welfare. In 2017 the company joined the "4 per 1000" initiative, which aims to increase the storage of carbon in the soil by 4 percent per year. In 2018, it made a commitment to contribute $6 million toward research on soil health. Unilever has also made commitments to regenerative agriculture, including the introduction of a Regenerative Agriculture Code for all their suppliers.

These giants are not the only ones waking up to regen-ag. Patagonia announced in 2020 that it is getting into food. Founder and CEO Yvon Chouinard, a self-confessed "doom-bat about humanity's prospects if we continue on the path we're on now," has concluded that selling more sustainable outdoor clothing and gear isn't going to be enough. Now Patagonia Provisions will champion regenerative organic agriculture to grow and sell "deeply flavorful, nutritious foods" that "build soil health, ensure animal welfare and protect agricultural workers." Patagonia's current offering includes not only fruit, vegetables, and grains from regenerative organic sources but also wild salmon, mackerel, mussels, and buffalo jerky. They want to provide "foods that are a key part of the solution instead of the problem," with a new triple bottom line: food, water, love.[20] Are you a fan yet?

Case Spotlight: Knepp Estate

Knepp Estate in the UK is showing that animal farming can also be regenerative. In her book *Wilding: The Return of Nature to a British Farm*, Isabella Tree tells the story of how she and her husband, Charlie Burrell, converted their 1,400-hectare farm from traditional livestock agriculture, which was losing money, into a thriving "wild farm," with free-roaming herbivores such as cattle, ponies, pigs, and deer. The result of rewilding the land is that biodiversity has gone up radically, attracting numerous rare species of birds, bats, and butterflies, while resource and carbon inputs have dropped massively, since there are no fertilizers or other chemicals and no high-energy feeding systems, farm machinery, or routine medication. What's more, the pasture-fed, wild-range meat is healthier.[21]

Despite these promising alternatives, we urgently need to look at what causes the biggest impacts in agriculture and how to lower them. For example, could insects be the key to reducing the ecological footprint of feeding our pets and livestock? Growing feed for meat production has huge impacts on carbon, water, pollution, and biodiversity. What if we substituted the crops we grow for livestock and the meat we produce for pets (which is 12 percent of total meat consumption) with insects? Dutch insect farmers Protix estimate that insect-based foods use 2 percent of the land and 4 percent of the water per kilogram of protein. Hargol FoodTech already makes livestock feed from grasshoppers, while the British Veterinary Association says insect-based foods are better for pets than prime steak.

The Power of Plants

Of course, the challenge is not just to feed pets and livestock. Can we feed 10 billion people and still meet the Paris Climate Agreement's net-zero carbon target in 2050? The World Resources Institute thinks we can, if we change how we eat, grow food, and protect and restore ecosystems. They map 22 actions in their "Creating a Sustainable Food Future" report, including extending food shelf life; keeping nitrogen in the soil; cultivating low-methane rice and cattle feed, high-yield oil palm, and algae-based fish food; and practicing massive reforestation. But the biggest positive impact, they conclude, will come from shifting to plant-based diets, which use 20 times less land and emit 20 times less carbon than meat.[22]

Plant-based company Impossible Foods shows, in a report called "Turn Back the Clock," that by removing the methane emissions associated with livestock and restoring the biomass lost to animal agriculture, we could achieve a net reduction in carbon emissions within 20 years, even if we did nothing to reduce carbon from other sources. Of course, this is a thought experiment—the meat industry will not suddenly disappear—but it does show how big a factor animal farming is in tackling climate change. A plant-based Impossible Burger uses 96 percent less land and 87 percent less water, and it generates 89 percent less CO_2 emissions than a burger made from beef.[23]

As a result of these resource and climate impacts, as well as animal welfare and health concerns, exposure to meat supply chains is now seen as a risk by institutional investors, according to a report called "Appetite for Disruption" by the $5.3 trillion investor coalition FAIRR. For example, did you know that over a period of 18 months in 2018 and 2019, a quarter of the world's pigs died from swine fever? We're talking about a livestock pandemic of epic proportions that wiped out 40 percent of China's pig population. The economic toll exceeds $140 billion, farmer livelihoods have been devastated, and the scale of animal suffering is unimaginable.[24]

There is an ethical issue here as well. Pigs are among the top 10 most intelligent animals on the planet, on a par with dogs. Nevertheless, they are factory farmed on an industrial scale to meet the world's insatiable appetite for pork. China leads with 310 million pigs, more than double the European Union. But change is coming. Not only has African swine fever decimated pork production in Asia and pushed up prices, but plant-based "alt-pork" products are poised to scale in the region, led by OmniFoods, Beyond Meat, and Impossible Foods. It's a small but significant victory in tackling animal cruelty and the environmental impacts of the meat industry.

Hot Trend: Plant Protein

As always, the greater the risks, the greater the opportunities. With livestock supply chains accounting for 14.5 percent of global carbon emissions and alt-protein predicted to capture 10 percent of the meat market in 15 years, there will be winners and losers. In the United States alone, veganism grew 600 percent between 2014 and 2017—and that was before the movement really got going. Alt-protein company Beyond Meat's stock price more than tripled in the three months after its listing in May 2019. The global market for plant-based meat grew to $13.6 billion in 2020 and is projected to reach $35 billion by 2027, growing at an annual rate of 14.4 percent.

Now we see Nestlé, IKEA, Burger King, McDonald's, KFC, and others gearing up for global growth in plant-based foods. FAIRR ranks 25 retail giants, identifying leaders (Unilever, Tesco, Nestlé, Marks & Spencer,

Conagra) and laggards (Amazon, Hershey, Costco, Saputo). Across the board, 87 percent are increasing own-brand plant-based products, and 67 percent mention plant-based or vegan in their annual reports or quarterly earnings calls. Why? Simply put, it's a "world-positive" solution. A plant-based diet is one of the top actions on climate change, according to Project Drawdown, plus it offers significant environmental, animal welfare, and health benefits. That's why, after more than 30 years of being vegetarian, I chose to go vegan more than five years ago.

Of course, there are some who believe that vegans and vegetarians are actually destroying the planet. This is linked to the production and consumption of soybeans, which have increased 15-fold since the 1950s and are often associated with tropical deforestation and other environmental impacts. But those who place the blame on the growth of plant-based diets haven't really done their homework. Only 6 percent of soy is consumed by humans; 90 percent is fed to chickens, pigs, and cows, and the rest goes into pet food and biofuels. Hence, it is the quadrupling of meat production in the past 50 years that has fueled soy expansion and its ecological damage.

As our focus switches increasingly to plant-based diets, we will be reminded that nature is rich in bounty, full of precious treasure, generous rewards, and—in accordance with the Latin root of the word *nature*—pure goodness. Yet most of nature's gifts go undetected, are ignored, or get squandered. How many people know that the winged bean of New Guinea contains more protein than cassava and potato; the wax gourd of tropical Asia grows an inch every three hours and reaches maturity in four days; the babassu palm from the Amazon (known locally as the "vegetable cow") can produce 125 barrels of oil from 500 trees; and the serendipity berry from West Africa is 3,000 times sweeter than sucrose?

Embracing Symbiotic Innovation

When I was running sustainability services for accounting firm KPMG in South Africa, I spent a lot of time visiting mining sites, and some of them were literally like moonscapes. Now, as many coal mines reach the end of their life or are retired early, we have a great transformation opportunity. An excellent example is Germany's Lusatian Lake District, which used to contain 60 coal strip mines supplying 90 percent of East Germany's electricity and heat. Today the area has been changed into a 60-square-mile wetland with 20 artificial lakes, providing a variety of nature habitats and ecotourism options. This is an example of symbiotic innovation.

Key Concept: Symbiotic Innovation

The challenge of restoration needs all kinds of innovation to lower our impact on biodiversity and increase the functionality of our ecosystems. I have focused on land use in general, and food production in particular, because of its outsized ecological footprint. But, as they say, necessity is the mother of invention. And the kind of creativity we need now is symbiosis—innovation that creates mutual benefits for nature, society, and the economy. Can we restore ecosystems and simultaneously create economic opportunities for poor communities, whether from ecotourism or harvesting of produce from the forest or the oceans? Can we protect key habitats that simultaneously increase well-being or resilience, since they may contain vital ingredients for new medicines or provide a buffer against the ravages of climate change? Symbiotic innovation means finding single solutions with multiple benefits.

Another example of symbiotic innovation is growing food in a way that protects or restores vital habitats. For example, cranberries grow best in boggy, water-soaked soil. Every acre of cranberries needs 5.5 acres of surrounding marshland, so in effect, you have farmers preserving precious wetlands. Ocean Spray Cranberries, a $2 billion cooperative, became the first agricultural company to have all its 700 farms certified as sustainable by the Sustainable Agriculture Initiative Platform. This is farm-to-fork regenerative agriculture in action. To be sure, cranberry farmers can also damage the environment, but there is the potential for symbiosis here.

We need to be open to new approaches and technologies, such as vertical farming or hydroponics. Happily, there are many positive examples to learn from. California start-up Iron Ox uses a "human led, robotics-first" hydroponic growing system that consumes 90 percent less water over traditional farming while growing 30 times the crops per acre of land. Antwerp-based social enterprise PLNT reuses shipping containers to create a climate-controlled environment for growing food that is CO_2 neutral, reuses 95 percent of the water needed, and runs on renewable energy.

A similar approach is taken by Square Roots, cofounded by Kimbal Musk (brother of the more famous Elon), as part of the urban farming, real food, and sustainable agriculture movements. Did you know that the best basil in the world comes from Genoa, Italy—and the best-tasting crop that chefs there remember was from 1997? So that's the microclimate that Square Roots simulates in their shipping-container hydroponic gardens. Hydroponic systems grow leafy greens in vertical stacks, drip fed by liquid nutrients with little water, no soil, no weeds, and no chemical pesticides or herbicides. If there is a pest infestation, they just simulate a Mojave Desert climate. Ingenious. This may feel like the antithesis of back-to-nature farming, but if technological innovation can radically reduce our footprint, then we should support it.

We need to apply innovation not only to the land but also to the oceans. In fact, we need to change from being ocean hunters to ocean farmers. The agro-industrial approach to fishing has decimated the oceans, as the *Seaspiracy* documentary makes painfully clear. Some fish stocks, such as Atlantic cod, already collapsed in the 1990s, while the global catch of wild seafood flatlined 20 years ago. One sustainable alternative is cultivating mussels in the ocean. Not only are they extremely healthy and packed with protein, fat, and essential nutrients, but they also grow fast with zero resource inputs—no feeds, no fertilizers, no freshwater. Mussels are the Buddhas of the deep, filtering and purifying 5,000 gallons a year as they breathe in and out.

At the same time, we need to be bolder and more creative with our government policies. In order to encourage more farmers to produce food from regenerative agriculture, we must create incentives. What if we paid landowners to protect nature? The Swiss are doing this—and it works. Since the 1990s farmers have been paid to keep at least 7 percent of their land as Biodiversity Promotion Areas. Quite simply, they let the land grow naturally into a meadow, with no fertilizer, and mowed just once a year. Meadows are one of the most biodiverse habitats in the world, so the result is thriving: These protected areas contain more diverse species and more species of concern, when compared with conventionally grazed, fertilized, and mowed farmland.

The UK is taking a similar approach with its new Agriculture Act 2020, which proposes "public money for public goods." This means that land managers (most often, farmers) will be paid for delivering environmental benefits and ecosystem services, such as species conservation, habitat restoration, or a reduction in greenhouse gas emissions. This move could transform agriculture and be a great boon for biodiversity. Another approach is adopting "no net loss" as a nonnegotiable biodiversity threshold. This means companies could make biodiversity offsets. Desperate times call for desperate measures.

Letting the Earth Thrive

I am super-excited by the restoration of ecosystems. Can you tell? I do not in any way want to minimize the scale and urgency of our environmental problems or the tragedy of the catastrophic obliteration of life on earth that we are carrying out every single day. But now, for the first time in my three decades of working in sustainable development, I see a ray of hope, a real chance for nature. I see companies prepared to pay billions for natural climate solutions, I see governments willing to make bold Green Deals, and I see citizen organizations such as Extinction Rebellion adamant to make the crusade for nature into a civil rights movement. Let us embrace the vision—and then take action to make it real.

REGENERATION

The news is good (have you not heard?)
For every insect, beast and bird
The Great Extinction's turning 'round
The seeds of change found fertile ground

The barren fields are set to bloom
The rivers sparkling crystal clear
New forests rise up from the gloom
The wild calls out for all to hear

The color's back in coral reefs
We heed the words of tribal chiefs
The farms are making healthy soil
The sun and wind's replacing oil

The news is good (don't you agree?)
Nature's back, it's not too late
Across the land, the air and sea
We're letting earth regenerate.

CHAPTER 4

Renewal

We see a world of abundance, not limits. In the midst of a great deal of talk about reducing the human ecological footprint, we offer a different vision. What if humans designed products and systems that celebrate an abundance of human creativity, culture, and productivity, that are so intelligent and safe, our species leaves an ecological footprint to delight in, not lament?

—William McDonough and Michael Braungart,
Cradle to Cradle

I am often asked why I made the film *Closing the Loop*, which was, at the time of release in 2018, the world's first feature-length documentary on the circular economy. There are two reasons. The first is that I was fed up with documentaries about the problems we face. To be sure, films like *An Inconvenient Truth*, *Cowspiracy*, *A Plastic Ocean*, *Seaspiracy*, and many others have their place. The public needs to be educated about the scale and urgency of the challenges. But I long ago learned that trying to scare or guilt people into action is seldom the most effective strategy for change. Where were all the films about solutions? They seemed to be in short supply, so I set out to change that.

The second reason that I got into moviemaking is summarized in my opening words in *Closing the Loop*: "Unless we go to circular, it's game over for the planet; it's game over for society."[1] Those are strong words, but I absolutely believe them to be true. It is logically, biologically, physically, and scientifically impossible to continue growing our economic activities on a finite earth. If we cherish even the remotest hope of avoiding exceeding this planet's capacity to supply raw materials and absorb our waste—and the collapse of our civilization as a result—we need to change from our linear extractive, throwaway economy to something that operates in cycles, as nature has done for 3.8 billion years.

I was fortunate to connect with American film director Graham Sheldon, an Emmy and two-time Telly Award winner. Together with a small crew, including Rin Ehlers Sheldon and Andi Beqiri, we traveled to Ecuador, South Africa, Italy, the Netherlands, Germany, and the UK to capture the stories of businesses that were rethinking products and how we make them. Some solutions were high-tech, such as the Infinity polyester fabric that was researched and developed to be recyclable eight times, or the Novamont bio-based and biodegradable plastics for agriculture and food packaging, or the Biogen plant that makes biogas and organic fertilizer from food waste.

Other cases were much more about social inclusion and creating business opportunities, such as EcoPak—which turns "trash into cash" by making Tetra Pak drink boxes into roofing, furniture, and jewelry—or the REDISA tire-recycling scheme that was creating jobs for waste collectors and small recycling businesses. Their approaches are fairly low-tech but worthy of our attention, because unless the circular economy becomes a solution for everyone—not only those in rich and technically advanced countries—we will still fail to avert ecological disaster. I return to some of their stories in the next chapter, because they remind us that thriving is an opportunity to improve lives while also giving nature a chance to flourish.

The film has been extremely well received by film festivals around the world and is now available free-to-view on YouTube with multilingual subtitles. I encourage you to check it out. It's 93 minutes long, so I recommend setting aside an evening and making some popcorn. If by the end you walk away a little inspired, thinking that creative solutions are not only possible but already being implemented, then my goal in making the film has been achieved. But, as you will discover in the rest of this chapter, when it comes to renewal of resources to counteract the forces of depletion, we have plenty of solutions to choose from.

Designing to Be Inherently Good

What if humans disappeared tomorrow? Alan Weisman, in his scientific book *The World without Us*, conducted a thought experiment to contemplate our human legacy.[2] His general conclusion—that the world would be better if humans disappeared and that the planet would, in time, recover from human impacts—is not surprising. The insights are more in the details: Most buildings, technologies, and cultural artifacts will not survive long. Instead, our lasting legacy will be plastics, heavy metals, and persistent artificial chemicals, many of which will toxify the environment for hundreds, and even thousands, of years.

The circular economy tackles the problem of resource depletion and waste from both ends: By producing goods sustainably, consumption matters less, and by consuming them differently, we ensure that products are shared, sustainable, and durable. The circular economy is not a new idea. Its roots go back to conceptions of Spaceship Earth in the 1960s, ecobalance assessments in the 1970s, industrial ecology in the 1980s, cleaner production and eco-efficiency in the 1990s, and cradle-to-cradle in the 2000s. William McDonough and Michael Braungart's concept of cradle-to-cradle was a real breakthrough, because it clarified the difference between natural nutrient cycles and technical nutrient cycles (bio-loops and techno-loops).[3] All of these concepts are about changing from a "take-make-use-lose" linear economy model, which extracts resources and creates waste, to a circular economy where we "borrow-make-use-and-return" resources, so that energy and materials flow in continuous, beneficial cycles.

Key Concept: The Circular Economy

Solutions that serve as a counterforce to depletion allow renewal of resources through the circular economy. The circular economy, therefore, includes all the expenditures and investments that decouple economic growth from environmental impact by "closing the loop" on resource and energy flows. Examples range from waste recycling and biodegradable plastics to renewable energy. It is about finding solutions that help us to operate within the limits of the planet by radically changing resource use and ecosystem impacts, with a focus on shifting to renewable energy and resources, achieving zero-waste production and consumption, and moving to a low-carbon society. The circular economy, using the Ellen MacArthur Foundation's definition, designs out waste and pollution, keeps products and materials in use, and regenerates natural systems.

The circular economy is about closing loops, but—as previously mentioned—there are two kinds of loops, and we shouldn't mix them up. For example, I decided to buy the world's first 100 percent compostable phone case from Pela. It comes from nature and harmlessly goes back to nature. That's loop type 1. But my wife received a pair of Adidas Parley sneakers for her birthday, made from 100 percent waste plastic collected from the ocean. It doesn't come from nature and can't go back to nature. But it turns waste back into a product and is also recyclable. That's loop type 2. We need both, separately: bio-loops and techno-loops.

The Ellen MacArthur Foundation built on the cradle-to-cradle concept and has done a sterling job to make the circular economy widely comprehensible and increasingly scalable. Dame Ellen MacArthur was inspired by her solo round-the-world sailing feat to apply the same principles to the economy that she needed to survive for more than 70 days on her yacht, which was to reuse, repair, and recycle everything possible. The foundation's definition of the circular economy is incredibly elegant and holistic: (1) Design out waste and pollution; (2) keep products and materials in use; and (3) regenerate natural systems. The zero-waste movement has largely neglected regeneration, but now that's changing.

We have only just begun to apply these principles in earnest. For instance, plastic straws are on their way out—already visibly so in Europe. But if we stop there, we may win the battle and lose the war on plastic pollution. Extending the single-use plastic bans beyond Europe, to countries where plastic pollution is worse, is a good start. But we also have to deal with up to a million metric tons of discarded fishing nets that some estimates say make up nearly half of all ocean plastic.

And rather than simply banning "bad" products and materials, we need to design them to be inherently "good." Gregory Unruh, sustainability guest editor at the *MIT Sloan Management Review*, calls designing out waste and pollution *premediation*.[4] We know all about remediation. It means cleaning up our mess, whether that be contaminated land, toxic emissions, or ocean plastic pollution. We certainly need a lot of that. But if we're going to create a thriving future, we need to design our products, processes, and services to be inherently benign or, better still, renewable and restorative. That means not having to clean up at the end of a product's life, because the product is already good for nature; it is biosphere positive.

Of course, designing out waste and pollution does not apply only to physical products. There is a circular economy for heat and carbon as well. That's where a new energy technology called quad-generation comes in, developed by National University of Singapore researchers. Quad-generation goes further than the more widely practiced co-generation and tri-generation. Co-generation uses excess heat to generate electricity as well as to warm up buildings, which is why it is called *combined heat and power*. Tri-generation does the same but uses waste heat for cooling as well as heating. Quad-generation adds CO_2 extraction as a fourth process, resulting in 30 percent less carbon emissions. It's a win-win: good for business and good for the climate. In fact, many industries—especially the food and drinks sector—use CO_2 as an input to their products and processes.

Beer is a good example. During traditional production, fermentation releases CO_2 into the atmosphere (bad for the climate); then the company buys commercially manufactured CO_2 to artificially carbonate the alcohol (bad for the climate); then CO_2 is released when we drink the beer (bad for the climate). Now Earthly Labs has innovated a circular economy technology to capture the CO_2 during brewing and convert it to a liquid for storage, ready for carbonating the beer. Using this process, Denver Beer Co. halved its costs and also sells some of its captured CO_2 to a cannabis greenhouse. A carbon revolution is brewing.

Keeping Products and Materials in Use

A key strategy for sustainability is product durability. In our throwaway world, we often think about recyclability. But it's far better to first reduce consumption and waste by extending the life of products. Durable materials—of which plastics are one—may be more sustainable, even if that is unpopular to say.

Unfortunately, many products have built-in obsolescence; they are designed to have a limited, short life. But that's finally starting to change. The EU's "right-to-repair" regulations apply to household appliances and electronic goods as of 2021 and require manufacturers to make their products easier to repair and reuse. France has announced plans to introduce product labeling that specifies the durability of products, and their repairability, on a scale of 1 to 10. And sustainability pioneer Patagonia has its Worn Wear platform for exchanging used clothes, plus a free repair service and DIY repair and care guides.

For this to work, we need to change how we view products that have multiple lives. I like the idea of a product being *pre-loved* rather than second-hand or used. And like the car that becomes Bumblebee in the *Transformers* movie, pre-loved doesn't mean second-rate. One of my favorite TV shows is a BBC program called *The Repair Shop*. All sorts of items are brought in for restoration—some neglected, some broken, many simply worn down by the passage of time. Each has a story and is wrapped in poignant memories, and each is lovingly restored by highly skilled experts. This is like so many things in life that may be worse for wear but can almost always be repaired. The point is not to try to make them new again but rather to make them functional, to revive and extend their life.

Key Concept: Urban Mining

Many technologies that we want to scale, such as renewable energy and batteries, are metal hungry. Urban mining is the necessary solution. Rather than mining ores from the earth, we can focus on recovering, reusing, and recycling metals from end-of-life products. That's what Umicore does with electronics products and industrial waste. This promotes the reuse of materials. Similarly, Google has just committed to all its products containing recycled materials by 2022. More companies must follow suit. But they will do so only if we as customers demand products with recycled content. If we don't, there will continue to be an oversupply of recycled material, and virgin materials will remain cheaper, as with plastic today.

Electronic waste is a significant problem, and it's only going to get worse as the world gears up for 5G networks. We risk being buried by an "e-valanche" of electronic waste. As it is, we only recycle 25 percent of our 50 million tons of annual global e-waste. What happens when 5 billion mobile-phone users upgrade to 5G and throw away their gadgets (or abandon them in a drawer or cupboard)? We must dramatically improve the circular economy for e-waste recyclability and recycling. This is not so much a technology challenge. Already Apple's Daisy robot can recycle 200 iPhones an hour. The challenge is more one of legislation, logistics, scaling, and (crucially) human behavior.

An innovation that will help is having material and product passports. Humans have passports, so why not the things we make and trade? For decades, supply-chain integrity focused on traceability and transparency, linked to fair-trade, conflict-free, organic, and cruelty-free standards. Now, as we transition from a linear to a circular economy, we need to up the game again. It is not enough to know where a product comes from and who made it. We also need to know what's in it and how to recycle it. Dutch company Circularise provides a window on the future, working with blockchain and injected tracer-DNA to allow product materials to be tagged and decoded.

As the circular economy gains traction, there's a new job category emerging: the materials broker. Much like a mortgage broker, who matches home buyers and banks, a materials broker matches the waste or by-product output from one company with the resource or feedstock needs of another company. Materials brokers are supported by secondary-materials design and engineering companies such as Miniwiz in Taiwan, which has created more than 1,200 sustainable materials from waste in their TrashLab.

Making Our Living Spaces Livable

There are many levels at which we can and must apply thriving, including where and how we live. Are you living in a city that's fit for the future? Depending on the index you choose, different cities top the tables: Oslo (UN City Prosperity Index), Vienna (EIU Livable Cities Index), London (Arcadis Sustainable Cities Index). But the more interesting question is: What is a thriving city?

In cities, renewal takes many forms, and one of the most fundamental is how green it is. I mean that quite literally: How much green space does a city have dedicated to parks, forests, lakes, rivers, and scenic nature spots? According to a ranking by the World Cities Culture Forum, Oslo has an incredible 68 percent of the city dedicated to public green space. Other leaders are Sydney (46 percent), Vienna (45.5 percent), Chengdu (42.3 percent),

Zurich (41 percent), Shenzhen (40.9 percent), and Nanjing (40.7 percent).[5] How much green space does your city have—and is it accessible? Do you have green islands, or is nature integrated throughout the city?

Greening a city is not only good for its citizens but also a smart investment. Did you ever notice that we willingly pay a green premium? Think of property prices. Houses or apartments in lush suburbs with tree-lined streets, near parks, or in the countryside cost more to rent or buy. The reason is simple: We value green space. Trees and parks improve our quality of life. We know from scientific studies that being in and around nature adds to our health and well-being. So why do we still have cities and towns that prioritize roads, parking, and pavements over trees, parks, and lakes? Spending on urban and suburban greening is an investment in thriving.

Hot Trend: Sponge Cities

One way to green cities is to design *sponge cities*, which are urban landscapes that use vegetation to act like giant sponges that passively absorb, clean, and use rainwater. I've been in Lagos, Nigeria, during rainy season, when the floods create mayhem. Now many cities face a similar challenge—and climate change makes it worse. Sponge cities are a solution. Professor Kongjian Yu is a sponge city architect (fabulous job title!) who is installing terraced wetlands in the heart of 250 Chinese cities. These are saving lives and billions of dollars. Why not ask your mayors and city leaders a new question: How spongy is our city?

Space is at a premium in cities, so we have reduced nature to pockets of green in the midst of patchwork farms, concrete buildings, and asphalt streets. But pockets can contain hidden treasures. Japanese botanist Akira Miyawaki has introduced the idea of planting pocket forests, which are dense clusters of diverse native trees. This has a remarkable effect. These mini urban forests grow 10 times faster, have 100 times more biodiversity, and store 40 times more carbon than conventional forests. The small, local scale of pocket forests means that they can be grown in schools, parks, campuses, corporate offices, or even on roofs, at factories, or in suburban gardens.

Even better is getting rid of some of that asphalt and concrete. Pedestrianization of urban space is a growing trend—and the benefits are enormous: healthier citizens, lower carbon, increased productivity, and stimulated retailers. Hamburg is planning a 17,000-acre system of green-ways, and Oslo has replaced more than 700 curbside parking spots with bike lanes, plants, tiny parks, and benches. Barcelona has car-free super-blocks, Ghent has closed 35 hectares to vehicular traffic, and Madrid and Copenhagen have carless downtown shopping areas. It's not just big cities: York in the UK (population 150,000) plans to be car free by 2023. With cars, less can be more.

One of the things we gain by going car free is clean air. The World Health Organization estimates 7 million people die every year from air pollution, and 9 out of 10 people breathe air containing high levels of pollutants.[6] If you want to know your local area's air pollution levels, Breezometer is a great app, with live updates. The craziest part is that these impacts are all totally preventable. The quickest and most scalable solution is renewable electrification—of grids, lighting, cooking, cars, and industrial processes. In the future, there will also be more high-tech solutions, such as Graphene Flagship's smog-eating photocatalytic coatings for pavements and walls, which passively remove air pollutants.

Water is another key to creating a renewable city. A new breakthrough in turning seawater into freshwater could finally make the process cheap and sustainable. The world's first land-based distillation desalination plant dates back to 1928 in Curaçao, in the Netherlands Antilles, and a reverse-osmosis plant was built in Jeddah, Saudi Arabia, in 1978. The problem with existing methods is that they are expensive and energy intensive. Now researchers at Monash University in Australia have cre-ated a type of nanotechnology that is responsive to sunlight and turns seawater into drinking water in 30 minutes.

Working in an Oasis

I often wonder why we don't model work life on campus life. Most university campuses are inspiring, rejuvenating places to be. With their green open spaces, trees, benches, and cafés, they feel like living oases in a desert of concrete and asphalt. Casually dressed students find quiet or social spaces, depending on their needs. Campuses are ideal for learning, collaborating, and innovating. Why, then, do we design office environments where the spirit goes to die? Why do we surround ourselves with cluttered cubicles instead of nurturing nature? Only the big tech companies, it seems, have understood the power of campus work-play spaces.

What we need to do is transform our work buildings from sterile mausoleums into living ecosystems. This means reinventing buildings to be less like economic factories and more like human communities. I am excited about three pioneering standards: *living, well,* and *active* buildings. Living buildings focus on creating thriving spaces that are self-sufficient, healthy, and beautiful, producing more energy than they use and treating all water on site. Well-certified buildings enhance human health and well-being. And active buildings, demonstrated at Swansea University in the UK, intelligently integrate renewable-energy technologies for heat, power, and electric vehicle transport.

These standards are important because, over their life cycle, buildings can generate nearly 40 percent of global carbon emissions. One solution, developed by engineers at Purdue University, is a new white paint that reflects 95.5 percent of sunlight. This keeps surfaces cooler than the temperature of the air that surrounds the building, which may reduce or eliminate the need for air-conditioning. Another innovation could be switching to wood as a construction material. A study for Europe shows that if 80 percent of new residential buildings in Europe were made from wood, they would store 55 million tons of CO_2 a year, equivalent to 47 percent of the cement industry's annual emissions in Europe.[7]

For now, concrete remains ubiquitous in construction. Unfortunately, its key ingredient, cement, accounts for about 7 percent of the world's carbon emissions. But McKinsey estimates that technology innovations could reduce the industry's CO_2 emissions by 75 percent by 2050.[8] For example, the Dutch demolition company New Horizon works to promote a circular approach to the reuse of resources tied up in existing buildings. Similarly, StoneCycling is taking steps to reduce building waste, using material from old construction projects to produce bricks with unique colors, shapes, and textures. The inputs for the products are waste ceramics, glass, and insulation, as well as rejected clay from traditional brick manufacturing—all locally sourced.

Breakthrough Solution: Living Concrete

What if we could build with concrete that is living rather than inert? That's what scientists at the University of Colorado, Boulder, have been working on. By mixing cyanobacteria with sand and gelatin, they have produced a material with the potential to self-heal, absorb pollution, and even glow in the dark. The bioconcrete's lower carbon footprint could help tackle the cement industry's climate impacts. These are the beginnings of regenerative construction.

Besides the materials we use to build our workplaces, roofs also create an opportunity for renewal. There is no adequate substitute for wilderness areas or protected biospaces where species can thrive. But a growing body of research suggests that living roofs (or green roofs) can help stem the extinction tide of insects and birds by providing a patchwork mosaic of habitats. A New York City law requires all new buildings to have living roofs or rooftop solar. Currently, the 730 green roofs in New York cover just 60 of the city's 40,000 rooftop acres. Imagine the impact when green and renewable-energy roofs become the new normal in New York. Then imagine other cities following suit.

If you think this applies only to office space and not to factories, you are wrong. Admittedly we often see beautifully designed headquarters (or campuses in the tech industry), but factories are generally functional, utilitarian, and designed to maximize production, with little or no thought given to aesthetics. Is it any surprise that the workers feel like cogs in a machine? What's lacking is architectural imagination. Spanish architect Ricardo Bofill gives an idea of what is possible: He transformed an old cement factory into his company's head office, known as La Fábrica or The Cathedral, complete with living roofs, trees, orchards, and green lawns.

We can also bring nature inside our offices and factories, making workplaces a green haven. Companies that are doing this—Interface, Google, Facebook, Amazon, and Microsoft—call this *biophilic design*. Biophilia literally means "nature love" but is associated with biologist Edward O. Wilson's philosophy that humans have an innate, biological affinity for the natural world.[9] I stayed at a Marriott hotel in Wroclaw, Poland, that used biophilia design principles: wooden floors and panels, curved lines, marble and stone, lots of plants, natural light, and posters of nature. Even though I was inside a building, I felt more relaxed and closer to nature. Research shows that biophilic design reduces stress, increases focus, boosts immunity, and reduces mental illness. Is your organization a fan of biophilia yet?

Making a Home for Nature

While our catastrophic loss of wildlife and insect populations is largely due to industrial agriculture, our cities have also wiped out ecosystem habitats. If you have a garden at home, no matter how small, you can be part of biodiversity renewal. Our suburban lawns (along with golf courses) are green deserts. They are biodiversity unfriendly by design—chemically treated, lacking diverse flora, water thirsty, and very poor carbon sinks. Time for some suburban rewilding.

Douglas Tallamy, in his book *Nature's Best Hope*, presents a compelling vision of homegrown national parks—comprising all the urban and suburban gardens in a country—which can provide refuge for insects, birds, and wildlife that have been crowded out of rural areas by agriculture and industry.[10] If American homeowners converted half their land to native plantings, it would create an area larger than all national parks in the lower 48 states combined. There are two simple guidelines: (1) Plant indigenous species, since these are evolutionarily suited to supporting your ecosystem, and (2) reduce (or get rid of) your lawn.

Scaling back on grass is only the first step. If we care about biodiversity, we should worry less about species and more about habitats. We are all familiar with Save the Species campaigns—and we should care enough to want to save them. But if we save or restore their habitats, the species will save themselves. Even in our gardens, we can create thriving habitats: water basins, leaf litter, bee hotels, wild patches, log piles, and native trees and flowers.

We can all make homes for wildlife. I recently discovered a hedgehog visiting our garden at night. It made me so happy. All gardens, farms, towns, and cities should be wildlife friendly. For too long, humans have been at war with nature—aiming to dominate and subjugate, to control and curtail, to tame and train out its wildness. Instead, by creating habitats (large or small) that attract and welcome other species, that include rather than exclude wildlife, we are affirming the right of all life to flourish. We are placing ourselves in the web of life rather than at the apex. We are being good neighbors.

Turning our home organic waste into compost is another simple action we can take to support renewal of resources. Composting reduces waste, increases soil fertility, fixes carbon, and enhances biodiversity. It also feels good to be a participant in nature's recycling process. Happily, there are composting bins and wormeries for every size of home and garden—and even compost-collecting programs for urban dwellers in some cities—so everyone can get involved.

Personal Tip: Switch Your Soap

Regenerating our homes is not only an outdoor activity. We can also change what's going on inside. For example, the humble bar of soap is enjoying something of a renaissance—and so it should. COVID-19 aside, the simple act of teaching children around the world to wash their hands can save a million deaths a year. There are also huge environmental benefits if we choose solid bars of soap, shampoo, and shaving cream rather than liquids or gels. A comparative life-cycle assessment found that we use six times more liquid soap per wash, and the bar has a carbon footprint 10 times lower. Factor in the impact of plastic packaging waste, and the soap bar becomes the clear sustainable choice.

There are many opportunities to make an impact by changing how we shop. One of the biggest is addressing the 1.3 billion tons a year of food that is wasted, costing nearly $680 billion. In Helsinki, Finland, the S Group, a retailing cooperative, has adopted a novel way to reduce food waste. Every day at 9:00 p.m. in its 900 stores, it's happy hour. But rather than offering cheaper alcohol drinks, food items that are nearing their sell-by date are discounted by 60 percent. And it works. After all, we're all suckers for a good deal. The customers win, the business wins (it costs money to get rid of waste), and the planet wins. Everyone's happy.

According to Project Drawdown, tackling food waste is the third most effective solution to climate change. There are many changes to make, from improved food packaging and cold-chains (refrigeration of produce from "farm to fork") to better ways of dealing with foods that have passed their sell-by or use-by dates. But I also have one simple, revolutionary idea, mainly targeting restaurants, hotels, and caterers, which waste enormous amounts of food by overproviding. Why not introduce small, medium, and large options on all menus? When I buy a coffee, I can choose the size that I want. Why not for food?

Unpacking the Issue of Food Packaging

Food packaging is a massive culprit in the crime of plastic pollution. But Nestlé—which sometimes gets a bad rap on sustainability—is promising to change that. Until now, snack-food packaging has been notoriously unsustainable. Our global $161 billion addiction churns out mass-produced plastic wrappers that are prone to becoming litter and are not generally recyclable. Now Nestlé has launched the world's first high-volume snack packaging using recyclable paper and high-speed, flow-wrap technology. The wrapping made its debut with YES! fruit and nut bars but should extend to other products too. This is part of the solution, but we need consumer education as well.

Besides snack packaging, single-use plastic shopping bags create ubiquitous litter and end up suffocating wildlife or blocking their digestive tracts. That's why Walmart, Target, and CVS Health are working with Closed Loop Partners on the Beyond the Bag Initiative, which is a call for innovators to reinvent single-use shopping bags.

Some innovators in the industry believe watermarks could help with recycling. We are used to seeing watermarks in our currency notes, but soon we may be seeing them in plastic packaging as well. More than 80 major brands—including P&G, PepsiCo, and Mondi—will collaborate in the HolyGrail 2.0 project in Europe to insert digital watermarks the size of postage stamps into consumer goods packaging. These watermarks can then be decoded using a standard high-resolution camera to aid sorting of waste into the right categories during recycling. They can also be used to identify manufacturer information, thus increasing accountability for moving to a circular economy by keeping materials in use.

Of course, even better than recycling plastic would be to reduce the need for it in the first place. Heineken is showing that this is possible. By replacing its six-pack plastic rings with a cardboard topper, the company expects to eliminate 517 tons of plastic packaging, equivalent to 94 million plastic bags. Heineken has also halved its carbon emissions since 2008. We must applaud steps like this but also keep the ultimate prize in mind, which is to achieve zero-waste shopping. One way is to create zero-waste shops, such as Robuust in Antwerp, where you bring your own containers and bags for refills.

Case Spotlight: The Loop Platform

Embracing the home-delivery model can help eliminate plastic waste, which is what the zero-waste shopping platform Loop is doing in the UK, France, and the United States. Loop is run by TerraCycle, which works with manufacturers such as Heinz, Coca-Cola, Unilever, Danone, and Nivea; retailers such as Tesco; and logistics companies such as DHL and DPD. The platform enables shoppers to purchase food, drink, health, beauty, and cleaning products online and then to return the packaging, either from home using an online request for pickup or at one of the DHL or DPD collection points. Tesco hopes this will help remove 1 billion pieces of plastic packaging from its UK stores by 2021.

Zero Grocery in San Francisco is eliminating the need to drop off used packaging. They deliver food in reusable (mostly glass) containers, which are picked up with the next delivery. To people of a certain age, this will not seem strange at all. It is how milk used to be delivered. Concerns about health and hygiene are unfounded. The returned containers are sterilized before reuse, and the groceries are handled less on average than the products bought in store.

Glass is one packaging alternative to plastic, but it is not the only one. What if food waste were viewed as simply another raw material and turned into packaging? In Italy, designer CRA has developed an innovative juice bar called Feel the Peel that 3D-prints leftover orange peels into disposable bioplastic cups. Every time we support these creative alternatives, we are leaving oil in the soil and taking climate-positive steps.

Turning the Tide on Plastic

These packaging challenges are part of a wider problem of plastic proliferation. "Breaking the Plastic Wave," a report by the Pew Charitable Trusts and SYSTEMIQ, concludes that if we fail to act, by 2040 the volume of plastic on the market will double, the annual volume of plastic entering the ocean will almost triple, and ocean plastic stocks will quadruple, reaching more than 600 million metric tons.[11] In contrast, the Ellen MacArthur Foundation shows that a circular economy approach could reduce the annual volume of plastics entering our oceans by 80 percent, generate savings of $200 billion per year, reduce greenhouse gas emissions by 25 percent, and create 700,000 net additional jobs by 2040.[12]

In Dusseldorf I took a step into the belly of the Big Plastics beast: K Trade Fair, the world's largest plastics industry event. My two takeaways were the following: First, plastics are here to stay. Let's not be naïve and think they will disappear; they are too useful. And second, the industry is deeply unsustainable and has to reinvent itself to regain its social license to operate. Judging from the more than 3,300 exhibitors, this is starting to happen. Companies are rapidly redesigning plastics to be low-carbon, nontoxic, bio-based, carbon-sequestered, recycled, recyclable, 3D-printable, compostable, and circular. And for whatever can't be composted or recycled, there's the option of transforming plastics back into their chemical building blocks, a process called *chemcycling*, which the BASF chemical company is championing.

Key Concept: Industrial Symbiosis

Industrial symbiosis is the practice of designing industrial parks or business zones so that the waste or by-product of one production process serves as input or feedstock to another. The classic case is Kalundborg Symbiosis in Denmark, which has been applying this principle since 1972. Today it is a partnership between 11 public and private companies in the city of Kalundborg. The BASF chemical company has a *Verbund* concept that is very similar. At six Verbund sites worldwide, production plants, energy and material flows, logistics, and site infrastructure are all integrated to save resources and minimize waste and pollution. Similarly, in China's Midong chemical park, 4.72 million tons of waste by-products are exchanged between companies.

Innovations like these are encouraging. They show that alternatives are possible. But we also need to transform the plastic industry itself. The task of the Alliance to End Plastic Waste and the New Plastics Economy could not be more urgent. Solutions already exist. For example, plastic-eating bacteria have been discovered near a bottle-recycling plant in Japan and a polluted site in Houston, Texas. These microbes digest PET, the most common plastic waste. And, more recently, German scientists have found bacteria that eat the polyurethane used in sneakers, a harder-to-recycle plastic. Researchers at Adelaide University have even invented nanoscale magnetic coiled springs that disintegrate microplastics.

But for these solutions to scale up, the companies need economic incentives: carbon pricing, waste taxes, circular economy subsidies, bottle-deposit schemes, and better collection and recycling systems. One of the biggest barriers to policy-driven reforms of this kind is negative lobbying by companies and their sector associations. That's why Coca-Cola and PepsiCo pulling out of the Plastics Industry Association was a significant move. Apparently, these food and beverage giants no longer want to support a group that continues to lobby against phasing out of single-use plastics. That's a positive sign, but we have to remain vigilant.

Still, I am optimistic about the changes we have seen on plastics in an incredibly short time. The great U-turn has already begun. Consider that on May 10, 2019, the UN added plastic waste to the Basel Convention, which regulates and restricts trade in hazardous materials. Plastic-waste flows will now have to be sorted and traced and cannot be dumped on poorer countries. It took the EU only nine months to approve their plastics strategy. We are witnessing a tipping point in action. In fact, it is an instructive case in what really drives sustainable transformation. Is it government, business, customers, media, scientists, entrepreneurs, the public?

In complex systems, the answer is *all of the above*. But some lead and others lag. We can learn lessons from the antiplastics movement. It started with nonprofits complaining but having no real impact. Business and government were content to make superficial responses (such as litter-education campaigns). Meanwhile, the science was building. But it took entrepreneurship (notably Boyan Slat with Ocean Cleanup) and media (numerous documentaries, including *Drowning in Plastic*, *A Plastic Ocean*, and *Plastic Is Forever*) to trigger consumer and public pressure. Legislation followed (plastic-bag bans, the EU plastics strategy, and the Basel Convention changes). Now we get serious innovation, investment, and change.

The Coming Boom of Biofabrication

What is solar powered, sequesters carbon, and can grow up to 12 feet a day? The answer is algae. In some forms, algae are a problem. In rivers, lakes, and estuaries, fed by nitrogen and phosphorous fertilizer runoff, algae blooms in excess, leading to suffocating eutrophication (depletion of oxygen in the water). But as a potential carbon sink and regenerative material, algae are almost miraculous. ALGIX is using it to create Bloom, a bioplastics foam used in sneakers for Adidas and TOMS. Similarly, Notpla makes edible, biodegradable water sachets; LOLIWARE has innovated hypercompostable straws; and Evoware turns algae into cups, wraps, and bags.

This shows us that the problem of plastics is challenging industrial innovators to get creative. Besides using bioplastics foam, Adidas topped the 2020 Sustainable Cotton rankings by sourcing 99 percent Better Cotton–certified and 1 percent organic material. Meanwhile, Nike is making a splash with its Space Hippie collection. That Nike shoe has a lower carbon footprint and incorporates recycled materials such as plastic water bottles, T-shirts, waste foam, and textile scraps. It doesn't pass the circular economy test—ultimately, we need to make techno- and bio-loops separate and continuous. But the direction is as important as the destination.

There is no doubt that the switch to regenerative fashion materials is well underway—and plant-based leather is the next big thing. Making alternatives to animal skin has brought eco entrepreneurs out of the woodwork, with faux leather materials being produced from mushrooms (Amadou and Mycoworks), pineapple leaves (Piñatex), cork (Corkor)—and the newest kids on the block—eggplant skins (chef Omar Sartawi), cacti (Adriano Di Marti), and apple peels (Beyond Leather Materials ApS). They will all have to demonstrate that they can be as versatile and durable as hide-based leather. But for the animals, the environment, and the climate, it's a challenge worth taking up.

Hot Trend: Biofabrication

What if, instead of using fossil fuels, minerals, and plants to make products, we worked with nature to grow the materials we need? That's what biofabrication is: literally fabricating with biology, or manufacturing using living cells. Biofabricated materials can replace textiles, plastics, and construction materials. Our future living factories include mycelium (from fungi), bacteria, yeast, and algae. Many are naturally fire retardant, hydrophobic (water resistant), and biodegradable. Biofabrication pioneer Suzanne Lee gives the example of Biomason, which grows carbon-positive bricks at room temperature that are three times stronger than kiln-fired concrete blocks, representing potential annual CO_2 reductions of 800 million tons.

To be naturally regenerative, these products and materials should be climate positive (absorb more carbon than they emit), bio-based (made from natural materials), and biodegradable (break down harmlessly to nature). Biotech company Newlight achieves all three, using microbes that turn methane (a more powerful climate-warming gas than CO_2) into a new material, which they call Air Carbon. This can be fashioned into straws, cutlery, or faux leather and breaks down naturally if it gets into our rivers or oceans. MIT researchers are hoping to do biofabrication with wood, now that they have grown wood-like plant tissue—without soil or sunlight—from cells extracted from the leaves of a zinnia plant.

Scientists are also finding biofabrication alternatives to dyes. No one wants a world without color, but textile dyeing uses 8,000 chemicals and is the second-largest polluter of water in the world. Colorifix wants—as its name suggests—to fix the problem. The company is led by Cambridge University researchers who have figured out how to insert pigment-forming genetic information into bacteria, which then literally grow colorful organic dyes. The result is a chemical-free dyeing process that also uses up to 40 percent less energy and up to 90 percent less water. (The fashion industry uses enough water for dyeing to fill 2 million Olympic-size swimming pools each year.)

Another way to avoid using toxic chemical dyes for textiles is a scientific breakthrough that allows cotton to grow naturally in different colors. According to Trusted Clothes, 10–15 percent of dyes are released into the environment during the dyeing process, causing 40,000 to 50,000 tons of annual chemical pollution by the global textile industry.[13] Now the Commonwealth Scientific and Industrial Research Organisation, in Australia, has discovered that adding certain genes can produce yellow, orange, and purple cotton. Surely this is an example of using genetic modification for a better, more sustainable solution. Isn't it time that our views on genetically modified organisms (GMOs) became more nuanced?

Another application of biofabrication is 3D bioprinting: literally printing three-dimensional living objects. One of the pioneers, Inventia Life Science, is printing living cells for pharmaceutical research and medical drug discovery. How does it work? Cells taken from a patient are cultivated and multiplied to create bio-inks, which are printed as microdroplets from a cartridge with an ink-jet nozzle onto a tissue-culture plate. Hence, 3D cancer cells can be printed with the same form and structure as in the body, and then different drugs can be tested on those cells. Soon tissues and organs may be 3D-printable too.

The advances in growing cells, whether through 3D printing or other methods, is about to revolutionize the food industry. Nature's Fynd, backed by $80 million from Bill Gates and Al Gore, has just started production of alternative protein grown from bacteria that live in Yellowstone's geothermal hot springs. And in Tel Aviv, at a new restaurant called The Chicken, you can order a meal that has been grown from cells in a bioreactor on a plot next door. The long-heralded innovation of cultured meat—also known as cellular agriculture or lab-grown meat—is about to take off.

In December 2020 Singapore became the first country to approve the sale of cultured chicken bites grown by Californian start-up Eat Just. The global meat market exceeds $330 billion and is a major cause of climate change, deforestation, chemical pollution, water stress, and animal cruelty. Cultured meat removes those impacts. When fully operational, a cultured-meat factory will be able to harvest half its total volume every day, forever. Now that's what I call thriving.

The Movement to Reinvent Movement

No matter how sustainably we manufacture the materials and products we need, they are useless unless we can get them to the customer. Hence transport and logistics is a sector that also needs renewal. How we move stuff and people around the world has never been more complex or more urgent to rethink. Freight and logistics cause 7 percent of global carbon emissions and jam up our transport networks. There are solutions in big data, the Internet of Things, artificial intelligence, drones, and electric vehicles. But in our drive for efficiency, let's not forget effectiveness. If regenerating cities is the goal, more cars or smarter technology, no matter how efficiently they are run, may not be better for nature or society. Perhaps carless cities are a better solution.

This is where national politics—with its binary choices, toxic rhetoric, and stalemate posturing—is increasingly ineffective. By contrast, many cities are showing both leadership and bold action. Austin, Texas, for example, is joining many cities around the world with plans to take cars off the road while increasing mobility for its citizens. It will invest more than $7 billion in a new transit system, and another $460 million in new infrastructure centered on walking and biking. The plan aims to remove 250,000 daily car trips, bringing down car commutes from 75 percent of the population to 50 percent by 2039.[14] Change is happening.

Besides cities, leaders at the state, provincial, or county level can also be progressive. For example, California is greening truck fleets. According to the Advanced Clean Truck rule, more than half of the trucks sold in California have to be zero-emission vehicles by 2035, and by 2045 all new trucks must meet this standard. In 2018 California already required that all new public transit buses sold must be zero-emission starting in 2029. And even earlier, in the 1990s, it was California's lower emission regulations that led to breakthrough innovations in passenger electric vehicles, first by Japanese manufacturers, then by American and German automakers.

Hot Trend: Shared Mobility

The mobility revolution is not only about reducing vehicle emissions but also about replacing private car ownership with shared mobility. According to research by the Transport Technology Forum, 50 percent of all new cars in the UK will be smart vehicles, connected to the internet.[15] Soon vehicle-access platforms driven by big-data algorithms will be the quickest and cheapest way to move around the city. Manchester, following in the footsteps of Copenhagen, estimates that each electric car-sharing vehicle can replace 11 vehicles on the road. Less congestion, less pollution, less cost, less inconvenience, and less carbon. What's not to like?

Electric vehicles are another obvious solution, to which we return in the chapter on resilient infrastructure. But it will take at least a decade for people to replace their fossil-fuel cars with electric vehicles, and if we want to avoid climate breakdown, we simply can't wait that long. In Greek mythology, Prometheus is a Titan who steals fire from the gods and gives it to humanity. What if we could "steal" carbon from the atmosphere and turn it into fuels? That is the mission of Prometheus Fuels, which launched its carbon-neutral fuel into the market late in 2020. Investor BMW i Ventures calls this a game changer, and they may be right.

Electrification is not only a solution for cars, of course. Electric trains go back to 1895, with the first high-speed rail system, the Tōkaidō Shinkansen, launched in Japan in 1964, and numerous magnetic-levitation trains following in the decades thereafter. The mag-lev train in Shanghai has a top speed of 430 kilometers per hour (270 miles per hour). Electric boats are also poised for rapid convergence (at least for short haul). ForSea now has two 100 percent electric ferries with 46 daily crossings between Denmark and Sweden, transporting 7 million passengers and 2 million vehicles a year. The switch from fossil fuel is saving 28,000 metric tons of CO_2 annually in a sector that still accounts for 3 percent of global carbon.

Decarbonizing maritime shipping is harder, but the industry is not shying away from the challenge. Today cargo ships burn climate-damaging heavy fuel oil, and there are no easy alternatives. The batteries that power new-generation electric ferries—such as Denmark's E-ferry Ellen—do not currently have the range to cross oceans. Shell has published its road map to net-zero shipping by 2050, and it is betting on hydrogen fuel cells and liquified natural gas. The sector plans to cut carbon-emission intensity by 40 percent by 2030.

Perhaps the hardest sector for renewal is air travel. Most airplane fleets were grounded during the height of COVID-19, and the airline sector is on its knees. But postpandemic, our appetite for air travel will return—and then how do we reconcile it with the existential threat of climate change? Commercial aviation accounts for 2 percent of global carbon emissions and has plotted a pathway to carbon neutrality by 2050. The bigger challenge is how to make the shift more rapidly. Sustainable aviation fuel can reduce CO_2 emissions by 70–100 percent but remains expensive.

Electric planes for short-haul flights and carbon offsetting can help. Electric planes are at a much earlier stage, of course, but the Solar Impulse 2's electric round-the-world flight in 2015–2016 has served as a vital catalyst. In the UK, Cranfield Aerospace Solutions is already working on developing the UK's first all-electric-powered aircraft, with commercial flights coming as early as 2023. Israeli aviation company Eviation Aircraft has its first customer for its electric airplane, Cape Air. Even Airbus is working on the E-Fan X hybrid-electric plane. But we need stronger government incentives and increased public pressure.

Case Spotlight: Net-Works Program

One of my favorite renewal examples is the Net-Works program of carpet manufacturer Interface. It showcases a fair and inclusive business model with the aim to have "less plastic, more fish." They work with 40 communities in the Philippines and Cameroon, with expansion to Indonesia underway. The goal is to successfully establish a community-based supply chain for discarded fishing nets—a major source of plastic pollution and a hazard to marine life. So far, they have collected more than 224 metric tons of nets—enough to go around the world more than five times. They then work with Aquafil to recycle the nets into high-quality nylon yarn, which Interface makes into high-design carpet tiles.

The project has also prototyped a community-based Marine Protection Area to replenish fish stocks, covering 627 hectares, with 202 hectares in a no-take zone in the Philippines. These areas include restoration of seagrasses, mangrove rehabilitation, and improved governance and enforcement. Net-Works has given 2,200 families access to finance through its community banks, with 1,200 members voluntarily making small weekly contributions to an "environment pouch," which is used to support conservation activities.

Overall, the Net-Works program has improved the marine environment for 64,000 people. Now it wants to go further, by developing an ecological and inclusive seaweed supply chain for carrageenan (seaweed extract) that simultaneously replenishes fish stocks in Southeast Asia. This is a farming practice that already benefits more than a million people in the Philippines alone.

Embracing Less Is More

I am extremely excited by all of the emerging business models and technological solutions that will help us to renew our finite resources. As you have read in this chapter, the innovations are already there; now it's time to scale these breakthroughs. Certainly government incentives will help, as will increasing customer demand for circular products and services. But it's also time for leadership from business—to show us that it is possible to decouple our environmental impacts from economic growth and to show that they really are committed to a regenerative future. Until Tesla demonstrated that electric vehicles can not only look good but also perform better and be safer than other cars, governments and customers were in wait-and-see mode.

Now it's time for creative action for renewal and giving up everything that stands between us and a more sustainable world.

GIVING UP

I'm giving up—
Not on life, but on those actions that threaten life
Not on living, but on those habits that distract from living
Not on loving, but on those fears that get in the way of loving

I'm giving up
Food that forges a chain of suffering and death
Clothes that weave a garment of exploitation and shame
Fuels that are harbingers of cancer and climate catastrophe

I'm giving up—
Not on people, but on the poor choices that people make
Not on freedom, but on the complacency that cripples freedom
Not on hope, but on the sense of impotence that kills all hope

I'm giving up
Words that break down rather than build up others
Work that lacks a larger purpose of improving society
Products that leave a trail of misery and waste in their wake

I'm giving up—
For the good of myself and those who have less than I do
For the good of the planet and those who share its blue-green
     bounty
For the good of the children and those who will inherit what we
     leave behind

I'm giving up
All these things and more—
In my best and brightest and bravest moments—
For good

SECTION III

REGENERATING SOCIETY

It's clear that the struggle for justice should never be abandoned because of the apparent overwhelming power of those who have the guns and the money and who seem invincible in their determination to hold on to it. That apparent power has, again and again, proved vulnerable to human qualities less measurable than bombs and dollars: moral fervor, determination, unity, organization, sacrifice, wit, ingenuity, courage, patience.

—**Howard Zinn**, "The Optimism of Uncertainty"

The revolution toward thriving would do well to learn from the mistakes of the sustainable development movement over the past 30 years. Among these has been to treat environmental and social issues as separate, distinct agendas, which of course they are not. Another has been to focus strongly on environmental issues while neglecting human development. For thriving to achieve its full potential, we need a *both-and* approach: thriving of both nature and society, both society and the economy, both the economy and nature.

Having already explored the restoration of ecosystems and the renewal of resources, in Chapter 5 we investigate the shift of turning disparity in society into responsibility by making the economy more inclusive. In Chapter 6 we look at the shift from disease to improving individual health through revitalization in the well-being economy. Both are a nod to the aphorism that "you can't succeed in a society that fails." And for the world to thrive, we must "leave no one behind." Thriving cannot become a game for rich, liberal folks to play; rather, it must set the new rules of the game for helping everyone in society.

CHAPTER 5

Responsibility

*The real tragedy of our postcolonial world is not that
the majority of people had no say in whether or not they
wanted this new world; rather, it is that the majority have
not been given the tools to negotiate this new world.*

—**Chimamanda Ngozi Adichie**, *Half of a Yellow Sun*

As night falls, the surrounding Borneo tropical rain forest has come
alive with noise—most notably the trill of frogs and the rhythmic
pulse of cicadas. I am with 10 others on the Sabah study tour
of the Emerging Leaders Dialogue Asia (ELDA). The previous day, after
a workshop for ELDA delegates on transformational leadership that I
co-delivered with Indira Kartallozi (my partner in business and life), our
group flew from Kuala Lumpur to Kota Kinabalu. This was the start of an
incredible journey, organized on behalf of ELDA by our fabulous friend
and colleague Kishore Ravuri.

In the next two weeks we would visit Forest Solutions Malaysia in Kota Marudu and learn about their "mosaic" model of commercial timber plantations mixed in among protected secondary rain forest. We would sleep in bamboo huts at Camp International's volunteer center in the village of Bongkud before driving to Mount Kinabalu, where we learned about the community's recovery from a terrible earthquake in June 2015 that killed 4 guides and 14 tourists, including schoolchildren. We also traveled to Tunku Abdul Rahman Park, a marine conservation area around five islands off the coast of Kota Kinabalu.

But undoubtedly the highlight for me was to discover the inspiring story of Barefoot College, which trains village grandmothers to be solar engineers. We heard about this project on our first evening of the tour, when we were welcomed for dinner in the beautiful family home of Jasmine, an ELDA alumna. We enjoyed a mini feast of banana fritters, pomelo, and langsat (a bit like lychees but more delicious) while getting a sneak preview into this incredible organization, which has partnered with the Sabah Women Entrepreneurs and Professionals Association (SWEPA) in Borneo.

Barefoot College is the brainchild of Sanjit "Bunker" Roy. As a postgraduate student, in 1972, Roy volunteered to live and work in one of India's poorest states and dreamed of bringing together the best of urban knowledge and rural wisdom. That dream became a reality when he started building Barefoot College in 1980. Today, the organization works in 96 countries and has provided 1 million people with access to light, while replacing 500 million liters of kerosene with clean energy for light, heat, and cooking; every year it also provides 1 billion liters of clean drinking water.

During our study tour, SWEPA arranged for us to meet one of Barefoot College's beneficiaries, a so-called *solar mama* in Borneo. She was part of the program that takes illiterate grandmothers from poor rural villages and within six months trains them at the college in India for their new job. They return to the village and install and maintain a full solar lighting system. The group especially targets grandmothers because of their commitment to the village they come from. Young people would most likely move to the city.

The story of the solar mamas captures many elements of what it means to harness the power of responsibility to create a more inclusive society and economy. So many barriers are being broken through, as these amazing women challenge stereotypes about age, gender, and rural capacity. Barefoot College shows that sustainable development—including adopting sustainable technologies—is an option for people living with low incomes in remote villages. The Barefoot model empowers people to be agents of their own destiny.

The Access Economy

In contrast to exclusion and discrimination, the access economy is about giving everyone fair access to economic opportunities. As the Emerald "Global Inclusivity Report, 2020" highlights, there are many societal barriers to inclusion, most notably gender and race discrimination, poverty, and workplace challenges, in which leadership attitudes and biases in recruitment or promotions play a key role. On the other hand, the benefits of inclusion are compelling: the promotion of different ways of thinking; a culture of openness and learning, creativity, productivity, and motivation; and the creation of economic value.[1] But to achieve these, we must make diversity an action, not an adjective. Inclusion of diverse groups in society and organizations doesn't just happen spontaneously. Quite the opposite. Tribal dynamics are pervasive in society—even in urban, developed settings—meaning that people often seek out others like themselves and exclude anyone different.

Key Concept: The Access Economy

The access economy includes all the expenditures and investments on shared services or inclusive approaches that increase diversity and efficient use of assets, resources, and capacity. Examples range from refugee employment to car-sharing and crowdfunding. It is about finding solutions that address issues of inequality and access

continued →

by being transparent about the distribution of value in society and working to ensure that benefits are fairly shared and diversity is respected. These inclusive solutions make up the counterforce to disparity and promote responsibility.

The right of women to vote is a cautionary tale in this respect. The first country to give women democratic voting rights was New Zealand in 1893, years ahead of Finland (1907), Canada (1917), the UK (1918), and the United States (1920); it took Portugal until 1976. Political inclusion for women, which is a necessary precursor to economic inclusion, was a long and hard fight. In the end, the success of New Zealand's suffragettes was partly due to their linking it to a social issue, which was alcohol abuse and its associated violence against women. The Woman's Christian Temperance Union argued that granting political power to women would help ensure their protection.

In Russia women also had to struggle to win their right to vote and similarly used the tactic of making it a social and economic issue. When we celebrate International Women's Day, few realize the link to Russia's February Revolution in 1917, when women from the textile factories in Saint Petersburg (then Petrograd) went on strike for "bread and peace." Seven days later Tsar Nicholas II abdicated, and the government granted women the right to vote. This is typical of complex systems: Political, social, and economic elements are inextricably linked.

Today, the World Economic Forum's *Global Gender Gap Report* shows we still have a long way to go to ensure equal opportunities for women. We have inspiring role models, such as climate activist Greta Thunberg; General Motors CEO Mary Barra; Finland's prime minister, Sanna Marin; former Patagonia CEO Rose Marcario; and New Zealand's prime minister, Jacinda Ardern. But we must continue to support the bottom-up people's movement for change—for example, the women who made "pinkie promises" with their kids in 2020 that they will #VoteLikeAMadre to fight climate change. This is a laudable rallying cry, but making the access economy a reality is hard.

Fresh Insight: Women Entrepreneurship

Investing in women entrepreneurs could boost global GDP by as much as $5 trillion, a 6 percent rise, according to a study by the Boston Consulting Group.[2] Yet across 100 countries analyzed, women-led start-ups attract less than half the investment compared to companies started by men. Why? Partly, it's that fewer women start new businesses. (The exceptions are in Vietnam, Mexico, Indonesia, and the Philippines.) And partly it is good old-fashioned discrimination, linked to "old-boy networks." These are sociocultural rather than business barriers, since start-ups founded and cofounded by women actually perform better over time, generating 10 percent higher cumulative revenue over a five-year period.

When we talk about the access economy, of course we are not only looking at access for women. We also need to include young people, old people, ethnic minorities, the LGBT community, poor people, and other neglected groups. One highly effective access economy strategy to achieve this is to use financial instruments, such as *social bonds*. Until now, environmental, social, and governance (ESG) bonds were largely focused on funding projects and investments with environmental goals—so-called *green bonds*—but social bonds started to surge in 2020. Leading the wave was Alphabet Inc., which made the largest corporate ESG bond sale, comprising $5.75 billion of bonds to fund organizations that support Black entrepreneurs, small and medium businesses affected by COVID-19, affordable housing, and other pressing societal issues. In 2019 the $285 billion in ESG bonds was spread across green ($220 billion), sustainability ($48 billion), and social ($17 billion) categories. In the first half of 2020 social bonds already accounted for $41 billion, up 373 percent from the same period a year before.

Underlying these economic-access issues is an unspoken critical success factor. To be included in the economy, people need the right knowledge and skills, the competencies to match market needs. An analysis of more than 660 million professionals and more than 20 million job listings on LinkedIn reveals a fascinating list of the top 15 skills in high demand. The hard skills are mostly to power the Fourth Industrial Revolution—blockchain, cloud and distributed computing, analytical reasoning, artificial intelligence, user-experience design, scientific computing—but also include more generic skills, such as business analysis, affiliate marketing, sales, and video production. The soft skills include creativity, persuasion, collaboration, adaptability, and emotional intelligence. For the access economy to flourish, we must develop these skills among those groups that are currently most excluded from the economy.

The Black Lives Matter Movement

Anyone who thinks that tackling racism and social injustice is not part of the sustainability agenda really does not understand sustainability. The same is true for thriving. The challenge of economic inclusion is very clear when viewed through the lens of race. The police brutality exposed by the Black Lives Matter movement is the ugly tip of a systemic-racism iceberg, where the underlying issue is economic exclusion. To heal our fractured societies, we need to start listening to people who have been marginalized and discriminated against. Apple's $100 million Racial and Equity Justice Initiative is a move in the right direction, with its goal of changing education, recruitment, partnerships, and investments to deliberately support and promote marginalized groups.

Case Spotlight: BASF Dialogues

We need more initiatives like BASF's Courageous and Compassionate Conversations, which were initiated in 2020 as a constructive response to the killing of George Floyd in the United States. During sessions with 5,000 North American employees of the global chemical company, the issues of social justice, racism, and discrimination were raised for open and honest discussion. Diversity, equity, and inclusion need such proactive, human-centered approaches to make real progress.

To create a more inclusive economy, it helps to have strong role models—and not only political leaders such as Nelson Mandela, Barack Obama, and Kamala Harris but also economic leaders. It is a sad indictment of Fortune 500 companies that, in 2020, they included only three Black CEOs: Kenneth Frazier of pharmaceutical company Merck & Co. (who retired from the role on July 1, 2021), Marvin Ellison of home improvement retailer Lowe's, and Roger Ferguson Jr. of insurance company TIAA. But there are others who have beat the odds and serve as inspiration, such as Sundar Pichai, CEO of Google; Indra Nooyi, former Pepsi CEO and now on the Amazon board of directors; Rajeev Suri, former CEO of Nokia and current CEO of Inmarsat; and Ursula Burns, former Xerox CEO and now an Uber board member.

When it comes to role models for aspiring young Black people, perhaps Hollywood can help too. I'm thinking here of *Black Panther*, which is more than just a superhero film. Based on a Stan Lee character who first appeared in the Fantastic Four comics in 1966, it has become the 12th highest-grossing film of all time since its 2018 release, collecting $1.34 billion at the box office. It is a brilliant film with a fabulous soundtrack, but its significance is much greater. Not only is the superhero Black, as is most of the cast; the action is set in Wakanda, a mythical African country with technology vastly superior to the West, challenging prevailing attitudes about Africa. Change begins with imagination.

Cultural symbols are also important in reinforcing the notion that all ethnicities can and should play a strong role in society. Sports have always been better at this than politics or religion, and I saw this again when South Africa won the Rugby World Cup in 2019. In 1995, when South Africa first won the trophy, the country was a fledgling democracy, and rugby was still the sport of the oppressors (white Afrikaners). Yet President Nelson Mandela used the occasion to unify a divided nation. In 2019, when Siya Kolisi led his team to victory as South Africa's first Black Springbok captain, the incredible societal transformation that began 25 years ago reached another milestone.

Governing for Better Inclusion

It is clear from the vexing array of inequality challenges that government has to play a strong role in stimulating the access economy. One promising avenue of policy intervention is the provision of a universal basic income. Germany is the latest country—following Canada, Finland, India, and Namibia—to conduct an experiment in this area; 120 volunteers will get €1,200 per month for three years, replacing means-tested social security payments. This is not a new idea; Sir Thomas More wrote about it in his sociopolitical satire *Utopia* in the 16th century. But since the 1980s it has become a recurrent proposal from those seeking to create a fairer and more sustainable economy. Interestingly, the Finnish experiment concluded that people supported by a basic income felt happier, even though it did not lead to higher levels of employment.

Another experiment, this time from Canada, found that providing financial assistance to those in need really does help but not if the amount is too small. The New Leaf Project gave a $5,600 one-off cash payment to 50 homeless adults and compared them to 65 homeless people who received nothing. The results were startling: After one month, the number of days these people spent homeless dropped from 77 percent to 49 percent, and food security rose to 67 percent, compared with 37 percent before. What's more, spending on alcohol, cigarettes, and drugs decreased 39 percent over 12 months.

Breakthrough Solution: The iThrone

Issues of inclusion are not simple; they are entangled problems. For billions around the world, the historic injustices of slavery and colonialism have stacked the odds against them. For example, 1.8 billion people still do not have access to adequate sanitation. Putting in water and sewage infrastructure is expensive, and even portable toilets are out of the economic reach of many low-income communities.

It is government's responsibility to address issues like this, but it does not need to provide the solutions. With the right policy incentives, innovation can step into the breach. For example, the social enterprise Change:WATER Labs has created the iThrone toilet, which uses membrane technology to evaporate raw sewage and turn it into pure water and urine salts that are good for fertilizer. The sustainable innovation requires no plumbing or electricity, making it five times cheaper than comparable toilets and with half the waste-collection costs.

Governments also have to look for the hidden connections between economic exclusion and other issues. For example, when you think about social justice, I bet you are not thinking about shade. Yet in a TED Talk, Los Angeles mayor Eric Garcetti, who is chair of the C40 group of cities tackling climate change, said something totally unexpected: "Shade is an equity issue."[3] Around the world, the poorest, most marginalized communities, most of which have Black and Brown populations, live in areas with no trees and high levels of environmental degradation and pollution. The lack of shade is a proxy for numerous other overlooked ecological injustices. In fact, environment almost always touches on social inequalities. Therefore, when governments set about greening their cities, they must take care to bring nature and a clean environment to economically deprived areas first.

To further illustrate how economic inclusion is a complex, systemic issue, consider the scourge of historic national debt in developing countries. More often than not, these are debts racked up by corrupt government regimes to fund ego projects and to wage local or regional wars. One creative solution is providing debt relief for poor countries in exchange for their protection of ecosystems and natural resources, which secures carbon sinks that the world desperately needs. This is a great example of governments pursuing sustainable, inclusive policies.

Responsible Innovation for Inclusion

Whenever I am in Bangkok, I try to visit Cabbages & Condoms—one of my favorite restaurants in the world. On one of those visits, in 2019, by chance I met its inspiring founder, social entrepreneur Mechai Viravaidya. While the place itself is quirky, with decor made from colorful contraceptive condoms and pills, it is the story behind the restaurant that is remarkable. For decades Viravaidya has used this business and other social enterprises to educate Thais and empower women and communities. The results are breathtaking: Family size in Thailand dropped from 7 to 1.5 since 1975, and new HIV cases fell by 90 percent from 1991 to 2003. The social innovation continues with his Bamboo School for sustainable development.

Case Spotlight: Freeplay

Technology innovation must be appropriate to the local context. For example, what if there is no electricity, and batteries are expensive and hard to come by? This was a problem that Freeplay tackled in Africa, when social entrepreneur Trevor Baylis invented the "clockwork radio." The motivation for designing a radio that worked without batteries or electricity, using "windup" kinetic energy, was to help halt the spread of AIDS in Africa by providing much-needed access to health information and advice in off-grid rural areas. Freeplay, now owned by Euro Suisse Group, went on to innovate windup flashlights and lamps that allow people to work and study at night, and even fetal heart-rate monitors for primary health-care workers.

Cabbages & Condoms and Freeplay are just two of many examples of using business and innovation to improve social and economic inclusion. Sometimes the technology that enables inclusion is more high-tech. For instance, if we can use sensors to guide autonomous vehicles, why not use the same technology to guide people who are blind? Strap Technologies is answering that question with a chest-worn device that uses radar, lidar, and ultrasonic sensors to replace the traditional white cane or guide dog. In much the same way as for self-driving cars, the combined sensors dynamically map the surroundings in real time. But instead of turning that data into vehicle navigation, the wearer receives haptic feedback—vibrating signals through its four straps—with essential information on the proximity and location of obstacles and how to avoid them.

Making society accessible for people who are blind is about giving dignity and economic opportunity to an otherwise marginalized group. Refugees are another such group. One champion for their cause is Hamdi Ulukaya, the son of nomadic sheep farmers from the Turkish mountains, who immigrated to America and started Chobani, which today is a $1.5 billion dairy products company. Ulukaya has made a point of using employment to bring about social change. A third of his employees are immigrants or refugees, and more than 20 languages are spoken at the company's plants—which include the world's largest yogurt facility—where they pay workers, on average, twice the federal minimum wage and give a portion of their profits to charitable causes. As an aside, Chobani is also rapidly expanding into providing plant-based dairy alternatives to decrease their environmental footprint.

Creating empowering technologies and implementing inclusive hiring policies are powerful approaches. Another is to build systems of socioeconomic exchange. In Indonesia, for example, Garbage Clinical Insurance invites poor communities to clean up trash in their neighborhoods, where local authorities are not providing adequate waste services, in exchange for health insurance. In China and Turkey reverse vending machines allow citizens to deposit recyclable bottles and receive public transport credit. And Plastic Bank works with low-income communities around the world to turn plastic recycling into livelihoods, labeling it "social plastic" to attract consumers' support. These are all ways to do trading up instead of trading off.

The Spark of Social Entrepreneurship

Many of the business examples shared in this chapter are social enterprises. One of the pioneers in this field is Bill Drayton, who founded Ashoka in 1980. The organization identifies *changemakers* who are "committed to championing new patterns of social good" and supports them with training and, in some cases, seed funding.[4] Today Ashoka has become the largest network of leading social entrepreneurs in the world, with more than 3,000 lifelong fellows. It turns out, for moving from disparity to responsibility by creating an access economy, one of the most effective strategies is to invest in social entrepreneurs.

Ashoka has data to back up this claim. In a 2018 survey of a quarter of their fellows from 74 countries, they found that they were having impacts on economic development, education, health, human rights, civic participation, and the environment.[5] More than half were focused on helping people living in poverty or children and youth. Other beneficiaries included women, people living in rural and remote areas, people with disabilities, migrants or refugees, and people treated unfairly because of their race, ethnicity, religion, sexual orientation, or gender preference.

Almost all of the social entrepreneurs (93 percent) had managed to influence public policy by achieving legislative change, providing research or previously missing data to policymakers, or advising policymakers or legislative bodies as experts. They were also active in representing marginalized populations, challenging laws in court, and convincing their governments to allocate funds to specific causes. Since government policy sets the rules of the game, this is a strong indicator that social entrepreneurs work on creating systemic change.

The survey found that 93 percent also altered market systems. For example, they increased the flow of market information about prices or products to different market actors, made it easier for people to trade or access certain goods or services in the existing market, or created a new market that allowed people to trade or access a product or service they previously could not. The social entrepreneurs also focused on creating value for a product or service where value previously did not exist, and on providing new ways for low-income people to generate income. Sometimes, their efforts involved changing the code of conduct or official policy of a large organization or industry, or encouraging for-profit organizations to include previously excluded people.

One way in which Ashoka fellows drive systems change is by trying to shift societal mindsets or cultural norms. They also strive to create a business model that can be replicated and scaled. In fact, 90 percent have seen their idea replicated and two-thirds have actively encouraged this, often by open sourcing their idea (in other words, not trying to copyright or patent protect their intellectual property). A key enabler in replication is to embrace partnership—and indeed, around four-fifths of fellows have partnered with governments, schools, or universities.

Hot Trend: B Corporations

A powerful catalyst for social entrepreneurship is the B Corporation movement, which is promoting and certifying companies that are purpose driven and that create benefit for all stakeholders, not just shareholders. The B stands for *benefit*. Certified B Corporations achieve a minimum verified score on the B Impact Assessment—a rigorous assessment of a company's impact on its workers, customers, community, and environment—and make their B Impact Report transparent on bcorporation.net. Certified B Corporations also amend their legal governing documents to require their board of directors to balance profit and purpose.

To date, they have certified more than 3,500 companies from 150 industries and more than 70 countries, including big brands such as Patagonia, Danone, Natura, and Ben & Jerry's. But this underestimates the impact the movement is having. More than 80,000 companies have used the free B Impact Assessment tool to gauge their impact on workers, customers, community, and environment. In the United States, there is Benefit Corporation legislation in 37 states, meaning that companies can choose the B Corp model as a form of legal incorporation. There are similar options in other countries, such as the Community Interest Company structure in the UK.

Muhammad Yunus, founder of the Grameen Bank and pioneer of the global microcredit movement, has introduced what he calls "social business"—a non-loss (meaning break-even or profit-making), nondividend, investor-owned organization, where 100 percent of its resources are for social good. All surplus (profit) is reinvested into the business for the pursuit of its social mission. In his book *Building Social Business* Yunus argues that this is different from a social enterprise, which may not be a business and may not meet the criteria he has set out.[6] In this respect, the Grameen

Group is leading by example, with 21 social businesses covering multiple sectors, from telecoms and energy to textiles and food.

We should also not forget a much older form of social enterprise and one that is still more ubiquitous than B Corps and other modern-day variations. I am referring to the 3 million cooperatives around the world, which represent 1.2 billion cooperative members. The key distinction with the cooperative structure is that the enterprise is owned, controlled, and run by and for its members (rather than shareholders). The members can be customers, employees, users, or residents, and each has an equal vote, regardless of the amount of capital they put in. The goal of cooperatives is for the economic and social benefits of their activity to stay in the communities where they are established, with profits either reinvested in the enterprise or returned to the members.

When Sharing Becomes Smart

Besides corporate diversity practices, government welfare policies, responsible innovations, and social enterprises, another business model that can help create economic inclusion is what is variously called the *peer-to-peer*, *collaborative*, or *sharing* economy. The idea of sharing resources is probably as old as civilization itself and was normal practice among subsistence communities for thousands of years. But more recently academics Marcus Felson and Joe L. Spaeth have been credited with introducing the notion of "collaborative consumption" and the "economy of sharing."[7]

The concept remained rather obscure, however, until it was popularized in two books: *Wikinomics: How Mass Collaboration Changes Everything*, by Don Tapscott and Anthony D. Williams, published in 2008, and *What's Mine Is Yours: How Collaborative Consumption Changes the Way We Live*, by Rachel Botsman and Roo Rogers, published in 2011.[8] In both cases, digital platforms such as Uber, Airbnb, Facebook, and Alibaba were seen as game changers that allowed assets to be shared more easily and cheaply.

Tapscott and Williams distilled these changes into four principles: openness, peering, sharing, and acting globally. Botsman and Rogers identified four key drivers behind these shifts in how we live, work, play, travel, bank, learn, and consume: (1) technology innovation, including better, faster internet capabilities; (2) a values shift, with trust shifting from institutions to distributed networks; (3) economic realities, notably the fallout from the 2008 global financial crisis; and (4) environmental pressures—such as the effects of climate change—on resources.

While most people use collaborative consumption and the sharing economy interchangeably, Botsman and Rogers suggest that there are nuanced differences, and they identify three systems:

1. *Redistribution*, which stretches the product life cycle, taking a used or pre-owned item and moving it from where it's not wanted or needed to somewhere or someone who wants it and can use it

2. *Collaboration*, which involves sharing resources such as time, money, and skills

3. *Product-service systems*, which allow users to pay for the benefit of the product without needing to own it

Within these systems, some will be business-to-consumer (B2C), such as Zipcar and Netflix; some will be peer-to-peer (P2P), such as Airbnb and TaskRabbit; and some will be business-to-business (B2B), such as Gettable. These alternative systems are significant not because of their novelty—buying secondhand clothes, using credit unions, and hiring taxis, for example, have all been around for a long time—but rather because digital technology has allowed these practices to scale. Netflix, which started in 1997, grew to more than 180 million subscribers in 2020; Uber took just 10 years from 2009 to reach 75 million global customers and contract with 3 million dedicated drivers in 83 countries.

Hot Trend: Nownership

Besides scale, the sharing economy is important because it challenges the notion of private property, one of the foundations of capitalism. It represents a seismic shift from ownership to *nownership*. An Expedia study found 74 percent of Americans now favor experiences over products or things. And a global survey by PwC found that 72 percent of people expected to become a consumer in the sharing economy in the next two years and see major benefits, including a more affordable and eco-friendly lifestyle, greater convenience and efficiency, and increased community building.[9]

To be clear, the sharing economy does not always work. The tough nuts to crack are cost and convenience. Taking an Uber or Lyft is easier than driving and parking in a congested city. But can renting a lawnmower, drill, fridge, washing machine, dress, or pair of jeans be as cost effective and hassle-free? The answer to this question has profound implications for how people will be working and consuming in the future.

From the perspective of inclusion, the sharing economy allows for more participation in the economy, both for producers and consumers. Whether it's the 60,000 independent workers on TaskRabbit or the 3 million Uber drivers, for many of them, the platforms have provided an economic opportunity and a potential route to financial independence. I have seen this for myself in many countries where I have taken an Uber and talked to the drivers. It is not a solution for everyone, and the system has also been abused (which I discuss shortly), but it does represent a genuine opportunity for economic inclusion that did not exist before.

Now for the caveat. Uber has come under heavy criticism and faced litigation for a variety of issues related to worker conditions (such as the safety of drivers), inadequate pay, and the lack of social security benefits, since drivers are contractors and not employees. Similarly, the so-called gig economy for freelancers has shown how vulnerable workers can be, especially if they reside in a country with a weak social welfare system. Times of economic hardship tend to impact independent workers far more than employees.

These are challenges for the sharing economy, but they do not invalidate the business model or extinguish the benefits that many derive from getting economic access. We can and must address the limitations, but we should also remember cases like Hello Tractor, founded by Jehiel Oliver with a mission to improve farmers' lives by becoming the world's best agricultural services platform. Use of its sharing app since 2014 has already helped more than 800,000 farmers in sub-Saharan Africa to have access to mechanized farming options that radically improve their productivity and profitability.

Reimagining the Winner-Takes-All Economy

All of these approaches and innovations are part of creating an access economy. But at a more fundamental level, they invite us to reimagine our current exclusive winner-take-all economy. For that reason, I would like to share my encounters with three remarkable economists who have inspired my views on what an inclusive economy is all about. They are Francis Wilson, Jeffrey Sachs, and Manfred Max-Neef.

Of these, Sachs is the most well known globally, while Max-Neef is more familiar in Latin America. I return to both of them later, but it was Professor Francis Wilson who had a seminal impact on me. He was head of the Southern Africa Labour and Development Research Unit at the University of Cape Town when I was studying for my business science degree. His title gives a clue to his perspective—liberal, prolabor, leaning toward socialist—which at that time in South Africa, around the late 1980s, meant anti-establishment.

It was Wilson who completely opened my eyes to the scourge of apartheid—using economics. He showed us how the degrading migrant-labor system worked. Most workers in the gold and platinum mines had to travel far from their homes (including from other African countries), stay in single-sex hostels, and work grueling and dangerous shifts for low wages. He explained *influx control*, where Black people had to carry passbooks that allowed them to work in the cities for a limited time before going back to their homelands, which were reservations of land (around 14 percent of South Africa's total area, where 55 percent of the population was meant to live).

Our core text for the course was *Uprooting Poverty*, a book that Wilson had coauthored with Mamphela Ramphele.[10] By appealing to our intellect and showing that the economic policies of apartheid were crazy, while educating us on the injustices and human indignities, Wilson changed me from a naïve, yet complicit, racist into a more conscious activist for a just economic system and a fairer society. That is the power of economics. This awakening was a big part of why my career took the direction it did, focusing on the social responsibilities of business. And ever since, I've had real respect for economists who use their knowledge to call for social justice.

Professor Jeffrey Sachs is one of these: an American economist and director of The Earth Institute at Columbia University. I had a chance to interview Sachs for a book I wrote for Cambridge University called *The Top 50 Sustainability Books*, and I have met him several times since, now that he is on the international advisory board of Antwerp Management School.[11] Sachs was very influential in setting up the United Nations Millennium Development Goals in 2000, under Secretary-General Kofi Annan, and the follow-up Sustainable Development Goals, which were set by the UN in 2015 and will run until 2030.

Sachs is famous for saying in 2005 that extreme poverty could be eradicated by 2025.[12] When I interviewed him at his home in New York in 2008, what impressed me most was his positive attitude, in contrast to the doom and gloom that is an occupational hazard if you work in sustainability. Sachs's main argument was that we now know how to end poverty. We have figured out the kinds of economic and social policies that are most effective. Of course, knowing the solutions and having the political will to implement them are two different things. I asked him if he thought he was being overly optimistic. His answer was very interesting. Rather than being in denial—he told me that 10 million children die every year from preventable causes—he took his hope from what is already being achieved.

Sachs gave me lots of examples of where our efforts are paying off: the dramatic drops in malaria deaths, the increases in food production—and all from simple policies such as spreading the use of insecticide-treated bed nets or fertilizers and high-yield seeds. He encouraged me to look beyond the stereotypes (such as Africa as an economic disaster zone, or the idea that aid doesn't work) and to look at the evidence. I think that's a really important lesson—and a great strength of economics: We have to cut through the political and ideological rhetoric and look at the numbers to see what works. He concluded that the problem isn't our lack of tools; it's our ability to manage the powerful tools that we have to human effect.[13]

Human-Scale Economics

But what does that mean: to human effect? An economist who understood this better than most was the late Professor Manfred Max-Neef, also known as the "barefoot economist." Max-Neef was a Chilean economist who lived in exile for many years during the 1960s and 1970s because of his opposition to the dictatorial governments of his own country and others in the region. In 1983 he was awarded the Right Livelihood Award (also known as the Alternative Nobel Prize), and in 1993 he stood as a minority candidate in the Chilean presidential election.

I interviewed Max-Neef by videoconference in 2008 and met him in 2010, when he invited me to spend three days at his home in Valdivia, Chile. He was one of the most inspiring people I have had the fortune to meet, partly because of his remarkable life story and his work among poor communities and also because of the model of fundamental human needs that he derived from that work. He was a musician too, and I was lucky to hear him play one of his piano compositions when I was there. He told me, "I sometimes even say (a little bit as a joke) that I have put music into economics."

One of the stories he told me about his early career left a lasting impression on me: He had joined the Shell Oil company at age 21 and quickly got promoted, first to executive trainee and then to executive. "The chief of personnel called me in," he recalled. "There was a great ceremony. I had many congratulations, and he handed me an envelope. So I opened it, and there was a key. And he said: 'That is the key to the executive toilet.' And I said, 'This is what [being] an executive is all about—having my own toilet?' Well, that's a joke."

After that, Max-Neef tried to imagine his future with Shell—having the power to negotiate oil deals with the Shah of Iran—and he realized, "That's not me; I don't fit here." He recalled his mother reciting Homer's *Iliad* to him when he was a child, including the combat between Achilles and Hector. He asked her to tell him the story over and over, and when she asked why, he said, "Because I hope that next time Hector will win." From the very beginning, "my sympathy was for the weak, not the strong." Shell, he said, "that's Achilles; I'm Hector."

As a result, Max-Neef's career turned to economics; he was the first economist in Chile to focus on the sociology of development. After more than 20 years of living as a grassroots economist in Argentina, Chile, and Ecuador (where he helped mobilize 300,000 peasant farmers to "do their own development"), he was given a grant by the Swedish Dag Hammarskjöld Foundation and asked to record his experiences and philosophies on development economics. This was then published as a groundbreaking book called *From the Outside Looking In: Experiences in Barefoot Economics*.[14] Most profoundly, it challenged Maslow's ideas about a hierarchy of fundamental human needs.

Smart Insight: Human-Scale Development

In Manfred Max-Neef's conception of "human-scale development," he presented a matrix of nine fundamental human needs: subsistence, protection, affection, understanding, participation, leisure, creation, identity, and freedom. These apply to four different states: being, having, doing, and interacting. Max-Neef argued convincingly from his work with poor people that, beyond eating and drinking to survive, there is no hierarchy of needs. Any of the nine needs can be satisfied by anyone, regardless of income or development, in any order, and they are common across cultures.[15]

Thinking in a human-centered way may even lead companies to innovate their recruitment practices. Imagine if companies hired the first person to apply for a job. No CV piles to trawl through, no background checks, no tortuous rounds of interviews. This is a novel hiring strategy to increase diversity and inclusion. It gives a chance to those who would normally get screened out because of discrimination, bias, or an unconventional past. In 2019 the New York social enterprise Greyston Bakery tried it in its North Carolina distribution center, reducing staff turnover by 60 percent. In 2020 the Body Shop adopted the same approach for its distribution centers. This may only work for low-skilled jobs, but it is an example of the kind of human-scale creativity we need to create an inclusive economy.

From Waste to Worth

In *Closing the Loop*, the circular economy documentary that I coproduced and presented, many of the cases we highlighted had features of socioeconomic inclusion. For example, in the city of Quito in Ecuador, the municipality was collaborating with the company EcoPak to upcycle Tetra

Pak cartons into furniture, corrugated roofing, kitchen tabletops, and even jewelry. For the sorting process, where the Tetra Paks were picked out from the general municipal waste, they chose to work with a group of women who had suffered domestic abuse. This is a classic inclusive approach.

Similarly, the tire-recycling case of REDISA in South Africa helped many previously disadvantaged people to become self-employed, some as waste pickers collecting the discarded tires in their communities, others as depot managers in sorting, cutting, and packing the tires for onward distribution. According to executive director Stacey Davidson, REDISA was responsible for the creation of 226 businesses and 3,000 jobs, which gave her great job satisfaction. For her, the idea of turning waste into worth also incorporates the nurturing of self-worth and human development. The circular economy is not just about a different way of production; it's about changing lives.[16]

Case Spotlight: Stanley's Story

One of the lives that REDISA changed was that of Stanley Mangoegape, manager of a tire-recycling depot just outside the city of Johannesburg. His story really touched me deeply during the filming of *Closing the Loop*. I asked him at one point what his entrepreneurial journey had been like and what motivated him to keep going in this work. This was his answer: "My life has changed completely. I got very, very sick, and at my age I couldn't get any job. I mean, if you look at me now, I'm one of the happiest. In life if you're not working it's very, very difficult. More especially if you're not a thief, and you don't know what to do, and then you get an opportunity like this. It has changed me forever, and I'm a better man. And my family enjoys the opportunities that I give them, and they benefit; we have food on the table. It's not only my family, there are other close families that benefit also, because I create jobs for these guys, and

continued →

they also support their families. So my life has changed to see other people happy, and also myself happy and healthy."

Stanley's concluding remarks were also very poignant, as he reflected on his life under the racist apartheid regime. "I grew up in a very strange environment, to be honest. And when I grew up it was 1976, where we burned these tires. But today I'm creating jobs with these tires. So, I'm very proud to say my end will be a better one, and I'm able to live in this South Africa that we are in today."

Khothatso Moloi, CEO of Waste Beneficiation, had a similar reflection on how tires turned into more than just an economic opportunity. He recalled in the film how discarded tires in their community used to be a health hazard. Either they trapped water and served as a breeding ground for mosquitos or they were burned for fuel or in protest of apartheid policies, giving off toxic fumes. Hence, the circular economy for tires is as much about improving health and well-being as about resource efficiency.

Shaping Our Future

This chapter is about taking responsibility for the inequality of our world—and I mean responsibility in the best sense of the word: recognizing our ability to respond. And yet, in order to respond to injustice or suffering, we need to care. We can find a hundred rational reasons and business arguments to take responsible action, but at some point, there must be a moral drive. We must act because we care.

BECAUSE I CARE

When I strike on the streets in mass protest
And warn you to change or beware
It's not because I'm foolhardy—

It's because I care
When I brood in the quagmire of worry
And greet your bright smile with a stare
It's not because I'm unhappy—
It's because I care

I care that the forests are burning
That the storms are grey prophets of gloom
I care that the children are yearning
For a future where nature can bloom

When I speak with the words of the voiceless
And lay my stark message out bare
It's not because I'm emotive—
It's because I care
When I spark with the flames of great passion
And hope that you'll take up my dare
It's not because I'm hot-headed—
It's because I care

I care that the homeless are growing
That the poor cannot flee from their pains
I care that the blood is still flowing
That the slaves are not free from their chains

When I strive for a future that's better
And look for a purpose to share
It's not because I'm a hippie—
It's because I care
When I burst with ideas for solutions
And tackle tough problems with flair
It's not because I'm creative—
It's because I care

I care that the animals suffer
That the farms are like factories of doom
I care that survival gets tougher
That the sixth mass extinction now looms

When I call for bold action on climate
And demand that you clean up the air
It's not because I'm dramatic—
It's because I care
When I speak of the need for more justice
And implore you to do what is fair
It's not because I'm a dreamer—
It's because I care

I care that all Black lives should matter
That the scourge of race-hatred remains
I care that the women get battered
That they still have to fight for their gains

When I wish for rewilding of nature
And the right to protect life so rare
It's not because I'm a "greenie"—
It's because I care
When I join in the movement for changes
It's not my intention to scare
It's just me shaping our future—
It's because I care.

CHAPTER 6

Revitalization

*When health is absent, wisdom cannot reveal itself, art
cannot manifest, strength cannot fight, wealth becomes
useless, and intelligence cannot be applied.*

—Attributed to **Herophilus** (ancient Greek physician)

I have been blessed with good health in my life—and it is not something I take for granted. In this chapter, I recount many stories of how innovation is bringing health and well-being to those who need it. But before I do, let me share a personal story. Picture a boy, aged six. He is a happy child, full of energy and always the first on the playground, eager to make new friends. One day he feels tired. He gets a fever and begins throwing up. At first the doctor diagnoses food poisoning. But he doesn't get better. His mother, a trained pediatric nurse, is concerned, especially because his pulse is very high. She takes him to the emergency ward of the hospital. The doctors run tests and find an infection of the heart valve.

While in the hospital, the boy goes into cardiac arrest. The doctors scramble to save him. In the coming days his heart will stop another two times, in one case for seven minutes. They install an artificial valve, but the heart fails to respond. A heart bypass machine is keeping him alive. Meanwhile, his other organs are failing. He is given multiple blood transfusions. He is put on dialysis to keep his kidneys working. His lungs are punctured so that they can drain off the fluids. After five days on the bypass machine, they have to turn it off, as his body can no longer cope. If the heart doesn't restart on its own, there is nothing more they can do.

They switch off the machine, and the boy's heart begins to pump on its own. The artificial valve is working. He will remain in an induced coma for two weeks, but his life is saved. He will need to learn to walk and talk again. He will need to take blood thinners for the rest of his life, and he can never get a tattoo or play contact sports. But apart from this, he can live a normal life. Today, this boy is a man of 30. He is fit and healthy. He eats nutritious foods and works out at the gym; sometimes he runs. But most of all, he loves basketball—and he's good; he even coaches an amateur team.

The boy is our son, Andi. Every day we are grateful that he is alive. But more than this, we are inspired by how he is making the most of his life and never taking his health for granted. His is a story of revitalization. He is living testimony to the power of science and technology, the care of medical workers, and the love of his parents. He is also an example to everyone of how a positive attitude to living is vital for well-being. The uncomplaining resilience and good spirits that he showed as a six-year-old going through such a traumatic experience are still the mark of the man.

When injury or illness strikes, our quality of life suffers too. We are not meant to be incapacitated. Our natural state as humans is to be full of energy, to enjoy vitality. When we suffer from physical or mental disease, the counterforce is revitalization. The fact that Andi not only recovered but has gone on to lead a productive life shows the potential of revitalization. And that same force for individual thriving is benefiting millions of people today, turning breakdowns in health into breakthroughs for well-being.

Drawing from the Well of Well-Being

The most obvious example of looking after well-being in recent times is the development and rollout of the COVID-19 vaccines. In 2020 around 160 COVID-19 vaccines were under development. The first to achieve government approval was the Pfizer-BioNTech vaccine, in December 2020, with others following swiftly in its wake. The speed with which the vaccines were researched, developed, and approved is unprecedented and should be applauded as an incredible achievement of the universities, pharmaceutical companies, and government agencies responsible.

Now governments, pharmaceutical companies, and multilateral agencies are rising to the unprecedented challenge of producing and distributing the vaccines. The World Economic Forum estimates that between 10 billion and 19 billion vaccines will be needed globally.[1] To put this in perspective, 1 billion children have been vaccinated in the world over the past 10 years. This may be a coming-of-age moment for blockchain technology. Since blockchain is a digital way to secure transactions without interference or manipulation, it could ensure traceability and prevent fraud.

Other innovations will also be necessary to ensure that the vaccine reaches all its intended beneficiaries. For instance, it's not only fresh fruit and vegetables that need refrigeration—so do COVID-19 vaccines. How will this be ensured in developing countries such as Sudan, where only 28 percent of the population have electricity, and temperatures climb over 100 degrees Fahrenheit (37 Celsius)? One solution is solar fridges, and UNICEF expects to install more than 65,000 around the world.[2] Another innovation is from Sure Chill, which makes fridges that use ice to keep vaccines cool for days, or even weeks, without a source of power. In time, Pfizer also expects to create a powder vaccine.

We have triumphed in many battles against infectious diseases—not only COVID-19 but also SARS, avian flu, swine flu, Ebola, and others—but the war is far from won. The difference between a battle and a war is mainly duration. When COVID-19 struck, many thought it was a battle easily won. But it turns out to be a war. That means changing tactics when the enemy changes—in this case, the virus mutated into more virulent strains. It also means having perseverance, staying the course, and doing what's necessary to win until the vaccine tips the scales in our favor. Other crises, such as climate change, are a war as well and will need similar trust in science, stoic patience, human resilience, social adaptation, technological innovation, and never-give-up attitudes.

Besides responding to infectious diseases, a large part of the well-being economy is about tackling noncommunicable diseases (NCDs)—such as strokes, diabetes, heart disease, and cancer—which kill more people than infectious diseases. To put this in perspective, while COVID-19 resulted in more than 4 million deaths by mid-2021,[3] NCDs cause 41 million global deaths annually (71 percent of all deaths), with 85 percent (28 million) occurring in low- and middle-income countries. The main killer is cardiovascular disease (including heart attacks and strokes), followed by cancers and respiratory diseases.[4]

Even one of the biggest corporate agents of disease, cigarette company Philip Morris, is doubling down on its commitment to a "smoke-free future," as set out in its 2020 Letter from the Board to Shareholders. The company claims cigarette sales can end within 10 to 15 years in many countries. The plan is to scale up "smoke-free alternatives," such as vaping, which Philip Morris admits are also "not risk free."[5] It's hardly revitalization, but, still, it's a big shift for an industry that kills 8 million people a year and damages the health of 1.1 billion customers.[6]

Many will find it easy to condemn tobacco companies. But what about pharmaceutical companies, which develop many of the treatments needed to ensure health and well-being? The fight for inclusive medicine is decades old, but it's far from being over. Take diabetes, which affects 415 million people. Over the past 60 years, the price of insulin has gone up from 77 cents to $250, 43 times more than US inflation. Such patent-driven predatory pricing is possible only because the $27 billion market is controlled by just three companies: Eli Lilly, Novo Nordisk, and Sanofi.[7] Now the Open Insulin Project of biotech company Counter Culture Labs is reverse engineering the drug to make open-source generic insulin. By publicly sharing the formula and manufacturing instructions, medical facilities around the world can make their own insulin. I hope they—and others like them—succeed.

The well-being economy is not all in the hands of Big Pharma. Universities are key players as well, and often we see them being more farsighted and less driven by short-term profits. For instance, academic researchers have recently discovered that the rise in modern diseases such as obesity, diabetes, asthma, and food allergies are linked to a loss of microbiota diversity (for example, healthy bacteria) in our gut. People who historically lived in forests and savanna regions—without access to modern medicine—have more diverse microbiota than those in industrial countries. At Rutgers University they are now creating a microbiota vault to preserve ancestral microbes for future generations, before they become extinct. Reintroducing these healthy bacteria into microbe-deprived humans will be part of our future health care.

Key Concept: The Well-Being Economy

Health-care solutions provide a counterforce to disease, creating revitalization through the well-being economy, which includes all expenditures and investments that increase human health and happiness in society. These may range from stress-relief practices and life coaching to plant-based diets and responses to social diseases (such as domestic violence). It is about finding solutions that satisfy our fundamental human needs, improve our health, and heal our diseases, enabling a lifestyle and culture that value quality of life, physical fitness, vitality, happiness, and other indicators of well-being. Well-being has become big business. The corporate wellness market is expected to grow to $87.3 billion by 2026.[8]

How Health Tech Is Helping

Necessity is the mother of invention, and the COVID-19 crisis is proof: Manufacturers such as Tesla, Ford, and GE retrofitted factories to produce ventilators; universities rapidly went virtual; and orchestras performed via videoconference. Now we need a new wave of creativity: innovation at low cost—or *frugal innovation*—so that what is needed can quickly scale and be accessible to all. For example, MIT created a ventilator that can be made for $100 as compared with $30,000 for commercial ventilators, and they open-sourced the design. Similarly, Maker's Asylum in India made a low-cost face shield. This is innovation for well-being and inclusion.

3D printing is a key enabler of frugal innovation. For example, at the height of the pandemic, a hospital in Chiari in northern Italy was running out of valves for respiratory machines. Ordering replacements would take time, and, meanwhile, people were dying. The digital manufacturing company FabLab heard about the problem, reverse engineered the valves, and was able to 3D-print 100 valves the next day. 3D printing is also being used to manufacture prosthetics at a fraction of the cost. Limbitless Solutions has reduced the cost of a myoelectric arm by 90 percent, from around $10,000 to $1,000, while e-NABLE is an online community that supports DIY 3D prosthetics, with some simple designs costing as little as $50.

Hot Trend: The Bio Revolution

Not all innovation is of the low-cost variety. In what McKinsey & Company calls the "bio revolution"—a confluence of advances in biomolecules, biosystems, biomachine interfaces, and biocomputing—innovation is set to deliver up to $1.3 trillion in annual economic benefits between 2030 and 2040 in the human health and performance domain. Applications will include cell, gene, and RNA therapies to treat or even prevent disease, a range of anti-aging

treatments to extend life spans, innovations in reproductive medicine, improvements to drug development and delivery, and new
predictive modeling of human health and disease. No wonder synthetic biology start-ups raised $3 billion in the first half of 2020
alone.[9]

Some of these innovations may be controversial, such as the release
of 750 million genetically modified mosquitoes in the Florida Keys. The
GMO mosquitoes will insert a gene into the mosquito population that
makes them infertile and especially targets the invasive *Aedes aegypti* mosquito, which transmits diseases such as dengue, chikungunya, and Zika.
With more than 400,000 people dying from mosquito-transmitted malaria
every year, we need to be open to scientific solutions that save lives.

In an analysis of "tech for good," McKinsey examines the possibilities of
artificial intelligence (AI)–powered drug research that is speeding up drug
discovery, robotics that help those with disabilities, lifestyle wearables that
monitor individuals' health and track improvements, and telemedicine
that uses telephones and computers to improve access to health-care services.
In India, for example, telemedicine could replace as many as half of in-person
outpatient consultations by 2025, saving $4–5 billion annually.[10]

The caveat to telemedicine is the *digital divide*—those that technology has left behind. We often think of this as the gap between developed
and developing countries. But there is also an age-related digital divide.
In the United States, for primary-care organizations such as Iora Health,
Oak Street Health, ChenMed, and Landmark Health, many of their mostly
elderly patients don't have electronic devices or an internet connection, and
even those who do are not necessarily competent in using them. For digital
inclusion to work in health care, therefore, telemedicine solutions must
include provision of devices, connections, and training for elderly patients,
especially during COVID-19 times.

Besides telehealth, advanced robotics—such as exoskeletons (external frames) and wheelchairs with computer and voice control—can help people with specific disabilities to communicate with others, and increase mobility. For example, Hoobox Robotics has developed a wheelchair that can be controlled by facial expressions, facilitating mobility using AI technology. And in a collaboration between Affectiva and Autism Glass, AI is used to automate the recognition of emotions and provide social cues to help individuals along the autism spectrum interact in social environments.

AI can also help with mental health. Three-quarters of workers think 2020 has been the most stressful year ever, and 85 percent find that mental health issues at work spill over into the home, according to an international survey by Workplace Intelligence and Oracle.[11] Technology has stepped in: Ginger is a chatbot that draws on 45 million chat messages and 2 million clinical assessments to give automated counseling. BioBeats gives an individualized employee mental well-being score, based on health-monitoring data, and Woebot uses AI, empathy, and therapeutic expertise to support mental health. This is technology with a human touch.

Many of these technology benefits are being felt around the world, including in developing countries. In Rio de Janeiro in Brazil, for example, Hospital Estadual Getúlio Vargas is using advanced analytics to help improve patient care and treatment, which has resulted in the length of stay for intensive-care patients being cut by three days. Meanwhile, in the United States, Partners HealthCare has been using at-home monitoring devices to track weight, blood pressure, and other metrics for congestive heart failure patients. The program reduced hospital readmissions by 44 percent while generating cost savings of more than $10 million over a six-year period.[12]

Opportunities for Revitalization

The UN's "Global Opportunity Explorer" report identifies many inspiring examples of innovation for revitalization, from combating NCDs with mobile technologies and innovative finance to everyday health enablers.[13] Let's take a look at some of these, as a way to emphasize how many possibilities we have for making a positive impact on human health.

In the United States, BlueStar by Welldoc aims to help chronic disease patients to better manage their conditions. It delivers clinically validated disease-management tools via mobile phones, reducing hospital admissions and health-care costs in the process. In the UK, a mobile microphone stethoscope, developed by Oxford University and the University of Cape Town, allows patients to record their own heart rhythms using only standard hands-free mobile microphones widely available in most countries. Data can then be sent to health professionals for inspection and diagnosis.

In India, the mDiabetes initiative, developed by Arogya World and Nokia Life—the "m" stands for *mobile*—generates population-level awareness about diabetes and encourages healthier behavior by sending millions of free and culturally relevant text messages available in many languages. Another inclusive technology, from Peek Vision, consists of a smartphone and low-cost adapter capable of capturing images of the retina, offering eye examinations to patients in remote areas. Results can be shared with doctors abroad, while GPS data keeps track of patients' locations for future treatment, inspection, and diagnosis.

In Nigeria and Ghana, the mPedigree network uses text messages to enable patients to verify drugs before using them. This helps tackle the problem of dangerous counterfeit medicines in developing countries. The network partners with legitimate drug manufacturers, who label their products with a scratch-off code that can be verified by means of a free text message. And the global Be Healthy, Be Mobile initiative orchestrated by the World Health Organization, the International Federation of Pharmaceutical Manufacturers & Associations, and the International Telecommunication Union seeks to scale up mobile health (mHealth) into existing NCD control activities (including smoking cessation) in various countries.

Key in health-care provision is to ensure that babies and children get access to the care and medicines they need. The New Cooperative Medical

Scheme is an innovative social health insurance mechanism in China to decrease the financial barriers for poor households to gain access to newborn health services.

Improving access to nutritious food is another important health strategy. Norway, Sweden, and Denmark have adopted a common Green Keyhole food-labeling scheme to help consumers recognize healthier food options. The program is voluntary for food producers; items bearing the symbol must conform to nutritional regulations in certain food groups. In French Polynesia a different kind of regulation is in place. The Etablissement Pour la Prevention uses revenue generated from a tax on alcohol and sweetened snacks and drinks to fund health promotion efforts, including obesity prevention.

Daily access to nutritious food is crucial for children's development. In Côte d'Ivoire, a "farmer-to-school" model called One School, One Canteen provides smallholder farmers with the technical and financial support they need to supply healthy school meals. The program benefits local economic development, child health, and the environment simultaneously.

Another initiative, the Healthy Food Financing Initiative in the United States, provides onetime grants and loans to improve access to healthy food in underserved areas. This is accomplished by developing or expanding corner stores, farmers markets, and other forms of healthy food retail. In Pennsylvania the model helped develop 88 healthy food retailers and created thousands of jobs.

Healthy food also means tackling the ineffectiveness of medicines that results from the ubiquity of antibiotics in the environment: They are in the meat that we eat, they leak into drinking water, and they are overprescribed by doctors. As a result, there is a big drive to get antibiotics out of the meat supply chain. In Chile, Nova Austral aims to achieve antibiotic-free salmon production, while the Norwegian Veterinary Institute has vaccines to replace antibiotics in farmed salmon. In the United States, Perdue completely removed all antibiotics from its hatchery, while Subway committed to serving antibiotic-free chicken and turkey at its restaurants. In Brazil, Korin was the first company to establish a large-scale production of antibiotic-free poultry, and California became the first American state to outlaw routine use of bacteria-fighting drugs in livestock.

The Rise of Plant-Based Health

A number of documentaries—such as *Cowspiracy*, *The Game Changers*, and *What the Health*—have raised public awareness about the negative health and environmental impacts of the meat and dairy industries and, by contrast, the virtues of plant-based diets. These claims have been hotly debated, and the proponents have been accused of cherry-picking scientific studies to support their vegan agenda. But it seems there is enough evidence to suggest that their main thesis is still broadly correct. A predominantly plant-based diet is on balance healthier than a predominantly meat-based diet. Let's look at some of the most credible studies that have been done.

Research from Oxford University concludes that a failure to increase plant-based diets and reduce meat consumption by 2050 would result in between 5.1 million and 8.1 million avoidable deaths and between 79 million and 129 million years of life lost.[14] Nine of the top 15 risk factors for global morbidity result from poor dietary quality, while diseases associated with poor dietary quality—including coronary heart disease, type II diabetes, stroke, and colorectal cancers—account for nearly 40 percent of global mortality. Consumption of sugar-sweetened beverages, unprocessed red meat, and processed red meat are consistently associated with increased risk across all of these disease categories.[15]

Smart Insight: Plant-Based Diets

Researchers at Oxford University compared a conventional omnivorous diet (including all types of meat, dairy, and plants) with three alternative diets—vegetarian (dairy and plants only), pescatarian (dairy, plants, and seafood only), and Mediterranean (dairy, plants,

continued →

seafood, and moderate amounts of poultry, pork, lamb, and beef). They found that, in the three predominantly plant-based alternative diets, incidence rates of type II diabetes were reduced by 16–41 percent and of cancer by 7–13 percent, while relative mortality rates from coronary heart disease were 20–26 percent lower, and overall mortality rates for all causes combined were up to 18 percent lower.[16]

Among the first companies to take a scientific approach to plant-based protein were Beyond Meat and Impossible Foods. By sourcing the five building blocks of meat—protein, fat, minerals, carbohydrates, and water—directly from plants, the companies were able to use heating, cooling, and pressure to create the fibrous texture of meat from plant-based proteins. Finally, by mixing in fats, minerals, fruit- and vegetable-based colors, natural flavors, and carbohydrates, they replicated the appearance, juiciness, and flavor of meat. The Beyond Burger and Impossible Burger made headlines because, among other claims, they appear to "bleed" and taste remarkably similar to animal meat. But are they healthier?

A clinical study using Beyond Meat's plant-based products conducted at Stanford University evaluated the impact of replacing animal-based meat with plant-based meat over an eight-week period.[17] The study found improvement in key health metrics—such as cholesterol levels, heart disease risk factors, and body weight. Beyond Meat products offer protein levels greater than or equal to their animal-based counterparts with no cholesterol, no antibiotics, and no hormones.

Beyond Meat's innovative approach has proved economically savvy, with revenues growing from $16 million in 2016 to $407 million in 2020, which equates to 2,444 percent growth over five years. The company is also poised for future growth. In September 2020, it became the first plant-based multinational that will have its own major production facility in China, where the government has committed to reducing meat consumption by

50 percent by 2030. It will compete with more established regional brands, such as Omni Foods, but there is a massive market, and research suggests 62.4 percent of Chinese are very or extremely likely to purchase plant-based meats, which is roughly the same as in India and almost double the United States (where it is 32.9 percent).[18]

The big food manufacturers, including Tyson Foods, Danone, Unilever, and Nestlé, are now scrambling to get skin in the game (to use a perversely nonvegan figure of speech). Food retailers from Tesco to IKEA (fun fact: IKEA sells more meatballs than any other company in the world) and franchises such as KFC and McDonald's are also rapidly scaling their plant-based offering. A lot of the innovation is coming from the Netherlands, which is the second-largest agricultural exporter after the United States. There are already more than 60 companies and research institutions in the Netherlands focused on plant-based protein—in what is called the Protein Cluster in Foodvalley NL (the Silicon Valley for plant-based food)—including the Vegetarian Butcher (a Dutch company that Unilever acquired), Beyond Meat, and Upfield.

Staying Healthy of Mind

Mental well-being is at least as important as physical health. Take a moment to pause and reflect. How do you feel right now? Has today been a good day or a bad day? What about yesterday? Did you experience a lot of enjoyment, feel well rested, smile or laugh a lot, and feel treated with respect? On average, across 143 countries, 7 out of 10 of us feel these emotions on any given day, according to Gallup's Positive Experience Index.[19] But where in the world are you most likely to feel positive? In the rich world? In Scandinavia? In fact, 9 out of the top 10 countries in the Index are from Latin America. Are you surprised?

This obviously has something to do with culture (and maybe weather too). But there are many facets to mental health. For example, according to "The Unengaged Mind," a paper by psychologist John Eastwood and colleagues, boredom can lead to overeating, depression, anxiety, drug and alcohol abuse, and more risk of making mistakes.[20] No wonder mental well-being has been such a challenge for so many during months of pandemic lockdown, social distancing, and self-isolation. For our own mental health, it is important that we stay stimulated and engaged rather than distracted and demotivated. One way is to alter our routines. We might change our work tasks, take a course, revive a hobby, cook a new dish, or plan an exciting project.

For organizations, it's important that leaders are supportive of employees' mental health. For example, at one point during the pandemic, all the staff of Antwerp Management School, where I am a professor and hold an academic chair, received a message from our dean, Steven De Haes, headlined "Hey, it's ok!" These words reassured, encouraged, and inspired us—and I think they should be a motto for our time. This simple message conveyed a commitment to remain human centered, no matter how difficult the times. Hey, it's okay to take a break from the screen when you need to. Hey, it's okay to reorganize your work from home around the needs of your family. The message is: We understand; we can be flexible. Hey, it's okay.

It may also help to reframe mental well-being as vitality. Vitality is about achieving good energy levels, holding positive attitudes, staying physically healthy, and cultivating mental resilience. This is quite different from other more commonly asked questions, such as how satisfied, motivated, happy, or engaged employees are. Vitality depends on being part of a supportive network of colleagues and loved ones. Nurturing whole-person vitality is an enabler of other goals, such as meaningful jobs and sustainable careers.

Case Spotlight: Lendlease

Lendlease, a multinational construction, property, and infrastructure company, demonstrates how to cultivate vitality and embed well-being into organizational culture. Besides having a workplace featuring "neighborhood tables," working walls, focus points for activities that require concentration, and enclosed pods and breakaway areas that foster collaboration and social interaction, the company also installed a Wellness Hub. This is a preventive care facility that occupies two floors of its corporate headquarters and has adjoining areas for physical activity and training, as well as a six-meter-high breathing wall with 5,000 plants that remove air pollutants, cool the surrounding space, improve energy efficiency, and reduce air-conditioning costs. Other initiatives include three annual well-being days for employees and extensive inclusive health initiatives around diet and exercise.

In contrast to vitality, many people feel mental strain, which is associated with work-related stress. The interference of work with private time is correlated with staff turnover, notably the intention to leave a job. According to the European quality of life survey conducted by Eurofound between 2007 and 2016, work-life balance has deteriorated—mostly after 2011—for all age groups and in particular for young women and women aged 35 to 49 years.[21] As the line between work and nonwork blurs, providing a robust suite of well-being programs focused on physical, mental, financial, and spiritual health is becoming an organizational responsibility and a strategy to drive employee productivity, engagement, and retention.

Another solution would be to work less. But is that even possible? Microsoft Japan has experimented with a four-day working week, and the results are (for some) surprising. For the month of August 2019, the company ran a new project called Work-Life Choice Challenge, giving its entire 2,300-person workforce five Fridays off in a row without decreasing pay. Naturally enough, almost all employees approved of this, since it allowed them extra time for family, self-development, and volunteering.

The surprising finding is that, despite working 20 percent less time, sales went up 40 percent compared to the same month the previous year.[22] So rather than working longer and harder, could we all shift to working smarter and more effectively? Could you deliver the same or more value in five hours a day?

Nurturing Resilient Employees

From a well-being perspective, a crisis like the COVID-19 pandemic highlights the importance not only of health services, pharmaceutical treatments, and technological solutions but also of developing individual resilience.[23] The more we can learn to cope with disruptive change, the better we will survive and thrive in the years ahead. Researchers have found that resilient individuals possess three common characteristics: an acceptance of reality, a strong belief that life is meaningful, and the ability to improvise. Other researchers emphasize the importance of problem-solving abilities, favorable perceptions, positive reinforcement, and strong faith.

Smart Insight: Skills Bricolage

Being able to improvise and problem solve in the face of disruption is another way to say that we need to adapt creatively. Some scholars call this *ritualized ingenuity,* and the work of French anthropologist Claude Lévi-Strauss is often cited, especially his concept of *skills bricolage*—"a kind of inventiveness, an ability to improvise a solution to a problem without proper or obvious tools or materials."[24] Resilient organizations tend to have many bricoleurs, but ingenuity is not a skill that comes naturally during crises, unless it is already a habit. Renowned organizational psychologist Professor Karl E. Weick puts it this way: "What we do not expect under life-threatening pressure is creativity."[25]

Emergence and improvisation have been shown to be important in response to shocks or crises: for instance, in the way that responders to the 9/11 disaster at the World Trade Center acted creatively to find solutions. Emergence in the context of disruption involves creating new relationships, processes, or ways to get things done in an unfamiliar context. Improvisation, on the other hand, is more like jazz, which entails composing in real time, adapting and responding like a live conversation to whatever happened before or is currently happening.

Let's also not forget that diversity increases resilience in living systems, whether that is a community, organization, or ecosystem. The simple reason is that diversity is more likely to produce creative solutions to problems and is less dependent on narrow bands of capability or perspective. Diversity is an antidote to the malaise of groupthink.

These factors suggest that resilience in the workplace requires vigor—in other words, high levels of energy and mental resilience while working, as well as the willingness to invest effort in one's work and to persist in the face of difficulties. If these elements are present, there is a positive correlation between resilience and job satisfaction, work happiness, and organizational commitment. Conversely, a lack of individual resilience can be associated with burnout and other health problems. So are there things that individual employees and their organizations can do to foster resilience?

According to industrial psychologists, there are four keys.[26] The first is to recognize that some people tend to experience enduring negative emotional states such as anxiety, guilt, anger, and depression more frequently, intensely, and readily and for a more enduring period of time. In psychological jargon, they experience neuroticism. By being aware of these individuals, more support can be given to them during periods of stress, such as a reduced workload or counseling.

The second key is to cultivate self-efficacy, which is an individual's belief that he or she can perform a selected task. This assurance can be shaped by a person's past experiences, their spiritual beliefs, or their ethical values. If a person believes that there is something that they can do about a stressful situation they face, they will be more likely to engage in effective active coping strategies, such as seeking social support and problem solving. Organizations can help with training that builds confidence and self-esteem.

The third key is to encourage mindfulness. Although this term is often used as a proxy for meditation, they are not the same thing. Meditation is one of many techniques that can improve mindfulness. Mindfulness itself refers to the ability of an individual to be conscious about their attitudes and behaviors. It may include nonjudgment and acting with awareness. By contrast, a lack of mindfulness results in an inability to step back and consider events from a distance. Employees in this state have a tendency to be reactive and inflexible when confronted with negative thoughts, emotions, or circumstances. Chris Laszlo and Frederick Chavalit Tsao, in their book *Quantum Leadership*, go even further to suggest mindfulness as the most effective way to achieve thriving in business, society, and nature.[27]

The fourth key is to support coping behavior. Coping is a process of adjustment following an adverse event. In the workplace, positive reframing of a problem and not being afraid to reach out for support are associated with more resilience and greater job satisfaction.

The Good Work Goals

One of the initiatives under my chair at Antwerp Management School is the Sustainable Transformation Group on the Well-Being Economy, which includes companies such as Randstad, Johnson & Johnson, AXA, and Golazo. The purpose of the group is to take collaborative action to promote well-being. In 2021 the group launched the Good Work Goals, its commitment to leadership for the creation of workplaces that value good employees and support good societies. This is a declaration that putting people first is essential for the health of the economy, society, and nature.

There are 10 goals, which are summarized in Table 6.1. All of the goals support improved well-being among employees, some directly (i.e., safe, healthy, resilient, happy, balanced, supportive, and meaningful work) and others indirectly (i.e., inclusive, sustainable, and responsible work).

TABLE 6.1: THE GOOD WORK GOALS

Theme	Motto	Goal	Examples
Safe work	We do not learn safety by accident	Striving to prevent incidents, accidents, or conditions that threaten or harm the physical health of employees	Providing the necessary workplace procedures, protective equipment, and training to minimize the risk of accidents, injuries, and fatalities
Healthy work	We take care of body, heart, and mind	Encouraging and enabling physical health and activity, ergonomic design, wholesome diets, and positive mental well-being among employees	Providing access to exercise and mindfulness facilities or classes, ensuring workspaces and jobs do not cause or make illnesses or diseases worse, and increasing plant-based food options in workplace cafeterias
Resilient work	We may fall, but we rise again	Supporting employees in their ability to positively manage stress and adapt to unexpected or significant changes	Providing access to stress-management training or coaches and multiskilling or reskilling employees for flexible jobs and careers
Inclusive work	We know our diversity is our strength	Supporting employee diversity and not discriminating on the basis of gender, race, religion, or other relevant characteristics	Setting inclusive recruitment targets, instituting antidiscrimination policies, and building partnerships that increase access to underrepresented groups in society as potential employees
Happy work	We do what we love and love what we do	Prioritizing job satisfaction, employee fulfillment, and a team-based culture.	Surveying employees to determine their level of job satisfaction, recognizing talent, training workers on team skills, and holding regular team-building exercises

continued →

Theme	Motto	Goal	Examples
Balanced work	We work to live; we don't live to work	Supporting a healthy balance between time spent working and not working, and relationships within and beyond the workplace	Offering flexible work options, discouraging excessive working hours or digital availability, and providing adequate maternity/paternity leave and workplace child-care facilities
Sustainable work	We take care of the earth so the earth can take care of us	Promoting environmental consciousness and action to reduce impacts on natural resources and ecosystems	Committing to science-based targets on climate and biodiversity, moving from a linear to a circular (zero-waste) economy, and acting to regenerate nature
Supportive work	We are the support you can count on	Supporting the personal and professional development of employees and rewarding employees fairly	Providing continuous learning opportunities and transparent performance appraisal, supporting living wages in the supply chain, and tackling the gender pay gap
Meaningful work	We work together to achieve a higher goal	Allowing employees to feel they are contributing positively to a larger societal purpose and the needs of all stakeholders	Conducting regular stakeholder engagement and setting ambitious strategic goals that address global social and environmental challenges
Responsible work	We leave the world better than we found it	Giving employees the opportunity to take action toward bettering society and the environment	Giving back to society through charitable donations, employee volunteering programs, and cross-sector partnerships

Given the timing of their release, the Good Work Goals also highlight that good workplace practices are a demonstrable responsibility not only during times of stability and prosperity but also—and likely even more so—during times of crisis and recovery, as the world is experiencing as a result of the COVID-19 pandemic.

For example, in COVID-19 times, new workplace designs, operating procedures, and working from home must not increase safety risks for employees; adequate personal protective equipment and hand sanitizer must be available for all employees; social-distancing rules must be respected in the workplace; and home workers must be supported in creating healthy workspaces. At the same time, levels of stress, anxiety, and burnout among employees should be regularly checked and mitigated, and attention must be paid to how the crisis is affecting different employee groups differently—some more than others.

During crises like this, keeping employees connected (virtually or in person), boosting morale, and showing empathy for workers' personal circumstances must be prioritized. There must be flexibility, understanding, and support to accommodate working at home where appropriate, while respecting employees' personal or family time. Every effort must be made to allow employees to continue to work and be paid, as well as to pursue further education and reskilling where appropriate. In addition, organizations can take action to help those who are worst affected by the crisis, which are often the most vulnerable, marginalized, and excluded in society. Looking out for the health and well-being of employees, customers, and other stakeholders in this way can give work an extra sense of purpose.

Answering the Question "Why?"

In the quest for revitalization, employee engagement has become an important indicator for HR leaders. Research suggests that 85 percent of workers globally are not engaged in their work, while in the United States only 14 percent strongly agree that the values of their employer match their own.[28] In today's knowledge economy, where human capital often represents an organization's main asset—and its source of competitive advantage—these are concerning numbers and translate into significant risks and costs.

Studies have found that decreased employee engagement leads to higher absenteeism; more errors, accidents, and defects; lower productivity; lower profitability; lower job growth; and 65 percent lower share price over time.

Smart Insight: Aspiration Deficit

The reasons given by employees for lower engagement is that they are feeling worn down by a combination of stress, boredom, and *aspiration deficit*—the feeling that their work lacks a sense of deeper meaning or purpose that might compensate for the heavy demands placed on them. These were among the findings of research some years ago by London PR agency The Fish Can Sing. They found that 66 percent of all 18–35-year-olds are unhappy at work, and the proportion rises to 83 percent among 30–35-year-olds. According to their results, one in 15 has already quit the rat race, and 45 percent are seriously contemplating a career change.[29]

They labeled this group of people TIREDs—which is an abbreviation for Thirty-something Independent Radical Educated Drop-outs. In analyzing this market segment, they discovered that these otherwise highly successful and motivated professionals were lacking something in their corporate life. This they called the "LDDR factor"—they wanted Less Demand (i.e., less work-related stress, shorter working hours) and Deeper Reward (i.e., more job satisfaction, higher quality of life).

According to the Worldwatch Institute, about a third of Americans report being "very happy," the same share as in 1957, when Americans were only half as wealthy. So what is going on here? Viktor Frankl, author of *Man's Search for Meaning* and a survivor of four Nazi concentration camps, suggests that our Western pursuit of economic growth may be to blame: "Consider today's society," he says. "It gratifies and satisfies virtually every need—except for one, the need for meaning. This spreading meaning vacuum is especially evident in affluent industrial countries. People have the means for living, but not the meanings."[30]

More recent research suggests that this is not an isolated phenomenon. In fact, around 50 percent of Americans report a lack of meaning and significance at work, which they believe is more important than feeling happy.[31] From other research we also know that the purposefulness of a job in itself is important for engagement and seeing growth possibilities, and it has a great effect on intrinsic job motivation.

One of the simplest ways for organizations to respond to employees' desire for purpose is to embrace thriving. The outdoor clothing and food company Patagonia shows how looking after employee well-being and advocating for sustainability can pay dividends. The company has been listed as one of the World's Most Innovative Companies by *Fast Company* in 2012, 2014, 2017, 2018, 2019, and 2020—and those accolades are consistent with Patagonia's creative compensation and rewards model that seeks to support employees both inside and outside of work.

The title of founder CEO Yvon Chouinard's autobiography is *Let My People Go Surfing*, which gives some insight into the organization's culture.[32] The company provides 23 three-day weekends per year, a well-being policy that allows employees to do recreational exercise during work hours, and extensive family benefits, such as on-site day care to support parenting and breastfeeding. The company encourages employees to treat work as play and regards its own workers as the ultimate customers, which means it places a special emphasis on how it treats and rewards them.

For Patagonia, reward is not only about financial incentives or giving time off but also about giving employees a sense of purpose or mission in their work. For example, since 1985 Patagonia has pledged 1 percent of sales to the preservation and restoration of the natural environment. It also has numerous programs to support corporate responsibility and sustainability; these include B Lab, Sustainable Apparel Coalition, bluesign, Fair Factories Clearing House, and Worn Wear.

One of the remarkable things about Patagonia is that being purpose driven is not a top-down directive. For example, when employees proposed that the company give away all of its 2016 Black Friday sales to grassroots environmental organizations, then-CEO Rose Marcario approved the plan within 30 minutes via text message. The company raised $10 million and signed up 24,000 new customers as a result. Meanwhile, the cumulative effect of all these innovations is that Patagonia has seen its performance and productivity continue to rise.[33]

Nature-Based Therapy

Something that Patagonia understands well—their founder, Yvon Chouinard, was a mountaineer after all—is that nature is a powerful healer. In fact, one of the most effective ways to deal with stress and improve mental well-being is to spend time in nature. The science to support this claim is getting stronger year by year. In a review of links between nature and mental health published in *Science Advances*, the researchers found considerable evidence already in existence.[34] In particular, they observed that an experience of nature leads to increased psychological well-being, a reduction of health risk factors, and a reduction of the burden of some types of mental illness. Let's look at these effects in a bit more detail.

In the first category, studies have produced evidence that links nature experience with increased positive emotions; happiness and subjective well-being; positive social interactions, cohesion, and engagement; a sense of meaning and purpose in life; improved manageability of life tasks; and decreases in mental distress, such as negative emotions. Nature experience has also been shown to positively affect various aspects of cognitive function, memory and attention, impulse inhibition, and children's school performance, as well as imagination and creativity.

In the category of benefits, nature experience has been associated with improved sleep and reductions in stress, which in turn are major risk factors for mental illness, especially depression. In addition, there is growing evidence that nature experience is associated with a decreased incidence of other disorders, such as anxiety disorders, attention-deficit and hyperactivity disorder (ADHD), and depression.

Given these benefits, we need to ask whether people are getting enough exposure to nature—or in other words, whether many are suffering from what the author of *Last Child in the Woods*, Richard Louv, calls "nature deficit disorder."[35] This is certainly a reasonable assumption, given that more than half the world's population now live in cities, and even the countryside is severely degraded by agriculture and industry. Many people today are effectively living in urban areas that are *nature deserts*. And even for those who have access to parks, we might question whether their visits are sufficient to gain the necessary health benefits.

Smart Insight: Nature Therapy

According to a study of 20,000 people, led by the European Centre for Environment and Human Health at the University of Exeter, people who spent two hours a week in green spaces—whether local parks or other natural environments, and either all at once or spaced over several visits—were substantially more likely to report good health and psychological well-being than those who did not. This conclusion held true regardless of people's occupation, ethnic group, income, or existing health condition (for example, whether they suffered from chronic illnesses and disabilities).[36]

Some call this effect *nature therapy*, since scientists have found that being in nature decreases blood pressure, heart rate, sympathetic nerve activity, and cortisol. In layperson's terms, nature destresses and detoxifies. For example, when I am in the mountains of Rugova in Kosovo, surrounded by green forests, flowing streams, and singing birds, I can literally feel my body relaxing and my mind clearing. You don't have to go that far. Scientists find the same effect from walking in the park, contemplating a flower, or gardening. Even having natural materials such as stone floors, wooden furniture, or plants in the office registers a positive physiological effect.

There is an informative book, beautifully presented with full-color photographs, called *Shinrin Yoku*.[37] It is written by Yoshifumi Miyazaki, one of the leading nature-therapy researchers. *Shinrin yoku* is a term that was coined by the Japanese Ministry of Agriculture, Forestry, and Fisheries in 1982 to mean "forest bathing"—a variation on the idea of sunbathing. The concept was developed in Japan in the 1980s, bringing together ancient wisdom from the culture with cutting-edge environmental health science. There are now forest-bathing centers and trails scattered throughout Japan.

I am grateful to have had many personal *shinrin yoku* experiences. Besides those already mentioned, there have been walks in the forests of Knysna in South Africa, in the Dandenongs just outside Melbourne in Australia, and in botanical gardens in Morocco and Singapore.

One particularly powerful experience took place at the Erawan National Park in west Thailand, which I experienced as a blissful moment of nature-induced *ecophoria*. Allow me to describe the scene: The weather is hot, but I am cool under the dappled shade of jungle trees. I am lounging in a refreshing rock pool, contemplating a cascading waterfall. Tiny fish are nibbling my feet, which is strangely pleasant, while larger fish swim all around me unafraid. My mind is at ease, my body is relaxed, and my spirit is soaring. Ecophoria reminds us what we are fighting so hard to protect and restore—and why.

The Healing Balm

In this chapter, we have explored how to move from disease to the revitalization of body and mind. Some of the solutions will come from innovation in science and technology, while others will require us to rethink our lifestyle choices and dietary habits. We have also looked to organizations to support health and well-being by providing "good work," work that makes us more able to cope and thrive. And finally, we have turned our gaze toward nature, as an enduring source of rest and rejuvenation, wonder and wisdom. And so, to end the chapter, I commend you into nature's embrace.

NATURE'S EMBRACE

Take me to the forests green
I need to feel their healing balm
To soak in groves of dappled sheen
And wallow in their soothing calm

Take me to the mountains high
I need to stretch and strain and strive
To rise up where the eagles fly
And burst with joy to be alive

Take me to the wilderness
I need the space to be alone
To tap the vein of nature's bliss
And slip into the mindful zone

Take me to the beaches gold
I need to feel the sun's warm rays
To dive into the oceans cold
And drift on lunar tidal sways

Take me to the valleys cool
I need to rest within their shade
To cast ideas into a pool
And watch them ripple till they fade

Take me to the desert sand
I need to clear my cluttered mind
To see the beauty in the bland
And treasure secrets that I find

Take me to the alpine snow
I need to breathe its pristine chill
To thaw my soul while embers glow
And feel the pure adrenal thrill

Take me into nature's arms
I need to feel her love embrace
To shelter from life's daily harms
And gaze upon her wizened face.

SECTION IV

REGENERATING THE ECONOMY

We must demonstrate that we can reinvent our economies and our businesses by putting values at the heart of a twenty-first-century economy. . . . Think of the doughnut as a visual compass for how to meet the needs of all people within the means of a thriving planet. The outer circle represents our ecological ceiling, consisting of nine planetary boundaries beyond which lie unacceptable environmental degradation and potential tipping points in Earth systems. The inner circle represents our social foundation, derived from internationally agreed minimum social standards, as identified by the world's governments in the Sustainable Development Goals in 2015. The space in between—where our needs are met and the earth's systems are protected—is where humanity can thrive.

—**Kate Raworth,** *Doughnut Economics: Seven Ways to Think Like a 21st Century Economist*

Contemporary economics is degenerative. It systematically disregards ecological limits and fails to ensure that fundamental human needs are met. The economy is good at creating jobs, products, services, and technologies, but what is the quality of these outputs? Do they create more harm than good? The impacts of economic activity are explained away as "negative externalities," as if environmental integrity and social justice exist in some realm outside of the economy. But that is not true—everything is interconnected.

There are two essential forces for the economics of thriving. In Chapter 7, I show how to shift from disconnection from technology and by technology toward innovation that serves the needs of people and the planet by metaphorically rewiring the economy. In Chapter 8, we look at the shift away from disruption linked to crises such as the climate emergency, and we examine how a thriving economy can be designed to promote resilience through activities that mitigate risks and turn them into opportunities.

CHAPTER 7

Rewiring

*We're already a cyborg. You have a digital version of yourself online. . . .
And you have superpowers with your computer and your phone and the
applications that are there. You can answer any question; you can video
conference with anyone anywhere; you can send a message to
millions of people instantly. You just do incredible things.*

—**Elon Musk,** remarks at Code Conference 2016

I first visited Kenya in east Africa in the early 1990s as an undergraduate business student. When I returned again in 2010, I was mightily intrigued by a new innovation called M-Pesa that was sweeping the country. It was developed by Vodafone in partnership with the local mobile operator Safaricom. By then I was living in the UK and was surprised to discover that Kenyans could transfer money simply by sending a text from their mobile phones. This was not something that was possible at the time in Britain or anywhere else that I knew of.

When M-Pesa first launched in 2007, an estimated 80 percent of Kenyans did not have a bank account. This simple service instantly gave access to basic financial services for the "unbanked" while empowering thousands of entrepreneurs to act as M-Pesa agents—often small mobile-phone stores or other retailers such as barbers, butchers, and bakers. Customers register with an authorized agent and then deposit cash in exchange for electronic money, which they can send instantly via text (or SMS, as it was more popularly known back then) to their family or friends throughout the country.

By 2019 M-Pesa was facilitating 12 billion annual transactions in seven countries, with 41.5 million customers and more than 430,000 agents.[1] This is a great example of rewiring: using technology to deliver on social or environmental goals. M-Pesa has also inspired other mobile solutions in Africa—for example, the M-Kopa "pay-as-you-go" solar system, which has allowed 3.7 million people to access solar lighting to power radios, televisions, fridges, and smartphones. This has saved $467 million in fuel costs and 2 million metric tons of CO_2 while connecting 47,000 individuals to the internet for the first time.[2]

The subsequent rise of tech start-ups in the region has earned Nairobi the nickname of Silicon Savanna—Africa's very own Silicon Valley. The region has seeded many inspiring social enterprises that are focusing their technology breakthroughs on service to society. For example, Twiga Foods connects farmers to markets using mobile phones, while Hope Tech Plus uses sonar and echolocation to assist the visually impaired. Sanivation converts sewage into biomass fuels to replace traditional firewood and curb deforestation, and Ushahidi is a data crowdsourcing platform that was developed to map reports of violence in Kenya after the postelection violence in 2008.

Innovation is not confined to Kenya, of course. Every year there are more than 3 million patent filings globally, so there is no shortage of new ideas for new "stuff." But just because something is innovative doesn't necessarily make it good for society. According to the multinational company Philips, which has been an invention powerhouse for 130 years, there is a "technology innovation gap": Only 54 percent of people they surveyed across the United States, Russia, China, Saudi Arabia, and the Netherlands were satisfied with existing innovations in the areas that were most important to them, such as environment, health, and education.[3]

Philips calls technological solutions to meet these societal needs "meaningful innovation"; I call it *synnovation,* which is short for synergistic innovation. It creates benefits for individuals and society and for business and the environment. It is innovation with purpose, which is the theme for this chapter on rewiring society by advancing the digital economy.

The Fourth Industrial Revolution

The digital economy ranges from basic access to computers, mobile phones, and the internet to participation in the so-called Fourth Industrial Revolution. Klaus Schwab, founder of the World Economic Forum, popularized the concept in 2016, explaining it as follows: "The First Industrial Revolution used water and steam power to mechanize production. The Second used electric power to create mass production. The Third used electronics and information technology to automate production. . . . [The Fourth Industrial Revolution] is characterized by a fusion of technologies that is blurring the lines between the physical, digital, and biological spheres."[4]

Key Concept: The Digital Economy

The world needs solutions that can act as a counterforce to disconnection, resulting in a symbolic rewiring of society through the digital economy. This includes all the technological expenditures and investments that increase connectivity and intelligence in society, from high-speed internet and the Internet of Things to massive open online courses and artificial intelligence. It is about finding

continued →

solutions that use technology to better connect us to one another, improve the efficiency and effectiveness of our economic activities, allow us to share what we value most, and facilitate more democratic governance by allowing us (as customers or citizens) to give direct, immediate feedback.

In practice, the Fourth Industrial Revolution is associated with the convergence of seven rapidly advancing technologies: 5G mobile broadband, cloud computing, blockchain distributed ledgers, 3D printing, the Internet of Things, automation and robotics, and artificial intelligence and (big) data analytics. These are all individually disruptive and collectively revolutionary. For example, Table 7.1 shows the World Economic Forum's top 10 emerging technologies of 2020, giving a glimpse into how the digital economy is finding new applications.

TABLE 7.1: TOP 10 EMERGING TECHNOLOGIES OF 2020

Technology	Description	Benefit
Microneedles	Needles 50–2,000 microns in length (about the depth of a sheet of paper) and 1–100 microns wide (about the width of human hair)	Painless injections and tests; increased access to medicines
Sun-powered chemistry	Sunlight-activated catalysts (photocatalysts) that convert waste carbon dioxide into chemical compounds for medicines, detergents, and textiles	Nonextractive production of useful chemicals; carbon sequestration
Virtual patients	"In silico medicine"—virtual organs or body systems used for testing drugs and treatments and predicting how a real person will respond to the therapies	Reduced cost of clinical trials; less need for human clinical trials

Technology	Description	Benefit
Spatial computing	A combination of virtual reality, augmented reality, and high-fidelity spatial mapping to enable physical objects to move and aid physical navigation	Increased mobility and safety for the elderly or disabled; efficient factories
Digital medicine	"Digital phenotyping" detection aids that flag health concerns, based on monitored biodata or ingestible, micro-bioelectronic pills	Early disease detection; quicker feedback on medical questions
Electric aviation	Electric airplanes, incorporating a variety of technologies, such as hydrogen-electric fuel cells or electric propellers	Low-carbon-emission flight; lower-maintenance airplanes
Lower-carbon cement	Methods to combat climate change via construction materials—this includes lower-limestone formulations, carbon capture and storage in the cement, and inclusion of carbon-absorbing bacteria	Lower carbon emissions
Quantum sensing	High-precision measurement based on subatomic particle behavior, such as weak electrical and gravitational effects	Improved health, navigation, and early warning systems
Green hydrogen	Electrolysis, powered by renewable energy, that splits water into hydrogen and oxygen, with no other by-products	Zero-carbon energy, useful in shipping, chemicals, and other manufacturing
Whole-genome synthesis	The use of genetic information—such as from a virus, bacteria, or yeast—to synthesize genomes and edit their genetic code	Medical applications (the basis for COVID vaccines); production of biomaterials

Source: *Adapted from World Economic Forum,*
"Top 10 Emerging Technologies of 2020."

The advances in the digital economy have major implications for the future of work. We know about blue-collar, white-collar, and even green-collar workers. Now we will see the rise of *new-collar* professionals, who work in the new job sector of digital transformation. There are exciting careers emerging in "Industry 4.0," which is shorthand for the Fourth Industrial Revolution. If we do it right, automation will replace many 4-D jobs (dangerous, difficult, dull, and dirty) and stimulate the growth of new STEAM roles (in science, technology, engineering, art, and mathematics). Without a doubt, companies and individuals will need to make significant investments in reskilling and upskilling to smooth the transition.

In fact, half of workers will need reskilling in the next five years. That's according to World Economic Forum's "The Future of Jobs Report, 2020."[5] Automation and COVID-19 are proving to be a highly disruptive combination, with an estimated 85 million jobs likely to be displaced by 2025. On the bright side, 97 million new jobs are predicted to emerge to take their place, while 84 percent of employers plan to rapidly digitalize working processes. Knowledge of "new tech" will be increasingly necessary, with a forecast skills gap in areas such as critical thinking and analysis, problem solving, and self-management, including active learning, resilience, stress tolerance, and flexibility.

That may seem daunting to many, but we face a choice. Either we can act like the Luddites of old—a secret oath-based organization of English textile workers in the 19th century who went around breaking machines in the Industrial Revolution as a form of protest—or we can embrace this brave new world. That does not mean ignoring the risks of new technologies or abandoning the precautionary principle; rather, it means identifying these risks, along with the opportunities, and improving the technologies to make them better.

The Promise of Artificial Intelligence (AI)

Of all the many digital economy technologies, AI, or machine learning, often gets the most attention. Ever since Karel Čapek introduced the word *robot* into our lexicon—in a 1921 science-fiction play called *R.U.R. (Rossum's Universal Robots)*—we have been fascinated and frightened by the prospect of machines becoming intelligent and taking over the world.

Whether it's the spaceship computer HAL in Arthur C. Clarke's *2001: A Space Odyssey* (made into a film by Stanley Kubrick), Philip K. Dick's *Do Androids Dream of Electric Sheep?* (which became Ridley Scott's movie *Blade Runner*), James Cameron's *Terminator* film franchise, or Steven Spielberg's *AI*, our imaginations seem to know no limits to the AI nightmares we can conceive.

The reality is less fantastical but no less interesting. Few are aware, for instance, that John Milton's epic poem *Paradise Lost*, published in 1674, played a part in the history of AI. When Milton named the capital of Hell *pandæmonium*—from the Greek meaning "all the little spirits"—he reinterpreted this as the place of swarming demons. Little did he know that this idea would inspire a 25-year-old researcher at MIT's Lincoln Laboratory to create the first model of machine-learning software almost 300 years later. Oliver Selfridge was experimenting in the 1950s with how to teach a computer to learn, when he was inspired by Milton's image of "a bunch of these demons shrieking up the hierarchy."[6] He reconceived this as bottom-up learning with feedback loops, which is the basis for AI.

Alan Turing, the British World War II code breaker who worked at Bletchley Park on cracking the German Enigma code using computational devices, is perhaps more well known and played his own part in AI history. On the question of whether machines can think, Turing proposed "The Imitation Game," in which a computer imitates a human during a series of five-minute keyboard conversations. The now famous "Turing test" was that if a computer is mistaken for a human more than 30 percent of the time during these conversations, it qualifies as being intelligent. Some claim that a computer program called Eugene Goostman, which simulates a 13-year-old Ukrainian boy, passed the Turing test at an event organized by the University of Reading in 2014.

It's hardly surprising, given its history and popular associations with science fiction, that any mention of AI makes us think of a humanoid robot or about machines taking over our jobs (if not our world). But AI comes in many forms and has great potential for tackling our social and environmental challenges. A report from McKinsey has identified 160 cases, covering all 17 Sustainable Development Goals, where AI—in the form of deep learning—is being used for social good.[7] The cases range from diagnosing cancer and identifying victims of online sexual exploitation to aiding disaster-relief efforts and helping to catch wildlife poachers. When used right, technology is our ally, not our enemy.

For instance, what do you think of when I say, "256 shades of gray"? (If you thought of *Fifty Shades of Grey*, I'm not telling.) That's the power that AI is bringing to health care in general and to tackling COVID-19 in particular. AI can analyze 256 shades in a grayscale image from a mammogram or ultrasonic lung scan in a fraction of a second and diagnose abnormalities far more accurately than a radiologist. What's more, AI is not necessarily about replacing doctors and nurses. In fact, a recent survey by MIT Technology Review Insights and General Electric found nearly half of US health-care professionals said AI is boosting their ability to spend time with and provide care to patients.[8]

AI can also take the pain and inefficiency out of recycling. Today, most municipalities and waste companies are still engaged in Sisyphean battles to cajole and convince people to separate their waste. And despite their best efforts, even with beautifully color-coded and icon-enriched bins, the wrong trash often ends up in the wrong containers, adding time, effort, and expense to the recycling process. Now CleanRobotics, a semifinalist in the IBM Watson AI XPRIZE, has invented the TrashBot, which automatically sorts waste into different categories at the disposal stage. ZenRobotics and MBA Polymers have similar high-tech solutions for waste depots. It seems Hollywood's WALL-E is coming to life.

Hot Trend: Autonomous Drones

AI is even helping to advance the capabilities of drones. We know that drones will soon be as ubiquitous as airplanes, but first we need to know that they are really useful and totally safe. A test of simultaneous autonomous (self-flying) drones in the Port of Antwerp shows what is already possible. The test was conducted in 2019 by SAFIR, a consortium with partners such as Amazon and Proximus, during which drones made deliveries, performed maintenance inspection of equipment, checked air- and water-pollution levels, and navigated around an impromptu simulated chemical accident. This is proof that multiple drones can fly safely in complex, unpredictable environments and deliver economic, social, and environmental benefits.

That's not to say that AI, like any technology, does not have its downsides. For instance, human biases have crept into AI and machine-learning technologies. Harrisburg University researchers are claiming they can use facial recognition to predict criminality. Yet a US National Institute of Standards and Technology study found that facial recognition software falsely identified African American and Asian faces 10 to 100 times more than Caucasian ones.[9] IBM is taking the issue seriously. Besides creating an AI ethics board and releasing open-source tool kits such as AI Fairness 360 to combat bias, in June 2020 the company also stopped offering its software for mass surveillance or racial profiling.

The Power of Data

Big Tech companies—such as Google, Amazon, Microsoft, and Facebook—already store 1,200 petabytes of data between them.[10] That's 1.2 billion gigabytes, and storing that data in server farms is projected to emit 3.2 percent of global carbon and consume a fifth of the world's electricity by 2025.[11] If we could find more efficient ways to store data, we would need less hardware and less energy. In the search for solutions, data scientists are studying how DNA packs information so tightly. It's a mind-boggling fact that if we managed to copy the data-storage technique used by our DNA, we could store all the internet's data on a device the size of a shoebox. No wonder tech companies are racing to develop ways to convert digital data into synthetic DNA-inspired storage.

Once you have data, there are all kinds of potential applications. Take hospitals, for instance. Without mission control, the Apollo mission to the moon would have been a catastrophic failure. Yet most hospitals are run without a data command center. Thankfully that's starting to change. After GE installed an integrated data control center at Maryland's John Hopkins Hospital in 2016, access to the hospital for very sick patients improved by 78 percent over 18 months, and waiting time for emergencies fell by 35 percent, even while inpatient occupancy increased 8 percent.[12] Now the UK's Bradford Royal Infirmary is getting its own mission control center, with real-time data on patient flow, ambulance arrivals, and more. They realize that data can save lives.

Smart Insight: Digital Twins

Data can also create eco-efficiencies. Just as prevention is better than a cure, sustainable design is better than retrofitting. That's where digital twins come in. By creating a detailed virtual representation of products, processes, factories, and supply chains (also sometimes called *value chains*), companies can simulate the performance of different designs and operating conditions. They are an extension of scenario planning but at the product and process level. Digital twins allow designers and operators to find efficiencies, radically reduce resource inputs, improve safety, cut emissions, and eliminate waste.

One of the leaders in the field, Dassault Systèmes, uses digital twins as a decision-making cockpit, enabled by the Fourth Industrial Revolution.[13] When I spoke at their Planning in a Disruptive World event in Barcelona, organized by the company's DELMIA Quintiq division, we were looking at smart solutions such as digital twins for operations, traffic simulation for better logistics, blockchain traceability in supply chains, and connected value networks to support a circular economy. It's exciting stuff, as long as we don't optimize the status quo and just make unsustainable companies more efficient.

Digital technologies can be applied at a nano scale (very small) all the way through to a cosmic scale (very large). For instance, cosmology researchers from Washington State University have identified 24 planets that are earthlike, some of which may be super habitable. There's just one small problem: They are all more than 100 light-years from our solar system.[14] Luckily, we won't have to wait for the invention of wormhole technology to study these planets. Instead, the EU is creating a digital twin of our own planet, called Destination Earth. The simulation will be detailed to a resolution of one kilometer, allowing us to model ocean circulation, food security, weather forecasting, and climatic events such as droughts, floods, and fires. It seems the connected consciousness of Gaia, the Greek goddess of the earth, is coming alive.

Of course, one of the richest sources of data is nature itself. By studying natural phenomena such as microorganisms, the health of soils, the acorn's encoded secrets, the pollination of lavender, the dance of honeybees, the flight of flamingos, the intelligence of pigs, and the respiration of forests, we cultivate awe and respect. We learn to value life more. Ignorance may be bliss, but knowledge is a well of discovery that never runs dry. To care about nature or people, first we need to know about them. And the more we know, the more we are inspired.

Learning from the encoded data in nature is not just a romantic notion. When *New Scientist* declared that CRISPR—a technology to edit genes—"will likely change the world," it was not wrong.[15] Tinkering with nature makes many people uncomfortable (and others downright outraged), but the fact is that we have been doing it for thousands of years, especially in agriculture. Today, genetically modified organisms (GMOs) have potential sustainability benefits that are increasingly compelling, even though many strongly oppose their use. For example, gene editing may help reduce methane emissions from livestock and rice farming and increase carbon sequestration of crops. We face a dilemma, and the sensible way through seems to be that we should apply the precautionary principle yet still remain open to new technology and innovation.

You never know, the next Google or Tesla or Alibaba could be a champion for thriving, although predicting these rare unicorns is hard—some might even say impossible. A *unicorn* in this context refers to a privately held start-up company valued at more than $1 billion. The term was coined in 2013 by venture capitalist Aileen Lee to indicate how rare these companies are. Even so, CB Insights has an algorithm that has scored a few hits in the past. Its 2015 Future Unicorns list included Postmates Inc., Dollar Shave Club, and HelloFresh, which all went on to become billion-dollar companies. The 2020 Top 50 list is dominated by tech start-ups, which is not unexpected—and I like the look of the digital-health contenders, such as Doctor on Demand, Lyra Health, and Capsule.

Smart Innovation for Thriving

The truth is we don't really know which new technologies and start-up companies will become unicorns—or even thoroughbred horses, for that matter. But we can place bets in areas that seem likely to produce world-changing innovation. Three that are particularly ripe for harvesting are nanotechnology, blockchain, and 3D printing. Nanotechnology is a revolution in progress that many are not seeing—literally, because nano-materials are really, really small. Already researchers are creating submarines small enough to deliver medicine inside the human body and molecule-size drills that kill cancer cells. It's a fairly safe bet that nanotechnology will transform the world in terms of health, sustainability, and energy.

One nano supermaterial is graphene, the thinnest and strongest material known to humans. It is flexible, transparent, and conducts heat and electricity 10 times better than copper, making it ideal for better fuel cells, water purification, and even electronic fabrics that harvest energy as we move. Something that sounds similar but is different is nanographite, which is used as a lubricant in items ranging from fire extinguishers to lithium-ion batteries. University of Wyoming researchers have demonstrated a method to convert pulverized coal powder—an abundant resource that we must avoid burning at all costs—into nanographite, which is a high-value material with ecological and economic benefits.

In other applications, scientists at Nanyang Technological University in Singapore have developed insulin nanoparticles that could be taken as an oral medicine, replacing insulin injections for 422 million diabetic patients globally. Meanwhile, at University of North Carolina–North Carolina State's Joint Department of Biomedical Engineering, they are investigating the use of perfluorocarbon nanodroplets that convert from a liquid to a gas when ultrasound energy is applied. Promising in-vitro testing suggests that this may be especially effective in breaking up tough blood clots that can cause strokes and other health problems.

Hot Trend: The Blockchain

Blockchain holds great promise in making our supply chains transparent and our products more traceable. As a technology, blockchain is a system of recording information in a way that makes it difficult or impossible to change, hack, or cheat the system. It is essentially a digital ledger of transactions that is duplicated and distributed across the entire network of computer systems on the blockchain. There are many applications. A lot of attention has been focused on cryptocurrencies, such as Bitcoin, that use blockchain. But besides securing financial transactions, blockchain can also give us confidence in data that tells us more about what we are consuming and its social and environmental impacts.

Besides health applications, smart technology can inform the choices we make as customers. Most of us are oblivious to the impact of our consumption patterns. Every day, we buy things, use things, and throw things away, often without knowing what they are made of, where they came from, or what will happen after they are discarded. A pioneering tech company called EVRYTHNG wants to change that by giving every product a virtual profile, accessible from the digital cloud. By simply scanning a QR code using our phone, we will learn more about the product's life story.

At the moment, EVRYTHNG ask us to trust their data. But for companies that use blockchain, products and the materials they are made of can be tracked and traced with confidence in the data. Provenance is a company built on this premise, using blockchain to make sustainable supply chains accountable. For example, they have worked with Royal Auping to create a product passport showing material transparency for the company's fully recyclable mattress. In sustainable fishing, they have worked with 12 pole-and-line-certified producers in Southeast Asia to track fish through the supply chain for UK, Japanese, and US markets. And for the 10,500 milk farmers in New Zealand's Fonterra Cooperative Group, Provenance has helped to prove and share the farmers' credentials around reducing their carbon footprint and using plant-based packaging.

Like nanotechnology and blockchain, 3D printing—which is also sometimes called additive manufacturing because of the method of adding successive layers of material in the printing process—has numerous breakthrough applications. We have mentioned some of these already, notably in the medical sphere. Besides rapidly manufacturing respiratory valves, face shields, and artificial limbs, a US consortium of academics, medical workers, and manufacturers was set up to 3D-print 4 million nasal swabs a week to relieve the bottleneck in production for COVID-19 testing.[16]

But the potential of 3D printing extends way beyond the medical field. For example, a start-up based out of Austin, Texas, has 3D-printed tiny houses for a community of 50 people living in poverty in southern Mexico, as well as for homeless people in Austin. There are environmental applications as well. Marine scientists and architects from the Swire Institute of Marine Science of the University of Hong Kong and its Robotic Fabrication Lab of the faculty of architecture have worked together to 3D-print terra-cotta tiles that will act as artificial reefs. There are also open-source design specifications for a RepRapable Recyclebot, which turns waste plastic into 3D-printing filament.

Context-Based Innovation

Technologies such as artificial intelligence, digital twins, blockchain, nanotech, and 3D printing represent the leading edge of smart innovation. But we must not forget the importance of the access economy. We should be asking: Are these technologies inclusive and affordable, or do they exacerbate the digital divide? Another way of phrasing the question is: Are the technology innovations appropriate to the context where solutions to our social and environmental challenges are most needed? In many cases, this context means developing countries, low-income communities, or places where there are groups excluded from society.

This is a topic that is close to my heart. Not only was I born and raised in Africa, but my work has taken me to more than 40 developing countries. For that reason, I was delighted to be commissioned by the United Nations Environment Program to do research on eco-innovation and technology transfer in developing countries and emerging economies. The report, called "Moving Ahead with Technology for Eco-innovation," was published in 2017 and includes many cases of what for decades has been called "appropriate technology" and that I call *context-based innovation*.[17] Let's look at a few examples featured in the research.

Drip irrigation is a technique that reduces water use by 30–70 percent and increases land productivity by 20–90 percent, depending on the crop. Making this technology more affordable for farmers in developing economies could address a key pressure point of agriculture—an industry that is responsible for 70 percent of freshwater use globally—and reduce current operational inefficiencies from evaporation, leakage, and seepage in open irrigation systems. In order to do this, the Indian State Tamil Nadu Drip Irrigation Project provided hands-on technical training to farmers to switch to drip irrigation. Results showed increases in crop yields by as much as 40 percent, as well as reduction in water use. For example, one banana farmer involved in the study reported cutting daily irrigation duration by half. At the same time, yields nearly doubled.

Hot Trend: Aquaponic Systems

Aquaponics is a system combining aquaculture and hydroponics in a symbiotic environment, whereby fish that are farmed in tanks provide water and nutrients for growing fruit and vegetables, after which the water is filtered and fed back into the tanks for reuse. A successful example is Bustan Aquaponics farm in Egypt. It was established as the first commercial aquaponics farm in the country, growing a large variety of lettuce, greens, herbs, and Nile tilapia fish. Because of Egypt's hot climate and many pressures on agricultural land, aquaponics has prevailed as a sustainable agricultural model. According to the founder, Faris Farrag, Bustan's aquaponic system saves 90 percent of water, compared to traditional irrigated farming, while growing pesticide-free produce.

Another way to innovate agriculture is to look at the crop itself. A good example is the Cassava: Adding Value for Africa Project (C:AVA). The project has developed supply chains for high-quality cassava flour in Ghana, Tanzania, Uganda, Nigeria, and Malawi to improve the livelihoods and incomes of at least 90,000 smallholder households as direct beneficiaries, including women and disadvantaged groups. C:AVA is led by the Natural Resources Institute of the University of Greenwich, working with a variety of local partners in each of these countries. In the case of Nigeria, C:AVA's partners are the Federal University of Agriculture Abeokuta and the Bill and Melinda Gates Foundation. Through the project, small farmers were able to increase how much flour they produced for each liter of fuel used by a factor of eighteen, thus decreasing their costs and increasing their profits dramatically.[18]

Frugal technologies that turn waste into value are another opportunity in developing countries. In Vietnam, a Sustainable Product Innovation Project introduced a gasifier stove (a form of biomass gasification technology) using rice husks as a feedstock for domestic and small industrial stoves. Given that annual rice production is around 500 million metric tons, the volumes of rice-husk waste are considerable. The gasifier stove has gone through several iterations to improve on its use, quality, efficiency, and cost effectiveness.

Also on the theme of turning waste into worth, by investing in electric-arc-furnace technology, Ecuadorian steel company Adelca was able to use 100-percent-recycled steel as a raw material, saving $12 million on the 20,000 tons of steel it produces every month. Each ton of recycled steel also saves 1.5 tons of iron ore, 0.5 tons of coal, 40 percent of the water used in production, and 75 percent of the energy needed to make steel from raw materials. In addition, it saves 1.28 tons of solid waste while reducing air emissions by 86 percent and water pollution by 76 percent.[19] To ensure an adequate supply of raw materials, Adelca invested in building up its network of recyclers, including paying for and delivering training, donating metal-cutting equipment, offering loans, and paying the best price for the scrap metals.

Solar energy is another increasingly viable technology for many developing countries. Without electricity, people living in rural areas are forced to use expensive and hazardous lighting and heating alternatives such as candles, batteries, and kerosene lamps, which can cost as much as a third of the net income of poorer households. Azuri Technologies is working to change this by installing pay-as-you-go solar home systems in sub-Saharan

Africa. For every 10,000 units installed, 50,000 people will enjoy clean energy access, $2 million will be saved over the life of the solar system, and 12,000 tonnes of greenhouse gas emissions will be offset.[20]

Enabling Technology Transfer

When entrepreneurs are contemplating their innovation options, one of the most crucial decisions is whether to develop technologies in-house or source them from the market. Developing a technology in-house is a time-consuming process, requiring brainstorming, intense desk research, investment into research and development (R&D), a testing phase, securing of intellectual property rights (IPR), and finally launching the product. Typical methods have involved the gleaning of information by reverse engineering products, analyzing patent applications, attending trade shows and conferences, reviewing technical journals, and taking advantage of "spillover" effects by engaging former employees of technology companies.

The returns of a customized technology solution developed in-house can be significant, strengthening the core competencies of the company and creating a competitive advantage in the market. A key determinant in the decision of whether to develop technologies in-house is the fit with the organization's existing portfolio of products, expertise, plant, and equipment. If the fit is weak, or if in-house development is not financially or technically feasible, as is the case for many start-ups or companies in developing countries, it is best to consider sourcing the technology from the market.

The bulk of market-based technology transfer is in the form of international trade, foreign direct investment, and licensing. For example, the Chinese company Jiangsu Redbud Textile Technology has developed and tested new varieties of jute, which are well adapted to growing in wastelands, saline ground, low-lying wetlands, and drought conditions. In order to share the technology more widely, the company established a platform called SS-GATE in Benin in Africa and built a "green jute industrial park" to strengthen technical cooperation. The product was innovated to fit environmental conditions, and the institution created a collaborative space for innovation.

Another example is LanzaTech, a US-headquartered company with a vision of turning our global carbon crisis into a feedstock opportunity. LanzaTech sees the potential to displace 30 percent of crude oil use today and reduce global CO_2 emissions by 10 percent. By recycling carbon from industrial off-gases, synthetic gas generated from biomass, and reformed biogas, the company can reduce emissions and make new products for a circular carbon economy. LanzaTech has used licensing to set up a plant in China that produces ethanol from carbon monoxide emitted by a steel plant, and another in India for the conversion of solid waste into biofuel.

For technology transfer to succeed, however, there are five barriers that need to be overcome. First, institutional capacity needs to be built among local companies, universities, government departments, and research institutes. Second, there needs to be sufficient market demand for the innovation that is being developed. Many solutions that have been parachuted in from the West have failed, since they do not fit the local needs, tastes, culture, or ability to pay. Third, there needs to be absorptive capacity—the extent that companies and individuals can create, learn, adapt, or use the new technologies. Fourth, intellectual property rights need to be respected, but these can be expensive. And fifth, there has to be access to funding.

The Southern Africa Innovation Support Programme (SAIS) is an example of how to overcome these barriers. It is supported by the Ministry for Foreign Affairs of Finland, in partnership with the ministries responsible for science, technology, and innovation of Botswana, Namibia, South Africa, Tanzania, and Zambia, and the Southern African Development Community Secretariat. SAIS describes itself as a regional initiative that supports the growth of new businesses through strengthening innovation ecosystems and promoting cross-border collaboration between innovation role players in Southern Africa. The program focuses on strengthening early-stage enterprises and young entrepreneurs, connecting innovation ecosystems, and promoting innovations serving socially or economically disadvantaged populations.

Key Concept: Crowdfunding

Access to finance is often the biggest barrier to overcome for technology innovators. This is where crowdfunding has emerged as a new model. Instead of relying on wealthy individuals and institutional investors making large financial commitments, crowdfunding seeks small financial commitments from a large number of people—that is, the crowd. There are three general models: reward based, debt based, and equity based. These platforms are typically more suited to new ventures but increasingly support a range of initiatives.

Crowdfunding platforms such as Kickstarter and Indiegogo are open to anyone who can get online. One of the most famous examples is Dutch entrepreneur Boyan Slat's Ocean Cleanup crowdfunding campaign on the ABN-AMRO SEEDS platform. With the support of more than 38,000 funders from 160 countries, more than $2 million was raised in 100 days, making it the most successful nonprofit crowdfunding campaign in history at the time.[21]

Fairphone is another good example of overcoming technology-transfer barriers. Claiming to be "the world's most sustainable smartphone,"[22] Fairphone has three design principles: (1) responsibly sourced materials, including fair-trade gold, recycled copper, and conflict-free metals; (2) support for living wages, including a bonus for factory workers of €1.85 per Fairphone 3 assembled; and (3) modularity, including six easily replaced components that boost longevity and minimize environmental footprint. In 2018 the company raised €20 million in funding and debt, including a €2.5 million equity crowdfunding campaign, a €4.5 million funding round from social-impact investors, and €13 million in debt financing from creditors, including the consortium of ABN-AMRO and the Dutch Good Growth Fund.[23]

Open Innovation

iNNpulsa is an example of a government-funded open-innovation program, created to support and promote business growth in Colombia. Colombian companies publish their challenges, sharing them with the general public and other companies in order to cocreate solutions. Typically, these co-innovators will share in the risks and the rewards. And these programs do not have to be government sponsored. More and more, we see private investors, corporate entities, and philanthropists setting up innovation prizes to crowdsource the most promising technology breakthrough ideas.

Key Concept: Open Innovation

The concept of open innovation—essentially crowdsourcing ideas—was articulated by American professor Henry Chesbrough as a more distributed, more participatory, more decentralized approach to innovation. It's the antithesis of the traditional approach where internal R&D activities lead to internally developed products that are then distributed by the firm. Instead, there is a two-way process: External ideas and technologies are brought into the firm's own innovation process, and underutilized ideas and technologies in the firm are allowed to go outside to be incorporated into others' innovation processes.

One of the most well known is XPRIZE, which has designed and operated 17 competitions since 1994 in the areas of space, oceans, learning, health, energy, environment, transportation, safety, and robotics. Their approach is to set ambitious future-positive goals and then invite innovators to compete for the prize money that will enable them to turn their designs into reality. They express their mission as wanting to inspire and guide innovators to create breakthroughs that enable a world of abundance—a world where every man, woman, and child can access all the energy, clean drinking water, shelter, education, and health care they require.

Among the current prizes are Feed the Next Billion XPRIZE ($15 million, to produce alternatives to chicken breasts or fish fillets that replicate or outperform conventional chicken and fish in access, environmental sustainability, animal welfare, nutrition, and health, as well as taste and texture); NRG COSIA Carbon XPRIZE ($20 million, to develop breakthrough technologies to convert CO_2 emissions into usable products); IBM Watson AI XPRIZE ($5 million, to demonstrate how humans can work with AI to tackle global challenges); Rainforest XPRIZE ($10 million, to enhance our understanding of the rain forest ecosystem); Rapid Reskilling XPRIZE ($5 million, to quickly reskill under-resourced workers for the digital revolution); and most recently, Carbon Removal XPRIZE ($100 million, sponsored by Elon Musk to find innovations that will remove CO_2 at a gigaton scale).

Another initiative is the Earthshot Prize, launched by Sir David Attenborough and Prince William in 2020, which will award five £1 million prizes each year for the next 10 years, providing at least 50 solutions to the world's greatest environmental problems by 2030. It takes inspiration from President John F. Kennedy's Moonshot, which united millions of people behind the goal to land a person on the moon, thus catalyzing the development of new technology in the 1960s. The Earthshot Prize is centered around five *Earthshots*—simple but ambitious goals for our planet, which, if achieved by 2030, will improve life for us all for generations to come (Figure 7.1).

IPRs and Open Sourcing

The World Intellectual Property Organisation (WIPO) argues that clear IPRs encourage innovation, since companies can earn returns on

Protect and restore nature

By 2030, we choose to ensure that, for the first time in human history, the natural world is growing—not shrinking—on our planet.

Clean our air

By 2030, we choose to ensure that everyone in the world breathes clean, healthy air, at World Health Organization standard or better.

Revive our oceans

By 2030, we choose to repair and preserve our oceans for future generations.

Build a waste-free world

By 2030, we choose to build a world where nothing goes to waste, where the leftovers of one process become the raw materials of the next—just like they do in nature.

Fix our climate

By 2030, we chooseto fix the world's climate by cutting out carbon, building a carbon-neutral economy that lets every culture, community, and country thrive.

Figure 7.1: *The five Earthshots of the Earthshot Prize*

their R&D investments and are therefore incentivized. However, the WIPO position has been strongly criticized, especially by advocates for those in developing countries. They argue that patents on food (such as Monsanto's "terminator seeds," which are sterile in the second generation) or lifesaving medicines (such as treatments for HIV/AIDs, malaria, or COVID-19) are unethical.

Key Concept: Open Sourcing

Many of the concerns around intellectual property rights—such as how they withhold life-enhancing products or lifesaving innovations from those who cannot afford them—can be addressed through open sourcing. This is a collaborative mode of production, testing, and distribution, often involving volunteers, where patents and related research are shared publicly through platforms. Open sourcing stands in stark contrast with legislation that seeks to protect intellectual property.

WIPO has responded to criticism by setting up WIPO Green, an online platform for technology exchange. The intention is to support global efforts to address climate change by connecting providers and seekers of environmentally friendly technologies. Through its database, network, and acceleration projects, it brings together key players to catalyze green technology innovation and diffusion.

Other initiatives have sought to go further, such as the Eco-Patent Commons, which was set up by the World Business Council for Sustainable Development to spur the diffusion of patented sustainable technologies. Between 2008 and 2016, the nonprofit initiative provided royalty-free access to 248 patents covering 94 green inventions.[24] Another example is the Medicines Patent Pool (MPP), set up in 2009 under Unitaid. Today, it has licenses from 10 patent holders related to 18 products, including treatments for HIV/AIDS (covering more than 92 countries), hepatitis C, and tuberculosis. A total of 22 generic companies and drug developers have licenses from MPP, resulting in more than 150 ongoing drug-development projects.[25]

On platforms like these, IPR is still handled by using licenses, but these are typically either a general public license or Creative Commons license.

The latter is innovative in and of itself. Creative Commons is a nonprofit organization that was set up in 2001 to help overcome legal obstacles to the sharing of knowledge and creativity that address the world's pressing challenges. To achieve their mission, they provide Creative Commons licenses and public domain tools that give every person and organization in the world a free, simple, standardized way to grant copyright permissions for creative and academic works, as well as to ensure proper attribution and allow others to copy, distribute, and make use of those works.

Many large companies struggle with this tension between patent protection and open sourcing. We've seen this battle play out among Big Tech, with Microsoft and Apple going the proprietary route, while Google has been more oriented toward open-source approaches (for example, with its Android and Chromium operating systems). Much of the inspiration for open-source software comes from the Linux operating system, developed by Linus Torvalds in 1991. Now even the likes of Microsoft are opening up. The company surprised many—given its reputation as the world's biggest seller of licensed software—by joining the Open Invention Network, a community dedicated to protecting open-source software from patent lawsuits by technology giants such as Google, IBM, and (ironically) Microsoft.

Another Silicon Valley giant, Elon Musk, came out in 2014 as a fan of open sourcing, when he declared that Tesla would no longer "initiate patent lawsuits against anyone who, in good faith, wants to use our technology." His blog of June 12, 2014, began, "Yesterday, there was a wall of Tesla patents in the lobby of our Palo Alto headquarters. That is no longer the case. They have been removed, in the spirit of the open-source movement, for the advancement of electric vehicle technology."[26]

Explaining his decision, Musk reflected: "When I started out with my first company, Zip2, I thought patents were a good thing and worked hard to obtain them. And maybe they were good long ago, but too often these days they serve merely to stifle progress, entrench the positions of giant corporations and enrich those in the legal profession, rather than the actual inventors. . . . We believe that Tesla, other companies making electric cars, and the world would all benefit from a common, rapidly-evolving technology platform."[27]

Open sourcing can help solve many of our most difficult challenges. The Deepwater Horizon oil spill is a case in point. Following an explosion on BP's oil platform in the Gulf of Mexico on April 20, 2010, the ensuing spill of 200 million barrels of oil that affected 1,300 miles of coastline is widely regarded as the worst marine oil spill in American history.[28] Initial efforts by disaster-response ships wasted tons of diesel and absorbed only a small fraction of the oil—about 3 percent.[29]

As a result, MIT appointed innovation engineer Cesar Harada to lead a team and come up with a better solution. They designed Protei, a remote-controlled, semi-autonomous, biomimetic (nature-inspired) marine sailing drone that is driven by the combined forces of the wind and waves. After sharing the design specifications online, sailors, scientists, and engineers from around the world contributed to improving the drone. Following the crisis, Protei resulted in the formation of Open H2O, which has a goal to develop open-source technologies to explore and save the oceans.

The Potential of Digital Platforms

Many of these digital solutions are commercial, but there is growing recognition of the public benefits that open or shared digital platforms could deliver. Hence, governments are using them more and more. For example, the District Health Information Software 2 is an open-source, web-based health-management information system platform, which is used by 67 low- and middle-income countries, benefiting 2.28 billion people. In another application, TaKaDu's software uses data from sensors to create actionable alerts about water-network anomalies sent to users via an easy-to-use online platform.

Waste management is another area of government that can benefit from collaborative data platforms. In the Indian city of Bengaluru, the government used digital mapping to improve its waste-collection and transportation systems, while Waste Ventures India uses an app to schedule doorstep waste pickup from households and businesses across India. It recycles the waste into compost and new materials, providing stable economic opportunities for workers in the process.

Case Spotlight: Kio Kit

Education is another natural fit for digital platforms. A nice example is the Kio Kit, which is a digital education toolbox enabling schools in emerging markets to access online educational tools. The kits come with 40 Kio computer tablets, preloaded with engaging educational content that is divided into three key sections: academic content aligned to the local curriculum, games that stimulate critical thinking, and content focused on responsible citizenship and environmental conservation. Along with the tablets, the Kio Kit includes a BRCK wireless router designed for mobile use even with unreliable electricity and internet access. The BRCK router also has solar-charging capabilities and a lockable case. Designed to be user-friendly, particularly for children, the tablets do not require individual cables for charging. Instead they are simply placed back into the Kio Kit, which charges them wirelessly.

These platforms do not have to be run by the government; nor do they have to be highly sophisticated. For example, 2degrees creates online networks for companies to share sustainable supply-chain-management expertise and best practices with others. Working with global corporations such as ASDA, GlaxoSmithKline, and Unilever, 2degrees facilitates knowledge sharing through "fully-linked collaboration," bringing all of a company's suppliers and partners together on a secure digital platform to help companies reduce risks, costs, and environmental impacts.[30]

Even Repair Cafés are benefiting from the digital economy. They self-organize volunteer-led workshops where people can learn to repair broken goods, from electronic appliances and bicycles to clothes and buildings. Using their RepairMonitor software, they collect data from Repair Cafés around the world, which can be used to make recommendations to manufacturers, regulators, and consumers about which consumer goods break most often and how that can be avoided.

Digital platforms can also help connect talent with jobs across geographic and sectorial borders. For the millions of unemployed youths globally, it opens a whole new perspective for seeking and landing jobs. By creating better matches or simply making matches possible, digital platforms can ensure that more positions are filled. It is estimated that as many as 540 million individuals could benefit from online talent platforms by 2025.[31]

As we move to a digital-platform world, facing the risk of data being compromised through cyberattacks becomes critical. The digital economy has its dark side. Cyber security is not only about malware on computer systems but also about physically screening and identifying potential criminals—and, conversely, ensuring that innocent users can securely access their computers, offices, and data. This is where behavioral biometrics has a big part to play. Biometrics refers to technologies that analyze patterns of human interaction with electronic devices to design new security tools unique to the individual. Standard biometrics include the use of fingerprints or face scans. Next-generation biometrics use concrete and measurable patterns of human traits, such as keystroke analysis, voice authentication, and body movement. For example, Blindspotter, a product from Balabit, collects user-related data and user-session activity in real time or near real time, to spot anomalies in behavior. Similarly, NuDetect from NuDataSecurity identifies the real user based on hundreds of behavioral attributes.

Time to Redesign

This chapter has been all about how technology innovation in the service of nature and society can bring us smart solutions. Now, it's time for us to take all this creativity and use it to rewire the economy.

IT'S TIME

It's time to redesign, to reconceive the world we leave
For those who follow in our wake, for each child's sake
It's time to spark and innovate, to syncopate with
New ideas, beyond the fears of failures past, at last
It's time to rise, with fire burning in our eyes
And change our ways to giving, for life and for the living

It's time to re-align, to reassess the mess we make
When what we take is more than need, is greed
It's time to halt life's slow decline, the heinous crime
Of ecocide, the plastic tide, the skies of smoke that choke
It's time to heal the dying soil, to ease the workers' toil
And make new waves of daring, with love and with great caring

It's time to redefine, to resurrect the hope that springs
With wings of acting boldly now, with minds that beam
It's time to dream of futures green, to reinvent our fate
To help the earth regenerate, where waste is food, renewed
It's time to turn from death, to take a breath, start afresh
And make a mighty pivot, for life and all who live it.

CHAPTER 8

Resilience

Adults keep saying: "We owe it to the young people to give them hope." But I don't want your hope. I don't want you to be hopeful. I want you to panic. I want you to feel the fear I feel every day. And then I want you to act. I want you to act as you would in a crisis. I want you to act as if our house is on fire. Because it is.

—**Greta Thunberg,** "Our House Is on Fire"

Imagine a village of 140 families where, over the short space of a few days, all the men of the families are killed. Sadly, this is not fiction. It happened in the farming village of Krushe e Madhe in Kosovo, where a massacre by Serb forces in 1999 left 500 children without fathers. How do you recover from that? If you are one of the widows left behind, how do you move past the trauma and keep food on the table for your family? My wife is from Kosovo and has spent time with some of these remarkable women. Theirs is a story of resilience, and strength of the human spirit. It is an inspiring testimony to how people can endure suffering and come back from disaster.

A documentary called *Hive* tells their tale through the eyes of one of the widows, Fahrije Hoti. At first, she relies on the family's beehives, but they do not produce enough honey to support them. So she gathers together some of the other widows, and together they start making *ajvar*, a smoky red pepper spread that is a staple of Balkan cuisine. At the same time, the women begin taking over the farming activities that used to be done by their husbands. They teach one another how to grow peppers, potatoes, onions, cucumbers, and other vegetables, and eventually they organize themselves into an agricultural cooperative called Krusha.

Apart from the psychological trauma, they also have to overcome social prejudice in a patriarchal society where women in general, and widows in particular, are often expected to stay at home, do housework, and look after the children. When the ajvar production starts in Hoti's backyard— including roasting, hand-peeling, grinding, and stewing large vats of the red peppers—they are met with derision from the men, who are also scandalized when Hoti learns to drive a car, another taboo in the culture at that time. "We had lost our husbands, our children, and they called us whores," she recalls. "That was the most hurtful."[1]

Today the cooperative employs around 25 women and supplies 28 markets around Kosovo with different products that are based on traditional recipes. This story reminds me of the remarkable resilience I have seen women demonstrate in so many countries, such as in Sri Lanka, another country that has been scarred by violence. When my wife and I were there in 2015, generously hosted by CSR Lanka, it had been only six years since their 25-year civil war had ended, and one place in particular left a lasting impression on me: the Bodyline factory, which makes almost all of Nike's sports bras, as well as supplying Victoria's Secret.

The scale of the factory is immense, with one work area housing around 1,500 women. I was impressed that they had chosen to locate the factory in a rural area rather than in a city. This meant that workers did not need to move from their villages or make long commutes to work. Once again, the women had self-organized to support one another, in this case via a program called Go Beyond. Through this network of solidarity, they could promote the opportunities of women in the workplace and also help one another to deal with cultural taboos and social prejudices they encountered as a result of being the main breadwinners in the household. They showed that, through resilience, even the worst kinds of disruption can be turned into opportunities for thriving.

The Risk Economy

The major forms of disruption that we see in the world today are all manifestations of stressed systems. In his book *Collapse*, as mentioned in Chapter 2, the American geographer, historian, and anthropologist Jared Diamond reviews the causes of historical and prehistorical instances of societal collapse, from the Maya civilization and Easter Island to Rwanda and Haiti.[2] He finds four main causes: environmental changes, the effects of climate change, hostile neighbors, and a breakdown of trade partnerships.

Key Concept: The Risk Economy

The counterforce to disruption is solutions that provide resilience through the risk economy, including all expenditures and investments that lower and respond to risks in society. These range from property insurance and health and safety controls to flood defenses and emergency response training. The strategies are about not only lowering risk but also aiding recovery and ensuring continuity. Thus, the risk economy is about finding solutions that help us prepare for and respond to emergencies and catastrophes, allowing us to survive and thrive through periods of breakdown, uncertainty, and volatility.

Today, the World Economic Forum's annual *Global Risks Report* gives some insight into what are perceived to be the major forces of disruption in the world (Table 8.1).

TABLE 8.1: TOP PERCEIVED GLOBAL RISKS IN TERMS OF LIKELIHOOD AND IMPACT (2017–2021)

Global risks	2017	2018	2019	2020	2021
Extreme weather (likely + impactful)	X	X	X	X	X
Climate action failure (likely + impactful)	X	X	X	X	X
Weapons of mass destruction (impactful)	X	X	X	X	X
Biodiversity loss (likely + impactful)				X	X
Infectious diseases (likely + impactful)					X
Natural resource crises (impactful)					X
Human environmental damage (likely)					X
Natural disasters (likely + impactful)	X	X	X	X	
Water crises (impactful)	X	X	X	X	
Human-made environmental disasters (likely)				X	
Data theft or fraud (likely)	X	X	X		
Cyberattacks (likely)		X	X		
Involuntary migration (likely + impactful)	X				
Terrorist attacks (likely)	X				

Source: *Data from World Economic Forum,* Global Risks Report, 2021

It is imperative that we learn from these crises, which is what the risk economy is all about. Let's take one of the most notorious disasters as a case in point. On April 14, 1912, at 11:40 p.m., the "unsinkable" HMS *Titanic* hit an iceberg and sank. I think we can draw four lessons from this tragedy, in terms of how we respond to crises: (1) Never believe you are unsinkable, or too big or too smart to fail; arrogance makes you blind. (2) Invest in early warning systems, and don't ignore alarm bells; believe the science. (3) What you see is only the tip of the iceberg; most of the problem is invisible. (4) Act early when facing a credible risk; changing direction takes time, and the bigger the organization, country, or economy, the longer change takes.

When it comes to preventing disasters—or at least minimizing the impact of risks—science matters, and the weather is proof. We like to joke about the weather forecasts always being wrong. But the truth is that meteorological science, supported by highly complex computer models, is twice as accurate today than in the 1980s. With each passing decade, meteorologists can see one day further into the future. The benefits of this additional foresight can be dramatic. For example, when Cyclone Fani struck India in May 2019, a million people had been evacuated. Although 89 died, a similar storm in 1999 had killed more than 10,000.[3] This global forecasting system works because of free and open data sharing between nations. Besides science, collaboration makes the difference.

The volatility of weather links to the wider challenge of climate change, which is probably the biggest focus area for the resilience economy. Besides the economic damage already in evidence, there are also human impacts that demand our urgent action. There are currently 21.5 million climate refugees who, until recently, had not been added to the 25.9 million political refugees that are afforded legal status and government protection.[4] The World Bank expects climate refugees to rise to 165 million by 2050, and in 2020, for the first time, they were given legal recognition.[5] In a landmark legal case (*Ioane Teitiota v. New Zealand Government*), the UN Human Rights Commission concluded that a person cannot be returned to their home country (in this case, the Pacific island of Kiribati) if climate change is threatening their life or critically endangering their health.

We all want to thrive in the future, but first we will have to survive. And in order to survive in a VUCA world (that is volatile, uncertain, complex, and ambiguous), we will need to develop resilience. A few years ago, when the World Bank asked me to share some thoughts on the subject at an event they were hosting, these were the 5-D strategies for resilience that I presented:

1. *Defend* your assets through intelligent design and financial buffers.

2. *Diversify* your people and products to increase creativity and lower risk.

3. *Decentralize* your infrastructure and markets to reduce single-source dependence.

4. *Decouple* your growth from scarce environmental resources.

5. *Define* your vision and purpose to give people something bigger to believe in.

Using this simple test, how resilient is your company, city, or country?

Raising Ambition on Climate Action

According to the Lloyd's Register Foundation World Risk Poll, 69 percent of people worldwide see climate change as a serious threat (28 percent say serious; 41 percent say very serious). That still leaves 13 percent who do not perceive a threat and 18 percent who don't know or refused to answer.[6] But knowing how complex systems change, this two-thirds-plus majority is more than enough to flip global society into a new way of behaving and doing business—despite diehard deniers, lobbyists, and laggards. We are social animals strongly influenced by what others believe.

Hot Trend: Carbon Neutrality

According to climate scientists, it is crucial to get carbon emissions on a downward trajectory by 2030 if we are to avoid dangerous climate change.[7] With that in mind, the GlobeScan-SustainAbility survey of sustainability experts on climate leadership makes interesting reading. Most (55 percent) believe we are already into the "irreversible damage" zone and that companies must be carbon neutral by 2030 or sooner (67 percent) to prevent the global temperature rising more than 1.5 degrees Celsius, which is considered the threshold beyond which climate damage will increase dramatically. The experts are relying on national governments (82 percent) and the private sector (75 percent) to scale efforts, set ambitious goals and targets, and advance technological solutions. Topping the list of perceived leaders on climate action are Unilever, Patagonia, Tesla, IKEA, and Alphabet/Google.[8]

In terms of government leadership, we naturally look to the rounds of climate negotiations at the so-called Conference of Parties meetings. Despite these ongoing talks, governments and business must now be judged on climate action. The UK was the first major government to enact a law for achieving net-zero carbon emissions by 2050, and the EU has since followed suit. Research by The Economist Intelligence Unit shows that 71 percent of senior executives surveyed from four energy-intensive sectors are confident of meeting this goal. Other promising findings are that energy self-generation by business is expected to rise and emission-reduction budgets have increased significantly, more than 20 percent for a quarter of respondents.[9]

The most persistent argument among climate action laggards is that it will cost too much. Leaving aside that we know it will cost more the longer we delay, let us look at the real price tag. First, the G20 countries expect to spend $6.3 trillion to tackle COVID-19, which is equivalent to 9.3 percent of their 2019 GDP. In contrast, a report from the Energy Transitions Commission—backed by multinationals (such as ArcelorMittal, Shell, Tata Group, and Volvo) and NGOs (such as the World Resources Institute)—estimates it could cost 0.5 percent of global annual GDP spending to reach net-zero carbon by 2050.[10]

So, yes, there is a short-term price tag, but it is entirely affordable and comes with numerous nonfinancial benefits. As politicians will tell you, if you want to win an election, be sure to use the words *job creation*. Research cited by McKinsey & Company shows that government spending on either energy efficiency or renewable energy is likely to create almost three times as many jobs as the same investment in fossil fuels.[11] Yet governments still spend $5 trillion every year in fossil-fuel subsidies worldwide as a result of corporate lobbying by coal, oil, and gas companies.

That is at least part of the reason why we have made slow and inadequate political progress to date. To meet the Paris Climate Agreement and avoid runaway climate change, we must all achieve net-zero carbon by 2050: households, businesses, industries, cities, and countries. According to the Energy and Climate Intelligence Unit, so far only one-sixth (16 percent) of global GDP is already covered by net-zero emissions targets set by nations, regions, and cities.[12] We need to up the ante and follow the example of those that are more ambitious: Norway and Sweden have net-zero emissions laws for 2030 and 2045, respectively. Meanwhile, We Mean Business has more than 900 companies with $17.6 trillion in market cap signed up to a zero-carbon economy transition. What are your country's, city's, or company's net-zero targets?

Many believe that the COVID-19 crisis will give us the Great Reset that we need. In fact, despite lockdowns around the world, economies stalling, and airplane fleets being grounded, global carbon dioxide emissions fell only by 5.8 percent, or almost 2 billion metric tons, in 2020.[13] Before being tempted to celebrate, think about the disruption we have experienced. We would need more than this level of reduction (7.6 percent) every year of this decade to stay within 1.5 degrees Celsius warming. The message is clear:

Carbon is still deeply embedded in our economy and our modern lifestyles, and reduced consumption is unlikely to secure a climate-safe future. We need radical innovation, supported by a carbon tax and strong government policies on clean tech.

Getting there will also require that companies pass my simple admission-ambition test for separating thriving-focused pioneers from pretenders. This means that, first, they admit the scale and urgency of our global challenges and their complicity in these, and second, they set bold strategic goals that will transform not only themselves but society as well. Here, the Climate Ambition Alliance gives us some hope, with 73 countries, 14 regions, 398 cities, 768 businesses, and 16 investors committing to achieve net-zero CO_2 emissions by 2050.[14] Combining ambition and societal consciousness leads to transformation.

Bursting the Carbon Bubble

The global economy is in transition—and many companies, industries, and even national economies will be economic losers in the process. This is the growing reality of transition risk. A study published in *Nature* estimates that a third of oil reserves, half of gas reserves, and more than 80 percent of coal reserves must remain unburned to meet the Paris Climate Agreement.[15] If these assets are left stranded, the carbon bubble will burst, wiping $1–4 trillion from the global economy, according to Cambridge University research.[16] Other sectors—such as automotive, chemicals, and transportation—face similar transition risks.

In fact, companies making their wealth from fossil fuels may go extinct sooner than we think. According to Christiana Figueres, former head of the United Nations Framework Convention on Climate Change, "The shelf life of these companies in their current form may be more than five years—but is certainly no more than 30."[17] I'm convinced they will adapt rather than die. How soon depends on pressure—from governments and civil society. Already we see Shell planning to be the world's largest electricity company by the early 2030s. But we urgently need a global carbon price to speed the necessary transition. This would mean that carbon-intensive industries are effectively taxed and their products are more expensive, which would act as a strong economic incentive to shift more quickly to a thriving, regenerative economy.

In response to these early signs of stranded assets and transition risk, we see adaptation and innovation. BP wrote down $17.5 billion in the second quarter of 2020. The reason, said BP, was that the pandemic weakened long-term demand for energy and will speed the transition to renewables. BP also revised its assumptions about the 2030 carbon emissions price from $40 to $100 per ton.[18] In August 2020 BP went further and committed to increase its low-carbon spending to $5 billion a year by 2030, as well as boost its renewable-power generation to 50 gigawatts while shrinking oil and gas output by 40 percent compared with 2019.[19]

Case Spotlight: BlackRock

The climate action writing is on the wall. And savvy investors have been adding some of their own script. Shareholder activism (which I like to call *shactivism*) has long been a strategy of the responsible and sustainable investment movement. But when BlackRock—the world's biggest investor, with $8.7 trillion assets under management—adopted this activist approach, it became clear that the game had changed. In his 2020 letter to CEOs, BlackRock chief Larry Fink stated: "Climate change has become a defining factor in companies' long-term prospects. . . . The evidence on climate risk is compelling investors to reassess core assumptions about modern finance. . . . And because capital markets pull future risk forward, we will see changes in capital allocation more quickly than we see changes to the climate itself. In the near future—and sooner than most anticipate—there will be a significant reallocation of capital."[20]

As part of this reallocation of capital, in its 2020 letter to clients, BlackRock announced that it would immediately pull out its investment in companies that generate more than 25 percent of their revenues from thermal coal production.[21] In its 2020 "Investment Stewardship Annual Report," it then disclosed how it had voted to replace directors or support shareholder environment, society, and governance proposals for 53 companies (with a combined market cap of $669 billion) and place another 191 on notice for action in 2021 if they do not make substantial progress. BlackRock's environmental shactivism (including on climate change) went up 289 percent in 2020 compared to the previous year.[22]

Making the shift that investors such as BlackRock and many others are now demanding is more difficult for some sectors than others. Industrial heating is a case in point. The kilns, reactors, chillers, crackers, and furnaces of the world are almost all powered by fossil fuels and emit 10 percent of our global CO_2. That's as much carbon as cars (6 percent), planes (2 percent), and ships (2 percent) combined. And because of the high temperatures required (over 500 Celsius/932 Fahrenheit), likely substitutes—including biodiesel, renewable electricity, renewable natural gas, solar thermal, geothermal, thermal storage, and hydrogen—are struggling to compete. According to the Center for Global Energy Policy at Columbia University, all these alternatives cost between 2 and 10 times more.[23] Decarbonizing is hard, but necessary.

That's true for the airline industry as well. Some believe that the only solution is for all of us to stop flying, or at least feel guilty when we fly, as per the Swedish notion of *flygskam*, or flight shame. But I am not convinced by this approach—first, because I do not think it will work. We have been trying to guilt people into sustainability for decades without success. Second, the airline industry can and must find technological pathways to carbon neutrality and is committed to achieving this. So what could the pathway to a resilient future look like for the airline industry?

One solution is biofuels, which the industry is calling *sustainable available fuels* and which produce 70–90 percent less carbon than conventional jet fuel. The problem is still the price; biofuels are up to four times more expensive. But economies of scale and policy incentives can fix this. Land-use competition with food is another concern, but there are alternatives, such as algae-based biofuels. Even better is to convert waste into biofuels. Virgin Atlantic flew the first waste-derived biofuels commercial flight in 2018. Now Velocys is building a waste-to-biofuels energy plant in the UK. Add natural climate solutions (such as investing in biocapacity, which are nature's carbon sinks), and a net-zero or net-positive carbon footprint looks possible.

To Net Zero and Beyond

The starting point for business leaders has to be committing to science-based targets that are in line with the Paris Climate Agreement. But those who really understand the science—and therefore the urgency of the next decade for averting climate catastrophe—strive to go further, aiming for net-zero carbon by 2030. The UK water industry, including the nine biggest utilities, are taking up this challenge. Their industry road map includes heating 150,000 homes by producing biomethane from sewage waste, adding three gigawatts of new wind and solar to meet 80 percent of the sector's electricity needs, converting to 100 percent electric vehicles, restoring 20,000 hectares of peatland and grassland, and planting 11 million trees.[24]

When it comes to net-zero carbon commitments like these, what to include is critical. Globally defined standards for measuring emission reductions distinguish between carbon from operational activities (called Scope 1 emissions), from electricity and heat used (Scope 2), and from the activities of suppliers (Scope 3). Microsoft, for example, has committed to be fully carbon negative by 2030, cutting emissions from its operations, electricity use, and suppliers to below zero. (This includes investing in carbon sinks, such as forests.) The company has also gone further than any other by promising to remove enough carbon to cancel all the operational- and electricity-related carbon they have emitted since the company was founded in 1975.

This is a great lead to follow. However, if we are going to resolve the climate crises, we must also change the discussion on carbon. That begins by realizing that all carbon is not the same. We need to start differentiating between good carbon and bad carbon. Unilever's Carbon Rainbow helps us to do that (Figure 8.1). The rainbow forms part of the company's Clean Future strategy, which includes an ambitious commitment to replace 100 percent of the carbon derived from fossil fuels in their Home Care cleaning and laundry products with renewable or recycled carbon by 2030. The rainbow excludes black carbon from fossil fuels and instead draws on regenerative and circular economy carbon sources, including gray carbon from plastic waste, green carbon from plants, blue carbon from marine sources, and purple carbon from CO_2.

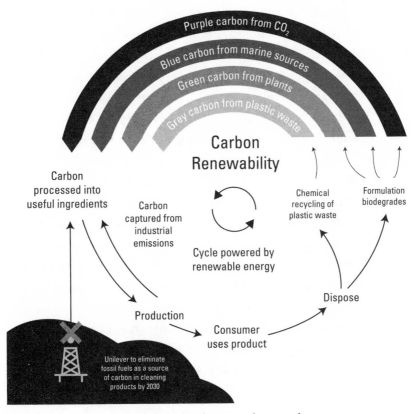

Figure 8.1: *Unilever's carbon rainbow*

The conventional purple carbon solution proposed by industry—and, not coincidentally, mainly by the oil and gas sector—is carbon capture and storage (CCS). A lot of research and development has gone into CCS, and I sometimes wonder how much carbon we would already have absorbed if that capital had been invested in natural climate solutions. Be that as it may, CCS technology is starting to show signs of breakthrough. For example, have you heard of tetraamine-functionalized metal organic frameworks? Me neither, until recently. This is the new wonder-material that university scientists working with ExxonMobil claim captures carbon dioxide emissions up to six times more effectively than conventional CCS technology.

Using a less conventional approach, one company is turning purple carbon into something very precious indeed. In fact, it seems too good to be true: making diamonds as a natural climate solution. Well, perhaps not entirely natural, but a carbon sink nevertheless. This is the new business venture of Dale Vince, the British environmental entrepreneur and founder of the UK renewable-energy company Ecotricity. A mined one-carat diamond requires digging up 1,000 metric tons of rock and earth, using 3,890 liters of water, and emitting more than 108 kilograms of carbon dioxide. Vince's new business, called Sky Diamonds, will extract CO_2 from the air to manufacture 1,000 carats of carbon-negative diamonds, all molecularly identical to mined stones. Thriving can sparkle.

Sky Diamonds may be a gimmick to ease the conscience of rich folks, but it also demonstrates that every industry needs to find a way to make their products carbon negative. The carpet-tile manufacturer Interface is another example. It has gone from being a fossil-fuel-intensive company to one that is striving to be climate positive through its four-part Climate Take Back strategy: (1) Live Zero—do business in ways that give back whatever is taken from the earth; (2) Love Carbon—stop seeing carbon as the enemy, and start using it as a resource; (3) Let Nature Cool—support our biosphere's ability to regulate the climate; and (4) Lead the Industrial Re-revolution—transform industry into a force for climate progress.[25] Importantly, this includes carbon-negative carpet tiles—part of the Embodied Beauty collection, which includes climate-positive CircuitBac Green backing, made from up to 87 percent recycled and bio-based content.

Staying with the indoor building environment for a moment, can you think of another product category that desperately needs reinvention? There are many, but consider this: As the planet warms, demand for air-conditioning (AC) goes up, warming the climate even further. How do we solve this conundrum? The International Energy Agency predicts that AC demand will rise from 1.6 billion units today to 5.6 billion in 2050.[26] Innovation needs to kick in, which is why the Rocky Mountain Institute has a $3 million Global Cooling Prize. Solutions are out there.[27] In Singapore, Reevac Deep Cooling technology delivers 24-degrees-Celsius airstreams using no refrigerants or compressors and producing negligible waste heat, and in Bangladesh eco-coolers are made from recycled PET bottles, a frugal innovation that drops indoor temperatures 5 degrees Celsius.

Another building-related innovation is lighting. The switch from incandescent to LED light bulbs is already world changing—and it's about to get even better. An average LED uses around 6 watts of electricity per hour and lasts 50,000 hours, compared with incandescent bulbs that use 50 watts and only last 1,200 hours.[28] That's a six-ton carbon savings per bulb. Now scientists have come up with a new biomimicry (nature-inspired) design modeled on the microscopic, jagged surface of firefly abdomens, which look like a series of lopsided pyramids or factory roofs when magnified. Creating the same uneven surface on LEDs could increase the light they emit by 50 percent.

The Race for Renewables

Since renewables rank so highly as a climate solution, let's look into this clean energy technology a little more. Solar energy, for example, is booming—and some of the places it is taking hold may surprise you. For instance, there's a quiet revolution in renewables happening in Texas, for decades a synonym for Big Oil. At first glance, it may not be obvious. With around

22 percent of total electricity sales coming from renewable energy, Texas ranks only 11th in the nation, a long way from Oklahoma, Iowa, Kansas, and North Dakota, which all had more than 45 percent renewable power in 2019. But a project called Renewables on the Rise 2020 shows that the Lone Star State is poised to leap forward, since it ranks first for wind-energy production, third for battery-storage capacity, fifth for solar-energy production, fifth for electric vehicles, and fourth for charging stations.[29] And that was all before Tesla decided to locate its next Gigafactory in Austin, Texas. Watch this space: Texas is about to go big on renewables.

Breakthrough Solution: Extreme Solar

We already know that distributed solar is a great solution for households and offices. But when it comes to powering industrial activity, this approach lacks punch. Solar panels simply don't generate enough heat to make cement, steel, or glass or to support other industrial processes. But that may be about to change, thanks to a concentrated solar technology breakthrough funded by Bill Gates. Clean energy company Heliogen has discovered how to use artificial intelligence and a field of mirrors to generate extreme heat above 1,000 degrees Celsius, a quarter of the temperature on the surface of the sun. The renewables race is heating up!

And then there's wind energy. Paradoxically, on most issues to do with thriving, when Donald Trump comes out against something, it's like a perverse endorsement. If he insists something is fake news, it is almost certainly a fact. And if he says something's bad, it's most likely good. During his turbulent presidency, he ranted against wind power. Yet wind energy is a highly effective solution to climate change, emitting 27 times less carbon per unit of energy produced over its full life cycle than coal, as well as 24 times less than hydropower and 20 times less than natural gas.[30] As if that weren't enough, every year the effectiveness of wind turbines goes up. For example, one Haliade-X wind turbine can now supply electricity to 16,000 homes. Fortunately, the world is opting for more wind and less hot air.

Even so, we should not get too self-assured. Renewable is not automatically the same as sustainable or regenerative. In the age of fossil fuels, it made sense to conflate. But that's no longer the case, especially for hydroelectric power. Advocates of thriving have become increasingly critical of the social and environmental impacts of hydro schemes. A recent example is Austria-backed KelKos Energy, which had three hydropower licenses revoked in the Decan Valley, a national park and protected zone in the Accursed Mountains of Kosovo. A consortium of 60 civil society organizations hailed this as a victory for sustainable development.

The solar, wind, and battery industries would do well to take note. For example, at the moment, most wind turbine blades are made from fiberglass and cannot be recycled or repurposed. Instead, they are piling up in landfills, where they will stay for thousands of years. DecomBlades, a consortium of Danish companies, is looking to change that and make wind turbines that are 100 percent recyclable. Solar panels are less problematic, since silicon solar modules are primarily composed of glass, plastic, and aluminum: three materials that are recycled in mass quantities. In fact, a study by the International Renewable Energy Agency estimates the recyclable materials in old solar modules will be worth $15 billion in recoverable assets by the year 2050.[31] Even so, the use and recycling of precious metals in renewable technologies remains cause for concern.

Once again, we must look to innovation for solutions. For example, can we find an alternative to hydropower that uses the same approach but without the negative impacts? The answer is yes, we can. And the clue is that what goes up must come down. That's the basic principle of gravity-driven renewable energy. And unlike solar, wind, tidal, and geothermal sources, gravity systems are able to synchronize energy generation with periods of peak demand. Edinburgh-based company Gravitricity is planning to use abandoned mine shafts to raise and lower weights of 500 to 5,000 metric tons, generating 1 megawatt to 20 megawatts of power. The company also expects its energy storage solution will cost less than lithium batteries.[32]

Driving the Electrification Trend

Another area of climate innovation is transportation. We are entering a perfect storm that is driving rapid change and rapidly changing how we drive. The confluence of climate change, renewable energy, and electric vehicle (EV) trends is powering another Industrial Revolution, at 10 times the speed. According to Bloomberg New Energy Finance, by 2040, EVs will account for 57 percent of global passenger car sales and 81 percent of municipal bus sales.[33] By the same date, 56 percent of light commercial vehicle sales and 31 percent of medium commercial vehicles in the United States, China, and Europe will be electric. A UK survey by *Business Car* magazine and E.ON echoed these trends, finding that 37 percent of fleet managers expect full electric vehicles to increase in their fleet in the next three years, and 24 percent of company car drivers anticipate their next company car will be fully electric or a hybrid.[34]

Hot Trend: Fleet Managers as Energy Brokers

The vision of electric vehicles linking to net-zero buildings (which integrate renewable energy for heat, power, and transport) as well as to the energy grid (so-called vehicles-to-grid) may completely transform the role of fleets and their managers. As Darren Gardner from the European energy company E.ON put it, in the future "fleets will become power stations and fleet managers will become energy brokers."[35]

The number of EV models coming onto the market (many of them in the more affordable range) is significant, and the charging network is rapidly expanding across many regions in the world. Charging speeds are also about to take a quantum leap, with Shell, for instance, having already demonstrated superchargers three times faster than Tesla's. But are EVs really more sustainable? The short answer is yes, they are, over the life cycle of the vehicle. Nevertheless, the batteries they use are resource intensive.

Global EV sales are forecast to rise from 1.7 million in 2020 to more than 50 million by 2040—and the vast majority of those cars will be run on lithium-ion batteries. For now, Chile has the largest reserves of lithium and is the second-largest supplier after Australia. But clean-tech investors and entrepreneurs want to change that, by injecting billions of dollars and creating thousands of jobs in the Imperial Valley—already being nicknamed Lithium Valley—an economically disadvantaged region in Southern California, where the Salton Sea has the potential to meet a third of global lithium demand.

That may address supply issues, but lithium extraction is not without its environmental impacts. And there are other metals to worry about as well. Tesla recently announced a big contract to source nickel from Indonesia, which holds a quarter of the world's reserves. Nickel makes EV batteries more efficient and reduces dependence on cobalt from the Congo, with its associated "conflict minerals" human rights issues. Yet nickel projects in Southeast Asia operate on fossil fuels and dump their waste in the ocean (technically, deep-sea tailings disposal). I am less worried about recycling the batteries; companies such as Umicore in Belgium are already set up for this. EVs still trump fossil-fuel cars, but the mineral extraction footprint needs addressing.

Despite these impacts, electric vehicles are an innovation that will improve our climate response. And it's not the only innovation on offer. Bill Gates provides an excellent summary of "the solutions we have and the breakthroughs we need" in his book *How to Avoid a Climate Disaster*.[36] Others are even more optimistic, suggesting that if we simply apply and scale sustainable technologies already in existence, we can meet the Paris Climate Agreement by the mid-2040s. This is the conclusion from think tank Project Drawdown in their 2020 review.[37] Their original 2017 publication *Drawdown*, edited by Paul Hawken, set out 100 existing climate solutions, evaluated scientifically and ranked in terms of their potential positive impact. The financial case is also compelling, with net operational savings exceeding net implementation costs four to five times over.

Daring to Draw Down Carbon

Let's dig a bit deeper into the solutions—and gain some perspective on the potential impact of each. Project Drawdown categorizes solutions that could keep us within 1.5 degrees Celsius of warming into those that reduce sources of carbon emissions, those that support carbon sinks, and those that improve society. Of these, the biggest impact is likely to come from reducing sources of carbon emissions, accounting for 70 percent of the necessary drawdown. The next most effective is supporting sinks, which can contribute 25 percent by absorbing carbon. Improving society can bring the remaining 5 percent.[38]

Regenerative Solutions: Project Drawdown Top Five

In case you get lost in the multitude of climate solutions or are not so interested in the detail presented in this section and want to skip over it, here are the top five climate solutions, out of the 100 innovations that have been researched in Project Drawdown. Ranked first is onshore wind turbines, second is utility-scale solar photovoltaics, third is reduced food waste, fourth is plant-rich diets, and fifth is health and education. Taken together, these account for a third (34 percent) of the overall carbon-reduction opportunity.

When it comes to reducing sources of carbon, the biggest potential solution is changing how we produce electricity, followed by our food, agriculture, and land-use practices. Industry, buildings, and transport account for less but are also important. As for supporting sinks, land sinks currently dominate—providing the second-largest overall solution category after electricity—followed by engineered sinks and coastal and ocean sinks. Improving society is all about health and education solutions.

Looking at electricity, the biggest bang for the buck comes by shifting production, and, within this, the potential of onshore wind turbines is highest, followed by utility-scale solar photovoltaics. Energy efficiency provides another set of solutions, especially the switch to LED lighting. Besides these, improving the electricity system can be achieved through grid flexibility, microgrids, distributed energy storage, and utility-level energy storage.

Moving on to food, agriculture, and land-use practices, the three categories of solutions are addressing waste and diets, protecting ecosystems, and shifting agricultural practices. Within waste and diets, the opportunities are fairly evenly spread between reducing food waste and shifting to plant-rich diets, while protecting ecosystems points (perhaps surprisingly) to peatland protection as most effective.

Looking to industry could yield an often-neglected solution, which is addressing refrigerants. These represent a disproportionate 72 percent of the overall opportunity for reductions from industry. The reason is because the fluorinated gases used as refrigerants have a potent greenhouse effect with a global warming potential of up to 13,900, meaning that one ton of CFC-13 in this case has the same effect on the climate as 13,900 tons of CO_2. In contrast, the potential for transportation to reduce climate impacts is less than most people think (13 percent of the overall opportunities) but nevertheless important, as is improving buildings.

In terms of supporting carbon sinks, the main categories of solutions are shifting agricultural practices, protecting and restoring ecosystems, and using degraded land. The biggest single opportunity is tropical and temperate rain forest restoration. Within shifting agricultural practices, the largest impact comes from silvopasture, which is an agroforestry practice that integrates trees, pasture, and forage into a single system. Incorporating trees improves land health and significantly increases carbon sequestration. Promoting perennial staple crops, such as bananas, avocado, and bread-fruit, is another solution. Compared to annual crops, they have similar yields but higher rates of carbon absorption.

Talking about climate solutions inevitably leads to the question of geo-engineering. The more controversial proposals, which I think are rightly dismissed for the most part, include stratospheric aerosol injection using sulphates to reflect more radiation, or ocean fertilization by adding vast amounts of iron or other nutrients to stimulate the growth of algal blooms that absorb CO_2. While these proposals may have merits, in that they could have a climate-cooling effect, the concern is about unintended consequences in such a complex living system. Project Drawdown, by con-trast, proposes just one engineered sink solution, which is the production of biochar. This is produced by slowly baking biomass, such as agricultural waste, in the absence of oxygen, thus retaining most of the feedstock's car-bon. It can be buried for sequestration and enrichment of soil.

The final major category of solutions is health and education. As levels of education rise (in particular for girls and young women), access to repro-ductive health care improves, and women's political, social, and economic empowerment expands. As a result, fertility typically falls. This means that we can expect our global population to stabilize in the coming decades and start to fall, with obvious long-term benefits for the climate, since cumula-tive impacts will go down.

What the insightful science-based research of Project Drawdown demonstrates is, first, that we can tackle climate change and reach the Paris Agreement's 1.5-degree target by 2050 or even earlier, even with today's existing technologies, techniques, and other solutions. Second, there is no silver-bullet solution. Even though some changes promise more impact than others, none of them get us to the finish line on their own. We are not faced with dichotomous choices of either-or—for example, investing in either reducing carbon emissions or growing carbon sinks. Rather, we are offered both-and opportunities, which in all likelihood will positively reinforce one another, causing a virtuous cycle of improvement.

Innovation for Climate Adaptation

Many of the solutions presented so far fall into the category of climate mitigation. They show us that we have many options to slow down and eventually reverse global warming. But that is only half of the story. The fact is that climate change is already happening, and it will almost certainly get worse before it gets better. That means that there are billions of people who will suffer from the impacts of climate change. We need solutions, therefore, that help us—as individuals, communities, organizations, cities, or countries—to cope with the effects of climate change. Here there is a place for innovation as well.

"Adapt Now" is a report by the Global Commission on Adaptation, led by Bill Gates, Ban Ki-moon, and Kristalina Georgieva. It warns that, without changes, the number of people who do not have enough drinking water will grow from 3.6 billion to more than 5 billion by the middle of the century. Hundreds of millions of people living in coastal cities could be forced to move, costing cities $1 trillion a year by 2050. And more than 100 million people could be forced below the poverty line by 2030. By contrast, investing $1.8 trillion over the next decade would lead to $7.1 trillion in benefits.[39]

The recommendations for investment center on five main areas: building new early warning systems for storms; creating more resilient urban infrastructure; changing water management; restoring and protecting mangrove forests, which protect communities from storm surges while helping boost fishing industries; and creating changes in farming, such as planting drought-tolerant maize that small farmers are now growing in Zimbabwe. If we invest in adaptation, the report argues, we reap a triple dividend:

avoided losses + economic benefits + social and environmental benefits. Let's look at some examples and how these dividends have been quantified.

In terms of avoided losses, early warning systems save lives and assets worth at least 10 times their cost. Just 24 hours' warning of a coming storm or heat wave can cut the ensuing damage by 30 percent, and spending $800 million on such systems in developing countries would avoid losses of $3–16 billion per year. Likewise, making infrastructure more climate resilient can add about 3 percent to the upfront costs but has benefit-cost ratios of about 4:1. With $60 trillion in projected infrastructure investments between 2020 and 2030, the potential benefits of early adaptation are enormous.[40]

Besides avoided losses, economic benefits include lower financial costs, increased security, and improved investment opportunities. For example, London's Canary Wharf and other developments in East London would not have been possible without the protection from the Thames Barrier. Investment in adaptation also improves the productivity of resources and people.

Flood-resistant varieties of rice in Orissa, India, not only reduced losses during times of floods but also boosted farm yields during normal years. Similarly, drip-irrigation technologies, first developed to address severe water scarcity, are spreading because they are also better and more efficient. There are benefits for cities too. Rotterdam enjoys social benefits, in the form of improved community cohesion and quality of life, from green spaces that are designed to slow floodwaters.

Regenerative Solution: Mangrove Forests

There are many social and environmental benefits of investing in climate adaptation. For instance, many nature-based actions that reduce flooding also increase biodiversity and make the air and water cleaner. Restoring coastal mangrove forests not only protects coastal communities from more dangerous storm surges but also provides critical habitat to sustain local fisheries. While mangrove forests provide more than $80 billion per year in avoided losses from coastal flooding—and protect 18 million people—they also contribute almost as much ($40–50 billion per year) in nonmarket benefits associated with fisheries, forestry, and recreation. Combined, the benefits of mangrove preservation and restoration exceed the costs by up to 10 times.

The "Adapt Now" report summarizes three basic elements of climate-change adaptation. First, we have to reduce and prevent the impacts. Solutions most often come from agriculture research and development, climate proofing buildings and infrastructure, land-use planning, nature-based solutions to protect people and assets, and permanent relocation (migration). The second element is to prepare and respond to the impacts. This includes early warning systems, forecast-based action (contingency planning), strengthening the capacity of first responders, and temporary evacuation. Third, we must restore and recover from the impacts. This is where insurance and risk-finance instruments can help, as well as social safety nets, recovery services (including health and education), and strategies or policies to build back better.[41]

Of course, it is not only humans that will be affected by climate change; there are also the myriad plants and animals that make up the web of life on which we depend for our own continued existence. That's why Brazil's National Institute for Amazon Research has started to look ahead in their ADAPTA project. They plan to house hundreds of species of plants, mammals, fish, and insects from the Amazon in climate-controlled rooms that represent the earth 25, 50, and 100 years from now. The project will, in effect, put these species through a real-life climate simulator, to see which ones are able to adapt. This will inform conservation efforts that may help weaker species to survive.

Innovation for Crisis Response

I have focused extensively in this chapter on climate change because it is perhaps the most serious risk—what Joe Biden rightly called, during his first week of presidency, an "existential risk."[42] As we have seen, the climate emergency is already causing global disruption and generating lots of innovation for resilience. But of course, there are many causes of disruption, including other natural and human-made disasters, from earthquakes and pandemics to industrial accidents and financial crises. Given the COVID-19 situation, pandemics have already received quite a lot of attention in this book—notably in Chapter 6, which focuses on shifting from disease to revitalization. So let me now look briefly at some resilience solutions to other areas of disruption.

Case Spotlight: Ushahidi's Disaster Response

One of my favorite examples of a resilience solution is Ushahidi's response to the devastating earthquake in Haiti in 2010, which killed 200,000 people. Ushahidi, which translates to "testimony" in Swahili, was developed to map reports of violence in Kenya after postelection violence in 2008. It has been headquartered in Nairobi since then, and thousands have used its crowdsourcing tools to raise their voice. In the case of the Ushahidi-Haiti project, they secured a free SMS short code from Digicel Haiti within 48 hours of the earthquake. The purpose of this short code, 4636, was to crowdsource information on urgent needs from the disaster-affected population and to map these text messages on a public map, called Crisis Map.

A second step was to rapidly launch an online platform to crowdsource Haitian-Creole–speaking volunteers from around the world to translate and geolocate text messages sent to Digicel's 4636 short code. This real-time translation of tens of thousands of text messages by some 1,100 volunteers helped to get vital information about the needs and location of victims to international aid agencies in languages that they could understand. After being contacted by the US Marine Corps, Ushahidi imported the data into Google Earth, which was then used in on-the-ground rescue efforts. As the crisis unfolded, the US Federal Emergency Management Agency declared that "the Crisis Map of Haiti represents the most comprehensive and up-to-date map available to the humanitarian community," and the US Marine Corps added that "it is saving lives every day."[43] Not bad for a tech enterprise from east Africa.

There has been a lot of innovation on the design of buildings to withstand earth tremors. Some designs are fairly low-tech and entirely appropriate for many of the communities affected by earthquakes, such as the bamboo houses designed by the engineering consultancy Ramboll in the wake of a quake that killed 560 people on the Indonesian island of Lombok in 2018. Another approach, developed by researchers from Stanford University and California State University, puts houses on sliding "isolators" that move along the ground. The design was tested in conditions four times the intensity of the earthquake that flattened parts of San Francisco in 1989, and the test house sustained almost no damage at all.

When it comes to earthquakes, it's not just houses that need solutions; bridges are affected as well. University of Utah professor Chris Pantelides has designed a new bridge-repair method that uses a thin doughnut-shaped composite shell, which is placed around damaged pillars and then filled with concrete. The innovation cuts repair time from weeks or months down to mere days. There is also research from the US Geological Survey, Caltech, the University of Houston, and others that shows how a crowd-sourced GPS-based earthquake warning system on smartphones could send out a message when it detects the initial rumbling of an earthquake.

In the state of Oklahoma, the earthquakes are caused by humans—or by fracking, to be more specific. Before 2008 Oklahoma had barely any serious seismic activity. The state averaged one to two earthquakes of 3.0 or greater on the Richter Scale each year. But then oil and gas drilling took off, and Oklahoma became the most seismic state in the country, even exceeding California. By 2013 there were 109 "plus-3" earthquakes, with 584 in 2014 and 850 in 2015. No wonder the residents began suing the fracking companies in 2016.[44]

The rapid land-use change associated with fracking—and the aftermath of the earthquakes it causes—is exactly the sort of situation that tech company Planet Labs is designed to spotlight. The company operates a fleet of more than 150 earth-imaging satellites that produce a detailed map of the world with a resolution that can be as high as 50 centimeters, and the map is updated daily. This provides all kinds of opportunities to increase resilience. The dynamic maps can show illegal logging or fishing operations, the emergence of slums and the spread of wildfires, the loss of key habitats or the patterns of urban development. In each case, near-real-time data allows policymakers or concerned NGOs to identify problems and respond quickly.

Acts of Courage

In the end, resilience is about surviving disruption and building back better. It is about caring enough for those who are affected by disasters and crises to want to help them. It means recognizing that, for billions of people around the world, staying alive is an achievement in itself. Therefore, let us embrace our role as guardians of all life, our own, our loved ones', and those of people whose lives are so much harder than ours but no less precious. Let us celebrate being alive.

ALIVE

I live
And therefore, I am victorious
Every breath is a triumph
Every step, an accomplishment

For living and breathing and walking
Are acts of defiance
Against dying and resigning and stopping

I am alive
And therefore, I am miraculous
Every emotion is an improbability
Every idea, an implausible feat
For living and feeling and thinking
Are audacious abilities
Against the odds of chance and chaos

I survive
And therefore, I am heroic
Every day is a battle won
Every year, a universe conquered
For surviving and striving and thriving
Are human superpowers
Against oblivion and entropy and meaninglessness

We live
And while we live, others die
Every life is an arc of light
Every death, a shooting star
For living and shining and fading
Are the black fate
Of each glorious being whose life we celebrate

We are alive
And therefore, we are guardians of life
Every heartbeat is a sacred gift
Every experience, a rare treasure
For living and laughing and loving

Are anti-spells
Against dying and darkness and desolation

We survive
And therefore, we are incredible
Every sunrise is another chance
Every moonrise, another bridge
For surviving and rising and connecting
Are acts of courage
That honor creation
And welcome living
And reaffirm life.

SECTION V

REGENERATING ORGANIZATIONS

You simply cannot expect to build a business with longevity and resilience if you don't embed ethical conduct in all you do. This is now a precondition for any successful company and if you do not move to a more responsible, sustainable and equitable way of doing business, then you don't deserve to have any business at all. . . . Those companies that embrace the long-term, multi-stakeholder model perform much better, as it helps them to earn their license to operate, reduce costs, attract and retain top talent, access new markets, accelerate innovations, and partner with key stakeholders to effect system-level change.

—**Paul Polman**, in R. A. Butler, "Putting Sustainability at the Center of Business Strategy"

Organizations are the way we collaborate to get things done in society. They have always existed, but the scale, scope, and power of today's governments, companies, and nonprofit organizations are unprecedented in history. That means, if we want to thrive, we need to do it through organizations and those that lead them. That may sound like a daunting task, but let's not forget that organizations are also complex living systems. Everything we have learned about thriving can also be applied to making organizations more effective.

In Chapter 9 we look at the organization itself, and especially at how the key to a thriving, regenerative business is integration. We explore six facets of integration, from rethinking patterns, realigning partners, and renewing principles to redefining purpose, reassessing performance, and redesigning portfolios. In Chapter 10 we look at what it means to be a thriving-driven leader. We identify the characteristics and competencies that leaders require in order to turn systems breakdown into breakthrough, including being more systemic, inclusive, strategic, caring, innovative, and courageous.

CHAPTER 9

Integration

The companies that survive longest are the ones that work out what they uniquely can give to the world—not just growth or money but their excellence, their respect for others, or their ability to make people happy. Some call those things a soul.

—**Charles Handy,** *The Age of Unreason*

Food for Thought

When I lived in Cambridge, UK, I would often drive to London and pass a site run by Biogen that had a massive green dome and several green tanks. Then, when I was filming *Closing the Loop*, I had the opportunity to visit the site. The first impression, as I stepped into Biogen's processing plant with the film crew, was the overwhelming stench of rotting organic matter. This was the receiving point for truckloads of food waste, sent by municipalities, farms, restaurants, and hotels. At the moment we arrived, a few tons of watermelons were being bulldozed into a corner. They still looked good to eat but must have passed their sell-by date.

After getting accustomed to the smell, we followed the process as the watermelons and other food waste were loaded onto conveyer belts to be pummeled and pulped before being pumped as a sludge into anaerobic digestor tanks and fermented. The biogas naturally created in the sealed tanks is used as a fuel in a combined heat-and-power unit to generate renewable energy. What's left from the process is a nutrient-rich biofertilizer that is applied twice a year on nearby farmland in place of fossil-fuel-derived fertilizers.

This is a great example of a business creating value through thriving, which is what we explore further in this chapter. Think about the forces of breakdown that this business is helping to reverse. We have the problem of food waste, which has major resource and energy impacts. We have the problem of fossil-fuel-derived energy, which is causing climate change and respiratory illnesses. And we have agro-industrial farming that is killing the soil and decimating biodiversity with its use of chemical fertilizers.

Biogen is turning the problem of food waste into a renewable energy source while simultaneously providing an organic fertilizer alternative for farmers. Every metric ton of food waste recycled by anaerobic digestion, as an alternative to ending up in a landfill, prevents between 0.5 and 1.0 metric ton of CO_2 entering the atmosphere. And at the same time, it starts to rebuild the soil and bring back biodiversity. According to Biogen, the biofertilizer achieves even better yields than chemical alternatives, so there is an economic regeneration effect as well.

This is the value of thriving. It turns forces of breakdown into counterforces of breakthrough. The risks of declining are transformed into opportunities for thriving. And most importantly, the solutions that are developed create multiple benefits. By supporting a circular economy for food waste, we can turn resource depletion into renewal and lower the risk of climate disruption, thus increasing resilience. Disease from fossil fuel pollution–related health impacts is turned into revitalization, while using sophisticated, digitally controlled anaerobic technology is a form of rewiring the economy.

Behind the scenes, Biogen's regenerative approach works because they have integrated it at every level of the organization, from strategy through to operations and from stakeholder engagement through to transparent reporting of performance. This approach is what I call *integrated value management* (or IVM), and I've found it is helpful for organizations that want to go on a journey toward becoming champions of thriving. It is an answer to the question: How can we achieve thriving through business and other societal institutions?

The Integration Imperative

The question of how to achieve thriving through business was one I had been wrestling with for some time. The answer came to me in a light-bulb moment in Ann Arbor, Michigan, in September 2014. I was working on a new sustainability market offering for the global consulting and training company Omnex. I had been recently appointed as senior vice president of sustainability services and was spending the week with Chad Kymal, founder and chief technology officer of Omnex. We were exploring what business and society needed most in order to make more rapid and real progress toward a sustainable future.

Happily, all my experience of developing new ways of thinking about corporate social responsibility (CSR) and "future-fitness" (which I have described in my books *The Age of Responsibility*,[1] *Sustainable Frontiers*,[2] and others) served as a fertile seedbed for something new to germinate. After Chad and I had spent a few days trawling through international sustainability codes, guidelines, and standards—of which there are more than 450—the answer to our market-gap question was suddenly forehead-slappingly obvious. Business needs a way to navigate the tidal wave of voluntary requirements and societal expectations. In short, businesses need integration; they need to create integrated value, the value of thriving.

This is not a novel idea. CSR and sustainable business thought leaders have been calling for integration of societal and environmental concerns for years, decades even. And many of the standards ask companies to integrate sustainability-related issues into their management systems, especially those from the International Organization for Standardization (ISO), such as

ISO 9000 (for quality), ISO 14000 (for environment), and ISO 26000 (for social responsibility). Academics have also been calling for various forms of integrated value, from stakeholder value (R. Edward Freeman) and blended value (Jed Emerson) to sustainable value (Stuart Hart and Mark Milstein) and shared value (Michael Porter and Mark Kramer).

Yet in practice, in most companies, the issues remain siloed. Health and safety have their own department with their own specialists; environment, if it is addressed at all, is another function with different experts; social responsibility is the job of corporate affairs, marketing, or the charitable foundation; human rights belongs to the managers in legal affairs, procurement, or supply chain; and so on. The challenge, in other words, is not the *what* or the *why* of integration; it is the *who* and the *how*.

Fresh Insight: SQuELCH Issues

After reviewing many of the CSR and sustainability guidelines, codes, and standards, it is evident that there is an 80:20 Pareto rule at work here: 80 percent of the requirements are more or less the same, and 20 percent give each standard its own distinctive focus. With some analysis, I identified 10 common themes, which I playfully nicknamed the $S_2QuE_3LCH_2$ issues: safety + social (S_2), quality (Qu), environmental + economic + ethical (E_3), labor (L), carbon or climate (C), and health + human rights (H_2). So the first imperative for integration is for the business to make sure that all the SQuELCH issues are on its radar and being addressed.

The second imperative is not to create separate management systems for each sustainability issue but rather to integrate them into one seamless SQuELCH management system—that is, to integrate across management silos. (Don't worry, I am not suffering under the delusion that my acronym will be widely, or even narrowly, adopted, but it makes me smile). For this, we built on Omnex's extensive consulting expertise, software systems, and standards knowledge.

The third imperative is to integrate across the issues and, more specifically, the opportunities that come from breakthrough innovation. If we do this, we create value in the form of thriving. Building on the six shifts to thriving, each has an innovation pathway: restoration, renewal, responsibility, revitalization, rewiring, and resilience create solutions that are, respectively, symbiotic, sustainable, shared, satisfying, smart, and secure. (You will have noticed by now that I'm never one to let an alliteration go to waste).

Integration Brings Innovation Synergies

The idea of creating value in the form of thriving is really simple. We must focus our economic institutions and channel our creative energies not only toward tackling the six areas of societal breakdown and turning them into breakthrough opportunities but also toward creating solutions that bring multiple, simultaneous, mutual benefits across the global system. These could be smart innovations that are also sustainable, or shared innovations that are also secure, or satisfying innovations that are also symbiotic.

Key Concept: Synergy

Thriving value highlights the importance of synergy, a key systems-thinking concept that organizational theorist Russell Ackoff and polymath Buckminster Fuller studied in great detail. Synergy is the phenomenon of the whole being greater than the sum of the parts. You may have seen it expressed as 1 + 1 = 3. In other words, something emerges from the interaction of the parts in a system that is new and valuable. This is why, in thriving, complexity of relationships and diversity of parts is so important, since it seeds creativity.

Let's revisit some of the examples that have been mentioned in previous chapters to illustrate the point about integration bringing innovation synergies. We saw how Planet Labs analyzes and indexes 1.4 million daily satellite photos of the surface of the earth to enable researchers to track physical changes over time, including the impacts of fires, floods, earthquakes, deforestation, and urbanization. From a thriving-value perspective, this is not only a *smart* solution (using sophisticated digital technologies) but also *secure* (helping us to anticipate or respond to disruption), *symbiotic* (tackling the degradation of ecosystems), and *sustainable* (reducing the depletion of natural resources).

Do you recall Garbage Clinical Insurance? They are bringing a *shared* solution (aiming to address poverty in Indonesia by working with underserved communities) that is also *sustainable* (the community is collecting waste, since municipal services are inadequate) and *satisfying* (since they get health insurance in return for the garbage they have collected). Provenance is another case we highlighted that is *smart* (using digital finance and blockchain technology), *shared* (empowering farmers and producers from developing countries), and *sustainable* (verifying environmental and social standards in the supply chain).

Similarly, Timeless is a *smart* and *satisfying* app, developed by 14-year-old Emma Yang, that uses face identification software to help Alzheimer's patients recognize their loved ones, while Planetarians is creating a *sustainable* and *satisfying* innovation by using extrusion technology to transform food waste into nutritious food products, creating high-fiber, high-protein snacks that it says can tackle childhood obesity.

The inevitable question is whether there is a company or a technology that incorporates all six elements of thriving value. Maybe there is, but I am not aware of one. However, I would suggest that Tesla comes close. Their electric vehicles have saved, at the time of writing, more than 3.6 million tons of CO_2, which tackles climate disruption and makes it a *secure* solution. Besides this, their solar and battery technologies are accelerating the renewable-energy transition. Despite legitimate concerns about the sourcing of precious metals and the recycling of batteries, I think it is safe to say they are net-positive on the *sustainable* dimension. Tesla's utility-scale pow-er-pack solar- and battery-storage installations in Puerto Rico in the wake of Hurricane Maria are another example of a *secure* and *sustainable* response.

When it comes to *smart*, Tesla cars are basically computers on wheels, with the most advanced AI-enabled autonomous driving software of any automotive company. Their renewables and battery packs are similarly managed for optimum efficiency by digital innovation. On the well-being dimension of *satisfying*, Tesla cars are the safest in all categories, scoring the maximum a car can score in the National Highway Traffic Safety Administration tests. This includes scoring nine times better than other safe cars, such as the Volvo S60, in the pole test and 50 percent better than any other car in rollover risk. On top of this, Tesla's semi-autonomous Autopilot feature results in nearly 10 times fewer accidents and fatalities than human-driven cars. On the *shared* dimension, Teslas are not cheap (not even the Model 3), but the company's strategy of moving to self-driving fleets may make it an accessible Uber-type service company in the near future.

Integrated Value Management

In 2017 I accepted an appointment as professor of integrated value and holder of the chair in sustainable transformation at Antwerp Management School in Belgium, supported by BASF, Port of Antwerp, and Randstad. This allowed me to further develop the concept and practice of integrated value. Specifically, I extended its scope of application in three directions: to complex problems, innovative solutions, and embedded management. This means that we need integration at three levels: (1) in our understanding of the forces of breakdown in society, especially how global economic, gov-ernance, societal, and environmental challenges are interconnected; (2) in our understanding of the forces of breakthrough in society, and how these opportunities are interconnected; and (3) in our management processes to turn breakdowns into breakthroughs.

Chapters 3–8 elaborate on the first two. Now let me touch on the third, integrated value management (Figure 9.1).

Rethinking patterns
Understanding the complex, dynamic system of which organizations are a part

Realigning partners
Listening to stakeholders and collaborating with partners

Renewing principles
Fostering human values that support thriving

Redefining purpose
Being mission-driven to make a positive difference through organizations

Reassessing performance
Adopting ambitious, science-based targets

Redesigning portfolios
Scaling products or services and investments that accelerate regenerative solutions

Figure 9.1: *Elements of integrated value management (IVM)*

Rethinking Patterns

Organizations are embedded parts in a larger global socioecological system. And one of the reasons why organizations go into decline or fail is that they do not have sufficient understanding of the complex, changing patterns that make up their operating context. For example, organizations may underestimate the significance of shifts in societal norms, or they may be unprepared for dramatic disruptive crises. They may fail to see how changes in complex supply chains or public policy frameworks are having ripple effects across their competitive landscape.

A key facet of IVM is continuously mapping and tracking megatrends and socioecological changes that may affect the long-term performance of the organization, paying particular attention to the relationships between these forces and factors. The main goal here is to reach a deeper understanding of these patterns of relationships and trends.

Key Questions for Rethinking Patterns

- What are the major socioecological trends that are shaping the organization's context, and how are they interconnected?
- Which thriving-focused aspirations (for example, those represented by the Sustainable Development Goals, or SDGs, such as gender equality or climate action) does the organization prioritize, and how are they related to other issues or SDGs?

Some tools or approaches that can be used for this facet are scenarios and systems mapping, together with an understanding of the six forces of breakdown, which should be seen as triggers for transformation. Let's start with scenarios, which are often mistaken for forecasts. Scenarios are not predictions; rather, they are stories of possible futures. The purpose of developing scenarios is to open our minds to different pathways that may lie before us, in order to prepare for these contingencies and attempt to shape the future toward more desirable outcomes.

I saw this firsthand in South Africa, where scenarios developed by the multinational mining company Anglo American in 1987 encouraged the nation to contemplate the "high road" of a negotiated transition to democracy versus the "low road" of a descent into a protracted, bloody civil war.[3] Anglo American was not the first company to use scenarios. They have been used more famously by Shell for 50 years, notably under the leadership of Arie de Geus, a Dutch business executive and management theorist who was the head of Royal Dutch Shell's Strategic Planning Group. For example, in 2008, they released their "Shell Energy Scenarios to 2050," in which they mapped out two possible pathways: the worlds of Scramble (where "events outpace actions" and the result is chaotic adaptation) and Blueprints (where "actions outpace events" and the result is coordinated transition to a more sustainable future).[4]

While this scenario thinking has not automatically made Shell the darling of sustainability advocates, it has certainly helped the company to be less defensive than many other oil and gas companies, as Shell gears up to support a Blueprints energy transition. Among their commitments, they aim to be a net-zero-emissions energy business by 2050 or sooner. In addition, in 2021 Shell "confirmed its expectation that total carbon emissions for the company peaked in 2018, and oil production peaked in 2019."[5]

Another technique is systems mapping. If you're not familiar with this method, let me illustrate with the example of COVID-19. Imagine a simplified system with three elements: infection rates, contact with others, and preventive behavior. What happens when contact between people goes up? Infection rates go up. We call this a *reinforcing* feedback loop and draw it as an arrow with a plus sign. What happens when we increase preventive behavior, such as self-isolation and social distancing? Contact goes down. We call this a *balancing* or *canceling* feedback loop and draw it as an arrow with a minus sign. And there you have a simple system map that helps us understand the dynamic consequences of our actions.

In practice, when working with organizations, we add more variables. For example, we used systems mapping in a workshop with Johnson & Johnson in Belgium (their Janssen subsidiary), where we took the 14 trends we had identified for the pharmaceutical industry and had their managers map the relationships between them. For instance, what is the relationship between a growing population and affordability of medicines, or between effective antimicrobials and artificial intelligence, or between reputation and protecting natural resources? We then went further and linked the trends to the 17 Sustainable Development Goals and looked for relationships between the most relevant SDGs.

Typically, systems mapping should show whether different elements of a system are linked, how strongly they are connected, the direction of the causal relationship, whether the relationship is reinforcing or balancing, and if there are delays between the cause and effect. The point of all of this is to get people thinking about the whole interconnected system of which the organization is a part. It's about understanding how the company fits into the broader, dynamic patterns of nature, society, and the economy.

Realigning Partners

As we've already noted, our global socioecological challenges are typical of entangled problems, meaning that they are difficult to solve because of their complexity and interconnectedness with other problems, multiple institutions, or related systems. Tackling these problems therefore requires a collaborative approach. For organizations, this means being open to multi-stakeholder perspectives on sustainability problems and solutions, as well as looking for strategic partnerships that can help shape systemic responses to these challenges.

Therefore, another key facet of IVM is regularly surveying and capturing the most important concerns and expectations of key stakeholders, as well as entering into cross-sector partnerships to advance progress on those priority sustainability issues. The main goal is to listen to the perspectives of these interested and affected parties on the most significant areas of impact associated with the organization, and to prioritize issues that could benefit from partnerships and strategic action.

Key Questions for Realigning Partners

- How has the organization engaged with its key stakeholders, and what are the issues they are most concerned about?
- What are the cross-sector or multi-stakeholder partnerships that the organization uses to tackle the challenges of thriving?

Some tools or approaches that can be used for this facet are stakeholder prioritization and materiality assessment methods, which can be linked to the 17 SDGs and the six shifts to thriving.

Once significant stakeholder issues have been identified, companies should look for cross-sector partnerships to help them make progress in those areas. Take Newmont, for instance, which is the world's largest gold-mining company and one often criticized for its environmental impacts. Newmont has entered into a partnership with the International Union for Conservation of Nature (IUCN) to help identify ways that the company can meet its global target to achieve zero net loss for biodiversity—and net gains, where possible. This includes conducting independent reviews at select mine sites using the IUCN Biodiversity Net Gain Protocol. The work links to broader collaboration between the IUCN and the International Council on Mining and Metals (ICMM), which has resulted in the production of the ICMM Good Practice Guidance for Mining and Biodiversity.

Another example is discount supermarket chain Lidl, which has developed a partnership with Fairtrade International. The goal is to improve the livelihoods of small-scale coffee farmers in Peru and Mexico, helping to build the producers' capacity and resilience to the adverse effects of climate change. The company also worked with the Fairtrade Foundation to launch its new "Way to Go!" range of Fairtrade chocolate bars, based on a partnership to support living wages for cocoa farmers in Ghana. The move builds on the German retailer's existing commitment to 100 percent certified sustainable cocoa and promoting Fairtrade product sales, which grew more than 50 percent in 2019.[6]

Renewing Principles

Sustainable development is based on societal expectations, which in turn emerge from collectively held values, attitudes, and beliefs. For example, there are values around justice or fairness and the sanctity of life. Organizations also have embedded values, which form the basis for how they behave as an institution and how their employees behave. Most large organizations have values statements, but these are not necessarily the "emergent" values that are widely held or are manifest in daily actions and behaviors.

A key facet of IVM is periodically checking what the organization's emergent values are and whether they are *synergetic*—that is, whether they contribute to the healthy functioning of the collective (the team, the organization, the society, the ecosystem). The main goal of this facet is to allow the real values of the organization to emerge through a process of dialogue and then to reinforce the desired values as part of the culture.

Key Questions for Renewing Principles

- Has the organization gone through a process of inclusive dialogue with employees and other stakeholders to identify its lived synergetic values?
- Does the organization do ethics training or use other approaches to embed synergetic values into the organization's culture?

Some tools or approaches that can be used for this are values surveys or ethics barometers, as well as facilitated dialogues among employees and other stakeholders, linking to typical synergetic values. Ethics training or whistleblower procedures are another option.

Values are strongly linked to culture. The World Values Survey, for example, maps the countries of the world across two axes: traditional values versus secular-rational values and survival values versus self-expression values. Similarly, psychologist Geert Hofstede proposes six cultural dimensions—such as individualism versus collectivism, and long-term versus short-term orientation—and derives scores for each country. To make this more relevant to companies, however, I like to use the six dimensions of organizational culture identified by Hofstede Insights (which is based on his country-oriented work), covering organizational effectiveness, customer orientation, level of control, focus, approachability, and management philosophy.

It is worth briefly reflecting on the question of why, given that values are a key driver of behavior, we often see a values-action gap, meaning we say or believe one thing and do another. Here are three reasons: (1) We face ethical dilemmas, or values conflicts. For example, if I pay more for sustainable products, there is less for something or someone else; perhaps I will be less able to provide for my family. (2) We suppress our individual values to conform with the group or a higher authority. For example, if I express compassion for animals, my friends or colleagues might tease me. (3) The consequences of our ethical choices are too complicated or too far away. For example, if I fail to take climate action now, who will suffer and when? If I'm not sure, it's easier to do nothing.

Redefining Purpose

One of the reasons for the unsustainable state of our world is the unsustainable economic model we have been using for the past 50 years, which is based on two flawed assumptions: (1) that economic growth can continue indefinitely on a finite planet, and (2) that companies that pursue narrow financial goals will automatically benefit wider society. In order to move to a thriving future, organizations need to redefine their purpose from short-term profit maximization or shareholder returns to the creation of long-term societal value. They need to be able to demonstrate that their processes, products, and services contribute to a fairer society and a more sustainable world.

Therefore, a key facet of IVM is reflecting on the strategic aspirations of the organization to ensure that they are aligned—in terms of focus and ambition—with whole-systems health, stakeholders' needs, and synergetic values. The main goal of this facet is to check whether the organization's purpose is clearly articulated as inspiring, ambitious strategic goals centered on the benefits the organization plans to deliver to society.

Key Questions for Redefining Purpose

- Do the organization's strategy and strategic goals clearly express the long-term value they deliver to society?
- Does the organization have policies dedicated to thriving that give substance to their wider societal purpose?

Some tools or approaches that can be used for this facet are best-practice benchmarking (finding and comparing examples of excellent purpose statements) and strategy workshops, which can be linked to the 17 SDGs and the six pathways to innovation.

It is significant that BlackRock CEO Larry Fink's 2019 open Letter to CEOs was titled "Purpose and Profit." Both the Business Roundtable Statement on the Purpose of a Corporation and the World Economic Forum's "The Universal Purpose of a Company in the Fourth Industrial Revolution" expressed a similar sentiment. The message is crystal clear: The purpose of business is important, and it's no longer just about fiduciary duty to shareholders (if it ever was). In practice, this means that business leaders can no longer use the self-serving mantra of shareholder value as a way to evade social responsibility and dodge public accountability.

One company that has shown the way on bold strategic goals is carpet manufacturer Interface. For 25 years Interface's Mission Zero has been inspirational. Now the results are in. So did they achieve zero negative environmental impact? Not quite, but what they achieved is remarkable: 100 percent renewable electricity and 89 percent renewable energy use. In addition, compared to 1996, the company has 96 percent lower carbon intensity, 92 percent less waste to landfill, 89 percent less water used, 69 percent cradle-to-gate carbon footprint reduction, and 46 percent reduction in energy use. Now, with the launch of its new Climate Take Back strategy—"Live Zero, Let Nature Cool, Love Carbon, and Lead the Industrial Re-Revolution"—Interface is pioneering what it means to be thriving.[7]

Another landmark effort has been the much-hailed Sustainable Living Plan of Unilever, set up under former CEO Paul Polman. This, too, has run its course, with some remarkable achievements. Between 2010 and 2020 1.3 billion people were reached through health and hygiene programs, and today around 50 percent of management roles are held by women, 100 percent of their electricity is renewable, and there is zero waste to landfill from their factories. Their greenhouse gas emissions are down 50 percent, their waste footprint was cut 32 percent, and 2.34 million women were given access to initiatives to improve their safety, skills, and opportunities.[8]

The Unilever Compass will take its place, with 15 multiyear priorities and nine imperatives. There was some concern that Polman's successor, Alan Jope, would give sustainability less priority. First indications are that those fears are unfounded. Along with establishing a €1 billion Climate and Nature Fund, Unilever has committed to having a deforestation-free supply chain by 2023, to having all its product formulations biodegradable by 2030, to implementing water stewardship programs for local communities in 100 locations, and to having net-zero emissions products by 2039.[9] These are ambitious goals. Let's hope others follow their lead.

There are many ways to engage in a larger purpose. For example, the organization might join a 100-club. There are several to choose from now, and they all signal ambitious leadership. The RE100 and EV100, both curated by The Climate Group, include companies that commit to 100 percent renewable energy and 100 percent electric vehicle fleets respectively. The EP100, also from The Climate Group, focuses on energy productivity, while the CE100, run by the Ellen MacArthur Foundation, features companies committed to the circular economy. These 100-clubs bring brand benefits, of course, but their impact is more about raising the bar on what is possible, making ambitious targets for thriving the new norm.

Reassessing Performance

How we measure success—at a global, national, organizational, or community level—often determines our actions and impacts. The dominance of economic and financial measures in the past 50 years has resulted in many unacceptable impacts on society and the environment. Organizations have begun to measure and report on "nonfinancial" impacts, but these still lack consistency, accuracy, and impact on investment decisions. There is now an urgent need to disclose total economic impacts, science-based targets for nonfinancial performance, externality valuations for socioecological costs to society, and proxies for intangible value.

So another key facet of IVM is determining and transparently reporting appropriate, holistic metrics that give an accurate picture of the total impacts of the organization on society and the environment, using science- and norms-based approaches. The main goal of this action is to check whether the organization's performance metrics are aligned with whole-systems integrity, as well as its stakeholder needs, synergetic values, and strategic purpose.

Key Questions for Reassessing Performance

- Is the organization using reporting standards and methods that are science-based (recognizing social and ecological thresholds) and norms-based (recognizing societal expectations)?

continued ➜

> • Does the organization have key performance indicators and associated targets that are ambitious enough to reflect the urgency of the changes required to address global challenges?

Some tools or approaches that can be used for this facet are benchmarking reporting standards, footprinting and life-cycle analysis tools, externality valuation methods that measure the social and environmental costs of economic activities, and science-based targets.

In fact, if a company has not publicly committed to science-based targets on carbon reduction, it is "faking it." These fakers can no longer claim that they are committed to sustainability, let alone thriving. When the scientific evidence of our climate emergency is so clear, unanimous, and devastating, there is no more room for excuses. Either a company accepts the science and acts boldly to prevent climate catastrophe, or it ignores the science while pretending to care. A similar argument can be made for other areas, such as biodiversity loss. But reassessing performance goes beyond carbon accounting.

Nonfinancial reporting (also called CSR, sustainability, ESG, or SDG reporting) is still not widely and consistently adopted, but not for lack of trying. There are now numerous guidelines and standards to draw on: the Toxic Release Inventory (established in 1986), the Eco-Management and Auditing Scheme (abbreviated EMAS, and established in 1993), the Global Reporting Initiative (GRI, 1999), AccountAbility 1000 (AA1000, 1999), Carbon Disclosure Project (CDP, 2000), Accounting for Sustainability (A4S, 2004), the International Integrated Reporting Council (IIRC, 2010), Sustainability Accounting Standards Board (SASB, 2011), Reporting 3.0 (r3.0, 2012), Future Fit Benchmark (2016), Value Balancing Alliance (2019), and Stakeholder Capitalism Metrics (2021).

Redesigning Portfolios

It is clear that our global challenges—many of which are getting worse, not better—will not be solved through incremental business-as-usual approaches. The scale, urgency, and complexity of the societal problems we face make innovation imperative. At the organizational level, this means changing from an approach of minimizing the negative impacts of existing products and services to reorienting the organization's core commercial offering so that it becomes a positive part of the solution, aligned with the larger societal purpose that it has articulated.

A key facet of IVM is applying innovative design thinking to products, services, processes, and business models to deliver high-impact and scalable solutions to our socioecological challenges. The main goal of this is to reorient the focus of R&D efforts toward designing solutions with societal benefits and to strategically shift the portfolio of products and services toward being inherently supportive of thriving.

Key Questions for Redesigning Portfolios

- Does the organization include thriving as a design principle for product, service, and process innovation?
- What proportion of the organization's portfolio of products or services provides a solution to socioecological challenges?

Some tools or approaches that can be used for this facet are exponential thinking and design thinking, linked to the six economic spheres (the ecoservices, circular, access, well-being, digital, and risk economies) and the six innovation pathways (symbiotic, sustainable, shared, satisfying, smart, and secure).

Exponential thinking—anticipating very rapid, radical change, such as we see with exponential growth curves—leads to what John Elkington calls *green swans* in his book of the same title, which he believes are a sign of "the coming boom in regenerative capitalism."[10] The metaphor is an elegant riff on Nassim Nicholas Taleb's black swans, which are unpredictable, rare, high-impact events with severe consequences. Green swans are the opposite—positive exponential changes. Elkington explains that, for now, we see more individual and technology green swans than companies, but there are many "ugly ducklings" (think of Hans Christian Andersen's fairy tale) that may yet prove their transformational beauty. Elkington plays with the concept, imagining black swans with green feathers and vice versa.[11]

But how to back potential green swans? I like BASF's approach, which it calls the Sustainable Solution Steering method and also makes available as a free-to-download manual for third parties. The company used a triple-bottom-line lens (looking at economic, social, and environmental benefits) to assess more than 50,000 "solutions"—which make up more than 96 percent of their product portfolio—engaging more than 2,500 experts worldwide in the process.[12] The outcome is a clustering of its product portfolio into four categories: Accelerator, Performer, Transitioner, and Challenged.

Accelerators, which made up 29 percent of BASF's total portfolio in 2019, make a substantial sustainability contribution in the supply chain. This includes, for example, chemicals that are essential for renewable-energy technologies or batteries. Performers are the second category, making up 62 percent; these meet basic sustainability standards on the market. Transitioners, accounting for 9 percent, are products that have specific sustainability challenges that are being actively addressed. And finally, Challenged products, responsible for 0.1 percent of sales, are associated with substantial sustainability concerns and are flagged for phasing out within five years of classification. BASF's ambition is to increase the sales of Accelerator solutions to €22 billion by 2025, up from €15 billion in 2019.[13]

Reshaping Playing Fields

As vital as these six steps of IVM are, organizations on their own cannot achieve the necessary transformation to a thriving future. Therefore, it is important to also support and promote government policies and market incentives that reward thriving-focused commercial behavior. We need companies to engage in positive lobbying that supports, rather than obstructs, policy reforms that are in line with science-based targets and norms-based societal expectations.

Hence, organizations should regularly review the policy (legislative) and market (financial) "rules of the game" to determine where they can actively promote legal or operational changes that are more likely to ensure sustainable and responsible outcomes. And there are plenty of good policies to support, such as the EU Green Deal, the US Green New Deal, and the BCG policy in Thailand.

Case Spotlight: EU Green Deal

The president of the European Commission calls the EU Green Deal "Europe's man on the moon moment"—an ambitious, world-changing plan. At face value, it looks like leadership to me. The 2030 goals include 50 percent reductions in carbon (up from 40 percent previously), 32 percent renewable energy, and 32.5 percent energy efficiency improvement.[14] To get there, Eurocrats will use policy reforms on the circular economy, mobility, building and renovation, pollution, food, ecosystems, and biodiversity. The EU Emissions Trading Scheme will also be extended and will help fund the economic transition. Make no mistake, the Green Deal is a big deal.

The Biden administration seems to be aware of the need for ambitious policy reform. At the time of writing, it is still early days, but the first signs are that America may yet become a credible force for thriving. We knew President Biden was going to rejoin the Paris Climate Agreement, but he has gone further, asking his domestic climate "czar," Gina McCarthy, to draw up plans to commit the United States to "the most aggressive" carbon cut possible, which turns out to be 50 percent by 2030, in line with the EU's commitment. Besides pulling the permit on the controversial Keystone XL oil pipeline, Biden intends to do away with fossil-fuel subsidies, ban new oil and gas leases on federal land, and set aside a third of all federal lands for conservation. The changes have already begun with approval of the nation's first major offshore wind farm, the Vineyard Wind project, off the coast of Massachusetts. He is also asking the Pentagon to assess the national security risks from climate change as part of what is being called his "whole-government" approach. At the same time, his executive actions cover discrimination, racial justice, immigration, and environmental justice.

Progressive policies are by no means limited to the rich West. For example, in Thailand, a bio-circular-green (BCG) economic model has been introduced by the research community and promoted by the Thai government as a new economic model for inclusive and sustainable growth. The BCG model aims at promoting four industries—agriculture and food; medical and wellness; bioenergy, biomaterials, and biochemicals; and tourism and the creative economy. It's an approach that aligns with the SDGs and builds on the Sufficiency Economy Philosophy, which was promoted by the late King Bhumibol Adulyadej.

China is also starting to be a leader for the thriving, regenerative economy. We should never forget that they have already lifted 700 million people out of extreme poverty and plan to end poverty for the remaining 50 million within five years. Since 2012 China has afforested nearly 70,000 square kilometers, and between 2000 and 2017, a quarter of newly afforested areas in the world were in China. And on climate change, China's aim to peak CO_2 emissions before 2030 and achieve carbon neutrality before 2060 will act as a global stimulus for low-carbon innovation. President Xi said that the total amount of wind and solar power that China generates will rise exponentially—from 500 million kilowatts to 1.2 billion kilowatts in a decade.[15]

Turning new economic stimulus packages green is the biggest opportunity to create a tipping point for thriving. In the EU the stimulus plan is €750 billion, and the government has already stated it will support sustainable growth and a green transition. How much of the United States' $4.5 trillion infrastructure plan and Japan's nearly $1 trillion recovery budget will be wisely spent is yet to be seen, but the potential for pivoting the global economy onto a path toward thriving is massive.

The Values Dividend

Thriving—including sustainable investments and climate solutions—will be worth trillions, according to a spree of reports: a $1 trillion energy windfall from renewables,[16] $7.1 trillion returns from $1.8 trillion invested in resilience,[17] $4.5 trillion from sustainable food by 2030,[18] and $23.9 trillion from low-carbon cities by 2050.[19] Are entrepreneurs queuing up? Are companies rewriting their strategies? Are investors overhauling portfolios? Yes, to some extent. And no, not really. Not yet. We need "show me the money" proof first. The real question is: Which will be the first trillion made from a sustainable business, sector, or investment fund? Place your bets. Mine is on Tesla.

Tesla's first-mover advantage on electric vehicles is already big. When Volkswagen launched its ID3 "to rival Tesla" in 2019, the bigger news was almost completely missed. To meet the EU's strict 2021 vehicle emissions requirements, Fiat Chrysler Automobiles will pay about $2 billion between 2019 and 2021 for the necessary emission credits to ensure that it avoids hefty fines for noncompliance. In 2020, $300 million of this went to Tesla, part of the $1.58 billion in revenue from sales of regulatory credits that Tesla generated in 2020, nearly tripling its 2019 figure of $594 million.[20]

Factor in the fact that Tesla's market cap increased by more than $500 billion in 2020 and is now worth as much as the combined market cap of the nine largest car companies globally, despite making less than 1 percent of the world's cars,[21] and there is a compelling case that Tesla is reaping what I call a values dividend.

The opposite is also true. When companies ignore the keys to thriving, they end up destroying rather than creating value. One example might be Bayer's toxic takeover of Monsanto in 2018.

Bayer's stock value declined 44 percent in the year following its €63 billion buyout in 2018. A US court granted $2 billion in damages to a couple who claimed that Roundup, the glyphosate-based weed killer, caused their cancer, which followed $2.5 billion in damages from two previous cases.[22] Then, in June 2021, Bayer agreed to pay almost $10 billion to settle thousands of similar pending US lawsuits.[23] Add the evidence of toxic lobbying revealed by the leaked Monsanto Papers, and Bayer's reputational damage starts to look as catastrophic as its mounting legal liabilities. We could be seeing the true cost of unsustainable business.

Often, the discussion around the values dividend gets phrased as the following question: What is the business case for sustainability? It's a question I've been asked for 30 years, so finally I distilled the economic benefits into the 10 Rs of return on thriving (Figure 9.2). Let me make each one clear by using an example.

Risk is lower. The costs of growing the business will be lower without expensive delays resulting from protests by angry activists or unhappy suppliers. Moving to a circular economy may also decrease potential disruption of resource supplies. Risk is the reason why 11 major shipping banks signed the Poseidon Principles, committing to assess the carbon intensity of their shipping investments and to incorporate climate goals into shipping vessels that they fund.

Reputation improves. The reason that Tesla is valued so highly by the market (and by its customers) is because it has gained a reputation for innovative solutions that will accelerate the world's transition to sustainable energy. Sustainable Brands has, since 2006, tapped into this understanding, bringing together companies that see social and environmental challenges as an essential driver of brand innovation, value creation, and positive impact.

Resilience is built. Companies such as Interface have done better during economic recessions because of savings from their sustainability programs, their innovation culture, and strong employee commitment. This is why

Risk
Risk is lower, especially because of better supply chain and stakeholder management.

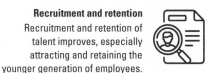

Recruitment and retention
Recruitment and retention of talent improves, especially attracting and retaining the younger generation of employees.

Reputation
Reputation improves, thus also increasing the intangible asset of brand equity.

Revenues
Revenues are boosted, especially because markets for ethical, responsible, and regenerative products are among the fastest growing.

Resilience
Resilience is built, especially the ability to anticipate and survive system shocks such as climate disruption, pandemics, or social unrest.

Returns
Returns are higher, with better access to finance and better long-term financial performance.

Resource efficiency
Resource efficiency increases, thus saving costs through less water, energy, and waste.

Research and development
Research and development are stimulated, especially since thriving opportunities require innovation to deliver.

Regulation
Regulation is anticipated, therefore allowing early adaptation and avoiding of fines and penalties.

Reason for being
Reason for being is clarified, because thriving provides a powerful purpose for organizations.

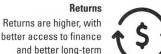

Figure 9.2: *The 10 Rs of return on thriving*

Randstad worked with Antwerp Management School to develop the Future Resilience Index, with 10 factors to assess individual, organizational, and societal resilience.

Resource efficiency increases. The Excess Materials Exchange among companies such as Schiphol Airport, Philips, and Sodexo discovered €64 million in financial value creation. According to the Waste and Resources Action Programme, savings of between 30 and 50 percent can be achieved by investing in no- and low-cost water-reduction techniques and technologies. A company with an annual turnover of £2 million could save up to £20,000 per year.

Regulation is anticipated. Eighteen countries have already committed to ban sales of new diesel and gasoline cars and move to 100 percent zero-emission vehicles, with Norway leading with a ban from 2025. In the EU the Plastics Strategy caught many producers and retailers off guard with its rapid ban of single-use plastics and its declaration that by 2030 all plastic packaging placed on the EU market must either be reusable or recyclable.

Recruitment and retention of talent improves. A Deloitte survey finds that 42 percent of Millennials and Gen Z are choosing relationships with companies whose core business has positive social or environmental impacts, while 38 percent are lessening ties with companies with a perceived negative impact.[24] In addition, research shows that sustainable and responsible companies also boost employee motivation, productivity, loyalty, and satisfaction.

Revenues are boosted. Sustainability-marketed products grew more than seven times faster than other products in 2015–2019,[25] with plant-based foods expected to grow annually at 11.9 percent from 2020 to 2027.[26]

Returns are higher. Analysis by S&P Global Market Intelligence and Morningstar shows that investments that are screened on environmental, social, and governance criteria are less risky and outperform the market in both the short and long term.[27]

Research and development are stimulated. The Business Commission on Sustainable Development estimates that meeting the SDGs will unlock $12 trillion in new market value,[28] while Accenture estimates that the circular economy is a $4.5 trillion opportunity.[29]

Reason for being is clarified. When Paul Polman was CEO of Unilever, around 1.7 million people applied to work at the company every year. Polman believes this had a lot to do with its inspiring Sustainable Living Plan. Similarly, IKEA is using its People & Planet Positive strategy to drive innovation, transform their business, shape their investments, and unleash new business opportunities.

The Time for Action Is Now

One of the things I most admire about business—and why I have so enjoyed my career in commerce—is that companies and their leaders have an incredible ability to act. I am reminded of a proverb that says business is like a wheelbarrow; if you want to get anywhere, you have to lift the load and push forward. Today, we stand at a threshold when bold action is desperately needed. In the face of intransigent politics, the world is looking more than ever to companies to bring solutions. It is time for business to stand up and be counted, to be praised for its actions or punished for its inaction. I hope and believe that many businesses will rise to that glorious challenge. Indeed, many already are acting now.

ACTING NOW

I'm acting now—for the future
For all the children and their children
For the powerless and the voiceless
Because the time for talking is over
And the time for action is now

I'm acting now—for the planet
For all species and their habitats
For the web of life that is fraying
Because the time for excuses is over
And the time for action is now

I'm acting now—for the present
For all leaders and their followers
For the fearful and the hopeless
Because the time for delaying is over
And the time for action is now.

CHAPTER 10

Leadership

*As a leader, I have always followed the principles I first saw
demonstrated by the regent at the Great Palace. . . . I always
remember the regent's axiom: A leader, he said, is like a shepherd.
He stays behind the flock, letting the most nimble go out ahead,
whereupon the others follow, not realizing that all along
they are being directed from behind.*

—**Nelson Mandela,** *Long Walk to Freedom*

Giants among Us

One of the highlights from my years of living and working in South Africa
was a special week in December 1999 when I had a chance to attend talks
by two great world leaders: Nelson Mandela and the Dalai Lama. The occasion was the Parliament of the World's Religions, which convened in Cape
Town to celebrate the diversity and fundamental unity of all faiths and
spiritual traditions.

The parliament began with the commemoration of World AIDS Day and the unveiling of the AIDS Memorial Quilt in the Cape Town Botanical Gardens. The quilt has continued to be added to, and today it weighs 54 tons and spans 1.2 million square feet.[1] We then joined in a walking procession to District Six, a residential area where 60,000 of its inhabitants were forcibly removed during the 1970s by the apartheid government.[2]

I delivered two papers during the parliament: one called "Better to Light a Candle Than Curse the Darkness," which traced the history of Unitarians in South Africa, and a second titled "Earth Spirit of Africa," which explored traditional African attitudes, folklore, and rituals about nature. Besides this, I reveled in the arts and culture on display, attending a flute recital, Native American singing, South African gumboot dancing, Japanese Taiko drumming, overtone chanting, and a performance by one of my favorite African bands, Amampondo.

The talk by Mandela was awe inspiring. I described it in my diary as "the wisdom and charm, the stature and humility, the grace and humor of the man we call Madiba." *Madiba* is an isiXhosa word for "father" and is a term of endearment most South Africans use when referring to Mandela. I also noted that, while his words were wise, what really made an impact was his presence and the courage and hope that he symbolized in our troubled world on the cusp of a new century.

By then, Mandela had already been South African president for more than five years and had become a global role model for what inspiring leadership means. For many, the Dalai Lama, who has served as Tibet's spiritual leader in exile since 1959, represents another great leader. As with Mandela, it was less what the Dalai Lama said and more the testimony of his life that inspired: his resilience in the face of persecution, his ability to forgive, and his ongoing mission to bring peace and unity to the world.

When Mandela died in 2013, I wrote a poem called "He Lived Among Us." It is too long to include in full here, but a few extracts give some idea of the impact he had on me personally, and on many millions in South Africa and across the world.

He lived among us—
And now it is for us to carry his torch onward
It is for us to follow his shining example
It is for us to fight for his unshakeable ideals—
Now that he is gone

He shared our days—
And now we must make the rest of our days count
We must work as he did to set others free
We must show that the spirit can triumph in the end—
Now that he is gone

He was one of us—
And now we are challenged to become one of him
We are inspired to be the best we can be
We are reminded that "I am because we are"—
Now that he is gone

Finding Your Inner Superhero

I have had the privilege of meeting so many inspiring leaders and champions of thriving in my travels to nearly 80 countries, many of whom are battling against the odds, motivated by the conviction that change is necessary and that they want to be part of the solution. Recognizing the power of this deep, existential desire to make a difference was one of the findings of my PhD research on what motivates people working for a more sustainable world.

Have you ever wondered what drives us to care? Why are you interested in thriving, or sustainability, or justice, or social responsibility? Most of us—whether we are professionals, academics, consultants, students, activists, or wannabes for the cause of thriving—could be pursuing different career paths. For my sins, having studied marketing, I could have become a spin doctor or an adman. So what makes us choose social and environmental progress instead? What makes us align our aspirations and energies with making the world a better place?

My research shows that there are deep psychological—even existential—reasons why we pursue thriving. And you may be surprised to know that it is not only because we want to save the world, or because we care about people, or even because we want to make a difference. At least, not directly. The real reason is because it gives us personal satisfaction, not of the sugar-rush or warm-cuddly variety but of the purpose-inspired, life-satisfaction kind.

If we dig a bit deeper, we find that six motivational forces drive our work in thriving. First, it allows us to feel that our efforts are aligned with our personal values, whether these are faith based, humanistic, or nature inspired. Second, we find the work stimulating. Thriving is a bit like Sudoku for hippies—it is complex, dynamic, and challenging, like an ultimate earth puzzle that needs solving. Most enthusiasts for thriving share these two motivations. Beyond this, we are motivated and satisfied by different things, which result in four types of thriving-driven leader.

Fresh Insight: Your Inner Superhero

What is your superpower as a thriving-driven leader? Some purpose-inspired leaders find meaning in giving specialist input, while others prefer empowering people. Some are motivated to come up with effective strategies, while others feel most satisfied if they are making a contribution to society. These drivers translate into a set of leader archetypes. Think of them as our very own Fantastic Four: namely, Experts, Facilitators, Catalysts, and Activists. Which one are you?

Experts tend to be focused on the details of a particular issue and have a deep knowledge and understanding, often of a technical or scientific nature. They like working on projects, designing systems, and being consulted for their expertise. Their satisfaction comes from continuous learning and self-development. They are most frustrated by the failure of others to be persuaded by the compelling evidence or to implement systems as they were designed.

Facilitators are most concerned with using their knowledge to empower others to act, using their strong people skills to make change happen. They like working with teams, delivering training, and giving coaching. Their satisfaction is in seeing changes in people's understanding, work, or careers. They become frustrated when individuals let the team down or when those in power do not allow enthusiastic groups to act.

Catalysts enjoy the challenge of shifting an organization in a new direction, using their political skills of persuasion to change strategies. They like working with leadership teams and articulating the business case for thriving. They are often pragmatic visionaries and are frustrated when top management fails to see—and more importantly, to act on—the opportunities and risks facing the organization.

Activists are typically passionate about impacts on society or the planet as a whole, using their strong feelings about justice to motivate their actions. Their satisfaction comes from challenging the status quo, questioning those in power, and articulating an idealistic vision of a better future. They tend to be great networkers and are mainly frustrated by the apathy of others in the face of urgent crises.

As you reflect on what type of leader you may be, I expect all four will resonate to a greater or lesser extent. This is because we are composite beings when it comes to making thriving happen. But we do gravitate more strongly to one archetype, based on what gives us the deepest personal satisfaction. And there are three good reasons why you should know which superhero cape and tights fit you best.

First, aligning with your inner superhero means embracing a mode of action in which you are most professionally effective and purpose inspired.

Second, it allows you to check that your formal role, or the direction of your career, is consistent with your archetype—the mask must fit the cape and tights. And third, it encourages you to consciously put together teams with a balance of Experts, Facilitators, Catalysts, and Activists—the ideal earth-crime-fighting force.

It is not enough that all change begins with individuals. For change to be sustained and transformational—for thriving to be a force for good in the world and to save the earth *from* humans and *for* humans—we need the joint efforts of the Fantastic Four, each with their particular superpower: the Experts' knowledge, the Facilitators' collaboration, the Catalysts' strategy, and the Activists' compassion. Will you join in the heroes' crusade?

The Lever of Leadership

Many of the crises we face in the world today are a result of a crisis in leadership. In contrast to the purpose-inspired leadership of Nelson Mandela and the Dalai Lama, we have too many leaders who are self-serving and power hungry, shortsighted and short-term oriented, myopic and misguided. We live in a time when the size, complexity, and urgency of our global challenges calls for a different kind of leadership. I call it thriving-driven leadership, but there are many other names that fit: ethical leadership, sustainability leadership, servant leadership, transformational leadership.

Key Concept: Leadership

What do we mean by leadership? The etymological Anglo-Saxon root of the words *lead*, *leader*, and *leadership* is *laed*, which means "path" or "road." The verb means "to travel." Thus, a leader is someone who takes us on a journey, who shows us the way, who inspires and supports us as fellow travelers to reach a common goal, who challenges and stretches us to pursue a destination in the distance.

Leadership is really "the art of mobilizing others to want to struggle for shared aspirations."[3] In my paper with Dame Polly Courtice, former director of the Cambridge Institute for Sustainability Leadership, we distilled the essence down to the notion that "a leader is someone who can craft a vision and inspire people to act collectively to make it happen, responding to whatever changes and challenges arise along the way."[4]

I also like the characteristics that Rob Goffee and Gareth Jones describe in an article discussing authentic leadership. Leadership, they observe, is relational. It is something you do *with* people, not *to* people.[5] Put simply, you cannot be a leader without followers. Like all relationships, it needs to be monitored and cultivated. Leadership is also nonhierarchical. Formal authority or a title doesn't make you a leader. Leaders can be found at all levels.

Is thriving-driven leadership any different? Do we need leaders with different characteristics, for example? In the research I have done at Cambridge University and at Antwerp Management School, we have put this question to the test, and the short answer is *yes*—and *no*. We reached the conclusion that thriving-driven leadership (or whatever label you prefer to use) is not a separate school of leadership but rather a particular blend of leadership characteristics and competencies applied within a definitive context.

Foundations of Thriving-Driven Leadership

The point about context really matters. For example, compare former General Electric CEO Jack Welch, who is often celebrated for his winner-take-all leadership, with Jeff Immelt, who took over from him just as global sustainable development challenges were rising up the agenda. Welch died in 2020, and praises rightly came pouring in. Welch certainly knew a thing or two about leadership. I especially like his "4 Es and a P" for effective leaders: energy (bring positive attitude to all situations), energize (be a catalyst for others), edge (make tough decisions; yes or no, not maybe), execute (get things done), and passion (care deeply).[6]

I think he was a man for his times. Jeff Immelt necessarily brought a different style—less "winning at all costs," more "innovation by collaboration"—one better suited to today's sustainability challenges. Immelt led with a far more inclusive and socially conscious approach, making major investments in environmental and health technologies that are still paying off today. Yet both were great leaders, suited to their particular context.

The changing context of global challenges may also be why we are seeing the emergence of a surprisingly young crop of leaders in business and politics, such as Mikela Druckman, founder and CEO of Greyparrot (33), and US Representative Alexandria Ocasio-Cortez (31). Elsewhere, other young leaders in power are taking bold actions on critical issues such as climate change and gender equality. These "juvenocracies" include Austria (led by Sebastian Kurz, 34), Finland (Sanna Marin, 35), Ukraine (Oleksiy Honcharuk, 36), El Salvador (Nayib Bukele, 39), and New Zealand (Jacinda Ardern, 40). Here springs hope.

Before we go into exploring the characteristics of thriving-driven leaders in more detail, it's worth adding a caveat. Leadership today is a paradox. Literally. The latest neuroscience suggests that the best leaders are those who can rapidly switch between paradoxical styles—such as directive or participative, rational or emotional, structured or innovative. This is the finding of decades of research by Professor Steven Poelmans, who serves as the Melexis-endowed chair on Neuroscience- and Technology-Enabled High Performance Organizations at Antwerp Management School. These different leadership modes use different parts of the brain—and switching between them is extremely demanding in terms of neural processing capacity. But paradoxical leadership also releases tremendous creative energy for solving entangled problems.

The Leadership Parable of Gulliver the Goose

This is the story of Gulliver, a young goose who gets lost on his way to leadership school. How embarrassing! But, as a result, he finds himself on an African adventure, meeting strange and wonderful creatures, each of whom teaches him a paradoxical lesson in leadership. The first lesson, shared with him by Cuthbert, a camel he meets in the Sahara Desert, is this: To find your path, you must lose your way. You can read about Gulliver's incredible journey—and find out the 11 other paradoxical lessons—in my book *Follow Me! (I'm Lost): The Tale of an Unexpected Leader.*[7]

What, then, about the characteristics of thriving-driven leaders? A combination of the six characteristics that I discuss shortly are not unique to thriving-driven leaders, but they are the most relevant and most visibly present in leaders who are effective in advancing the agenda of thriving. In the case of the Cambridge research, we identified 10 contexts, 20 characteristics (including traits, styles, knowledge, and skills), and 10 actions that shape and define sustainability leaders.[8] In the Antwerp research conducted for the European Petrochemicals Association, we found five characteristics and five competencies.[9] For the sake of elegance and readability, I have distilled these into six thriving-driven leadership characteristics (Figure 10.1).

Systemic Leadership

Being a systemic and holistic thinker encompasses the ability to appreciate the interconnectedness and interdependency of the whole system, at all levels, and to recognize how changes to parts of the system affect the whole. Thriving-driven leaders must have skills that support systemic thinking. They must be able to manage complexity. This means analyzing, synthesizing, and translating complex issues; responding to risk, uncertainty, and dilemmas; recognizing and seizing opportunities; and resolving problems or conflicts.

Systemic

Appreciates the interconnectedness and interdependency of the whole system; promotes interdisciplinary solutions

Inclusive

Is self-aware and empathetic, with high levels of emotional intelligence; empowers others and encourages diversity

Strategic

Thinks and plans for the long term, using foresight tools to open minds to alternative possibilities, while not discounting the future

Caring

Is concerned for the well-being of humanity and all other forms of life; is guided by a moral compass

Innovative

Plays the role of creative destroyer and transformer, for the improvement of nature, society, and the economy

Courageous

Is prepared to fight for a higher cause and challenge the status quo, despite personal or professional sacrifices

Figure 10.1: *Characteristics of thriving-driven leadership*

As Geanne van Arkel, former head of sustainable development at Interface, puts it, "If you are able to find the bridge where your talents and your own purpose connects with what is needed in this world, that is exactly when you become a sustainability leader."[10] By implication, thriving-driven leaders must also have broad and deep knowledge about our global challenges and dilemmas. They must understand the social and ecological system pressures and the connections between these systems and political and economic forces. This requires that they appreciate interdisciplinary thinking, which recognizes the links between the physical sciences, the social sciences, technology, business, and other disciplines.

Key Concept: Synthesizers

In a world desperate for systems thinking, people who can span disciplines, cross boundaries, and spot synergies will thrive. The remarkable biologist E. O. Wilson called these people *synthesizers*. They are all the more important because, as Wilson observed, "We are drowning in information, while starving for wisdom."[11] Synthesizers have three essential characteristics: (1) They are *open-minded*, which means they are able to listen to others, especially those they disagree with; (2) they are *unifiers*, since they search for common ground and trace hidden connections; and (3) they are *innovators*, since creativity comes from novel combinations of seemingly disparate fields.

Two examples of systemic leaders are Elon Musk, CEO of Tesla and SpaceX, and Anu Sridharan, cofounder of NextDrop. Musk's leadership of Tesla in particular has been systemic, with no small measure of strategic, innovative, and courageous elements as well. His audacious vision and ambition from the start was to disrupt an entire sector, based on the clear understanding that fossil-fuel-powered cars, as a significant cause of climate change and air pollution–related diseases, are unsustainable. But changing a complex system such as the automotive sector, which is deeply entrenched with the oil and gas industry, needed a number of breakthroughs.

First, he had to choose a technology alternative that would significantly reduce the negative impact of internal-combustion-engine cars. The answer, of course, was electric vehicles (EVs), but he had to prove they could compete with (or even outcompete) gas-fueled cars. At the same time, he needed to build out a charging infrastructure, bring down the price by scaling production, and clean up the electricity grid by bringing solar and battery technologies into play. Only by changing all these complex elements of the transport and energy system has Tesla become a successful catalyst for the EV and renewables revolution currently underway.

Anu Sridharan is another great example of a systemic leader. In India, it's not uncommon for women to stay at home for hours, waiting for water to come out of the faucet so they can drink, cook, and clean. NextDrop, which Sridharan founded, connects the vast network of valve operators, engineers, and citizens to maintain up-to-date information on where the water supply is (and isn't), and then it passes that information on to residents via text messages. By finding a solution to a dysfunctional part of the water-distribution system, Sridharan was able not only to ensure a more reliable source of water for 70,000 villagers but also to save them more than 13 million hours of waiting time.

Inclusive Leadership

Thriving-driven leaders are inclusive leaders. This requires that they are self-aware and empathetic, with high levels of emotional intelligence. Equally important are sincerity, personal humility, and reflexiveness, which requires a leader to be able to see their own place in and influence on a situation. Being inclusive means that collaboration and participation are the default mode of leadership, including building commitment through dialogue and consensus. These leaders embrace democratic approaches, coaching, and nurturing a culture and structure that ensures peer support, provides encouragement, and recognizes achievement.

Inclusive leaders also celebrate diversity in the teams and organizations that they lead. There are many kinds of diversity, from gender and ethnicity to ability and lifestyle choices. What inclusive leaders understand is that embracing diversity is not only the fair thing to do but also good for performance. According to the recruitment platform SocialTalent, for every 1 percent increase in gender diversity, company revenue increases by 3 percent, while high levels of ethnic diversity can result in increases in revenue of 15 percent.[12]

When I think of inclusive leadership, two people immediately come to my mind. The first is Wangari Maathai, who started the Green Belt Movement in East Africa. The second is Bunker Roy, the founder of Barefoot College, which I discuss briefly in Chapter 5. In both cases, these thriving-driven leaders chose to empower rural women first and foremost, many of whom were living in poverty. This is an important reminder that inclusion is also about economic empowerment and working with people living in nonurban areas.

Case Spotlight: Wangari Maathai

The late Wangari Maathai, through the Green Belt Movement that she started in 1977, ensured that more than 30,000 women became trained in forestry, food processing, beekeeping, and other trades that helped them earn income while preserving their lands and resources. In recognition, she was awarded the Nobel Peace Prize in 2004, in part for the more than 51 million trees that had been planted through the Green Belt Movement. She reflected, "I'm very conscious of the fact that you can't do it alone. It's teamwork. When you do it alone you run the risk that when you are no longer there nobody else will do it."[13]

In Bunker Roy's case, since he founded Barefoot College in 1972, the organization has trained more than 2,200 rural women in 93 countries to become Barefoot solar engineers who have solar electrified their own communities, providing over a million people with lighting.[14] This is as much about restoring dignity to those who are traditionally excluded as it is about developing or transferring practical skills. Roy, who confesses that he had a very elitist, snobbish, expensive education in India—and that it almost killed him—reflected: "Who is a professional? A professional is someone who has a combination of competence, confidence and belief. A water diviner is a professional. A traditional midwife is a professional. A traditional bone setter is a professional. These are professionals all over the world. You find them in any inaccessible village around the world. You have to have a dignity of labor. You have to show that you have a skill that you can offer to the community and provide a service to the community. So we started the Barefoot College, and we redefined professionalism."[15]

Strategic Leadership

Thriving-driven leaders need to think long term. This entails having a strategic perspective and using foresight tools to help others see the whole while not discounting the future. McKinsey research shows that long-term-oriented companies deliver 47 percent higher revenues and 36 percent better returns, as well as generate on average $7 billion more in market capitalization.[16] But with the short-term orientation of financial markets and shareholder speculators, focusing on long-term value is easier said than done. And yet that is what defines strategic leadership.

Paul Polman, on his first day as the new CEO of Unilever in 2010, told shareholders not to expect quarterly reports. Speaking with *Forbes* magazine, Polman explained his rationale:

> To solve issues like food security or climate change, you need to have longer-term solutions. You cannot do that on a quarterly basis. . . . It's the same for companies. . . . So what I said when I came here is I need to create this environment for the company to make the right longer-term decisions. So we stopped giving guidance. We stopped doing quarterly reporting. We changed the compensation for the long term.[17]

Tellingly, when Polman made his shock announcement about no longer reporting financial results quarterly, Unilever's share price dropped 8 percent. But that didn't stop him from building a new long-term corporate strategy, which became their much-heralded Sustainable Living Plan. What shareholders should have noted was that Polman was not against creating value and sharing wealth with the company's shareholders. In fact, he planned to double the size of the company within 10 years. And in the end, the "gamble" (if that's what it was) paid off. During his tenure as CEO, Unilever delivered a total shareholder return of 290 percent.

Not surprisingly, Polman became the poster child for what the former global managing partner of McKinsey, Dominic Barton, called "nothing less than a shift from what I call quarterly capitalism to what might be referred to as long-term capitalism."[18]

By implication, being a strategic leader means being visionary while still remaining driven to produce results. These leaders possess the ability to balance passion and idealism with ambition and pragmatism. A visionary style brings energy and charisma into the mix, focusing on challenging and transforming people's perceptions and expectations and motivating people to transcend narrower forms of self-interest. As Catherine Girard, expert leader of energy and raw materials for Renault, put it, "A big part of individual sustainability leadership is the capacity to anticipate future challenges, the capacity to convince and to mobilize, while always relying on facts, data and scenarios."[19]

Caring Leadership

A thriving-driven leader is caring. They care for the well-being of humanity, as well as all other forms of life, and are guided by a moral compass. They are altruistic leaders who focus on transcending self-interest and on promoting the collective or the good of the whole; they are servant leaders.

Of course, we care for others only when we feel empathy. But empathy is not automatic; it is a learned behavior, cultivated from a young age. We ask our children: How would you feel if someone did that to you? Empathy is inconvenient; it takes effort. We have to step out of our selfish bubbles, leave aside our own needs. Empathy is proactive; it means connecting with others emotionally or mentally walking in their shoes. If we are to care for people who are vulnerable, animals that are suffering, or a planet that is threatened, we must begin by kindling empathy.

Two people I consider to be caring leaders are Vandana Shiva and Muhammad Yunus, both of whom I've had the good fortune to meet. Yunus told me that, in order to care, we have to give up on our "bird's-eye view" and embrace a more grassroots "worm's-eye view."[20] He was reflecting on the time when he was an economics professor in Bangladesh, and the country was hit by a famine. "I felt totally empty. All of the economics theories sounded so hollow and useless," Yunus said. "So I thought why don't I go out and see if I can reach out to another human being. Be next to him or her and help the person to overcome any difficulty for that particular day."

That led to Yunus founding the Grameen Bank in 1983—and by the time it was awarded the Nobel Peace Prize in 2006, it had granted loans to more than 7 million borrowers. The average amount borrowed was $100, and the repayment percentage was very high. More than 95 percent of the loans went to women or groups of women. Yunus says:

> To me, the poor are like bonsai trees. When you plant the best seed of the tallest tree in a six-inch-deep flower pot, you get a perfect replica of the tallest tree, but it is only inches tall. There is nothing wrong with the seed you planted; only the soil-base you provided was inadequate. Poor people are bonsai people. There is nothing wrong with their seeds. Only society never gave them a base to grow on.[21]

Vandana Shiva has a similar attitude when it comes to caring for the world's poor rural women, but she combines this with caring for nature. Today, she is one of the leaders and board members of the International

Forum on Globalization, but her rise to prominence really started in the 1970s and 1980s when she became deeply involved in the Chipko movement. *Chipko* literally means "hug," and this was an activist movement by the Himalayan communities of Uttarakhand in India to protect the forest. Today what she cares about most deeply is how agro-industrial methods being imposed by food multinationals wreak havoc with farmers' livelihoods and nature.

What is interesting is that when leaders care, there is often a spillover effect. This manifests in two ways. First, people who are engaged in one socially conscious or environmentally responsible behavior will tend to adopt a positive attitude toward other behaviors that support thriving. Second, there is an opportunity to inspire thriving-focused actions in the workplace that also create a beneficial spillover effect at home. For instance, Andrew Griffiths, head of value chain sustainability at Nestlé UK, noted that "the more embedded sustainability becomes within the workplace, [the more] our employees are taking it home. Not only to their family and friends, but also into their communities."[22]

Innovative Leadership

Realizing a thriving future will almost certainly be impossible without breakthrough innovation, and therefore we need innovative leadership. Leaders with a creative style enjoy playing the role of designer, architect, innovator, game changer, and transformer of systems. This can mean adopting a radical persona, which is certainly not for everyone. Leaders such as Anita Roddick (founder of The Body Shop) and Yvon Chouinard (founder of Patagonia) are associated with this style. Their highly visible leadership includes taking risks; acting like a revolutionary, campaigner, crusader, or activist; and challenging the status quo. Sometimes we call this missionary leadership.

I could literally choose hundreds of great examples of innovative leadership. For inspiration, just check out Ashoka or the Skoll Foundation's fellows. Or cast your eyes over *Fast Company's* Top 50 Most Innovative Companies. Let me tell the stories of just two of them: Keller Rinaudo and Ethan Brown.

Keller Rinaudo is CEO and cofounder of Zipline, a company that builds autonomous drones designed for delivering medical supplies to remote parts of the world. The Harvard-educated Rinaudo started his career as a software engineer and a professional rock climber. For a time, he worked at Harvard University in biotechnology, building what are called molecular automata, or DNA computers. Then he discovered the wonderful world of logistics and the possibilities of using new technologies to deliver medical supplies to all of the world's inhabitants, wherever they may live.

To get an insight into how innovative leaders like him think, here's why Rinaudo first launched Zipline's technology in one of the smallest countries in Africa. "We wanted to find a country that was small enough that we could get to national scale quickly and had a government that was making active investments in technology and healthcare for its citizens. Rwanda really fit that bill. So, in partnership with Rwanda's administrative health [ministry], we've been able to turn Rwanda into the first country to achieve universal healthcare access for all. They have been able to put every single one of their citizens within a 15- to 25-minute delivery of any essential medical product."[23]

The CEO of Beyond Meat, Ethan Brown, is also bringing innovation to disrupt a traditional industry, in this case the food sector. He shows how the combination of childlike curiosity and fundamental biological science can lead to innovation. He reflects that he had a wonderful opportunity as a kid to grow up in the city and spend a lot of time in the countryside, including on a dairy farm his father started.[24]

Fast-forward, and Brown started a career in the energy sector, working for the leading company in the world on proton-exchange membrane fuel cells, which he describes as "a terrifically elegant technology." So what changed? He really wanted to make an impact on the climate crisis and realized that livestock was a big part of the solution. "So here I returned to this issue that I had as a child," he says, referring to his time spent on his father's farm.

> Once you start thinking about human health and the use of water, land, energy, it became clear to me that if you could figure out a way to separate meat from animals you could make a difference. I started thinking about, "What is meat and how do we build meat differently?" And that was the genesis of the company.[25]

There's a technical science-based side to innovation, but there's also the human side of what drives the innovator. Brown says his motivation is twofold: First, there's the desire to turn plant-based meat from a cottage industry into an innovation powerhouse. He compares food companies such as Kraft, which might have one or two scientists working on meat substitutes, with the energy sector, where billions of dollars and hundreds of scientists are working on renewable and sustainable alternatives. The second driver is a sense of urgency to what Beyond Meat is doing: bringing a scalable solution to climate change, biodiversity loss, and health crises such as diabetes and heart disease.

Courageous Leadership

Thriving-driven leaders also require moral courage. They need to be certain that they are fighting for a higher cause and be prepared to challenge the status quo, or even make personal and professional sacrifices to pursue their purpose. For some, this conviction comes late, as it did for Interface founder Ray Anderson during his "spear-in-the-chest" moment, when he realized that someday CEOs like him would be put in jail for theft of our children's future.[26] And for some, such as Greta Thunberg, moral courage comes early.

According to Christoph Jäkel, vice president of sustainability strategy at BASF, true sustainability leadership is intrinsically motivated, not something that is specified in a job description. As Immanuel Kant put it, "The starry heavens above me and the moral law within me."[27] Courageous leadership is often the hardest in entrenched industries and behemoth corporates. Annette Stube, head of sustainability at Maersk, observes, "It really takes a lot of courage to stand up in such a culture and say, 'Well, this is what I believe we have to do.'"[28]

That's why I think Henrik Poulsen is a great example of moral leadership. He joined Ørsted in 2012—when it was still known as Danish Oil and Natural Gas, or DONG Energy—and over eight years spearheaded a fundamental transformation of the company into the largest offshore wind developer in the world and one of the most coveted investments in renewable energy. Although DONG Energy had started building wind farms at sea years before Poulsen came on board, he led the company's exit from coal-fired power plants and oil and gas production, as well as its rebranding to Ørsted. Its share price has roughly tripled since DONG Energy was first listed on the Copenhagen Stock Exchange in June 2016.

Jakob Bøss, senior vice president for corporate strategy and stakeholder relations, recalls the moment of change at Ørsted: "The first major turning point in our transformation from fossil fuels to renewable energy was in September 2008 when our CEO at the time announced a new vision. When we started talking about this vision, 85 percent of the company's power and heat production came from fossil fuels and 15 percent came from renewables. The vision was that by 2040, this would have flipped around."[29]

There was major resistance, not only from the market but also internally, as Martin Neubert, CEO of Ørsted Offshore Wind, recalls. The transformation was seen as an "engineering dream"; yes, you can technically do it, but it comes at a huge cost, and it's not really something that's going to change how we power societies. Those in the business were effectively asking: Is the world really changing so much around us? Not only that, but the first commercial-scale wind farm that they built in Denmark was not a success. It was an expensive and challenging learning curve. But Poulsen believed you have to go "all in" and "put yourself and your capital to mobilize behind that opportunity."[30]

The moral courage comes from believing in the vision that the leader is pursuing. But Poulsen says that many companies make the mistake of making their vision about what the company would like to achieve or what the company would like to be:

> For [a company's vision] to be truly aspirational, it has to make a bigger contribution. It's not about the company. It's about what the company can contribute to a more sustainable world. . . . We must be ready to make near-term sacrifices to get it done. We cannot tell our grandchildren that we failed to protect the planet because we were too focused on protecting our own wellbeing. We must act now.[31]

Ethical convictions give us a pathway through an age of obfuscation, where truth is turgid, morals are malleable, and compromise is commonplace. That's why clarity has become a rare and precious gift. I was reminded of this when listening to Greta Thunberg's poignant podcast. The power of her message is not its novelty or nuance but its simplicity and sincerity. Thunberg brings clarity: The climate emergency is crystal clear; so, too, the farcical failure of leadership. In her words, nature doesn't negotiate, the laws of physics don't compromise, and science does not lie. Such clarity gives focus—and focus must lead to bold action.

Regenerating Yourself

To be a leader in the revolution toward thriving, you also need to regenerate yourself. Partly this is about being the change you want to see in the world. But more than that, personal thriving is about looking after yourself and ensuring that you have the perspective and passion, the inspiration and vision, the energy and support, and the imagination and focus that you need to continue the work of changing the world for the better. This is a quest of existential magnitude; for many of us, it consumes our careers, our relationships, our life. So we need to make sure that we, too, are in balance, healthy, and hearty.

It begins with bliss. Have you heard the phrase "Follow your bliss"? You might recognize this mantra from mythologist Joseph Campbell. The fact is that we are all searching for meaning in life—an answer to the eternal *why*. And the good news is that we can and do create our own meaning. How? There are many paths to purpose, according to existential psychologists. One way was spotted by Abraham Maslow, well known for his hierarchy of needs. He discovered a paradox—namely, that self-actualization requires self-transcendence. In other words, making our lives personally meaningful requires that we pursue something beyond ourselves. Something bigger. Something that makes a positive difference in other people's lives. It could be at work, in the community, or elsewhere.

Part of discovering our purpose is also realizing that we have choices. One of my favorite books is *Illusions* by Richard Bach, which is about a messiah who decides to quit. It reminds me that change is always a choice. We may feel trapped by responsibilities (real and imagined) and expectations (those we have of ourselves and those we think others have for us). But we can still choose to act differently, to change our default routines, to explore alternative paths. Those choices will have consequences, but our unconscious choices to reinforce the status quo have impacts as well—especially on our time, our energy, and our spirit.

What choices will you make today? Every day we encounter doors—doors to new rooms, new directions, or even new worlds. And in most cases, only we can open those doors. Doors are decision points in our life. We must choose: to open or not to open. Some doors are locked, of course, which means we have to discover (or make) keys. Keys are most often forged from new knowledge, new ideas, new experiences, new connections, and new perspectives. From these malleable materials, we find a way to open doors—in our work, relationships, or personal life—and thereby change the path we are on.

Fresh Insight: Ikigai

It helps to know what gets you out of bed in the morning. The Japanese have a word, *ikigai*, which translates as our "reason for being alive." The importance of finding a purpose for our life has long been recognized by philosophers and "doctors of the soul." Austrian psychiatrist Viktor Frankl (himself a Nazi concentration camp survivor) discovered that the search for deeper meaning is a powerful motivator, especially through periods of suffering. Existential psychologists have found that the greatest sources of meaning are healthy relationships, altruism, achievement, creativity, pleasure, and religious faith or spiritual beliefs. How would you describe your ikigai?

That path, in turn, may lead you to your craft. I'm betting nobody ever asked you: What is your craft? That's a different question from "What is your job, your career, or your profession?" A craft is any activity that requires a high level of skill, which you patiently hone over time. A craft is also something that you love doing for its own sake, where you derive joy from the process and take pride in the outcome. Once again, the Japanese are helpful. They call a craft your *takumi*. It is no coincidence that we often refer to "master" crafters, because pursuing a craft is inherently a journey toward mastery, not only of your chosen activity but also of yourself.

Rise Up, New Leaders

The biologist E. O. Wilson says that an ideal scientist must think like a poet, work like a clerk, and write like a journalist.[32] I believe that applies to anyone trying to make a positive impact on the world, as all thriving-driven leaders are. We need to think creatively, to imagine better solutions to complex problems. Then we need to work systematically, to gather the evidence and build a compelling case for action. And finally, we need to be effective storytellers when we communicate about the benefits of changing the status quo. The question is not *whether* to lead but *what*, *where*, *why*, and *how*.

TO LEAD

To lead or not to lead?
That is the wrong question
For in our hour of need
It's what to lead that matters more
The core of values and their strength
The door of possibilities
The planted seeds and fruits they bear
It's there true leadership resides
For tides are changing quickly now
It's not the who, it's where and how

Leaders come and leaders go
But which will show a better way
A brighter day because they led
A lighter tread upon the earth
The birth of purpose in our lives
And work in which our spirit thrives
Let's not ignore the children's voice
The choice is ours, to lag or lead
To make the world more green and fair
In ways that care, that hope and dare

Don't tell me that you lead, for I
Will never be impressed
It's how you lead that interests me
And what you strive for without rest
It's where your dreams are taking us
And who will thrive the best
It's why you lead that tells me more
Than all the feathers in your nest
To lead is nothing special, for
To serve's the real test

To lead or not to lead?
The question's quite absurd
For leadership's the path that freed
The slaves and we need so much more
From shore to shore, where chains remain
And oceans rise, yet leaders' lies
Support charades and barricades
That cling to glories of the past
Rise up new leaders who can shape
A future that is built to last.

EPILOGUE

Witness

*After a rain mushrooms appear on the surface of the
earth as if from nowhere. Many do so from a sometimes
vast underground fungus that remains invisible and largely
unknown. . . . Uprisings and revolutions are often considered
to be spontaneous, but less visible long-term organizing
and groundwork—or underground work—often
laid the foundation.*

—Rebecca Solnit, *Hope in the Dark*

Giving Our Witness Statement

In David Attenborough's *A Life on Our Planet*, he describes the documentary film and accompanying book as part "witness statement," part
"vision for the future." This is one of the most powerful things any of
us can do: to bear witness. What is your world like? Not *the* world, but
your world. Your country, your city, your town, your community, your

workplace, your university, your school, your family life. How has it changed? What has improved and what has deteriorated? Then add your vision for how you want your world to be, and you have an agenda for change, a call to action.

This book is the latest installment in my own witness statement and vision for the future. As it turned out, writing the book was a personal test of thriving. Most of my books take about two years to write and publish. This one had been in incubation since 2017, and I began writing it in earnest around the middle of 2019. A year later, in the middle of lockdown and having written about 50,000 words, I managed to irrevocably erase my computer hard drive and its backup in the cloud. Not the smartest thing I've ever done, it has to be said. There was nothing to do but to begin writing the book again.

I realized immediately that I could not—and should not—try to write exactly the same book. So I changed my approach, the title and focus changed, and that gave me the energy and inspiration I needed to start again. I think that is true of all kinds of thriving. We should not imagine that we can recreate nature, society, and the economy as it was before, whether that be a few years ago or centuries or millennia in the past. The world will thrive; I am convinced of that. But it will be a different world. A world in which humans and cities and livestock and farms and climate damage all live in a complex and changing web of adaptation.

My witness statement—the testimony of this book—can be summarized in the table of fundamental elements of thriving: the six sixes (Table E.1). As a thought experiment, since each element could be related to every other element—for example, applying purpose to restoration, or the circular economy to disparity, or convergence to rewiring, or innovative leadership to resilience—there are 630 potential combinations of the fundamental elements of thriving. That suggests that there is a tremendous potential for synergy, creativity, innovation, and inspiration.

TABLE E.1: THE FUNDAMENTAL ELEMENTS
OF THRIVING (THE SIX SIXES)

Keys to thriving	Forces of breakdown	Forces of breakthrough	Market opportunities	Aspects of integration	Qualities of leadership
Complexity	Degradation	Restoration	Ecoservices	Patterns	Systemic
Circularity	Depletion	Renewal	Circular	Partners	Inclusive
Creativity	Disparity	Responsibility	Access	Principles	Strategic
Coherence	Disease	Revitalization	Well-being	Purpose	Caring
Convergence	Disconnection	Rewiring	Digital	Performance	Innovative
Continuity	Disruption	Resilience	Risk	Portfolios	Courageous

Living the Questions

Inspiration is one thing. But what that future world looks like depends on our actions. So let me recap how each of us is faced with questions that lead to choices, which in turn can make thriving a reality in our lifetime. First, there are questions about our focus in life and work, about how we can turn systemic breakdowns into breakthroughs. Which of these questions trigger your interest the most? Ask yourself:

- Am I passionate about restoring ecosystems or renewing resources?

- Am I committed to treating people responsibly, with dignity and respect, or revitalizing their health and well-being?

- Am I curious about using technology to rewire the economy or ensuring resilience in the face of crises?

You don't have to do everything; it is better to be focused and to follow your bliss.

Then there are questions that make us better leaders and effective agents of change, drawing on the keys to thriving. You may ask:

- How can I increase my networks and connections (the key of complexity) or find ways to renew the materials or energy I use (the key of circularity)?

- How can I be more innovative in addressing entangled problems (the key of creativity) or increase a sense of shared purpose (the key of coherence)?

- How can I add my work or my voice to the trends transforming the world for the better (the key of convergence) or ensure that the institutions that serve society best are able to survive and thrive through times of crisis (the key of continuity)?

Finally, there are the questions that remind us how to maximize our chances of success, that turn thriving from a naïve wish into a credible possibility. Ask yourself:

- Can I create or support solutions that bring simultaneous benefits to nature, society, and the economy (innovations that are symbiotic, sustainable, shared, satisfying, smart, and secure)?

- Am I investing in my own personal thriving by keeping my body, mind, and spirit refreshed and rejuvenated, thereby giving me the strength, focus, and motivation to do my vital part for the revolution toward thriving?

In the end, thriving will be society's collective journey toward a better future. It is a quest that is of vital importance for the world, and I hope you will join the fellowship of thriving adventurers. If we do not embark on this perilous trail, with all its high mountains and dark valleys, its traps and monsters, its false summits and dead ends, we will not avert disaster, of that

I am sure. The well-being of nature, society, and the economy is at stake, and the collapse of civilization as we know it is a very real possibility. But unlike fantasy stories, there is no holy grail or "one ring to rule them all." This is a journey that will last forever.

Reasons for Hope

Personally, I have never been more excited about the future in all my years working for sustainable development. Yes, the challenges and risks are dire and urgent. But there has been a visible awakening, a palpable shift in consciousness in the past few years—among leaders and citizens, scientists and journalists, teachers and children. We have passed a tipping point from talking into action, from posturing into investment, from risk management into innovation scaling. The Great Reset is already underway. The butterfly effects are already rippling through the system. But I won't lie—we are in a race for our lives.

I am often asked what keeps me optimistic that thriving will carry the day. There are three reasons. First, it is because I am a student of complex living systems. I understand how their tightly interlinked networks are optimized to maintain life and restore balance. I see how feedback loops can cause systems to break down, but also how they can bring about rapid breakthroughs. I observe how convergence is happening between technological innovation, social movements, new business aspirations, and political expectations. I celebrate that self-organization happens when there is a compelling common purpose.

My second reason for hope is that I have worked with advocates of sustainability and thriving for more than 30 years, and they are smart, passionate, and resilient people—indefatigable champions of life who will never give up in the fight for a thriving planet, a healthy society, and a fair economy. As guardians of thriving, we have moved collectively beyond education about the problems into implementation of the solutions. And we are no longer lone voices crying in the desert. We are a powerful movement, hundreds of millions strong. We are the purpose-inspired flock that is changing the direction of society. And we are increasingly connected and organized.

Fresh Insight: Thriving as a Superorganism

I like to think of the movement toward thriving as a superorganism, because it is. We can take inspiration from the Trembling Giant, which has lived in the Fishlake National Forest of Utah, in the United States, for the past 80,000 years. This is no fantasy giant—it is the living, breathing kind. Its name, Pando, from the Latin meaning "I spread," gives us a vital clue. Pando is a superorganism comprising 45,000 quaking aspen trees, all genetically identical and sharing the same root system, spanning 107 acres and weighing 6,615 tons. I believe the movement toward thriving is becoming its own kind of Pando.

My third reason for hope is hope itself. It's the fact that hope comes from within. It is not dependent on circumstances beyond our control. Hope is a way of being in the world. It is an expectation of resilience in the face of change, of solidarity in times of distress, of positive action in the midst of negative rhetoric. I'm saying that we choose hope not because everything is perfect or because a better future is guaranteed, but because hope is more productive. It is more effective. It is more joyful. Hope is not the same as denial. Rather, hope is an action verb—a commitment to help, to be part of the solution, to be an activist for thriving.

And all of this confirms to me that the thriving train is picking up incredible speed, while the incumbent institutions and leaders are huffing and puffing, making a lot of noise and smoke, but chugging to a standstill and even starting to roll backward. If you prefer a less mechanical metaphor, think about fields of mushrooms sprouting and consuming the decay of old, dead wood and discarded leaves. These mushrooms are connected underground in a vast living network. Besides creating fertile humus for the soil, they are facilitating the exchange of vital nutrients and information between the trees of the forest, ensuring that they survive and thrive.

Change the World

We are all part of the web of life, and the more we tug at its threads, the more we realize that everything is connected. As Chico Mendes—a Brazilian rubber tapper, trade union leader, and environmentalist—reflected, "At first I thought I was fighting to save rubber trees, then I thought I was fighting to save the Amazon rain forest. Now I realize I am fighting for humanity."[1]

That is what the challenge of thriving is all about. And it comes with a sobering warning, which has been attributed to the Cree Native American Indians: "Only when the last tree has died and the last river been poisoned and the last fish been caught will we realize we cannot eat money."

That is what is at stake. Nothing less than life itself—our own life and the life of others, the life of the millions of organisms that share our precious planet, and the life of all future generations. Knowing this, it only remains for me to invite you to join together with me and countless others in the movement for thriving. It's time to change the world.

CHANGE THE WORLD

Let's change the world, let's shift it
Let's shake and remake it
Let's rearrange the pieces
The patterns in the maze
The reason for our days
In ways that make it better
In shades that make it brighter

That make the burden lighter
Because it's shared, because we dared
To dream and then to sweat it
To make our mark and not regret it
Let's plant a seed and humbly say:
I changed the world today!

Let's change the world, let's lift it
Let's take it and awake it
Let's challenge every leader
The citadels of power
The prisoners in the tower
The hour of need's upon us
It's time to raise our voices
To stand up for our choices
Because it's right, because we fight
For all that's just and fair
For a planet we can share
Let's join the cause and boldly say:
We'll change the world today!

Let's change the world, let's love it
Let's hold it and unfold it
Let's redesign the future
The fate of earth and sky
The existential why
Let's fly to where there's hope
To where the world is greener
Where air and water's cleaner
Because it's smart to make a start
To fix what we have broken
Our children's wish unspoken
Let's be the ones who rise and say:
We changed the world today!

Acknowledgments

To the team at Antwerp Management School, including Steven De Haes, Ilse Daelman, Lars Moratis, Eva Geluk, Jan Beyne, and Rozanne Henzen, and colleagues at BASF, Port of Antwerp, Randstad, Johnson & Johnson, and all the organizations we partner with, thank you for making me part of your sustainable transformation journey.

To the team at the University of Cambridge Institute for Sustainability Leadership, including Polly Courtice, Martin Roberts, Theo Hacking, Jemma Cobbold, Bruce Haase, Elspeth Donovan, Beth Knight, John Isherwood, Louise Nicholls, Louisa Harris, Hemma Varma, Alex Base, Munish Datta, Chris Urwin, David Lawrence, Laura Gherasim, Christele Delbe, and the many others I work with, teach, or tutor, thank you for making my work in sustainability such a collaborative labor of love.

To my editor, Joan Tapper, and the team at Greenleaf Book Group, thank you for supporting my vision of conveying the promise and practice of thriving to a wider public.

Notes

Foreword

1. Christiana Figueres, "The Case for Stubborn Optimism on Climate," TED Talk, October 2020, https://www.ted.com/talks/christiana_figueres_the_case_for _stubborn_optimism_on_climate?language=en.

Prologue

1. A. Gore, *An Inconvenient Truth: The Planetary Emergency of Global Warming and What We Can Do About It* (New York: Rodale, 2006).
2. World Commission on Environment and Development, "Our Common Future," 1987, https://sustainabledevelopment.un.org/content/documents/5987our-common-future.pdf.
3. R. Solnit, *Hope in the Dark: Untold Histories, Wild Possibilities* (Chicago: Haymarket Books, 2016).
4. V. E. Frankl, *Man's Search for Meaning: An Introduction to Logotherapy* (Boston: Beacon Press, 1962).
5. H. Rosling, A. Rosling, and A. R. Rönnlund, *Factfulness: Ten Reasons We're Wrong about the World—and Why Things Are Better than You Think* (London: Sceptre, 2019).

Chapter 1

1. P. Hawken, *Regeneration: Ending the Climate Crisis in One Generation* (London: Penguin, 2021).
2. T. Carlyle, "Goethe," in *The Works of Thomas Carlyle*, vol. 26, *Critical and Miscellaneous Essays I*, ed. Henry Duff Traill (Cambridge: Cambridge University Press, 2010), 198–257.
3. J. C. Smuts, *Holism and Evolution* (London: Macmillan, 1926), 317.
4. Smuts, *Holism and Evolution*, 1.
5. Smuts, *Holism and Evolution*.

6. Smuts, *Holism and Evolution*, 99, 86.

7. M. Gandhi, *The Essential Gandhi*, ed. Louis Fischer (New York: Random House, 2002), 98.

8. F. Capra, *The Science of Leonardo: Inside the Mind of the Great Genius of the Renaissance* (New York: Doubleday, 2007).

9. F. Capra and P. L. Luisi, *The Systems View of Life: A Unifying Vision* (Cambridge: Cambridge University Press, 2014).

10. F. Capra and P. L. Luisi, *The Systems View of Life: A Unifying Vision* (Cambridge: Cambridge University Press, 2014), 65.

11. P. Hawken, *The Ecology of Commerce: A Declaration of Sustainability* (New York: HarperCollins, 1993).

12. K. E. Boulding, "The Economics of the Coming Spaceship Earth," in *Environmental Quality in a Growing Economy: Essays from the Sixth RFF Forum*, ed. H. Jarrett (Baltimore: John Hopkins University Press, 1966), 3–14.

13. E. Elhacham et al., "Global Human-Made Mass Exceeds All Living Biomass," *Nature*, December 9, 2020, https://www.nature.com/articles/s41586-020-3010-5.

14. T. M. Lenton et al., "Tipping Elements in the Earth's Climate System," *Proceedings of the National Academy of Sciences of the United States of America* 105, no. 6 (2008): 1786–1793.

15. J. C. Smuts, *Holism and Evolution* (London: Macmillan, 1926), 18.

16. S. Johnson, *Emergence: The Connected Lives of Ants, Brains, Cities and Software* (London: Allen Lane, 2001).

17. University of Leeds, "Sheep in Human Clothing: Scientists Reveal Our Flock Mentality," *ScienceDaily*, February 16, 2008, https://www.sciencedaily.com/releases/2008/02/080214114517.htm; E. Yong, "The Tipping Point When Minority Views Take Over," *The Atlantic*, June 7, 2018, https://www.theatlantic.com/science/archive/2018/06/the-tipping-point-when-minority-views-take-over/562307/.

18. Johnson, *Emergence*.

19. T. Seba, *Clean Disruption of Energy and Transportation: How Silicon Valley Will Make Oil, Nuclear, Natural Gas, Coal, Electric Utilities and Conventional Cars Obsolete by 2030* (Silicon Valley, CA: Tony Seba, 2014).

20. *The Economist*, "Cutting the Cord," *The Economist*, October 7, 1999, https://www.economist.com/special-report/1999/10/07/cutting-the-cord.

21. W. Mathis, "Building New Renewables Is Cheaper than Burning Fossil Fuels," *Bloomberg Green*, June 23, 2021, https://www.bloomberg.com/news/articles/2021-06-23/building-new-renewables-cheaper-than-running-fossil-fuel-plants.

22. J. McMahon, "New Solar + Battery Price Crushes Fossil Fuels, Buries Nuclear," *Forbes*, July 1, 2019, https://www.forbes.com/sites/jeffmcmahon/2019/07/01/new-solar--battery-price-crushes-fossil-fuels-buries-nuclear/?sh=12e31cec5971.

23. Bloomberg New Energy Finance, "Battery Pack Prices Cited below $100/kWh for the First Time in 2020, while Market Average Sits at $137/kWh," December 16, 2020, https://about.bnef.com/blog/battery-pack-prices-cited-below-100-kwh-for-the-first-time-in-2020-while-market-average-sits-at-137-kwh/.

24. *Renewable Energy World*, "BNEF: Energy to Storage Increase 122X by 2040," *Renewable Energy World*, July 31, 2019, https://www.renewableenergyworld.com/storage/bnef-energy-storage-increase-122x-by-2040/#gref.

25. J. M. Diamond, *Collapse: How Societies Choose to Fail or Succeed* (New York: Viking, 2005).

26. R. Krznaric, *The Good Ancestor: How to Think Long Term in a Short-Term World* (London: W. H. Allen, 2021).

27. D. Barton et al., "Measuring the Economic Impact of Short-Termism," McKinsey Global Institute, February 2017, https://www.mckinsey.com/~/media/mckinsey/featured%20insights/long%20term%20capitalism/where%20companies%20with%20a%20long%20term%20view%20outperform%20their%20peers/mgi-measuring-the-economic-impact-of-short-termism.ashx.

28. D. Barton, "Capitalism for the Long Term," *Harvard Business Review*, March 2011, https://hbr.org/2011/03/capitalism-for-the-long-term.

Chapter 2

1. N. Klein, *The Shock Doctrine: The Rise of Disaster Capitalism* (Toronto: Alfred A. Knopf Canada, 2007).

2. J. Elkington, "25 Years Ago I Coined the Phrase 'Triple Bottom Line': Here's Why It's Time to Rethink It," *Harvard Business Review*, June 25, 2018, https://hbr.org/2018/06/25-years-ago-i-coined-the-phrase-triple-bottom-line-heres-why-im-giving-up-on-it.

3. C. W. Churchman, "Wicked Problems," *Management Science* 14, no. 4 (1967): B141–B146.

4. H. W. J. Rittel and M. M. Webber, "Dilemmas in a General Theory of Planning," *Policy Sciences* 4 (1973): 155–169.

5. J. C. Camillus, "Strategy as a Wicked Problem," *Harvard Business Review* 86, no. 5 (2008): 98–106.

6. Y. N. Harari, *Sapiens: A Brief History of Humankind* (New York: Harper, 2014).

7. J. M. Diamond, *Collapse: How Societies Choose to Fail or Succeed* (New York: Viking, 2005).

8. Intergovernmental Science-Policy Platform on Biodiversity and Ecosystem Services, *The Global Assessment Report on Biodiversity and Ecosystem Services* (Bonn, Germany: IPBES, 2019).

9. C. Sagan, *Pale Blue Dot: A Vision of the Human Future in Space* (New York: Ballantine Books, 1997).

10. *The Blue Planet*, narrated by David Attenborough (BBC, 2001).

11. A. Sen, *Development as Freedom* (New York: Alfred Knopf, 1999).

12. R. D. Wilkinson and K. Pickett, *The Spirit Level: Why More Equal Societies Almost Always Do Better* (London: Allen Lane, 2009).

13. United Nations Development Programme, *Human Development Report 2019: Beyond Income, Beyond Averages, Beyond Today; Inequalities in Human Development in the 21st Century* (New York: UNDP, 2019).

14. United Nations Department of Economic and Social Affairs, *World Social Report, 2020: Inequality in a Rapidly Changing World* (New York: United Nations, 2020).

15. World Inequality Lab, "The World Inequality Report, 2018," 2018, https://wir2018.wid.world/.

16. World Economic Forum, *Global Gender Gap Report, 2020* (Geneva: World Economic Forum, 2019), http://www3.weforum.org/docs/WEF_GGGR_2020.pdf.

17. World Economic Forum, *Global Gender Gap Report, 2020*.

18. World Health Organization, "Noncommunicable Diseases," April 13, 2021, https://www.who.int/news-room/fact-sheets/detail/noncommunicable-diseases.

19. World Health Organization, "The WHO Special Initiative for Mental Health (2019-2023): Universal Health Coverage for Mental Health," 2019, https://apps.who.int/iris/handle/10665/310981.

20. Centers for Disease Control, "Up to 40 Percent of Annual Deaths from Each of Five Leading US Causes Are Preventable," May 1, 2014, https://www.cdc.gov/media/releases/2014/p0501-preventable-deaths.html.

21. M. Springmann et al., "Health and Nutritional Aspects of Sustainable Diet Strategies and Their Association with Environmental Impacts: A Global Modelling Analysis with Country-Level Detail," *The Lancet* 2, no. 10 (2018): E451–E461.

22. D. Carrington, "UK Health Professions Call for Climate Tax on Meat," *The Guardian*, November 4, 2020, https://www.theguardian.com/environment/2020/nov/04/uk-health-professions-call-for-climate-tax-on-meat.

23. World Health Organization, "The WHO Special Initiative for Mental Health."

24. Gallup, "Gallup's Perspective on Employee Burnout: Causes and Cures," 2000, https://www.gallup.com/workplace/282659/employee-burnout-perspective-paper.aspx.

25. United Nations Conference on Trade and Development, *Digital Economy Report, 2019: Value Creation and Capture; Implications for Developing Countries* (New York: United Nations, 2019).

26. Alliance for Affordable Internet, "2019 Affordability Report," 2019, https://a4ai.org/affordability-report/report/2019/.

27. United Nations Conference on Trade and Development, *Digital Economy Report, 2019*.

28. M. Muro, R. Maxim, and J. Whiton, "Automation and Artificial Intelligence: How Machines Are Affecting People and Places," Brookings Metropolitan Program, January 2019, https://www.brookings.edu/research/automation-and-artificial-intelligence-how-machines-affect-people-and-places/.

29. Johns Hopkins University and Medicine, "COVID-19 Dashboard," https://coronavirus.jhu.edu/map.html (accessed July 27, 2021).

30. Munich Re, "Record Hurricane Season and Major Wildfires—the Natural Disaster Figures for 2020," January 7, 2021, https://www.munichre.com/en/company/media-relations/media-information-and-corporate-news/media-information/2021/2020-natural-disasters-balance.html.

31. H. Rosling, O. Rosling, and A. R. Rönnlund, *Factfulness: Ten Reasons We're Wrong about the World—and Why Things Are Better than You Think* (New York: Flatiron Books, 2018).

32. E. László, *The Chaos Point: The World at the Crossroads* (London: Piatkus, 2006).

33. R. Carson, *Silent Spring* (Boston: Houghton Mifflin, 1962).

Chapter 3

1. R. Costanza et al., "Twenty Years of Ecosystem Services: How Far Have We Come and How Far Do We Still Need to Go?" *Ecosystem Services* 28 (2017): 1–16.

2. R. Costanza et al., "The Value of the World's Ecosystem Services and Natural Capital," *Nature* 387 (1997): 253–260.

3. R. Costanza et al., "Changes in the Global Value of Ecosystem Services," *Global Environmental Change* 26 (2014): 152–158.

4. R. Costanza et al. "Twenty Years of Ecosystem Services."

5. Convention on Biological Diversity, *Global Biodiversity Outlook 5* (Montreal: Secretariat of the Convention on Biological Diversity, 2020).

6. World Economic Forum, "The Future of Nature and Business," 2020, http://www3 .weforum.org/docs/WEF_The_Future_Of_Nature_And_Business_2020.pdf.

7. Union for Ethical BioTrade, "The Big Shift: Business for Biodiversity," August 2020, https://www.ethicalbiotrade.org/resource-pages/the-big-shift-business-for-biodiversity.

8. J. Muir, *John of the Mountains: The Unpublished Journals of John Muir*, ed. Linnie Marsh Wolfe (Madison: University of Wisconsin Press, 1979), 439.

9. J. Claes et al., "Valuing Nature Conservation: A Methodology for Quantifying the Benefits of Protecting the Planet's Natural Capital," McKinsey & Company, September 22, 2020, https://www.mckinsey.com/~/media/McKinsey/Business%20 Functions/Sustainability/Our%20Insights/Valuing%20nature%20conservation/ Valuing-nature-conservation.pdf.

10. G. Monbiot, *Feral: Rewilding the Land, the Sea, and Human Life* (Chicago: University of Chicago Press, 2014).

11. Beaver Solutions, "What Good Are Beavers?," https://www.beaversolutions.com/ beaver-facts-education/what-good-are-beavers/ (accessed July 23, 2021).

12. S. Deinet et al., *Wildlife Comeback in Europe: The Recovery of Selected Mammal and Bird Species* (London: Birdlife International and European Bird Census Council, 2013).

13. Walmart, "Walmart Sets Goal to Become a Regenerative Company," September 21, 2020, https://corporate.walmart.com/newsroom/2020/09/21/ walmart-sets-goal-to-become-a-regenerative-company.

14. Natural Climate Solutions, video featuring Greta Thunberg and George Monbiot, September 19, 2019, https://www.naturalclimate.solutions/.

15. A. N. Zerbini et al., "Assessing the Recovery of an Antarctic Predator from Historical Exploitation," *Royal Society Open Science*, October 16, 2019, https:// royalsocietypublishing.org/doi/10.1098/rsos.190368.

16. P. Christiani et al., McKinsey & Company, "Precision Fisheries: Navigating a Sea of Troubles with Advanced Analytics," McKinsey & Company, December 2019, https:// www.mckinsey.com/~/media/McKinsey/Industries/Agriculture/Our%20Insights/ Precision%20fisheries%20Navigating%20a%20sea%20of%20troubles%20with%20 advanced%20analytics/Precision-fisheries-Navigating-a-sea-of-troubles-with -advanced-analytics-vF.ashx.

17. World Economic Forum, "By 2100, Coral Reefs Might Completely Disappear," February 20, 2020, https://www.weforum.org/agenda/2020/02/ coral-reefs-climate-crisis-environment-oceans.

18. M. Liebman and M. Woods, "Marsden Long-Term Rotation Study," Iowa State University, https://www.cals.iastate.edu/inrc/marsden-long-term-rotation-study (accessed July 29, 2021).

19. J. Lovelock, "James Lovelock on Biochar: Let the Earth Remove CO2 for Us," *The Guardian*, March 24, 2009, https://www.theguardian.com/environment/2009/ mar/24/biochar-earth-c02.

20. Y. Chouinard, "Why Food?" *Patagonia Provisions*, April 23, 2020, https://www .patagoniaprovisions.com/pages/why-food-essay.

21. I. Tree, *Wilding: The Return of Nature to a British Farm* (London: Picador, 2019).
22. World Resources Institute, "Creating a Sustainable Food Future: A Menu of Solutions to Feed Nearly 10 Billion People by 2050," July 2019, https://files.wri.org/d8/s3fs -public/wrr-food-full-report.pdf.
23. Impossible Foods, "Turn Back the Clock: 2020 Impact Report," December 2020, https://downloads.ctfassets.net/hhv516v5f7sj/54h9AkKqqLK8FEJ2cnFZ5D/ 4bf80ecb3589923dc6d0aba02e0a7cd2/Impossible_Foods_Impact_Report_2020.pdf.
24. FAIRR, "Appetite for Disruption: A Second Serving," July 2020, https://www.fairr .org/article/appetite-for-disruption-a-second-serving/.

Chapter 4

1. *Closing the Loop*, dir. Graham Sheldon (Kaleidoscope Futures Lab and Stand Up 8 Productions, 2018).
2. A. Weisman, *The World without Us* (New York: Thomas Dunne Books/St. Martin's Press, 2007).
3. W. McDonough and M. Braungart, *Cradle to Cradle: Remaking the Way We Make Things* (New York: North Point Press, 2002).
4. G. C. Unruh, *The Biosphere Rules: Nature's Five Circularity Secrets for Sustainable Profits* (Altadena, CA: Global Leadership Academy Press, 2019).
5. World Cities Culture Forum, "% of Public Green Space (Parks and Gardens)," http:// www.worldcitiescultureforum.com/data/of-public-green-space-parks-and-gardens (accessed July 30, 2021).
6. World Health Organization, "Air Pollution," https://www.who.int/health-topics/ air-pollution#tab=tab_1 (accessed July 29, 2021).
7. A. Amiri and J. Ottelin, "Building European Cities with Wood Would Sequester and Store Half of Cement Industry's Current Carbon Emissions," Aalto University, November 2, 2020, https://phys.org/news/2020-11-european-cities-wood-sequester -cement.html.
8. T. Czigler et al., "Laying the Foundation for Zero-Carbon Cement," McKinsey & Company, May 14, 2020, https://www.mckinsey.com/industries/chemicals/ our-insights/laying-the-foundation-for-zero-carbon-cement.
9. E. O. Wilson, *Biophilia* (Cambridge, MA: Harvard University Press, 1984).
10. D. W. Tallamy, *Nature's Best Hope: A New Approach to Conservation That Starts in Your Yard* (Portland, OR: Timber Press, 2020).
11. Pew Charitable Trusts and SYSTEMIQ, "Breaking the Plastic Wave: A Comprehensive Assessment of Pathways towards Stopping Ocean Plastic Pollution," July 2020, https://www.pewtrusts.org/-/media/assets/2020/07/ breakingtheplasticwave_report.pdf.
12. Ellen MacArthur Foundation, "The Circular Economy Solution to Plastic Pollution," July 2020, https://plastics.ellenmacarthurfoundation.org/ breaking-the-plastic-wave-perspective.
13. Trusted Clothes, "Impact of Dyes," June 23, 2016, https://www.trustedclothes.com/ blog/2016/06/23/impact-of-dyes/.

14. A. Peters, "Austin, Texas, Just Voted to Spend $7 Billion on a Transportation Revolution," *Fast Company*, November 5, 2020, https://www.fastcompany .com/90572127/austin-texas-just-voted-for-a-transportation-revolution# :~:text=Austin%2C%20Texas%2C%20where%20drivers%20spend,centered%20 on%20walking%20and%20biking.

15. Transport Technology Forum, "The State of the Connected Nation," July 2020, https://ttf.uk.net/wp-content/uploads/2021/06/TTF_State_of_the_Nation_2020_ Ed-1.pdf.

Chapter 5

1. Emerald, "Global Inclusivity Report, 2020: The Power of Diverse Voices," 2020, https://www.emeraldgrouppublishing.com/sites/default/files/2020-06/emerald-global -inclusivity-report_0.pdf.

2. S. Unnikrishnan and C. Blair, "Want to Boost the Global Economy by $5 Trillion? Support Women as Entrepreneurs," Boston Consulting Group, July 30, 2019, https://www.bcg.com/publications/2019/boost-global-economy-5-trillion-dollar -support-women-entrepreneurs.

3. T. Arango, "'Turn Off the Sunshine': Why Shade Is a Mark of Privilege in Los Angeles," *New York Times*, December 1, 2019, https://www.nytimes.com/2019/12/01/us/los -angeles-shade-climate-change.html.

4. Ashoka, "Ashoka Venture and Fellowship," https://www.ashoka.org/en-il/program/ ashoka-venture-and-fellowship (accessed July 27, 2021).

5. Ashoka, "The Unlonely Planet: How Ashoka Accelerates Impact; Results of the 2018 Global Fellows Study," 2018, https://www.ashoka.org/en-us/story/2018-global-study -finds-ashoka-fellows-change-policy-market-dynamics-and-how-people-think.

6. M. Yunus, *Building Social Business: The New Kind of Capitalism That Serves Humanity's Most Pressing Needs* (New York: PublicAffairs, 2010).

7. M. Felson and J. L. Spaeth, "Community Structure and Collaborative Consumption: A Routine Activity Approach," *American Behavioral Scientist* 21, no. 4 (1978): 614–624.

8. D. Tapscott and A. D. Williams, *Wikinomics: How Mass Collaboration Changes Everything* (Toronto: Penguin Group, 2008); R. Botsman and R. Rogers, *What's Mine Is Yours: How Collaborative Consumption Changes the Way We Live* (New York: HarperCollins, 2011).

9. PricewaterhouseCoopers, "The Sharing Economy," 2015, https://www.pwc.fr/fr/ assets/files/pdf/2015/05/pwc_etude_sharing_economy.pdf.

10. F. Wilson and M. Ramphele, *Uprooting Poverty: The South African Challenge* (Cape Town: David Philip, 1989).

11. W. Visser, *The Top 50 Sustainability Books* (Abingdon, UK: Routledge, 2009).

12. J. Borger, "US 'Could End World Poverty by 2025,'" *The Guardian*, March 6, 2005, https://www.theguardian.com/world/2005/mar/07/usa.books.

13. See W. Visser, *The Top 50 Sustainability Books* (Abingdon, UK: Routledge, 2009). See also J. D. Sachs, *The End of Poverty* (New York: Penguin, 2006).

14. M. Max-Neef, *From the Outside Looking In: Experiences in Barefoot Economics* (London: Zed Books, 1992).
15. M. Max-Neef, *Human Scale Development: Conception, Application and Further Reflections* (New York: Apex Press, 1989).
16. *Closing the Loop*, dir. Graham Sheldon (Kaleidoscope Futures Lab and Stand Up 8 Productions, 2018).

Chapter 6

1. P. Shukla, A. Rajput, and S. Chakravarthy, "How the Massive Plan to Deliver the COVID-19 Vaccine Could Make History—and Leverage Blockchain Like Never Before," World Economic Forum, July 17, 2020, https://www.weforum.org/agenda/2020/07/blockchain-role-in-distributing-covid-19-vaccine-could-make-history/.
2. A. Peters, "Solar Fridges and Powdered Vaccines: How to Get a COVID-19 Vaccine to the Developing World," *Fast Company*, November 12, 2020, https://www.fastcompany.com/90574433/solar-fridges-and-powdered-vaccine-how-to-get-a-covid-19-vaccine-to-the-developing-world.
3. Johns Hopkins University and Medicine, "COVID-19 Dashboard," https://coronavirus.jhu.edu/map.html (accessed July 27, 2021).
4. World Health Organization, "Noncommunicable Diseases," April 13, 2021, https://www.who.int/news-room/fact-sheets/detail/noncommunicable-diseases.
5. Philip Morris International, "Taking the Lead: PMI's Board Reaffirms the Company's Corporate Purpose," June 9, 2020, https://www.pmi.com/smoke-free-life/pmi-board-reaffirms-companys-corporate-purpose.
6. World Health Organization, "Tobacco," July 26, 2021, https://www.who.int/news-room/fact-sheets/detail/tobacco.
7. G. Burningham, "The Price of Insulin Has Soared: These Biohackers Have a Plan to Fix It," *Time*, October 24, 2019, https://time.com/5709241/open-insulin-project/.
8. ReportLinker, "Global Corporate Wellness Industry," May 2021, https://www.reportlinker.com/p05895920/Global-Corporate-Wellness-Industry.html.
9. M. Chui et al., "The Bio Revolution: Innovations Transforming Economies, Societies, and Our Lives," McKinsey Global Institute, May 13, 2020, https://www.mckinsey.com/industries/pharmaceuticals-and-medical-products/our-insights/the-bio-revolution-innovations-transforming-economies-societies-and-our-lives.
10. J. Bughin, "'Tech for Good': Using Technology to Smooth Disruption and Improve Well-Being," McKinsey Global Institute, May 15, 2019, https://www.mckinsey.com/featured-insights/future-of-work/tech-for-good-using-technology-to-smooth-disruption-and-improve-well-being.
11. Oracle and Workplace Intelligence, "Mental Health at Work Requires Attention, Nuance, and Swift Action," 2021, https://www.oracle.com/a/ocom/docs/hcm-ai-at-work-volume-2.pdf.
12. Milken Institute School of Public Health, "Telemedicine: Using Remote Monitoring to Reduce Hospital Readmissions," October 24, 2015, https://onlinepublichealth.gwu.edu/resources/telemedicine-reduce-hospital-readmissions.
13. United Nations Global Compact, "Global Opportunity Explorer, 2019," 2019, https://www.unglobalcompact.org/library/1171.

14. M. Springmann et al., "Analysis and Valuation of the Health and Climate Change Cobenefits of Dietary Change," *Proceedings of the National Academy of Sciences of the United States of America*, March 21, 2016, https://www.pnas.org/content/113/15/4146.

15. M. A. Clark et al., "Multiple Health and Environmental Impacts of Foods," *Proceedings of the National Academy of Sciences of the United States of America* 116, no. 46 (2019): 23357–23362.

16. D. Tilman and M. Clark, "Global Diets Link Environmental Sustainability and Human Health," *Nature* 515 (2014): 518–522.

17. A. Crimarco et al., "A Randomized Crossover Trial on the Effect of Plant-Based Compared with Animal-Based Meat on Trimethylamine-N-Oxide and Cardiovascular Disease Risk Factors in Generally Healthy Adults: Study with Appetizing Plantfood— Meat Eating Alternative Trial (SWAP-MEAT)," *American Journal of Clinical Nutrition* 112, no. 5 (2020): 1188–1199.

18. C. Bryant et al., "A Survey of Consumer Perceptions of Plant-Based and Clean Meat in the USA, India, and China," *Frontiers in Sustainable Food Systems*, February 27, 2019, https://www.frontiersin.org/articles/10.3389/fsufs.2019.00011/full.

19. Gallup, "Gallup Global Emotions, 2020," 2020, https://www.gallup.com/analytics/324191/gallup-global-emotions-report-2020.aspx.

20. J. D. Eastwood et al., "The Unengaged Mind: Defining Boredom in Terms of Attention," *Perspectives on Psychological Science* 7, no. 5 (2012): 482–495.

21. Eurofound, "European Quality of Life Survey, 2016," 2017, https://www.eurofound.europa.eu/surveys/european-quality-of-life-surveys/european-quality-of-life-survey-2016.

22. L. Eadicicco, "Microsoft Experimented with a 4-Day Workweek, and Productivity Jumped by 40%," *Business Insider*, November 4, 2019, https://www.businessinsider.com/microsoft-4-day-work-week-boosts-productivity-2019-11.

23. W. Visser and S. Jacobs, "Multi-level Resilience: A Human Capital Perspective," AMS Sustainable Transformation Paper Series No. 4, 2019, http://www.waynevisser.com/wp-content/uploads/2019/07/STL_paper4_visserjacobs_resilience_2019.pdf.

24. D. L. Coutu, "How Resilience Works," *Harvard Business Review*, May 2002, https://hbr.org/2002/05/how-resilience-works.

25. Coutu, "How Resilience Works."

26. C. S. Rees et al., "Understanding Individual Resilience in the Workplace: The International Collaboration of Workforce Resilience Model," *Frontiers in Psychology* 6 (2015): 73.

27. C. Laszlo and F. C. Tsao, *Quantum Leadership: New Consciousness in Business* (Stanford, CA: Stanford University Press, 2019).

28. S. Buck, "The Business Challenge of Our Time Is Creating Meaningful Work," *Fast Company*, July 30, 2018, https://www.fastcompany.com/90208459/the-business-challenge-of-our-time-is-creating-meaningful-work.

29. M. Caper, "Are You One of the Tireds?" *Evening Standard*, September 8, 2003, https://www.standard.co.uk/hp/front/are-you-one-of-the-tireds-7228495.html.

30. V. E. Frankl, *Man's Search for Meaning: An Introduction to Logotherapy* (New York: Simon and Schuster, 1984).

31. J. Amortegui, "Why Finding Meaning at Work Is More Important Than Feeling Happy," *Fast Company*, June 26, 2014, https://www.fastcompany.com/3032126/how-to-find-meaning-during-your-pursuit-of-happiness-at-work.

32. Y. Chouinard, *Let My People Go Surfing: The Education of a Reluctant Businessman* (New York: Penguin, 2006).

33. J. Beer, "How Patagonia Grows Every Time It Amplifies Its Social Mission," *Fast Company*, February 21, 2018, https://www.fastcompany.com/40525452/how-patagonia-grows-every-time-it-amplifies-its-social-mission.

34. G. N. Bratman et al., "Nature and Mental Health: An Ecosystem Service Perspective," *Science Advances* 5, no. 7 (2019), https://advances.sciencemag.org/content/5/7/eaax0903.

35. R. Louv, *Last Child in the Woods* (London: Atlantic Books, 2010).

36. M. P. White et al., "Spending at Least 120 Minutes a Week in Nature Is Associated with Good Health and Wellbeing," *Scientific Reports* 9 (2019), https://www.nature.com/articles/s41598-019-44097-3.

37. Y. Miyazaki, *Shinrin-Yoku: The Japanese Way of Forest Bathing for Health and Relaxation* (London: Aster, 2018).

Chapter 7

1. Vodafone, "M-PESA," https://www.vodafone.com/about-vodafone/what-we-do/consumer-products-and-services/m-pesa (accessed July 28, 2021).

2. M-KOPA, "Impact," https://m-kopa.com/impact/ (accessed July 28, 2021).

3. Philips, "Philips Meaningful Innovation Index: Making Innovation Matter; The People's View," January 23, 2013, http://www.newscenter.philips.com/pwc_nc/main/standard/resources/corporate/press/2013/Survey-WEF/2013-01-23-Philips-Meaningful-Innovation-Index-Report.pdf.

4. K. Schwab, "The Fourth Industrial Revolution: What It Means, How to Respond," World Economic Forum, January 14, 2016, https://www.weforum.org/agenda/2016/01/the-fourth-industrial-revolution-what-it-means-and-how-to-respond/.

5. World Economic Forum, "The Future of Jobs Report, 2020," October 2020, http://www3.weforum.org/docs/WEF_Future_of_Jobs_2020.pdf.

6. S. Johnson, *Emergence: The Connected Lives of Ants, Brains, Cities and Software* (London: Allen Lane, 2001), 54.

7. M. Chui et al., "Notes from the AI Frontier: Applying AI for Social Good," McKinsey Global Institute, December 2018, https://www.mckinsey.com/~/media/mckinsey/featured%20insights/artificial%20intelligence/applying%20artificial%20intelligence%20for%20social%20good/mgi-applying-ai-for-social-good-discussion-paper-dec-2018.ashx.

8. MIT Technology Review Insights and GE Healthcare, "The AI Effect: How Artificial Intelligence Is Making Health Care More Human," 2019, https://www.gehealthcare.com/campaigns/research/ai-insights.

9. P. Grother, M. Ngan, and K. Hanaoka, "Face Recognition Vendor Test (FRVT), Part 3: Demographic Effects," NISTIR 8280, December 2019, https://nvlpubs.nist.gov/nistpubs/ir/2019/NIST.IR.8280.pdf.

10. G. Mitchell, "How Much Data Is on the Internet?" *Science Focus*, https://www.sciencefocus.com/future-technology/how-much-data-is-on-the-internet (accessed July 28, 2021).

11. *The Guardian*, "'Tsunami of Data' Could Consume One Fifth of Global Electricity by 2025," *The Guardian*, December 11, 2017, https://www.theguardian.com/environment/2017/dec/11/tsunami-of-data-could-consume-fifth-global-electricity-by-2025.

12. GE Healthcare, "Ground Control to Major Growth in Hospital Command Centers," September 11, 2019, https://www.gehealthcare.com/article/ground-control-to-major -growth-in-hospital-command-centers.

13. Dassault Systemes, "Digital Twin Technology Generates the Insights to Drive Growth Post-pandemic," https://www.3ds.com/3dexperience/cloud/digital-transformation/ digital-twin-technology (accessed July 28, 2021).

14. S. Zaske, "Some Planets May Be Better for Life than Earth," *WSU Insider*, October 5, 2020, https://news.wsu.edu/2020/10/05/planets-may-better-life-earth/.

15. *New Scientist*, "What Is CRISPR?" https://www.newscientist.com/definition/what-is -crispr/ (accessed July 28, 2021).

16. E. N. Brown, "The Race to 3D-Print 4 Million COVID-19 Test Swabs a Week," *Fast Company*, April 24, 2020, https://www.fastcompany.com/90495332/ the-race-to-3d-print-4-million-covid-19-test-swabs-a-week.

17. United Nations Environment Programme, "Moving Ahead with Technology for Eco-innovation," 2017, https://www.oneplanetnetwork.org/sites/default/files/ unep_156_movingaheadwithtechnology_web_180328.pdf.

18. W. Visser, "Sustainable Tech in Africa: 10 Lessons from a Cassava Company," *The Guardian*, August 26, 2014, https://www.theguardian.com/sustainable-business/2014/ aug/26/sustainable-tech-africa-10-lessons-cassava-flour-production-company.

19. W. Visser, "Closing the Loop on Steel: What We Can Learn from a Manufacturer in Ecuador," *The Guardian*, November 20, 2014, https://www.theguardian.com/ sustainable-business/2014/nov/20/steel-recycling-circualr-economy-manufacturer -ecuador-adelca.

20. Azuri, "Life Changing Technology: Solar Is Impacting Lives and Local Economies," http://azuri.wpengine.com/impact/#metrics (accessed July 28, 2021).

21. Ocean Cleanup, "Crowd Funding Campaign the Ocean Cleanup Successfully Completed," September 15, 2014, https://theoceancleanup.com/press/press-releases/ crowd-funding-campaign-the-ocean-cleanup-successfully-completed.

22. See the company's home page, at https://www.fairphone.com/en.

23. Fairphone, "Fairphone Surpasses Investment Target with €7 Million from Impact Investors," November 12, 2018, https://www.fairphone.com/wp-content/ uploads/2018/12/Investment-Round-Press-Release-1.pdf.

24. J. L. Contreras, B. H. Hall, and C. Helmers, "Assessing the Effectiveness of the Eco-Patent Commons: A Post-mortem Analysis," CIGI Paper No. 161, February 20, 2018, https://www.cigionline.org/publications/ assessing-effectiveness-eco-patent-commons-post-mortem-analysis/.

25. Medicines Patent Pool, "About Us," https://medicinespatentpool.org/who-we-are/ about-us (accessed July 28, 2021).

26. E. Musk, "All Our Patent Are Belong to You," *Tesla* (blog), June 12, 2014, https:// www.tesla.com/blog/all-our-patent-are-belong-you.

27. Musk, "All Our Patent."

28. A. Borunda, "We Still Don't Know the Full Impacts of the BP Oil Spill, 10 Years Later," *National Geographic*, April 20, 2020, https://www.nationalgeographic.com/ science/article/bp-oil-spill-still-dont-know-effects-decade-later.

29. Smithsonian, "Gulf Oil Spill," April 2018, https://ocean.si.edu/conservation/ pollution/gulf-oil-spill.

30. S. Allidina, "Collaboration: Future Is Fully Linked," *Raconteur*, June 16, 2016, https://www.raconteur.net/collaboration-future-is-fully-linked/.

31. J. Manyika et al., "A Labor Market That Works: Connecting Talent with Opportunity in the Digital Age," McKinsey Global Institute, June 2015, https://www.mckinsey.com/featured-insights/employment-and-growth/connecting-talent-with-opportunity-in-the-digital-age.

Chapter 8

1. *Hive*, dir. Blerta Basholli (Ikonë Studio and Industria Film, 2021).
2. J. M. Diamond, *Collapse: How Societies Choose to Fail or Succeed* (New York: Viking, 2005).
3. World Meteorological Organization, "Disaster Preparedness Limits Toll from Cyclone Fani," May 2, 2019, https://public.wmo.int/en/media/news/disaster-preparedness-limits-toll-from-cyclone-fani.
4. T. Ida, "Climate Refugees—the World's Forgotten Victims," *Race to Zero*, June 21, 2021, https://racetozero.unfccc.int/climate-refugees-the-worlds-forgotten-victims/.
5. World Bank, "Climate Change Could Force over 140 Million to Migrate within Countries by 2050," March 19, 2018, https://www.worldbank.org/en/news/press-release/2018/03/19/climate-change-could-force-over-140-million-to-migrate-within-countries-by-2050-world-bank-report.
6. Lloyd's Register Foundation, "The Lloyd's Register Foundation World Risk Poll," https://wrp.lrfoundation.org.uk/explore-the-poll/the-majority-of-people-around-the-world-are-concerned-about-climate-change/ (accessed July 28, 2021).
7. J. Watts, "We Have 12 Years to Limit Climate Change Catastrophe, Warns UN," *The Guardian*, October 8, 2018, https://www.theguardian.com/environment/2018/oct/08/global-warming-must-not-exceed-15c-warns-landmark-un-report.
8. GlobeScan and SustainAbility, "The Climate Decade: Ten Years to Deliver the Paris Agreement," November 2, 2020, https://globescan.com/report-2020-climate-survey-evaluating-progress/.
9. Economist Intelligence Unit, "Ready for Change: Pathways to a Low-Emissions Future," 2019, https://futurepresent.economist.com/wp-content/uploads/2019/11/readyforchange.pdf.
10. Energy Transitions Commission, "Making Mission Possible: Delivering a Net-Zero Economy," September 2020, https://www.energy-transitions.org/publications/making-mission-possible/.
11. McKinsey & Company, "How a Post-pandemic Stimulus Can Both Create Jobs and Help the Climate," May 2020, https://www.mckinsey.com/~/media/McKinsey/Business%20Functions/Sustainability/Our%20Insights/How%20a%20post-pandemic%20stimulus%20can%20both%20create%20jobs%20and%20help%20the%20climate/How-a-post-pandemic-stimulus-can-both-create-jobs-and-help-the-climate.pdf.
12. Energy and Climate Intelligence Unit, "Countdown to Zero: Plotting Progress towards Delivering Net Zero Emissions by 2050," June 2019, https://ca1-eci.edcdn.com/reports/ECIU_Countdown_to_Net_Zero.pdf.
13. International Energy Agency, "Global Energy Review: CO2 Emissions in 2020," March 2, 2021, https://www.iea.org/articles/global-energy-review-co2-emissions-in-2020.

14. United Nations Framework Convention on Climate Change, "Climate Ambition Alliance: Nations Renew Their Push to Upscale Action by 2020 and Achieve Net Zero CO2 Emissions by 2050," December 11, 2019, https://unfccc.int/news/climate -ambition-alliance-nations-renew-their-push-to-upscale-action-by-2020-and -achieve-net-zero.

15. C. McGlade and P. Ekins, "The Geographical Distribution of Fossil Fuels Unused When Limiting Global Warming to 2°C," *Nature* 517 (2015): 187–190.

16. J.-F. Mercure, et al., "Macroeconomic Impact on Stranded Fossil Fuel Assets," *Nature Climate Change* 8 (2018): 588–593.

17. C. Figueres, "For Our Future, the Oil and Gas Industry Must Go Green," *New York Times*, September 23, 2019, https://www.nytimes.com/2019/09/23/opinion/climate -change-fossil-fuels.html.

18. D. Kirka, "BP Takes $17.5B Hit as Pandemic Accelerates Emissions Cuts," *AP News*, June 15, 2020, https://apnews.com/article/europe-health-coronavirus -pandemic-2019-2020-coronavirus-pandemic-business-57b7078c0f1c8bddfcca2b4 a7479d5e3.

19. BP, "From International Oil Company to Integrated Energy Company: BP Sets Out Strategy for Decade of Delivery towards Net Zero Ambition," August 4, 2020, https://www.bp.com/en/global/corporate/news-and-insights/press-releases/from -international-oil-company-to-integrated-energy-company-bp-sets-out-strategy -for-decade-of-delivery-towards-net-zero-ambition.html.

20. L. Fink, "A Fundamental Reshaping of Finance," 2020, https://www.blackrock.com/ uk/individual/larry-fink-ceo-letter.

21. BlackRock Global Executive Committee, "Sustainability as BlackRock's New Standard for Investing," 2020, https://www.blackrock.com/corporate/ investor-relations/2020-blackrock-client-letter.

22. BlackRock, "Investment Stewardship Annual Report," September 2020, https:// www.blackrock.com/corporate/literature/publication/blk-annual-stewardship -report-2020.pdf.

23. J. Friedmann, Z. Fan, and K. Tang, "Low-Carbon Heat Solutions for Heavy Industry: Sources, Options, and Costs Today," Center for Global Energy Policy at Columbia University, October 2019, https://www.energypolicy.columbia.edu/research/report/ low-carbon-heat-solutions-heavy-industry-sources-options-and-costs-today.

24. Water UK, "Net Zero 2030 Routemap," https://www.water.org.uk/routemap2030 (accessed July 28, 2021).

25. Interface, "Lessons for the Future," 2019, https://interfaceinc.scene7.com/is/ content/InterfaceInc/Interface/Americas/WebsiteContentAssets/Documents/ Sustainability%2025yr%20Report/25yr%20Report%20Booklet%20Interface _MissionZeroCel.pdf.

26. International Energy Agency, "Air Conditioning Use Emerges as One of the Key Drivers of Global Electricity-Demand Growth," May 15, 2018, https://www.iea.org/ news/air-conditioning-use-emerges-as-one-of-the-key-drivers-of-global-electricity -demand-growth.

27. A. Kalanki and C. Winslow, "Global Cooling Prize: A Pathway to Net-Zero Residential Cooling by 2050," Rocky Mountain Institute, April 20, 2021, https:// rmi.org/global-cooling-prize-a-pathway-to-net-zero-residential-cooling-by-2050/.

28. LEDified, "How LEDs and Incandescents Differ," http://www.ledified.com.au/leds
-vs-incandescents-the-ultimate-comparison (accessed July 28, 2021).

29. Environment America Research and Policy Center, "Renewables on the Rise 2020:
A Decade of Progress toward a Clean Energy Future," October 21, 2020, https://
environmentamerica.org/sites/environment/files/reports/AM%20Renewables%20
on%20the%20Rise%20-%20Merged.pdf.

30. M. Pehl et al., "Understanding Future Emissions from Low-Carbon Power Systems
by Integration of Life-Cycle Assessment and Integrated Energy Modelling," *Nature
Energy* 2 (2017): 939–945.

31. International Renewable Energy Agency, "End-of-Life Management: Solar
Photovoltaic Panels," June 2016, https://www.irena.org/publications/2016/Jun/
End-of-life-management-Solar-Photovoltaic-Panels.

32. Gravitricity, "Fast, Long-Life Energy Storage," https://gravitricity.com/technology
(accessed July 28, 2021).

33. Bloomberg New Energy Finance, "Electric Transport Revolution Set to Spread
Rapidly into Light and Medium Commercial Vehicle Market," May 15, 2019,
https://about.bnef.com/blog/electric-transport-revolution-set-spread-rapidly-light
-medium-commercial-vehicle-market/.

34. *Business Car*, "Now and Next: Fleets, Company Car Drivers and Plug-In Vehicles,"
Business Car, November 1, 2019, https://www.businesscar.co.uk/analysis/2019/
now-and-next-fleets,-company-car-drivers-and-plug-in-vehicles.

35. W. Visser, "Wayne Visser: A Perfect Storm Is Driving Change and Changing
Driving in Business," *Business Car*, November 20, 2019, https://www.businesscar.co.uk/
blogs-and-comment/2019/wayne-visser-a-perfect-storm-is-driving-change-and
-changing-driving-in-business.

36. B. Gates, *How to Avoid a Climate Disaster: The Solutions We Have and the
Breakthroughs We Need* (New York: Alfred A. Knopf, 2021).

37. Project Drawdown, "The Drawdown Review, 2020: Climate Solutions
for a New Decade," 2020, https://drawdown.org/sites/default/files/pdfs/
TheDrawdownReview%E2%80%932020%E2%80%93Download.pdf.

38. Project Drawdown, "Table of Solutions," https://drawdown.org/solutions/table-of
-solutions (accessed July 28, 2021); Project Drawdown, "Drawdown Framework,"
https://drawdown.org/drawdown-framework (accessed July 28, 2021).

39. Global Commission on Adaptation, "Adapt Now: A Global Call for Leadership on
Climate Resilience," September 2019, https://gca.org/wp-content/uploads/2019/09/
GlobalCommission_Report_FINAL.pdf.

40. Global Commission on Adaptation, "Adapt Now."

41. Global Commission on Adaptation, "Adapt Now."

42. *Washington Post*, "Biden Calls Climate Change an 'Existential Threat,'" *Washington
Post*, January 27, 2021, https://www.washingtonpost.com/video/politics/biden-calls
-climate-change-an-existential-threat/2021/01/27/b82690c7-eda6-48b4
-babd-6de0094ee9b1_video.html.

43. Ushahidi, "Haiti: Taking Stock of How We Are Doing," February 6, 2010, https://
www.ushahidi.com/blog/2010/02/06/haiti-taking-stock-of-how-we-are-doing.

44. B. Schiller, "Oklahoma Now Has More Earthquake Activity than California, Thanks
to Oil and Gas Drilling," *Fast Company*, December 16, 2015, https://www
.fastcompany.com/3054683/oklahoma-now-has-more-earthquake-activity-than
-california-thanks-to-oil-and-gas-drilling.

Chapter 9

1. W. Visser, *The Age of Responsibility: CSR 2.0 and the New DNA of Business* (London: Wiley, 2011).
2. W. Visser, *Sustainable Frontiers: Unlocking Change through Business, Leadership and Innovation* (Abingdon, UK: Routledge, 2015).
3. C. Sunter, *The World and South Africa in the 1990s* (Cape Town: Tafelberg Human and Rosseau, 1987).
4. Shell, "Shell Energy Scenarios to 2050: Signals and Signposts," 2011, https://www.shell.com/energy-and-innovation/the-energy-future/scenarios/new-lenses-on-the-future/earlier-scenarios/_jcr_content/par/expandablelist/expandablesection_680706435.stream/1519772516187/787285b3524a8522519a5708558be86cd71a68b2/shell-scenarios-2050signalssignposts.pdf.
5. Shell, "Shell Accelerates Drive for Net-Zero Emissions with Customer-First Strategy," February 11, 2021, https://www.shell.com/media/news-and-media-releases/2021/shell-accelerates-drive-for-net-zero-emissions-with-customer-first-strategy.html.
6. A. Myers, "Lidl Shows 'Way to Go!' with New Range of Fairtrade Chocolate Bars," *Confectionary News*, July 13, 2020, https://www.confectionerynews.com/Article/2020/07/13/Lidl-shows-Way-to-Go!-with-new-range-of-Fairtrade-chocolate-bars.
7. Interface, "Lessons for the Future," 2019, https://interfaceinc.scene7.com/is/content/InterfaceInc/Interface/Americas/WebsiteContentAssets/Documents/Sustainability%2025yr%20Report/25yr%20Report%20Booklet%20Interface_MissionZeroCel.pdf.
8. Unilever, "Unilever Sustainable Living Plan, 2010 to 2020: Summary of 10 Years' Progress," March 2021, https://assets.unilever.com/files/92ui5egz/production/16cb778e4d31b81509dc5937001559f1f5c863ab.pdf/USLP-summary-of-10-years-progress.pdf.
9. Unilever, "Unilever Sets Out New Actions to Fight Climate Change, and Protect and Regenerate Nature, to Preserve Resources for Future Generations," June 15, 2020, https://www.unilever.com/news/press-releases/2020/unilever-sets-out-new-actions-to-fight-climate-change-and-protect-and-regenerate-nature-to-preserve-resources-for-future-generations.html.
10. J. Elkington, *Green Swans: The Coming Boom in Regenerative Capitalism* (New York: Fast Company Press, 2020).
11. Elkington, *Green Swans*, 3.
12. BASF, "Sustainable Solution Steering," https://www.basf.com/global/en/who-we-are/sustainability/we-drive-sustainable-solutions/sustainable-solution-steering.html (accessed July 29, 2021).
13. BASF, "Sustainable Solution Steering."
14. E. S. Nicolás, "Von der Leyen: 'Green Deal Is Our Man-on-Moon Moment,'" *euobserver*, December 11, 2019, https://euobserver.com/environment/146895.
15. X. Jiang, "How China Is Implementing the 2030 Agenda for Sustainable Development," *OECD Development Matters*, February 28, 2020, https://oecd-development-matters.org/2020/02/28/how-china-is-implementing-the-2030-agenda-for-sustainable-development/.
16. Carbon Tracker, "The Trillion Dollar Energy Windfall," September 5, 2019, https://carbontracker.org/reports/the-trillion-dollar-energy-windfall/.

17. Global Commission on Adaptation, "Adapt Now: A Global Call for Leadership on Climate Resilience," September 2019, https://gca.org/wp-content/uploads/2019/09/GlobalCommission_Report_FINAL.pdf.

18. Food and Land Use Coalition, "Growing Better: Ten Critical Transitions to Transform Food and Land Use," September 2019, https://www.foodandlandusecoalition.org/global-report.

19. L. Lazer, C. Haddaoui, and J. Wellman, "Low-Carbon Cities Are a $24 Trillion Opportunity," World Resources Institute, September 19, 2019, https://www.wri.org/insights/low-carbon-cities-are-24-trillion-opportunity.

20. L. Kolodny and M. Wayland, "Fiat Chrysler Spent over $300 Million on Green Credits in Europe Last Year—Mostly from Tesla," CNBC, March 3, 2021, https://www.cnbc.com/2021/03/03/fiat-chrysler-spent-eur-300-million-on-green-credits-mostly-from-tesla.html.

21. M. Wayland and L. Kolodny, "Tesla's Market Cap Tops the 9 Largest Automakers Combined—Experts Disagree about If That Can Last," CNBC, December 14, 2020, https://www.cnbc.com/2020/12/14/tesla-valuation-more-than-nine-largest-carmakers-combined-why.html.

22. D. Meyer, "Bayer Has Now Lost over 44% of Its Value since Its Monsanto Merger," Yahoo! Finance, May 14, 2019, https://finance.yahoo.com/news/bayer-now-lost-over-44-110259769.html.

23. L. Burger and T. Bellon, "Bayer to Pay up to $10.9 Billion to Settle Bulk of Roundup Weedkiller Cancer Lawsuits," Reuters, June 24, 2020, https://www.reuters.com/article/us-bayer-litigation-settlement/bayer-to-pay-up-to-10-9-billion-to-settle-bulk-of-roundup-weedkiller-cancer-lawsuits-idUSKBN23V2NP.

24. Deloitte, "The Deloitte Global Millennial Survey, 2019," 2019, https://www2.deloitte.com/content/dam/Deloitte/global/Documents/About-Deloitte/deloitte-2019-millennial-survey.pdf.

25. New York University Stern Center for Sustainable Business, "Sustainable Market Share Index, 2020," 2021, https://www.stern.nyu.edu/experience-stern/about/departments-centers-initiatives/centers-of-research/center-sustainable-business/research/research-initiatives/csb-sustainable-market-share-index.

26. Meticulous Research, "Plant Based Food Market Worth $74.2 Billion by 2027," October 2020, https://www.meticulousresearch.com/pressrelease/53/plant-based-food-market-2027.

27. E. Whieldon and R. Clark, "ESG Funds Beat Out S&P 500 in 1st Year of COVID-19: How 1 Fund Shot to the Top," S&P Global Market Intelligence, April 6, 2021, https://www.spglobal.com/marketintelligence/en/news-insights/latest-news-headlines/esg-funds-beat-out-s-p-500-in-1st-year-of-covid-19-how-1-fund-shot-to-the-top-63224550.

28. Business & Sustainable Development Commission, "Better Business, Better World," January 2017, https://sustainabledevelopment.un.org/content/documents/2399BetterBusinessBetterWorld.pdf.

29. P. Lacy and J. Rutqvist, Waste to Wealth: The Circular Economy Advantage (London: Palgrave Macmillan, 2015).

Chapter 10

1. T. Machemer, "You Can Now Explore All 48,000 Panels of the AIDS Memorial Quilt Online," *Smithsonian Magazine*, July 21, 2020, https://www.smithsonianmag.com/smart-news/aids-memorial-quilt-now-online-180975370/.

2. South African History Online, "District Six Is Declared a 'White Area,'" https://www.sahistory.org.za/article/district-six-declared-white-area (accessed July 29, 2021).

3. J. Kouzes and B. Posner, *The Leadership Challenge* (San Francisco, CA: Jossey-Bass, 1995).

4. W. Visser and P. Courtice, "Sustainability Leadership: Linking Theory and Practice," Social Science Research Network, October 21, 2011, https://papers.ssrn.com/sol3/papers.cfm?abstract_id=1947221.

5. R. Goffee and G. Jones, "Authentic Leadership," *Leadership Excellence*, May 2009, https://strategy-leadership.com/wp-content/uploads/2012/10/Authentic_Leadership_Goffee_Jones-1.pdf.

6. A. Serio, "The Ingredients to Great Leadership: 4Es and a P," Jack Welch Management Institute, April 26, 2018, https://jackwelch.strayer.edu/winning/leadership-4es-p-energy-energize-edge-execute-passion/.

7. W. Visser, *Follow Me! (I'm Lost): The Tale of an Unexpected Leader* (London: Kaleidoscope Futures, 2019).

8. Visser and Courtice, "Sustainability Leadership."

9. R. Henzen and W. Visser, "Characteristics, Competencies and Employee Benefits of Individual Sustainability Leaderships," Antwerp Management School, August 28, 2019, https://blog.antwerpmanagementschool.be/en/characteristics-competencies-and-employee-benefits-of-individual-sustainability-leaderships.

10. Henzen and Visser, "Characteristics, Competencies and Employee Benefits."

11. E. O. Wilson, *Consilience: The Unity of Knowledge* (New York: Knopf, 1998).

12. SocialTalent, *How To: Increase Diversity through Improved Recruitment and Hiring Processes* (Dublin: SocialTalent, 2016), https://www.socialtalent.com/blog/recruitment/how-to-increase-diversity-through-improved-recruitment-and-hiring-processes-free-download.

13. W. Maathai, *The Green Belt Movement: Sharing the Approach and the Experience* (New York: Lantern Books, 2006), 138.

14. See the Barefoot College website, at https://www.barefootcollege.org.

15. B. Roy, "Learning from a Barefoot Movement," *TEDGlobal 2011*, July 2011, https://www.ted.com/talks/bunker_roy_learning_from_a_barefoot_movement?language=en.

16. D. Barton et al., "Measuring the Economic Impact of Short-Termism," McKinsey Global Institute, February 2017, https://www.mckinsey.com/~/media/mckinsey/featured%20insights/long%20term%20capitalism/where%20companies%20with%20a%20long%20term%20view%20outperform%20their%20peers/mgi-measuring-the-economic-impact-of-short-termism.ashx.

17. A. Boynton, "Unilever's Paul Polman: CEOs Can't Be 'Slaves' to Shareholders," *Forbes*, July 20, 2015, https://www.forbes.com/sites/andyboynton/2015/07/20/unilevers-paul-polman-ceos-cant-be-slaves-to-shareholders/?sh=1289aff4561e.

18. D. Barton, "Capitalism for the Long Term," *Harvard Business Review*, March 2011, https://hbr.org/2011/03/capitalism-for-the-long-term.

19. European Petrochemical Association and Antwerp Management School, "Individual Sustainability Leadership," 2019, https://www.antwerpmanagementschool.be/en/research/sustainable-transformation/research-1/individual-sustainability-leadership.

20. For more on this, see T. Zin, "Seeing Poverty in a Worm's Eye View: A Public Talk by Professor Muhammad Yunus," ActionAid Myanmar, May 21, 2019, https://myanmar.actionaid.org/publications/2019/seeing-poverty-worms-eye-view -public-talk-professor-muhammad-yunus.

21. M. Yunus, *Creating a World without Poverty: Social Business and the Future of Capitalism* (New York: PublicAffairs, 2007), 54.

22. European Petrochemical Association and Antwerp Management School, "Individual Sustainability Leadership."

23. D. Maloney, "High-Flying Bird: Interview with Keller Rinaudo," *DC Velocity*, January 14, 2019, https://www.dcvelocity.com/articles/30385-high-flying-bird-interview -with-keller-rinaudo.

24. N. Patel, "The Business of Meatless Meat: Decoder Interview with Beyond Meat CEO Ethan Brown," *The Verge*, December 22, 2020, https://www.theverge .com/22193672/beyond-meat-ceo-interview-ethan-brown-decoder-podcast.

25. Patel, "The Business of Meatless Meat."

26. R. Anderson, "The Business Logic of Sustainability," *TED2009*, February 2009, https://www.ted.com/talks/ray_anderson_the_business_logic_of_sustainability.

27. I. Kant, *Critique of Practical Reason* (Cambridge: Cambridge University Press, 1997), 133.

28. European Petrochemical Association and Antwerp Management School, "Individual Sustainability Leadership."

29. Ørsted, "Our Green Transformation," *YouTube*, January 25, 2021, https://youtu.be/ N0jja0TrzQ4.

30. Ørsted, "Our Green Transformation."

31. Ørsted, "Our Green Transformation."

32. E. O. Wilson, *Biophilia* (Cambridge, MA: Harvard University Press, 1984).

Epilogue

1. Justice and Conservation Observatory, "Legacy Chico Mendes, the Rubber Tapper Leader Who Gave Life to the Fight against Environmental Devastation," May 11, 2021, https://www.justicaeco.com.br/en/legado-chico-mendes-o-lider-seringueiro -que-deu-vida-pela-luta-contra-a-devastacao-ambiental/.

Bibliography

Adichie, Chimamanda Ngozi. *Half of a Yellow Sun*. New York: Anchor, 2006.

Alliance for Affordable Internet. "2019 Affordability Report." 2019. https://a4ai.org/affordability-report/report/2019/.

Allidina, S. "Collaboration: Future Is Fully Linked." *Raconteur*, June 16, 2016. https://www.raconteur.net/collaboration-future-is-fully-linked/.

Amiri, A., and J. Ottelin. "Building European Cities with Wood Would Sequester and Store Half of Cement Industry's Current Carbon Emissions." Aalto University, November 2, 2020. https://phys.org/news/2020-11-european-cities-wood-sequester-cement.html.

Amortegui, J. "Why Finding Meaning at Work Is More Important Than Feeling Happy." *Fast Company*, June 26, 2014. https://www.fastcompany.com/3032126/how-to-find-meaning-during-your-pursuit-of-happiness-at-work.

Anderson, R. "The Business Logic of Sustainability." *TED2009*, February 2009. https://www.ted.com/talks/ray_anderson_the_business_logic_of_sustainability.

Arango, T. "'Turn Off the Sunshine': Why Shade Is a Mark of Privilege in Los Angeles." *New York Times*, December 1, 2019. https://www.nytimes.com/2019/12/01/us/los-angeles-shade-climate-change.html.

Ashoka. "Ashoka Venture and Fellowship." https://www.ashoka.org/en-il/program/ashoka-venture-and-fellowship (accessed July 27, 2021).

Ashoka. "The Unlonely Planet: How Ashoka Accelerates Impact; Results of the 2018 Global Fellows Study." 2018. https://www.ashoka.org/en-us/story/2018-global-study-finds-ashoka-fellows-change-policy-market-dynamics-and-how-people-think.

Azuri. "Life Changing Technology: Solar Is Impacting Lives and Local Economies." http://azuri.wpengine.com/impact/#metrics (accessed July 28, 2021).

Barton, D. "Capitalism for the Long Term." *Harvard Business Review*, March 2011. https://hbr.org/2011/03/capitalism-for-the-long-term.

Barton, D., J. Manyika, T. Koller, R. Palter, J. Godsall, and J. Zoffer. "Measuring the Economic Impact of Short-Termism." McKinsey Global Institute, February 2017. https://www.mckinsey.com/~/media/mckinsey/featured%20insights/long%20term%20capitalism/where%20companies%20with%20a%20long%20term%20view%20outperform%20their%20peers/mgi-measuring-the-economic-impact-of-short-termism.ashx.

BASF. "Sustainable Solution Steering." https://www.basf.com/global/en/who-we-are/sustainability/we-drive-sustainable-solutions/sustainable-solution-steering.html (accessed July 29, 2021).

Beaver Solutions. "What Good Are Beavers?" https://www.beaversolutions.com/beaver-facts-education/what-good-are-beavers/ (accessed July 23, 2021).

Beer, J. "How Patagonia Grows Every Time It Amplifies Its Social Mission." *Fast Company*, February 21, 2018. https://www.fastcompany.com/40525452/how-patagonia-grows -every-time-it-amplifies-its-social-mission.

BlackRock. "Investment Stewardship Annual Report." September 2020. https://www.blackrock .com/corporate/literature/publication/blk-annual-stewardship-report-2020.pdf.

BlackRock Global Executive Committee. "Sustainability as BlackRock's New Standard for Investing." 2020. https://www.blackrock.com/corporate/investor-relations/2020 -blackrock-client-letter.

Bloomberg New Energy Finance. "Battery Pack Prices Cited below $100/kWh for the First Time in 2020, while Market Average Sits at $137/kWh." December 16, 2020. https://about.bnef .com/blog/battery-pack-prices-cited-below-100-kwh-for-the-first-time-in-2020-while -market-average-sits-at-137-kwh/.

Bloomberg New Energy Finance. "Electric Transport Revolution Set to Spread Rapidly into Light and Medium Commercial Vehicle Market." May 15, 2019. https://about.bnef.com/blog/ electric-transport-revolution-set-spread-rapidly-light-medium-commercial-vehicle-market/.

The Blue Planet. Narrated by David Attenborough. BBC, 2001.

Borger, J. "US 'Could End World Poverty by 2025.'" *The Guardian*, March 6, 2005. https://www .theguardian.com/world/2005/mar/07/usa.books.

Borunda, A. "We Still Don't Know the Full Impacts of the BP Oil Spill, 10 Years Later." *National Geographic*, April 20, 2020. https://www.nationalgeographic.com/science/article/ bp-oil-spill-still-dont-know-effects-decade-later.

Botsman, R., and R. Rogers. *What's Mine Is Yours: How Collaborative Consumption Changes the Way We Live*. New York: HarperCollins, 2011.

Boulding, K. E. "The Economics of the Coming Spaceship Earth." In *Environmental Quality in a Growing Economy: Essays from the Sixth RFF Forum*, edited by H. Jarrett, 3–14. Baltimore: John Hopkins University Press, 1966.

Boynton, A. "Unilever's Paul Polman: CEOs Can't Be 'Slaves' to Shareholders." *Forbes*, July 20, 2015. https://www.forbes.com/sites/andyboynton/2015/07/20/unilevers-paul-polman-ceos -cant-be-slaves-to-shareholders/?sh=1289aff4561e.

BP. "From International Oil Company to Integrated Energy Company: BP Sets Out Strategy for Decade of Delivery towards Net Zero Ambition." August 4, 2020. https://www.bp.com/en/ global/corporate/news-and-insights/press-releases/from-international-oil-company-to -integrated-energy-company-bp-sets-out-strategy-for-decade-of-delivery-towards-net-zero -ambition.html.

Bratman, G. N., C. B. Anderson, M. G. Berman, B. Cochran, S. de Vries, J. Flanders, C. Folke, et al. "Nature and Mental Health: An Ecosystem Service Perspective." *Science Advances* 5, no. 7 (2019). https://advances.sciencemag.org/content/5/7/eaax0903.

Brown, E. N. "The Race to 3D-Print 4 Million COVID-19 Test Swabs a Week." *Fast Company*, April 24, 2020. https://www.fastcompany.com/90495332/the-race-to-3d-print -4-million-covid-19-test-swabs-a-week.

Brundtland, G. H., P. Ehrlich, J. Goldemberg, J. Hansen, A. Lovins, G. Likens, S. Manabe, B. May, H. Mooney, K.-H. Robert, et al. "Environment and Development Challenges: The Imperative to Act." 2012. https://www.conservation.org/docs/default-source/publication -pdfs/ci_rioplus20_blue-planet-prize_environment-and-development-challenges.pdf.

Bryant, C., K. Szejda, N. Parekh, V. Deshpande, and B. Tse. "A Survey of Consumer Perceptions of Plant-Based and Clean Meat in the USA, India, and China." *Frontiers in Sustainable Food Systems*, February 27, 2019. https://www.frontiersin.org/articles/10.3389/fsufs.2019.00011/ full.

Buck, S. "The Business Challenge of Our Time Is Creating Meaningful Work." *Fast Company*, July 30, 2018. https://www.fastcompany.com/90208459/the-business-challenge-of -our-time-is-creating-meaningful-work.

Bughin, J., E. Hazan, T. Allas, K. Hjartar, J. Manyika, P. E. Sjatil, and I. Shigina. "'Tech for Good': Using Technology to Smooth Disruption and Improve Well-Being." McKinsey Global Institute, May 15, 2019. https://www.mckinsey.com/featured

-insights/future-of-work/tech-for-good-using-technology-to-smooth-disruption
-and-improve-well-being.

Burger, L., and T. Bellon. "Bayer to Pay up to $10.9 Billion to Settle Bulk of Roundup Weedkiller
Cancer Lawsuits." *Reuters*, June 24, 2020. https://www.reuters.com/article/us-bayer
-litigation-settlement/bayer-to-pay-up-to-10-9-billion-to-settle-bulk
-of-roundup-weedkiller-cancer-lawsuits-idUSKBN23V2NP.

Burningham, G. "The Price of Insulin Has Soared: These Biohackers Have a Plan to Fix It." *Time*,
October 24, 2019. https://time.com/5709241/open-insulin-project/.

Business & Sustainable Development Commission. "Better Business, Better World." January 2017.
https://sustainabledevelopment.un.org/content/documents/2399BetterBusinessBetterWorld
.pdf.

Business Car. "Now and Next: Fleets, Company Car Drivers and Plug-In Vehicles." *Business Car*,
November 1, 2019. https://www.businesscar.co.uk/analysis/2019/now-and-next-fleets,
-company-car-drivers-and-plug-in-vehicles.

Butler, R. A. "Putting Sustainability at the Center of Business Strategy." *Mongabay*, October 19,
2020. https://news.mongabay.com/2020/10/putting-sustainability-at-the-center-of
-business-strategy-an-interview-with-paul-polman/.

Camillus, J. C. "Strategy as a Wicked Problem." *Harvard Business Review* 86, no. 5 (2008): 98–106.

Caper, M. "Are You One of the Tireds?" *Evening Standard*, September 8, 2003. https://www
.standard.co.uk/hp/front/are-you-one-of-the-tireds-7228495.html.

Capra, F. *The Science of Leonardo: Inside the Mind of the Great Genius of the Renaissance*. New York:
Doubleday, 2007.

Capra, F., and P. L. Luisi. *The Systems View of Life: A Unifying Vision*. Cambridge: Cambridge
University Press, 2014.

Carbon Tracker. "The Trillion Dollar Energy Windfall." September 5, 2019. https://carbontracker
.org/reports/the-trillion-dollar-energy-windfall/.

Carlyle, T. "Goethe." In *The Works of Thomas Carlyle*, vol. 26, *Critical and Miscellaneous Essays I*,
edited by Henry Duff Traill, 198–257. Cambridge: Cambridge University Press, 2010.

Carrington, D. "UK Health Professions Call for Climate Tax on Meat." *The Guardian*, November
4, 2020. https://www.theguardian.com/environment/2020/nov/04/uk-health-professions
-call-for-climate-tax-on-meat.

Carson, R. *Silent Spring*. Boston: Houghton Mifflin, 1962.

Centers for Disease Control. "Up to 40 Percent of Annual Deaths from Each of Five Leading US
Causes Are Preventable." May 1, 2014. https://www.cdc.gov/media/releases/2014/p0501
-preventable-deaths.html.

Chouinard, Y. *Let My People Go Surfing: The Education of a Reluctant Businessman*. New York:
Penguin, 2006.

Chouinard, Y. "Why Food?" *Patagonia Provisions*, April 23, 2020. https://www.patagoniaprovisions
.com/pages/why-food-essay.

Christiani, P., J. Claes, E. Sandnes, and A. Stevens. "Precision Fisheries: Navigating a Sea of
Troubles with Advanced Analytics." McKinsey & Company, December 2019, https://www
.mckinsey.com/~/media/McKinsey/Industries/Agriculture/Our%20Insights/Precision%20
fisheries%20Navigating%20a%20sea%20of%20troubles%20with%20advanced%20
analytics/Precision-fisheries-Navigating-a-sea-of-troubles-with-advanced-analytics-vF.ashx.

Chui, M., M. Evers, J. Manyika, A. Zheng, and T. Nisbet. "The Bio Revolution:
Innovations Transforming Economies, Societies, and Our Lives." McKinsey Global
Institute, May 13, 2020. https://www.mckinsey.com/industries/pharmaceuticals
-and-medical-products/our-insights/the-bio-revolution-innovations-transforming
-economies-societies-and-our-lives.

Chui, M., M. Harryson, J. Manyika, R. Roberts, R. Chung, A. van Heteren, and P. Nel. "Notes
from the AI Frontier: Applying AI for Social Good." McKinsey Global Institute, December
2018. https://www.mckinsey.com/~/media/mckinsey/featured%20insights/artificial%20
intelligence/applying%20artificial%20intelligence%20for%20social%20good/mgi-applying
-ai-for-social-good-discussion-paper-dec-2018.ashx.

Churchman, C. W. "Wicked Problems." *Management Science* 14, no. 4 (1967): B141–B146.

Claes, J., M. Conway, T. Hansen, K. Henderson, D. Hopman, J. Katz, C. Magnin-Mallez, et al. "Valuing Nature Conservation: A Methodology for Quantifying the Benefits of Protecting the Planet's Natural Capital." McKinsey & Company, September 22, 2020. https://www .mckinsey.com/~/media/McKinsey/Business%20Functions/Sustainability/Our%20Insights/ Valuing%20nature%20conservation/Valuing-nature-conservation.pdf.

Clark, M. A., M. Springmann, J. Hill, and D. Tilman. "Multiple Health and Environmental Impacts of Foods." *Proceedings of the National Academy of Sciences of the United States of America* 116, no. 46 (2019): 23357–23362.

Closing the Loop. Directed by Graham Sheldon. Kaleidoscope Futures Lab and Stand Up 8 Productions, 2018.

Contreras, J. L., B. H. Hall, and C. Helmers. "Assessing the Effectiveness of the Eco-Patent Commons: A Post-mortem Analysis." CIGI Papers No. 161, February 20, 2018. https://www.cigionline.org/publications/assessing-effectiveness-eco-patent-commons -post-mortem-analysis/.

Convention on Biological Diversity. *Global Biodiversity Outlook 5.* Montreal: Secretariat of the Convention on Biological Diversity, 2020.

Costanza, R., R. D'Arge, R. de Groot, S. Farber, M. Grasso, B. Hannon, K. Limburg, et al. "The Value of the World's Ecosystem Services and Natural Capital." *Nature* 387 (1997): 253–260.

Costanza, R., R. de Groot, L. Braat, I. Kubiszewski, L. Fioramonti, P. Sutton, S. Farber, and M. Grasso. "Twenty Years of Ecosystem Services: How Far Have We Come and How Far Do We Still Need to Go?" *Ecosystem Services* 28 (2017): 1–16.

Costanza, R., R. de Groot, P. Sutton, S. van der Ploeg, S. J. Anderson, I. Kubiszewski, S. Farber, and R. K. Turner. "Changes in the Global Value of Ecosystem Services." *Global Environmental Change* 26 (2014): 152–158.

Coutu, D. L. "How Resilience Works." *Harvard Business Review*, May 2002. https://hbr .org/2002/05/how-resilience-works.

Crimarco, A., S. Springfield, C. Petlura, T. Streaty, K. Cunanan, J. Lee, P. Fielding-Singh, et al. "A Randomized Crossover Trial on the Effect of Plant-Based Compared with Animal-Based Meat on Trimethylamine-N-Oxide and Cardiovascular Disease Risk Factors in Generally Healthy Adults: Study with Appetizing Plantfood—Meat Eating Alternative Trial (SWAP-MEAT)." *American Journal of Clinical Nutrition* 112, no. 5 (2020): 1188–1199.

Czigler, T., S. Reiter, P. Schulze, and K. Somers. "Laying the Foundation for Zero-Carbon Cement." McKinsey & Company, May 14, 2020. https://www.mckinsey.com/industries/ chemicals/our-insights/laying-the-foundation-for-zero-carbon-cement.

Dassault Systemes. "Digital Twin Technology Generates the Insights to Drive Growth Post-pandemic." https://www.3ds.com/3dexperience/cloud/digital-transformation/digital -twin-technology (accessed July 28, 2021).

Deinet, S., C. Ieronymidou, L. McRae, I. J. Burfield, R. P. Foppen, B. Collen, and M. Bohm. *Wildlife Comeback in Europe: The Recovery of Selected Mammal and Bird Species.* London: Birdlife International and European Bird Census Council, 2013.

Deloitte. "The Deloitte Global Millennial Survey, 2019." 2019. https://www2.deloitte.com/ content/dam/Deloitte/global/Documents/About-Deloitte/deloitte-2019 -millennial-survey.pdf.

Diamond, J. M. *Collapse: How Societies Choose to Fail or Succeed.* New York: Viking, 2005.

Dickens, C. *A Tale of Two Cities.* London: Chapman and Hall, 1859.

Eadicicco, L. "Microsoft Experimented with a 4-Day Workweek, and Productivity Jumped by 40%." *Business Insider*, November 4, 2019. https://www.businessinsider.com/ microsoft-4-day-work-week-boosts-productivity-2019-11.

Eastwood, J. D., A. Frischen, M. J. Fenske, and D. Smilek. "The Unengaged Mind: Defining Boredom in Terms of Attention." *Perspectives on Psychological Science* 7, no. 5 (2012): 482–495.

The Economist. "Cutting the Cord." *The Economist*, October 7, 1999. https://www .economist.com/special-report/1999/10/07/cutting-the-cord.

Economist Intelligence Unit. "Ready for Change: Pathways to a Low-Emissions Future." 2019. https://futurepresent.economist.com/wp-content/uploads/2019/11/readyforchange.pdf.

Elhacham, E., L. Ben-Uri, J. Grozovski, Y. M. Bar-On, and R. Milo. "Global Human -Made Mass Exceeds All Living Biomass." *Nature*, December 9, 2020. https://www .nature.com/articles/s41586-020-3010-5.

Elkington, J. *Green Swans: The Coming Boom in Regenerative Capitalism.* New York: Fast Company Press, 2020.

Elkington, J. "25 Years Ago I Coined the Phrase 'Triple Bottom Line': Here's Why It's Time to Rethink It." *Harvard Business Review*, June 25, 2018. https://hbr.org/2018/06/25-years-ago -i-coined-the-phrase-triple-bottom-line-heres-why-im-giving-up-on-it.

Ellen MacArthur Foundation. "The Circular Economy Solution to Plastic Pollution." July 2020. https://plastics.ellenmacarthurfoundation.org/breaking-the-plastic-wave-perspective.

Emerald. "Global Inclusivity Report, 2020: The Power of Diverse Voices." 2020. https://www .emeraldgrouppublishing.com/sites/default/files/2020-06/emerald-global-inclusivity -report_0.pdf.

Energy and Climate Intelligence Unit. "Countdown to Zero: Plotting Progress towards Delivering Net Zero Emissions by 2050." June 2019. https://ca1-eci.edcdn.com/reports/ECIU _Countdown_to_Net_Zero.pdf.

Energy Transitions Commission. "Making Mission Possible: Delivering a Net-Zero Economy." September 2020. https://www.energy-transitions.org/publications/making-mission-possible/.

Environment America Research and Policy Center. "Renewables on the Rise 2020: A Decade of Progress toward a Clean Energy Future." October 21, 2020. https://environmentamerica .org/sites/environment/files/reports/AM%20Renewables%20on%20the%20Rise%20-%20 Merged.pdf.

Eurofound. "European Quality of Life Survey, 2016." 2017. https://www.eurofound.europa .eu/surveys/european-quality-of-life-surveys/european-quality-of-life-survey-2016.

European Petrochemical Association and Antwerp Management School. "Individual Sustainability Leadership." 2019. https://www.antwerpmanagementschool.be/en/research/ sustainable-transformation/research-1/individual-sustainability-leadership.

Fairphone. "Fairphone Surpasses Investment Target with €7 Million from Impact Investors." November 12, 2018. https://www.fairphone.com/wp-content/uploads/2018/12/Investment -Round-Press-Release-1.pdf.

FAIRR. "Appetite for Disruption: A Second Serving." July 2020. https://www.fairr.org/article/ appetite-for-disruption-a-second-serving/.

Felson, M., and J. L. Spaeth. "Community Structure and Collaborative Consumption: A Routine Activity Approach." *American Behavioral Scientist* 21, no. 4 (1978): 614–624.

Figueres, C. "For Our Future, the Oil and Gas Industry Must Go Green." *New York Times*, September 23, 2019. https://www.nytimes.com/2019/09/23/opinion/climate -change-fossil-fuels.html.

Fink, L. "A Fundamental Reshaping of Finance." 2020. https://www.blackrock.com/uk/individual/ larry-fink-ceo-letter.

Food and Land Use Coalition. "Growing Better: Ten Critical Transitions to Transform Food and Land Use." September 2019. https://www.foodandlandusecoalition.org/global-report.

Frankl, V. E. *Man's Search for Meaning: An Introduction to Logotherapy.* Boston: Beacon Press, 1962.

Friedmann, J., Z. Fan, and K. Tang. "Low-Carbon Heat Solutions for Heavy Industry: Sources, Options, and Costs Today." Center for Global Energy Policy at Columbia University, October 2019. https://www.energypolicy.columbia.edu/research/report/ low-carbon-heat-solutions-heavy-industry-sources-options-and-costs-today.

Gallup. "Gallup Global Emotions, 2020." 2020. https://www.gallup.com/analytics/324191/gallup -global-emotions-report-2020.aspx.

Gallup. "Gallup's Perspective on Employee Burnout: Causes and Cures." 2000. https://www.gallup .com/workplace/282659/employee-burnout-perspective-paper.aspx.

Gandhi, M. *The Essential Gandhi*. Edited by Louis Fischer. New York: Random House, 2002.

Gates, B. *How to Avoid a Climate Disaster: The Solutions We Have and the Breakthroughs We Need.* New York: Alfred A. Knopf, 2021.

GE Healthcare. "Ground Control to Major Growth in Hospital Command Centers." September 11, 2019. https://www.gehealthcare.com/article/ground-control-to -major-growth-in-hospital-command-centers.

Global Commission on Adaptation. "Adapt Now: A Global Call for Leadership on Climate Resilience." September 2019. https://gca.org/wp-content/uploads/2019/09/ GlobalCommission_Report_FINAL.pdf.

GlobeScan and SustainAbility. "The Climate Decade: Ten Years to Deliver the Paris Agreement." November 2, 2020. https://globescan.com/report-2020-climate-survey -evaluating-progress/.

Goffee, R., and G. Jones. "Authentic Leadership." *Leadership Excellence*, May 2009. https://strategy -leadership.com/wp-content/uploads/2012/10/Authentic_Leadership _Goffee_Jones-1.pdf.

Gore, A. *An Inconvenient Truth: The Planetary Emergency of Global Warming and What We Can Do about It.* New York: Rodale, 2006.

Gravitricity. "Fast, Long-Life Energy Storage." https://gravitricity.com/technology (accessed July 28, 2021).

Grother, P., M. Ngan, and K. Hanaoka. "Face Recognition Vendor Test (FRVT), Part 3: Demographic Effects." NISTIR 8280, December 2019. https://nvlpubs.nist.gov/nistpubs/ ir/2019/NIST.IR.8280.pdf.

The Guardian. "'Tsunami of Data' Could Consume One Fifth of Global Electricity by 2025." *The Guardian*, December 11, 2017. https://www.theguardian.com/environment/2017/dec/11/ tsunami-of-data-could-consume-fifth-global-electricity-by-2025.

Handy, C. *The Age of Unreason.* Boston: Harvard Business School Press, 1990.

Harari, Y. N. *Sapiens: A Brief History of Humankind.* New York: Harper, 2014.

Hawken, P. *The Ecology of Commerce: A Declaration of Sustainability.* New York: HarperCollins, 1993.

Hawken, P. *Regeneration: Ending the Climate Crisis in One Generation.* London: Penguin, 2021.

Henzen, R., and W. Visser. "Characteristics, Competencies and Employee Benefits of Individual Sustainability Leaderships." Antwerp Management School, August 28, 2019. https://blog .antwerpmanagementschool.be/en/characteristics-competencies-and-employee-benefits -of-individual-sustainability-leaderships.

Hive. Directed by Blerta Basholli. Ikonë Studio and Industria Film, 2021.

Ida, T. "Climate Refugees—the World's Forgotten Victims." *Race to Zero*, June 21, 2021. https://racetozero.unfccc.int/climate-refugees-the-worlds-forgotten-victims/.

Impossible Foods. "Turn Back the Clock: 2020 Impact Report." December 2020. https:// downloads.ctfassets.net/hhv516v5f7sj/54h9AkKqqLK8FEJ2cnFZ5D/4bf80ecb358 9923dc6d0aba02e0a7cd2/Impossible_Foods_Impact_Report_2020.pdf.

Interface. "Lessons for the Future." 2019. https://interfaceinc.scene7.com/is/content/InterfaceInc/ Interface/Americas/WebsiteContentAssets/Documents/Sustainability%2025yr%20 Report/25yr%20Report%20Booklet%20Interface_MissionZeroCel.pdf.

Intergovernmental Science-Policy Platform on Biodiversity and Ecosystem Services. *The Global Assessment Report on Biodiversity and Ecosystem Services.* Bonn, Germany: IPBES, 2019.

International Energy Agency. "Air Conditioning Use Emerges as One of the Key Drivers of Global Electricity-Demand Growth." May 15, 2018. https://www.iea.org/news/air -conditioning-use-emerges-as-one-of-the-key-drivers-of-global-electricity -demand-growth.

International Energy Agency. "Global Energy Review: CO2 Emissions in 2020." March 2, 2021. https://www.iea.org/articles/global-energy-review-co2-emissions-in-2020.

International Renewable Energy Agency. "End-of-Life Management: Solar Photovoltaic Panels." June 2016. https://www.irena.org/publications/2016/Jun/ End-of-life-management-Solar-Photovoltaic-Panels.

Jiang, X. "How China Is Implementing the 2030 Agenda for Sustainable Development." *OECD Development Matters*, February 28, 2020. https://oecd-development -matters.org/2020/02/28/how-china-is-implementing-the-2030-agenda-for -sustainable-development/.

Johns Hopkins University and Medicine. "COVID-19 Dashboard." https://coronavirus .jhu.edu/map.html (accessed July 27, 2021).

Johnson, S. *Emergence: The Connected Lives of Ants, Brains, Cities and Software.* London: Allen Lane, 2001.

Justice and Conservation Observatory. "Legacy Chico Mendes, the Rubber Tapper Leader Who Gave Life to the Fight against Environmental Devastation." May 11, 2021. https://www .justicaeco.com.br/en/legado-chico-mendes-o-lider-seringueiro-que-deu-vida-pela-luta -contra-a-devastacao-ambiental/.

Kalanki, A., and C. Winslow. "Global Cooling Prize: A Pathway to Net-Zero Residential Cooling by 2050." Rocky Mountain Institute, April 20, 2021. https://rmi.org/ global-cooling-prize-a-pathway-to-net-zero-residential-cooling-by-2050/.

Kant, I. *Critique of Practical Reason.* Cambridge: Cambridge University Press, 1997.

Kirka, D. "BP Takes $17.5B Hit as Pandemic Accelerates Emissions Cuts." *AP News*, June 15, 2020. https://apnews.com/article/europe-health-coronavirus-pandemic -2019-2020-coronavirus-pandemic-business-57b7078c0f1c8bddfcca2b4a7479d5e3.

Klein, N. *The Shock Doctrine: The Rise of Disaster Capitalism.* Toronto: Alfred A. Knopf Canada, 2007.

Kolodny, L., and M. Wayland. "Fiat Chrysler Spent over $300 Million on Green Credits in Europe Last Year—Mostly from Tesla." *CNBC*, March 3, 2021. https://www.cnbc.com/2021/03/03/ fiat-chrysler-spent-eur-300-million-on-green-credits-mostly-from-tesla.html.

Kouzes, J., and B. Posner. *The Leadership Challenge.* San Francisco, CA: Jossey-Bass, 1995.

Krznaric, R. *The Good Ancestor: How to Think Long Term in a Short-Term World.* London: W. H. Allen, 2021.

Lacy, P., and J. Rutqvist. *Waste to Wealth: The Circular Economy Advantage.* London: Palgrave Macmillan, 2015.

Laszlo, C., and F. C. Tsao. *Quantum Leadership: New Consciousness in Business.* Stanford, CA: Stanford University Press, 2019.

László, E. *The Chaos Point: The World at the Crossroads.* London: Piatkus, 2006.

Lazer, L., C. Haddaoui, and J. Wellman. "Low-Carbon Cities Are a $24 Trillion Opportunity." World Resources Institute, September 19, 2019. https://www.wri.org/insights/ low-carbon-cities-are-24-trillion-opportunity.

LEDified. "How LEDs and Incandescents Differ." http://www.ledified.com.au/leds-vs -incandescents-the-ultimate-comparison (accessed July 28, 2021).

Lenton, T. M., H. Held, E. Kriegler, J. W. Hall, W. Lucht, S. Rahmstorf, and H. J. Schellnhuber. "Tipping Elements in the Earth's Climate System." *Proceedings of the National Academy of Sciences of the United States of America* 105, no. 6 (2008): 1786–1793.

Liebman, M., and M. Woods. "Marsden Long-Term Rotation Study." Iowa State University. https://www.cals.iastate.edu/inrc/marsden-long-term-rotation-study (accessed July 29, 2021).

Lloyd's Register Foundation. "The Lloyd's Register Foundation World Risk Poll." https://wrp .lrfoundation.org.uk/explore-the-poll/the-majority-of-people-around-the-world -are-concerned-about-climate-change/ (accessed July 28, 2021).

Louv, R. *Last Child in the Woods.* London: Atlantic Books, 2010.

Lovelock, J. "James Lovelock on Biochar: Let the Earth Remove CO2 for Us." *The Guardian*, March 24, 2009. https://www.theguardian.com/environment/2009/mar/24/ biochar-earth-c02.

Maathai, W. *The Green Belt Movement: Sharing the Approach and the Experience.* New York: Lantern Books, 2006.

Maathai, W. Nobel Lecture. December 10, 2004, Oslo, Norway. https://www.nobelprize .org/prizes/peace/2004/maathai/26050-wangari-maathai-nobel-lecture-2004/.

Machemer, T. "You Can Now Explore All 48,000 Panels of the AIDS Memorial Quilt Online." *Smithsonian Magazine*, July 21, 2020. https://www.smithsonianmag.com/smart-news/aids-memorial-quilt-now-online-180975370/.

Maloney, D. "High-Flying Bird: Interview with Keller Rinaudo." *DC Velocity*, January 14, 2019. https://www.dcvelocity.com/articles/30385-high-flying-bird-interview-with-keller-rinaudo.

Mandela, N. *Long Walk to Freedom: The Autobiography of Nelson Mandela.* Boston: Little, Brown, 1995.

Manyika, J., S. Lund, K. Robinson, J. Valentino, and R. Dobbs. "A Labor Market That Works: Connecting Talent with Opportunity in the Digital Age." McKinsey Global Institute, June 2015. https://www.mckinsey.com/featured-insights/employment-and-growth/connecting-talent-with-opportunity-in-the-digital-age.

Mathis, W. "Building New Renewables Is Cheaper than Burning Fossil Fuels." *Bloomberg Green*, June 23, 2021. https://www.bloomberg.com/news/articles/2021-06-23/building-new-renewables-cheaper-than-running-fossil-fuel-plants.

Max-Neef, M. *From the Outside Looking In: Experiences in Barefoot Economics.* London: Zed Books, 1992.

Max-Neef, M. *Human Scale Development: Conception, Application and Further Reflections.* New York: Apex Press, 1989.

McDonough, W., and M. Braungart. *Cradle to Cradle: Remaking the Way We Make Things.* New York: North Point Press, 2002.

McGlade, C., and P. Ekins. "The Geographical Distribution of Fossil Fuels Unused When Limiting Global Warming to 2°C." *Nature* 517 (2015): 187–190.

McKinsey & Company. "How a Post-pandemic Stimulus Can Both Create Jobs and Help the Climate." May 2020. https://www.mckinsey.com/~/media/McKinsey/Business%20Functions/Sustainability/Our%20Insights/How%20a%20post-pandemic%20stimulus%20can%20both%20create%20jobs%20and%20help%20the%20climate/How-a-post-pandemic-stimulus-can-both-create-jobs-and-help-the-climate.pdf.

McMahon, J. "New Solar + Battery Price Crushes Fossil Fuels, Buries Nuclear." *Forbes*, July 1, 2019. https://www.forbes.com/sites/jeffmcmahon/2019/07/01/new-solar--battery-price-crushes-fossil-fuels-buries-nuclear/?sh=12e31cec5971.

Medicines Patent Pool. "About Us." https://medicinespatentpool.org/who-we-are/about-us (accessed July 28, 2021).

Mercure, J.-F., H. Pollitt, J. E. Viñuales, N. R. Edwards, P. B. Holden, U. Chewpreecha, P. Salas, et al. "Macroeconomic Impact on Stranded Fossil Fuel Assets." *Nature Climate Change* 8 (2018): 588–593.

Meticulous Research. "Plant Based Food Market Worth $74.2 Billion by 2027." October 2020. https://www.meticulousresearch.com/pressrelease/53/plant-based-food-market-2027.

Meyer, D. "Bayer Has Now Lost over 44% of Its Value since Its Monsanto Merger." *Yahoo! Finance*, May 14, 2019. https://finance.yahoo.com/news/bayer-now-lost-over-44-110259769.html.

Milken Institute School of Public Health. "Telemedicine: Using Remote Monitoring to Reduce Hospital Readmissions." October 24, 2015. https://onlinepublichealth.gwu.edu/resources/telemedicine-reduce-hospital-readmissions.

Mitchell, G. "How Much Data Is on the Internet?" *Science Focus.* https://www.sciencefocus.com/future-technology/how-much-data-is-on-the-internet (accessed July 28, 2021).

MIT Technology Review Insights and GE Healthcare. "The AI Effect: How Artificial Intelligence Is Making Health Care More Human." 2019. https://www.gehealthcare.com/campaigns/research/ai-insights.

Miyazaki, Y. *Shinrin Yoku: The Japanese Way of Forest Bathing for Health and Relaxation.* London: Aster, 2018.

M-KOPA. "Impact." https://m-kopa.com/impact/ (accessed July 28, 2021).

Monbiot, G. *Feral: Rewilding the Land, the Sea, and Human Life.* Chicago: University of Chicago Press, 2014.

Muir, J. *John of the Mountains: The Unpublished Journals of John Muir.* Edited by Linnie Marsh Wolfe. Madison: University of Wisconsin Press, 1979.

Muir, J. *My First Summer in the Sierra.* Boston: Houghton Mifflin, 1911.

Munich Re. "Record Hurricane Season and Major Wildfires—the Natural Disaster Figures for 2020." January 7, 2021. https://www.munichre.com/en/company/media-relations/media-information-and-corporate-news/media-information/2021/2020-natural-disasters-balance.html.

Muro, M., R. Maxim, and J. Whiton. "Automation and Artificial Intelligence: How Machines Are Affecting People and Places." Brookings Metropolitan Program, January 2019. https://www.brookings.edu/research/automation-and-artificial-intelligence-how-machines-affect-people-and-places/.

Musk, Elon. Interview by Kara Swisher and Walt Mossberg. Code Conference, June 2, 2016, Rancho Palos Verdes, CA. https://www.youtube.com/watch?v=wsixsRI-Sz4&list=PLKof9YSAshgyPqlK-UUYrHfIQaOzFPSL4&index=9.

Myers, A. "Lidl Shows 'Way to Go!' with New Range of Fairtrade Chocolate Bars." *Confectionary News,* July 13, 2020. https://www.confectionerynews.com/Article/2020/07/13/Lidl-shows-Way-to-Go!-with-new-range-of-Fairtrade-chocolate-bars.

Natural Climate Solutions. Video featuring Greta Thunberg and George Monbiot. September 19, 2019. https://www.naturalclimate.solutions/.

New Scientist. "What Is CRISPR?" https://www.newscientist.com/definition/what-is-crispr/ (accessed July 28, 2021).

New York University Stern Center for Sustainable Business. "Sustainable Market Share Index, 2020." 2021. https://www.stern.nyu.edu/experience-stern/about/departments-centers-initiatives/centers-of-research/center-sustainable-business/research/research-initiatives/csb-sustainable-market-share-index.

Nicolás, E. S. "Von der Leyen: 'Green Deal Is Our Man-on-Moon Moment.'" *euobserver,* December 11, 2019. https://euobserver.com/environment/146895.

Ocean Cleanup. "Crowd Funding Campaign the Ocean Cleanup Successfully Completed." September 15, 2014. https://theoceancleanup.com/press/press-releases/crowd-funding-campaign-the-ocean-cleanup-successfully-completed.

Oracle and Workplace Intelligence. "Mental Health at Work Requires Attention, Nuance, and Swift Action." 2021. https://www.oracle.com/a/ocom/docs/hcm-ai-at-work-volume-2.pdf.

Ørsted. "Our Green Transformation." *YouTube,* January 25, 2021. https://youtu.be/N0jja0TrzQ4.

Patel, N. "The Business of Meatless Meat: Decoder Interview with Beyond Meat CEO Ethan Brown." *The Verge,* December 22, 2020. https://www.theverge.com/22193672/beyond-meat-ceo-interview-ethan-brown-decoder-podcast.

Pehl, M., A. Arvesen, F. Humpenöder, A. Popp, E. G. Hertwich, and G. Luderer. "Understanding Future Emissions from Low-Carbon Power Systems by Integration of Life-Cycle Assessment and Integrated Energy Modelling." *Nature Energy* 2 (2017): 939–945.

Peters, A. "Austin, Texas, Just Voted to Spend $7 Billion on a Transportation Revolution." *Fast Company,* November 5, 2020. https://www.fastcompany.com/90572127/austin-texas-just-voted-for-a-transportation-revolution#:~:text=Austin%2C%20Texas%2C%20where%20drivers%20spend,centered%20on%20walking%20and%20biking.

Peters, A. "Solar Fridges and Powdered Vaccines: How to Get a COVID-19 Vaccine to the Developing World." *Fast Company,* November 12, 2020. https://www.fastcompany.com/90574433/solar-fridges-and-powdered-vaccine-how-to-get-a-covid-19-vaccine-to-the-developing-world.

Pew Charitable Trusts and SYSTEMIQ. "Breaking the Plastic Wave: A Comprehensive Assessment of Pathways towards Stopping Ocean Plastic Pollution." July 2020. https://www.pewtrusts.org/-/media/assets/2020/07/breakingtheplasticwave_report.pdf.

Philip Morris International. "Taking the Lead: PMI's Board Reaffirms the Company's Corporate Purpose." June 9, 2020. https://www.pmi.com/smoke-free-life/pmi-board-reaffirms-companys-corporate-purpose.

Philips. "Philips Meaningful Innovation Index: Making Innovation Matter; The People's View." January 23, 2013. http://www.newscenter.philips.com/pwc_nc/main/standard/resources/corporate/press/2013/Survey-WEF/2013-01-23-Philips-Meaningful-Innovation-Index-Report.pdf.

PricewaterhouseCoopers. "The Sharing Economy." 2015. https://www.pwc.fr/fr/assets/files/pdf/2015/05/pwc_etude_sharing_economy.pdf.

Project Drawdown. "Drawdown Framework." https://drawdown.org/drawdown-framework (accessed July 28, 2021).

Project Drawdown. "The Drawdown Review, 2020: Climate Solutions for a New Decade." 2020. https://drawdown.org/sites/default/files/pdfs/TheDrawdownReview%E2%80%932020%E2%80%93Download.pdf.

Project Drawdown. "Table of Solutions." https://drawdown.org/solutions/table-of-solutions (accessed July 28, 2021).

Raworth, K. *Doughnut Economics: Seven Ways to Think Like a 21st Century Economist.* London: Random House Business, 2017.

Rees, C. S., L. J. Breen, L. Cusack, and D. Hegney. "Understanding Individual Resilience in the Workplace: The International Collaboration of Workforce Resilience Model." *Frontiers in Psychology* 6 (2015): 73.

Renewable Energy World. "BNEF: Energy to Storage Increase 122X by 2040." *Renewable Energy World*, July 31, 2019. https://www.renewableenergyworld.com/storage/bnef-energy-storage-increase-122x-by-2040/#gref.

ReportLinker. "Global Corporate Wellness Industry." May 2021. https://www.reportlinker.com/p05895920/Global-Corporate-Wellness-Industry.html.

Rittel, H. W. J., and M. M. Webber. "Dilemmas in a General Theory of Planning." *Policy Sciences* 4 (1973): 155–169.

Rosling, H., A. Rosling, and A. R. Rönnlund. *Factfulness: Ten Reasons We're Wrong about the World—and Why Things Are Better than You Think.* London: Sceptre, 2019.

Roy, B. "Learning from a Barefoot Movement." *TEDGlobal 2011*, July 2011. https://www.ted.com/talks/bunker_roy_learning_from_a_barefoot_movement?language=en.

Sacks, J. D. *The End of Poverty.* New York: Penguin, 2006.

Sagan, C. *Pale Blue Dot: A Vision of the Human Future in Space.* New York: Ballantine Books, 1997.

Schiller, B. "Oklahoma Now Has More Earthquake Activity than California, Thanks to Oil and Gas Drilling." *Fast Company*, December 16, 2015. https://www.fastcompany.com/3054683/oklahoma-now-has-more-earthquake-activity-than-california-thanks-to-oil-and-gas-drilling.

Schwab, K. "The Fourth Industrial Revolution: What It Means, How to Respond." World Economic Forum, January 14, 2016. https://www.weforum.org/agenda/2016/01/the-fourth-industrial-revolution-what-it-means-and-how-to-respond/.

Schwab, K. "It's Time for a 'Great Reset' of Capitalism." *Private Equity News*, June 9, 2020. https://www.penews.com/articles/its-time-for-a-great-reset-of-capitalism-20200609.

Seba, T. *Clean Disruption of Energy and Transportation: How Silicon Valley Will Make Oil, Nuclear, Natural Gas, Coal, Electric Utilities and Conventional Cars Obsolete by 2030.* Silicon Valley, CA: Tony Seba, 2014.

Sen, A. *Development as Freedom.* New York: Alfred Knopf, 1999.

Serio, A. "The Ingredients to Great Leadership: 4Es and a P." Jack Welch Management Institute, April 26, 2018. https://jackwelch.strayer.edu/winning/leadership-4es-p-energy-energize-edge-execute-passion/.

Shell. "Shell Accelerates Drive for Net-Zero Emissions with Customer-First Strategy." February 11, 2021. https://www.shell.com/media/news-and-media-releases/2021/shell-accelerates-drive-for-net-zero-emissions-with-customer-first-strategy.html.

Shell. "Shell Energy Scenarios to 2050: Signals and Signposts." 2011. https://www.shell.com/energy-and-innovation/the-energy-future/scenarios/new-lenses-on-the-future/earlier-scenarios/_jcr_content/par/expandablelist/expandablesection_680706435.stream/1519772516187/787285b3524a8522519a5708558be86cd71a68b2/shell-scenarios-2050signalssignposts.pdf.

Shukla, P., A. Rajput, and S. Chakravarthy. "How the Massive Plan to Deliver the COVID-19 Vaccine Could Make History—and Leverage Blockchain Like Never Before." World Economic Forum, July 17, 2020. https://www.weforum.org/agenda/2020/07/blockchain-role-in-distributing-covid-19-vaccine-could-make-history/.

Smithsonian. "Gulf Oil Spill." April 2018. https://ocean.si.edu/conservation/pollution/gulf-oil-spill.

Smuts, J. C. Holism and Evolution. London: Macmillan, 1926.

SocialTalent. How To: Increase Diversity through Improved Recruitment and Hiring Processes. Dublin: SocialTalent, 2016. https://www.socialtalent.com/blog/recruitment/how-to-increase-diversity-through-improved-recruitment-and-hiring-processes-free-download.

Solnit, R. Hope in the Dark: Untold Histories, Wild Possibilities (Chicago: Haymarket Books, 2016).

South African History Online. "District Six Is Declared a 'White Area.'" https://www.sahistory.org.za/article/district-six-declared-white-area (accessed July 29, 2021).

Springmann, M., H. C. J. Godfray, M. Rayner, and P. Scarborogh. "Analysis and Valuation of the Health and Climate Change Cobenefits of Dietary Change." Proceedings of the National Academy of Sciences of the United States of America, March 21, 2016. https://www.pnas.org/content/113/15/4146.

Springmann, M., K. Wiebe, D. Mason-D'Croz, T. B. Sulser, M. Rayner, and P. Scarborough. "Health and Nutritional Aspects of Sustainable Diet Strategies and Their Association with Environmental Impacts: A Global Modelling Analysis with Country-Level Detail." The Lancet 2, no. 10 (2018): E451–E461.

Sunter, C. The World and South Africa in the 1990s. Cape Town: Tafelberg Human & Rosseau, 1987.

Tallamy, D. W. Nature's Best Hope: A New Approach to Conservation That Starts in Your Yard. Portland, OR: Timber Press, 2020.

Tapscott, D., and A. D. Williams. Wikinomics: How Mass Collaboration Changes Everything. Toronto: Penguin Group, 2008.

Thunberg, Greta. "Our House Is on Fire." Speech at World Economic Forum, September 20, 2019, Davos, Switzerland. https://www.youtube.com/watch?v=U72xkMz6Pxk.

Tilman, D., and M. Clark. "Global Diets Link Environmental Sustainability and Human Health." Nature 515 (2014): 518–522.

Transport Technology Forum. "The State of the Connected Nation." July 2020. https://ttf.uk.net/wp-content/uploads/2021/06/TTF_State_of_the_Nation_2020_Ed-1.pdf.

Tree, I. Wilding: The Return of Nature to a British Farm. London: Picador, 2019.

Trusted Clothes. "Impact of Dyes." June 23, 2016. https://www.trustedclothes.com/blog/2016/06/23/impact-of-dyes/.

Unilever. "Unilever Sets Out New Actions to Fight Climate Change, and Protect and Regenerate Nature, to Preserve Resources for Future Generations." June 15, 2020. https://www.unilever.com/news/press-releases/2020/unilever-sets-out-new-actions-to-fight-climate-change-and-protect-and-regenerate-nature-to-preserve-resources-for-future-generations.html.

Unilever. "Unilever Sustainable Living Plan, 2010 to 2020: Summary of 10 Years' Progress." March 2021. https://assets.unilever.com/files/92ui5egz/production/16cb778e4d31b81509dc5937001559f1f5c863ab.pdf/USLP-summary-of-10-years-progress.pdf.

Union for Ethical BioTrade. "The Big Shift: Business for Biodiversity." August 2020. https://www.ethicalbiotrade.org/resource-pages/the-big-shift-business-for-biodiversity.

United Nations Conference on Trade and Development. Digital Economy Report, 2019: Value Creation and Capture; Implications for Developing Countries. New York: United Nations, 2019.

United Nations Department of Economic and Social Affairs. World Social Report, 2020: Inequality in a Rapidly Changing World. New York: United Nations, 2020.

United Nations Development Programme. Human Development Report 2019: Beyond Income, Beyond Averages, Beyond Today; Inequalities in Human Development in the 21st Century. New York: UNDP, 2019.

United Nations Environment Programme. "Moving Ahead with Technology for Eco-innovation." 2017. https://www.oneplanetnetwork.org/sites/default/files/unep_156 _movingaheadwithtechnology_web_180328.pdf.

United Nations Framework Convention on Climate Change. "Climate Ambition Alliance: Nations Renew Their Push to Upscale Action by 2020 and Achieve Net Zero CO2 Emissions by 2050." December 11, 2019. https://unfccc.int/news/climate-ambition -alliance-nations-renew-their-push-to-upscale-action-by-2020-and-achieve-net-zero.

United Nations Global Compact. "Global Opportunity Explorer, 2019." 2019. https://www .unglobalcompact.org/library/1171.

University of Leeds. "Sheep in Human Clothing: Scientists Reveal Our Flock Mentality." *ScienceDaily*, February 16, 2008. https://www.sciencedaily.com/releases/2008/02/ 080214114517.htm.

Unnikrishnan, S., and C. Blair. "Want to Boost the Global Economy by $5 Trillion? Support Women as Entrepreneurs." Boston Consulting Group, July 30, 2019. https:// www.bcg.com/publications/2019/boost-global-economy-5-trillion-dollar-support -women-entrepreneurs.

Unruh, G. C. *The Biosphere Rules: Nature's Five Circularity Secrets for Sustainable Profits*. Altadena, CA: Global Leadership Academy Press, 2019.

Ushahidi. "Haiti: Taking Stock of How We Are Doing." February 6, 2010. https://www .ushahidi.com/blog/2010/02/06/haiti-taking-stock-of-how-we-are-doing.

Visser, W. *The Age of Responsibility: CSR 2.0 and the New DNA of Business*. London: Wiley, 2011.

Visser, W. "Closing the Loop on Steel: What We Can Learn from a Manufacturer in Ecuador." *The Guardian*, November 20, 2014. https://www.theguardian.com/ sustainable-business/2014/nov/20/steel-recycling-circualr-economy-manufacturer -ecuador-adelca.

Visser, W. *Follow Me! (I'm Lost): The Tale of an Unexpected Leader*. London: Kaleidoscope Futures, 2019.

Visser, W. *Sustainable Frontiers: Unlocking Change through Business, Leadership and Innovation*. Abingdon, UK: Routledge, 2015.

Visser, W. "Sustainable Tech in Africa: 10 Lessons from a Cassava Company." *The Guardian*, August 26, 2014. https://www.theguardian.com/sustainable-business/2014/aug/26/ sustainable-tech-africa-10-lessons-cassava-flour-production-company.

Visser, W. *The Top 50 Sustainability Books*. Abingdon, UK: Routledge, 2009.

Visser, W. "Wayne Visser: A Perfect Storm Is Driving Change and Changing Driving in Business." *Business Car*, November 20, 2019. https://www.businesscar.co.uk/ blogs-and-comment/2019/wayne-visser-a-perfect-storm-is-driving-change-and -changing-driving-in-business.

Visser, W., and P. Courtice. "Sustainability Leadership: Linking Theory and Practice." Social Science Research Network, October 21, 2011. https://papers.ssrn.com/sol3/papers .cfm?abstract_id=1947221.

Visser, W., and S. Jacobs. "Multi-level Resilience: A Human Capital Perspective." AMS Sustainable Transformation Paper Series No. 4, 2019. http://www.waynevisser.com/wp-content/ uploads/2019/07/STL_paper4_visserjacobs_resilience_2019.pdf.

Vodafone. "M-PESA." https://www.vodafone.com/about-vodafone/what-we-do/consumer -products-and-services/m-pesa (accessed July 28, 2021).

Walmart. "Walmart Sets Goal to Become a Regenerative Company." September 21, 2020. https://corporate.walmart.com/newsroom/2020/09/21/walmart-sets-goal-to-become -a-regenerative-company.

Washington Post. "Biden Calls Climate Change an 'Existential Threat.'" *Washington Post*, January 27, 2021. https://www.washingtonpost.com/video/politics/biden-calls-climate-change-an -existential-threat/2021/01/27/b82690c7-eda6-48b4-babd-6de0094ee9b1_video.html.

Water UK. "Net Zero 2030 Routemap." https://www.water.org.uk/routemap2030 (accessed July 28, 2021).

Watts, J. "We Have 12 Years to Limit Climate Change Catastrophe, Warns UN." *The Guardian*, October 8, 2018. https://www.theguardian.com/environment/2018/oct/08/global-warming-must-not-exceed-15c-warns-landmark-un-report.

Wayland, M., and L. Kolodny. "Tesla's Market Cap Tops the 9 Largest Automakers Combined—Experts Disagree about If That Can Last." *CNBC*, December 14, 2020. https://www.cnbc.com/2020/12/14/tesla-valuation-more-than-nine-largest-carmakers-combined-why.html.

Weisman, A. *The World without Us*. New York: Thomas Dunne Books/St. Martin's Press, 2007.

Whieldon, E., and R. Clark. "ESG Funds Beat Out S&P 500 in 1st Year of COVID-19: How 1 Fund Shot to the Top." S&P Global Market Intelligence, April 6, 2021. https://www.spglobal.com/marketintelligence/en/news-insights/latest-news-headlines/esg-funds-beat-out-s-p-500-in-1st-year-of-covid-19-how-1-fund-shot-to-the-top-63224550.

White, M. P., I. Alcock, J. Grellier, B. W. Wheeler, T. Hartig, S. L. Warber, A. Bone, M. H. Depledge, and L. E. Fleming. "Spending at Least 120 Minutes a Week in Nature Is Associated with Good Health and Wellbeing." *Scientific Reports* 9 (2019). https://www.nature.com/articles/s41598-019-44097-3.

Wilkinson, R. D., and K. Pickett. *The Spirit Level: Why More Equal Societies Almost Always Do Better*. London: Allen Lane, 2009.

Wilson. E. O. *Biophilia*. Cambridge, MA: Harvard University Press, 1984.

Wilson, E. O. *Consilience: The Unity of Knowledge*. New York: Knopf, 1998.

Wilson, F., and M. Ramphele. *Uprooting Poverty: The South African Challenge*. Cape Town: David Philip, 1989.

World Bank. "Climate Change Could Force over 140 Million to Migrate within Countries by 2050." March 19, 2018. https://www.worldbank.org/en/news/press-release/2018/03/19/climate-change-could-force-over-140-million-to-migrate-within-countries-by-2050-world-bank-report.

World Cities Culture Forum. "% of Public Green Space (Parks and Gardens)." http://www.worldcitiescultureforum.com/data/of-public-green-space-parks-and-gardens (accessed July 30, 2021).

World Commission on Environment and Development. "Our Common Future." 1987. https://sustainabledevelopment.un.org/content/documents/5987our-common-future.pdf.

World Economic Forum. "By 2100, Coral Reefs Might Completely Disappear." February 20, 2020. https://www.weforum.org/agenda/2020/02/coral-reefs-climate-crisis-environment-oceans.

World Economic Forum. "The Future of Jobs Report, 2020." October 2020. http://www3.weforum.org/docs/WEF_Future_of_Jobs_2020.pdf.

World Economic Forum. "The Future of Nature and Business." 2020. http://www3.weforum.org/docs/WEF_The_Future_Of_Nature_And_Business_2020.pdf.

World Economic Forum. *Global Gender Gap Report, 2020*. Geneva: World Economic Forum, 2019. http://www3.weforum.org/docs/WEF_GGGR_2020.pdf.

World Economic Forum. *Global Risks Report, 2021*. Geneva: World Economic Forum, 2021. http://www3.weforum.org/docs/WEF_The_Global_Risks_Report_2021.pdf.

World Economic Forum. "Top 10 Emerging Technologies of 2020." November 2020. http://www3.weforum.org/docs/WEF_Top_10_Emerging_Technologies_2020.pdf.

World Health Organization. "Air Pollution." https://www.who.int/health-topics/air-pollution#tab=tab_1 (accessed July 29, 2021).

World Health Organization. "Noncommunicable Diseases." April 13, 2021. https://www.who.int/news-room/fact-sheets/detail/noncommunicable-diseases.

World Health Organization. "Tobacco." July 26, 2021. https://www.who.int/news-room/fact-sheets/detail/tobacco.

World Health Organization. "The WHO Special Initiative for Mental Health (2019–2023): Universal Health Coverage for Mental Health." 2019. https://apps.who.int/iris/handle/10665/310981.

World Inequality Lab. "The World Inequality Report, 2018." 2018. https://wir2018.wid
  .world/.

World Meteorological Organization. "Disaster Preparedness Limits Toll from Cyclone
  Fani." May 2, 2019. https://public.wmo.int/en/media/news/disaster-preparedness
  -limits-toll-from-cyclone-fani.

World Resources Institute. "Creating a Sustainable Food Future: A Menu of Solutions to Feed
  Nearly 10 Billion People by 2050." July 2019. https://research.wri.org/sites/default/
  files/2019-07/WRR_Food_Full_Report_0.pdf.

Yong, E. "The Tipping Point When Minority Views Take Over." *The Atlantic*, June 7, 2018.
  https://www.theatlantic.com/science/archive/2018/06/the-tipping-point-when-minority
  -views-take-over/562307/.

Yunus, M. *Building Social Business: The New Kind of Capitalism That Serves Humanity's Most Pressing
  Needs*. New York: PublicAffairs, 2010.

Yunus, M. *Creating a World without Poverty: Social Business and the Future of Capitalism*. New York:
  PublicAffairs, 2007.

Zaske, S. "Some Planets May Be Better for Life than Earth." *WSU Insider*, October 5, 2020.
  https://news.wsu.edu/2020/10/05/planets-may-better-life-earth/.

Zerbini, A. N., G. Adams, J. Best, P. J. Clapham, J. A. Jackson, and A. E. Punt. "Assessing the
  Recovery of an Antarctic Predator from Historical Exploitation." *Royal Society Open Science*,
  October 16, 2019. https://royalsocietypublishing.org/doi/10.1098/rsos.190368.

Zin, T. "Seeing Poverty in a Worm's Eye View: A Public Talk by Professor Muhammad
  Yunus." ActionAid Myanmar, May 21, 2019. https://myanmar.actionaid.org/
  publications/2019/seeing-poverty-worms-eye-view-public-talk-professor
  -muhammad-yunus.

Zinn, H. "The Optimism of Uncertainty." *The Nation*, September 2, 2004. https://www
  .thenation.com/article/archive/optimism-uncertainty.

Index

About the Author

Photo by Joke Emmerechts Fotografie

DR. WAYNE VISSER is a globally recognized Cambridge "pracademic." An idea-monger, storyteller, and meme weaver, he is the author of 40 books. His work as a champion for thriving, strategy analyst, sustainability academic, documentary filmmaker, poet, and professional speaker has taken him to more than 75 countries. He has been listed as one of the world's top 10 most influential faculty thinkers on social media on issues of responsible business (by University of Bath #thinklist), a top 100 thought leader in trustworthy business (by Excellence and Trust across America), a top 100 sustainability leader (by ABC Carbon), and a top 500 influencer on CSR and business (by SustMeme).

Dr. Visser currently serves as head tutor, fellow, and lecturer at the University of Cambridge Institute for Sustainability Leadership, as well as professor of integrated value at Antwerp Management School, where he holds the world's first academic chair in sustainable transformation, supported by BASF, Port of Antwerp, and Randstad. He is also a director of the think tank and media company Kaleidoscope Futures Lab and founder of CSR International. Previous roles include director of sustainability services for KPMG and strategy analyst for Capgemini in South Africa.

Besides work, Dr. Visser is a biophile—a lover of nature—with a penchant for *shinrin yoku,* forest bathing. He is also a diarist, having kept a journal for more than 30 years, and a poet with seven volumes of published poetry. He lives with his wife, Indira, in Norfolk, England.

For more about Dr. Visser and his work, or to book him to deliver a speech or training workshop, visit http://www.waynevisser.com.

AUTHOR'S NOTE

This works contains content that may be triggering for some readers, including on-page violence and mild gore, on-page abuse, off-page or implied child abuse and sexual abuse, discussions of sexual assault, discussions of marital abuse, and graphic sexual scenes. If you would like more information, a detailed list can be found on the author's website.

www.liliantjames.com

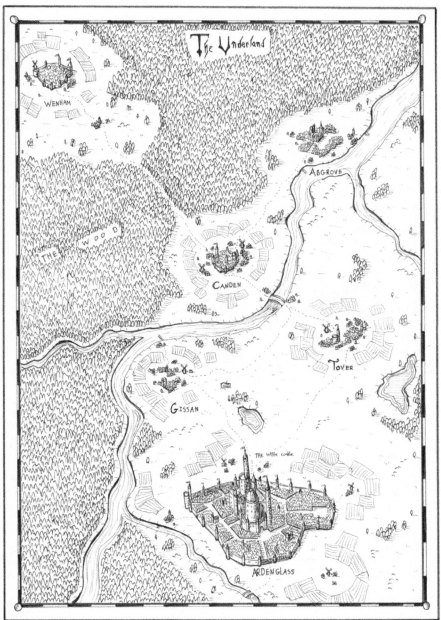

The Underland

WENHAM

ABGROVE

THE WOOD

CANDEN

TOVER

GISSAN

THE WHITE CASTLE

ARDENGLASS

PART ONE
THE UPSIDE
...MOSTLY

ADELAIS

CHAPTER ONE

AGE 8

The first thing I saw was the blood. It dripped from the metal spikes, staining the fur more red than white. Running through the woods with the single-minded focus of avoiding the "party" Mother had set up for me, I'd barely seen the rabbit's prone form in time to avoid tripping over it and ruining my clothes.

I likely would've caught my own leg in the trap if it hadn't already been filled. I shuddered. Father didn't usually put them so close to the house. Not for fear of me injuring myself or anything, but rather that his hunting dogs might do so. It'd happened once to his favorite hound, years ago, when it'd stepped on one mid-chase, and Father still cursed up a storm anytime someone made the mistake of mentioning it.

He'd carried the poor beast home only to put it down in a fit of rage two weeks later when it was still limping and had failed to bring down an injured doe. Although there hadn't been a single flicker of guilt in his eyes when he'd done it, he'd been more careful about where he laid his traps ever since. At least, he had been until now.

My lungs compressed rapidly as they attempted to heave in air from my sprint through the trees, and it made the bodice of my dress squeeze my chest uncomfortably. Mother had tied it so tight, it felt like my insides were trying to pop out, but even still, I didn't move. I just stared down at the broken corpse, mind awhirl and limbs frozen in place.

I'd known Father liked to hunt, but I'd only ever seen his kills after he'd brought them back to the estate. And even then, it'd typically been through the cover of whatever shrub I was hiding behind.

The sight of the mangled rabbit intrigued me. I knew what death was, of course—had learned about it during Sunday sermons. I understood it was a natural occurrence we'd all experience, eventually. A necessary steppingstone on our path to the afterlife. A better life.

That's what our priest always said. It had always sounded like flowery and poetic nonsense to me. I couldn't comprehend how dying could ever be better than living. It was hard enough trying to wrap my head around the concept of death as it was. Like how I could be alive and laughing one minute, and then, *poof,* gone the next.

Staring at the bloodied rabbit at my feet, I couldn't help but question whether it was truly as peaceful as everyone claimed. *He* definitely didn't look peaceful with his broken neck.

Our priest made it sound easy, like falling asleep under a warm blanket when God was ready to greet our souls, but that's not what I'd always pictured.

Knowing most adults, death was probably agonizing and gruesome, and they'd all congregated one day and agreed to make up a lie about peace and eternal joy to keep their children from bothering them with ridiculous questions. That's certainly what Mother had said after Grandmother's funeral last year.

I remembered being forced to attend even though I'd never met her, shuffling behind Mother in a stiff, scratchy black dress and too-tight shoes I'd desperately wanted to kick off. Mother had gone into detail about how happy Grandmother was now, mostly for the benefit of the crowd around us, but I'd just stood there, preparing myself to see an old woman covered in blood.

Of course, Grandmother hadn't looked anything like this poor rabbit, and I'd been shocked to find her looking merely asleep, just as everyone had said. No blood. No wounds. No visible reason for her to no longer exist. In truth, the only difference between her and the portraits I'd seen had been the amount of powder caked on her face.

The image of her had plastered itself in my head, popping to the forefront of my mind, night after night. I'd asked Mother a hundred questions about death, about Grandmother, and about where we went when we closed our eyes for the last time. Because how could we see heaven if our eyes were closed?

But Mother had only grown angry with my interest, and when she'd looked at me with that narrowed, disapproving frown she wore when she failed to hide her hatred, I'd known better than to tell her the truth. That *this* had been what I'd expected to see when I'd peeked over the edge of Grandmother's casket. Death in the way that I'd always imagined it in my head when I secretly sketched by my window at night.

Raw, bloody, and grotesque.

I glanced around to make sure no one had followed me, and then eased down into a squat, tucking my dress beneath my bottom and sitting back on my heels. Confident I was alone, I tilted my head, allowing my eyes free rein to observe the rabbit more closely.

It was hard to tell how long it'd been dead, but by the lack of a smell, I'd guess it hadn't been more than a few hours. The animals Father brought back always made the entire area around his shed smell horrid if the staff didn't take care of them fast enough.

Just a handful of hours ago, this little one had been running by as carelessly as I'd been, minding its own business when it'd come upon Father's trap. In the wrong place at the wrong time.

There and then gone.

I hesitantly reached out but paused, hovering my fingers a hairsbreadth from its fur, watching the strands twitch in the light breeze. Biting my lip, I craned my head around and glanced over my shoulder one last time toward the house to make sure I was still alone.

No one was there, but Mother would notice me missing soon, if she hadn't already, and would send someone to come looking for me if I didn't hurry. She hated it when I wandered into the woods behind our house.

Such behavior isn't fitting of a lady.

But it was the thought of Father finding out that truly frightened me. My mother was cross and knew just where to land her verbal strikes to have my eyes stinging and nose burning, but Father would give me a lashing ten times worse than her hatred if he caught me.

He always made the staff clean up and prepare his kills, not wanting to get his hands dirty, but when it came to my punishments, he was always the one to administer them. Sometimes, I pretended it was because he didn't like the thought of someone else hurting me, but then the little voice in the back of my head would laugh at me, knowing it was because he just didn't want the staff to go easy on me.

Shaking my head and deciding my discovery of the rabbit wasn't worth the risk, I made to stand, planning on running back home and pretending I'd never come. But I stopped mid-raise, unable to help myself, and stared down at the body that lay mere inches from my polished shoes.

I wasn't sure why, but the thought of running away immediately made my chest feel like Mrs. Gayle had slammed a bag of potatoes into it. It hurt to draw in breath, and my hands began to tingle like they were begging me to linger a little longer. Just the one extra second it'd take to reach out again. I was practically vibrating from the effort of resisting.

Logically, I knew enough to understand that wasn't normal, but I also didn't have the strength to fight the sudden, unexplainable pull. Confused, I continued to stare wordlessly at the rabbit for another moment, inspecting where the metal of the trap had embedded into its body, its reddened fur dried and matted beneath.

And then I slowly stretched out my hand again, hesitating for only a second, worried about getting its blood on my baby blue dress, before finally letting the tips of my fingers brush against its small, white foot.

I'd expected it to feel like the stray cats that sometimes wandered around our estate—fluffy or maybe silky—but instead of soft fur, I felt only an uncontrollable, agonizing heat.

The second my fingertips made contact, pure fire shot up my hand. It needled into my veins, scorching my muscles and boiling my bones as it zigzagged up my arm, continuing into my shoulder at a speed I couldn't escape.

I balked, panicking, and attempted to lurch away. But it was like my fingers had melted, merging with the animal's fur until we were one and the same, and I was unable to break away as the invisible flames reached my chest.

My spine arched, and my knees slammed to the dirt, my jaw popping as my mouth widened painfully, and I threw my head back and screamed.

But just as quickly as it'd happened, it was over.

I heaved in air, yanking my hand away so violently I toppled backward, crashing onto my bottom and smearing even more dirt across my dress. If whatever just happened didn't kill me, Mother was going to finish the job when she saw me.

Leaning up onto my elbows, I looked past my splayed legs at where the rabbit had been, expecting the corpse to be engulfed in the unholy flames of the devil. But there was nothing there.

The place where the trap and body had been was now nothing but an unmarked spot on the ground, decorated with only a few dried leaves gently shifting back and forth in the breeze.

Heart still pounding in my chest from the lingering memory of pain, I pushed up onto all fours and crawled toward the tree base, cautiously sliding my hands through the dirt. When I still felt nothing, I frowned and sat back onto my heels, rubbing my hands over my face and focusing on the granules of dirt digging into my skin to center my thoughts.

Maybe I was losing my mind? Mother had always sworn mine didn't work quite right, and Father didn't believe I possessed one at all.

In the past, anytime I'd begun to believe them, Mrs. Gayle had always clucked her tongue and said I just had a healthy imagination. But now, I wondered if maybe my parents had been right all along. Either way, this was definitely my sign that I should head home.

I sighed, not looking forward to what awaited me there, but it wasn't until I'd lowered my hands and looked behind me toward the estate that I suddenly realized I didn't recognize where I was. Heart leaping into my throat, I scrambled to my feet and spun in a circle, my eyes wide and mouth agape.

The trees around me that had been thick and overgrown only a moment ago were now thin and sharp, stretching out in every direction like spider legs. The branches that'd been covered with green foliage were now barren, their brown, brittle leaves blanketing the ground.

Adrenaline pumped through my body, and I craned my neck back to see that the sky, which had been a clear, cloudless blue through the thick canopy, had lost all its color. I could see more of it now with the trees no longer maintaining their leaves, but the blue had dulled and was barely visible through the shelf of darkened, gray clouds.

I knew every inch of the woods behind our estate. As much as my parents tried to pry my love for it out of me, they couldn't. I flocked to it every chance I got, just like today. But these…these weren't *my* woods. I wasn't sure where I was, but what I did know with certainty, was that it wasn't home.

And something about that idea, as unbelievable and unrealistic as it was, had something warm and jittery fluttering in my belly. A small smile pulled at my lips. *I wasn't home.*

Although I had no desire to run away from my family, I also wasn't afraid of being alone. Being alone meant no pain, no yelling, no tutor or governess, and no high expectations I could never meet.

Being alone meant I could be whoever I wanted and do whatever I wanted. It was why I loved the woods so much. Why I slipped into its embrace even when it poured or snowed. It was a place where I could disappear for a few minutes or hours and go on an adventure.

Pushing up to my feet, I readjusted my dress, brushing off as much dirt as I could, and cringed at the torn hosiery over my knees. An adventure this may be, but it wouldn't end that way when Mother caught sight of the condition of the clothing she'd purchased for me for the party.

Something crunched behind me, and I whipped around, fully expecting her to have heard my thoughts and appeared out of thin air. But no one was there.

My eyes darted back and forth between the trees, looking for whoever—or whatever—had made the sound, but still I saw nothing. Not even the flicker of a butterfly's wings.

And it belatedly dawned on me, that although my woods held mostly smaller, nonaggressive animals, I had no idea what these strange woods held. Poachers? Highwaymen? Bears that would tear my intestines from my body?

Another snap of a twig sounded, and I squeaked, dropping to the ground to snatch up the closest stick I could find—which was little more than an overgrown splinter.

Straightening my spine, I held my thin weapon like a sword and bared my teeth in a way I could only hope looked ferocious and brave. Then I spun, fully expecting someone to be lying in wait, ready to pounce.

Instead, I found a rabbit staring up at me.

A very much alive, white rabbit.

I tilted my head and stared back, dropping my weapon behind me so I wouldn't risk frightening him. With a twitching nose and a set of adorable ears extending high above his head, I wouldn't have thought a thing about the sweet creature, if it weren't for the dried streaks of blood caked in his fur.

He watched me for another moment like he was feeling me out as well, considering what danger I might present. I stood statue-still, my eyes darting over his body for any hint that he was a different rabbit. But I was positive he was the same one I'd just seen.

Focused as I was, I nearly flinched back when he suddenly dropped his head to the ground to nose at the leaves beneath his feet. He'd apparently decided I posed little enough of a threat that he could search for a meal. Which was a good sign. The poor thing had clearly been through a lot today.

"It has to be you," I murmured, roving my eyes over his stained body once again.

I wouldn't have believed it if I wasn't looking at him with my own two eyes, but there was no way this wasn't the same rabbit I'd just seen dead in Father's trap. No wounds were present, but the blood smears were identical. He'd come back to life like the princesses in my fairytale book. The ones who'd been cursed before being kissed by their true loves.

Excited beyond measure, I crouched slowly, remembering how nervous the stray kittens around the estate could often be.

"Come here, little one," I whispered, shuffling an inch closer. The rabbit froze, his body locking up except for the slight shifting of his large ears.

"It's okay. I won't hurt you," I said, daring to scoot another inch closer. He lifted his head to eye me again, his body now tensing, readying to run if I made the wrong move.

"Are you magic?"

The possibility had excitement filling my chest and running over, flowing through every crevice of my body until I felt almost nauseated. He had to be magic. Unless I'd officially gone completely bonkers, there was no other explanation as to how he'd not only come back to life, but also escaped Father's trap.

I smiled, wondering if he could understand me, and desperately hoping he could. It was certainly possible. Who knew what all a magical rabbit was capable of?

"It's okay. I promise I'm not going to hurt you," I said, quickly glancing around us and seeing nothing but more spidery trees. "There's got to be some kind of pond or river around here. We can find one, and I'll help you wash all that icky blood off of you. Wouldn't that be nice?"

I held my breath, eyes fixed on him, half expecting the rabbit to open his mouth and answer. But after several long seconds, my eyes began to burn, and the instant I lost the battle and blinked, the rascal leaped up and bounded past me, a cloud of dirt billowing behind him.

My smile widened until my cheeks hurt, and I giggled, twisting to give chase. The wind whipped at my shoulders, further tangling my already knotted hair as I ran, dodging trees and tripping over various roots and stones in my effort to keep up.

I pumped my arms harder, laughing with unfiltered joy at the feeling of pure freedom, even as I fell behind and lost sight of the ornery thing. Wherever I was, wherever my resurrected little friend had taken me, it was somewhere fantastical.

There was no father here to punish me, no mother to scream in my ear. No red-faced tutors calling me stupid, and no disgusting tea parties with awful girls and pointed stares and whispers.

There was no one around at all.

After several minutes, I finally slowed to a stop, realizing there wasn't much point in continuing to chase an animal I could no longer see. I rested my hands on my thighs, gulping in lungfuls of air and winced, feeling bites of pain at the back of my heels.

My stiff, hideous shoes had already been insufferably uncomfortable while I'd only been standing at attention behind Mother in the house. They definitely hadn't been made for sprinting through the woods over uneven ground, and I'd done that exact thing twice now.

I shifted my weight around to test the damage and winced again. The dreadful things. I'd have blisters by tomorrow, for sure.

Straightening back up, I took in measured breaths to calm my racing heart and gazed around me. The trees were thicker and more numerous here than in the area I'd first arrived at, but they were still bare and spindly enough to allow some light in.

What light, I wasn't sure, since there was no sun or moon that I could make out through the wooden web above me. But it wasn't the quality of light or lack of an obvious source that had me frowning, unease making the hairs on the back of my neck stand at attention.

It was the total and utter silence.

This deep into any woods—magical or not—I should've spotted other creatures by now, small or large. Squirrels darting up branches to hide their acorns, birds singing to one another from their nests, insects buzzing about and flying in my face, worms and spiders lounging on the roots. *Something.*

But I was still completely alone.

Well…except for the little white and red ball of fluff I now spied hiding behind a tree to my left. I giggled. He looked like a giant cotton ball.

"Are you hiding from me, Cotton?" I whispered, although the silence made me feel almost like I was yelling. He ignored me, continuing to nibble on a root he'd found at the base of the tree.

I moved slowly, raising my hands out in front of me, and he dropped it, warily watching my approach. "Come on, you don't want to chew on that nasty dead stick. Maybe we can find something better to eat together after we find a way to wash you off."

His eyes never left me, but he didn't run again as I grew closer and sidestepped around the tree. Would touching him again take me home? I hadn't considered it before, but if the last time brought me here—wherever *here* was—it made sense that touching him again would take me back. Right?

I chewed my lip, suddenly unsure if I wanted to pick him up after all. I really didn't want to go home yet. Not before I had the chance to explore a little. But leaving the poor thing all matted and gross was cruel, especially when the blood was sure to attract the attention of a larger animal.

Not letting myself second-guess my decision, I nodded firmly and scooped him up, eyes squeezing shut and my muscles seizing in anticipation of the blinding hot pain that would take me home. But Cotton just settled into my arms and nosed at my hand calmly, like he hadn't just run from me a few minutes ago.

I peeked one eye open, and then the other, releasing my held breath with a whoosh. We were still there. Curious. I glanced down at Cotton, stroking my fingers through a small section of clean fur.

Maybe he could only use magic once a day? It seemed like it must be a lot of work to transport to an entirely new place. Maybe he needed to eat or sleep first?

I looked around, noting that there wasn't really anything green or soft for him to eat where we were at. There was likely plenty of grass outside of the woods, but I had no idea which direction to go to leave. There was no clear path anywhere around us.

"Do you know how to get out of here, Cotton?" I asked, hoping he'd at least nod his head, but he only nibbled at his foot.

I sighed. "Well, all right. Guess it's up to me then."

Praying I didn't stumble upon a bear or an angry fox; I chose the direction that looked a smidge brighter than the rest and crossed my fingers that I wasn't about to get even more lost.

I made it all of two small steps before stopping again.

"Ugh, these shoes are the worst," I whined, clenching my jaw to keep from crying when it felt like the backs of them were scraping against raw skin. "Be thankful you'll never have to wear any."

Cotton, however, did not appear at all concerned with my pain. Careful not to drop him, I shifted my weight and toed the contraptions off, examining the damage. Sure enough, two bleeding wounds peeked out through tears in my hosiery.

"See what I mean."

Angry with my mother for making me wear them, I kicked them to the side and sagged in relief as my feet sank freely into the loose dirt. Even stepping on a sharp stone was bound to feel better than those godforsaken things.

I wasn't sure how long I walked, but rather than get brighter and less dense, the air began to chill as I walked and the sky darkened considerably, sending gooseflesh across my neck and down both arms.

I shivered, snuggling Cotton closer, and nervously eyed the fog that seemed to be sliding in heavier through the trees with each step I took. My excitement over having a magical rabbit quickly began to lessen the colder and darker it got, replaced by a sudden urge to sprint back the way I came.

"I think maybe we went the wrong way," I whispered.

"I'd think so."

ADELAIS

CHAPTER TWO

I lurched to a stop, staring wide-eyed at my fluffy new friend. "I *knew* you could talk," I squealed, smiling and hefting him higher, ready to ask if he knew where in the world we were, when someone—who definitely wasn't Cotton—snorted behind me.

The sound had me nearly jumping out of my skin, almost dropping Cotton in the process. Spinning fast enough to give myself whiplash, I froze like a caught deer when I saw who had snuck up behind me.

A man, or at least I assumed so from the low tone of his snort, leaned against a tree a few feet away. His posture was casual, but his features were concealed in shadow beneath a deep hood, which immediately set me on edge.

Although he appeared to be an adult from size alone, his cloak hid the majority of his body so that the only details I could make out were his dark trousers, black boots, and a single hand spinning a glinting, silver object in front of his chest.

I squinted, trying to make out what he held, only for my eyes to fly open in alarm when I realized what it was.

The man straightened, and I instinctively retreated a step. Slipping an arm out from under Cotton, I kept my eyes on the stranger and slowly ran my hand over my hair, searching for one of the sharp hairpins Mother had twisted into it to keep the brittle, blonde mess pulled back.

Errant strands screamed and tore as I dug one out, but I bit my lip and ripped it from my scalp, brandishing it in front of Cotton and me.

His posture was relaxed and unthreatening and, for some reason I couldn't explain, even though I felt fear, it wasn't the same crashing wave of undulating terror I experienced whenever Father stalked toward me. It was more like soft laps at the shore, like my body was simply waiting, still unsure if it should flee or fight.

However, that didn't mean I trusted the shadowed stranger, nor did it mean I wasn't aware of what the spinning silver knife in his hand could do to my skin.

Observing my frozen form for another moment, he seemed to come to some conclusion and stepped away from the tree, reaching up to knock the hood back off his head. Even as it dropped, revealing his face, I swore he still appeared more like a moving shadow than a man.

From his black hair, cut short on the sides yet unruly on top, to his dark cloak and clothes, he was entirely colorless. It was no wonder I hadn't noticed him until he'd spoken.

What truly caught my attention and held it, though, were his eyes. Even from several feet away, there was no *not* noticing them once he'd dropped his hood. I could see streaks of blue in their depths, but the hue was so dark, they almost appeared black. It was as if they drew in the darkness around him and stored it within his irises.

He had lightly tanned skin and clear, distinct features, more like stone than flesh. His jaw and cheekbones, and even his nose, were sharp and brutal, and he was tall, possibly even more so than Father.

His lips, the bottom fuller than the top, were pressed firmly together with distaste as I continued to stare wide-eyed at him, but I couldn't tear my gaze away. He appeared human, and yet somehow not, at the same time.

Fascination crawled through me until it was equal to my fear, and I squeezed my fist around my hairpin, my fingers itching to hold a piece of charcoal and paper instead.

"And what, pray tell, are you going to do with that?" he asked, his voice deep and graveled. It was mixed with just a hint of amusement as his dark eyes darted down to my outstretched hand, like he found the notion of me defending myself to be adorable.

I swallowed, glancing down at my pathetic excuse for a weapon and then back up at him, lifting my chin. This man wasn't my father and had no right to try to frighten me. "If you come any closer, I'll stab your eye out."

He huffed a laugh and crossed his arms, his spinning blade disappearing in the blink of an eye.

"Stab my eye out?" He tilted his head, lips twitching. "Somehow, I don't think a little thing like you has it in her to remove an eyeball from a skull. It's actually quite difficult."

My left arm ached with the effort of holding onto Cotton, and I shifted, trying to rest the bulk of his body on my hip. "Maybe so, but I don't need to remove your eyeball to make it hurt."

Surprise flickered in his eyes, but it was gone so fast, I wasn't sure I'd even seen it. "Big words from someone so small."

I opened my mouth to tell him his tiny knife had been no more impressive, but a sharp shriek echoed in the distance. I jolted, struggling to keep ahold of Cotton, who was now actively wiggling in my arms.

The man's lips curled in the corner, so slight I wouldn't have noticed if I hadn't been staring so rudely. "Does the Wood scare you?"

I frowned at his tone, aware that he was patronizing me, but I still found myself pausing and considering his question. Because the truth was, I *wasn't* scared. Not really.

Alone in an unknown place with an armed man, predators prowling, and the light quickly fading from the sky, I knew I should be utterly terrified, but I wasn't. I'd felt true fear many times, and although I did feel a flicker of it, it was fading by the second.

"I don't want to get eaten alive or anything," I admitted, "but no, not really. I think it's kind of beautiful here, weird noises and all."

In its own way, it was. The trees, though barren and thin, were striking and unique, and the cloud-covered sky cast a somber light that was enough to move by but not enough to burn your brow or make you sweat. It made me want to curl up at the base of the nearest tree and draw for hours.

The man blinked slowly before lowering his arms to his sides and considering me closer. "There's nothing beautiful about this place. If you're not scared of the Wood, you're a fool."

I shrugged, adjusting Cotton in my arms, his wiggling having turned into full bucking the closer the man got. It wasn't the first time, or even the hundredth, I'd been called such. The word had long ago lost its bite.

Pursing my lips in thought, I said, "Well, I disagree. You're here, and although you don't seem all that nice, I think your eyes are beautiful."

They flared at that, something akin to bewilderment crossing their depths for the briefest of seconds. He took another step closer to me and squatted down to my level, his cloak bunching over his thighs as he did. "What's your name, little rabbit?"

I frowned, dropping my eyes to the filthy creature in my arms. "I don't think he can talk. I already tried. I named him Cotton because he's so white. Well, apart from the blood. That's there because my father killed him."

I glanced up, expecting him to nod at my explanation, or at least admire Cotton, but he just raised a dark brow and pointed a finger at me, making Cotton buck even harder in my grasp. "Not him. You."

"Oh." Then why did he ask about the rabbit? Adults were so weird sometimes. "I'm Adelais."

"Ace?"

"No. Ad-eh-lace."

His fingers flicked back and forth, like he wasn't sure what to do with them when they weren't filled with tiny, glinting knives. "What are you doing out here, Ace? You should know the Wood is forbidden."

"*Adelais*. And I followed him," I said, giving Cotton a soft pat. "I think he might be magical. He was dead, squeezed to death in one of my father's traps, and now he's not."

His mouth twitched again, the tiniest curl pulling at the corner. "And what about you?" he asked. "How did you die?"

I frowned and scrunched my nose up tight. I knew my dress was dirty and torn, but I didn't think it looked quite that horrid. "I'm not dead."

"Right," he muttered, running an irritated hand through his hair until it stood up every which way. "Let me rephrase that. How did you get so deep into the Wood, Ace? Were you looking for someone?"

I rolled my eyes but didn't correct him again. I was starting to think he couldn't hear all that well. "I told you. I followed Cotton here. He was dead, and I touched him. Except it didn't work when I touched him again, that's how I'm holding him. We're friends now."

However, Cotton didn't appear to feel the same way, because as soon as I relaxed my hold to give him another pat, he leaped from my grasp. His claws dug into my arm, and I yelped, watching as he crashed hard to the ground. But just as fast as he'd jumped, he was up again and moving, bounding through the trees and out of sight.

"Great," I sulked, rubbing my hand over the stinging scratches now adorning my forearm. There was no way I'd catch up to him, and I had no idea how to get home without his magic.

A firm grip on my shoulder startled me, and I staggered back, instinct telling me to put distance between us. But the man held on, his eyes roving over my face and alighting like I imagined mine did whenever I was trying to work out a particularly confusing puzzle.

"Where are you supposed to be right now, Ace?"

I rolled my eyes again, and his narrowed. For some reason I couldn't explain, though he made me nervous, I didn't think he planned to cause me harm. However, that didn't mean I was naïve enough to tell a strange man where I lived.

I pulled at his hold again, darting my gaze around in the foolish hope of catching sight of Cotton poking around somewhere close. "Why should I tell you? I don't know who you are. For all I know, you're asking because you plan to go to my house and rob my family."

He glared down at me and didn't answer right away. I swallowed, fidgeting under the heat of his stare, and prayed that my gut feeling about his intentions wasn't wrong.

"Terek."

I quirked my head to the side, not recognizing the word, and wondered if it was perhaps another language or something. "What?"

He released me, stepping back and wiping his hands on his cloak, as if touching me had dirtied him. "My name. You can call me Terek."

"Oh." I rolled the name around in my head and pursed my lips. *Terek.* What an odd name. Then again, he didn't seem to find mine all that normal either.

I looked around as the wind picked up, slapping yellow strands of hair across my face. It was starting to get particularly dark, and I had no idea how I was going to get home. I chewed my lip, the realization of just how much trouble I was in settling like a rock in the pit of my stomach. My parents were going to be furious.

As if sensing my thoughts, Terek shifted back until he could lean against another tree, his dark eyes somehow seeming to focus on me and scout the landscape at the same time. Like even though he was eyeing me like a hawk, he was also aware of the movement of every leaf that fluttered within the entire wood.

"Where are you supposed to be?" he asked again. "I'm sure your guardians are worried sick searching for you."

I scoffed, earning me a frown. "They're not searching for me. They'd just send a servant out to do it." I toed at the ground, drawing a circle with my already filthy feet. "I wasn't supposed to be at anything important. Just some stupid tea party. I *told* Mother I didn't want to go. It's not my fault she didn't listen."

His expression shuttered in an instant. "Let me get this straight. You entered the Wood, against her majesty's decree, because you didn't want to attend a damned children's party?"

Majesty? My brow furrowed. Who was he talking about? "I always go into the woods." I paused, gesturing around me. "Well, not these woods, I guess. The girls who showed up to the party are awful and pull my hair, and I hate sitting there pretending that drinking boiling hot, leaf water is fun. It's not."

I crossed my arms, refusing to feel guilty. I'd like to see Terek drink the tea Mother always had shipped in and keep a straight face. It was like pouring water on the ground and slurping it up. But worse.

"Crimson take me, I'm not meant to deal with children," he muttered, pressing the pads of his thumb and forefinger into his eyelids. "Come on, let's get you home. Are you from Ardenglass?"

I shook my head. He was absolutely dreadful at listening. "No, I live at Ellington Estate," I said, still unwilling to tell him where exactly that was. "I told you, my father killed Cotton with a trap, and I found him. He was all bloody and dead, and when I touched him, he brought me here. To these woods, or the Wood, or whatever you called it."

Terek's face tightened, similar to how Father's did when he read something in the paper he didn't like, usually right before he started yelling about money and *idiots in power*. "You're saying you touched a dead rabbit at home, and it brought you into the Wood?" he repeated slowly.

His tone irritated me. "Yes," I snapped, shoving my hair out of my face before planting my hands on my hips like Mrs. Gayle did when she was being stern with me. Why was it that adults thrived on demanding answers from children but never actually believed any of the answers we gave?

"Cotton was going to take me home after he'd washed up and eaten. That's why you should've been nicer and not scared him off."

His flat expression didn't waver. "I'm not a nice man, little rabb—" He straightened, his muscles going taut as his words died, and his long fingers were suddenly clasped tightly around a knife I hadn't even seen him retrieve.

Still as stone, his dark eyes darted back and forth above my head before flaring slightly as they latched onto something behind me.

I attempted to turn to see what had caught his attention, but his free hand gripped my shoulder painfully, preventing me from moving. He yanked me toward him until I nearly bounced off his chest and leaned down into my face.

I tried to pull away, the first touch of true fear sliding into my veins at the look of fury on his face.

"You need to go home, right now, Ace."

I tried again to shrug off his hand, that icy feeling creeping into my chest and wrapping around my heart when his grip only tightened. "Ardenglass is to your left. When I let go of you, I expect you to sprint home as fast as you can. Do not look back or stop for anything."

His gaze flicked above my head again, his jaw clenching, and my eyes and nose began to burn. "I can't," I said, desperately trying not to cry. "I don't know how to go home without Cotton!"

He cursed, yanking me after him and causing me to trip over my feet before shoving me behind the nearest tree. The contact sent a jolt through my dress and up my spine, the wood almost seeming to push against me.

Then he was back in my face, his knife mere inches from my chest as he snarled under his breath. "If you do not fucking leave right now, you will die, little rabbit. Forever. Do you understand?"

I nodded, hiccupping. I understood, but that didn't change the fact that I couldn't do what he was ordering me. Terek could threaten to kill me all he wanted, but I couldn't make Cotton appear out of thin air.

Trying not to antagonize him further, I squeezed my eyes shut, imagining Cotton with his gaping wounds and bloody fur and wishing on every star I'd ever seen that he was with me again. I focused on the feeling of his fur beneath my fingers and let my tears fall as I silently begged him to come back.

Fire lanced through my chest, engulfing me, and I threw my head back, my skull slamming into the trunk just as I screamed. I couldn't open my eyes or so much as move a single finger to escape. All I could think about was the pain and wonder what I'd done to make Terek decide to bury his knife in my heart.

Then, like the snap of someone's fingers, or the flicker of a sconce blowing out, the pain was gone. I collapsed back against the tree, my limbs numb and barely holding my weight for several minutes.

I just stood there, frozen against the bark, and waited. If this was what death felt like, I'd been right, and it wasn't nearly as peaceful as everyone said. Because I could still taste the tang of fear on my tongue and feel the pressure in my core as my bladder begged me to release it.

Daring to open my eyes, I blinked rapidly, unprepared for what felt like the hundredth time that day, for the sight before me. Of Cotton, bloodied and dead at my feet, his body crushed within a trap, surrounded by lush, green trees.

I was...*home?*

My hand flew up to my chest, and I stared down, heart heaving as I rubbed at the uninjured spot Terek's knife had hovered over. The thought of him had me shoving off and spinning in a circle, whipping my head back and forth in search of him. He'd been holding onto me just a second ago.

Had he come with me? Or had he been the one to send me back? Or had I fallen asleep and dreamt the entire thing?

I dropped my hand and glanced down at myself, relief washing through me that I wasn't losing my mind. The bodice of my dress was streaked with dried blood, my hosiery more torn than intact, and my feet were filthy and bare, with no shoes in sight.

"It was real," I whispered, grinning and squatting down toward Cotton's poor form.

Would we go back if I touched him again? I reached out a hand but hesitated. I wanted to test it out and see if I was right, but the memory of the promise of death in Terek's eyes had me immediately pulling my hand back and tucking it into my lap.

As much as I wanted to see if it was possible to magic there again, I had no desire to have the beautiful man continue to scream and threaten me for wandering *the Wood*.

I looked toward the estate and the darkening horizon and winced. Mother and Father were bound to do plenty of that on their own.

TEREK

CHAPTER THREE

I didn't pause to let my mind grasp what the actual fuck I'd just witnessed. Didn't allow myself a chance to second-guess the fact that I'd told the girl to run to Ardenglass, and instead she'd straight up disappeared like a goddamn spirit.

I couldn't, not if I wanted to survive the next few beats. Or, as close to surviving as one could get rotting down here in the bowels of hell. The moment her body disappeared from within my grasp, I was moving, the dagger I'd held to her small form flying from my palm like a shooting star.

A six-legged beast came in fast from my left, an almost frustrated-sounding growl erupting from his maw as she disappeared. Its head swiveled from side to side like it was looking for something, and then it snarled and shoved off the ground, lunging for my neck.

Claws extended from all six paws as hundreds of needlepoint spikes erupted from its fur-covered back, only for its warning snarl to turn into a howl when the razor-sharp tip of my dagger embedded itself into its eye.

I lurched back to avoid the bulk of its momentum as it fell and then spun, ramming my elbow into the hilt of my blade and driving it even deeper into its skull. The Creature's piercing wail as it slammed to the ground grated over my open senses, slicing at my eardrums and immediately making me wish I could kill it a second time over.

But before I could contemplate taking its other eye out of spite, my peripheral caught the movement of the second Creature I'd spotted. Attempting to take advantage of my distraction, it rushed low, its jaw frothing with green, poisonous drool as it extended to rip open my thigh.

Unfortunately for it, I had more than enough experience with how these fuckers liked to hunt, and I'd already anticipated it'd do exactly that the moment the first had drawn my attention. And it might've worked.

If I'd been anyone else.

Darting forward, I jumped, planting my boot against the crumbling bark of a tree, and kicked off, unsheathing the second blade from my side as I flipped over its body. It didn't even have time to register I was gone before I'd landed smoothly behind it, its teeth snapping empty air.

My cloak slipped from my shoulders and crumpled to the ground, the clasp giving out from the sudden force of my action. I glared at the Creature, fucking irritated. There were very few garments that could withstand the regular use of my abilities, but goddamn it, I'd just bought that one. Avoiding the next snap of its teeth, I released my second dagger, answering the Creature's snarl with one of my own as it twisted out of the way with a speed that nearly matched mine.

Crimson, I fucking hated the Wood.

It tilted its head, its lizard-like snout almost appearing to laugh at me as my blade sank into the bark behind it rather than through its hideous face. But I only smirked in answer, dropping my gaze to the third blade I'd already whipped from my boot.

The one now buried deep in the center of its throat.

The Creatures of the Wood were the only beings within this world that came close to matching what the Underland had cursed me with, but while many were fast, I was always faster.

The demented lizard blinked, its glassy, yellow eyes slow to take in the sudden death it hadn't been expecting. Blood gurgled past its teeth, and then it fell, crashing next to the first. The thud of its body echoed around me, warning off any others that might've been watching from just outside my senses, considering the same ill-conceived choice.

The entire ordeal lasted mere minutes, but I didn't move a muscle even after they'd both fallen. Not until several more weighted breaths had gone by while their own chests ceased to utter a single heartbeat.

The Creatures of the Wood had always been intelligent. Anyone who thought otherwise was a goddamn fool. And with them now also getting bolder in the last year, I didn't dare risk falling prey to the possible ruse of one playing dead.

The sole fact that they'd challenged me, especially in the presence of another, child though she'd been, filled me with a dark sense of foreboding. The queen would set the entirety of the Wood on fire in retribution if she so much as even thought they were fighting back again.

And as someone with a memory of the first war, that was a mess I had no desire to clean up.

When I was certain neither beast was of this world, I cracked my neck and sauntered toward them, walking across my now ruined cloak to retrieve the dagger that'd landed in the tree. Tucking it back into its sheath, I crouched at the needled Creature, its remaining red eye unseeing yet somehow glaring reproachfully at me.

I wrapped my hand around the dark leathered hilt protruding from its other and yanked, barely registering the squelching sound it made as it popped free.

Black blood coated the metal, the scent pungent and impossible to block out. I grimaced, using its fur to wipe the residual gore from my weapon before I moved to the other body, kicking it between the horns to knock its head back and reveal the fatal blade in its throat.

After I'd cleaned that one as well, I carefully slipped it back into my boot and stepped over the putrid corpses, ready to make haste out of this miserable place.

The smell of their spilled blood, sharp and overwhelming to my own nose, would quickly draw the attention of the larger, more dangerous Creatures. They may hunt in packs, but everything needed to eat, and I had no intention of still being within the borders of the Wood when it happened.

Every person—well, those with an old enough memory—knew there were no two Creatures alike, both in appearance and abilities. Not the ones residing deep within these neglected trees, at least. And it was those unpredictable differences that made them so goddamn lethal.

This far in, it was pure fucking luck that the two stupid enough to attack me hadn't possessed the ability to steal my sight or boil the blood in my veins until my skin melted.

On any other day, I'd have appreciated the challenge such a skirmish could bring to my otherwise worthless existence. Would've craved and relished the change, *any* change, to this cursed eternity I was forced to live day in and day out.

Fighting a Creature hungry enough to defy the queen's order was the only excitement I saw, and it was the only way to keep my mind and body busy. Well…that and picking fights at Tweeds after a few rounds of Duma's ale. But until recently, instances like today had been rare; occurring maybe a few times a year at most.

Once bold and impetuous during the first months of their uprising, the Creatures of the Wood had eventually tired of their slaughter. They'd surrendered, learning to stay deep within their borders, and thus turning my assignment into a mindless, tedious waste of time over the decades.

But as much as I usually relished a good hunt and a bloody kill, the act held no such interest for me today. There'd been no rush, no thrill. My heart hadn't so much as increased a single beat. Not when my mind had been too busy reeling from what had occurred seconds prior to their arrival.

I frowned, running a hand through my hair and staring at the empty space behind the tree I'd last seen that random girl.

Ace.

She couldn't have been more than nine or ten, and she'd come so close to her end without even knowing it. Traipsing through the fucking Wood with a goddamn pet rabbit like it was a walk in the park. Like she hadn't been seconds away from watching her pet be eaten while she was slowly disemboweled.

If she'd been found by anyone other than myself when these pieces of shit appeared, the Creatures would've found a far more lucky end. I shook my head. Ace's time in the Underland would've been as good as done, just like every other unlucky, dead fool who found themselves within these trees.

The only difference between her and them was that, although the girl had been an absolute fucking fool, she hadn't been a *dead* one.

Spearing my gaze around me, I sent my hearing further and double-checked the area. When I heard nothing warranting concern, I tucked my hands into my pockets and minimized all my senses to as close to normal as I could get.

I glared down at my soiled cloak, tempted to abandon it since I had no intention of ever wearing it again with their blood forever embedded into its fibers. However, in the end, I snatched it up and crumpled it in my fist. I may not wear it, but that didn't mean I couldn't sell it for some much-needed coin.

Beginning the trek back toward the border, my mind immediately went back to Ace, the image of her disappearing right in front of me playing on repeat. I couldn't wash it from my mind, nor the feeling of my fingers clutching nothing but air where they'd just been wrapped around her bony shoulders.

The girl had been a goddamn Upsider—a living, breathing, completely unaware Upsider. I had no proof, but I'd bet the future of my soul on it.

Never, in all the years I'd been chained to the Underland, had I come across a living person before. Not here in a land where the dead both ruled and served. Even now, my mind was wrapping itself around the memory of her, attempting to convince itself I'd imagined the entire ordeal.

I might've allowed myself to believe it, blaming it on my inability to sleep most nights, had it not been for the child-sized footprints in the dirt.

For decades, I'd wandered the edge of the Wood, monitoring the tree line between it and the precious city of Ardenglass. Not because I actually worried about the Creatures within truly fighting back again, but because the queen did. And serving her bloody fucking majesty was my sole purpose in this misery of a second life.

And just like every other day of that enraging fact, today had been no different. I'd woken up cold and alone, scarfed down a dry, tasteless breakfast, and bathed just long enough to loosen my muscles and fist out a quick release. Then I'd set out on my rounds, fantasizing about a true death that would never come.

Same shit. New decade.

But unlike every other day, for some inane reason I couldn't explain, with every step I'd taken along the border, my body had itched and screamed at me to venture into the trees. I'd fought it at first, thinking it was just my senses telling me there were Creatures closer than normal.

But even after I'd opened my hearing and confirmed there was nothing large that I could sense within miles of the tree line, that fucking urge refused to abate.

The harder I'd resisted, the stronger it'd seemed to ignite across my body until every hair had risen to attention, demanding I submit. And although my logic protested the idea, fully aware only threats lingered in the dark, my body hadn't listened, all but forcing me deeper into the Wood against my will.

Soon after, I'd heard her. Or rather, her quiet steps.

Assuming it was a smaller Creature attempting to venture past the allowed border, I'd pulled a dagger and prepared myself to slash its throat open before it had any chance at using some horrific ability to render me boneless, or worse.

I'd just thrown my hood up and slipped farther into the shadows, silencing my breathing and readying for the kill, when she'd come into view. And only years of experience hiding my emotions kept me from stumbling forward in surprise.

She'd been a plain, gangly thing with hazel eyes and stringy, yellow hair knotted beneath a hideous ribbon. Her blue dress had been torn along the hem and her bare feet were filthy, giving her the overall impression of a struggling, lost soul.

I'd almost turned away, content to let the Wood have her if it wished—child or not, she wouldn't be the first it'd taken, nor the last—but there'd been a strange light about her that I'd struggled to walk away from. Something I couldn't quite explain or put my finger on, but that had drawn my undivided attention, regardless.

At first, I'd just wanted to observe her more closely, to see if the light emanating from her was an indicator that she was a Creature trying on a new skin, in an attempt to leave the Wood. It wouldn't be unheard of.

There was already at least one such Creature who could do exactly that, and it was one of the most intelligent and deadly beings I'd ever had the misfortune of meeting.

But Ace had just been a human girl. A *living*, human girl. Only now that she was gone, did I realize that the light I'd seen had to have been her unblemished, intact soul shining through.

It wasn't possible. The living didn't come to the Underland. *Couldn't* come here. Yet somehow, she had, and that knowledge had me questioning everything I'd ever known about this place. Had it always been possible, and I'd never known, or was she the first?

She'd claimed the rabbit had brought her when she'd touched its dead body, but I wasn't so sure that's what'd happened. When I'd touched her, it was like my hands went fucking numb, a sense of familiarity flowing through me like a crashing wave.

Crimson hell, I'd touched the girl without even thinking when I'd sensed the beasts coming. I wasn't sure who Ace was, or how she'd come to be here, nor did I know what all she was capable of. And it was that part that set me on edge.

Attempting to shake off the uneasy feeling that line of thinking gave me, I lengthened my strides, keeping my wits about me as I weaved through the last of the trees. But I neither heard nor saw even the smallest of Creatures as I finally approached the edge of the Wood, the lush, green grass on the other side coming into view.

Just a short, easy trip along the well-used road after that, and the white outer wall of Ardenglass would appear on the horizon. The home of thousands of souls, including the Crimson Queen and her White Guard.

The laughing notion of the sharp, cruel walls of Ardenglass ever being a home to someone had my thoughts drifting toward the Upside and the last time I'd felt even a hint of that foreign feeling. A sense of belonging. Of purpose.

And like a house of cards, those treacherous thoughts cascaded down, bringing with them longing and images best left untouched.

Memories of my own time in the Upside flashed behind my eyes. Moments so long ago, they were more like foggy gray images than anything solid or real. A pointed finger and disgusted yelling, a smiling face lined with age, a quiet walk before sudden pain.

I shuddered, clutching the cloak in my hand hard enough to crack my knuckles, and shoved those thoughts as far away as I could. My history in the Upside didn't matter. What mattered was the possibility of this girl—hell, of anyone—being capable of traveling between our worlds as she pleased.

Plenty of people in the Underland had abilities. Nothing like what many Creatures possessed, but still abilities that had never existed for them in the Upside. A so-called *gift* for reasons no one quite knew. Some were helpful, like sensing metal or growing large crops, while others were more decorative and showier.

To my knowledge, I was the only one who possessed more than one, but even that was nothing compared to what Ace could do. If she'd been dead and could simply transport around the Underland, I'd have thought nothing about it. She wouldn't even have been the first. I'd have simply sent her on her way and warned her to stay far from Ardenglass.

But to transport to the Underland while still *alive?* I shook my head again, waving away an insect intent on buzzing around my face. Whatever Ace's secret was, I could only hope the queen never heard a whisper about it. And not just for the young girl's sake.

ADELAIS

CHAPTER FOUR

I knew I was in a heap of trouble the moment I ran out of the woods. The high noon sun, which had been straight up in the sky when I'd made my desperate dash across the grounds, was now hovering noticeably closer to the western horizon.

What I'd hoped would be a quick run through the trees to clear my head and avoid at least part of the horrid party had somehow turned into several hours, thanks to my unintentional trip with Cotton. One hour gone, and Mother still might not have noticed. But several?

There was no way she hadn't by now, and it was ridiculously unfair that I was going to be in so much trouble for it. I might've left the house on purpose, and sure, I hadn't exactly been in any hurry to return once Cotton had magicked us away, but that didn't mean I'd planned to be gone so long.

Even now, I wasn't sure how that much time had passed. I'd been so delighted over my discovery that magic was real—really, truly real—my entire trip had only felt like minutes to me, not hours. I frowned, maybe time worked differently where I'd been.

Not that either of my parents would care, or even believe me.

I glanced over my shoulder as I made my way along the path back up to our estate. That same pull, the one that'd gripped me in its lull and demanded I reach out and touch Cotton, was duller now, but it still lingered, begging me to spin around and go back.

I ignored it this time, biting the insides of my cheeks and trudging along. I was reckless on my best days, but I wasn't *that* reckless.

Distant shouting graced my eardrums just as the heart of the estate came into view. I paid the noise no mind at first, keeping my attention on my bare feet to make sure I didn't slice them on a rogue rock.

Yelling wasn't uncommon around here. My mother, the Mrs. Margarette Ellington, was only a lady in public. In private, she was rarely demure and always vocally angry about something or other.

But when the voice rang out again, my head shot up. It wasn't my mother's voice I could hear but our head housekeeper, Mrs. Gayle. And it was my name her scratchy, hoarse voice was shouting.

Grabbing at the muddy, torn hem of my dress, I ran for the back of the house, praying I could locate her before anyone else saw me. If I found her fast enough and made sure to look as apologetic as possible, maybe the aging, gray-haired woman would sneak me inside and help me into clean clothes before Mother saw me. She'd done it before.

One of the plus sides to the number of cocktails Mother consumed most days was that as long as I was clean, Mrs. Gayle and I stood a chance at convincing her I'd been around the grounds all along. It wouldn't be the first time we'd pulled it off to help me avoid her wrath.

Our home lay in one of the finest parts of the country and had stood there proudly for generations. The estate was grand, encompassing more acres than I was privy to, including the main grounds that surrounded the house and a portion of the woods I loved so much.

The line of trees wasn't incredibly distant by any means, but it was just far enough away that the house disappeared from view by the time I reached it, hiding me from any prying eyes from even the highest windows whenever I snuck off.

The house itself lay right in the center of it all, and although handsome to me, it was said to be a little out of style. At least, according to the comments I'd once overheard from a few of Mother's guests. She'd stepped away to yell at the cook for serving the wrong dish, and the women she'd invited had begun talking under their breath, forgetting I was present.

Something I'd discovered over the years was that if we sat quietly enough, children were easily ignored. It was almost like its own sort of magic, blending us into the background even as we sat in plain sight.

And while that might bother those desperate to be considered grown, I, for one, enjoyed it immensely when adults forgot about my existence and gossiped freely.

It was something they tended to do often in the breathtaking garden located just within the grounds, directly between the house and the path to the woods. Mother's ultimate pride—which I was now beelining to hide behind.

Large enough to fit an entire party during her regular luncheons, the garden was something Mother loved to show off and brag about but was never willing to work on herself—or even sit in, if she had no one to show off for.

But she always made sure to keep up on the latest trends, screaming at the staff at the turn of each season to adjust it to whatever was popular. Even if it meant ripping out hundreds of perfectly healthy flowers.

This season, it was various shades of green. The edge of the garden had been turned into a chaotic, yet somehow still beautiful, maze of ivy-covered trellises. They'd had to be brought in already grown since Mother had refused to see the trellises bare while the ivy matured, and I could still picture how red Father's face had become when he'd discovered the cost.

Every inch of the garden was something to be admired and observed, but never touched. It was a lesson I'd learned the hard way when I'd been little and had wandered in, pretending to be a princess from one of my storybooks and had dared to pick a single red rose.

The memory of how Mother had caught me and forced me to stand within the sharp bushes while she'd walked off and forgotten about me was permanently ingrained in my mind even two years later.

"If you like the roses enough to steal from me, you can stay with them."

She'd had an entire bottle that day, something she did anytime

Father turned his wrath on her instead of me. She'd left me crying for hours, terrified to move, with my legs covered in small red cuts that burned and itched.

Mrs. Gayle had been the one to dry my tears and clean me up before tucking me into bed. It was a lesson fresh in my mind as I crouched and moved awkwardly up to the outer hedge that bordered the garden. I kept my body low and peeked over slowly, careful not to be seen.

By that point, there were more voices calling my name in the distance, but only Mrs. Gayle had any emotion in her voice. The others, hired help who cared for the estate, sounded more bored than anything. It was to be expected, given I ran off to play at least once a week and was never in any real danger.

However, it wasn't Mrs. Gayle's call that caught my attention and held it, but the soft, lilting voice of my mother, just on the other side of the hedge. I pressed my ear to the rough, waxy leaves, trying to catch her words.

"Oh, she'll arrive soon, I'm certain of it. Our Adelais is a…a dreamer, that's all. Her little head is always off in the clouds somewhere."

Another voice, a high-pitched feminine one I didn't recognize, scoffed. "Margarette, you should strongly consider sending that one to Vincent's Finishing School before it's too late. No man wants a wife with an airy disposition. Dean Turner's firm hand will fix that little problem in no time. He's especially good with the girls."

Mother gave a stuttered hiccup that sounded more like the beginning puff of a tea kettle than a laugh. The staff always joked it was her telltale sign that she was set to erupt the moment company was gone.

Mother may not care for me, but she'd never publicly admit to the other high-standing families that there was something off about me. *"Notions like that percolate until they infect people's opinions of our entire family name, Adelais."* If there was anything Mother felt strongly about, it was the way people viewed our family's reputation.

"I have certainly heard positive things about both Vincent's and

Dean Turner," Mother agreed, gently clearing her throat. "Shall I have more tea brought out? Or perhaps we could step into the drawing room upstairs. The view of the trellises is quite lovely from the open windows."

I dropped down to all fours as the severity of my predicament dawned on me. I'd known there were girls inside since Mother had invited them over for a tea party under the guise of helping me make friends, but I hadn't known all their mothers would be in attendance.

I sucked in my cheeks and pinched my arms until tears formed, frustration making me want to scream. I should've known Mother's excuse was a lie. She didn't care about me making friends. She'd only wanted a reason to invite over their mothers to show off the garden and her newly renovated drawing room.

Which meant both the house and the garden were full of people who'd love nothing more than to see me humiliate her.

I looked down at my dress and let out a whine, knowing my hair, which rarely looked nice even on my good days due to the dye Mother used on it, likely looked even worse than the garment did. "Oh God, she's going to kill me," I whispered, pressing the heels of my palms against my eyes.

I needed to find Mrs. Gayle and get out of sight before the women meandered out. Staying low, I rounded the hedge as fast as I could, aiming for the little alcove on the side of the house, crossing my fingers she was nearby.

Sure enough, the short, round woman stood in front of the plain kitchen door, her hands clasped over her stomach and her brow furrowed as she looked out across the grounds in the direction of the woods.

Her wrinkled chin twitched back and forth, something she did subconsciously whenever she was nervous or anxious. I'd never been so happy to see it.

"Mrs. Gayle!" I called out, rushing to her and flinging myself into her arms. They barely opened in time to catch me, and she staggered back with a pained grunt. Her quivering hands tightened around my shoulders a beat later in a quick embrace before she gently pushed me back.

"Young mistress, where have you been?" she asked, keeping her voice low and motioning for me to do the same. Her gaze dropped from my face before I could answer, her warm brown eyes twin pools of horror as she took in my disheveled state.

"Goodness, child, what have you done to yourself? And where on earth are your shoes?" She clicked her tongue at me, still not giving me a chance to answer, and turned toward the door, pressing a hand to my back. "Come now. Hurry. Let's see what we can do with you before—"

"Adelais."

The cold, curt voice shot across the yard, low and sharp as a whip, cutting through the air and severing any chance I had at making it inside unscathed. Mrs. Gayle side-stepped away, her hand dropping from my back like I were a stove flame she'd accidentally stuck it in.

I stiffened, forcing my body to freeze and fighting the knee-jerk instinct to sprint for the door. Anything to avoid speaking to him. But like the good girl he expected me to be, I buried the dangerous temptation deep in my gut, knowing such behavior would only make things worse.

I was brave. I'd survived the burning pain of Cotton's magic and threatened to stab a shadow man in the eye. I could survive this, too. Straightening my shoulders and turning, I tilted my chin up and repeated it in my head, attempting to convince myself I wasn't terrified of the man standing behind me.

I was brave. I was brave. I was brave.

George Ellington strode toward us, his tall form made even more imposing by the navy suit he wore, impeccably tailored to his broad, muscular form. He was a man who prided himself on his physical prowess, and it showed in every long stride his thick legs took to reach me.

His blonde hair was trimmed short, the strands smoothly styled in a straight combover that was as perfect and flat as his hazel eyes. Eyes that were narrowed at me just above his wide nose and thinned lips, barely visible beneath his full, coarse mustache.

The second he came to a stop, his hand shot out, and I flinched, resisting the urge to hide behind Mrs. Gayle's skirts. The last thing I wanted was to get her into trouble, too. Instead, I stood statue-still, biting the insides of my cheeks and fighting back a wince when his fingers overlapped around my wrist and squeezed.

"Thank you for detaining my daughter, Mrs. Gayle," he said, the words low and clipped as he worked to keep his rage from seeping into them with us still standing out in the open for anyone to see.

Mrs. Gayle hesitated, her mouth opening and shutting like a fish, before she dipped her head and stepped out of the way. My heart sank, but I didn't fault her for her dutifulness. We all knew there was nothing she or I could do, not when George Ellington was both her employer and my father.

But as she raised her face, her warm, tender eyes met mine and held as Father tore me away and half-dragged me along the side of the house.

"Must I shackle you to the floor, Adelais?" he growled, punctuating his words with harsh jerks of my wrist. The bones ground together, and I bit my cheeks harder to keep my reaction subdued. I'd be lucky if I didn't have a bracelet of finger-shaped bruises tomorrow.

Stumbling over a loose stone, tears burned in my eyes and I hiccupped, feeling something sharp cut into one of my feet as I tried in vain to keep up with my father's strides.

"Just look at you. And today of all days." His eyes darted around us, and he cursed, a foul word I knew better than to ever repeat. "Your mother went out of her way to plan this party for you, and you thank her by—"

"It wasn't for me," I mumbled, my lips moving before I could think better of it. The last word hadn't even fully passed my lips before I slapped my free hand over my mouth. But the damage had already been done.

Father's grip tightened even more, and he yanked hard, popping my wrist and pulling me in until he was bearing down on me. Spittle flicked up into his mustache.

"William Corbett's son is in attendance today, which you'd know if you ever bothered to use the head on your shoulders. What sort of impression do you think you're going to make covered in filth and with the mussed hair of a common whore?"

I wasn't sure what a whore was, but I knew better than to ask based on the way he'd spat the word at me. Although I had no memory of Mother telling me who would be at the party today, I did recognize the name.

The Corbetts owned a portion of land my father wanted to expand his business onto, on top of being one of the wealthiest families in the region. I'd overheard my father tell my mother on more than one occasion that it was a family he wanted to "bring closer."

Apparently, he'd meant through me.

"I'm sorry, Father," I said in a rush, wanting to ease his anger. "I didn't mean to be gone so long. I only wanted some fresh air, but then there was this rabbit, and—"

"Didn't mean to?" he said, hatred burning through his eyes until the hazel color seemed to leach right out of them. "Did you suddenly lose control of your own two legs?"

"No, sir."

He continued to stare down at me, lip curled like he was truly contemplating if I was worth the effort anymore. His next words only furthered that thought. "One of these days, Adelais, you're going to run away, and I'm not going to allow you back."

I swallowed the lump in my throat, letting his words sink into the pit of my stomach where I shoved all my emotions when he was around. It wasn't the first time I'd wondered if my parents wanted to get rid of me, but it was the first time Father had ever voiced the possibility to my face.

Regardless of what he accused, and as mean as my parents could be, I had no desire to run away forever. Not anymore. I'd tried once, years ago, after the first time Father had taken a cane to me. I'd gone so far as to pack a bag and march through the woods, hoping to find a kind family on the other side. It'd been one of the worst mistakes I'd ever made.

I'd been six and had gotten scared once night fell. I'd been cold and had raced home, missing my parents. The second caning I'd received when I'd walked through the door, on top of the first that'd still been swollen, had ensured I'd never tried again.

"I wasn't running away," I whispered, knowing the words were as useless as my childish hopes had been. He'd never listened to me before, and he certainly wouldn't now. I could only imagine his reaction if I told him the truth.

Sure enough, he only continued to glare at me, his expression unyielding until I dropped my eyes to the ground. Then he scoffed and stepped back, rising to his full height.

"That's what I thought. Rest assured, I'll deal with you later," he said, his warning ringing through my ears and sinking into my skin as the footman opened the front door for us.

As old and outdated as the outside of our home might be, the inside was the true gem. At least, according to my mother. The foyer was a large, circular room with dark wood floors and vibrant, eccentric rugs. The columns lining the room were thick and white, extending to the vaulted ceiling and almost seeming to pop in contrast to the dark floor and paint.

Right in the center of it all was a wide staircase with a deep maroon runner leading up to dozens of rooms. Apart from mine and my parents', most went unused. The house had been built generations ago, meant to hold a large family with numerous children and visiting relatives. Yet, besides the expected social parties, it was only ever the three of us here.

And it was that exact grand staircase that my father stopped at, finally releasing my throbbing wrist to straighten his suit jacket and cuffs. "Go upstairs and clean up. I'll send Mrs. Gayle to help you dress. Be quick about it, because so help me God, Adelais, there will be hell to pay if you cost us a match with Corbett's son."

I nodded, my eyes burning so badly, I was afraid they'd melt right down my face in place of my tears. Not from the idea of costing myself a match—I couldn't have cared less about marriage—but from disappointing my parents, yet again.

I knew a betrothal would come eventually, and that when it did, it would be because Mother and Father had organized it, but that was all the mind I'd ever paid to it. I'd choose running through the woods or sitting at my window drawing fantastical pictures than ever think of marriage. Which only added to all the reasons I made my parents unhappy.

And as I ascended the stairs with my father's eyes on my back, I couldn't help but wonder if I weren't so good at being everything they *didn't* want, if maybe, just maybe, they'd love me a little bit more.

ADELAIS

CHAPTER FIVE

My punishment for disrespecting the guests by avoiding Mother's party was that I'd been forced to sit through the rest of it with Mother's angry eyes on me from across the room, knowing where I'd be taken the moment everyone left.

Knowing that after Father was done parading me in front of Mr. Corbett and his son—who didn't seem to want to be there anymore than I did—his smile would fall away, and he'd follow me to his study, his heavy steps behind me a countdown to what was coming.

The fear had made me unable to enjoy anything, and although I hadn't minded being unable to taste Mother's horrific tea, it would've been nice to have at least enjoyed the sweets. Especially given the awkward silence I'd endured sitting across from Mr. Corbett's son for hours.

I hadn't known what to say, and I'd been so out of it, I couldn't even remember the boy's name. I only knew that he was four years older than me and appeared permanently bored.

Father had brought me to his study after the party, just as I knew he would, and promptly sent me to my room after, advising Mrs. Gayle to lock it behind me. In his eyes, it was another punishment. In mine, it was my only haven outside the woods.

For over an hour, I just laid across my bed in only my chemise, listening to the sounds of the staff begin to settle down as I tried to think of anything other than the throbbing pain of my back. I'd deserved every bit of it, as much as it'd hurt. I'd known better than to be gone so long, knew better than to embarrass my parents on a day company was around.

But even now, aware of all of that, I struggled to care.

I cared about disappointing them, of course, but I just couldn't bring myself to care what the other girls, or Corbett's sour-faced son, thought of me. They didn't like me, but I didn't like them all that much either. It was nearly impossible to when I'd been taught my entire life to distrust every single one of them. We all had.

Even the girls who acted like the best of friends at every gathering and spent all their time together were more than happy to stab each other in the back if it'd move them up the social ladder and impress their mothers. I couldn't imagine how much worse they'd be when we were older.

I didn't want some rude girl who only smiled to my face to be my friend. I wanted a *real* friend, someone who liked me for me.

Hissing at the burn of the fabric sliding across my skin, but thankful for the freedom my room offered me to express it, I slid forward until I could see my ruined dress piled on the floor. Mrs. Gayle had tried to carry it out of my room, clucking her tongue at the stains and tears, but I'd practically tackled her, unable to fully bite back my scream of pain as I did.

I'd scared the life out of her, but I hadn't wanted to risk her throwing out the only evidence I had that today had been real. That the magical woods—*the Wood*—had been real. The one with the thin, spidery trees, the fog-blanketed sky, and the strange man who lurked within its shadows.

Alone in my room, darkness growing as night cloaked over the grounds, I stared down at Cotton's bloodstains, finding myself missing him a little.

I waited for the trickle of fear to slide through me at what had happened to me today. Apprehension about a dead rabbit coming back to life, confusion about being somewhere I'd never been, terror over finding a man standing behind me. Something. But I felt only a curious excitement.

Because even with an undead Cotton and Terek's sharp knife, neither had caused me harm. Sure, Terek had yelled at me, and I'd definitely thought he'd stabbed me when the pain of transporting had happened, but the fact was, he *hadn't*. It wasn't until I'd come home to my father that the pain had come.

Where home often felt like a prison, the Wood Cotton had taken me to had felt freeing in a way I'd never experienced before. Like I was so far from my parents' reach and expectations that they no longer existed anymore. Like I was safe.

Careful to keep my back straight, I sighed and continued sliding forward until I slunk onto the floor, trying to move as silently as possible. My parents would've retired by now, Mother to her room and Father to his study, both of which were far from my room. Still, I had no desire to risk their wrath by being caught awake just in case they'd assigned someone to listen for me sneaking about.

Once I was flat on the wood planks of my bedroom floor, I stretched my arm under my bed, groping blindly until my fingertips located the crooked edge of the loose board. Wincing with the movement, I pried it up and set it to the side before reaching in to remove my two most treasured items in the entire world.

I'd discovered the loose board last year when I'd been attempting to slip under my bed to hide, and it'd been the perfect spot to keep the papers and charcoal I used daily. Mrs. Gayle had gifted them to me in secret after I'd cried for hours when Mother had forbidden me from drawing.

She'd shown an interest at first when she'd stumbled upon my sketches and realized I had a "natural talent" for it. It was the first time she'd ever seemed pleased with me. When she'd realized that maybe her useless daughter actually possessed a skill worth something.

Mother had purchased me everything I could possibly need to draw portraits of her guests in the garden and showcase my skill at her events. Until, of course, the day she'd flipped through my pages and had seen what I'd been drawing.

The made-up creatures of my imagination rather than a kitten sleeping. Blood raining from the sky rather than a group of ladies smiling. Mother's garden with every flower dead.

She'd had the staff take it all away that same day and had immediately begun dyeing my hair a yellow color to match her natural blonde, claiming the black in my hair was a sign of the devil. As if removing it would make me and my drawings more like her.

"You have no one to blame but yourself. You're a poison, Adelais. You ruin everything you touch."

She hadn't stayed to see me cry, to watch me curl up and shed all the tears I'd never given her before. But Mrs. Gayle had. She'd returned a few days later to slip me a stack of battered pages and chunks of charcoal on the promise that I be careful to never get caught.

Luckily for me, my parents never ventured into my room anymore, and even if they did, they'd certainly never do something as horrific as crawl beneath my bed.

Carefully climbing to my feet, I snatched a pillow from my bed and walked stiffly over to my window, propping it up to support my tender back. Then I tucked my legs up close to my chest and rested my stack of pages against them, charcoal pressed between my fingertips and at the ready.

I looked out over the property, toward the hill hiding the line of trees, everything silver and black under a full moon. But it was the other trees I pictured in my mind's eye. Their coiling roots and reaching branches seemed so unlike the woods of my home, and I wanted to get them out of my head and onto the page while I could still remember.

Yet, when I put my charcoal to the fresh white sheet, drawing sharp lines and dragging my thumb over spots to get the shading just right, it was Terek I began to sketch. His angry eyes and harsh features, the clench of his jaw and the glint of the knife in his palm.

I drew the angles of his face in a few ragged strokes, my hands seeming to remember the small details better than I could picture my own father's. My fingers moved faster and faster, sketching out his straight nose and furrowed brow, his unruly hair and his narrowed gaze.

When I'd finished his portrait, I kept going, moving on to Cotton and then finally the trees. I sketched by moonlight and the barest flicker from my bedside lantern until fatigue inevitably pulled at me, and my vision began to blur.

The welts on my back were still tender but had gone mostly numb for the time being. Thankful for the reprieve, as small as it was, I stood and rolled up the pages, shuffling back to my bed and dropping to the floor to store them.

Father might actually murder me if he ever caught sight of the drawing of Terek and learned that I'd been with a grown man without a chaperone. But secured beneath my floorboards, along with my charcoal and memories, Terek and the Wood could stay my little secret.

Curling myself around my pillow, I left my covers off, so as not to cause more friction against my skin than necessary, and closed my eyes, praying that come tomorrow, I'd remember whatever magic had occurred today.

And that somehow, I'd be able to find Cotton and go there again.

8—⚷

MY BEATING SHOULD'VE made me penitent. Every throb of the harsh welts along my back should've encouraged me to stick to my lessons and strive to be the well-behaved girl my parents expected me to be. And I tried. I really did.

I sat through my entire piano lesson without fidgeting or doodling, endured my tutor's harsh tone without making a single face behind his back, and successfully stayed awake even though my tender skin had made it nearly impossible to sleep the night before.

Granted, it was probably that same pain that was helping to keep me awake all day as well. Even now, every time I shifted, pain sliced across my back in hot, angry waves. The swelling had gone down sometime during the night, but the still-pink skin was no less sensitive.

But even with all my good intentions, by the time I'd made it through French and had my embroidery project shoved into my hands—a hideous thing resembling more of a melting heart than a flower—my resolve to be a perfect lady for my parents had all but disintegrated.

My right knee bounced as I watched my tutor, waiting for him to turn his attention to the young housekeeper eyeing him and wiping the already sparkling clean windows. Something that occurred every time she worked during my lessons with Mr. Jenkins.

My knee bounced faster and faster, and the moment he turned to lean over the woman, I dropped my project and ducked out of the room. Since he had a whole lot more interest in her mouth than he did in my worthless sewing skills, it'd be minutes before he bothered to check on me and notice I was missing.

Sprinting down the stairs, I slipped through one of the servants' halls and made my way to the kitchens, aiming for the back door out of the house. The one I'd tried and failed to sneak into the previous day. My hand had already wrapped around the doorknob when Mrs. Gayle rounded the corner and spotted me.

"Adelais!" she called, her voice hitching on the last syllable. My fingers tightened as I continued to fling the door open. I had no desire to ignore her, but I also had no desire to face her either.

I hated to be rude, but if I stopped to talk to her, she'd only fret until she guilted me into going back upstairs to my lesson. As if embroidery was a necessary skill one needed to survive. I rolled my eyes, the idea utter rubbish.

So instead, I shouted an apology behind me and dashed out, letting the door slam shut behind me. I didn't stop, pumping my legs as fast as my back would allow until I'd safely made it across the grounds and over the hill to the canopy of trees.

The ties of my dress made me feel like my lungs were being squeezed in half, but the fresh air rushed across my cheeks and rustled my short, unbound hair, waking me more than anything else had all day.

I inhaled as much as the confining clothing allowed and smiled up at the sky, reveling in the perfume of the wildflowers mixed with the bitter undertone of damp leaves and dirt. This was my happy place.

Resting my shoulder against the closest trunk, I watched the leaves along the branches sway above me and waited until my chest slowed its rapid movements.

I shifted this way and that, feeling my dress stick to my back and crossed my fingers, praying it was only sweat and that Father hadn't broken my skin this time. I hadn't had a mirror in my room to see, but since it was only minor discomfort rather than blistering pain, I was semi-confident it was the first.

I hoped. The damage may have been courtesy of my father, but Mother would blame me all the same if I ruined another dress.

Glancing back to make sure Mrs. Gayle hadn't tried to follow me, I added an extra prayer that my tutor would be too embarrassed about losing me again to report me to my parents, and I walked deeper into the cover of the trees.

I moved slowly, carefully watching my feet as I neared the general area where I'd previously found the trap. I'd gotten lucky the first time, but since I didn't actually know where my father placed all his traps, it'd be foolish to assume I'd be lucky a second.

For all I knew, there were several lying in wait to snap my toes off within the underbrush, and if there was anything my parents would never forgive, it'd be causing unfixable harm to myself and ruining my future marriage prospect with No Name Son Corbett.

But after several minutes of looking, I finally found it—or at least, one of them. The lack of a dead body made it hard to tell if it was the same one, since all I could see were the iron teeth glinting up through the brush. Not that it mattered. The rabbit had clearly already been removed by either a predator or my father.

Disappointment gnashed at my stomach, but I pushed it down to join every other disappointment I'd felt in my measly eight years. I'd known finding the rabbit again would be a slim possibility, but I still couldn't completely swallow back my heavy sigh.

I stepped around the tree, squinting my eyes and gazing out around me for any other full traps. I'd already risked punishment to come out here so soon after last time, so I might as well keep looking. I didn't even plan on being gone long. I just wanted more proof that it *had* happened. That both the magical, strange woods and Terek had been real.

To my dismay, I succeeded at nothing other than wasting my time and risking my father's wrath before I'd had to sprint back home, empty-handed and hungry. The good thing about always dining alone was that slipping back in unnoticed during the afternoon meal was unlikely to be an issue.

Mother would be dining with whichever ladies she was trying to impress this week, and Father would either be in his study or traveling somewhere for work.

I didn't bother going back out after that, opting to rest my sore back and finish my embroidery while Mr. Jenkins glared at me, his lips swollen, and a small red bruise now present on his neck. Although I hadn't bled all over my dress, the friction from running had chafed the skin until even the barest brush of fabric stung.

The next day, however, I snuck out again right before breakfast, stopping only to steal a boiled egg from the kitchen before rushing out the door. If I was fast, I could find the proof I was looking for, confirm I wasn't crazy, and be back around the same time as yesterday without anyone being the wiser.

⸻

TWO HOURS AND depleted confidence later, I'd nearly given up when I spotted what I was looking for. An unmoving, fur-covered form lying at the base of a tree.

I sprinted over, my heart doing flips and tingles shooting down my spine as excitement flowed through me, only for it to turn to stone in the pit of my stomach when I got close enough to make out the small, gray squirrel.

My nose crinkled as I stood over it, and I slapped a hand to my face, plugging my nose. Where Cotton's body had been bloodied but intact, this one was absolutely wretched. Its body appeared to have already been discovered and ripped open by something, its insides playing tag with its outsides, while flies swarmed in and out for a taste.

But I didn't move, questions circling in my head in time with the horrid smell. What if it wasn't just Cotton, or even rabbits? What if it was any animal here that could do it? What if it was the woods, themselves, that were magical?

I looked around, as if hoping for some sign from the trees that they were the ones who'd magicked me somewhere, but only the leaves answered, whisking across the ground toward me. Well, here went nothing.

Filling my cheeks with air, I held my breath and squatted, reaching out a hand to brush against the squirrel's tail—the only undamaged part of its body—and braced myself for the scalding pain.

Nothing happened.

I tried again, gripping its paw and then its head, ignoring the feel of something soft and mushy sliding against my fingers. The body was simultaneously stiff and goopy, but it wasn't until something gave way beneath my hand that I yanked it back, gagging and wiping my palm along the grass at my feet.

My crushing failure tasted almost as bad as I imagined this rotting squirrel did. My nose and eyes burned, and I raised my head, hoping another body would suddenly appear.

"I know the Wood was real," I whispered.

I may not have known how I'd gotten there, or where I'd gone, apart from Terek calling it the Wood, but I'd gone *somewhere*. My face heated, and I placed my clean hand over my eyes, sniffing back tears and trying to remember what exactly I'd done the last time.

Maybe it *was* only rabbits that could take me? Or perhaps it was the time of day that was important, or the weather? I arched my head back and glanced at the sky, noting the weather didn't look all that much different than it had before.

Maybe it had something to do with me? What I wore or what I'd eaten for breakfast? I kicked my feet, wanting nothing more than to plop on the ground and have a good cry. The possibilities were endless. It could be anything or everything that affected the magic.

Determined to try once more since I had no idea what else to do, I squeezed my eyes shut and held my breath as I reached out my hand. But again, nothing happened.

Fuming and now reeking of all manner of putrid liquids, I stomped back to the house, my mood black and with no intention of finding Mr. Jenkins, regardless of the consequences. I had no desire to see anyone at all.

Sadly for me, the stern, older woman standing just within the kitchen door didn't care what I wanted. She turned away from the table she'd been leaning over, wiping her hands on her apron and shuffling toward me with a speed I didn't even know she could manage.

"There you are! Where have you been, girl? Mr. Jenkins has already been in looking for you. You're going to get yourself into a heap of trouble if you don't stop sneaking away from him," Mrs. Gayle said, her wrinkled hands dropping to rest on her hips as she watched me trudge in, cranky and disheartened.

I shrugged, earning me a clucking tongue and narrowed glare.

"It's only a matter of time before that man loses interest in his newest infatuation and starts lecturing your mama about you. Then what?" She gestured me farther into the kitchens, waving at someone to fix up a plate for me.

I shrugged again, and she lowered her head, her expression softening as she briefly rested her hand on my spine. "You should care. It'll be hard to find a husband with scars all over your back, Miss Adelais."

I blinked and shot my face up, surprise pushing back a few of my dark clouds. Mrs. Gayle loved me in her own way and always cared for me afterward, but she never brought up my punishments. Ever.

It was like she hoped if she ignored them, she could pretend they didn't happen. Sometimes, I resented her for it, because I'd give anything to be able to do the same, but most days, I just couldn't bring myself to hold it against her. If she dared to speak up, she'd only be let go, and then I'd truly be alone. And maybe she knew that, too.

"I'm unmarriageable anyway," I said, patting her hand when her lips pressed thin. "Mother has said it to both me and Father a hundred times by now."

She always said it in a way to hurt my feelings, but it didn't bother me. My parents were married, and they were both terribly unhappy. Why would I want a life like that when there was an entire unexplored world outside my home?

"Please, Adelais. Just attend your lessons. For me."

I sighed, brushing my hair back out of my face and stepping away to wash up at the large sink. "Fine," I said. "But if I die from boredom and can't even be married off to a hat maker, you'll be to blame."

I didn't keep my promise, but in the end, it hadn't mattered. Because over the next few days, although I'd found several other animals decaying in Father's traps, and even a bloated mouse around the estate, not a single one had taken me anywhere.

Not that week, nor any of the five weeks that followed.

TEREK

CHAPTER SIX

The thick, grotesque body slumped to the side, the sudden motion flicking flecks of blood all over my trousers from its broken jaw. Which was currently hanging loose with my dagger shoved through the roof of its mouth to kiss the inside of its head.

The handful of teeth that'd pierced my forearm pulled at my muscles, and I bared my own, kicking the dead beast harder than necessary. It flew back, and its bulk crashed into a tree a few spans away, sending bark cascading to the ground.

I glared down at it, irritation flaring. It was the twelfth one in five damn weeks that'd come sniffing around the border, far past where it should be. They hadn't been the small ones that were as close to harmless as Creatures of the Wood could get, but huge, deep-dwelling beasts that hadn't been seen this far out in years. *Many* years, at that.

What I'd yet to discover was what was bringing them out of their nest from within the heart of the Wood in the first place.

Though none of the twelve I'd come across had wasted a second before attacking once they'd caught my scent, they hadn't appeared to be on the hunt prior to that. Each one had just seemed to be...searching for something. *What* they were searching for was the question.

My lip curled as I stared down at the black blood steadily dripping from my blade. As much as I enjoyed the thrill of a good fight, which this one had given in spades, I fucking hated the goddamn stench they left on me the remainder of the day. It lingered in my nostrils even after the last trace was scrubbed clean.

This particular Creature had been the size of a bear and covered in rough, leathered skin, so I couldn't even wipe my dagger over fur. I'd either have to use my cloak, or suck it up and hold my breath until I could get to the river to wash it. Neither option was appealing.

Crimson take me, I hated the Wood.

I'd been just on the other side of the trees, patrolling as usual, when I'd heard it. It'd had its snout to the ground, casually lurking as it followed some trail I could neither see nor scent, even with my abilities wide open.

Distracted as it was, I'd expected it to be an easy kill, despite its size. Instead, I'd spent the better part of an hour going head-to-head with the fucker that I'd painfully discovered could harden its skin to solid stone at will. I'd nearly snapped my blade in half when I'd leapt on its back and attempted to remove its head from its body.

The entire ordeal had been strange. Fuck, all of them had. The Creatures with those types of abilities never came out of hiding anymore. Huka made sure of it, refusing to risk losing what little population they had left that possessed such skills.

I'd been patrolling the same route for so long, I'd long since stopped counting the years, yet I could count on two hands the number of Creatures I'd come across that had more than a generic ability of speed or poison.

Up until the last year—specifically the last few weeks—there hadn't been a point to my designated daily servitude since the end of the war. Minus the small fact that I didn't have a choice in the matter. That'd always remained the same.

Once free to roam the Underland at will, it'd been at least fifty years since the queen banished the Creatures to the Wood and built her high, thick walls around Ardenglass. Forty years since we won the war against them.

And while the last few decades had been calm and quiet, those first months following her decree had been a horror the likes of which I'd never known Upside. It'd taken the queen's entire White Guard to keep them back, and even then, the war had been bloody.

Souls were ripped from the Underland at an unprecedented rate, and while some had been fortunate enough to move on to their final resting place unscathed, most hadn't been so lucky. It'd terrified everyone, and utter panic had ensued, leading to mobs, theft, and chaos on top of the mass killings and disappearances the Creatures had still been causing around every corner.

In those months, I'd had hope. It'd been a foolish hope, but one that'd taught me to be quick and brutal. For Liz. For our future. To take whatever shots I had without hesitation, and to teach the Creatures that the border the queen had enacted would not bend or break, no matter how they battered at it.

They may have had more strength and abilities at the time, but we'd had the unending numbers. And while they'd been careful to leave the Wood otherwise whole and uninjured, we'd had no such compunction.

So, after months of bloodshed and the smell of burning wood, they'd eventually surrendered, tucking tail and disappearing deeper than we were willing to traverse. Every year since, my patrol of the Wood had been unnecessary. The guards stationed at Ardenglass's gate were more than enough of a deterrent for any stray Creature reckless enough to wander too close to the queen's precious city.

I was an unneeded middleman. Not that the queen would hear of it. She'd rather her White Guards stand around with nothing better to do than terrify her citizens, than ever see me relieved of my servitude.

Her fear of another war, of *them*, was far too great, and my abilities far too useful for the task. I had no doubt she'd use me to wipe every Creature from the face of the Underland, one by one, if she truly thought she could.

I couldn't fault her for it, much as I loved to fault her for anything and everything else after what'd happened. Not when I'd personally seen what the worst of the Creatures could do when triggered.

Not when I'd seen grown men beg for mercy, eyes fogged over, as they'd been forced to cut out their own hearts. When I'd witnessed a friend being turned inside out less than two spans away from me.

No, I didn't fault the queen for her fear of the Creatures, but I could, *and fucking would*, fault her with every false breath within my lungs for putting the goddamn problem on my shoulders.

Her Majesty claimed I was the only soul for the job—the term being her own cruel sense of humor—but she and I both knew the truth. That although she feared the Wood, she also sought to punish me.

Even so, the truth was that my unique possession of more than one ability had made me the best candidate for the job. Well…at least now that I could control them.

When I'd first arrived in the Underland, soaking wet and gasping for breath, I'd gone into shock, much like a gaping fish tossed up onto solid land. Most souls did when they realized they were dead, but mine had been far worse.

Because unlike the others, I'd barely had a chance to understand the bitter knowledge that I'd fucking died on my way to work before the Underland had slammed into me, shoving up my nostrils and burning my eyes from their sockets.

It'd been the Underland's version of spring, and the trees outside the Wood had been covered in pale blossoms that would've been breathtaking had the sound of their leaves rustling not made me slap my hands over my ears in agony.

The wind, a soft, fluttering breeze, might've been cool against my skin had my ability to smell a campfire's smoke miles away not made me nearly pass out.

The sight, the sound, the fucking smell of everything had overwhelmed me, to the point that I'd immediately puked within minutes of my new life. Or lack thereof, I supposed. I huffed a laugh at the thought.

I'd puked twice more before I'd even taken a step and had fallen unconscious a moment later.

When I'd finally awoke, I'd dragged myself to the nearest water source, only to pass out yet again when I'd dared to drink from a stream where I could taste every fucking thing that'd ever fallen into it.

Thinking back on it, it was honestly pure fucking luck, from a God I didn't believe in, that no Creature had stumbled upon me in my pathetic state.

For weeks, I'd languished under my suddenly heightened senses before I'd slowly begun to teach myself to withstand them. To shut them out until they were livable, and to drown myself in alcohol when I couldn't.

It'd been a painful, miserable process.

I'd only just begun to accept my fate and build myself a new life when *she'd* found me. Liz. The young, beautiful woman with the untamed curls, piercing green eyes, and an endearing blanket of freckles over her slightly pointed nose.

Liz's smile had radiated such warmth she'd immediately reminded me of the sun. The real, radiating sun of the Upside I'd so desperately missed.

She'd been as close to perfection to me as physically possible, and her demeanor, her laughter, her view of everything around her had been the tip of the bucket. Knocking me down a well I'd never wanted to climb out of.

She'd given me a new resolve to not just survive with my abilities, but to understand and master them. To accept and allow them to enhance my new life—*our* new life—rather than hinder it.

With Liz's patience and her humor, her soft touches and encouragement, I'd learned to control every one of my abilities until the barest whisper no longer felt like a shout, the slightest breath no longer an abrasion on my skin.

Not unless I willingly drew upon them and sent them out into the world. To sense danger, listen for game, or feel her lips against mine. Feel her body—

I growled, fisting my hands until I tore bloody crescents into my palms, clearing my mind and calming the wreckage those thoughts brought upon it. I had no business wandering down the path of those painful memories, and certainly not when I was still in the Wood.

Shaking them off, I cracked my neck and peered around me, stiffening when I realized I'd been subconsciously wandering deeper into the trees, rather than out.

"What in the crimson?" I muttered, spinning around and sending my hearing out to make sure I wasn't being led by one of the exact Creatures I'd just been thinking about. Though I heard nothing but a soft patter of steps far away, something in my chest lifted its head, urging me to keep going.

Unsheathing my second dagger, I tilted my head and focused on my surroundings, letting the almost animalistic instinct I had locate that pull. It only took me a second to find it. I narrowed my eyes, determined to keep my wits about me as I followed it.

I had no idea what the hell would be at the end of it, but a warning was clawing at the inside of my ribcage, demanding I seek it out. I wasn't sure if it was my memories playing with my mind or something else, but with all the weird shit going on the last few weeks, I'd be damned if I didn't find out.

I may have hated my abilities when I'd first arrived, but I'd learned the hard way to never ignore that fucking voice.

Because the only time I had, I'd lost everything.

ADELAIS

CHAPTER SEVEN

AGE 9

O ver a month had passed, my birthday along with it, before I stepped foot back in the Wood. At that point, I'd all but given up on ever returning, assuming Cotton had simply been a uniquely magical rabbit I'd never find again.

My crushing disappointment mellowed my mood, but it didn't keep me from going into the woods behind our estate whenever I could. Nor did it keep me from worrying Mrs. Gayle or infuriating Mr. Jenkins, but I'd stopped skipping my lessons.

I tried harder to be the best daughter I could, doing everything in my power, other than waking up the son my father wished me to be, and attempted to make the best of my non-magical existence.

It wasn't until I was walking past Father's shed one afternoon, headed to the trees to draw outside and skirt Mother's line of sight so she wouldn't force me to attend her luncheon, that everything changed.

I hadn't known he was in there. Father was rarely ever home in the middle of the day, and I'd nearly dropped my basket of snacks and supplies when his deep voice had cracked through the silence, snapping my name out like a whip.

"Adelais! Come here."

I glanced left and right, as if there was the smallest possibility that he could be speaking to anyone else, and then leaned into the open doorway, careful to drop my basket out of sight.

"Yes, sir?"

"Why aren't you with Jenkins right now?"

His back was to me with his head bowed, and his white sleeves were rolled up to his elbows as he worked on something over the table before him. Skinning some unlucky animal from the sound of it. I winced. I may have spent weeks searching for dead things, but that didn't mean I liked to see the poor things hurt. Unlike my father.

Hunting and prepping the animals he either caught or shot down were the only hands-on activities he seemed to thoroughly enjoy. When I'd been little and still believed he'd love me one day if I tried hard enough, I'd assumed it was because he enjoyed being the one to prepare food for our family.

Now that I was older and understood the way of the world and the limits to his affections, I knew better. My father simply enjoyed the power that killing gave him to own something else so completely.

"Mr. Jenkins retired due to a headache, sir. He gave me the afternoon off." What I didn't add was that one of the cooks, a handsome young man with a mustache that reminded me of a caterpillar, had *assisted* my tutor to his room. The housekeeper he'd been kissing just weeks prior had watched them go with painfully pinched lips.

My father turned then, just enough to look at me over the wide slab of his shoulder. "And where are you heading now?"

I swallowed, blurting out the first lie I could think of while I toed my basket even farther from the doorway. "I was looking for a shady spot to read, sir. My French could always use the practice."

Whether he believed my lie or not, I couldn't tell, since his stoic face always held that unimpressed air with me. But he nodded and turned back, grabbing something off the table and holding it out to me by its ears.

The *something* being the limp body of a gray, baby rabbit.

"Do me a favor and toss this in the kennels on your way. Idiots brought it in with the others, as if I could do anything with such a worthless thing." He gave it a shake, its little feet shifting back and forth in the air.

"You want...*me* to take that?" I asked.

It wasn't the act that gave me pause—the rabbit likely died from a broken neck since there was no blood that I could see—but the request, itself. My father had never asked me for a favor a day in my life, let alone something so unbefitting of his expectations of me.

His naturally flat expression twisted, morphing into the flare of irritation I was accustomed to. "No, Adelais, I asked my strong, capable son behind you. Yes, you. Take the damn thing and do what I asked."

I flinched, his jab about a son hitting me exactly where he'd intended it to. We both knew there'd never be one standing in my place. Mother hadn't been able to birth another child after me, no matter how much they wished for one, and it was my father's greatest disappointment.

Misunderstanding my reaction, he scoffed and twisted away again, flinging the rabbit in my direction with far more strength than was necessary. "Go on."

I lurched back and threw my arms up on instinct, not wanting something dead touching my face, no matter how much I dreaded angering him. His aim was impeccable, but rather than bounce off me and fall to the ground where I could grab it and scramble out, the rabbit slapped directly into my hands.

The burn was instantaneous. Like a flaming torch thrown on dry kindling, it seared into my palms and up my arms, aiming for my chest and engulfing my soul.

I didn't even have time to scream. One second, I'd been watching the limp rabbit flying at me, and the next, I was standing in the Wood, staring at a very real gray rabbit with a small, twitching nose.

My knees crashed to the ground, and my chest heaved in and out, a ragged cry erupting from my throat. I flipped my hands over, my heart running a race inside my ribs, expecting black burn marks but seeing only my unscathed palms.

I'd forgotten how much it'd hurt the first time, but with every second that passed as I knelt on the ground, the pain diminished, tucking itself into the back of my mind to be overshadowed by my utter elation.

"I did it."

The rabbit seemed to tip its head at me, its ears shifting this way and that, like it took offense to my exclamation. I giggled, mimicking its movements.

"No, I guess it was you who did it, wasn't it?"

But just like Cotton, it didn't answer. It just dropped its nose to the ground and began searching for something more interesting than me. I watched it wander off with a ridiculously large smile on my face. I was here. It was *real.*

I didn't bother following it as it caught the scent of something and took off, knowing I could get home by myself. Sure, I wasn't confident on how I'd done it last time, but I'd figure it out eventually, along with what was required to magic here in the first place.

I knew not all rabbits worked, since I'd touched two dreadful smelling ones over the past few weeks that hadn't. And it seemed their color didn't matter either. It was all rather confusing.

But it was my next thought that had me frozen in place, my stomach dropping to smother a little of my joy. I'd traveled next to Father. Right there in his shed. Cotton's body hadn't left when I'd come the last time, so I doubted this rabbit's had either.

Was my body just laid out across the doorway to his shed while he worked? Would he even notice if it was? I closed my eyes, letting my imagination run wild. Maybe he'd turn and see me on the ground and panic that I was dead. He'd race toward me and scoop me up, realizing how awful he'd been, and how much he loved me and wanted me to live.

Maybe—

"Crimson take me, I should've known it was you."

I squeaked, spinning on my heels and whipping my hand to my chest to keep my heart from leaping clean out of it. First, the ordeal with father, and now this? At this rate, my heart was just going to up and stop before I turned ten.

At first, I saw nothing, and I squinted my eyes, searching the darkness behind me. Then a small glint to my left caught my eye, and my visitor's outline became clearer, his body leaning against a tree a few strides away. The same man as before.

Terek.

The shadows seemed to cling to him, hiding the details of his face, but I didn't need them to know. Even if I hadn't recognized his voice, I'd have recognized the sharp knife spinning in his hand.

"What do you mean?" I asked when he said nothing else. I hadn't done anything loud or crazy to draw his attention. Had I? I frowned. Maybe magicking here was loud to other people? God, I had so much to learn.

Terek spun the knife twice more and then pushed off the tree in one smooth movement, the blade disappearing seamlessly at his waist as he finally stepped into view.

He wore the same dark trousers and tunic as before, and a black, scuffed-up cloak pushed back over his shoulders to reveal not one, but two knives tucked into some kind of belt at his waist.

I took a hesitant step back at the sight, not necessarily scared he'd suddenly use them, but still aware I was alone with a strange man who had a habit of sneaking up on me.

I wasn't sure what it was, but there was something about him that was almost comforting when I knew he should feel dangerous. But it was like, though logic screamed he was, he just didn't seem dangerous toward *me*.

Then again, I'd also trusted my father, once upon a time.

"Tell me something, Ace," he said, my name sounding more like a curse with the way he spit it out. "Why is it that I've only ever been drawn into this godforsaken Wood *twice* in my entire existence, and both times, I've found you here."

He continued forward, his long strides bringing him to me so quickly, I instinctively shifted back, barely able to track each of his movements.

"Where's here?" I asked, daring to take my eyes off him long enough to glance around. I wasn't one-hundred percent positive, but it looked like we were in a different part of the Wood than last time. The trees seemed thinner here, baring more of the overcast sky.

It was hard to tell, but it looked like daytime. It certainly wasn't as dark as it'd been the last time I'd run into Terek.

"I mean, I know this is the Wood," I said, circling my hands out to gesture around us and watching his eyes track them. "But what Wood? Where are we? Is this Wood magical? Or is it just the rabbits that are magical? Wait. Are *you* magical?"

The words poured out of me with no stop, like a waterfall that'd been blocked for almost two months. I'd been wanting to come back and ask him all these things from the moment I accidentally went home last time. I wanted to know if this entire place was magical, or if it was…me. If *I* was the one who was special.

His brow furrowed until he was somehow simultaneously glaring and frowning at me. "Are you saying you risked your life coming here after I specifically told you you'd die, and you don't even know where the hell you are?"

When I only blinked at him, a sheepish blush crawling up my neck, he cursed and ran a hand through his dark hair, mumbling something about stupid children and worthless instincts.

"I'm not stupid," I snapped, the words coming out before I could think better of them. I'd been called many names in my life, but stupid was one I really detested. I wasn't stupid.

He twisted back at an unnatural speed and eyed something behind me, a few loose strands of hair falling across his sharp face. "Maybe not, Ace, but that doesn't mean you won't be dead before you're even given the chance to leave."

In the next blink, he'd pulled a knife from his side and was flinging it at me. I squeezed my eyes shut and dropped to the ground, slapping my hands over my head while my heart shot up into my throat. Oh God, he was trying to kill me!

But instead of feeling my life drain from my body as his blade ripped through my flesh like I expected, I heard a sharp keening, and then the thud of something crashing to the ground behind me.

I shot my head up, twisting back to look at whatever Terek had just thrown his weapon at to see a crumpled, fur-covered body slumped a few yards away. Not abnormally large, but definitely not a small, gray rabbit either.

My eyes widened, and I slowly turned back around to stare up at the man now towering above me, the sliver of blue in his eyes focused on my face. "Never give your back to a Creature of the Wood, little rabbit. It'll be the last thing you ever do. That is the second life debt you owe me, so, unless you're interested in collecting enough for a lifetime of servitude, I suggest you go home."

I frowned at him. Second? Is that what he'd been yelling at me for last time? Because he'd seen a wolf or something? I glanced around us, peering into the distance for a sign of another animal, but there was nothing. Not even the quiet chattering of crickets, much like last time.

My frown deepened. It didn't seem unsafe here. For all he knew, maybe that poor thing had only been running by like Cotton. He'd killed it without even checking! Besides, he had no right to kick me out, he didn't own the entire Wood.

I mean, I supposed it was possible he did, since he clearly knew a lot about it, but still. I wasn't hurting anything, *unlike him*, and it's not like I'd come here on purpose. I just wanted to have a small look around.

There was no way Father hadn't noticed me gone by now, so with the punishment I knew awaited me, I might as well make the most of my trip before I went home.

Plastering the sweetest smile on my face that I could, the one that always made Mrs. Gayle back down on whatever she was cross about, I clasped my hands in front of me. "I think I'm going to stay for a little bit longer, but thank you, sir."

Silence settled between us, so long and uncomfortable that I began to fidget, rocking back and forth onto my heels. Okay…so was I allowed to go exploring now? I really, really wanted to before it got dark, but I also didn't want him to yell in my face again.

Finally, after what felt like an eternity of him analyzing my bones through my skin, his nostrils flared like an angry bull, and he took another step closer to me, tucking his hands into his pockets. The act itself wasn't menacing, but the sudden lack of blue in his eyes was.

"Let me rephrase that. You have no business being here. I don't know how it is you're getting here, but you need to stop. Go home."

"I didn't come here on purpose," I snapped, putting my hands on my hips. "My father threw a dead rabbit at my face."

A slow blink was his only sign that my answer surprised him. Well, he could join the party, I hadn't exactly expected it to happen either.

"Anyway, I only want to look around. I'm not going to cut down a tree or something," I said, showing him my weaponless hands.

"I have better things to do than babysit you while you skip around the fucking Wood."

"You shouldn't curse like that. It's impolite," I said, pursing my lips up like I'd seen my mother do when Father said something exceptionally unpleasant.

"Besides, I don't need a babysitter to walk around for a few minutes. I'm nine, not *five*," I added, rolling my eyes and turning to walk away from him. I had no desire to talk anymore. He was in a terrible mood, and he had no right to tell me what to do.

Before I could move even an inch to the side, Terek growled and shot forward. I squeaked and stumbled back, expecting him to tackle me to the ground, only to gape when the spot where he'd just been standing was empty.

I blinked rapidly, twisting my head side-to-side to see if he'd somehow darted behind a tree. I'd never seen anyone move that fast. Maybe he could disappear and magic somewhere else, too? It would explain how he was always sneaking up on me so well.

There was a slight whoosh of air along the back of my neck, and then something pressed into my lower back, just beside my spine. Something that caused a quick bite of pain to lance through my dress and into my skin, like the sting of a needle.

"What did I just tell you about turning your back?"

ADELAIS

CHAPTER EIGHT

T he low, gravelly voice just over my head made me jump, causing the biting pain at my back to worsen for a split second.

My breath hitched when Terek's woodsy smell hit me, like cedar and rain, and I realized it was the tip of one of his knives I could feel pressing dangerously close to my spine.

He hadn't actually cut me that I could tell, but he was making it very clear he could if I tried anything. Not that I'd have any idea what to try. How did you run away from someone who moved faster than you could blink?

"Are you saying…" I took a deep breath, lowering my voice when it came out squeakier than I hoped. My bridge of confidence that he wouldn't hurt me was starting to wobble over the rushing river a little. "Are you saying you're one of them? The Creatures?"

He drew closer, leaning down until his head rested just over mine, his arm coming around to position the point of his knife at my stomach. "No, little rabbit. I'm far fucking worse. They kill because they're hungry. I kill because *I like it*."

I swallowed, my body beginning to tremble when he stopped it just under my ribs, the tip aimed up at my heart. "Are you going to kill me?"

His arm stiffened, like he was considering doing something just to prove his point, but then he huffed out through his nose and straightened his arm to point his blade at the fallen animal. "No. I have no interest in murdering defenseless children, but a starving Creature has no such morals."

Something on his outstretched arm caught my attention, and I stared at it, my eyes widening in horror when I spotted the multitude of puncture wounds on it. Like something had tried its best to bite his entire arm off. "Terek, you're hurt!"

He pulled the bleeding limb back and stepped away from me, sheathing his knife. His face fell back into that stoic expression he always wore, but I could've sworn he looked the faintest bit embarrassed. Much like my father always did when his hunting partners returned with bigger game than he did.

"It's nothing. I'll heal."

"Because you're magic?" I asked, the words coming out before I could stop them. I knew he was trying to scare me so I'd leave, just like last time, and I'd be lying if I said he hadn't frightened me. But as much as I didn't like how mean he was trying to be, I couldn't help but find him fascinating anyway.

He didn't treat me like a pretty flower that was only worth something as long as I continued to bloom anytime a light was shined on me. That was more than I could say for my parents or Mr. Jenkins. It also helped that I still had a hundred questions, and there was no one else here to ask, but that was neither here nor there.

Terek scoffed and looked away, combing his hair out of his face. "Only simple-minded fools believe in magic. Stay long enough, and you'll learn the hard way that only curses exist here."

I pursed my lips, exasperated. He couldn't stand there and call me a fool for believing in magic when he could move like that and throw knives like shooting stars. And how else could he explain how I was getting to the Wood?

"Then how do you move so fast? Because I've seen my father's hounds run at full speed, and even they don't move as fast as you can. That's a gift, not a curse."

"My abilities are no gift," he seethed. "The Underland speaks to me whether I want it to or not. I had no choice but to learn how to listen."

The Underland? Is that what this world was called? My heart leapt in my chest, excitement burning so hot that for a moment I feared I was somehow magicking myself home.

"Teach me!" I yelled, my voice far louder than I'd meant it as excitement surged in my gut. I lowered it, clasping my hands in front of me. "Teach me how to listen."

He huffed a quiet laugh, rolling his eyes to the sky like he was contemplating every life choice he'd ever made that'd led him to stand there with me. "Like you listened when I told you to leave? Twice?"

"Please," I said, ignoring his jab. "I just want to know more about this place. The…Underland. I'll behave, I promise. I just want to learn how to use magic like you do."

I could use magic back at the estate to come here, so maybe, if Terek taught me how to listen to the other gifts, maybe I could use them there as well. I smiled, picturing my father's face if he tried to punish me, only to fall onto his face when I shot across the room as fast as Terek could.

He cocked a brow, clearly not believing me when I said I'd behave. "It doesn't work like that. There are those who arrive to the Underland and live much like they did Upside, and there are those of us who must learn how to live all over again. Some more so than others. I cannot teach you such a thing, so stop being a petulant child and be thankful you're not yet one of us."

"But I am," I said, the words coming out more like a question. Because although I was, I also wasn't. If the magic of this world was a curse, what did that make me?

"I want to learn more about the ma—the ability or curse or whatever that brings me here. Sometimes it works and sometimes it doesn't. What if I'm walking home and step on a dead bug by accident? Will I find myself here? Because if it *draws* you into the Wood like you claimed, that sounds like a really inconvenient—"

"Crimson take me, I get it. Stop talking." His head tilted, and his eyes went slightly out of focus, like he was listening for something.

When he apparently heard nothing, he looked back at me and frowned. Probably thinking about the last thing I said and very much not wanting that to happen.

He sighed. "What do you mean, it doesn't always work?"

8—ᴎ

TEREK LEANED AGAINST a tree as I talked, one foot tucked up underneath him, and his face contemplative. I sat on the ground with my dress pooled around me, resting against another tree a few feet across from him, and poked at the ground.

To anyone else, we likely looked like an odd pair, but it was the first time in my life that I felt important—not with my family, but with this strange man in the middle of the Wood, with Creatures supposedly prowling about, waiting to eat us. Or, at least me, according to him.

Terek still didn't look all that happy to be there with me, and he definitely appeared on edge with his eyes constantly darting about, but he listened as I explained everything I'd tried over the last five weeks.

The more I spoke, the more questions he began to ask, clarifying my story and checking for plot holes. I told him all of it. The rabbits that had worked, all the animals that hadn't, and the burning pain that scorched my insides when it happened.

"And you have no idea how you went home?" he asked, glancing down with a furrow in his brow.

I shook my head, cheeks turning pink. "The only thing I remember is wishing Cotton hadn't run away and thinking how badly I wanted to get away from you."

He gave me a deadpan look and waved a hand between the two of us. "Yet here you sit, desperate for my attention."

I scrunched my nose up tight. "Desperate for answers, not for you. There's a difference. You're just my only source of information at the moment."

He scoffed and looked away like I was the most annoying person he'd ever met, but I could've sworn his eyes softened ever so slightly.

"So, if this place isn't magical, which I still don't believe by the way, what is it? Is it nothing but trees forever?"

I liked my woods and this one more than most people, and especially more than Terek, but even I would miss a real bed eventually. A grin pulled at my lips at the thought, picturing Terek living in a treehouse somewhere.

"Don't get that ridiculous look on your face. It isn't exciting, and it isn't magical." He paused, as if considering whether he should continue. Luckily for me, he did. "What you're standing in is the Wood, Ace. It's just one small part of a much larger world."

"The Underland," I said, practically salivating with my desire to keep him talking. "So, there's more to it than this? More than trees? People?"

He stared at me for a long moment, his expression one I couldn't quite read. "The Underland is the in-between that hovers between the Upside and true death. A middle ground, if you will. This is where souls go after death when things are still being…decided," he said, tucking the dagger he'd been fiddling with back into what I now knew was called a sheath.

I shot up straight, my mouth falling open. Terek was *dead?* I wasn't sure why, but something squeezed in my middle at that. At the thought that something awful had to have happened to kill him so young. He couldn't have been older than mid-thirties.

"Decided?" I asked when I'd quieted the voice that immediately wanted to ask how he'd died and refocused on what he was saying. "As in, between heaven and hell?"

His face darkened, and his knuckles whitened over the handle of his blade before he tucked his hand back into his trouser pocket. "Hell is not what you think it is, little rabbit."

When I only stared at him, unsure what he meant, he leaned the back of his head against the tree and sighed. "If what you say about the bodies is true, it sounds like only beings whose souls are still residing in the Underland can bring you here."

I sat up straighter, dropping the long-stemmed weeds I'd been forming into a necklace over my lap. "So, any dead body could work? As long as their soul or whatever hasn't decided to move on?" My eyes widened, my thoughts going from one crazy place to another until I felt almost dizzy.

"I wonder if my grandmother's body would've brought me if I'd reached into her casket. She hadn't been dead for very long." Come to think of it, I wondered if she was here right now. It was a strange thought, one that hurt my brain a little.

His head slowly tilted back down to give me an incredulous look. "I would assume so, yes, but unless you plan on murdering a family member and trying it out, there's no way to know for sure."

My nose crinkled at the thought. I had no desire to touch a dead human, related or not. "How long do souls stay here before they move on?" Most importantly, how long did I have when something died before it no longer brought me? A day? Up until they began to rot or were eaten?

Terek's face shuttered in an instant, and he shoved off the tree, his jaw feathering like the wings of a hummingbird and his eyes suddenly black. "Story time is over."

"But I—"

"It wasn't a request, Ace. We're done. I have better things to do than sit here and answer small-minded questions from a spoiled brat who believes herself magical just because her body is desperate for death."

I shot up, my stomach clenching tight and making the contents swirl uncomfortably. "I *am* magical. If it's not the rabbits, that means it's *me*. I'm the special one."

He laughed, the sound dark and wretched and nothing like a laugh should sound like. "Special? Open your eyes. The only thing special about you is the fact that the world hates you so much it's trying to kick you out of it early."

"Stop. That's a horrible thing to say." The tears came fast, burning hot and making my eyes and nose sting like a hundred sneezes hitting me at once. Terek didn't stop. If anything, he only looked angrier at my welling eyes.

"You call it magic—"

"You're wrong!"

"—but I call it stupidity."

"I'm not stupid!"

"In reality, you're even more fucked up than the rest of us, because the Underland didn't even wait until death to curse your soul."

"Stop!"

"Do your parents know the daughter they've given everything to secretly begs for death?"

You're a poison, Adelais.

This hair is the sign of the devil.

You ruin everything you touch.

"I wonder if—"

"Stop!" I slapped my hands over my ears and screamed the word at the top of my lungs, feeling my tears pour over like a broken dam. I curled in on myself, squeezing the sides of my head as hard as I could just as fire exploded in my chest.

The last thing I glimpsed before my knees slammed into the cement floor of an empty shed, was a pair of midnight blue eyes staring down at a glinting blade with enough hatred to set both of our worlds on fire.

ADELAIS

CHAPTER NINE

AGE 11

When I was eleven, Mother and Father held a birthday party for me. It was a 'spare no expense' sort of affair that meant three different, horrifically tight, itchy dresses and a menagerie of ridiculous hats, for which dozens of helpless birds had given up their feathers.

The first warning sign should have been how invested and active Mother was in the planning. She spent an entire afternoon with me, longer than we'd been around each other in months, making me try on all manner of gloves and shoes.

The only time she hadn't been glued to my side, stating her opinion on this or that, was when she was glued to the seamstress's, insisting the periwinkle was not, in fact, the *right* periwinkle.

"That dull shade will wash out her skin and make her look ill. Do you think anyone will want their son marrying a girl with an unimpressive countenance? No, I'd think not."

Prior to that, she'd sat down with me for an hour several times a week for an entire month, forcing me to drink cup after cup of tea while she'd quizzed me on the families that would be in attendance. Who was whose son, who had money, and who to avoid, filling my head with all the things I was, and was not, allowed to talk about in polite company.

"We cannot risk another...*incident* with your unseemly imaginations."

The party wasn't for me at all, of course. Every housekeeper, servant, and cook walking the halls of the estate knew that. It was an opportunity for Margarette and George Ellington to show off the recent changes they'd had made to the property and pretend we were a perfect family that didn't scream and want to strangle each other daily.

Above all, it was an opportunity for them to show *me* off. After my continued disastrous meetings with the young Corbett, they were eager to reclaim my good standing and show that I was not only blooming into a *beautiful flower*, but that I also now possessed all the qualities a future suitor would wish for in a wife.

Basically, that I was a quiet, demure girl who didn't frolic in the woods or spend my free time drawing all manner of unladylike things.

"I'm not ready to be married," I grumbled the first time she'd sat me down, reaching forward to grab a biscuit and hoping it'd disguise the flavor of the tea.

In all honesty, I had no desire to be married, period. My parents might hate me, but they also hated each other, and I'd rather live unmarried forever than ever be like them.

Mother smacked my knuckles with the back of her spoon, making me hiss and yank my hand back. "What does being ready have to do with anything? Besides, no one's sprinting to sign a contract tomorrow," she said, sounding resigned to the fact. "We are planting seeds, Adelais. Vital seeds."

"Can't we just celebrate with Celia Alford's family? She has three brothers," I asked, a trickle of hope bleeding into my words. Celia was the daughter of one of Father's business connections, and although I hadn't actually ever had a real conversation with her, she'd never sneered at me.

I didn't want to marry her brothers either, but at least her family didn't seem completely vile.

Mother snorted, the sound causing her eyes to flare and her hand to flutter over her mouth. Clearing her throat, she folded both hands back into her lap. "The Alfords are barely eligible to be invited, let alone build lifelong ties to."

I frowned. Had she already forgotten that Father hadn't come from a high social standing before he'd made something of himself and married her?

"We're going to land you a match far better than *that*," she added, pursing her lips like even mentioning the Alfords had soured her tea. "Now, should we invite the Bellingfords? Of course, we should. Although, there *is* a rumor that they're secretly drowning in debt." She frowned, or as close to it as she ever allowed her delicate skin to wrinkle.

I stared down at the hand I had wrapped around my teacup, tuning out the rest of her rambling. Every meeting with her since had been the same, and as my birthday drew nearer, my anxiety over the event grew until I thought I'd vomit. If it didn't go perfectly, if I didn't make every single right move, I wasn't sure Mother would ever forgive me.

My anxiety grew to panic attack levels the morning of my eleventh birthday. I was woken at the crack of dawn, shoved into a cold bath, and scrubbed until my skin pinkened and stung. One of the younger maids touched up my hair color and twisted it into a semblance of elegance on the top of my head, while another yanked and pulled on the ties of my dress, drawing a suffocated groan from me.

I tried to sit still, but it was impossible not to fidget as I watched the morning sun rise higher and higher from my window. I could be a proper lady for Mother and Father. I could make them proud for once. I could do it. I drilled the words into my head, even while a louder voice laughed at me.

No, you can't.

"You never know," Miss Irene—the maid breaking my ribs off—said as she spun me around to look into the mirror. "Perhaps you'll make friends today, Miss Adelais."

I couldn't help but roll my eyes, at both her claim and the outfit she'd squeezed me into. The idea of making friends was nice, of having someone who enjoyed the same things and would make me feel a little less lonely. But Mother couldn't have cared less about inviting girls who were nice enough to be my friend unless said friendship would result in a future marriage contract.

Now I stood just within the entryway to our ballroom, dressed in a light shade of blue that made my yellow hair stand out sharply. I was sure Mother had arranged the combination on purpose to make me look like their perfect doll, and I hated it.

The sleeves were puffed up with lace that immediately itched, my scalp stung from all the snagged hairs, and the shiny, black shoes were a size too small, in an effort to make my feet appear daintier.

But I bit my tongue like a good girl and ignored all of it, just as a lady should. I smiled and kept my spine straight, even after it began to ache, with my hands clasped just so as I welcomed all of Mother's guests. Again and again, until my cheeks hurt, and my feet screamed at me.

It's lovely to see you.

Thank you so much for joining us.

You look splendid in that hue of salmon, Miss Addy.

Each child gave the perfunctory curtsy or bow required of them and then promptly disappeared into the ballroom to meet up with the other children they actually cared to see.

By the time I was excused and able to join my own party, each corner of the room was filled with distinct circles of bodies, both the children and the adults. Everyone had quickly congregated with others within their allowed social groups and were now having all manner of hushed conversations whispered behind gloved hands.

Prodded by Mother, along with a fierce look that brokered no room for argument, I approached one circle of children after the other, attempting to draw myself into their conversations, though I had no idea what most were talking about.

But no matter how I smiled, or what I said, I was met with only silence and perplexed looks. Either because they'd already forgotten who I was, since I'd never joined in before, or because they did know, and they very much didn't want me to.

Not a single one made room for me within their circle or at their table, and I was left to wander back and forth across the room like an unwanted puppy, eavesdropping on whatever pieces of gossip I could hear, all while Mother's eyes bore into the back of my head.

"I thought Miss Lewis's party was so droll, but this one truly makes hers seem..."

"...and Jim just returned from holiday. He said they spice their tea there, can you imagine..."

"...abominable drive. I cannot fathom why anyone would live way out here on these ill-equipped roads."

I bit my lip and stood off to the side of the largest group, surprised Mother's gaze hadn't caught my dress on fire yet and partly wishing it would if only to get me out of this room. I highly doubted it'd hurt any more than the fire I endured to go to the Underland anyway.

Father, at least, was deep in discussion about recent weather on the harbors and the effect it'd been having on cargo ships. He hadn't spared me a second glance since he'd entered, and he probably wouldn't until the event was over and Mother had informed him of my failure.

The thought of his face when she did made my spine tighten and nausea surge in my stomach. I just needed to try harder, smile at a few important people, and appear like I was included—even if I wasn't. I could do this.

With renewed vigor, I walked up to a circle of girls from the wealthiest families in attendance, including Beatrice Bellingford, whom Mother had made sure was coming, and who, at thirteen, was rumored to already be promised to a man twice her age.

The thought made me shudder, thankful the young Corbett—whom I hadn't spotted yet—was only a few years older than me.

Beatrice stood in the center, wearing a rose-pink dress with glimmering sheer sleeves and a perfectly styled updo, several stiff, blonde curls hanging about her face. Her cheeks had a little too much rouge, and she was merrily telling a story when I approached, every head around her leaning in to listen intently.

"So, I picked up the handkerchief and handed it to him, and he *winked* at me." She beamed, touching her fingertips to her lips while the crowd giggled.

I fought a frown, confused why everyone seemed so excited about that. I assumed she was likely talking about her promised, but it didn't seem like such an exciting story to me. Winking was just blinking one eye without the other. What was so special about that?

But I knew Mother was still watching, so I stepped closer, plastering a forced smile on my face. "How lovely! Did he say anything to you?"

"My poor heart. I thought I'd faint right there," Beatrice continued, her gray eyes skipping right over me like I hadn't spoken at all.

Tingles, and not the good kind, bubbled up my spine, but I tried again, raising my voice to be heard over the tittering of the other girls. "That sounds very exciting."

Rather than respond to my remark, she pointedly glanced at the two girls directly in front of me, who immediately shifted closer together until their shoulders brushed one another. She smirked and tossed her head, her blonde curls swaying back and forth.

"Is he terribly handsome?" a girl to my right asked, patting her hand over the lavender, silk scarf tied over her braids, her brown eyes sparking with barely concealed anticipation. Like she was living vicariously through Beatrice's story, hoping and praying her turn was next.

"Deplorably so, which was probably why my mouth stopped working the moment his eyes landed on me," Beatrice said with a giggle.

She leaned forward conspiratorially, and the others followed suit. "Luckily, Father noticed and immediately introduced himself. And...well, we all know how that ended for me," she added, smiling wide and waving her left hand in front of her, like she was imagining a ring upon the bare finger.

Realizing the girls in front of me weren't going to make space, I shuffled my way around and tried to squeeze in between two others, but they did the same, pressing their shoulders together and shutting me out. When a third pair also did it, my cheeks grew hot, belatedly understanding they were doing it on purpose.

Beatrice's smile grew. "That's why Father didn't bother coming today. He's quite good at telling the difference between those of good quality and those who are playing at it." She twisted, slanting her gray eyes at my parents across the room. More titters.

The heat in my cheeks burned down my neck and into my chest as my embarrassment swiftly turned to anger. My father may not have been born into as much money as the Bellingfords, but he wasn't playing at it. He'd earned his title through hard work, which was more than I could say about most of the families here.

Squaring my shoulders, I shoved between two bodies, ignoring their gasps of surprise and snapped, "Are you saying my family's not good enough?"

That got a few of the girls to finally glance at me.

Beatrice, however, continued to act as though I'd said nothing. She looked down at her hands, picking at an invisible string on the hem of her sleeve. "Does anyone else hear that wretched buzzing? It's incredibly annoying, and I wouldn't be surprised if it was some kind of ghastly insect. I'm sure there are copious amounts of them out here."

She looked down to their discarded teacups on the table beside them, her perfect, button nose crinkling. "Honestly, it's probably the tea that draws them in. Quite dreadful. It just goes to show, you can buy your way into a party, but you can't buy good taste."

She flicked her gaze away from the table, and her eyes locked with mine over the line of heads between us. Her lips quirked, and when the girls began laughing again, the heat on my skin bled deeper, driving straight for my heart and throwing my mouth open.

"Considering your hand is promised because a man twice your age agreed to buy *you*, I'd have to say I agree."

Almost as if in slow motion, every single girl turned to face me, looking like porcelain dolls with their wide eyes, frilly dresses, and painted lips. I should've noticed the cues and apologized, or simply spun away and run out of the room, but I was angry beyond the point of reason.

Angry that I'd had to come here in a scratchy dress and shoes that blistered my feet, angry that my parents hated me, angry that the other families hated *them*, and angry that I was expected to smile and be grateful through it all.

Stepping through the throng, the girls quick to let me in this time, I leaned into Beatrice's appalled face and let all that anger pour from my throat, using something I'd overheard Mother say and striking her in the face with every vile word.

"Everyone here knows your father sold you off because he's up to his neck in debt, so stop twirling your dress and pretending like you're better than us when your only redeeming quality is that you're a finely dressed, prized cow."

A muffled snort echoed out behind me in the suddenly heavy silence, and I balked, realizing with growing horror just how loud my voice had been.

Beatrice didn't move a muscle. She just stared around the room with her hands fisting her dress and her throat bobbing as her gray eyes filled with glinting silver.

I immediately stepped back, a stuttering apology materializing on the tip of my tongue, but it was too late. Mrs. Bellingford was already hurrying across the room, looking an unhealthy shade of white, while my mother followed directly after, every inch of her ready to commit murder.

It didn't take magic to know there was no way I'd be able to dig myself out of the trench I'd just created, but it was the pair of hard, hazel eyes of my father from across the room that had me bending forward and vomiting on Beatrice Bellingford's shoes.

WHEN THE LAST guest stepped out of the house, and the lingering whispers of gossip flittered past the slamming door, Mother's smile fell like a theater curtain. It hadn't taken long, most guests eager to make haste as soon as the delicious drama settled, and Beatrice's mother had rushed her out without so much as a quick wipe for her ruined shoes.

I'd been dismissed to clean up, and then promptly forced to enter again with every set of eyes pinned on me. Mother stuck to my side like a thorned burr, ordering me to *keep my foul mouth closed* and apologizing again and again on my behalf, while Father had disappeared entirely.

Which was far more terrifying than if he'd stayed and glared at me over his cup.

Now that it was all over, Mother just stared at the closed door, incapable of even looking at me as she spoke. Probably because she was too busy convincing herself not to kick me out right along with the guests. "You're a poison, Adelais. You know that, right?"

I flinched, her words finding their mark and burrowing in deep. "Beatrice started it," I tried, my voice pleading as I was finally given the chance to tell my side of the story. Surely, Mother would understand and explain it to Father. "She was so cruel, and she was saying horrible things about you and Father. I was only trying to stand up for you."

"Just stop," she said, disgust and disappointment warring for dominance on her wine-flushed face. "We do not stand up for ourselves or anyone else, Adelais. We are women. We smile, we bear it, and we ignore how it cuts."

ADELAIS

CHAPTER TEN

I t was dark by the time I'd stumbled from Father's study, but rather than go to bed and sleep it off as I usually would, I found myself tucked against a tree in the Wood, crying into my hands.

Once I'd figured out that my body completely disappeared from the real world when I traveled—or the Upside, as Terek called it—and that any freshly dead animal could take me, it'd become a lot easier to come and go to the Underland as I pleased.

I still wandered into the woods behind the house sometimes when I needed a little extra time to calm my churning thoughts, but nights like tonight, when it was dark out and my back was screaming, I just searched the mouse traps the staff hid around the estate. They were rarely all empty.

Thankfully, tonight had been one of the times I'd found an unfortunate little guy by the second trap. I didn't hesitate to crouch down and reach out, barely feeling the burning pain through the pulsing inferno Father's cane had already left on my skin. I'd just bit my tongue through it and dropped to the ground right where I'd appeared, pulling my knees up tight.

And that's where I'd stayed, unmoving, until a hand wrapped over the top of my shoulder. I jolted back, fresh tears slipping down as my skin pulled taut, only for a scream to follow them when I saw who stood behind me. Or, rather, *what* stood behind me.

It hadn't been a hand I'd felt, but a scaled face leaning down over me, inspecting the pathetic, wailing intruder curled up on the ground like a dying animal.

I tensed, remembering everything Terek had told me about the Creatures of the Wood, and waited for my inevitable death as it lunged for me. But to my surprise, it made no move to rip out my throat, nor did it seem angry, or all that hungry. The odd-looking animal hadn't even growled when I'd darted away like a spooked deer. It only tipped its head as if to ask, *"And what are you supposed to be?"*

My muscles slowly loosened, and I settled back onto the ground, wincing. It reminded me of a lizard almost. Well…if a lizard was the size of a house cat and had a baby with a bat, that is. It was the strangest, most fascinating thing I'd ever seen. It had four identical legs ending in sharp claws, but it only stood on the back two, its front ones pulled into its body like miniature arms.

Large, black eyes blinked up at me, and its head tilted to the other side, like it was trying to decide if I was a threat. It took a small step forward, its dark, webbed wings tucking in tight over its back, the iridescent sheen of its scales shifting from turquoise to chartreuse to violet as it moved.

It took a few more steps, pausing a foot away and extending its squared snout just enough to sniff my shoe. I sat stiffer than a church statue, partly because I wasn't sure my back could handle another sudden movement, and partly because Terek's warnings were still circling in the back of my mind.

A second later, it was ambling onto my lap, its claws thankfully retracted, and circled twice, padding at my thighs. I gaped, staring at it in shock as it happily made itself a nest in the middle of my crossed legs. I slowly raised my hand, so as not to startle it, and wiped the residual dampness from my cheeks.

"Well, hello to you, too. Aren't you a curious-looking thing."

Its pointed, oversized ears twitched, and it huffed as if to say, *"You're one to talk,"* before revealing a mouth of razor-sharp teeth as it yawned.

I froze at the sight, realizing God, or whoever had created the

Underland, wouldn't have given a Creature teeth like that if it consumed plants for food. Sure, it didn't seem aggressive, but the best predators never did.

Though I was fairly certain starving predators didn't make a habit of curling up on random laps like stray kittens looking for a good nap.

Continuing to move slowly, just in case, I lowered my hand and held it in front of its face to sniff. When it didn't seem the least bit worried, I curled my fingers under its chin and gently scratched the bared section of leathered skin not covered by its gem-like scales.

It tensed, like it was waiting for *me* to attack *it*, and when I only continued to scratch, it made a deep rumbling in its throat and closed its eyes.

"Wow," I whispered, smiling when it continued its odd purring with each scratch I gave beneath its chin. "At least someone likes me today."

I leaned back as much as I could and observed my new friend. I'd never seen anything like it, and I wondered if it was because animals like it didn't live in the woods at home, or if they didn't live in my world at all. Either way, he was amazing. At least, I thought it was a him. Its huffs certainly sounded a lot like Terek's.

I'd just closed my eyes, trying my best to push all the memories of today to the back of my mind where I could ignore them, when the happy purring suddenly turned to a sharp, warning hiss.

I wrenched my hands away and sat ramrod straight, biting back my own hiss when the Creature's entire body was yanked from existence. Its claws, which had shot out with its warning, ripped into my dress and dug into my thighs. Clenching my teeth, I slapped my hands over the shallow cuts just as a pair of black boots entered my line of vision.

"What the crimson hell are you doing?"

Tucking a few hairs behind my ear that had fallen loose from my updo, I glanced up to see Terek towering over me, brows drawn low, while my little friend dangled from his outstretched hand, snapping and clawing to get to him.

"Stop!" I shouted, pushing up to my feet, even as nearly every inch of me burned. "You're going to hurt him!"

His glare deepened, and he squeezed its neck harder, causing its eyes to bulge as it fought harder. "It's a Creature of the Wood," he said, as if that was all the explanation needed to choke the poor thing.

I was about to demand he release it at once when Terek turned away from me, and his arm whipped back, hurling its body almost as far as I could see, like it weighed no more than a feather.

I cried out, slapping my hands to my mouth to keep from outright screaming as I watched it barrel toward its likely death. But just before it could slam into the ground, its wings unfurled and swept wide, carrying it up into the canopy.

I watched it disappear and then whipped around, pointing a finger at the horribly mean man who'd decided to terrify it for no reason. "Shame on you. He was only sleeping. He didn't do anything to you."

Terek stared down at me, unfazed by my anger. "No, but it would've done something to you. Have you learned nothing over the years? There is not a single Creature of the Wood that is harmless, Ace. Even the smallest ones can be vicious. It'd have just as soon ripped out your throat as it would've slept in your lap."

I glanced at the bits of sky I could see between the branches, crossing my fingers the Creature was long gone and not lingering anywhere near Terek. Then I carefully sank back to the ground, biting my tongue to keep from visibly wincing at the throbbing in my leg. I didn't want Terek seeing the cuts and blaming the Creature since it'd been his fault it happened in the first place.

Although Terek had never been quite as cruel as the day my father had thrown the rabbit at me, I'd also never once seen him happy to see me. I considered his best days like today, when he seemed more apathetic rather than malicious. And I wasn't sure what it said about me that I found launching animals into the sky by their throats to be an example of his better days.

"What?" Terek asked, crouching down to sit beside me and resting his long arms over his knees. "No lecture about how wrong I must be?"

"I'm not talking to you."

He reclined his head against the tree, rolling his face toward me and leveling me with a flat look. "Sounds like you are."

"No, I'm—" I stopped, pressing my lips flat and glaring at him. God, he was so miserable sometimes. He knew what I'd meant.

He sighed and rolled his face back forward. "I must admit, when I'd awoken this morning, I didn't anticipate spending my time sitting next to a child, arguing over something as worthless as a Creature of the Wood. And they say eternity is dull," he murmured, more to himself than to me.

I frowned. "Just because he wasn't a person doesn't mean he was worthless. Besides, he was just trying to comfort me." I waited for him to make fun of me again for talking, but he just closed his eyes, his body loosening beside me.

"Comforting you about what?" he asked, his nostrils flaring slightly as he inhaled. "The scratches currently bleeding on your legs?"

I immediately crossed them, pulling my dress farther down, as if that would hide the accidental wounds he'd somehow noticed. "No. I had a bad day."

"Bad day," he muttered, his face losing some of the hardness that always made me a little nervous around him. "Well, go ahead and tell me then. You know you want to."

His words were slow, like he was already half asleep, but he was right, I did want to tell someone. I'd have told my little Creature friend if Terek hadn't been so awful, but now, he was the only one to tell.

"I ruined my birthday party."

"Oh?"

I told him about the horrible Beatrice Bellingford and her pack of friends and how they'd ignored me and said those dreadful things about my parents. All I wanted was someone—just one person—to agree that it'd all been unfair, and that I hadn't deserved Father throwing out my presents when I'd only been defending him. I wanted someone to tell me happy birthday and actually mean it.

But I should've known better than to think a man who hid in the shadows and killed innocent Creatures with no remorse would do such a silly thing.

He cracked an eye open, looking completely and utterly disinterested. "So what? They mocked your family because they don't like you and didn't want to be there. When was the last time you were nice when you were forced to be somewhere you didn't want to be?"

I bristled. "That's a mean thing to say."

"Don't ever expect me to be anything else, little rabbit. I'm no more your friend than they are. The question you should be asking yourself isn't why everyone is mean to you. It's why you're so set on being friends with those who are."

Because Mother told me to. Because I was tired of being lonely all the time. Because sometimes, I laid in bed and imagined what my life could be like if I didn't have to leave the estate in order to feel a flicker of happiness.

Because I'd thought, mean though he could be, that Terek might've been my friend, too.

I leaned forward and carefully pulled my knees up close, resting the side of my face on them and wishing I'd taken the time to change out of the tight, party dress before coming.

"Terek?"

"Hm?" he mumbled, eyes closed again and head lulling softly to the side.

"If you're not my friend, why do you always come to see me when I visit? Are you all alone out here too?" He'd said almost everyone who died ended up in the Underland until they moved on, but I'd never seen or heard another person other than him.

He didn't open his eyes, but his jaw tightened, and his fingers curled over his knees, knuckles white. When he said nothing, my heart dropped, and I twisted my head to lay on my other cheek, facing away into the Wood and hoping another curious Creature would wander into my lap.

When Terek finally spoke, his voice was gruff, like the words had leapt from his chest and shoved out of his mouth without permission. "I don't know, but I can't seem to fight it, and I can't explain it. Trust me,

I've fucking tried."

He sighed heavily, and I turned back to find his dark blue eyes open and staring up at the sky. "I suppose I'd rather sit in this godforsaken Wood, irritated by a scrap of a girl I can't seem to get rid of, than be out there, forced to thank the devil for granting me the chance to wipe her ass."

He slanted me a look. "But only barely."

It wasn't meant as a compliment, but I smiled anyway, beginning to learn that Terek tended to get meaner and nastier when his emotions got a little too close to the surface. Much like I'd done today with Beatrice.

Later, after we'd sat in comfortable silence and he'd eventually gotten up and I'd gone home to bed, his words stuck with me, following me over the next two years.

"The question you should be asking yourself isn't why everyone is mean to you. It's why you're so set on being friends with those who are."

Every time Mother forced me to attend a party or sit down with the girls who made no attempt to like me, I ignored their barbed comments and let their sneers and hushed gossip slide over me like I was a river stone. They could spew whatever they wanted. I refused to pretend to be friends with anyone who treated me that way anymore.

It wasn't always easy, and it only dug my loneliness deeper, but I had Terek, surly though he was, the small Creatures that'd slowly begun to edge out of the trees to introduce themselves to me, and the drawings I did of them.

Occasionally, I'd secretly add another page of Terek's likeness to my stack of drawings, too, knowing he'd rip them to shreds if he knew. But I felt an intense need to capture every angle of his sharp face, just in case there ever came a day when his soul moved on and I never saw him again.

I wanted to make sure I could remember him forever, because even though I wasn't his friend, he was mine.

ADELAIS

CHAPTER ELEVEN

AGE 13

Vincent's Finishing School was known for three things: having a high fence to keep its girls from running away, being operated by a man named Frederick Turner, who was feared by not only the girls but also the adult women who worked there, and magically *fixing* girls who failed to fit into society the way obedient, good girls should.

After Mr. Corbett cut ties with my father and announced his intentions of having his son marry Celia Alford, even though her family was socially beneath ours, it was the latter-known fact that got me sent there.

I'd begged and pleaded with my parents not to send me, swearing I could be perfect if they'd only give me one more chance, but my father refused to speak to me on the matter. He refused to speak to me at all.

He'd already begun to ignore me after the day he'd asked me to help with the rabbit, only to turn and see it on the floor and me nowhere in sight. But once Mr. Corbett had stopped by for the last time, all but shunning our family, my father stopped acknowledging my existence at all.

Mother still spoke to me when necessary, but she'd avoided any more parties not long after I'd stopped trying to talk to anyone, taking my lack of desire as a personal affront against her and her time. I hadn't minded that part so much, but in truth, I'd happily go to a dozen parties a week if it meant not attending Vincent's.

When it was clear that wasn't an option and neither of them were going to change their minds, I sprinted to the kitchens and threw myself into Mrs. Gayle's arms, uncaring that she was covered in flour and specks of dough.

"Come now, Miss Adelais. What's all this about then?"

I hiccupped, sucking in gulping breaths as my eyes flooded and my nose dripped over her apron. "Father is sending me away because no one wants to marry me."

She wrapped her hand around the back of my head, gently patting my hair down, and made soothing noises. "Oh, that's not true. Let's stop those tears before your poor face swells."

"It *is* true. Mr. Corbett told Father so. It's all my fault." Slowly, in-between wet sniffles, I told her what had happened and that I would be picked up the following day, the servants already packing my belongings as we spoke.

Mrs. Gayle took me to the side away from the other staff and sat down with me, listening quietly and pushing biscuits and tea at me. The first, I accepted; the second, I studiously ignored.

"Mr. Corbett didn't change his mind because you're unlovable, girl, no matter what your mother says. Men's minds are like giant caverns filled with nothing but echoes of their own making. They change them willy-nilly based on whichever echo is the loudest that day. Money, prestige, convenience, the list goes on."

"Tell that to Father."

She sighed, her full chest expanding beneath her blush dress as she watched me wipe at my nose and take another biscuit. "Your father is a very complicated man, Miss Adelais."

I glared down at the buttery goodness in my hand, the ones I'd already eaten suddenly feeling like rocks in my stomach. "He's not complicated. He's evil and vile and selfish and all the things he claims I am."

I paused, setting the biscuit down and tucking my clenched fists in my lap, unable to meet Mrs. Gayle's kind eyes. "I hate him. I hate them both."

The emotion had been growing over the years with each strike of Father's cane and each wine-infused insult from Mother, but I'd never voiced the words out loud. Now that I had, I felt the truth of them in every syllable.

I expected her to admonish me, or to flutter her hands and try to shush me so the walls wouldn't report my proclamation back to my parents, but she didn't do either of those things. She only pulled me closer and tucked my head beneath the soft underside of her chin.

"You know what? Every time I watch you walk out of that man's office, I hate him a little bit more, too."

Her quiet confession only made me cry harder. For me, for enduring the pain, and for her, for being helpless to do anything about it.

"I don't want to go," I whispered once my tears had finally run dry and my chest and throat ached.

I'd tried. I'd tried so hard to be brave, to be as strong and uncaring about others as Terek had once believed I could be, but I didn't feel strong right now.

I didn't want to go somewhere filled with people who would only seek to erase everything unique about me until they broke and molded me into whatever shape they wanted. I didn't want to be away from Mrs. Gayle or Terek.

"I know, but it'll be okay, Miss Adelais."

It wouldn't, and we both knew it.

"Maybe you could go with me?" I asked, even though I knew there was no excuse in the world Father would accept to send his head housekeeper to school with his greatest mistake.

Mrs. Gayle shifted beneath me, her fingers leaving my head to dig around in her apron. Then she pressed something hard and cold into my hand.

I sat up, blinking rapidly to clear my cloudy vision, and took in the round pocket watch resting in my palm. It had a small loop at the top, but it bore no chain, and the dark metal was dull and distressed, evidence of the many years it'd been used.

I held it up to my face to see it better, amazed to make out an intricate lace design circling around it. Some of the design was chipped and scratched, but it was still one of the most beautiful things I'd ever seen. Darting a look at Mrs. Gayle to make sure it was okay, I pressed the dial at the top to pop it open and immediately gasped.

Although only a used watch stared back at me, all I could see were Terek's eyes in the deep, midnight blue of its face. The two hands matched the lace of the top, but neither moved, their positions marking its last useful second like a gravestone. Much how I believed Terek often felt wandering the Underland.

I turned it over reverently, admiring the flowers etched into the back. "What is this?"

Mrs. Gayle smiled at me, but it was a sad smile, much like the one she always gave me after I'd gotten in trouble. "This was a gift from my husband, many years ago," she said, closing the top and tapping her stubby nails along it.

"He'd spent our entire savings on it after the physician told me I couldn't have children." She gave a quiet laugh, one that sounded happy but also like her heart was being squeezed a little too tight. "I'd been cross with him for days, demanding he return it, even as I secretly slipped it out of my drawer every night to stare at it in wonder."

Using my sleeve, I wiped at my eyes and nose, frowning down at the beautiful gift and wondering what it must be like to be loved so thoroughly. Was she wanting me to fix it? I knew nothing about cogs and wheels, and surely, she didn't think Father would help me?

"I'm sorry, Mrs. Gayle, I don't know how..." I stretched my arm out toward her, but she wrapped both of her roughened, wrinkled hands around mine, curling my fingers back over the worn watch.

"Take it with you, dear. I think it'll help you."

My nose crinkled, furrowing my brow. "But it doesn't work."

"Not to tell time, maybe." She smiled again, and this one was as warm and soft as her bread rolls. "But my husband gifted it to me when I thought my life was over, to remind me I was still loved. So, every time you look at this, I want you to remember that someone here loves you, too."

Fresh tears pooled, and I swallowed the lump in my throat, trying to see her face through the blur. "But he bought it for *you*. Don't you want it to remember him by?"

"My sweet girl, my husband threaded his love into every part of my body and soul long before he died. I feel it with every breath I take, something you'll experience yourself one day."

I blinked faster, my eyes beginning to burn with the effort not to cry again. "No one will ever love me that way."

Her lips tightened, pressing together so hard, they disappeared, and she inhaled deeply before reaching out to pull me back into her arms.

"That's your mother talking. You have a kind soul, Adelais. One that isn't made for this world. And someday, you're going to find where it fits. I promise."

※

A FEW HOURS later, after the servants had successfully packed up my necessary belongings and toiletries, I carefully tiptoed around the house until I found an occupied mouse trap in the back corner of the pantry.

Careful not to touch the body, I carried it to my room and shoved a chair beneath the doorknob, not trusting that Father wouldn't send someone to check on me to make sure I hadn't run away. I was betting on the fact that whoever checked would rather risk me running off than wake my father to admit they couldn't open my door.

The explosion of burning pain was the best feeling I'd had all day, even more so than Mrs. Gayle's hug. It was a promise spearing through every one of my veins that no matter how awful my life got Upside, I would always be safe in the Underland.

I wandered around for a few minutes, my yellow dress making me feel like a beacon in my otherwise neutral surroundings. I wondered what spring looked like here, if color ever grew, or if it was like this always. Not that it mattered. I loved even the spidery reaches of the trees, but adding a few splotches of color would sure be a sight to see.

Finding a tree with a fairly clear base, I crossed my legs and leaned back, closing my eyes and enjoying the way the trees always seemed to creak and lean into me. And it wasn't until I felt it, that the comfort I'd expected twisted into a flood of nausea.

This place was my home, more so than the estate had ever been. It was a place where I could be me, express my thoughts and feelings, draw pictures in the dirt, and play with Creatures who thought I was wonderful.

The chance that I wouldn't see it again was terrifying. I still didn't understand where my ability came from, though Terek was always quick to reinforce his belief that I was cursed. But the fact remained that I wasn't sure if it was a magic in *me*, or in the land our property was on.

And even if it was me who held the power to come here—an idea both Terek and I shared since my father and the staff regularly touched dead animals—what were my chances of finding a way to the Wood while at a finishing school?

I may have never been to one, but I was confident they didn't leave dead mice in the girls' rooms or bloody rabbits out in the grass. I'd be locked in a school where the only subjects taught were dancing and smiling, and all the girls hated themselves as much as they hated each other.

I'd be more alone than I'd been in years, and I couldn't help but wonder if I'd be happier dead. Not because I didn't actually want to be alive anymore, but because I could be *here*. In whatever towns and homes existed here.

As if sensing my dark thoughts, I felt a pushy nudge on my left arm, and I glanced down to see a furry, quirked head looking up at me. Its eyes gave off the same emotions I'd just been feeling, like it wasn't sure if I would love it or kick it to the curb.

"You're not appreciated either, are you, little one?" I asked, reaching down to scratch behind its pointed ears. "If I stayed here forever, maybe we could take care of each other."

It nuzzled into my armpit, bringing a scratchy giggle to my lips. Its fur was a mixture of rust and a brown that made me think of chocolate, and its long face reminded me almost of a fox. Minus the fact that it had six legs and three small, slitted eyes.

A second later, another nudge came, this time on my right, quickly followed by a rattle. I turned to see who the newcomer was and flinched back a little when a snake stared accusingly at me, the majority of its body disappearing around the tree.

I laughed again, feeling almost happy for those few quick moments. The unimpressed look it was giving me reminded me of my mother, like the snake was personally insulted that I'd agreed to take care of the fox and not it.

"Forgive me. You are, of course, welcome as well."

I leaned back to give the snake more space, and it slithered over my legs, its long body not nearly as heavy as I had imagined.

Its scales shifted, turning different shades of red and orange like the flickering embers of a fire, and its curved mandibles poked at my dress as if to say, *"Shed this weird skin, and I'll allow it."*

I smiled at its playfulness, running my free hand over its nose. "I wish so much that I could. I'd rather die tonight and stay right here with you than ever go back." But that wasn't entirely true either.

The desire to stay in the Underland was, but the fear that I'd simply die and go straight to the final afterlife was too high to ever risk my life on the chance. Not when even Terek didn't believe all people came to the Underland after death.

The snake rattled again, and the wind whipped through my hair, smacking it into my face like its own form of agreement.

I sniffed, tucking the stringy, yellow strands behind my ears again. At least, if I was at Vincent's for the next five years, Mother wouldn't be able to dye my hair this awful color anymore.

It didn't exactly take away my dread, but it was a positive I was determined to cling to like a lifeline. Even if I couldn't be myself at Vincent's, at least I could *look* like myself.

ADELAIS

CHAPTER TWELVE

I heard him before I saw him this time. Embarrassment coiled inside me, knowing his steps only reached my ears because he'd heard what I'd said and was giving me time to mask my face so we could both pretend he hadn't.

But as embarrassing as it was, it was proof that he cared, I supposed. In his own messed up, slightly demented way. He'd deny it if I ever pointed it out, but his suddenly loud steps, when he'd always snuck up on me in the past, were all the proof I needed. Not that it made any difference in the end since I had to tell him goodbye tonight, whether he cared or not.

The snake sprawled across my lap snapped its head toward the noise, its body tensing and pulling in like an accordion while its mandibles clicked loudly in warning.

"He hasn't got the friendliest face, I know," I said, running my hand down its flickering scales in soothing motions, "but he's not going to hurt you, I promise."

"You know better than to make promises you can't keep, little rabbit."

His voice was as flat and devoid of emotion as it always was, but each word calmed my frantic emotions all the same. I didn't know why, but something always seemed to settle inside me when Terek was near. A comfort and safety that didn't make sense but that I felt all the same.

My fox friend, however, didn't seem to agree and shot up, pushing off me and sprinting through the trees without a backward glance. I watched it go, sensing Terek standing directly beside me, and smiled down at my angry lap companion, prodding it to slide off.

"Go on," I whispered when it only coiled tighter and hissed at Terek. "I'll be all right. He's dreadfully mean and has never smiled a day in his undead life, but he won't hurt me either."

The man in question muttered under his breath, but I ignored the comment, well used to his ill-tempered demeanor by now. He was like a grumpy old man, and I'd become quite fluent in his mannerisms over the years.

He frowned when he found something I said interesting and didn't want me to know, spun his knives when he was lost in thought or semi-relaxed, and glared when he thought I was being unsafe. Much like right now.

"Come on now, don't make him angry. I only just got here," I said, tapping the snake on its tail to lower its barbed stinger.

It hissed at Terek one last time and then looked up at me, its triangular head almost seeming to bow in farewell before taking off through the brush.

"How many times must I tell you to leave the Creatures of the Wood alone?" he growled, his jaw tightening when I only crossed my arms over my bent knees and stared back at him.

"The same number of times I have to tell you they're fine with me, I guess."

Smaller Creatures of all types had begun coming up to me more often over the years, sometimes one at a time and sometimes grouped all together. Yet not once had one ever so much as nipped me, let alone hurt me in a serious manner. Nevertheless, Terek showed up every time, without fail, and was always quick to scare them away just before lecturing me.

But I wasn't in the mood for it today. I didn't have it in me to argue at all. I'd just wanted a few moments of peace before I was forced out of everything I'd ever known tomorrow.

"They are not *fine* just because you've been lucky enough to only encounter the small ones. You've fucking seen the full-grown ones. Stop encouraging them."

I pulled my legs up and wrapped my arms around them, resting my chin on my knees. "Not really. You always murder them before I even know they're there and then don't allow me to go see."

He scoffed, as if me admitting I couldn't sense them from afar only proved his point.

"Maybe you're the one who's wrong, Terek. Not all of them are as bad as you claim. It's okay to love peo—Creatures and things who are different than everyone else."

"I wasn't aware that your sporadic trips made you more knowledgeable about a world you don't belong in and Creatures I've seen friends slaughtered by. But by all means, keep defending them, Ace. You're only reinforcing my opinion about your presence here."

It wasn't the worst thing Terek had ever said to me. He had a tendency to say really horrid things anytime I irritated him too much and he wanted me to leave. Not so much to hurt me I'd learned, but because he knew I had a habit of magicking back Upside whenever I got overly upset.

Like a solid kick to my flight mode.

But unlike all the other times, I wasn't able to roll my eyes and brush his barb off as usual. Not when his words hit a nerve my parents had flayed wide open today. And I promptly burst into tears.

There was a heavy silence, or as silent as it could be with me crying on the ground at Terek's feet. A second later, his black boots disappeared from my line of sight, and then he heavily dropped down beside me, audibly exhaling.

"All right, go ahead."

I sniffed, wiping my sleeve over my swollen eyes. Mrs. Gayle would be appalled. "Go ahead and what?"

"*Leave*," I expected him to say. "*Leave and stop coming back, before even the Creatures you love betray you."*

"Tell me what's wrong."

I looked away, blinking rapidly to hide my surprise and try to slow the steady trek of tears. I was so tired of crying. "Why? So you can tell me for the thousandth time how stupid I am?"

"Probably."

My head shot up, hurt burrowing under my skin despite the expected reply. But his face held no malice as he stared down at me. He tipped his head, his lips twitching ever so slightly.

"Come on, Ace. Tell the dead man why you're so unhappy with your living, breathing life."

He'd meant it more as a pointed dig to me being childish than a joke, but I still found myself telling him anyway.

I'd never been able to keep anything from Terek when he gave me his full attention like he was doing now. I didn't have experience with love, but sometimes, I wondered if my inability to withhold sharing everything in my heart with Terek was because part of me loved him and just wanted him to love me back.

"They're sending me away."

"Who?"

"My parents," I clarified, fisting my hands in the pleats of my skirt and hiccupping. "They're sending me to finishing school because Mr. Corbett didn't want his son to marry me anymore."

And also because I played in the woods, drew creepy pictures, and embarrassed them at every turn by opening my mouth or not drinking tea correctly, but he didn't need to know all that.

Terek unsheathed one of his knives and inspected the handle, rubbing the pad of his thumb over the dark leather. "You're what, twelve?"

"Thirteen."

"Crimson hell. How is it people have evolved past selling off children under the guise of marriage in this stagnant world, but the Upside still hasn't fucking figured it out?"

He didn't say it like he expected an answer, so I just shrugged and continued. "There are no other suitors lined up, so I'm to attend Vincent's Finishing School to learn how to be a lady and a wife."

His lip curled, and he looked away from the handle to eye me up and down, as if the entire concept of me marrying horrified him. "Did you even want to marry this boy?"

I shook my head vehemently. I'd run into Corbett's son numerous times over the years and still didn't know his name. He never spoke to me if he could help it and was always introduced as *the young Corbett*.

"Then why are you upset?"

"Because my parents hate me for it."

Neither my mother or my father truly believed Vincent's could fix what they deemed wrong with me, nor had they wanted to spend the money to send me for lessons I could learn at home under Mr. Jenkins and a governess based on that idea alone. They simply wanted to get rid of me.

And as I sat in the shadows of the Wood, I realized I couldn't blame them.

Terek went so silent next to me that I might've thought he'd disappeared had I not been aware of every dancing movement of his silver blade. He had one knee drawn up, his arm flung across it, and stared out into the trees, lost in his own thoughts.

"Sometimes, it seems like our parents hate us when they're really only trying to do what's best for us."

I bristled, my eyes narrowing as I crossed my arms. "That's easy for you to say. You weren't born a girl. The only good thing I can do is get married to someone I don't love and birth babies I don't want to have."

Exactly how my mother and Beatrice's mother, and every other woman I knew, had. And I didn't think a single one of them had felt even a fleeting moment of happiness since.

"I'll never be what they want," I whispered.

Terek turned his head to look at me straight on, his hands stilling as if he already knew what I was going to say. "And what is that?"

"A boy."

I'd never voiced the words out loud, but they'd been my constant companion my entire life, a living entity that rested beneath my skin and poked its head up every time my parents were near.

I'd spent so many years pushing it down and believing if I stayed quiet, took my punishments, and continued trying even after each failure, I could make them forget what I'd been born. I could satisfy them.

Unfortunately, it was hard to convince people of your worth when it was measured by what men you could bring into their lives to replace you. A husband who would relieve the burden of you from your parents. New heirs to take over the family business to make up for the inconvenience of you being born the *inferior* sex.

Regardless of the obvious fact that men wouldn't even exist without the hard work of women.

Terek said nothing to my naked truth, knowing there was more and waiting for me to elaborate. I started slowly, staring at the dirt as I sketched out a rose in it with a twig.

"They never wanted children. Not in the sense that parents should. They only wanted the required heir to appease society and carry on Father's name. But they got me." The words scraped up my throat, the memory of Mother ranting and accusing me of poisoning her body digging its nails into the back of my mind.

From what Mrs. Gayle had once told me, Mother's pregnancy had been hard. She'd puked all nine months and had barely survived my birth when I'd come out feet first. Only to discover she'd suffered through all of it just to be handed a dark-haired *daughter*.

I wasn't sure how many times they'd tried for a son after me, but I did remember when they'd stopped. I'd been six and had sneaked to her bedroom door to press my ear against it after Father had rushed a physician in. I hadn't understood most of what was said, except for two things: Mother had lost several babies since me, and the physician was firmly advising her to stop.

Father's dreams had died that day, and it'd shown in his eyes every time he'd looked at me since. Because even dyeing my hair to look like the perfect child couldn't take away his belief that I'd somehow ruined his wife.

"I'm a constant reminder of what I stole from them. Mother says I owe it to them to marry a respectable man, but apparently pretty dresses and fine parties aren't enough to hide poison. I leave tomorrow." I huffed a laugh, one that sounded as wretched as I felt.

Terek stared at me, as if seeing me for the first time. Or maybe seeing himself in me. I wasn't sure, but something flickered in the blue of his eyes, an emotion I'd never seen from him before. Empathy.

"They're trying to break you, little rabbit. Don't let them."

I scoffed, breaking the connection and continuing my poor excuse for a drawing. "I don't have a choice. I can't just disobey my parents." Not on something like this. They could just as easily throw me onto the streets, and then what would I do?

"I didn't say disobey them. I said, don't let them *break* you." He twisted until his torso was fully facing me. "If you ever learn anything, learn this. You are stuck with yourself for eternity, Ace. Not your parents, not a husband or a lover. *You*."

He gave me a long look, waiting for me to meet his eyes before continuing. "You are the only person you can never escape and are therefore the only voice that matters. Submit to no one else."

"You make it sound easy."

"Nothing in life is easy."

"Or after?" I asked, attempting a small smile. To my surprise, Terek returned it with the barest one of his own.

"Or after."

I leaned back, dropping the stick and enjoying the small opening he'd finally allowed in the stone wall he kept erected around himself. "Is that what you did? Refused to submit to your parents?"

He nodded, surprising me again by opening the door a little wider. "I grew up in a wealthy family not all that different from yours for the time period. My father made his fortune in a…trade I didn't approve of," he said, pausing on the word like whatever he was speaking of didn't deserve the title. "I had no desire to be involved. I preferred to work with my hands."

I glanced down to his knives and back up, catching a glint in his eyes. It made me smile. "I'd have never guessed."

He huffed out his nose. It wasn't quite a laugh, but since he rarely even gave me that, I was going to take it as one. "Instead of working under my father, I took an apprenticeship under a milliner."

I practically shot up off the tree, my eyes bulging from their sockets. "*You* made *hats?*"

His gave me a flat look, shifting slightly away from me like he feared I might climb into his lap like a toddler ready for story time. "Like I said, I enjoyed working with my hands. Experimenting, creating things, and giving life to things that wouldn't have existed otherwise."

He flicked his free hand in a lazy wave, quickly shuttering the spark I almost missed crossing his eyes. "Needless to say, my father didn't approve, and when I refused to come running back to him with my tail between my legs, he did what any rich, prideful man would do. He disowned me and never looked back."

Terek stopped and ran a hand through his messy hair, clearing his throat uncomfortably. I sat back, speechless. I'd always been so jealous of the freedom boys got that it'd never dawned on me they might not want what their parents did either.

It should have, since the young Corbett never once looked happy to sit across from me at a table, but all my whiney self could see was the daily attention he got from his father. And the small-mindedness of that made me feel a twinge of shame.

For several minutes, Terek and I sat in an awkward silence. Me because I wasn't sure what to say to his story when he was now dead and could do nothing about his relationship with his father, and him because it was clear by the deep furrow in his brow that he wasn't sure why he'd shared it in the first place.

When I couldn't take it anymore, I blew a loud raspberry and did us both a favor by changing the subject to something far less personal. "Terek? What if I can't come back once I'm at school?"

"We can only hope."

I shot him a glare. "*Terek.*"

He sighed. "Why would you be unable to come back? Because you'll be watched too closely?"

Considering I'd be sharing a room with numerous other girls, that was definitely part of it. "That, and maybe I can only do it from my parents' estate."

Terek was already shaking his head before I finished. "It's you, little rabbit. You take yourself home every time, and I believe you could bring yourself here without a dead body, if you really tried."

I nodded, but what I didn't tell him was that I'd already wondered the same and tried. I'd just never been able to make it happen.

The conversation lapsed again, but unlike the previous one, this one wasn't forced, and it made me feel as if I might actually be okay. Because if this terrifying man believed I could be strong enough not to let anyone break me or change me, then maybe, just maybe, I could.

I stared at his side profile, noting each sharp angle of his face, the arm muscles his cloak didn't always hide, and the knives I'd seen him kill with more than once, and I couldn't help but giggle. "I really can't picture you sitting at a table making hats."

He cleared his throat again and shifted his weight, refusing to meet my gaze. "One can't live multiple lifetimes without expecting to change."

Multiple? "How long have you been here?" *How long have you been dead?* My heart squeezed, sorrow for this man who, unlike me, hadn't known a world existed after death. How terrifying it must have been.

Terek sighed, and I swore I could feel the weight of his weariness from the sound alone. "I don't know, Ace. I stopped counting a long time ago."

WHEN I CLOSED my eyes and returned to my room that night, a feat that'd been far harder than any previous time, I didn't cry. I just quietly sank to the floor, crawled beneath my bed, and pulled out the hidden sketches I'd created over the years. Creatures with sharp teeth, trees that hummed and curled around lonely girls, and Terek, the man who believed in me when no one else did. Even when I didn't, myself.

Then I plodded over to my packed bags, tucked the sketches safely beneath my folded clothes, and prayed to whatever god there was that the stack of pages wouldn't be my only window into the Underland for the next five years. But now knowing I'd make it through either way.

And although I was right.

I was also very wrong.

 TEREK

CHAPTER THIRTEEN

S ensing Ace had always been something I struggled to find the right words to describe, even to myself. It was hard to say I was drawn to her without sounding like a fucking creep, but there was no other way to explain it.

There was just something about her that had always called to me, no matter where I was. An innate sense of protection, frustration, and annoyance that billowed into a weird sort of connection that didn't make sense, yet one I hadn't realized I'd miss until it was suddenly gone.

It'd been two years since I'd seen Ace. Two years since I'd felt any hint of her presence, and I'd found myself staring into the Wood on more than one occasion—often after yet another fight—wishing to feel that spark of familiarity.

It hadn't always felt the same, yet it'd always somehow felt like *her*. Some days, it'd been like a miniature sun flaring in my chest and guiding me toward her. Those days, I'd usually find her singing lullabies to crimson only knew what Creatures or making necklaces with random weeds she'd found.

Other times, it wasn't so much a warmth as a string connected to my sternum, gently tugging me forward. On those days, I'd either find her moping next to a tree, puffy-eyed or brow furrowed while she drew in the dirt, or aimlessly wandering around, eyes closed and face to the sky.

But after two years of neither, when I'd finally sensed her today, I'd barely felt anything at all. I'd dismissed the light pressure in my chest for nearly an hour before I'd found my feet drawing me into the Wood. As if the string was still there but had gone limp and weak.

The thought made me hasten my steps, and when I finally delved deep enough and spotted the small form on the ground, something reached into my ribs and squeezed.

She wore a hideous gray frock of some kind, pulled tightly around her body with her legs tucked up somewhere beneath. I frowned, noting the worn, black, lace-up boots peeking out from the hem. Ace rarely ever kept her shoes on.

Her hood was pulled down so low, I could see nothing of her face from where I stood, to the point where I might've second-guessed that tug, had it not been for the two Creatures curled at her sides, hissing at me.

But it was the dimness of her glow that gave me pause. It almost made her look like she belonged here, and the possibility had my instincts on edge.

"Ace?"

Her posture stiffened at the sound of my voice, but she didn't look up, nor stop the methodical petting motions of her hand along the back of the two-headed feline at her right. "I wondered if you'd show."

Her voice was flat and rough, as if, although she'd wondered it, she hadn't actually cared if I did or not. I bristled, not sure why the idea instantly pissed me off.

"Have I ever not?"

She shrugged, the movement barely discernible under the woolen fabric. I wasn't even sure why she was wearing it. The Underland was never hot, but it wasn't cold today either.

"I wasn't sure if you were still here or not."

I tensed, tearing my eyes from her odd clothing as the desire to lash out at her coiled and snapped inside me. I shoved it down, aware she only said so because she had no fucking idea the truth of my soul.

Which was no one's fault but mine. She'd never needed to know the truth of it. She still didn't.

I took a deep breath and stretched my neck to the side, determined not to be an ass for once. "Likewise, little rabbit. It's been a while since I've been forced to suffer through these damn trees."

A lie. Possibly the first one I'd ever given her. Crimson knew, I'd made denial and avoidance a full-time occupation, but I'd never outright lied to her before.

But I'd actually found myself within the Wood far more over the last two years than I wanted to dwell on. The Creatures had been getting more and more restless with each passing year, and though none had dared approach the edge of the trees near Ardenglass yet, it was only a matter of time. But I didn't want to get into that with her, not when she and I viewed the Creatures so differently.

I eyed the two at her sides but didn't bother ridding her of them. There was no point anymore, not when she'd never listened, and more would just show right back up the next time she was here. However, that didn't stop me from unsheathing one of my daggers and spinning it in my hand. Just in case.

When Ace said nothing to my obvious tease, I took a step closer and nodded back the way I'd come. "I passed a mangy-looking, orange cat just over there. Since animals don't tend to last long in the Wood, I can only assume it's a new arrival and your designated carrier today."

Still nothing.

I frowned. She hadn't stepped foot here in years that I knew of, yet she had nothing to say? The Ace I knew had no idea how to keep her mouth shut. She shared her opinions and thoughts even when I openly chided her for them. It drove me insane, but it was also one of her best qualities.

Then again, she was around fifteen now. A couple years might've been a blink in eternity for me, but it wasn't for her. I remembered the last time I'd seen her, the despair she'd had over being sent away and the determination that had painted her expression as she'd said goodbye to me.

"Ace? Did you kill that poor cat just to come see me? Because I must say—"

"No. I found it. And I don't feel like talking."

My lips pressed together at her blatant dismissal, and I narrowed my eyes, crouching into a squat so that I could finally make out the planes of her face beneath the hood. She looked the same as she had last time, with her round features and soft cheeks, but her clenched jaw and dull hazel eyes were something I'd never seen before.

Her voice had come out raspy, yet her eyes were dry and hollow, not a single tear glistening against her cheeks. As if, rather than crying, she'd been screaming instead.

Something was wrong, but not like the tantrums she used to have or even the pity parties that had become her normal. This felt different, like she was fading away, and I was about to see her soul get crushed behind long, crimson-painted nails. The image made something yawn open inside me that I hadn't felt in a long time.

Panic.

Closing my eyes, I let my senses expand and inhaled deeply to get a better feel on her. Sadness, anger, joy, they all had specific underlying notes that were easy to distinguish once you understood their differences. But as prepared as I was for the smells of the Wood to shove up my nostrils, I was not at all prepared for the weight of her scent to hit me like a fucking hammer to the face.

There was a hint of a metallic tang coming from somewhere on her body, though dull and not too worrisome. Probably nothing more than a scrape on the knee or elbow. But it was the lingering bite of fear hovering over her like a cloud that had me nearly stumbling back when it hit my nose.

I inhaled again, my eyes slamming open. Though potent, the scent of her fear and pain wasn't fresh enough to have been caused by something within the Wood. It'd happened Upside, which meant her fear had to have been at overwhelming levels for me to still scent it here so strongly.

And then I noticed her hands. More specifically, the angry, red welts that crisscrossed over them.

Something rumbled in my chest, and the demon I fought daily to contain raised his head and snarled, sending needles of ice through my veins. "What happened to your hands, little rabbit?"

"I'm not a little rabbit," she snapped, but even then, there was only a flicker of her usual fire. No eye roll, no crossed arms, or pressed lips. Nothing. Like everything about her that had made her, *her*, had been almost completely snuffed out.

Closing my senses back to try to keep myself from losing my shit, I took a much more calming breath and focused in on her face, which was still pointed down toward her lap.

"I want to know who hurt you, Ace, and where. Because I know there's more than those I can see upon your hands."

Another lie. I didn't know anything for a fact, but the sight of those welts had me questioning the smell of dried blood I'd noticed before. Especially when combined with the too-big frock she was hiding most of her body within.

For a second, I thought she'd continue to ignore me. Her shoulders curled in, and she tucked her hands into her lap, ignoring the mewls of protest at her sides. But then she swallowed and spoke, her eyes still not meeting mine.

"I took your advice, you know."

What the crimson did that have to do with who hurt her? I wasn't even sure what advice she was referring to, but I assumed she must've meant she'd stayed away the last few years because of all the times I'd yelled at her to stop coming.

"To stay away from here?"

"To be strong for myself and not let anyone break me."

It wasn't at all what I thought she'd say, but nonetheless, it made pride simmer just under my skin. I pressed the tip of my dagger into the dirt and twirled it about a foot away from her boots. "That's good, Ace.

I'm—"

"Dean Turner enjoys the strong ones the most."

Everything went dead silent inside my head, and my hand froze, my gaze snapping back to her face. "What the fuck did you just say?"

She only hugged her legs tighter to her body, as if to shield herself from me and anyone else who might consider touching her. "I came here to be alone."

The fuck she did. My eyes flicked down to the Creatures plastered to her sides like a second skin of protection, and for the first time ever, I found myself thankful for their presence. I white-knuckled the pommel, using every minuscule amount of patience in my body to keep my voice calm while my body radiated fury.

"Ace, I need you to tell me—"

"I don't care what you need, Terek," she whispered, her voice cracking over my name. "Please, just leave me alone. I don't want to talk anymore."

I stared at her downturned face for several long moments, the demon screaming and thrashing at me to snatch her up and demand she tell me what this goddamn Dean Turner did to her. But I fought it down, refusing to be yet another man who took something from her against her will, when it was clear too much had already been taken.

Sheathing my dagger, I raised both palms to the Creatures baring their teeth at me and straightened up. "All right, then, Ace. We don't have to talk."

Trying not to punch every tree I passed, I walked just far enough away that I'd be secluded in the growing shadows of the quickly falling night, and tucked my hands into my pockets, opening my senses.

I no longer believed the smaller Creatures would cause her harm, sensing a kinship with her I didn't understand, but I watched over her all the same, listening for any larger ones that might catch her scent.

It wasn't until she'd finally stood an hour later, and gently shooed her companions away, that her eyes finally flicked up to where I stood.

She wouldn't have been capable of making out my form in the

darkness, but somehow, I knew she understood that I was still here, keeping her safe. Just as I always had.

But just as quickly, she looked away again, pulling her frock tighter around her body and squeezing her eyes shut. And then, in a blink, she was gone.

I expected her to return over the following days or weeks, now that she'd proven it could be done from her school, but she didn't. And after years without even a hint of that tug, I'd all but given up on ever seeing her again.

ADELAIS

CHAPTER FOURTEEN

AGE 20

A proper finishing school didn't take kindly to any of its students being viewed as flawed. And given the purpose of the institution was to make perfect ladies out of girls who were often less so, it was safe to say they took kindly to very few of the girls who were admitted.

For those of us who'd tried, whether for days or years, to stand up for ourselves when Ms. Mildred whacked our hands during piano lessons or when Ms. Helen screamed at us in French when we mispronounced something, it went beyond that.

We weren't viewed as flawed. We were viewed as *broken*. And the thing about broken dolls is it's easy to add new cracks when you believe they cannot be fixed anyway.

I sighed, trying for the hundredth time in two hours to force my mind on my future and not everything I'd been through over the last seven years. It didn't matter anymore. After thinking I'd be released when I turned eighteen and being painfully wrong, I'd finally aged out the moment my twentieth birthday arrived.

I was free. Or, as free as a woman could be sitting in the back of a coach headed toward the very people who'd sent her away to begin with.

As if hearing my thoughts, the coach took a sharp turn, making me plaster my hand to the window to keep from smashing my cheek against it. The trees immediately thickened on either side of us, and the road grew rougher with each turn of the wheels, nearly bouncing me off the bench.

I cursed as I whacked the back of my head during an exceptionally deep pothole and silently apologized for ever getting angry at Beatrice for the comments she'd made about where my family lived. She may have had a point.

Seeing the beginning of the property enter my line of sight, nerves swirled in my gut like an unruly group of butterflies. I pressed a hand to my torso and tried not to puke, letting my eyes go unfocused until the scenery disappeared and all I could see was my reflection staring back at me in the glass. My skin looked pale and my hazel eyes too wide, giving away exactly what I felt.

I closed them and took a deep breath as the coach began to slow, forcing my face to slacken. *Shove it down. Hide it. Do not let them win.* I took another breath and opened my eyes again, feeling no less likely to puke, even as a confident woman stared back at me.

It may have been a ruse, but only I would know that. To be honest, I looked so different than I had at thirteen when I'd been shoved out the door, I doubted my parents would recognize me if they weren't already expecting my arrival.

My cheeks had lost most of their roundness, giving me more of a heart-shaped face than an oval one, and though my nose was still the same, the smattering of freckles that'd always decorated it were now hidden beneath layers of powder. But it was my hair that was going to give them heart attacks.

Now reaching several inches below my shoulders, my hair had taken months to recover from the aggressive dye my mother had used to hide its natural black. I'd been ridiculed daily during those months, but it hadn't bothered me as much as the other girls had wanted it to.

I *had* looked ridiculous with the horrific half-and-half color, and I'd only let the black reach my chin before I'd taken my embroidery scissors and chopped the yellow off, earning me a fast trip to the dean's office.

He'd taken a measuring stick to my fingers, but it'd been worth it.

I'd nearly wept the first time I'd stood in front of a mirror and had finally seen *me* staring back.

Years without Mother's interference, and it was now soft and wavy, and absolutely nothing like the stringy, dry strands I'd had prior. By the time I'd climbed into the coach to head to Ellington Estate, I'd already ripped out the tight band we'd been required to hold our hair back with, and let it fall about my shoulders, enclosing me in the comforting embrace of the devil's shade.

I couldn't wait for Mother to see it.

⸻

A FEW MINUTES later, I stood before my childhood home, staring at its familiar, unchanged appearance, yet feeling like a complete and total stranger. The lack of a warm welcome mixed with the unknown butler staring at me like I was there to deliver the post definitely wasn't helping.

The man didn't move to approach me. He had graying brown hair, slicked back to hide a bald spot I was sure would be there, and wore a stiff suit that made his already short neck look nearly nonexistent. He had a wide, smooth-shaven face with a cleft in his chin, and his lips were pressed flat, as if he had a myriad of other duties he'd rather be attending to than welcoming me home.

I wasn't surprised my parents had needed to hire replacements over the years I'd been gone, but that inevitability didn't take away the disappointment that a stranger was the only person out here to greet me. My parents' absence didn't bother me so much, but Mrs. Gayle's did.

"You must be Miss Adelais," the man finally said when I'd stepped close enough to the front steps that he wouldn't have to raise his voice. He took a single step forward and gave a curt bow. "I am William Adler. If you'll follow me, the Mister and Missus Ellington are waiting for you in Mister Ellington's study."

I balked, the mention of Father's study immediately making my muscles tense up and my heart wither like a dying rose. I'd only just arrived, and Father was requesting me…there? I didn't move to ascend the stairs, the butterflies in my gut turning into a vicious swarm.

Instead, I twisted my hands in front of me and turned to glance back at my belongings that the coachman had set just beside a large wheel. There was no longer anything of importance inside of them since my drawings had long ago been confiscated and destroyed, but I still didn't like the idea of leaving them out here.

"I will, of course, have your belongings taken up to your quarters," Mr. Adler added with the same detached formality he'd used to welcome me.

I looked up at him again to see he hadn't moved a muscle, including those in his face. I was beginning to wonder if he even knew how to smile. If I hadn't already felt like a stranger pulling up to my childhood home, this man would've succeeded at making me feel as such all on his own.

Then again, knowing my parents, it was also probable they had instructed him to remain impassive.

Realizing I had no choice unless I wished to make a scene, I ascended the stairs but paused at the front door, attempting a smile that felt awkward and foreign on my face. "Does Mrs. Gayle know I've arrived?"

Mr. Adler extended his gloved hand to gesture me inside, his other tucked flush across his lower back as his face furrowed with confusion. "Miss?"

I frowned. How new was he to the estate that he didn't recognize the head housekeeper's name? "Mrs. Gayle," I repeated, my smile twitching. "Does she know I've arrived? I would like to see her before heading to the study, please."

Mr. Adler eyed me up and down, clearly assuming I meant I required assistance freshening up. Before I could correct him, he'd already flicked his fingers to someone standing just within the house and asked them to fetch a vaguely familiar-sounding name.

"Mrs. Gayle is no longer with us, Miss. Adelais, but I will send someone else up to assist you, and I will inform Mister Ellington you are making yourself presentable and will be right down."

Although still cold and formal, I could hear the warning in his words. My father had demanded my presence, and he was not a patient man. Still, I didn't enter the house. All I could do was stand there and stare blankly at Mr. Adler, his words like knives in my ears.

"Mrs. Gayle was let go?" What on earth could she have done for my father to choose to replace her? Sure, she'd been getting old, but she'd handled everything about the estate, and I hadn't even been there to get her in trouble for helping me.

I'd missed her dreadfully. She'd been the only one I'd actually been excited to see today. I slipped my hand in my pocket, wrapping my fist around the small watch that never strayed far from my person. I didn't know Mrs. Gayle's address, or how to find her, or if she had anyone who might take care of her, but I'd figure it out.

"No, Miss Adelais. I'm afraid Mrs. Gayle passed away about two summers back. Heart failure, I believe. Now, if you'll please follow Miss Irene—"

Everything around me went quiet, and I let him finally guide me into the house as he continued to speak, handing me over to Miss Irene to continue leading me up to my room. I stood frozen in the center of it, barely taking in the musty, unused scent that permeated the space, and let her peel the clothing from my body and drag a brush through my hair.

All the while feeling and hearing nothing but Mr. Adler's words as they lashed and bit at my mind, stirring something raw and bitter inside me.

My mother knew how much I loved Mrs. Gayle. Everyone in the estate did. Yet, she hadn't bothered to spend the few seconds it'd have taken to have someone write and inform me she had died.

I hadn't bothered my mother or demanded a single letter over the course of my stay at Vincent's. Not once. Even over holidays or when my eighteenth and nineteenth birthdays passed, and they still hadn't permitted me to leave. Yet, she hadn't cared enough to tell me the woman who'd practically raised me was gone.

I stared at myself in the mirror, feeling nothing but raw misery as Miss Irene shoved and squeezed me into a dress that, if I'd cared enough to notice, should've set off red flags about what my father wanted to see me about. But I was trying too hard not to break into a million pieces to take in more than its physical appearance.

The dress was snug across my torso and scooped low over my chest, baring more skin than I'd ever shown before. It was an iridescent pastel color that clashed with my hair, with a delicate ribbon tied between my breasts and a thick, blue one wrapped around my entire stomach to tie at the back. The sleeves were open and airy, cascading from my shoulders like waterfalls, and the skirt flowed from my hips in exaggerated waves.

I heard Miss Irene saying something, but all I could do was nod and silently accept the sheer gloves she was handing me, all while the hatred for my parents grew until I feared I might choke on it. A small part of me hoped I would, just so I wouldn't have to face them. So I wouldn't have to hold in my agonizing sorrow over Mrs. Gayle and pretend I was fine.

"Miss?" the girl asked, her face heavily furrowed and her hands held toward me like she feared I might faint at any moment.

I cleared my throat and forced myself to focus on the kind worry in her face, shoving my roiling emotions into the deeply buried box I'd been using over the years, and reminded myself to smile. *Shove it down. Hide it. Don't let them win.*

"Miss?" she asked again, gently touching my elbow. "Are you ready?"

I nodded again and forced my lips to form the word 'yes', even though the only thing I was ready for was the overwhelming desire to set my parents, and the entire estate, on fire.

ADELAIS

CHAPTER FIFTEEN

I stared at the door to my father's study, my hand hovering over the wood as I listened to the muffled sound of male voices on the other side, unable to cross the last inch of space to knock. Of all the rooms in the house, including several sitting rooms specifically for guests and quiet luncheons, and the drawing room with the view of Mother's precious garden, Father had chosen for me to meet them here.

If I dared bring it up, he'd only smile and turn the conversation to make me feel as if I was imagining things, making me question both myself and his intentions. But he and I both knew he'd brought me here for one reason, and one reason only. To make sure, after all these years, I hadn't forgotten my place.

I wasn't sure how much or how often my parents had been informed of what went on at Vincent's, but it was safe to assume they'd been told the basics of my supposed "behavior." That I'd arrived with my nose in the air, believing myself above every instructor and child, and that I'd argued and openly refused to participate in several required activities.

How Dean Turner had been considerate enough to take me under his wing and give me, and a few other girls, the special instruction we needed to *grow as women*. How his instruction had worked, and that after two years of fighting back, I'd finally given up my horrible ways.

What my parents wouldn't have been told was that I'd had to keep my nose in the air to contain the constant sting of tears from spilling over, and I'd avoided the other girls, not because I'd thought myself better than them, but because most of us at Vincent's had no idea how to make friends.

They wouldn't have been told that I'd only refused to participate in the activities that required cruelty to other girls, and that those of us who'd been brave enough to argue against it had all been immediately referred to the dean's office.

That after two years of trying my hardest not to break, I'd finally submitted, because not doing so would've cost me much more than my pride.

I still remembered my last trip to the Underland, the day I'd left Dean Turner's office from a private *lesson* and had found a cat at the bottom of the outside stairs, its neck clearly broken. I'd slipped and fallen down them in my hurry, scuffing up both knees as I'd launched myself at it.

And then Terek's appearance. The fury in his voice before his quiet understanding. The way part of me had wanted to scream at him to leave me alone while the other part had wanted to cry the moment he did.

So many times, I'd wanted to go back and tell him everything, but after one of the girls had hung herself with knotted bedsheets after a private lesson with Dean Turner, we'd been watched too closely for me to ever have the chance. I wondered if Terek had worried about me over the years. If he'd fretted and hoped I was okay.

If he'd show up if I went there later tonight.

I shook my head and tossed the thought from my mind. It wouldn't matter if Terek was willing to show if I infuriated Father. I was too old for him to take a cane to me like a child, but that didn't mean he wouldn't lock me in my room as punishment.

Taking a deep breath and reminding myself that whatever my parents wanted to talk to me about was better than being at Vincent's, I crossed that inch of space and knocked.

The talking cut off instantly, and for a moment, I considered sprinting out into the woods right then and saying to hell with everything. But just as my hand dropped, my father's voice rang out, cementing my fate.

"Come in, Adelais, and shut the door behind you."

Father's desk sat off to the right, the top covered in all manner of parchment, folders, and ink, with an overbearing wooden cabinet directly behind his velvet-upholstered chair, its doors closed and a large key sticking out of them.

On the adjacent wall to the right of his desk was a single, two-pane window with thick, red velvet curtains and two portraits: one of Father and the other of a grandfather I'd never met. The window was partially covered and allowed in little natural light, but it was made up for by the massive fireplace that burned bright and hot on the far left.

Before it, where my father always stood as he waited for me to rest my hands on the mantel for my punishments, sat a high-backed, brown couch, two red leather armchairs, and three small, mahogany tables, each with glasses of amber liquid.

My parents occupied the two armchairs, both dressed in their finest, but each receiving me quite differently. Father wore a pristine, black evening suit, his muscular body filling it out in a way that told me he hadn't changed one bit. His blonde hair was combed over as usual, and his stoic expression, obscured only by his mustache, gave away nothing as he took me in for the first time in seven years.

My mother, on the other hand, visibly stiffened the moment I walked through the door. She wore a deep red gown with gold jewelry accenting her ears, neck, and wrists, and her eyes, which were lightly painted and showing a few more wrinkles in the corners than I remembered, narrowed on me. More specifically, on my hair.

I might've dared to flash her a smile, if it hadn't been for the third individual sitting on one end of the couch across from them. A man in his early forties who smiled at me, like I imagined a wolf might a rat, as he stood and gave a shallow bow.

He wore a dark blue suit pulled taut over his stomach, and his hair was combed back rather than loose over his sweating forehead, but even cleaned up, I'd recognize that oily smile anywhere. My heart beat faster, and my lungs fought against the fastenings of my dress as it took everything in me not to whip around and sprint from the room.

My father sat back and took a sip from his glass, stretching his free hand out toward the only available seat. The right side of the couch next to the Dean of Vincent's Finishing School, Frederick Turner.

"I expected better from you than to keep company waiting," my father said, not even trying to conceal his irritation. "Come sit down."

Dean Turner roved his eyes down my dress, stopping for several beats too long on my chest before straightening his suit jacket and chuckling. "It's no worry at all, Ellington. I appreciate your daughter's desire to look her best. Something I'm proud to say she learned at Vincent's."

I felt nausea coil in my stomach, and I had to swallow hard, twice, before I could pull in a full breath without vomiting all over my father's study. I shouldn't have knocked. I should've followed my intuition and run to the woods when I'd had the chance.

"Thank you, sir, but I am feeling suddenly quite faint, and I think I'd better—"

"Sit down, Adelais."

I snapped my mouth closed and dipped my face to the floor, feeling the heat of all three sets of eyes as I nodded. For a split second, I considered holding my breath until I lost consciousness, but the thought of Dean Turner being the one to touch me as he picked me up off the floor had me immediately throwing out the idea.

Avoiding the dean's eyes like my life depended on it, I slowly made my way across the room and lowered myself to the couch, perching as close to the edge as possible when he reclaimed his seat and spread his thighs wide. Oh, God. Why? Why was he here?

Father grabbed one of the amber-filled glasses from the table beside him and wordlessly handed it to Mother to give to me. I took it from her on instinct, frowning when I caught the scent emanating from it. Liquor?

"Are we…" I took a steadying breath. "Are we celebrating something, sir?"

There was no way they were celebrating my return, but with the dean in attendance, I couldn't think of any other reason. Dean Turner only smiled and lifted his own glass, downing the majority in one audibly wet gulp.

"We are," my father said, leaning back again to cross an ankle over his knee as he stroked his thumb and forefinger down his mustache. A mustache that should've been speckled with gray by now but was a suspiciously uniform shade of yellow.

"Frederick here was just telling us how suitable of a wife you now are," he said, nodding at the dean like they were old buddies agreeing on the weather.

My furrow turned into a frown. Suitable? He'd certainly never said anything of the sort to me. I shifted even farther away from the man until I was practically melting into the side of the couch. Whatever he was up to, I didn't trust it. "I'm happy to hear that, Father."

"However," he said, barely letting me finish before he continued, "your suitability means very little when all the suitors we'd had lined up for you have now already been wed."

I tensed. Yes, that tended to happen when one was expected to marry young, and I was now several years older than I should've been. If I was suitable for anything at this point, it was becoming a governess for another young girl who'd eventually be bred for a loveless marriage.

But I nodded, indicating I was listening, and clasped my hands around the glass of liquor. "If there are no suitors lined up, may I ask what it is I have been brought in here for?" I finally darted a look over to Turner, a shudder of revulsion working through me when I again caught his eyes below my chin. "Am I being sent back to Vincent's?"

My mother, who had thus far been silent, sat forward when my father waved a hand at her, and smiled at me. A smile that was far too forced. "Not quite. We have come to an arrangement with Mister Turner that we believe will benefit all involved."

Somehow, with the way she said the words *not quite* and *arrangement*, I highly doubted that. A cold sweat prickled on the back of my neck, and my hands suddenly felt clammy beneath my gloves.

"What kind of arrangement?"

To my dismay, it was Turner who answered. "Your parents have agreed to make regular, sizable donations to the school in exchange for one thing."

Dots blurred my vision, and I pressed a hand to my stomach, suddenly feeling like I couldn't breathe. No. They couldn't be sending me back. I'd aged out, Turner had told me so, himself. I was free from that godawful man and that godawful torture of a school. I sucked in air, desperate to keep calm and show my father I was capable of control now. I was capable of perfection.

"Surely, there are still suitors who could fit your requirements, Father. I'm confident—"

He brandished his hand around, waving me off like a pesky insect. "There's no need to prance you around like a peacock when you're far too old, and Frederick has already agreed to take you."

My entire body froze, my father's meaning dropping inside me and sinking its teeth into every limb, organ, and vein. I didn't even flinch when Turner slid his palm over my leg to take my glass, which had dropped from my slackened grasp onto my thighs.

"Wh-what?"

"Isn't it wonderful?" my mother asked, the smile in her voice ripping me from my panicked stupor and pulling my eyes to her in time to catch the gratified smirk she hid behind her gloved hand. "Mister Turner owns a grand property right next to the school. Surely you've seen it."

I had. I'd also seen him take the worst of the troublemakers there, only to return the empty-eyed girls the following morning. One of whom had been the same girl to hang herself later that day.

I shoved out the image of her body swaying side-to-side and focused back on my mother's too-sweet voice, which was still babbling about how fortunate I was.

"You'll be so comfortable, and although your first son would, of course, take after his father at the school, Mister Turner has agreed that your second son would be sent here to make up for—"

I shot to my feet and took several steps away from the couch before my mind even comprehended what my body was doing. They wanted me to have a child with a monster and then watch that same child grow up to be just like him? The idea had bile burning up my throat, and fury exploded from my lips before I could stop it.

"No."

My mother's lips pressed thin. "The decision has already been made, Adelais. What else would you have us do? No one has shown even a minuscule amount of interest while you've been gone. Be thankful Mister Turner was willing to take you."

"Of course, no one was interested!" I snapped, gripping my dress to hide how my hands shook. "What parties was I supposed to attend while locked away hours from here? How many available, high-standing men do you know who go to finishing schools and knock on the door to see the stock of possible brides?"

"Watch your tongue," my father said, right as my mother said, "Plenty of young women who go to Vincent's are engaged by the time they leave. You can't keep hiding your failures behind excuses, Adelais."

My breath came harder, my chest straining beneath my gown until it felt like the edges were digging into the tops of my breasts. "You can't make me."

Father slowly set his glass down and rose, a dangerous look in his eye. "Until you are legally bound to Frederick Turner, you belong to me, and I will do with you what I wish. It's about time you earned your place."

There was a loaded beat of silence in which I stared at the floor, trying to think of anything to change their minds. But I could think of nothing as Turner pushed to stand, his suit jacket bunching up over his stomach before he yanked it down and tipped his head at my father.

"Ellington, could I have a moment alone with your daughter? I've found she's much more pliant and willing to listen when she's not so overwhelmed by groups of people."

I stiffened, understanding the hidden meaning for me behind his use of the word *pliant*. This man was delusional. In no version of this world or the Underland would my father ever let a man be alone with me and risk my virtue—or whatever was left of it. But as if I was truly as cursed as Terek had always claimed, my father straightened out his cuffs and nodded.

"Of course. It's past time for Margarette to have retired, anyway," he said, not even bothering to look at my mother as he snatched her glass from her hands and set it on the table. He raised his hand out and shook Turner's, looking all too pleased. "We can discuss more of the details tomorrow. Will you make sure my daughter gets to her room safely?"

"No," I said, my voice cracking on a higher pitch. "That's far from appropriate, Father. Dean Turner can speak to me tomorrow." *Please don't leave me alone with him.*

"Save me the dramatics, Adelais. Not only is Frederick a man of honor, but he deals with young girls all the time. You will be fine."

I knew exactly how he dealt with young girls. The memory of gagging and the pungent smell of sweat hit me all at once, and panic surged. I darted forward, wrapping my hand around my father's wrist. "Please, Father. I promise I will marry whoever else you choose, without complaint. Anyone. Please."

But I might as well have whispered my plea to the flickering fire for all the good it did. He only lowered his gaze to my fingers, his silence louder than if he'd screamed at me. I swallowed and dropped my hand, shuffling to the side to add even more distance from where Turner still stood by the couch.

My father gave one last nod behind me and opened his study door, pressing a hand to my mother's lower back and leading her out without sparing me a second thought.

I tensed in time with the click of the door, every bone in my body feeling ready to snap as I fought back tears and waited for Turner to approach me. To force fresh nightmares on me here as well, so that no home I ever slept in would be safe.

Instead, he just walked toward the fireplace and stared at it for two agonizingly long minutes, dragging out my misery in a way he'd always been far more skilled at than my father. Then he slowly reached into his pocket and pulled out something small and round I couldn't make out. He gave it a cursory glance and then tossed it next to the burning wood, discarding whatever it was like my father's office was his own personal rubbish bin.

"Why?" I asked, my voice hoarse and ragged, like my throat was already attempting to hide away. It's all I wanted to know. My parents' motivation was obvious. They were getting rid of their burden of me and guaranteeing Father someone to take over his business, while also tying a respected name to theirs.

But I couldn't wrap my head around the belief that Turner had agreed for nothing more than a yearly donation to the school.

"Why?" he repeated, ambling toward me and reaching out to caress his hand down my hair. "I am a great man, Adelais, but even I cannot live forever."

I jerked away and clenched my fists at my sides, digging my nails into my palms until I got both my breathing and tears under control. *You've made it this far. Don't let him win now.* I glanced at the closed door and took a small step toward it, considering my options.

Frederick Turner hadn't been physically disgusting to me until he'd shown his true colors; however, that didn't mean he was a fit man. If I made a run for it, there was a good chance he could catch up to me in a quick sprint, but I doubted he could keep up all the way to the woods. Then again, I wasn't sure I could either in this dress.

I took another step toward the door, and he matched it, clicking his tongue against the roof of his mouth like he was calming a skittish animal. "Now, now, Adelais. You know better."

"What I know," I hissed, leaning away when he closed another foot between us, close enough I could make out the pores across his prominent nose, "is that you will bear no child with me. I would rather beg on the streets than ever feel a child from you grow inside me."

"I figured you'd say that."

He lunged for me, but I'd already been anticipating it and lurched back, aware I only had seconds to get across the room and out the door before he'd regained his balance and overpowered my shorter strides. I just needed to get outside, and then it was a straight shot across the grounds and into the woods.

But as I spun, the hem of my dress, far longer than I'd worn in years, caught on my shoe, and I stumbled, my arms waving to keep myself from landing on my face. My heart hammered, but I threw myself forward, my fingertips brushing the edge of the doorknob just as thick fingers knotted into my hair and yanked, drawing a sharp cry from my lips.

He dragged me back toward the sitting area, his gait and expression unperturbed as I hit and thrashed in his hold, earning nothing but his satisfaction and a screaming scalp.

"You have two options, Adelais," he said, pulling me up before the fireplace and arching my neck back until I had no choice but to stare up at him. "The easy way or the hard way."

I shoved and slapped at his chest, yelling for anyone to come help me, but he just chuckled, knowing as well as I did that no one would dare enter my father's office without his permission. No matter what they heard.

So, I did the only thing I could think of to do, and I spit in his face. The second the glob hit his cheek, I squeezed my eyes shut, expecting him to slap me or throw me to the ground, ready to make a run for it the moment he did. Instead, he smiled at me, the sheer excitement in the expression freezing my movements and sending ice through my veins.

"That's more like it. We both know I like you far better when you choose the hard way, and I brought something special just for you, for this exact occasion."

Wrapping my hair around his fist until I couldn't budge an inch without crying out, he casually grabbed my father's fire tongs from beside the poker and lowered them toward the fireplace. Fresh tears pooled, and fear coated every inch of me as he pulled something out I couldn't see and held it up beside my head.

Oh God, oh God, *what was he doing?* I couldn't even twist my face.

All I could see against the study's ceiling were Turner's muddied brown eyes and his satisfied smile.

"I can treat you like my wife or breed you like cattle, Adelais. The choice is yours. If these beautiful lips want to continue denying that inevitability, that's perfectly fine by me. Let's see just how much you enjoy being cattle."

The tears poured free, coursing down into miniature puddles in my ears. "Please, Dean Turner." It was the first time I'd ever begged him for anything, and by the glint in his eyes, it was the wrong thing to do.

"It's Frederick or dear husband," he cooed, hovering the tongs just over my chest. "And I'd suggest holding very still."

ADELAIS

CHAPTER SIXTEEN

S itting unmoving on the end of my bed, I stared down at the watch in my ungloved hands, the worn metal still warm from how hard I'd squeezed it when I'd crashed into my room.

I ran my thumb over the lace design over and over, listening to the house close up for the night, knowing the countdown until morning would begin the second the last footfall of the staff sounded. The small window was my only chance for an escape before my future would be set in stone as permanently as it was now set in my skin.

It was well past midnight, and I could barely see my own hands when I finally dashed down the stairs on my tiptoes, careful to keep my heels from clacking against the wood and avoiding all the spots I could remember that made creaking noises.

My chest burned, the small section between my breasts hot and angry, but it was the humiliation and utter despair roaring to life far deeper that had my eyes and nose burning. I pushed it back, gritting my teeth. If I could suffer being alone with Turner in a room I hated more than any other, without losing my sanity just yet, I could make it out of this goddamn house before I let it go.

Turner had strolled to his prepared quarters with a bounce to his gait and a hum on his lips after forcing me to the couch to allow him to tend to a wound *he'd* caused, cooing at me like a well-behaved pet. I'd just sat there with my unlaced dress falling over my shoulders, feeling his fingers brush across the swell of my breasts, and stared at the flickering fireplace behind him, wishing I had the strength to shove him into it.

After covering the coin-sized burn with ointment and a small square of wrapping he'd requested from Mr. Adler to prevent an infection, he'd sent me on my way to bed with a pat on my ass, warning that I was to be ready to leave by morning.

"A wife rides in the coach. Cattle are pulled behind. You have until we break our fast to decide which you'll be, Adelais."

I didn't plan on being either. I'd been vibrating with the desire to run out of the house from the moment I watched him retreat toward his chamber, whistling a giddy tune like he hadn't just ruined me.

I'd told Turner I'd rather beg on the streets than marry him, and I'd meant it. He'd scoffed, believing himself capable of keeping a firm hold on me anywhere, but what he didn't know was that I hadn't meant any streets here. I hadn't meant this diseased world at all.

Still wearing my silver heels and the iridescent dress Turner had blessedly left untied in the back, I sprinted across the shadowed grounds, tripping and falling over hidden roots and holes more than once as my lone candle failed to light more than a few inches in front of me.

My hair whipped about my face, the majority of my scalp still numb at the base of my neck. The long strands lashed at my eyes and shoved between my parted lips, but I didn't bother pushing them back, too focused on keeping myself upright.

I didn't stop when I hit the first line of trees, instead urging myself faster with each foot I crossed. Unlike the Wood I was headed to, these ones had always been loud, all manner of insects and animals calling out to one another, living their lives unaware of the crack spearing through my chest and echoing in my ears.

Something with glinting eyes scurried across my path as I delved deeper, and I jumped, barely choking back my cry, the delusional, broken part of my mind afraid it was Turner coming to drag me back. But I shook it off and forced myself to keep going, ignoring the sting of errant branches as they scratched at my arms and snagged my hair.

It only made me move faster, my eyes scanning the underbrush with a desperation so acute, it felt like madness.

I hadn't searched for traps in more years than I could remember, having depended mostly on the estate mice once I'd discovered they worked, but my desperation refused to accept that there wasn't one out here. Because staying in the house long enough to find a mouse hadn't been an option, not with Turner within its walls.

Reaching one of the locations that'd been a favorite of Father's, I slowed and held out my only source of light, lowering the minuscule flame as close to the ground as I could manage without setting the brush on fire.

"Come on, where are you?" I said, my voice scratchy and raw from the scream I'd been unable to keep at bay in Father's office. I squinted into the dark, searching the base of a tree I'd been at a hundred times for the barest flash of metal. But it was like looking for a splinter in a stack of kindling.

I shoved up, a sharp pain lancing beneath my ribs with each inhale as I began to run again, beelining to the next of his usual hunting spots. And then the next. Sweat beaded across my brow, and I reached down and yanked the torn hem of my skirt from another snag, the quickly shortening candle indicating it'd been well over an hour.

And I'd still yet to find even an empty trap.

I could feel the crack within me growing with every minute I stayed in this world, and my chest felt like it was going to explode from the pressure of every emotion I'd forced down over the years. I dug my fingers into my hair and fell to my knees, letting the last struggling wisp of my candle flame burn out.

I didn't know if Father had stopped using traps over the years I'd been gone, or if he put them deeper now, or if I just couldn't see them. All I knew was that Turner was curled into his pillow right now, laughing at me, and I couldn't fucking breathe. Tears dripped down my cheeks as the crack began to split wide open. I dashed them away, but they only fell faster and harder.

And when I curled my legs into my chest and my knees smacked against Turner's raw marking, the tears turned into a soul-crushing scream. One that held all my pain, my rage, my fear, and my bitter loneliness. I let it pour out of me like a crashing wave for the first time in my life, tearing open my throat and ripping my control to pieces.

"*Please,*" I cried, digging my nails into the dirt and squeezing my eyes shut. I wasn't even sure what I was begging for. A trap to appear? A savior? Actual death? All I knew was that I'd give anything in the entire world to be anywhere but where I was.

I curled into a ball at the base of a tree, ignoring the pain between my breasts, and imagined myself lying in a different Wood. A place where I could run free beneath a comforting gray sky while troublesome Creatures startled me and nosed onto my lap. I could smell the wet dirt hidden beneath the blanket of dead leaves, feel the chill breeze against my skin, and hear the way the trees groaned as they leaned in to greet me.

My scream turned to soft cries as I pulled that feeling deep into my lungs, letting the clawing desire fill every part of me until I felt my entire body shake with the severity of it. I wanted to feel safe. I wanted to feel free. I wanted to be *home*.

The center of my chest began to burn hotter until it seeped into the rest of my body, extending through every muscle, organ, and vein faster and sharper than it ever had before, until it became all I knew. I thrashed on the ground, my body instinctively trying to escape the pain, even while my mind latched on with all its might.

Like it had always done before, the pain vanished as fast as it'd began.

My eyes flew open, and I staggered to my feet, barely registering the pull of inflamed skin on my chest that existed even in a world of death. Fresh tears streamed down my cheeks as I took in the gnarled branches and the soft gray peeking out from the canopy, and a choked sob ripped straight from my heart.

A small voice in the back of my head wondered if I'd somehow laid on an animal beneath the brush and hadn't noticed it, but it quieted soon after it'd spoken. There hadn't been anything but dirt beneath me. I'd done it myself. I'd come here without a body to help me, just as Terek had always believed.

I couldn't believe it. He'd been right.

A smile stretched across my face, and I hiccupped, the sound turning into a broken laugh that scraped up my ravaged throat. I began to wander aimlessly, tipping my head back and allowing the cold air to coat the crack in my soul and soothe it back together.

The estate's woods were comforting to me from a childhood of running to them as my safe haven, but the Wood was a home to me in a way I'd never had anywhere else. This was the home I'd been missing when I'd sat in the coach and made the journey back from Vincent's. *This* had been where I'd wanted to be.

My parents' expectations, the miserable years at school, Turner's triumphant smile—none of it mattered in the Underland. Of all the dangers that might exist here, not a single one of my very real nightmares did. And that knowledge made my lungs instantly inhale easier, like a weight had fallen from where it'd begun to grow on top of me.

Even the trees appeared to feel the same weightless joy, their branches almost seeming to bend in toward me as I walked, the wind whispering in my ears, reinforcing the notion that I was *safe.*

"What in the crimson hell are you doing way out here?"

The deep, graveled voice, sounding more shocked than angry, made my heart soar, and I spun, my swollen cheeks aching from how hard I smiled as that crack stitched up even more. I'd been so lost in my misery the last time I'd seen him, so set on the belief that all men sought to cause me harm, that I'd wanted nothing to do with him.

I'd regretted it after, wishing I'd have stayed and confessed everything, but I'd never had a chance to return and apologize. Between my wretchedness and how many years had passed, I wasn't sure if he'd come back to see me, and the fact that he had, filled me with warmth.

Unlike me, Terek was as unchanged as he'd always been. He stood only a few spans behind me, his muscular arms crossed beneath his black cloak. Shadows hid part of his face, but I could still make out the sharp features of his nose and jaw, and the speckling of what appeared to be blood across his forearms.

His shock seemed to turn to confusion as he took in my expression, and the likely clashing combination of happiness on my otherwise distraught face. "Why are you way out here?"

My smile fell, and my brow pinched. What? Did he mean because I'd wandered rather than immediately sat down, or had he thought I couldn't come at all anymore because of how long it'd been?

"I don't know. This is where I appeared."

Understanding lit his features, though he still looked slightly unnerved at the sight of me, like he hadn't sensed me at all and had come upon me on accident after whatever fight he'd clearly just had with a Creature. He glanced around us and tilted his head, listening for more, I assumed.

"Are you all right?"

I nodded, wiping the last trace of wetness from my cheeks and hoping I didn't look too horrible when he looked as perfect as always. Nothing that had happened mattered anymore. Not my parents, not Turner, not the throbbing pain of what they'd all done to me.

"Yes, I'm all right. It's just been a long day," I said, sighing and giving him as honest of a smile as I could. That was putting it mildly, but I didn't want to lay out my baggage at his feet to dig through and judge when he was looking at me like a normal human being without a single, disapproving glare.

"I can imagine," he said, his lips tipping up into an almost teasing smile that had my heart skipping a beat. Terek had never smiled at me before. Hell, I'd always considered myself lucky when I'd earned the barest twitch of those usually flat lips.

Something warm curled around my abdomen, and a tingle slid up my spine as he continued to watch me with an unwavering focus. I'd always known Terek was a handsome man, even as a young girl, but seeing him now, through eyes far older than they'd been before, it felt like the first time all over again.

And I realized, with a start, just how breathtakingly, sinfully beautiful he was.

He slid his hands into his pockets and made his way toward me, his eyes flicking to my loose bodice and pausing before slowly coming back up to my face. I flushed, forgetting how visible the swells of my breasts were in my haste to leave. I could only guess what he assumed I'd been doing.

I wanted to blurt out that I had absolutely not been doing what it looked like, but he took another step toward me, and my mind went fuzzy, my mouth forgetting how to form words. Terek wasn't looking at me like I was a stupid little girl, but like he found me just as attractive and enticing as I'd just realized I found him.

As if noticing my reaction to his perusal, his lips curled up even farther, and that tingling warmth grew, tightening around the base of my spine and spreading between my thighs in a way I'd never experienced before. I instinctively squeezed them together, suddenly feeling like I needed to splash cold water on my face.

What the hell was happening right now?

His nostrils flared, and he immediately closed another step between us until he was so close, I had to arch my neck back to see his entire face. "The first day is the hardest, but you'll get the hang of it soon and figure it all out," he said, tipping his head down to meet my eyes with his deep blue ones. "However, you should know that while the Underland is vast, the Wood is strictly forbidden."

I frowned, my confusion helping to clear my mind from whatever his proximity was doing to me. First day of what? I glanced around, wondering if I'd somehow arrived in a different Wood than I usually did. It didn't look different.

Then again, knowing Terek's general dislike of my presence here, this could just as easily be his new attempt at convincing me to leave. Sadly for him, I was too old for his mind games to upset me to the point of accidentally sending me Upside. This was the only place in any world I wanted to be.

I placed my hands on my hips, reveling in the way his eyes dropped down my body again. "Since when is walking through the trees forbidden?"

"Since you stepped foot in one teeming with unholy demons lurking within it."

I faltered, the sarcastic smile I'd been about to plaster on my face dying off as the voice in the back of my mind popped up. Terek seeing me differently was possible; I didn't exactly look the same anymore, but something was off about the way he was talking to me. And not only because he'd made it over five minutes without insulting me.

He was talking to me like I was a complete stranger.

Deciding the worst that could happen if my intuition was wrong was a jump start to that less than ideal, yet inevitable, part of our interaction, I darted my gaze around like I'd never been there before. "What do you mean by demons?"

"Exactly what it sounds like. Monsters like no animal you're used to, I can assure you." He watched my face for another moment, and when I failed to respond the way he expected, a small crease formed between his brows. "Are you sure you're okay?"

I gave a light shrug. "Yes. I guess I'm just so used to monsters that the idea doesn't frighten me all that much anymore." Another careful answer, not quite a lie, but not quite the truth either. For a moment, I thought he had to have finally recognized me, but then he tipped his head to gesture to the area to my right.

"Many here are, though most aren't quite as unlucky as you to be dropped in the Wood. However, if you head straight that way, you'll hit the edge of the trees in about a half hour. Then it's just a few hours north, and you should begin to see others."

My hands fell to my sides, and I stared at him, dumbfounded. If anything had convinced me that Terek absolutely, one hundred percent, didn't recognize me, it was his willingness to tell me how to leave. Something he'd adamantly—and usually quite angrily—refused to do.

The entire idea seemed ludicrous, but I could think of no other explanation. I understood that it'd been years, and the last time he'd seen me without me hiding beneath a massive coat I'd been seven years younger, but still, the man was supposed to have uncanny senses. I ran my hands over my dress, wondering if I should be insulted.

Then again, Terek had also never seen me without Mother's horrible yellow hair dye, nor did I have any memory of telling him what my natural color was. She'd had me too convinced as a child that it'd been the mark of the devil and something I'd needed to hide.

A mild sense of guilt and the manners I'd had drilled into me at Vincent's demanded I tell Terek the truth, but the heat coiling tighter each time his eyes traced over me smashed the idea into the ground and stepped right over it.

Taking my silence for either nerves or discomfort, he twisted his body away from me and took in our surroundings again to make sure we were still alone. "Come on. I'll make sure you get out in one piece. I'm headed out anyway. What's your name?"

Shame that Terek had always been honest with me, even when it hurt, yet I was openly deceiving him, dampened some of the heat, but not enough to pull the truth from my lips. I had no desire to see that smile flatten and his eyes harden. So, I shook my head.

"You don't have one, or you're just not going to give it to me?"

I fidgeted, suddenly nervous of saying something wrong and ruining whatever was going on between us. I didn't exactly have experience in the social department, but I sure as hell wasn't going to admit my name yet. "I don't make a habit of giving my name to unknown men who tell me I'm not safe and then offer to take me somewhere."

Normally, my refusal to listen would've earned me an immediate glower and muttered curse, but instead, he chuckled, making my heart do a weird fluttering in my rib cage.

"Good for you. However, in this case, I can promise you I mean you far less harm than what will find us if we don't leave."

I glanced around us again, wondering if that meant he could sense some smaller Creatures shuffling close by. I shamefully hoped not, since they'd give me away in a second if any came out to greet me. Thankfully, most of them hated getting close to Terek, but I didn't want to push my luck.

Lord knew it rarely treated me well, even on my best days.

"All right, but only because I quite like the idea of leaving this Wood and going somewhere with people and beds," I said, trying not to blush when I'd basically just admitted I wanted him to chaperone me to a bed while my dress hung unlaced at my back.

His darkening eyes told me he'd noticed, and a second later, I felt his long fingers wrap around my wrist. The contact instantly sent sparks flying across my skin, and his eyes followed mine to where we touched, his jaw feathering.

My breath hitched, and his eyes snapped up at the sound, lingering on my parted lips as his brow furrowed deeper this time. The expression reminded me of the niggling sensation I got when I'd walk into a room only to forget what I'd gone in there for.

I subconsciously ran the tip of my tongue over my bottom lip, watching him track the movement and step closer until his cloak brushed against my arms. I wasn't sure what had come over me, but his touch caused the sensation to explode, and whatever it was, he was definitely feeling it, too.

Without releasing my wrist, he slowly raised his other hand, giving me every chance to pull away, and threaded his fingers through the hair that'd fallen over my shoulder. The single, gentle touch swept through me, officially rendering me unable to function.

"There's something about you," he murmured, almost to himself, as he lowered his face to hover over mine. His eyes seared into my very soul, the blue brighter than I'd ever seen it, and for the briefest second, I tensed beneath that penetrating gaze.

The reaction was over as fast as it'd come, caused by the sudden realization that he was about to kiss me, and I had no idea how to kiss a man. But it was enough. Terek immediately pulled up, his face flattening as he began shutting down to the stoic version of him I was so used to. The way he always did when he gave something away of himself that he hadn't intended.

"I'm sorry," I started, trying for a small smile to halt the wall he was erecting between us.

He cleared his throat and released my wrist to run the hand through his hair. "Don't be. I'm not sure what..." He trailed off and cleared his throat again, his eyes hard. "Crimson hell, you just died, and I—"

"No, it's not like that," I said, reaching out to grasp his hand and smashing my lips together to keep from blurting out that I wasn't actually dead. His eyes snapped down to mine and then dropped to where we touched, but he didn't pull away.

"There's no need to explain yourself," he said, running his hand through his hair again and making it even more unruly. He looked more ruffled than I'd ever seen him before, and it made him appear younger somehow. Softer. "I shouldn't have done that. I won't claim to be a saint, but I don't usually make a habit of taking advantage of women lost in the Wood."

I could see the desire in his eyes beginning to fade as he regained control over his emotions, and I knew if he raised the wall around himself now, he'd never lower it back down again.

Staring at the familiar lines of his face, I focused on the way his midnight eyes had made me feel when they'd seen me, not as a possession or cattle, but as a woman he'd been about to kiss simply because he'd wanted to.

I was still hurting, bitter, lost, and a hundred other things kissing Terek wouldn't fix that I'd need to eventually work through. But two things I knew without a shadow of a doubt were that I felt a connection to him I couldn't explain, and that I wanted the power to choose something for the first time in my life.

Locked away at Vincent's, I hadn't been allowed to choose who saw the skin beneath my bodice for the first time, or who'd touched me beneath my skirt or entered my mouth, but I could choose whom I *willingly* gave myself to. And right now, I wanted Terek to kiss me more than I'd ever wanted anything in my life.

I gave a light squeeze of his hand, but he just shook his head and frowned, reaching up to subconsciously rub his free hand over his chest. "What is it about you that feels so..."

He trailed off and stared at my neck, as if he was listening to my heart and wondering if he recognized the beat, and something akin to panic shot through me. Acting without thought, I released his hand and wrapped both of mine around his neck, enjoying the look of surprise that hit his eyes right as I pulled his face down to mine.

I had no idea what to do other than the obvious fact of smashing our lips together. I didn't know if the first kiss was supposed to be open mouth or closed, or what the hell I was supposed to do with my tongue. All I could do was hope and pray that instinct would take over and I wouldn't embarrass myself beyond repair.

In the end, it hadn't mattered, because the second his lips made contact with mine, Terek's control *snapped*. Whatever thoughts had been creeping into his mind and hints he'd begun to pick up about me disintegrated with the low growl that slipped up his throat.

One hand wrapped around my lower back while the other dove into my hair like he'd been imagining doing it from the moment he saw me. I waited for the bite of pain across my scalp, but instead of fisting it and yanking the way Turner had, Terek only curled his fingers at the base of my skull to position me exactly where he wanted.

His lips were somehow soft and demanding at the same time as he worked them over mine, and I lifted higher onto my toes, trying to close the last of the distance between us. He responded in kind, pressing the flat of his palm against my spine just as his teeth nipped at my bottom lip.

I gasped at the mild sting only for the sound to drop into a positively indecent groan when his tongue took advantage of my parted lips and swept into my mouth. My fingers tightened around his neck, and I found myself pushing my hips flush against him, no longer in control of my body.

All I could feel was the raging inferno inside me, one Terek seemed to burn from as well as he slid the hand on my back to my hip and squeezed. The world faded away until there was nothing except his heat, his touch, and the feel of his tongue sliding against mine. God, I'd had no idea kissing could be like this. Like the entire world could crumble down around us, and I wouldn't care, just as long as Terek's lips never left mine.

Something hard pressed into the inside of my thigh, and I instinctively dropped a hand from his neck to grasp it, not wanting one of his knives to ruin the moment by slicing open one of my arteries. But the deep growl that erupted from Terek as my fingers wrapped around the firm length told me that was not at all what I'd just gripped.

His chest vibrated against me, and his kiss grew more frantic, the hand at my neck dropping to squeeze my breast in reprimand. The first touch had my nipples hardening beneath my bodice, but the second had me sucking in a gasp of pain instead, my body flinching back from where Terek's thumb had slid between my breasts.

His chest heaved in and out as he stared down at me, one hand still wrapped firmly around my hip and his eyes pitch black. "Did I hurt you?"

"No, it's not you," I said, pushing the pain to the far back of my mind, not wanting to give him any reason to pull away. "It's just this ridiculous dress. I'm fine."

"Are you sure?"

I smiled and nodded, my heart squeezing at the concern laced within his voice. "Yes, Terek, I'm sure."

I realized my mistake the second I uttered his name, but it was too late. In a blink, Terek had thrown me back, pinning me to the nearest tree so fast and hard, the back of my head audibly bounced off the bark. I blinked rapidly to clear the dots in my vision and tried to pull air into my lungs only to find him glaring down at me, one hand wrapped around my throat while the other held the point of a knife over my heart.

"Who the crimson fuck are you?" he spat, all traces of desire and heat gone, replaced by a cold fury that made my heart sink to the ground at my feet.

"T-Terek" I gasped, trying to force the words up my throat and past his hold. "It-it's...me."

His hands immediately dropped away, and he shoved back several feet, his shock a physical, tangible thing between us as he stared at me, his weapon now pointed at the ground.

"Ace?"

TEREK

CHAPTER SEVENTEEN

I gaped at the woman slumped against a tree, her chest contracting quickly to regain the breath I'd stolen from her, lips still swollen and red from our kiss. If what had just happened could be called something as simple as a kiss. Fucking life-altering was more like it.

Beautiful in a way that was as stunning as it was lethal, she'd all but obliterated my defenses with nothing more than the mild scent of vanilla and the touch of her wrist, instantly ensnaring me in a thrall I'd had no plans to try to understand or escape from.

It'd sparked throughout my entire body before homing in at my chest to settle into the empty void that'd once housed my soul.

Foolishly believing I knew what that feeling meant, I'd let instinct take over, only for fate to backhand me across the face, cackling all the while. Because not only had I been wrong about the connection I'd thought I felt, but I'd done so with fucking Ace.

Ace. The gangly girl who couldn't take a hint and never knew how to stop talking, with stringy yellow hair and a round face that bunched up whenever she felt slighted. Which was all the time.

Crimson. Fucking. Take me.

She flushed a deep red and reached up to tuck her hair—now a lush curtain of black waves—behind her ear. Even now, the similarities were few and far between. Her skin was paler than it'd ever been, her freckles hidden beneath powder, and her face had slimmed down, losing the softness of youth.

The only thing soft about the woman in front of me were the curves I'd had squeezed against me just a moment ago. The fullness of her breast in my hand and those goddamn thighs I'd been seconds from wrapping around my waist.

It was like the instant I saw her staring up at the sky in wonder, wearing a dress that accentuated everything about her, I'd needed to touch her. But doing so had only strengthened the feeling. I couldn't get her close enough, taste her thoroughly enough. I'd nearly flung my abilities wide open, inviting the entire world to rain down upon me, just to satisfy that urge.

Of course, the first woman to ever make me consider believing the bullshit the romantics here spouted about connections, would wind up being her. I'd had a multitude of adept partners over the decades, but not even Liz had made me question it. No, it had to be Ace. Fate, it seemed, was a meddling, cockblocking bitch.

"Terek?"

I tensed at her voice, rough and thick from an arousal *I'd* put there. It was still coating her, a heady scent that'd almost made me lose all sense of what was happening and do much more than kiss her.

It was Ace, and I hadn't noticed.

"I can't fucking believe this," I muttered, sheathing my dagger while I subconsciously ran a hand over my mouth, the taste of her still lingering on my lips.

She hesitated and fidgeted awkwardly, fisting her hands in the shimmering folds of her dress. "What part?"

"*What part*—" I closed my eyes and inhaled deeply, the last flicker of heat dying out as my frustration spiked. It would seem, even after all this time, I still didn't know how to keep myself far away from lying, deceitful women.

But it was the fact that I hadn't realized it was her, regardless of her intent on keeping it from me, that fueled my rising frustration into anger. No amount of curves, powdered skin, or dark hair should've been enough to blind me to who she was. Maybe if I'd been anyone else, but

I couldn't understand how I hadn't *felt* her.

The only explanation that came even close was that I hadn't sensed her in years, and that for once, I'd already been in the area when she'd arrived. I'd been preoccupied with pushing back an entire horde of Creatures that'd come sniffing around, so it was possible I just hadn't noticed.

But even now, though I could hear her heartbeat and feel that familiar tug now that my head was no longer stuck up my goddamn ass, it was different. Like it was fading somehow.

The idea needled at me, but I promptly ignored it, shoving any worry over her back to the pit where it belonged. I had no right to want any kind of connection to her. Not just because I'd known her when she was still missing teeth, but because she still possessed a beating heart and didn't belong here.

"Why the fuck didn't you say anything?" I finally spat, my harsh accusation startling her. "You knew damn well I didn't recognize you."

"Why didn't I say anything?" she repeated back to me, propping her hands on her hips and huffing a forced laugh. "Are you seriously asking me that while standing there glaring at me like I murdered you and sent you to the Underland myself?"

"I have a damn good reason to glare at you."

She rolled her eyes. "Terek, we both know you would've done so even if I'd have told you right away."

When I said nothing, which only proved her point, she shook her head and looked away, releasing a heavy sigh. "Look, I'm sorry for not telling you who I was. I should have. But I won't apologize for wanting you to treat me like a human being with feelings for once."

"You wanted a whole lot more from me than to be treated nicely," I growled, the twitch of my cock only further pissing me off. *No, goddamn it.*

Ace's face heated even more, the bright shade of red spreading to engulf her neck and collar. But she straightened her spine and tipped her chin up, acting completely unbothered, as if her heartbeat didn't give away just how badly she wanted to run from this entire confrontation.

"Be an ass all you want. I'm used to it. But you're just as much of a liar as I am if you claim you didn't feel the same thing I did. You were the one who tried to kiss me first, so I know you felt something, too."

Her hand contracted at her side, as if remembering how the evidence of my want had felt gripped in her palm. Evidence that was only too happy to make itself known again with barely a thought if I made the mistake of touching her again.

I seethed, fighting the urge to rip out every tree around me at the humiliating fact that no lie I told would hide what she'd felt. Her lips curled up, like she could read every word on my face and truly thought she'd won. As if my physical reaction meant what happened between us was okay when it was anything but.

"Oh, you're tasty, little rabbit. I won't deny it," I said, wanting nothing more than to wipe that arrogant smile from her pretty red lips. "But you're still just that. *A little rabbit.* I'd enjoy the flavor, but I'd leave the meal still hungry and looking for something better."

I let my eyes rove down her body again, like a bored merchant shopping for common spices, and she flinched back. Hurt filled her expression before she was able to fight it down, and her eyes blinked just a little too fast to be unbothered. When she spoke again, her voice was hard.

"I didn't ask for you to show up, Terek. I never have. You've always been the one to make that choice, so just leave if you don't want to be here. I can find my way on my own."

She twisted away from me, but I'd already anticipated it and easily blocked her. Pissed off at her or not, there was absolutely no way in hell she was leaving this Wood alone.

Just the idea of someone coming across her with her dress unlaced down her back had me carving my nails into my palms. I wanted to choke her and scream at her, while also taking those fucking lips against mine and feeling her writhe beneath my touch.

The clash of the two overwhelming desires made me hate her.

"Choice? You think I've ever had a choice when it comes to you? That I'd choose to wander into this godforsaken Wood over and over for a fucking child?" I laughed, the sound waking up something inside me I usually kept a tight restraint on. Something dark and cruel.

"I've tried to rid myself of you more times than I can count, but you're like a relentless weed, returning again and again, no matter how many times I rip you out. All because coming here makes you feel *special*."

"That's not why I come here, you insufferable ass," she snapped, her own anger rising to cover up the flare of hurt I could see pooling in her eyes. She sniffed and looked away, crossing her arms over her stomach. "I come here because it makes me feel safe."

I scoffed, beseeching the sky for patience. Was she kidding me? "You only feel safe because I kill all the precious Creatures you beg me not to. If I stopped, you'd never make it back home." And how I wished that fact didn't make me feel the way it did.

"The Upside is no home of mine. I'd rather take my chances with the monsters down here than the monsters up there," she said, her eyes glaring daggers at me as if I were the real monster here rather than the actual ones who harbored this Wood.

What was left of my restraint splintered at that look, and I shot forward, slamming her back against the tree. A whimper slipped from her lips, and her heart took off like a drum, her lungs pulling in air like she was preparing for me to steal her ability to use it.

I hovered my face over hers, caging her in with a hand on either side of her head. "Are you so desperate for death, little rabbit? Because I can make that happen, if you're so keen," I whispered, letting my breath coast over the shell of her ear and watching gooseflesh erupt down her neck.

"You speak of monsters, yet you've no idea what the real ones look like. You stay here, and I will show you just how miserable your life can truly be." Just like mine and everyone else trapped in this forsaken world.

Ace had always seen the Underland from a child's eye as some magical haven no matter how many times I told her otherwise. She had no fucking idea what most of the people here had been through. Part of that was my fault for not telling her, but I'd never seen a reason for a living person to know the details.

Outrage sparking in her eyes, Ace raised both hands between us and futilely shoved against my chest with all her strength, only to immediately suck in a sharp breath and yank them back.

My nostrils flared at her wince and caught a light medicinal scent mixed in with hers, barely noticeable, but there. My eyes fell to where her hands hovered over her breasts, and I had to swallow back the urge to rip them away and demand what was wrong.

Catching me looking, she gripped the top of her bodice and pulled it higher, flattening it to her collar and only furthering my suspicion. My fingers dug into the tree, the wood protesting as the bark cracked beneath my nails and crumbled over her shoulders.

"You know what I think, Ace? I think you're still lying. I think you come here not to be safe, but to feel important. I think you kissed me for the same reason. To feel like you mattered."

I scoffed, letting my self-loathing broil and rise at the way her entire face shut down with each word, until the hatred drowned out everything else inside me. "There's nothing special about you, Ace. As for today," I shrugged, "you were simply...convenient."

Her eyes flared, and for a moment, I wondered if she might actually slap me. Part of me hoped she would, but she only tipped her head back and met my eyes. "I'd rather be convenient than spineless. Because you can spout your threats all you want, but we both know you won't kill me."

She leaned closer, and I tensed, refusing to show my hand by pulling out of reach, but not wanting her to touch me either. I didn't know what it had done to me before, but I couldn't risk hindering my focus again.

"And you want to know the best part?" Her breath coasted over my neck, and my teeth clenched so hard I thought they'd shatter.

"What?" I gritted out.

"Whether it makes me special or not, this is my ability, not yours. I can come here whenever I please, no matter how much you hate me for it, and there's not a thing you can do about it."

"I won't have to. I'm not babysitting you anymore, Ace," I said, tasting every word of the lie as they flicked off my tongue. "And something tells me you won't make it past your first trip without me before you inevitably cuddle the wrong pet and go straight to the afterlife."

I tilted my head. "Then again, wanting to die has always been something you're obsessed with, so maybe you'd enjoy that, too."

Her eyes shuttered in an instant, a solid wall slamming down over them until they appeared as empty as those belonging to some of the oldest citizens here. "There are worse things than death, Terek."

"You have no fucking idea how true that is."

She smiled then, and it was the utter lack of life to the expression that finally gave me pause, dampening my anger like a wet blanket. It was a look I knew all too well, and one that made a memory from years ago spring to the front of my mind. Of Ace when she was about fifteen, curled into herself with swollen welts on her hands and the hint of blood on her body.

"You're wrong, you know," she said, the lifelessness to her voice so similar to how she'd spoken back then. "I didn't kiss you because I wanted to feel special. I kissed you because I've never had choices either, and I wanted you to be my first one."

"Adelais—" Her name was like a delicacy on my tongue, but she didn't seem to hear me as she turned away and closed her eyes, a single tear slipping down her cheek. Then she was gone, leaving me with nothing but uncertainty, hatred, and the lingering scent of vanilla in my nose.

It stayed with me long into the night as I continued to walk deeper into the Wood, my senses wide open and my daggers raining blood, seeing nothing but her empty eyes, and leaving slaughtered bodies in my wake.

ADELAIS

CHAPTER EIGHTEEN

It'd been less than a full day since I'd stepped out of a coach, and already I was sitting in another one, this particular one preparing to take me back to a place I'd only just escaped. At least, to a home nauseatingly close by to it, which I knew in my bones would be so much worse.

Turner's personal coach was a rich black color that reminded me of a man I was adamantly shoving from my mind with both hands and was far nicer and roomier than the first I'd taken to the estate. Yet, it somehow felt like a box closing in on me, threatening to squeeze the life from my chest if I let my guard down.

But that was probably due more to the horrible man sitting across from me than anything else.

I could still remember the way my parents had looked at me like their prize mare as I'd sat next to Turner at the table this morning, dark purple splotches under my eyes from my sleepless night and my pressed lips cracked from my abuse of them.

They'd seen none of that, of course, as they'd given me their quick acknowledgments before my father had given Turner a firm handshake and my mother had sipped her wretched tea, looking more eager than I'd ever seen her.

Besides the unyielding, clammy grip of a hand over my knee to control the nervous fidgeting Turner had always hated, no one paid me any attention as they'd discussed the details of their deal. My parents' donation amount, everyone's desire to do this quietly and without a grand affair, and the timeline of when they expected my womb to be shooting out children for them like a factory.

I took it all in stride. The less anyone looked at me or acknowledged my existence, the better. I'd been mere background décor most of my life, so that kind of future, at least, I knew I could survive just fine. I simply sat there and nibbled on my food, saying absolutely nothing.

Not as they finished breakfast and Turner guided me out with a hand on my lower back. Not as my bags, which never even made it to my room, were packed into the trunk of the coach. And not as I'd walked past George and Margarette Ellington to climb into it.

Not because I'd come home from the Wood suddenly deciding to give in and be a dutiful daughter—they could choke and die for all I cared—but because if I allowed even a sound to slip between my lips, I'd scream until the entire estate collapsed around us.

I had no more tears remaining in my body after I'd left Terek and had fallen to the ground in the estate woods, letting my broken heart crumble to pieces.

I'd cried well into the night until the soil had soaked up every bit of self-pity I'd had inside me, and only my hate and determination remained. Then I'd staggered to my feet and began the trek back to the house with nothing but the glow of the moon and the fire inside me to guide my way.

I wouldn't give Turner the power to break me, not again. I'd survive him just like I had last night and all the years before. He may have control over my future and the places I could go Upside, but he had no control over the places I could go that weren't. And neither did Terek.

Midnight eyes flashed in my mind, but I pushed them back again, refusing to let him get another moment of my thoughts. Terek couldn't keep me out of the Underland either, no matter how much he despised me and wished to.

He may have been right that neither of us knew what would happen if I died while in the Underland, but that wouldn't stop me from continuing to visit whenever I wished, especially now that I knew I could do it on my own. As long as I had that and found a way to sketch whenever Turner wasn't around, I could survive this.

Because I'd be damned if I let any of these overbearing assholes win in the end.

The coach lurched, the wheels grumbling and crunching over loose gravel as the horses pulled them into motion. I sighed, feeling Turner's smug gaze on the side of my face as I turned to look out the window.

I ignored him and stared out of the slightly fogged pane, wishing with all my heart to see Mrs. Gayle standing in the grass, waving farewell to me. Although the lawn stood empty where she'd once snuck me away and cleaned me up, I heard her voice whispering to me as I squeezed the small watch hidden within my coat pocket.

"Every time you look at this, I want you to remember that someone here loves you."

I smiled, and as Ellington Estate disappeared from view, I could've sworn I felt her arms wrap around me as I did.

"What are you smiling about?" Turner asked, irritation to his tone.

"Nothing. I just thought I saw a white rabbit."

TEREK

CHAPTER NINETEEN

Passing the walls of Ardenglass had always felt like willingly walking into a prison. A white, beacon of a prison that reached out and ripped apart another piece of my sanity every time I did. Walking through the city and into the heart of the White Castle was even worse.

Bloodthirsty Creatures, bounty hunters, and idiotic White Guards who couldn't shut their mouths I could handle, but stepping foot into the colorless abomination the queen had erected in her honor always made me feel like I was drowning all over again.

Whether that was because of what had happened the first time I had, or because of who I had to become every time I returned, I wasn't sure, and I didn't much care. I'd tear the entire thing down with my bare hands if I could.

Ardenglass, once a small town like Gissan or Abgrove, had flourished under the queen's rule, quickly becoming the primary refuge for new souls against the Creatures of the Wood back when they still wandered the Underland freely. Or so, history claimed.

Signs had been nailed to trees all along the main roads, pointing new souls toward the town with the promise of safety and supplies until they got settled and worked through whatever they needed to be ready for their final afterlives.

The more souls that arrived, the more Ardenglass grew, until it was a city three times the size of any other within several days travel. It became vastly overpopulated, and the queen, terrified the very people she claimed to want to save would be the ones to draw the attention of the Creatures, wanted them gone.

It was during that time I found myself here. People began being organized into smaller populations based on their skills and interests and sent out to join other towns or make new ones, such as Tover and Wenham. Though Wenham was only built within the last decade or so, and for very different reasons.

The White Castle itself, the one I was currently strutting through with a smirk on my face like every step didn't make me want to slowly peel my skin off, was built after. A gift the queen had built for herself for winning the war.

She'd earned her title of Crimson Queen around the same time— not for what she'd had us do to the Creatures, but for how she'd repaid all of us who'd fought for her. Once she'd started her new war against her citizens, the signs had been torn down, and new souls were warned to stay far away.

Now, only those who'd already lost everything they could lose stayed within the walls of Ardenglass, living out their eternal lives with no purpose other than hers. Not that the queen would ever admit it. She was too busy believing herself the savior of all, forever protecting them from the horrors the Creatures would have done to them, in exchange for only one small payment.

Personally, I'd take that which lurked *outside* of Ardenglass to that which lurked *within* any day. And if the whispers were true, more and more citizens were beginning to agree.

Now, here I was, walking the last few halls to the throne room, wishing the Creatures would storm from the Wood and attack, if only to keep me from having to enter that damn room. I clenched the royal letter in my fist, wishing I'd have followed my urge to gut the White Guard who'd brought it to me so I could feign ignorance to the queen's summons.

I'd just exited the Wood and had been walking along the river, having wasted yet another day searching for signs of Ace, when he'd come up behind me. My senses had been closed tight, my mind fogged over by the full week with no sign of her, and I hadn't sensed him before that moment. To his unluck.

I'd left the pathetic man alive, if not soiled and bleeding, only to instantly wish I hadn't once I'd read the letter he'd brought to me.

Her Royal Majesty requests your immediate presence.
Make haste.

With the foul mood I'd been in for a week, I would've ignored it, if not for the uneasy feeling the unwarranted summons gave me. There were a lot of things I ignored in life, but my instincts were not one of them. And they were screaming at me that something was wrong.

I shook the memory off, but the feeling clung to me like a bur. I needed to keep my focus. This was the last place I could afford to not be at my best, especially when those same instincts were reminding me that the queen would easily be able to tell if I wasn't.

Once through the main gate, which was swarming with White Guards twiddling their thumbs, I didn't pass many more within the castle walls themselves. Most of them spent their days tracking down any new souls desperate enough to attempt to run from the queen's orders.

Those who did stay within the castle were barely noticeable. Wearing all white, from their helmets down to their feet, they practically blended into the walls behind them, looking more like décor than useful defenses. Only the blood-red pommels of their swords and the small rose insignia in the center of their breastplates gave any color to their forms.

The same was true of every inch I walked. Everything was varying degrees of white: the tiled floor, the ceiling, even the portrait frames on the walls. Everything. The only exception being the large vases of thorned, red roses that adorned either side of the last hall leading to the throne room.

All visitors who wished an audience with the queen—which weren't many these days—or those who'd been tracked down and brought in by her guard, wore white if they could help it. The queen had never made an official decree requiring it, but it was well known that wearing anything else was asking to be thrown even further out of favor.

So, as usual, I stalked up to the six decorative men standing in front of the throne room doors, wearing solid fucking black.

Although four of them didn't move a muscle, other than to hover their hands a little closer to their pommels, two stepped forward, their armor clanking obnoxiously as they outstretched their arms toward me.

The woman on the left cleared her throat and gestured to my waist. "Weapons."

I glared at her, tempted to stab my daggers through her palms if she wanted them so badly, but somehow refrained. I was well aware the queen didn't allow anyone but her guards to have weapons near her. It was an order I'd be all too happy to ignore, if not for the fact that the two guards who'd stepped forward could detect even my hidden ones. The first guard with the ability to sense metal, the other, wood.

I clenched the summons even harder, hearing it tear inside my fist before stuffing it into my pocket and making quick work of my black-leathered daggers. The ones in my sheaths and the two smaller ones in my boots. I slapped them into their waiting palms, using more force than necessary and enjoying their grunts of pain.

"Do not. Lose. Those."

They both nodded and immediately retreated to their original posts at my order, while the guards who'd stayed back wrapped their hands around the large, opal handles and heaved open the doors to reveal the room that still haunted my nightmares.

I inhaled and exhaled slowly, letting myself sink into the darkest corner of my mind. Once I was confident my emotions were tucked as far away as possible, I rolled my shoulders and passed through, feeling the lack of my daggers with each step.

Where the rest of the palace had been a collection of varying shades of whites and creams, the throne room was what gave the massive eyesore of a castle its name. From the plastered ceiling down to the pristine tile of the floor, the expansive room was bright, stark fucking white.

Candelabras bordered both sides of the ornate, woven runner down the center of the room, while dozens upon dozens of sconces lined the walls. The light efficiently and effectively refracting off the surfaces and putting anyone entering at an immediate disadvantage.

My eyes burned, the feeling similar to walking into a lit room after being in a pitch darkness, but I forced them to stay open, unwilling to rein in my senses for even a split second. Something I was sure the queen was eagerly hoping I'd do.

Instead, I kept my face blank and moved at a steady pace, my boots thudding across the runner as I walked between the empty court seats toward the raised dais at the back of the room. And the single, massive throne of bones that sat in the center of it.

Although smooth as a river stone around the white, velvet cushions and armrests, every other inch of the throne was crafted by various sizes and shapes of bleached bones. Each one torn from the bodies of Creatures that had fought back in the war.

The queen had forced men and women alike to haul the slain bodies from the Wood, even though the war had barely ended, and their own bodies were still bruised and their wills broken.

The desecrated bones made up the four legs holding it upright while also extending several feet out on either side across the dais, the pieces perfectly cut and placed to create detailed sculptures of thorned branches growing from the high back of the seat. To represent not only that the Creatures had died at her hand, but that new life would grow from it.

Or whatever stupid shit she'd spewed at her citizens. Not that anyone but her faithful guards believed it.

And sadly for me, the monstrosity was occupied by the devil herself. With her pale skin and delicate, snowy dress, the woman sitting within its arms was barely discernible, apart from her thick mane of auburn curls, red lips, and the emerald eyes boring into me even from across the distance.

I forced my senses to span wider, fighting back the flinch that always came when I did so in public, and analyzed her features, looking for any hint as to her mood or what this sudden meeting could be for.

Freckles covered her skin, but unlike the sporadic dusting Ace had along her nose, the queen's were a smattering that continued down her cheeks and across her shoulders and arms, both of which were visible through the slits in her sheer sleeves. She wore no powder or added color of any kind, except for two blood-red slashes across her lips and painted over her nails.

Even after all this time, after everything she'd done, the woman was still painfully beautiful. Not in the stunning, jaw-dropping way Ace now was, but enough that even hatred couldn't protect me from noticing. And I wasn't sure if that made me hate her or myself more.

The White Castle's court was not in attendance, though that was no surprise since the topics the queen typically brought up with me weren't ones she wanted her subjects to know. But neither was she alone.

A second woman stood at the bottom of the dais just off to the right, dressed in trousers and an overly large tunic that I assumed were once white, but were now discolored with age and overuse. I recognized her long before she turned her face to me, and the uneasy feeling that had flickered to life now roared with a vengeance.

Why the crimson hell was Hara here?

Locked into an eternal age of eighteen, Hara had been in the Underland for a handful of decades now, but you'd never know it upon seeing her. With hollowed cheeks and shadowed eyes that looked even darker against her tan skin, combined with her unwashed blonde hair, she looked more like she was still toeing the line of death in the Upside than wandering freely here.

She was a self-serving, lying bitch on her worst days, and a wily, skittish one on her best. She always looked seconds from bolting from wherever she was, her eyes often darting about like she was either waiting for someone to attack her or just realized she was late for something important.

As someone in possession of an extremely useful ability, Hara also happened to be one of the queen's most trusted Soul Seekers. A job for which I hated her for, almost as much as the Underland seemed to.

The possibility of her being here at the same time as me by pure coincidence was slim, especially with the arrogant look currently tainting her gaunt face.

Stopping at the foot of the dais, I lowered myself into a deep bow, fisting my hands and nearly clawing through my palms to keep from grabbing uselessly at my empty sheaths. I didn't trust either of these women not to stab me in the back during the drawn-out seconds my bow forced me to take my eyes off them.

The Crimson Queen sat forward and slowly uncrossed her legs, allowing the side panels of her skirt to rest against the cushion and reveal the freckled skin of her upper thighs.

"Terek, my love. When they'd said you'd arrived at the gate, I must say, I was pleasantly surprised. You so rarely come to visit me anymore. I can't even remember how long it's been since your face has graced this room. A whole year?"

Her voice was smooth and sultry, echoing lightly in the open room and stabbing my sensitive senses like venom-coated needles to my eardrums. I bit my tongue hard enough to bleed to keep myself from scoffing. She said it like I'd come here of my own free will, rather than by a cursed letter delivered by a guard unbefitting of his job.

"Ten months, Your Majesty, and the pleasure of your summons is all mine. As always," I said, rising up to pin my gaze on her emerald one, each word tasting like ash on my tongue.

She *tsk*ed and waved a red fingernail at me. "Although your dedication to showing respect is acknowledged, we are far too close for such formality, *as always.*"

Her warning was clear, but I was in no mood to heed it today. Not when half my mind was still on the hazel-eyed woman who'd yet to come back since I'd seen her a week ago, and I was standing in Ardenglass, unable to go if that tug appeared. *If* it appeared.

The Crimson Queen frowned at my silence and then leaned to the side, drumming her nails on the armrest and making a show of looking behind me. "Where is Cain? The guard I sent to you. He was to escort you here and see to your needs."

See to my needs, my ass. He'd been sent to deliver a message and make sure I followed through. The first he'd succeeded at. The second, not so much. "The last I saw of him, Your Majesty, he was still writhing on the ground, squealing like a pig."

The guards just within the door behind me shifted, their armor clanking slightly, and the queen's eyes snapped to mine. "Did you kill yet another member of my White Guard, my love?"

I shook my head, feeling no remorse. "Of course not, Your Majesty. I simply removed his ability to speak after he chose to misuse it and ignore my warning."

The guard, Cain, had handed over the royal letter with a cocky gait and pinched face I'd immediately wanted to punch. I'd attempted to take the letter and ignore him, but then he'd made the poor choice to run his mouth about how inadequate I must've been in the queen's bed to be banished from her righthand to the Wood.

In truth, I was used to the comments, but I'd just finished a long day searching for Ace and finding only Creatures that'd been irritatingly difficult to kill, and I'd been in no mood to be reminded of my history of blind loyalty.

So when Cain failed to heed the silent warning in my eyes and continued talking, I'd taken it upon myself to slice my dagger through his tongue like the snake he so desperately wanted to be.

The queen sighed, pushing to stand and taking her time brushing out invisible wrinkles from her dress. "Why must you always pick on my favorites? He had such a lovely ability, too."

"As long as his ability had nothing to do with the skill of his tongue, he'll be fine. If he deserts, it will be from no fault of mine, Your Majesty."

She squinted at me for a long moment, and then huffed a breath and turned to Hara. "Why must men be so difficult? It's a wonder I keep any of them around at all."

Hara nodded, as expected, and the queen's eyes flashed as they met mine again. "Teaching a man a lesson, I can respect. However, ignoring my request to drop formality, I cannot."

The tone of her voice brooked no argument, and I stiffened. "My apologies, Lizbeth."

She clicked her tongue again. "Come now, I do so prefer it when you call me Liz."

TEREK

CHAPTER TWENTY

The sound of the nickname I'd once whispered to her at night, back when I'd longed to trace my lips over her skin and hear her laughter in my ear, made that darkness inside me sit up higher.

There was a time when I'd wanted nothing more than her. To protect her and care for her the way she had when she'd first found me. When I'd been at my lowest, medicating with alcohol to help drown out my senses and the sudden, overwhelming anger I couldn't seem to control here.

I couldn't fight a man without punching a hole through his chest, couldn't bed a woman without causing irreversible damage. I hadn't wanted to be alive anymore, not if life in the Underland was the only one offered to me.

Then she'd arrived with that piercing gaze that saw the dying soul within me, and she'd helped me figure it out, one day, one week, one month at a time. Her patience had been unending, and I'd loved her unconditionally.

Unfortunately for me, Queen Lizbeth, a title she'd kept hidden until I was so deep in her waters, I could no longer see the surface, had only ever wanted one thing from me. And I'd given it to her without a second thought, only to discover her beauty had been a mask for the corruption beneath.

Forcing me to verbally recognize our past and my idiocy each time she dragged me before her only furthered that fact and enraged me, just as she knew it would. My nostrils flared, and I dipped my head again, if only to hide the way I knew death leached into my eyes.

For what had to be the millionth time, I wished with everything I was that I could throw a blade through her heart and be done with it. Or run up and snap her neck before she even knew what was happening.

But the light tapping of her fingers over her chest as she watched me straighten up, and the knowing smirk curling her red lips, leashed the desire back down. Because while I may have possessed more abilities than any other, that did not include *her*.

Lizbeth flashed me a beaming smile and waved me off, as if my clear desire to torture her slowly was of no concern. She began making her way down the dais, clicking her heels loudly on each step, knowing it would grate across my eardrums.

"Now that that's settled, I'll get straight to the point, my love. For as we know, every hour you are away from the border increases the chance of war at our gate."

I internally sneered at her dramatics, but nodded to show I was listening. She paused two steps above the floor, maintaining the higher ground compared to my height.

"I requested to see you mostly because I missed you dearly, but also because of something rather…distressing that Hara has brought to my attention regarding you."

What the fuck? The uneasy feeling grew again, overshadowing the anger Lizbeth had attempted to distract me with. I tilted my head to the side, letting my gaze land on Hara, and watched her fidget beneath my attention as she fought to keep her expression controlled.

"Did she now?"

"Indeed. She claims to have seen you with a woman just within the Wood, which is, as you're aware, strictly forbidden to all citizens not under orders."

The second the word 'woman' left her mouth, the unease in my gut immediately dropped away as a lethal calm washed over me. It swept through like a wave, wiping away every reaction from my face and controlling the heartbeat I knew Lizbeth was listening for. All while every other part of me went on high alert.

I had no idea why the hell Hara would've been anywhere near the Wood, but there was only one woman I'd ever been with there, and she was someone I'd do anything to keep Lizbeth from finding out about. Knowing the temperamental bitch, this was likely just one of her jealousy fits, but the knowledge of Ace's ability, and what Lizbeth would do to obtain it, burned in my chest, my instincts screaming at me to tread very, very carefully.

Keeping my breathing steady, I tucked my hands in my pockets, watching both of them follow the movement with keen gazes like they didn't quite trust that I hadn't made it in there without a hidden blade.

"I'm afraid Hara will have to be a little more specific, but if the question is whether I have fucked a woman against a tree, the answer is yes. I wasn't aware the right to personal pleasure had been banned from me, as well."

Lizbeth's eyes flashed. "Be very careful how you speak, *my love*. You and I both know I quite like your brand of pleasure. However, it does become a problem when it interferes with your duty. Since random fucks, as you so eloquently put it, are not where your attention should be."

She paused, taking another step down. "Especially when the location is cause for punishment…for them."

I shrugged, knowing my indifference would infuriate her. "I'm assuming this is in reference to my latest company, and if so, I can guarantee that my attention was perfectly fine. She was a new soul, pretty enough, and convenient."

Repeating the disgusting word I'd used to Ace's face made me taste bile, but I shoved it down. If Lizbeth thought for even a moment that I felt anything other than lust for another woman, alive or not, she'd track her down and send her straight to the dark abyss.

"Is that so?" Lizbeth asked, raising a single brow and taking the last step off the dais, her nearness making revulsion crawl under my skin. "Is that why you didn't sense Hara? Whom I can only assume wasn't sneaking up on you given I had been the one to send her. Because your attention was…perfectly fine?"

I bristled, having no comeback other than to admit that I'd been so caught up in the taste of Ace, I'd been unable to sense anything other than her. Lizbeth sighed, tucking a few wayward curls from her face. "You carry so much unnecessary resentment, my love, but I do hope, beneath it, you remember how I feel about you lying to me."

I met her eyes, feeling the demon inside scream and thrash at the cage of my ribs. The demon *she'd* created. "Yes, Liz. I remember your history with honesty exceedingly well."

All traces of her mask fell away, and the queen I'd come to hate took its place, her green eyes hardening to ice. She advanced until only a foot separated us, her long nails tapping over her chest again, like a thief patting a purse of stolen coin.

"Hara, repeat for Mr. Terence Crowell what you saw."

She may as well have slapped me across the face. My hands went to my sheaths on instinct, and a growl worked up my throat, the desire to rip out her vocal cords so strong, it made every muscle in my body vibrate. She had no right to utter that name anymore after what she'd done.

What were the chances I could tear her head from her body before she could do the same to me? Because while Lizbeth was currently capable of it, I had far more experience.

She watched my hands twitching over my empty sheaths and leaned closer, as if daring me to try, and for a moment, I almost considered risking it. But then Hara spoke, and her words snapped my head to her instead, confirming my worst fear and freezing the blood in my veins.

"When I found you, you were fighting with a woman who didn't look like a new soul. I wasn't close enough to make out your argument, but there was something off about her. Like there was a…light to her or something. And when I edged closer to get a better look, she completely disappeared."

Hara cut a look at me like she hoped her pale blue eyes could slice me open where I stood. "And you didn't appear *remotely* surprised at her show of an ability."

I suddenly felt like I couldn't breathe, but I urged that wave of calm to sweep in and keep the panic hidden from view. I knew exactly what light she was referring to. Ace's inner light had been nonexistent when I'd run into her, one of the excuses I'd clung to as to why I hadn't recognized her, but for a few moments, while I'd had her mouth against mine, I'd seen a hint of it again, like her soul was waking up.

And fucking Hara seeing it was one of the exact reasons Ace should never have been here in the first place.

"Curious, isn't it?" Lizbeth asked, still far too close for my comfort as she absently twirled a ring around her finger. "And what do you have to say about that? About this…ability."

The hairs along the back of my neck rose. She said it without a flicker of interest in her voice, but after years of dealing with her moods, I knew better. Lizbeth wasn't just interested; she was fucking ecstatic.

Shit, shit, *shit*.

I smirked, scrambling for anything that would wipe away her excitement and remove Ace from Lizbeth's attention. *She doesn't know what she can do.* "I'd say whatever light Hara believes she saw was only the poor woman's irrational anger when she realized I had no intention of courting her." I shrugged. "In my experience, furious women tend to burn quite hot."

Hara's eyes narrowed and her lips pressed thin, making her appearance even more unflattering. "I know what I saw. She had an ability, Your Majesty. A strong one. And he didn't even try to bring her to you."

I opened my mouth to snap back, contemplating just how much trouble I'd be in if I snapped her neck instead, but Lizbeth cut in, raising her hand to caress my cheek. "I will always have a soft spot for you, Terek, but if you lie to me again, there will be consequences."

My body turned to granite, and my jaw tightened beneath her touch as I actively fought to keep my emotions locked away at the feel of her skin against mine.

"I have not lied to you, Liz. Yes, I was with a woman who possessed some kind of ability," I admitted, no longer able to claim otherwise, "but I was not aware of it until she'd used it. At that point, she was gone, and it was too late."

I shrugged again, like all my focus wasn't on keeping the demon contained to my chest, who's thrashing increased with each second Lizbeth touched me. "I assumed her gift was similar to Hara's, but like I said, she was gone."

Hara snorted, her reedy arms coming up to cross over her chest. "If she was a random fuck like you claim, what, pray tell, were you fighting about so animatedly? I got close enough to hear you say her name before she left. *Adelais*. Doesn't sound like a random fuck to me."

Ace's real name rang out through the room so loudly, I swore every citizen in Ardenglass could hear it, and my nostrils flared. I was going to burn Hara alive. Slowly, starting at her fucking toes. "What you view as animated and what I do, differs vastly. The woman was no one."

Lizbeth's nails instantly curled in, dragging my face back to hers as the pointed tips cut into my cheek with a heightened strength that didn't belong to her. "That, my love, is where you're wrong. I am quite good at seeing souls, in case you've forgotten."

"I haven't," I bit out, feeling the sting of my skin splitting.

"They shine to me," she continued like I hadn't spoken, digging her nails in deeper and tracking each line of blood as it dripped over my jaw. "Like a beautiful, soothing light that pulses around a body, telling me who has one and who does not."

I struggled not to break her wrist, knowing what she was about to say and wishing upon whatever god or fate existed that I could prevent the words before she spoke them.

She stopped, dragging her eyes back to mine. "Yet this woman didn't shine for me, Terek. She *glowed* like the Upside sun itself, calling out to me." Her voice sounded far away, and her eyes fogged over like she could picture that glow, and it hit me then like a punch to the face.

Why Lizbeth was confident enough in a random Soul Seeker's claim that she'd risk calling me away from the Wood to discuss it. A

Soul Seeker I already had a negative history with.

Because Lizbeth had seen Ace.

Sometimes, it was hard to remember just how many souls Lizbeth had taken over the years. How many abilities she'd sent her Seekers after and now had at her disposal. Like the young woman who could see a person's most recent memories, or the man who could pull an image straight from someone's mind and turn it into ink on parchment.

And then there were times like this, when she reminded me just how she'd come to power, and how she'd kept it. Because Lizbeth couldn't just take people's souls. She could *use* them.

I swallowed, letting enough of my disgust and dread out to mimic confusion. "What are you insinuating, Liz?"

"An Upsider," Hara whispered, finally catching on like the unwanted piece of shit she was. "You believe that woman was still alive? Holy shit. But…how could that even be possible?"

Lizbeth released my face, her eyes so bright she looked near feverish in the blinding white of the room. "How are any of our abilities possible? I don't know for sure what this Adelais is, but something tells me…" She trailed off, dragging her teeth along her bottom lip. "Either way, I want her soul."

She turned to say something to Hara about lowering her required quota, and I tuned it out, my heart feeling like it was about to seize with the effort to keep it from pounding and giving me away.

Crimson hell, I should've never come here. *It would've only implicated you if you hadn't,* a voice whispered. *She'd already seen her and made the assumption. At least now, you're aware of it.* Fuck, I needed to—

"Terek."

I whipped my head toward the two women now standing side by side, the size of Lizbeth's smile immediately making my stomach fall. "Are you listening to me?"

No. I nodded, unable to speak.

"Good. As I said, let's make a game of it then, shall we? Anyone may play." Her smile grew in time with the dread in my stomach. What the hell was she talking about?

"Whoever brings me this Adelais, the woman who can jump between worlds, will be given a reward." Lizbeth met my eyes, making sure I held her gaze, as she placed a hand over her chest. She made a humming sound, and a soft, blue light built beneath her hand, pulling away from her chest and casting shadows across her neck and jaw.

"The reward being the permanent return of their soul."

Time stopped, every one of my senses freezing. I heard nothing. Felt nothing. Saw nothing, except for the radiating light of my soul tucked within Lizbeth's chest.

My body lurched forward, and she immediately lowered her hand, the light snapping out of existence as quickly as it'd come. I blinked, watching her lips curl in amusement, while to my right, Hara looked ready to vomit or pass out.

Not once since Lizbeth had ended the war and begun taking souls as payment for her protection had she ever given one back. Not even to those whose abilities she deemed worthless. And especially not to those of us whose abilities she coveted with venomous glee.

It was Hara who recovered first, her slim body practically vibrating as she struggled to keep a rein on her own ability long enough to ask, "Rules?"

"No rules, except not to fatally injure her," Lizbeth said. "Bring her in relatively unharmed and earn your soul."

Hara's body flickered in and out of focus as she bowed deep. "Thank you, Your Majesty. I won't disappoint you." She shot me a glare, and in a blink, she was gone. Most likely reappearing somewhere outside the castle gate to make her way through the city before Lizbeth could spread the word to any others.

Lizbeth didn't even bother watching her disappear, her eyes too busy taking in every inch of my expression. The bitch could keep right on looking. She may have had my soul within her chest and my abilities running through her veins, but she'd get nothing else from me.

"If there is anyone in the Underland who wants their soul back more than you do, my love, it's Hara. I suggest not underestimating her."

"I underestimate no one," I said, my voice flat. I'd only done so once, and it'd cost me everything.

Lizbeth feigned a pout, pretending not to feel the hatred seeping from every pore in my body. "I suppose it's not quite a fair game with everyone playing and you tucked away within the Wood, but I'm sure you'll manage, won't you?"

I didn't react, refusing to rise to her bait. She wanted me to ask to stay, but I'd rather carve my heart out and hand it to her myself before I ever did that. She and I both knew what her answer would be anyway.

Patrolling the Wood for eternity was my punishment for not supporting her when she'd started taking souls and chaining people to the Underland. When she'd done so to *me*. However, what she didn't know, was that, for once, I had no desire to leave it.

"Is that all?"

Her smile changed, softening around the edges as she looked at me under hooded eyes. "Maybe. Why don't you escort me back to my rooms? Surely a few hours won't make a difference, and I can practically see the tension in your muscles."

She lifted her hands as if to curl them around my neck, and I immediately stepped back, letting her arms fall to her sides.

Lizbeth had always been selfish, even when she'd still been Liz to me, but she'd been growing steadily more delusional over the years. Her believing I would ever willingly lay a hand on her again, let alone my cock, only proved just how much worse that delusional world was growing.

"If there is nothing else you would like to accuse me of, I'd like to get back. I don't much appreciate being pulled away over the impracticability of a living woman being here, especially given the rise in Creature activity lately."

Her body stiffened, any hint of lust dropping from her face as doubt took its place. I could practically feel her focusing her stolen senses on me for any sign I was lying. She'd find none.

"Very well, you may go," she finally said, twirling the ring around her finger again. I dipped my head and spun away, hearing her voice continue from behind me. "But when you find this World Jumper, my love, I highly suggest you keep your clothing on this time. I'd hate to have to punish her for that, too."

I didn't bother turning back or answering as I stalked back out of the throne room, a black storm brewing inside of me that I needed to let out. *Now.*

I'd lost any hope of regaining my soul a long time ago, and no matter what bullshit Lizbeth spouted, I couldn't get myself to believe that she'd ever give it back. I could hand her Ace on a silver platter tomorrow and divulge every fact I knew about her ability, and Lizbeth would still find a way to go back on her promise.

But even if she didn't, I'd be trading my soul for Ace's, and the thought of Lizbeth in possession of her soul, and what she might possibly be able to do with her ability, made nausea coil inside me. That was a fate no one, Upside or Under, should want to risk.

And damn me to the dark abyss, as much as I wanted to escape Lizbeth, as much as I wanted to end the eternal misery of the fucking Underland, there was something else I suddenly wanted more. Some*one*, now more than ever, I needed to stay far away from.

While sacrificing Ace might earn me the one thing I'd waited decades to get back, it would also shatter it into a million pieces.

And wasn't that just the cruelest fate of all.

PART TWO
THE UNDERLAND

ADELAIS

CHAPTER TWENTY-ONE

AGE 27

Staring at the repulsive sight before me, I fidgeted, my nose scrunching up at the putrid smell of vomit radiating from the unconscious body slumped over the table.

It was close to midnight, the dining room barely lit since Frederick hadn't bothered to light any of the lanterns, and the fire was now only dying embers.

I'd waited patiently, perched on the edge of my bed, staring at the wall until the house went quiet, and I was sure he'd gone to sleep. Then I'd tiptoed back into the room to double-check, only to discover him still there, face plastered to the wood.

For a too-quick second, between the dried vomit at his lips and his sweat-soaked shirt, I'd blessedly thought him dead. But that dream had been crushed to dust when a loud, wet snore rumbled out of his open mouth.

I hesitated in the doorway, unsure what to do. I wanted to go to the Underland tonight—*needed* to—but doing so with him still downstairs was just asking to get caught. Then again, after the very real threat he'd promised over dinner, staying in my room wasn't exactly safe either.

Nowhere was anymore as long as I was still married to the bastard, and clearly, the medication I'd been crushing up in his food wasn't going to relieve me of that burden anytime soon.

Besides, even if he did wake up, there was a chance he'd just stumble off to his bed. A small chance, given his predilection to visit mine on his way, but still a chance, nonetheless.

In truth, he'd downed so many glasses of liquor tonight, his face ruddy and swollen, he might not notice my absence even if he did barge in. I could just picture him rutting into my pillow, spewing slurs at it and thinking he'd taught me a lesson, before teetering off half-naked to his own chambers.

Daring to take a step into the room, I snapped my fingers to see if he'd wake, but he didn't so much as flinch. I took a deep breath and held it, twisting my body sideways and readying to sprint out of the room in case he suddenly shot up.

"Frederick." Nothing.

"*Frederick.*" Still nothing, not even a hiccup in his snoring.

I released the trapped air from my lungs and staggered back, smacking my left shoulder into the doorframe. He'd never been so gone before, at least, not where I could see him. He'd always disappeared to his room once he'd passed the line of 'just drinking' to 'drunk'.

Gripping the doorframe so hard my nails screamed, I stared at my unconscious husband, feeling my hatred for him rip at my skin until I pictured it tearing from my body one bloody layer at a time.

It would be so easy to cross the last few steps between us and sink a knife into his back. To wrap my fingers around the one resting on his plate and bury the tip into whatever organs I could reach, twisting it back and forth until he howled and begged for mercy.

A mercy he had no right to.

My fingers twitched around the wood, the desire to sprint across the room and follow through making every tendon in my hand spasm. But as glorious as it would feel to quickly kill the man who thought so little of me that he could fall asleep next to a sharp blade and think nothing of it, Frederick didn't deserve that.

Not when I'd been forced to walk through life seeing everything as a possible weapon that could be used against me.

He deserved to suffer slowly, just like I had these last seven years.

He deserved to see the demented satisfaction in my eyes while I rammed a splintered rod into his body and forced him to experience the chafed, tortuous misery I felt every time he entered me. To glimpse the monster he'd created and nurtured inside me while I stabbed him in the gut over and over again, praying that his soul was far too tainted to be allowed to step foot in the Underland.

No, Frederick didn't deserve a lick of mercy a quick death would give him. And as much as the snarling voice in my head begged me to do it, I had no intention of spending another second of my life here in this cursed house.

Not when I could spend my days walking among the trees instead, and certainly not when killing my husband might ruin my own chance of my soul finding its way into the Underland after death. I wasn't actually sure if the purity of one's soul mattered, but until I knew for certain, I'd dare not risk it.

Knocking my knuckles against the wall just to be absolutely positive Frederick was out, I twisted and dashed back to my bedroom, all but ripping off the itchy, tight garment he always made me wear. Instead, I yanked on a thick, boneless dress that blessedly didn't attempt to rearrange my ribs, tucked the watch I went nowhere without into a pocket, and tossed my wedding band into a jewelry box.

Then I ripped every pin and band from my head and ran a comb through my unbound hair, roughly tearing through the knots until it was a dark waterfall flowing down over my unstrapped breasts.

With my hair uncurled and my potato sack of a dress hiding my figure, I was as far from a *perfect wife* as one could get. Granted, it didn't really matter since no one would see me other than a few curious Creatures interested in a lap to lay on. I certainly knew I wouldn't see a pair of midnight eyes. Not after seven years of their blatant absence any time I'd visited.

Skipping shoes since I didn't own a single pair that wouldn't give me blisters within an hour of walking, I took one last look around my room, listening for movement downstairs. When I still heard nothing,

I allowed myself to close my eyes and breathe, welcoming the scorching burn as I finally left this wretched world for the last time.

§——⚷

THE WOOD WAS dark when I arrived, but not quite the deep black of night it could sometimes be. There was a sharp, icy bite to the air, but the trees and underbrush were still illuminated by dull, silver streaks of light that slipped through the branches.

Time didn't always work the same way here as it did in the Upside, sometimes aligning with it and sometimes not, but if I had to guess, I'd say it was sometime around late evening, rather than the midnight I'd just left. Not that time mattered all that much here.

I stretched my arms and grinned up at the visible pieces of cloudy sky, slowly spinning as I breathed in the scent of pine and wet moss. I did it again and again, my chest feeling looser with each inhale of the comforting smell.

I wasn't sure if I'd ever truly feel at peace, if the bitter resentment and hatred swirling in my veins would someday abate, but being here, being *free*, was a damn good start.

And as much as I knew I'd wake up one day missing the warmth of the sun on my face, I loved the embrace of the Underland and the Wood more. Dreary and dark as it was, coming here had never once failed to bring me joy, even on the occasions when I'd come to escape the memory of Frederick's taste, or his touch, wishing for death.

It felt like finally finding my way home after wandering around lost my entire life.

Leaves danced around me as a gust of wind pushed through, and I shuddered, crossing my arms over my body as gooseflesh erupted across it. I may not miss the sun just yet, but I definitely hadn't anticipated it being quite so cold here already. The fabric of my dress was thick, but the short sleeves did little to keep the biting breeze at bay.

I couldn't help but feel a little silly for not having thrown on a coat before I'd left, but I'd been in such a hurry to disappear before Frederick awoke, I hadn't even considered it. I'd never really needed to since my previous visits had always been short. But now that I was staying, it'd been irresponsible and impulsive not to consider what long-term necessities I'd need to survive here.

I shivered again, wondering if I could go back to grab a coat and some stockings, but if there was anything I knew about my life, it was that I had rotten luck. If I went back now, Frederick would somehow be awake, and I'd get caught and would panic too much to concentrate on returning. And I'd rather freeze to death than take that chance.

Still, that didn't mean I *wanted* to freeze to death in the middle of the Wood. I might love it in all its weird, creepy glory, but I also loved bathing and a soft bed. The thought had a wide smile stretching across my face. Because for the first time ever, I wasn't going to go back to Frederick, but I also didn't have to stay within the Wood as I'd always done before.

I could do whatever I wanted.

I'd spent every miserable year of my life listening to men who believed they knew better. I'd knelt on the floor of every bedroom I'd ever had, tears on my cheeks, and prayed for my life to change, while not actually doing a thing to change it myself. And I refused to be that scared little rabbit anymore.

Damn my father for making me fear the creak of floorboards, damn Frederick for making me feel less than human, and damn Terek for making me think I didn't have the freedom to go wherever I wanted here.

I had the power to come to the Underland, not him. Terek didn't own it, and I was a grown ass woman. If I wanted to leave the shelter of the trees, I would.

Maybe I'd finally go to Ardenglass and see what was so terrifying about the city that the mere mention of it had always had Terek turning into a glowering statue. He'd given the impression it was a prison, but if it was truly a city full of new people just like me—just…more dead—it was sure to be more than that and have all the supplies I'd need to begin my life here.

People died every day, which meant there were constantly new souls arriving who didn't have currency or a single belonging to their name. There had to be some kind of setup or guidelines in place to help them get situated. Right?

I'd do whatever was necessary to be allotted a place here. I wasn't afraid of hard work if that was the requirement, and no one but Terek knew I wasn't technically dead.

Granted, there was a high chance of running into said asshole given his proclivity of finding me, but since he'd been decidedly absent for the last several years, I doubted he'd show even if he sensed me. Besides, what did I care if he did? He didn't like me, and he'd made sure that any feelings I'd had were buried long ago. It didn't matter what he thought.

I sniffed, lifting my chin and placing my hands on my hips like Terek was standing before me, begging me to listen. If he showed his stupidly perfect face, I wouldn't flatter him with so much as a glance. I had no desire to hear whatever his soft lips would say to me, nor watch the way his hands dove through his hair when I frustrated him.

If I wanted to visit a city and meet more people here, I had every right to.

Freshly motivated from my internal pep talk, I set off, humming to myself as I carefully made my way over the rough terrain. There were a whole lot more dried leaves and broken branches than I'd remembered, but my pride and determination kept me moving even when the underbrush poked and scraped at my bare feet. Another choice that hadn't been my smartest one.

And unfortunately for me, it didn't appear as if my pride or determination was going to magically point me in the right direction. Grown ass woman or not, I had no idea where I was heading or which way to go to leave the Wood.

They should honestly consider nailing direction signs to random trees. With the amount of people who died every day, I couldn't be the only one who popped up in the Wood, regardless of what Terek believed.

"You're fine. You'll figure it out. You always do," I whispered, squinting my eyes to try to make out which way looked like the best option. I wasn't scared of wandering around in the dark, but wandering around in the *freezing* dark wasn't high on my list of favorites.

I huffed a laugh, wondering if I'd even notice if I froze to death. Would I disappear and reappear in another area of the Underland, or would I just continue walking around lost, unaware that I'd died along the way? I had to admit, the thought was kind of humorous, albeit a little morbid and dark.

The Wood seemed to grow wilder with each step I took until the trees were so close together, I couldn't squeeze past without their branches scratching my arms. The few jagged ones my skin avoided ripped and yanked at my hair or dug into the bottom of my heels, drawing angry hisses from my lips. Every time I changed directions, trying to retrace my steps until the trees thinned out again, I somehow only stumbled deeper.

It was like the Wood was trying to force me toward something, twisting and turning so that no matter which way I walked, I toed farther into its belly. If I'd had a ball of string to mark my way, I surmised it'd be decorating the entirety of the Wood by now, zigzagging between the trees like a desperate spiderweb, showcasing my failure.

After what felt like another hour, I lurched to a stop and cursed, glaring down at my feet. The abused extremities had gone numb a while ago, along with my fingers, and as much of a blessing as it'd been to no longer feel the stabs against the pads of my feet, I knew it was a bad sign.

I fisted my hands in my dress, attempting to warm them back to life as the first seed of doubt crept in. Maybe coming here had been a mistake. For all I knew, I was miles away from any form of civilization. Hell, maybe even days. I never appeared in exactly the same place whenever I visited, and who knew how large the Underland was.

But even as I thought it, I immediately shoved the thought away. Staying Upside would have been the mistake. I just needed to stay positive and keep going.

I winced at the burn in my fingers as the blood worked its way back through them and forced my legs to move again. But after another half hour, when almost every lick of light had vanished from the sky and my teeth were audibly chattering, I finally slumped to the ground.

Pulling my knees up to my chest, I yanked my dress down over them like a makeshift blanket and rested my chin on top.

"Okay, Terek," I mumbled, closing my eyes and fighting back a yawn. "I changed my mind about not wanting to see you. Feel free to show up anytime."

I chuckled, feeling like my sanity was beginning to splinter. I'd raced off in the middle of the night with no coat or shoes, desperate to escape all men and live on my own, only to wind up lost and in need of assistance from one. The irony was cruel.

"Hello."

The word fluttered past my ear like a whisper on the wind, the tone soft and childlike. I froze, snapping my head up and whipping it around, craning my neck to locate where the voice had come from. But I saw nothing except the outline of loose leaves twitching in the breeze.

I huffed out a nervous laugh. Forget beginning to splinter, my sanity was apparently already past that point. The fact that it'd been so long since I'd slept wasn't helping either. I'd just rested my cheek back on my knees when the voice came again, stronger and clearer this time.

"Have you come to play? Or are you here to hurt us, too?"

The questions had me scrambling up, nearly tripping and faceplanting when my tingling feet threatened to give out. I pushed away from the tree I'd leaned against and spun, eyes darting from shadow to shadow, trying to distinguish a form within them.

There was no way I'd imagined it that time. Someone had definitely spoken, and it'd sounded like a child.

"Hello?" I called out, keeping my voice steady even as the hairs on the back of my neck rose. Whoever it was, they were clearly hiding because they worried I meant them harm.

Raising my hands in front of my chest, I tried to show I held no weapon of any kind. Although, in the Underland where people like

Terek existed, I supposed weapons weren't always physical objects that could be seen. "You can come out. I promise, I'm not going to hurt you."

A twig cracked behind me, and I whirled around, stumbling back and smacking my head on a branch when something sharp shot up between my toes. I rubbed at my bruised skull, blinking back spots to make sure I wasn't imagining the little girl standing a few feet away from me.

She was so small and frail, it wouldn't have surprised me that she'd been able to hide so easily, were it not for the blindingly white nightdress she wore that practically glowed against the dark landscape.

Where my hair was a soft, satin black, hers was a starless night sky at midnight, stick-straight and falling loosely to her hips. A thick section rested over her shoulder and obscured her face, but I could make out the corner of her lips and one brown eye that was just a little too big for her face. She couldn't have been older than six.

What the hell was a child doing out here? Was she from the Underland like Terek, or was she possibly like me? She didn't look scared, so it was likely the former, but I couldn't help but hope I was wrong since that would mean the poor girl had died at such a young age.

Having zero experience with children and unsure what to say or do to make her feel safe with a stranger, I squatted down until I was her height and smiled. She didn't look scared of me, but I'd learned to hide my fear by that age, too, so I knew better than to assume she was all right.

"Hello there. Are you lost?" I asked, trying to keep my voice gentle and warm. But rather than answer, she just continued staring at me, unblinking.

Perfect, Adelais. You've sent her into shock.

God, I had no idea how to interact with children. My own experience with my parents hadn't taught me anything except what *not* to do. Was I supposed to hug her? That didn't feel like the best thing to do for someone in shock. Maybe pat her on the head? That always seemed to calm the little Creatures who climbed into my lap.

Her skin was pallid and tight around her bones, and she was barefoot, but she didn't appear wounded or dirty, so she couldn't have been in the Wood for long. She was either a traveler like me or—more likely—she'd very recently died. I tried again.

"Do you need help? Did…did something happen to you?"

The question felt as stupid as it sounded. Of course, she needed help. Whether she was dead or not, the girl clearly wasn't happy to be in the Wood. That, or she'd just died in a horrific way, and instead of comforting her, I'd just reminded her of it. This was going splendidly.

She didn't answer either question, and I belatedly realized there was a good chance she might not speak the same language as me. She cocked her head to the side, causing her hair to fall away from her face and reveal pale lips, a button nose, and another round, brown eye.

Other than that, the girl didn't move, and I was fairly positive she also hadn't blinked once. Definitely traumatized.

My thighs were screaming at me from my squatted position, and I was considering dropping to my knees and offering a hug after all when her face suddenly twitched to life. Her large eyes seemed to spark, and the corners of her lips tipped up into a crooked smile as she finally spoke.

"Silly heart, all kinds of things happen here."

Okay…because *that* wasn't creepy or anything. I took a deep breath, remembering how awkward I'd been at making friends and talking to adults at her age, especially when I'd been scared or put on the spot.

"Well, I promise I'm not going to do anything to you. My name's Adelais. What's your name?"

"Chesie," she said, her head still tilted to the side with that odd smile as she glanced down to my bare feet and then to hers, curling her toes into the brush.

"It's nice to meet you, Chesie," I said, glad she was talking and appeared to be somewhat coherent, if just a little out of it. I pushed off my straining thighs and straightened, glancing around us to make sure no other random children hid nearby.

I didn't want to be unsympathetic and bluntly ask a child if she was dead, but her odd reply made it sound like she was familiar with the Underland. "Do you live nearby, Chesie? In Ardenglass, maybe? Shall we find your...mother or father?"

I trailed off, realizing that probably wasn't the right thing to say either since it was unlikely that her entire family had dropped dead and arrived here together. But Chesie just tipped her head to look up at the sky and grabbed the sides of her nightdress with both hands, swishing the fabric back and forth.

"We're not allowed within the White City," she said, the long strands of her hair swaying behind her with her movements.

"Yeah, me neither," I mumbled. "Did a man hiding in the shadows tell you that?"

"No. A woman painted in our blood did."

I blinked, darting my eyes nervously around us. If a woman covered in blood came wandering by, I was going to second-guess every life choice I'd ever made. A bloody rabbit I could handle. A full-grown woman? That sounded like a nightmare waiting to happen.

"All right," I said, more determined than ever to get Chesie somewhere safer. "So, where are you from then? Did you accidentally wander too far from home?"

"No," she answered, dropping her chin to look at me like I'd lost my mind. "But I am hungry."

"Oh." I patted my sides on instinct as though food might magically appear in my pockets. "I'm sorry, I don't have anything." *The dead still needed to eat?* "But I'll walk you home if you'd like so you can find something to eat there."

Please say you live nearby. Please say you live nearby. I had no intention of pulling a Terek and abandoning the girl either way, but if she lived far, I really wasn't sure how much help I'd be. It's not like I'd had any luck with finding my way out of the trees so far.

Chesie stopped swaying and leaned toward me, her hair falling forward until it hid half her face again. "There's plenty to eat right here, silly heart."

I frowned, wondering why everyone I met here seemed to feel the need to give me a weird nickname, and looked at the ground. I'd never seen any kind of mushroom or edible berry in all my visits, but that didn't mean such things didn't exist. There were probably miles of the Wood I hadn't explored or seen. Who knew what all was here.

However, I didn't see anything around us that she could be referring to, and by the way she was smiling at me, I was becoming more and more sure that she wasn't quite right in the head. Dying before you were old enough to understand it could do that to someone, I supposed.

She giggled at whatever expression was on my face and brought her hands up to circle her thin fingers around her eyes like binoculars. "What's your favorite food?" she asked, twisting her hands back and forth like she was zooming in to look at me closer.

"Um..."

"I like fingers best."

I blinked. "Do you mean like, ladyfingers?" I asked, unease trickling into my chest at the way she kept looking at me. She couldn't help whatever ailment she had or whatever had happened to her, but that didn't change the fact that she was starting to creep me out.

"I like ladyfingers too," I continued, taking a step to the side and hoping she'd start to walk with me if I kept the conversation going. "Although tarts are my favorite."

Chesie slowly lowered her hands to just beneath her chin and wiggled her fingers. Her eyes somehow appeared even larger than before, and I swore they took up most of her face. The movement of her fingers picked up in speed, and I bit my lip, taking another small step away.

"Maybe we should—"

"I wouldn't mind trying a tart," she said, her voice growing a little stronger and emphasizing each syllable of the words, "but no one ever brings me anything. I doubt its better than your fingers, anyway. All the delicate little bones. They snap so easily, you know."

Her sing-songy voice never faltered while she spoke, and her smile had turned sweet and innocent, but neither overshadowed the way her eyes dipped to my hands and flared.

Ice shot through my chest and into my veins as horror speared into every inch of my body. Oh God, I was so incredibly stupid. Shuffling closer, she started humming a tune, and I immediately retreated another step, keeping my eyes on her and refusing to blink, even as they began to sting.

Never give a Creature of the Wood your back, little rabbit. Terek's words replayed in my mind like he was right there with me, cursing at how idiotic and naïve I was. I took yet another step, but Chesie matched them, placing her feet exactly where I'd had mine, and showing just how well she could see in the dark.

"Finger bones have three small joints. Crack, crack, crack," she sang, stretching her arms out and waggling her fingers directly in my face, long black nails breaking through her skin and curling out like talons.

"I bite the tips and suck out the blood. Crack, crack, crack."

Oh God. Oh God, oh God.

"Don't…" I started, although I had no idea what I was asking her not to do. Not to sing that horrifying rhyme with her sweet, melodic voice? Not to eat my fucking fingers? All of the above?

Chesie tilted her head, watching me, and for a moment I thought maybe she'd listen. I pulled in a shuddering breath to calm my racing heart, only to choke on it when her head began to disappear.

A scream lodged in my throat, and before I could even process what I was seeing, her entire body vanished into thin air. I whipped around, feeling like my heart might give out at any moment as she continued to sing, her voice echoing all around me.

"The chest is made with twenty-four ribs. Snap, snap, snap. It houses your heart but only so well. Snap, snap, snap."

Where the hell was she? *What* was she?

Terek had warned me about the larger Creatures of the Wood having abilities, but I never had the chance to see any before he would kill them from afar, so I hadn't truly believed him. I'd grown so used to the small, quiet ones that approached me for comfort, I'd begun to think of the others as nothing but a scare tactic Terek had used to keep me from wandering off before he'd arrive.

I wouldn't have put it past him, but I also couldn't deny what my own eyes had just witnessed. I turned in a circle, squinting into the darkness for any sight of Chesie's white dress among the shadows.

"Be wary of the trees."

I whipped around at her soft, lilting voice, frantically searching all around me, desperate for a flash of movement. Anything that would hint at where she'd gone.

"Why?" I asked, wanting to keep her talking. As long as she was talking, she wasn't biting my fingers off or ripping open my ribcage, or whatever other horrible things she'd been singing about.

"Because," she said, giggling, "they've been watching you. Waiting."

I spun faster, my neck cracking with how roughly I twisted. I couldn't tell where her voice was coming from. It was like it was all around me, caging me in exactly where she wanted. "Waiting for what?"

"To harvest you, of course. Humans aren't really on top of the food chain when you think about it."

How had I ever mistaken that for a child's voice? Her tone was still soft and sing-songy, but it could no longer hide the *otherness* beneath it.

Something sharp scraped against my leg, and I spun to face her, my lungs all but giving out, but nothing was there. "What do you mean?"

"You think you use the trees for oxygen, but they use you right back. Humans think themselves powerful, yet you all eventually rot into the soil to feed their ever-growing roots." Another giggle. "They're quite patient."

"You're mad."

"You're wrong, little rabbit," she replied, her whispered words tickling my ear. I lurched away, more taken aback by her use of Terek's nickname than anything else. I hadn't heard it in years.

"How do you know that name? Where are you? Show yourself," I demanded, the quiver in my voice giving away my fear. I swallowed, trying to wet my throat, but my entire mouth felt thick, and the urge to vomit was overwhelming.

I turned slower this time, following the sound of Chesie's soft laughter.

"No one's mad here. No one at all."

Breath coasted over the arch of my ear and across my cheek. I twisted, swiping my hand up only to be met with nothing but open air. "Stop that."

"You'll find, silly heart, that those of us who've been caged in the unending darkness within the heart of the Wood aren't mad." Her voice now came from my right. "We're positively insane."

I felt fingers slide down the nape of my neck, and I twisted again, expecting to find nothing but air, only to tumble onto my ass when she stood not a foot away, grinning with those eerily large eyes.

My chest heaved in and out, but each desperate breath did nothing to fill my lungs as I forced myself back to my feet. "What do you want from me? I'm sorry if I trespassed somewhere I shouldn't have. I'll leave, I promise. Please."

Chesie flared her nostrils and inhaled deeply, her eyelids fluttering as if in ecstasy. Like my pleas were a fine wine she'd been craving for years and had finally been gifted a taste of.

"I want to play a game."

I shook my head vehemently. Whatever game she wanted to play, there was no way it'd end well for me. And as strong and fearless as I'd tried to act when I'd first arrived, I had no desire to be eaten by a little girl in the Wood.

Knowing I no longer had a choice if I wanted to survive, I tried to clear my thoughts and picture my room in Frederick's house. All I needed was one solid image, and the fire would carry me away like it always did. But no matter how much I grasped at it, I couldn't make the image form. All I could see was Chesie as she began taking slow steps toward me.

"My favorite game is hide and seek."

I shook my head again, surprised it wasn't falling off my shoulders. "I don't want to play."

She just smiled again, and this time, she didn't stop, even when the corners of her mouth began to tear.

The sight of her cheeks splitting open had my flight mode kicking into high gear, screeching at me to *fucking move*, but I couldn't breathe, let alone work my body. It was like an invisible hand had reached out and gripped me by the throat, forcing my muscles to tighten and freeze.

Blood poured over her jaw and dripped down, splattering across her chest, but she didn't seem to notice. She just smiled wider, flashing bits of bone and tissue, and I could do nothing but stand there as my bladder released itself down my legs.

Chesie stared at the trails of warm liquid racing down my shins and giggled, the sound now warped and gurgled. I tasted bile but could do nothing except watch in horror as she snapped her head back and opened her mouth, her jaw cracking like gunfire as it dislocated. It dropped to her collar, revealing two rows of jagged teeth that tipped out of her mouth like stalactites.

Staring at me with giant eyes, now bright yellow with thick, vertical pupils, Chesie blinked for the first time and curled her spine into a low crouch.

"Run, run, little rabbit. Ready or not, here I come."

And then, she lunged.

ADELAIS

CHAPTER TWENTY-TWO

Screaming, I threw myself to the ground and flung my arms over my head, barely registering the resounding sting when my forehead bounced off a rock. Honestly, I was too busy thanking God that my body had actually obeyed this time.

Something warm trickled down into my eye, but I didn't dare wipe it away, instead squeezing both shut as I waited for the agonizing pain of a slow death. But rather than feel those razor-sharp teeth dig into my flesh and tear, I felt only a whoosh of air above me before a keening wail broke the thick silence.

I flinched and slapped my hands over my ears, the soul-crushing cry reminding me of broken nails dragging across glass. *What the hell was that?*

When still nothing attacked me, I finally risked opening my eyes and blinked through what I could only assume was blood given the pain beginning to throb above my eye. Ignoring the slight hinderance of my sight, I frantically ran my hands over the ground, searching for anything I could use as a weapon.

Other than dried leaves, my fingers found only the partially embedded stone that'd cut me, but I wrapped my fist around it anyway and yanked. I may have had no desire to hurt anyone or any*thing* in this world, but I'd bash her head in with a damn pebble to defend myself, if necessary. It'd taken me seven years to have the courage to leave

Frederick, so I'd be damned if I died without a fight.

I was so goddamn tired of not fighting.

Although it felt like a lifetime, only seconds had passed since I'd fallen, and I was readying to leap up and lash out with my weapon when a dark voice cut through the air, halting not only my movements but the very blood in my veins.

"Did no one ever teach you it's poor manners to play with your food?"

Even calm and barely audible over the continued high-pitched screaming, that gravelly tone speared through me, somehow freezing my muscles and lighting me on fire at the same time. Years without so much as a whisper, and I'd still recognize that rough, baritone voice anywhere.

My head snapped up, shock—and something I didn't want to touch with a ten-foot stick—overshadowing every other emotion when Terek's tall, foreboding frame entered my line of sight.

Dressed from head to toe in the same black I'd only ever seen him in, he closed the distance between us in three long strides until he stood directly between Chesie and me. His arms were outstretched on either side of his cloak, just enough that I could see the glinting tip of a blade in each palm.

He didn't look at me, preoccupied with eyeing the Creature several paces away who was now leaning back against a tree, glaring at him with such hatred, it colored the air between them.

"Did no one ever teach you it's poor manners to barge into a woman's home uninvited?" she finally seethed, each word raw and guttural.

My brow furrowed at her use of the term *woman*, but I didn't have a chance to ruminate further before a grotesquely loud crack echoed out. I openly gaped, my eyes widening and my jaw falling slack as her own popped back into place.

I blinked furiously, my brain attempting to process what I was seeing as her bloody cheeks began to seamlessly knit together. The thick, curved nails protruding from her fingertips retreated, and her eyes darkened in color, morphing her in seconds back into the little, brown-eyed girl I'd first seen.

What the hell was she? And how many Creatures were there like her? Could all of them transform into people? My imagination went wild at the thought, picturing child-like Creatures wandering cities and towns in the Underland, partaking in everyday activities while the people around them stood oblivious.

My glowering companion huffed a laugh, completely unaffected by what we'd just witnessed. Like Chesie's ability to rip open her face and magically sew it back together at will was nothing new to him. I supposed, depending on how long he'd been in the Underland, maybe it wasn't. For all I knew, this wasn't even the first time he'd met one like her.

His next words confirmed it.

"I normally wouldn't care to disrupt your meal, Chesie, especially when said meal willingly, and idiotically, traipses into your personal borders. But this particular meal is off-limits."

Was he referring to me? Because if he seriously just referred to me as an idiotic meal within seconds of seeing me for the first time since our fight, I was going to throw this stone at his head. My eyes cut to him, glaring daggers at the side of his face while I squeezed my weapon.

The fluttering along his jaw told me he could feel my zeroed-in attention, but he studiously ignored me.

Chesie smiled, her teeth stark white in the dark, contrasting against the blood all over her face. She tilted her head to look around him at me. "Finder's keepers, I'm afraid."

Realizing I was still prostrate on the ground, I took a deep breath to calm the organ still rapidly beating within my chest and scrambled to my feet. I stepped to the side, wanting to keep her within my line of sight, but Terek matched my steps, keeping his body directly between us.

"This is the last time I will warn you. This one may have trespassed, but she doesn't know the borders and is under the queen's protection. Touch her, and the next one will go between your eyes."

I blinked. Um, what? The queen's protection? And his next *what* will go between her eyes? I frowned, glancing back at Chesie for any hint as to what he meant, only to notice what I hadn't been able to see from my position on the ground.

More specifically, the black handle protruding from the center of one of her palms, her skin stained with fresh, dripping blood.

Oh God, she hadn't been leaning against the tree. Terek had literally pinned her to it like some messed-up version of an insect collection. Creature or not, my stomach roiled, and nausea pushed up my throat at the sight of the gaping wound on what physically appeared to be a child.

I slapped my hand to my mouth, fighting back the urge to spew what little contents I had in my stomach. I absolutely refused to vomit, if only to save myself the humiliation of adding that smell to the one already coating my legs.

"You have no say in what I do here," Chesie snarled, her eyes growing bigger and yellowing as her temper rose. "Besides, I wasn't going to hurt her. I only wanted to play a game."

"Wrong," Terek growled, knuckles whitening around the knives still within his possession. "I have every say when you touch something that belongs to me."

Excuse me? I most surely did not, regardless of whatever weird palpitation my heart just did inside my ribs. I might've agreed that I owed him for saving my life, but that didn't mean he owned me. Arrogant asshole. Now I was definitely going to throw my rock at his head.

Just as soon as we were safely out of whatever borders I'd accidentally wandered into.

Chesie bared her teeth and reached across her body with her free hand to wrap it around the hilt of the knife. Letting out another horrifying wail, she ripped it from her hand, eyes now solid yellow and teeth sharp.

"Nothing here is yours, *Soulless*" she heaved, fresh blood gushing out and making me sway on my feet. "She belongs to the Wood."

Faster than lightning, Terek crossed the distance and slammed into her, crushing her small form against the gnarled bark. Several cracks split through the air, but I couldn't tell if the sounds came from the groaning tree or Chesie's bones.

Terek towered several feet above her, his eyes betraying no sympathy as he shoved the same blade back through her injured hand and pressed the tip of a second to the underside of her jaw. Her responding scream shook the leaves around us, and I stumbled back a step, latent survival instincts finally kicking in.

Holy shit.

I'd known Terek possessed abilities no human on the Upside ever could, even when he'd tried to pretend otherwise. It'd always been obvious that his senses were superior to that of a normal human being, but I'd had no idea he could move like that.

Growing up, I'd never once believed he'd harm me, not even when he'd held a blade to my body and made empty threats to kill me. But staring at him now, there was no denying that while Chesie was a predator hidden beneath a mask, so was he. And I couldn't help but feel slightly ashamed of how very little I knew about the man I'd once thought to give my heart to.

"You'd do well to remember who holds the power here, *Creature*," Terek snarled, digging the tip of his blade in harder when she hissed and tried to wrench away. I dropped my gaze, unable to stomach the sight.

Chesie had wanted to scare me—something she'd succeeded at ten-fold—and very likely would've hurt me, regardless of what she claimed, but something just felt wrong about torturing her when she wasn't even fighting back. She hadn't actually done anything wrong yet.

Terek, however, seemed to feel the opposite. "One word from me, and your measly borders will halve. Can't imagine Huka would be too happy with you about that."

The unfamiliar name drew my eyes back up to them. Who was Huka? Was that the queen's name? More importantly, who the hell was Terek if he had the power to take lands and change borders?

Chesie gnashed her teeth, clearly knowing whom he spoke of and not liking the threat one bit. "Careful what you give away, Soulless. You wouldn't want anyone to realize just how badly your queen wants a new little rabbit for her collection. Especially one whose insides shine so beautifully."

Terek's entire body went preternaturally still, and I swore not even his lungs dared to inflate for several moments. When he finally spoke, his words were heavy with warning. A warning for what, I wasn't sure.

"The queen desires nothing but a reason to push you and your putrid ilk farther."

Chesie's head tipped back against the tree, and a wet rattle worked up her throat as she let loose an uncontrolled cackle. "Your Wood-blessed eyes may see well, human, but mine see better. I wonder, if I break her open, will her soul stay here?"

The growl that rumbled up Terek's chest was nothing short of animalistic, and I felt my heart drop to my feet as his shoulders tensed. In that split second, I knew he was done with the conversation and had absolutely zero intentions of leaving her alive. He was going to murder her, right here in her home, all because I'd been foolish enough to wander into it.

Before I could second-guess it, or question my sanity, I cocked my arm back and launched the rock at his head, genuinely surprised when it hit its mark. The stone bounced off the center of Terek's skull, just above his ear, with a much too satisfying *thunk*.

Although it didn't appear to have hurt him, he whipped his head to the side, keeping Chesie in his peripheral as his midnight blue eyes met mine for the first time in years. A vicious darkness swirled in their depths, causing my lungs to momentarily forget how to work.

In all the times I'd dreamed of seeing those eyes again and had sketched them onto pages, I'd forgotten just how cruel they could be when filled with resentment. I swallowed, hating how small I felt beneath that glare. "Don't kill her."

His nostrils flared, his lip curling up like my request was a heinous crime to every single one of his senses. Considering how I smelled, that was saying something.

"Please, don't kill her," I repeated, straightening my spine and smoothing my hands down my dress, attempting to look more confident than I felt. "It's my fault for walking where I shouldn't have."

He scoffed, as if to say *yeah, no shit*, and I took a step toward them, hands raised. His eyes softened the barest amount, taking in every one of my movements, and I swore the hand at Chesie's throat shifted back a half inch. But then his eyes flicked up to my forehead, and he growled, his next words low and meant for me, even though he'd twisted back to Chesie.

"If this is anyone's fault, it's mine for ever having entertained your presence here."

The words fell between us and swelled, reaffirming that the wall he'd thrown up last time was still strong and stable, and he had no intention of tearing it down. The meaning behind the statement stinging as much as it had the first time. That I didn't belong here.

"Please, Terek, just let her go. You've hurt her enough, and she hasn't once tried to hurt you back," I pushed, pretending I hadn't heard him.

I crossed the last few feet and after only a second of hesitation, placed my hand on his upper arm, over his tunic. His eyes darted down to my fingers and then up to my face, pinning me in place so thoroughly I could've sworn it was me he held at knifepoint.

I could feel Chesie's attention on me, and I cut my gaze from Terek's long enough to meet hers instead. Her head was quirked to the side, her lips pursed and brown eyes narrowed, like I was a puzzle she was still trying to figure out.

The expression was so child-like and innocent, I might've thought I'd imagined the whole 'turning into a monster to eat me' part if she hadn't still been drenched in blood from her jaw to her chest.

Terek murmured several things under his breath that I didn't catch, and by the look he was giving me, I had a feeling I didn't want to know. Slowly, like he was wading through a sea of honey, he lowered the knife from her throat.

I released a breath and dropped my hand, shifting back so he could remove the other and step away. But he took his time, staring directly at me as he wiped the bloodied tip across a clean section of Chesie's dress. It wasn't until he'd slipped it back into the sheath at his waist that he finally fisted the other and leaned down over Chesie's contemplative face.

"Run, run," he whispered, ripping it from her flesh and parroting her words back at her. "Because if I ever catch sight of you around her again, there's not a word she can say that will save you."

He moved to wipe the second blade on her dress, but she darted to the side, almost as fast as Terek had moved. Flashing me a wide smile, like his threat and her mangled hand were nothing but annoying inconveniences, she grabbed the sides of her dress and curtseyed. I choked, a startled laugh catching in my throat at the deranged sight.

She just winked at me, raising her uninjured hand to give Terek a vulgar gesture that had his nostrils flaring, and then, in a blink, she was gone.

ADELAIS

CHAPTER TWENTY-THREE

I twisted, looking around for any hint as to where she'd disappeared to, but not even a leaf twitched. And with her absence came an eerie silence. The same silence that had likely surrounded us the second I'd stepped within her border, but I'd been too lost in my head to notice.

Aware that I was now alone with a man who detested me, I fidgeted behind Terek's back, feeling as contrite as I used to when Mrs. Gayle would catch me sneaking into the house as a kid, covered in dirt and sticky with sweat.

I had no idea what to do with my hands, let alone what to say to a man I hadn't seen in years. One who'd wanted to kill that Creature, but who had released her simply because I'd asked. One who had kissed me passionately and made me feel beautiful and wanted for the first time in my life, only to stomp on me like every other man afterward.

What I wanted to do was drum up the bravado I'd been sipping on when I'd first arrived and throw it at him as hard as I had the rock. But if there was anything I had to finally admit to, it was that I was never going to get out of this Wood without his help.

Honestly, knowing my luck, Chesie was still lurking somewhere nearby, waiting for Terek to depart so she could come play another morbid children's game.

I may not hate the Creatures of the Wood with the vehemence

Terek clearly did, but that didn't mean I had any desire to run into that particular one again. My best course of action would be to appeal to Terek's nicer side, small though it was, and see if maybe he'd at least lead me out.

"So," I started, filling my lungs and releasing the air slowly. "I suppose this is when you get to say, *I told you so.*"

I honestly didn't expect him to answer, fully prepared to chase after him when he ignored me and walked away, pretending he hadn't just gone back on his promise to never help me again.

So, when he whirled on me instead, moving faster than I could track, I yelped and reared back, nearly toppling to the ground. My reaction only seemed to make him angrier, and he glared at me, his jaw feathering.

"Not that I thought you were lying about the Creatures or anything," I added, raising my hands in front of my chest to ward off his foul mood, even though I had definitely believed he'd been exaggerating about the larger Creatures possessing such terrifying abilities. "I just meant—"

"What in the crimson hell were you thinking?"

"—that I hadn't expected...excuse me?"

"What? Have your ears stopped working in time with your common sense? What the fuck are you doing this deep in the goddamn Wood?"

Fuming, I opened my mouth, but he plundered on, swiftly stomping out the lie that'd been on the tip of my tongue. "Don't you dare say this is where you appeared. This is nowhere near where you've ever shown up before."

I didn't answer, assuming he wouldn't let me anyway. Not that it mattered. I had no answer to give that wouldn't piss him off. He ran a hand through his already messy hair, making pieces stand on end before they flopped back down across his forehead.

"You know, I actually second-guessed my own senses when I noticed where they were leading me," he said, looking away from me with a small shake of his head. "Because after all the times I've told you about the dangers of coming here, I never expected you to be stupid enough to wander straight into a Creature's nest."

"Wow," I said, clapping twice and drawing his attention back to me. "That might just be the longest you've ever made it before calling me stupid." Technically, he'd called me idiotic, but he hadn't said it to my face, so I wasn't going to count it.

His nostrils flared, and he shifted toward me like he wanted nothing more than to throttle me. "Nice to see you're still a brat."

"Disappointing to see you're still an ass."

His lips twitched. "You know, I've yet to hear a thank you slip past those pretty red lips of yours, considering this ass just saved you from an extremely gruesome death."

I scoffed, mentally slapping myself for the way my heart fluttered when his eyes flicked to my mouth. Later, when I was alone in a warm bed, I'd nurse my wounded pride at how pathetic that flutter made me feel. "I don't have to say anything. *You* chose to save *me*."

"Yeah, and my day would've likely gone a hell of a lot better if I hadn't," he said, his lips pressing thin again.

Only years of learning how to hide my reactions kept my face from crumbling in front of him. I wouldn't cry over this man. Not again. He didn't deserve it any more than Frederick had, and if I could hold my tears back with that monster, I could hold them back with this one, too.

"Fine. Then do us both a favor and scurry off," I said, blinking back the burn in my eyes and crossing my arms. *Please don't leave, please don't leave.* If he listened and abandoned me here, I was going to slam my head into a tree.

Terek's eyes immediately narrowed, and he stepped closer, forcing me to tip my head back to maintain eye contact. I planted my feet and kept my expression firm, even as his proximity sent unwanted trails of gooseflesh up and down my arms.

"Are you sure about that? I can sense no less than three Creatures prowling just out of sight, drawn to the lingering scent of your fear."

I swallowed, unsure whether or not to believe him, and somehow fighting the urge to glance behind me. "I don't need you coming to my rescue."

"The reek defiling your legs says differently."

My face burned, any hope that his senses somehow hadn't noticed dying a cruel death in the pit of my stomach. "I've done perfectly fine every other time without you up until now, but congratulations for being useful today, I guess," I snapped, my humiliation rekindling my anger.

He growled and ate the last foot between us until his firm torso almost brushed against my chest, the heat of his own anger clashing with mine.

By the way the black in his eyes ate up the blue, I thought he might actually strike me, but he just pressed the pad of his thumb to my forehead, swiping across my cut. The contact made me suck in a breath, and he whipped his hand back like he'd touched a scalding stove.

Lowering it, he held the blood-smeared digit in front of my face and said, "You call this doing just fine?"

I winced. I'd blessedly forgotten about hitting my head, but now that he'd pointed it out, I was suddenly painfully aware of the way the broken skin throbbed like it had its own heartbeat, his touch aggravating it further.

Asshole. The man hadn't changed one bit.

"I do," I said, swatting his hand away and feeling my irritation spike. "But even if I didn't, it's none of your business. I'm fine."

"Says the woman who's been stalked every time she's stepped foot in this Wood yet has been exceedingly, embarrassingly, unaware each time."

I blanched, my eyes widening before I could smother the reaction down. I'd lost count of how many times I'd felt like someone was watching me during my trips over the years. It'd been a telltale feeling that'd raised the hairs on the back of my neck, but I'd never caught sight of anything more than small Creatures and shadows.

And then I remembered, Chesie had called me little rabbit.

I must've said the last part out loud because Terek's nostrils flared. "I don't know how it knew that name, but I can assure you, that Creature has never been present anytime I have. If it ever watched you, it was in the moments before I'd arrive."

But even as he said it, we both knew that couldn't be true. Because Terek had been the only one to ever use that nickname. He twisted his head to stare behind him, his long fingers twitching toward his sheaths.

"So then who, pray tell, has been stalking me all these years? The tiny four-winged birds that like to perch above my head? Or how about," I tapped my finger to my lips, "the two-headed felines that always want scratches. They were quite ferocious."

So much for making him want to help me. I was doing a pretty damn good job of the opposite. But damn him, he was so frustratingly good at getting under my skin and pressing every single button.

He turned back toward me slowly, as if giving me every chance to run, and I swore I could feel my heart crashing against my sternum in response. His eyes dropped to the beating pulse point in my neck and lingered, like he was fighting the desire to wrap his hands around it and shake me.

"I never said it was a Creature."

I frowned. He'd literally just said I hadn't noticed I was being—I froze, blinking slowly like he'd just told me the sky was actually pink. *No.*

"You're lying," I blurted.

"I am many things, Ace, but a liar isn't one of them."

"So, you're saying you've been…watching me all this time?" That didn't make any sense. None at all, actually. With his ability to blend into the shadows, it didn't surprise me that I could go without seeing him, but why hadn't he said something?

Why had he let me spend the last seven years thinking he didn't care and that I was alone in this world, too?

"Yes, well, someone had to," Terek snapped, unaware—or more likely, uncaring—of how shaken I was by his admittance. "And go figure, the one time I'm late, you decide to stumble directly into one of the Underland's oldest Creatures."

He shook his head, pinching his thumb and index finger over the bridge of his nose. "If I let you out of my sight again, where will I find you next? Climbing into one of their gaping maws?"

"Oh, piss off," I said, finally snapping. "We both know the only time you've ever cared was when you didn't know who I was."

The last word had barely passed my lips before his hand gripped my throat, his fingers wrapping around it in an unyielding hold. Nearly lifting me up onto my toes, he glared down at me, his body pressing flush against mine as his pupils encompassed his eyes.

"If I didn't give a shit, I'd have let that thing tear you apart and watched from the shadows." His grip tightened, his breath coasting over my cheeks and lips as he leaned down over me. "If I didn't give a shit, I'd kill you right now and grant both our wishes."

"Yeah?" I asked, lifting onto my toes to try to shift some of the pressure from his hold but failing miserably. Terek's grip might as well have been pure stone. "What could you possibly know about my wishes?"

He smiled down at me, but the expression was edged with the same cruelty he'd had after our kiss. "Well, I, for one, would no longer be stuck babysitting you every time your privileged, spoiled ass got bored."

His fingers pressed in on the sides of my neck, making my blood pound and my face flush. "And you'd get exactly what you want. An eternity here, clinging to the old scraps of your life, wondering why the pieces no longer fit."

I inhaled slowly, trying to keep my breaths steady and give him zero reaction. His goal was to hurt me, and the truth was that he was right. But although I had grown up a privileged, lonely little girl seeking affection and adventure, she was long gone. She'd died years ago beneath a hot, searing brand, and she'd never come back.

"If you really wanted to kill me," I breathed, sucking in small gulps of air in between words even as my brain began feeling fuzzy, "you'd be pushing in to stop my flow of air...not squeezing to limit...my blood flow. Stop making empty threats...you won't follow through."

Terek's eyes flashed, and he squeezed harder, making stars dance in my vision. "Have a lot of experience with breath play, do you, little rabbit?"

Although hearing my nickname in his deep, graveled voice warmed me where it shouldn't, the insinuation behind his question killed any fake confidence I'd had with one, quick whoosh. The image of Frederick's face as he held me down and choked me flashed across my mind unbidden. The way his bloodshot eyes would twitch, and the way I'd curl up on the floor, waiting for it to be over.

I didn't reply, but my eyes must have answered for me because before I could blink again, Terek had launched himself away from me, chest heaving and gaze intent on my face.

"You've changed."

I rolled my eyes, pushing out the unwanted images of Frederick as I gently massaged my neck. I'd have finger-shaped bruises by tomorrow. "Yeah, seven years passing tends to do that."

He shook his head. "No. It's more than that."

I *had* changed, in more ways than I'd ever wanted to. I wasn't sure which one he could see, but I hated that he could see anything at all. If there was anyone, in any world, I absolutely did not want knowing all my weaknesses and failures, it was Terek.

So, I shrugged, brushing it off like it didn't matter. Because in the end, it didn't. I was standing in the middle of the Wood barefoot, bleeding, cold, and still very much lost. All I cared about right now was getting somewhere warm and alone.

Terek sighed, irritation evident in every line of his face. "Go home, Ace. Coming here was bad enough when you were a child, but you're too old to still believe this ability will do anything but ruin your life. You say you've grown up? Then act like it."

Was he kidding me? I'd been taking a walk minding my own damn business, not throwing eggs at someone's house. I may have begrudgingly accepted that he'd been right about the dangers lurking within these trees, but that didn't give him the right to stand there and patronize me.

"If I didn't listen to you before, I'm curious why you think I'd suddenly do so now," I said, attempting to walk past him, but every time I tried to side-step around his broad shoulders, he matched my steps, blocking my path.

"You don't belong here, Ace."

Laughter bubbled up, as bitter and dead as I felt on the inside, but I couldn't help it. I was hungry, cold, exhausted, and so fucking tired of hearing him tell me that. Everyone seemed to believe it, yet no one could seem to agree on where exactly I *did* belong.

"Something funny?"

I didn't bother answering. I was done. With him. With the conversation. With everything. I raised my hands to rub my aching temples only to drop them back to my sides when I saw the dirt caked beneath my nails.

My shoulders curled in, and I released a heavy sigh, suddenly weary all the way down to my soul. I wasn't sure how long it'd been since I'd last slept, but the longer we stood here bickering, the less energy I had for anything at all. Chesie could come back and gnaw on my fingers, and I'd probably let her.

"No offense, Terek, but we both know you have somewhere else you'd rather be. I appreciate that you had enough of a heart to keep me from being eaten, but you're under no obligation to do it again."

He stayed silent, but I could've sworn something that looked a lot like regret flashed across his face before he tucked his features back into their perfectly stoic positions.

"I'm not going back. Yell and threaten me all you want. There's nothing you can say that I haven't already heard. It'll just be a waste of time for us both. I'm staying here."

The wind picked up, pushing strands of hair across my face in an almost welcoming caress to my declaration. I shivered from the cold and pushed them back, trying not to think about the fact that I'd never had to style my own hair before and had no idea how to do anything other than brush it and tie it back in a bun.

Terek's eyes snapped down to my chest, where my pebbled arms were crossed over my body, and then back up before they fluttered closed for a beat. He cursed under his breath.

"Here," he said, unlatching the clasp at his neck and swinging his cloak off.

I stared at the proffered garment, not making any move to take it. Terek may not be the worst man I'd ever met, but he'd also just willingly admitted that killing me would make his life abundantly easier. Doing something nice, for the sole purpose of being nice, made me instantly suspicious.

For all I knew, it was a magical cloak that would restrain me or knock me unconscious the moment I slipped it on.

"Crimson take me, Ace, it's not going to grow teeth and bite your hand off. Your shivering is an incessant rattling that's making me want to claw my ears off. Take the fucking cloak."

Narrowing my eyes at his infuriating ability to somehow insult me with every breath, I snatched the cloak from his grasp and threw it over my shoulders. It swamped me, the fabric still warm from his body, and it took everything in me not to melt into the smell of him. Like cedar and the faintest hint of rain. And why the hell was I noticing that?

I yanked it tighter around me and stomped around him, feeling the hem catch as it dragged along the ground.

"Unless you still desire to befall a tortuous death, you might want to redirect your tantrum this way. You're heading even deeper into the Wood."

I raised my eyes to the sky, cursing the starless darkness. Of course, I was. Apparently, the heart of the Wood was the only direction my intuition knew how to lead me. Pride withering somewhere near my feet, I turned and stomped back, holding my head high in the air.

As much as I wanted to tell him to piss off again and figure my own way out—Creatures be damned—I knew for a fact he'd follow me, waiting for me to fail.

And a woman could only pee herself in front of a gorgeous man so many times before etiquette demanded she walk off the nearest cliff.

TEREK

CHAPTER TWENTY-FOUR

W alking at the pace of someone with both short legs and the inability to see her surroundings in the dark, not to mention the fact that she was fucking barefoot, meant the walk out of the Wood took three times longer than it had going in.

Granted, I'd all but flown through the Wood once I'd realized she was nowhere near where she was supposed to be, but still. An hour into our awkwardly silent walk, I was seconds away from throwing her over my shoulder and running the rest of the way out.

God, I hated this place.

Filling my lungs with a breath that smelled like death, wet moss, and her, and was anything but calming, I rubbed a hand over my face. Seriously, what the hell was I thinking? No. Scratch that. What in the crimson fuck was I *doing?*

After all the shit in Ardenglass with Hara and the goddamn bounty, I knew better than to be anywhere near Ace, especially out in the open. Knew better but was apparently still doing it anyway like a fucking idiot.

I dared a glance out of the corner of my eye at the woman in question—for the third time in five minutes—not wanting her to catch me looking.

Because I definitely shouldn't be looking.

Although her head hadn't stopped swiveling as she took in what she could of the dark landscape, she'd made sure to keep a full arm's width of space between us the entire time.

She'd changed so much over the last few years, proof that while my life was nothing but a frozen hand in a dead watch, hers had kept moving. I'd have had to be blind not to notice the changes prior to today, but it was different being this close to her.

Her hair was longer now, the tips brushing just above her elbows, and her body had filled out even more, leaving no hint of the sharp, gangly girl she'd been once upon a time.

But it wasn't those skin-deep differences that had my blood simmering and my jaw feeling like it'd break from how hard I clenched it. It was the deeper changes, the ones I hadn't noticed at first, but that now made her feel…wrong.

It'd taken me all three stolen glances to realize what it was about her that felt off, and once I did, I couldn't focus on anything else. It wasn't the way her body had changed that had warning signals blaring in my head, but rather, the utter lack of color to her at all.

I'd watched Ace grow progressively more somber over the years, but she'd still had a natural shine to her, her soul melting from her body in vibrant waves that had spoken to me across the distance, luring me through the Wood to wherever she'd appeared. No matter how far I was.

It'd been that way since the first time I'd met her. Happy or furious with me, Ace had been a glimmering light in my otherwise, pointless existence. My small window to the Upside and the fading memories of home.

I'd been addicted to it, to the tiny glimpses she'd always given me of what life had been like back when my biggest worry had been disappointing my family. Before the water had poured down my throat and into my lungs, ripping me from everything I'd known and tossing me here.

But as I looked at her, there was no sign of that light now. It was as if the Ace walking silently beside me was just a faded, worn-out version of herself. Like a painting that'd been left out in the elements too long. Her usually bright hazel eyes were now dull and lifeless, the dark circles beneath making them look sunken and heavy against her pale skin.

She looked like a walking corpse, less alive than the actual inhabitants of the Underland, and I fucking hated it. It made me want to shove her against a tree and grasp that pretty little throat again, refusing to release her until she told me what the hell had happened. I needed to know what, or who, had reached in and doused a soul as strong and radiant as hers.

My jaw popped. The possibility of it being the latter enraged me far more than it should, and I dropped my gaze to her left hand, currently grasping the edge of my cloak like her life depended on it.

Her delicate fingers were bare of jewelry, but that didn't mean she wasn't engaged or actively being courted. It might've been decades since I'd stepped foot on the Upside, but I wasn't fool enough to believe a woman of her age and beauty wouldn't be heavily sought after.

I glared at her hand, suddenly wishing she'd tuck it behind my cloak and out of sight. The thought of a wealthy man with a beating heart getting to wake up beside her every morning shouldn't put such a sour taste in my mouth. Ace wasn't mine to be jealous over, nor did I want her to be, no matter how much a single touch of her body still affected mine.

Hell, I didn't even want her in the Underland, period. Beautiful or not, she was quite literally one of the most infuriating women I'd ever met in my life, Upside or Under. Yet, even as I thought it, I couldn't fully contain the thread of satisfaction that burned through my veins at the knowledge that when she finally tired of this game and left, she'd go back home smelling like *me*.

The feeling didn't last long, though, when I raised my eyes from her hand to discover her face now twisted toward me, eyes pinned to my mouth. Which I belatedly realized was curled in an unguarded smirk.

Irritated for an entirely new reason, I let my lips fall, and her brow furrowed, drawing my attention to the gash on her head. It was no longer actively bleeding, but that didn't stop the sight from making me grind my teeth to the point of pain lancing up my jaw and reverberating through my skull.

It infuriated me beyond anything I'd ever known that the Creature who'd drawn both blood and terror from her was still walking this godforsaken world. Alive and free as a fucking bird to do it all over again.

"You know," I forced out, tucking my hands in my pockets and tearing my gaze away. I didn't mind the silence, it was better than listening to her complain, but I needed a distraction. Anything that would keep me from turning around and tracking Chesie down to put ten more holes in its body.

"What?"

I felt her attention still on me, but I kept my face straight ahead, calculating how much longer we had before the Wood edge came into sight. By the growing distance between the trees, I'd guess less than half an hour. "We've been walking for a while now, and I've still yet to hear a thank you."

If silence could speak, hers was screaming at the top of its lungs.

I chuckled. "Unless of course, your desired method of thanks doesn't involve using your lips to speak. In which case, I'd have to tell you, that'd be much preferred."

I'd never been the type of man to request physical payments for anything, nor would I ever, but she didn't need to know that. I plastered another smirk on my face, intentionally this time, to hide the fact that I was having to picture every horrific Creature I'd ever seen to refrain from imagining her lips doing anything other than pressing into a thin line.

Much like they were doing now.

"What? Fox got your tongue, little rabbit?"

She sniffed, pointedly ignoring me and sticking her nose in the air only to stumble and knock into me. I gripped her shoulder to hold her steady, but she yanked away from me like I'd burned her, her face so red the shade would've been obvious in the dark even to someone with no abilities at all.

"I have absolutely nothing nice to say to you, so I figured it was more polite to say nothing at all."

I couldn't help but smile, enjoying the flare of anger that lit up her eyes. Good. I liked her anger. It was better than the empty, dead look she carried otherwise. "Since when do you care about being polite? If memory serves me correctly, the first time I met you, you were avoiding an entire party of people who'd showed up just for you."

"I don't care, but since I'm stuck with you until the nearest town, I figured telling you how much I still hate you might make it awkward." She gripped my cloak tighter around her body. "Besides, that was a long time ago. I'm not a child anymore, in case you hadn't noticed."

Oh, I'd fucking noticed.

"What makes you think I have any inclination to help you once we make it outside these trees?" I asked, aware I had no intention of letting her leave my sight, even if she demanded it. Not when every White Guard and bounty hunter had received a perfect rendering of her appearance, thanks to a guard whose ability allowed him to pull the image of her face from Hara's mind and put it to parchment.

It'd been years since the bounty had been issued, but the prize was too great for anyone to forget. Ace's face would be seared into the mind of every single one of them more vividly than their fucking mothers.

"I *belong* to you, remember?" Ace answered, drawing out the word and lifting her hands to make curling motions with her fingers.

I scoffed, hoping the sound hid what those words did to me. The thought of owning this woman, of tasting those lips again, felt a lot like madness. And if history was anything to go on, nothing pulled me in to a woman like a little madness.

"Scoff all you want. You're the one who claimed I was to be protected because of it," she said, an arrogant smile on her face. "Your words, not mine."

"To best a predator, you have to be a bigger one, little rabbit. It's a lesson you'd do well to remember if you intend to continue overstaying your welcome."

She glared at me, but I pretended not to see it, grabbing her arm and dragging her out of the path of the branch she was about to walk straight into. "The Creatures of the Wood do not respond to pleas and begging. Fear has a specific smell, and they encourage it, feed on it like the greatest delicacy."

"What do they respond to, then? Being tortured against a tree?" she snapped, a sudden lash of anger lacing her tone and making it clear what she thought of my methods. What had she expected me to do? Sit down and offer to share my travel fare with it?

"Wouldn't you?" I asked, quirking a brow and enjoying the hue of pink that filled her cheeks when her emotions got the best of her. "They respond to aggression and possession, Ace. The choice was either to verbally claim you or stake my claim by pissing on you. Since you'd already done the latter, I figured the first would be more fitting."

That delicious pink burned hotter, continuing to her ears and down her neck. I wondered how much darker it'd get if I mentioned just how rancid she smelled.

"You speak as if Chesie was a mindless animal following basic instincts, but she wasn't." Ace shivered and grabbed the edges of my cloak again, wrapping it tightly around her body. "She recognized you, and she knew things about me, too."

Goddamn Chesie. The knowledge that it'd somehow watched Ace and seen us interact at some point over the years, without me sensing it, made me want to burn the entire fucking Wood to the ground. Even now, I couldn't comprehend how it'd gotten close enough to hear me utter her nickname, undetected.

It may have possessed the ability to cloak itself at will, but it still breathed and moved like any other. I should've sensed it. Then again, I hadn't sensed Hara all those years ago either.

Apparently, I became just a touch above utterly worthless whenever Ace was around.

"That's exactly what the Creatures of the Wood are. Chesie is simply old enough to have learned how to camouflage it behind an intricate façade. That's why it, and every other walking nightmare, is banished here."

"That's not true," Ace said, wincing and shifting her weight off whatever she'd stepped on. "I mean, obviously she can turn invisible and everything, but she was intelligent, Terek." She frowned up at me. "Why didn't you ever tell me some of them could talk? You'd acted like I was foolish when I'd thought Cotton could."

I shrugged and forced my legs to move faster, as if I could outrun the way her tongue wrapped around my name and the way flames licked at my chest at the sound of it. Crimson hell.

"You *were* foolish. And why would I?"

She ran after me, cursing quietly when she stepped on yet another broken branch. When we finally found her some damn shoes, I was going to whack her upside the head with them right before permanently adhering them to her feet.

"Oh, I don't know," she said, tapping a finger to her lips like she'd done before. "Maybe so I wouldn't assume a random little girl in the Wood was lost and offer help only for her face to rip open when she decided to eat my fingers?"

"I guess I assumed telling you to your face that you weren't wanted and shouldn't come back would've been enough to keep you away from anything like Chesie. Clearly, I was wrong."

I expected her to stand tall, raising her little nose in the air again and snap back at me, but she didn't. Instead, her body almost seemed to deflate at my words, her shoulders curving in and her arms tightening around her body. A stab of guilt tickled in my throat, but I swallowed down the urge to apologize.

Ace had no idea just how dangerous the Wood truly was and of how close she'd come to losing her life today. If she'd walked just a little farther, there would've been nothing I could've done to save her. And I'd rather her continue to believe I despised her than ever experience what some of the other Creatures were capable of.

Because while Chesie was indeed dangerous, Huka was far, far worse.

Over the decades I'd been in the Underland, I'd run into Chesie on several occasions, and up until today, I'd had no problem with it. Older than most human residents by more centuries than even the Crimson Queen knew, it was one of only a handful of Creatures we were aware of who could communicate in a human tongue.

When the queen had enacted her decree against them and war had broken out, Chesie had been one of the, albeit few, Creatures who'd refused to partake in the fighting. Instead, for reasons I'd never been sure of, a portion of their population had willingly gone deeper into the Wood. A decision I was almost positive they now regretted.

Whatever the reason, Chesie's choice not to murder myself or my comrades had meant that I'd respected its boundaries ever since. As long as it stayed within them, it wasn't any of my business what, or who, it ate.

Until now.

I still couldn't believe I'd fucking listened to Ace's naïve and reckless demand to let it live. I'd thought, after all these decades, that I'd finally cured my knack for blindly obeying selfish women, but apparently, I still hadn't.

I shook my head. That wasn't fair, nor was it true. A selfish woman wouldn't have bothered saving that thing's life in the first place, let alone admitting accountability for the situation. Ace may have been a brat and a pain in my ass, but her bleeding heart was caring to a fault.

It was me who'd been selfish. Me who could've kept a closer watch and continued urging her to stop coming. Me who could've done literally anything other than hide in the shadows and observe her from a distance.

I'd convinced myself it was what was best for her after what had happened last time, both with Hara and that cursed kiss. But the truth was that I couldn't stomach being this damn close to her. Couldn't stand seeing her lips part and remembering the hum that'd filled my entire body when they'd pressed to mine. Couldn't stand the heavy look in her eyes and not knowing what had put it there.

Avoiding her had always been for me.

"You keep saying I'm not welcome here, yet you told Chesie I was under a queen's protection. You can't have both, so which is it?"

Her question pulled me out of my musings, and I all but sewed my lips together, avoiding the answer. What was it about this damn woman that made my tongue run off like I was an adolescent with zero control over my body or words?

Saying that in front of her, hell, mentioning Lizbeth at all, had been monumentally stupid. I'd sworn to never let Ace find out about her, yet there I went, fucking it up within minutes of being around her. I was going to blame it on the blind rage that had filled me at the sight of blood on Ace's face and the smell of her fear saturating the air.

My claim hadn't been a lie, the bounty on Ace's soul meant that no one but the Crimson Queen was allowed to harm her. But since Ace had no idea about the bounty, the words never should've left my mouth. Just another notch on my list of reasons to go back and murder Chesie.

I glanced down at her, my eyes catching on the specks of dried leaves stuck to the long, dark strands of her hair before falling to her face, taking in the shape of her nose and the hard clench of her jaw. But it was the flat, expressionless look in her eyes that made me nearly trip over my feet.

Anytime they weren't flashing with anger, it was like all the will left her body. As though, even if she wasn't actively seeking death, she also didn't much care if it enveloped her. And I wasn't sure why the hell it bothered me so much.

I was dead. Everyone here was fucking dead. What was one more person to add to the growing list? She'd wind up here in the end, eventually. But for some inane reason I'd never known, the thought of her being dead felt like it could break me. Maybe because I'd known what would happen to her soul once she died.

The only thing I knew with certainty, was that fate seemed determined to keep slapping us together whether we wanted it to or not.

Sensing my attention, or more likely, irritated at my silence, Ace's hazel eyes met mine, and if I wasn't mistaken, the dark circles had grown over the last hour. "Is that how this trip is going to be? You either insulting me or ignoring me the entire way to Ardenglass in the hope that I'll burst into tears and leave?"

Ardenglass. My hands instinctively fisted at my sides. Just the thought of her in that city made me want to choke her again, shaking the smallest seed of common sense into her. I may have agreed to allow her out of the Wood to help her scratch the adventurous itch she had, but I'd chain her to a tree before I took her anywhere near the White Castle.

Forcing my hands to relax, I tucked them into my pockets and cut her a cruel smile. "That depends. Is it working?"

"You're such an asshole," she whispered, and I wasn't sure whether she'd meant it for me to hear or not since I was confident she had no problem saying it directly to my face. Either way, she should know by now that nothing slipped past my notice, especially in regard to her.

"Such vulgar language from a lady. You should be careful; if you keep saying that word to me, I'm going to think you're hinting at something, little rabbit."

Her shoulders tensed, and I bit back a smirk, knowing she was likely now calling me much worse things in her head. She shifted away from me, adding several extra inches of space between us. "What is it with men making everything about sex? If I called you an asshole a thousand times, it'd be because you're being an asshole a thousand times. That's it."

Apprehension sliced into my skin, and my steps faltered. Only my hands being stuffed in my pockets prevented me from snatching her wrist and yanking her back toward me. The thought of any man talking about sex to her enough to make her uncomfortable made me want to punch something. Hard.

"What the fuck does that mean?"

She stared at anything other than me, chewing the inside of her lip like her life depended on it and enforcing the bad feeling in my gut. "It didn't mean anything, Terek. I just meant in general."

Bullshit. She was about to duck under the branch ahead of us, but I reached out and gripped it, cleaving it from the tree with more force than necessary. "Don't lie to me unless you can do a better job of it."

She lurched to a stop, her gaze slowly moving from the severed branch to my face, eyes wide. "You just…" she looked down at it again and then back at the tree, "ripped that off like it was a piece of parchment."

"And?"

"And I'm starting to realize, I don't actually know you at all."

No, little rabbit, you really don't. I tossed the branch to the ground. "Don't change the subject."

She rolled her eyes. "What? I'm supposed to relive my entire life story for you, but you've never had to tell me a single thing? I'm sorry to be the one to break it to you, but that's not how trust works."

My fingers itched to wrap around her throat again, finding their home on the bruises already blooming against her soft skin and show her just how much she shouldn't trust me. But goddamn me, as much as I welcomed Ace's anger, the thought of her no longer trusting me made me nauseated.

"I don't need trust to make you do what I want, little rabbit."

"Stop calling me that."

"No."

We stood there watching each other for several long, agonizing seconds, both waiting for the other to concede to something. Anything that would remove the thick tension hanging in the air between us.

It was me who broke first. Stretching my arm out, I gestured to the thick, fence-like trees she'd yet to notice a few yards away. "Lucky for you, we're here."

She whipped around, hands shooting up to clench the cloak tightly around her neck as she took in the straight row of enormous trees that marked the edge of the Wood.

Jaw falling slack, she shot past me, her bare feet flying across the ground at a speed I didn't know her short legs possessed. She shoved past the reaching branches and squeezed between two trunks, her lungs sucking in air hard enough for me to hear each heavy breath as I walked up behind her.

It was too dark for her to make out the details, but that didn't keep her eyes from darting back and forth across the grass and open river, her fingertips twitching like she was desperate to take everything in and file it away to sketch out later.

If the thought of her stepping out into the open didn't make me feel like crawling out of my skin and shaking the fuck out of her, I might've smiled at the wonder on her face.

"Welcome to the Underland, little rabbit."

TEREK

CHAPTER TWENTY-FIVE

The river stretched out before us, the gentle lapping of the water against the shore loud compared to the quiet that had encompassed us within the trees. It was a sound I usually enjoyed; the melodic trickle a warm welcome after the eerie silence that always followed me in the Wood.

Ace walked closer, her steps hesitant and careful over the damp rocks that bordered the river. Squinting, she peered left and then right, taking in the unending water in both directions.

The river itself wasn't very wide, easily crossable as long as one was prepared for the cold, but it went on in both directions for miles. If she was hoping for a way around it, she was going to be disappointed.

"Do we just follow this? Or is there like a bridge or something?" She frowned, like she was suddenly questioning whether things like bridges and boats existed here.

"Yes, Ace. Believe it or not, the dead still know how to cut down trees and build things to survive. We don't live in caves."

She rolled her eyes, but I continued on before she could make some sarcastic comment that would only irritate me. "The closest bridge is too far to walk to tonight." Truth. But it was also way too close to Ardenglass for my comfort.

I pointed to the left, where the river squeezed between the Wood and a small hill surrounded by a grove of trees. Unlike the thick trees of the Wood, which never held onto their leaves, trees outside of its borders were richer and covered with various shades of orange and red around this time.

"That section just over there is crossable when the weather is calm. It'll probably reach your waist and be absolutely freezing, but it's that or nothing," I said, running my gaze down her legs. "Consider it a free bath."

I expected to see life flare behind her eyes as she glared at me, but instead, the woman shocked the hell out of me by twisting back and ramming her elbow into my side. Between having a close hold on my senses and not at all expecting her to have the energy to hit a leaf, let alone me, I made no move to block it.

But hearing the beautiful string of curses she let out as she hugged her arm to her chest and stomped off made it well worth it. Because sadly for her, she'd landed her elbow against the hilt of my dagger rather than my flesh.

Fighting a smile at her expense, I let her have a private moment to nurse her wilted pride and focused my attention to the grove on the other side of the water. I rarely stopped around here since I always traveled alone, and Ardenglass was so close, but if I remembered correctly, there was a natural outcropping of rocks hidden within it where we could stop at for the night.

It wouldn't be comfortable by any means, but it'd at least protect us from the worst of the chill, which was going to be especially desirable after submerging half our bodies in the river.

Given our proximity to the main path into the city, we wouldn't be able to risk a fire for longer than the time it'd take to dry our clothes, but since I wasn't expecting Ace to make it across the river before calling it quits, I—*holy fuck*.

"What the crimson are you doing?" I choked out, turning to see my cloak folded on the ground and Ace with her dress hiked up to her hips, exposing two perfectly shaped, pale legs that were not covered by stockings of any kind.

She popped her head up, her face heating as she gripped the fabric to her stomach, the hem barely extending a few inches below her hip bones and doing nothing to hide the way her inner thighs pressed together.

"Aren't we getting ready to cross?"

"Not fucking naked you're not," I snapped, cutting across the distance between us to snatch the skirt of her dress from her hands and drop it back to the ground. The last thing I needed was a gust of wind to come out of nowhere and reveal anything higher than what I'd just seen. The image of her legs alone was going to be scorched in my mind for a solid week. The sight of her undergarments would send me straight to the final afterlife.

Crimson take me, why did she have to have curves like that?

She smacked my hands off and stepped away, futilely smoothing out the now-crumpled fabric. "I wasn't getting naked, you ass. I was seeing how hard it'd be to hold my entire dress up out of the water. You may be fine sleeping like a wet dog, but I'd much rather not, if I can help it."

"You can help it. Go home."

Her hands turned to fists over her dress, and her face hardened to granite. "I'm not leaving, Terek. Whether you stay with me or not, is your choice, but I'll be here either way."

"Tell me why."

"No."

I glowered at her, still mentally scrubbing my mind with a wire brush. I was half tempted to grip her just above the curve of her hips and toss her in the middle of the river, wash my hands of her childish games, and sleep in my own bed. But almost as soon as the thought hit the front of my mind, that tug thrummed to life in my chest, urging me to stay.

"Fine," I said, reaching down to unlace my boots. "Follow behind me and pay attention. If you fall, or otherwise float down the river, I'm not helping you."

"Fine."

I removed one boot and then the other, soaking up the silence between us as I waited for the angry, whispered comment I knew she'd give. Another second ticked by.

"Asshole."

There it was.

IF SHE'D BEEN filthy before, slamming into the mud twice as she'd attempted to yank her feet from the squelching riverbed and walk up the shore hadn't done her any favors.

I watched Ace struggle from several feet away, my trousers soaked to my skin, boots and socks dangling from one hand, and my cloak draped over my forearm.

"So much for not sleeping like a wet dog," I said, staring at the hem of her dress, which was currently dragging through the dark brown water. I almost felt bad considering she'd successfully kept it out of the river up until the end. Almost.

"You know," she seethed, her teeth audibly clacking together as she finally clambered up the shore to stand next to me, "a gentleman would've offered his arm to help me after the first time I fell."

I dropped my boots and shoved my wet feet back into them, not bothering to lace them, and raised a brow. "A lady wouldn't be spending the night in the wilderness with a man she doesn't know."

To my delight, instead of cursing me again, a shadow of a smile teased her lips. The first hint of one I'd seen since she'd arrived. "I've never been very good at being a lady."

I stepped closer. "That doesn't surprise me in the least. Is that why you have no ring on your finger? Too busy sleeping under the stars with random men?"

I'd meant it in a teasing way, hoping to kindle the spark and see it brighten further, but instead of smiling at me and teasing back, Ace's face fell. Her lips pressed together as she glanced away from me. "You said there's shelter in there?" she asked, pointing toward the grove.

I nodded, watching her make her way to the trees, her steps slow and careful over the dark terrain. After a moment, I followed, torn between pressing her about the topic until she eventually caved and ignoring it completely.

In the end, I decided it didn't fucking matter and opted for the latter, showing her the small overhang of stone and gathering what branches I could for a fire. Partly because the thought of Ace getting married made me painfully aware of all the normal things in life I'd never have, and partly because I honestly just didn't want to hear her talk, period.

Not that she'd ever cared about the last part.

Crouching so I wouldn't crack my head on the roof of the shallow cave, I dropped my armload of branches and reached into the small pack tied to my waist to remove my flint. Ace was sitting at the mouth of the shelter, leaning against the wall with her knees bent and feet tucked beneath her dress, her hair a mess of dark, tangled strands over one shoulder.

I could feel her watching me, but I shifted so that my back was to her, focusing on the fire and positioning the sticks the way I needed to hopefully get a little bit of warmth in our bones.

I'd just gotten the smallest flicker when a breeze blew through, stinging my skin and saturating my nose with the smell of burning wood. I clenched my teeth and walled my senses off, allowing only the smallest trickle out so I wouldn't completely lose my head in front of her. That was the last thing I needed.

The second the flickers grew to arm-sized flames and the thick smell of smoke invaded even my dulled sense of smell, I immediately wanted to stomp it out, certain everyone within a twenty-mile radius could smell it as well. Between it and Ace's presence, I'd never felt more exposed.

Although I'd hadn't run into anyone actively searching for her in the last few years, that wasn't definitive proof that they weren't out there. Nor was it proof that I was the only person in the entire Underland who could feel the call of her soul.

For all I knew, the only reason I'd been the only one so far to find her in the Wood was because no one else's senses rivaled mine. But now that she was out of the trees and closer to civilization? I had no idea who all might sense her, or whether those who did would know of the bounty.

A bounty every citizen would kill to have, regardless of what it took to get it.

However, as on edge as the fire made me, I could hear Ace's hands sliding up and down her arms, ineffectively trying to warm herself. Avoiding the risk of smoke was pointless if she died of hypothermia. Things like disease and illness didn't naturally exist in the Underland, but technically, neither did she.

I had no idea if she could get sick here, but given her body and organs were still alive, it was logical to assume she very much could. And as much as it'd serve her right, the last thing I needed was her staying longer than she already was if she became too sick to take herself home.

"I know you were joking earlier, but I've actually never slept outside before. It's kind of calming, in a weird way."

I brushed my hands on my thighs and sat back a few feet away from her, closing my eyes and resting my head against the wall. "You say that now, but you're not used to this weather. I walk these borders every night, Ace. I know how cold it gets."

She shrugged like she wasn't worried, even though I swore her lips had a slight blue tint to them. I again fought the urge to ask her why the fuck she was still here. Why would a woman used to a high-quality life be so willing to sleep on the hard ground, wet and cold, when she could be tucked into a warm bed instead?

I knew her life Upside hadn't been perfect. Knew that while there were plenty of things she *had* told me that had enraged me on her behalf, there was also more she had not. Still, that didn't explain why she'd suddenly chosen death over being alive.

"So, is that why you were late?"

My eyes popped open at her question, and I tilted my head toward her. What the hell was she talking about now? "What?"

She cleared her throat and pulled her legs tighter to her chest, wrapping her arms around them. "Earlier you said, 'the one time I'm late.' Was that why? You were busy patrolling the border?"

I narrowed my eyes, the reminder instantly pissing me off. "Why?"

She leaned forward to rest her chin on her knees and began lazily drawing something in the dirt with her fingers. "Curiosity, boredom, and a need for something other than silence."

The last one I believed. "No, I hadn't been patrolling." *Even though I should've been.* "I'd...been with someone."

Her eyes shot up to mine, and something flashed across them too fast for me to catch before she cut them away again. She chewed on her lip, glancing back down at her swirling fingers like I was the last person she wanted to be around. That made two of us.

"I was talking with someone I hadn't seen in a long time," I added, though I wasn't sure why. "A friend."

If trusting someone just enough to know they wouldn't stab you in your sleep could be called friendship. None of us here dared become closer than that, not when we could all be used against each other like mindless, obedient chess pieces at any time.

Duma hadn't been dead as long as I had, but he and his brother had settled in far quicker, making a home in Tover and running a successful business. It was why I rarely saw him. It wasn't often that I had a need to travel there. But I'd run into him on the road out of Ardenglass.

He'd been heading out as well, having gone to pick up a shipment of herbs he could only acquire in the city for double what they were likely worth. We'd been discussing the lack of new faces arriving in Tover lately when I'd felt that familiar warmth in my chest. The vibrating tug that slithered through my veins and always made me feel incapable of denying it, of following it wherever it wanted me to go.

I'd known what it meant. What it *always* meant.

Ace.

The tingling had increased until it felt like a fire burning just beneath my skin, switching every one of my senses to high alert. But I'd ignored it. For ten solid minutes, I'd ignored her call and continued my conversation with Duma until I felt like my ribs would tear from my chest and walk off without me.

Those ten minutes almost cost Ace her life.

Now that I was stuck sitting out here with her, I couldn't help but wonder if fate had shoved its fingers into that run-in with Duma as well. Because the more I thought about it, if Ace made it through the night without giving up this charade, Tover was the only place I could take her where she might stay hidden until she did.

The town of Gissan was closer, but where Tover was clean and its people far from the Wood, Gissan was not. It was where the poorest citizens of the Underland resided, the majority fighting for the barest scraps to get by. Living worse in the Underland than they'd ever lived in the Upside, yet unable to pass on.

It was comical, really. So many Upsiders spouted religion and peace after death, creating their own deities and versions of heaven while ignorantly unaware that the afterlife could be so much worse than living.

Taking Ace to Gissan could, indeed, work in my favor, frightening her into believing all the towns were like that, but I didn't dare risk it when I was almost certain there'd be bounty hunters around every corner and at every inn.

Since I knew Ace could sleep here without disappearing, from the numerous occasions I'd found her napping on the ground over the years, all anyone would need to do was knock her unconscious and keep her that way long enough to drag her body to the White Castle. And I'd give anything to keep that from happening.

Mostly because the idea of Lizbeth getting her hands on Ace's ability was more terrifying than every Creature within the Wood, but also because, against all logic, I cared about Ace when I fucking shouldn't.

So, Tover it would be. As long as Duma didn't make any extra stops, he should easily beat us there, and the man still owed me a life debt. He and his brother could figure out what to do with her, and I'd wipe my hands clean and step away.

For good.

ADELAIS

CHAPTER TWENTY-SIX

I stretched my hands out in front of me, putting them as close to the open flames as possible without scorching my flesh. Damn, it was cold. Every part of me facing the fire was warm and comfortable, but anything that shifted even the smallest inch away instantly hit the air like a wall of ice.

Terek sat beside me, seeming completely unaffected by the weather as he stared up at a gouge in the rock, his dark eyes faraway, but his face losing none of its hardness, even as his mind wandered. I was beginning to wonder if it even could at this point, or if he was now as solid and unfeeling as the stone we sat beneath.

He'd said he'd been speaking with a friend, but there was nothing about this man that made me believe that. He looked ready for war just sitting around a fire with an unarmed woman. I couldn't imagine him sitting around a table, playing cards, and laughing with friends. Just trying to had an involuntary snort slipping out before I could contain it.

He blinked, as if coming out of a fog, and twisted toward me at the unladylike sound. "Hm?"

I shook my head, fighting a smile. "Nothing. I was just sitting here thinking about how I can't really picture you hanging out and talking with friends. It seems too," I paused, running my gaze down to the knives at his waist and back up, "normal for someone like you."

To my surprise, his lips twitched. "You're one to talk. Somehow, I don't think sitting in a garden, drinking tea while you gossip about Lady Dimwit's most recent indiscretion at the spring luncheon, counts as hanging out either."

A weird fluttering took off in my chest, a giggle threatening to escape at hearing his deep, gravelly voice say any of those words. But before it could grace the air, my stomach beat it to it, rumbling loud enough to wake anything within a mile radius of us.

I felt my face heat, and I tucked my hands into my lap, pressing them against my stomach in the hopes that the single touch would stop the horrid sound from repeating.

The hint of a smile immediately fell from Terek's lips, and he dropped his gaze to my torso, hidden behind my arms and bent knees. "When was the last time you ate?"

"Right before I left," I said, figuring he wouldn't appreciate the honest answer of, *I have no idea, nor did I even consider what I would eat once I got here.* I'd been in such a rush to leave before Frederick woke, the thought hadn't even crossed my mind.

"What did I tell you about lying to me, little rabbit?"

God, why was he so intent on still calling me that? He could just be trying to irritate me, but I couldn't help but wonder if it was his way of forcing himself to see me as less than the grown woman he'd kissed. To wipe away any connection we'd once shared, no matter how accidental and brief it'd been.

I rolled my eyes, but I didn't waste my breath lying again. "It's fine. I know you don't have to worry about things like that anymore. I'll figure out what to do about food when we get to the city." Hopefully.

Rather than ease his irritation, my mention of Ardenglass only seemed to anger him further. "You assume a lot for a woman who knows so little."

He pushed up off the wall and leaned around the fire to grab the travel pack I'd seen him untie from his waist. Then he sat back and tossed something at me. I squeaked and threw my hands up to shield my face, but the small, wrapped object landed perfectly in my lap.

I picked it up hesitantly, holding it out with my fingertips as I slowly unknotted the twine around it and peeled the wrapper off. A faint peppery smell hit my nostrils, and I crinkled my nose at what appeared to be ruined leather.

"Fancy, gourmet dinners are hard to come by out in the middle of nowhere, I'm afraid."

I glanced between Terek's face and the item—food, apparently—in my hand. "Wait. You mean you still have to eat down here? But you're all…"

"Dead?"

I nodded.

"Yes and no. We can't die of starvation or anything, but we experience the pain of hunger." He pulled another from his pack and ripped it open, tearing off a piece with his teeth.

I shuddered. I couldn't imagine my stomach feeling as if it was caving in on itself, only to never die from it. Forever. So much for a peaceful and loving afterlife.

"Honestly, our bodies still function about the same as before," he said, stretching his legs out as much as the space allowed and tucking an arm behind his head like he couldn't have been more comfortable. "We can eat, shit, sleep, and fuck just the same as we did on the Upside. Maybe even better."

Every inch of my body flared beet red, the image of Terek fucking anyone making me want to crawl straight into the fire at our feet. Common sense had always told me he'd been in the Underland far longer than I'd been alive, and he was, by far, the most beautiful man I'd ever laid eyes on, so of course he'd had sex.

But imagining him naked with someone was absolutely not something I should be doing. *Especially* not sitting a foot away from him. Alone and at night.

He smirked, and I knew he'd said it only to get a rise out of me, assuming me to be some delicate, virgin flower who'd yet to kiss another man other than him. I ignored the bait, refusing to give in to his taunt, and took a small bite of the brown hunk of food.

The second it touched my tongue, I immediately regretted it. What the hell was that? Instinct had me wanting to spit it into the dirt, but Terek's dark chuckle kept it in my mouth. I glared at him, which only earned me another laugh, this one deeper, with what I could've sworn was the faintest dip of a dimple.

"It's not poison, Ace. I eat to keep the pangs at bay and my body moving, not for the flavor. It's just dried meat."

He said it like that explained the awful, pungent taste against my tongue, but I'd eaten my fair share of game and— My jaw fell slack, and my eyes widened in horror as my mind finally caught up to what he'd just said.

"Oh my God," I said, holding my hand to my mouth and trying with every fiber of my being not to vomit all over my lap. "Is this...from a *Creature?*"

His lips pulled tight, like he was fighting another laugh, and I narrowed my eyes, swallowing hard. If he let out even a whisper of one, I was going to throw this horrid thing at his face.

"Crimson hell, Ace, no. I've never once eaten a Creature of the Wood. Given the lethal qualities some of them seep from their pores, I wouldn't advise anyone else to either. It's just venison."

He took another bite, but all I could do was stare at the piece in my hand, my mind awhirl with confusion. So, I was eating a dead...dead deer? How was that even possible?

"They don't, I don't know, *disappear* when you kill them? In the Underland, I mean?" I rubbed at my temple with my free hand. I was way too tired for this.

He finished off his food and wiped his hand on his thigh, pushing up into a crouch. "I told you, bodies work almost the same here. We may not die of starvation, but that doesn't mean we can't move on early. Same for animals. Their souls leave, and their bodies simply decompose like they do Upside."

"Okay, but how do you move on—"

"We have a long walk tomorrow, Ace," he suddenly said, face guarded and cold. He reached over to grab what looked to be a flask and then pushed up to his feet. "Starve if you prefer, but I wouldn't recommend it."

Without another word, he was gone, not even the quiet pad of his steps hitting the air. I blinked slowly, staring at the space he'd just occupied. Well, okay then.

If he thought using his stupid abilities and running away on the guise of getting water was going to make me stop asking questions, he was going to be extremely disappointed when he returned.

Like what the hell was this twice dead deer going to do to my insides? And why had he said we'd be traveling for an entire day? Terek might not know the answer to the first question, but he certainly knew the second.

He'd already mentioned before that Ardenglass wasn't very far, so he was either assuming I'd walk at the pace of a lethargic snail, or he was hiding something. I glared at the shadows beyond the trees, knowing there was a good chance he was watching me as well.

Terek might've been right about needing to eat in order to have energy tomorrow, but if the man thought I was going to go traipsing off with him without knowing where we were going, he had another thing coming. I'd worked too hard for my freedom to blindly follow yet another man.

Incensed and cold, I faced the fire again and shoved the rest of the meat into my mouth, holding my breath and picturing the sticky, flaky texture of the sweetest tarts as I forced it down.

If I survived Frederick only to die via a hunk of deer corpse, I was going to be really pissed off.

⚷—⟶

"SO," I STARTED, gesturing back toward where Terek had come from the second he re-entered my sight, some ten minutes later. "Ardenglass is only a few hours south from here, correct?"

His steps paused for the briefest moment, and then he sighed heavily and maneuvered past the fire to sit next to me. When he finally answered, the word was clipped, like he already knew what I was insinuating and was running different scenarios in his head of what he could say to keep me from talking.

"Yes."

"Are we making a pitstop on the way there?"

"No."

Maybe it was because wherever he was taking me was on the far side of the city then. Between the size and the congestion of people, who knew how long it would take to travel through the entire thing.

"Where are we—"

"I'm taking you to a town called Tover."

I huffed out a breath, counting to ten in my head. If this man did not stop interrupting me, I was going to lose it. How had I ever been attracted to anything other than his face? He had no patience and certainly no respect.

"Am I allowed to know why?"

"Because I'm not taking you to Ardenglass. End of discussion." He crossed his arms and tipped his face up, causing shadows to dance along his sharp features. From the angle I was at, it almost made him look more Creature than human.

I crossed mine as well, mimicking his arrogant mannerisms. "You can't truly think I'm gullible enough to believe there are only two cities in this entire world."

"You don't want me answering that."

"You're an ass."

"So you've said."

His moods were going to give me whiplash. "Terek, please."

He sighed. "No, there aren't only two. There are likely thousands of cities and towns across the Underland, Ace. This world isn't solid like the Upside, no matter how real it might feel to you."

He took a drink from the now-full flask before holding it out for me. "The Underland is alive, in a way. Ever-changing. This is where souls come to rest until they're ready to move on. The more souls arrive, the larger the Underland grows. I've been here a long time, and even I don't know more than a handful of the towns."

I took a long drink, not realizing how parched I was, and considered his answer. "What would happen if fewer souls arrived? Would some of the towns just disappear?"

The idea seemed preposterous. Would an entire town just poof out of sight one day? What would happen to the people who were there?

"In theory, I suppose," he said, tilting his head in an almost predatory way and glancing past me out of our shelter, eyes narrowing at whatever he saw.

"What does that mean?"

He didn't reply at first, listening to something outside I couldn't hear. When he was convinced whatever it was wasn't worthy of concern, he ran a hand through his hair and yawned. "It means thousands of people arrive every day, but very few leave. From what I know, the Underland hasn't shrunk in decades, and I doubt it ever will."

I took one last drink and handed the flask back to him, his yawn drawing out one of my own. "I wonder why no one's moving on," I said, reaching my hands out and hovering them over the flames, hoping the bite of the heat would help keep me awake a little longer. This was the most I'd ever gotten Terek to say in one sitting.

"Do you think it's because they're scared to move on, or because they're just that happy here?"

"You're so fucking blind." Terek scoffed, flinging out a hand and leaning toward me as he all but growled. "Do you truly believe people want to be here as long as they have? Twice their lifespans? Triple? Living their monotonous lives, day in and day out, because they *want* to?"

I blinked at the sudden fury coating his tone and fisted my dress, trying to calm my breathing with his sudden nearness. *He wasn't Frederick. He wasn't going to hurt me.*

"I didn't mean anything by it, Terek."

He sneered. "No one wants to be here except for you, Ace, and yet you're the only one capable of leaving whenever you want. If there is a so-called God, he sure has a fucked-up sense of humor."

"That's not fair," I said, feeling naked and defenseless. I hadn't asked for the ability to come here. It'd been gifted to me, just the same as Terek's abilities had been gifted to him.

"I may have the ability to go to the Upside, but that has nothing to do with people choosing not to move on to their final resting place. That's their choice, just as coming here is mine."

He leaned down even farther until his face was only inches from my own, every angry line visible in the orange light. "It's pretty fucking hard for your soul to move on when you're no longer in control of it. Choice doesn't exist here, little rabbit, and you'd do well to remember that. Those of us who wander for eternity only do so because of *her*."

The hatred laced within each word had my hackles rising. There was no second-guessing that whoever he was talking about was bad news. Someone he hated even more than the Creatures he sneered at. "Who?"

"The Crimson Queen." He kicked a log, causing sparks to fly up that barely missed my skin. "She's been in control of the Underland since before I arrived and will continue to be until all this is nothing but a forgotten memory."

"Is that who you were talking about with Chesie?"

"Yes, and I suggest you stay far away from her. For she is," he cut himself off and ran a hand through his hair again, making it stand all on end. "Let's just say, she would be very interested in your ability, and she is not known for her kindness."

"What is she known for?"

"For taking things that don't belong to her."

I recognized what he wasn't saying, the emotion hiding within his words—because I'd experienced the same thing every single day. Self-hatred. Whatever this Crimson Queen had done or had made him do, he utterly despised himself for it.

"Terek…"

He snatched his cloak off his lap and tossed it at me, smacking me directly in the face before it plopped onto my legs. "Go to sleep."

The sudden wall he erected felt like a slap in the face, and I gripped his cloak, eyes burning and wishing I had the privacy of my room to let them loose. Not because he'd hurt my feelings, but because his hot and cold behavior was really starting to piss me off, and I had a bad habit of crying when I was angry. Especially when I was exhausted.

I pushed up onto my feet, sacrificing the blessed heat in favor of moving as far away from him as our lodgings allowed. I'd yet to sleep next to an undeserving prick, and I wasn't about to start tonight.

Maintaining eye contact, even though every survival instinct told me to look away, I plopped to the ground and wadded his cloak into a pile on the dirt, stuffing it under my head as a makeshift pillow rather than a blanket.

"Just so we're clear, I'm tired, not obedient."

He didn't reply, but as my eyelids grew heavy, I could've sworn I heard the faintest huff of laughter.

 TEREK

Chapter Twenty-Seven

Now that Ace had finally curled up and stopped asking a hoard of fucking questions I had no interest in answering, I'd intended to let the flames die down a little and get a few measly hours of sleep.

Although the warmth was comforting and had done well to dry our clothing, allowing a fire to go unwatched was not on my list of stupid decisions to make. I'd made quite enough of them today as it was without attracting who knew what to our camp while I was out. My senses may have been unmatched, but even they had their limits.

As much as I'd suffered from them when I'd first arrived, I depended on my abilities heavily most days, so used to them now that I couldn't imagine how I'd ever functioned without them. But what only two people in the Underland knew, besides myself, was that my abilities went dead the second I lost consciousness.

They shut down the moment my body did, allowing anything or anyone to sneak up on me without a single hair rising on my body. I hadn't been aware of it until it'd been discovered and exploited by the first person here I'd dared to trust.

Being someone who didn't fear the dark abyss that supposedly existed if I died without my soul, I'd long since stopped caring if anything happened while I slept. But sitting here with Ace's body mere feet from my own, the thought of being without my senses, no matter how short-lived, filled me with unease.

I'd sat there for who knew how long, looking between her shivering form and the flames, debating which option was the lesser risk. Sacrificing any rest and allowing her to stay as warm as possible with the fire, or letting it die and getting as much sleep as possible.

In the end, I'd opted for the latter. I was fucking exhausted, and if I was lucky, the cold might send Ace home before I'd even awoken. Win-win.

But with every inch the flames lowered and the temperature dropped, Ace's body curled into a tighter ball, and my resolve splintered. I stared at her, lying as far away from me as she could without running into the other wall, desperately pressing her knees into her chest with her arms between them.

I'd given the woman my cloak to cover herself, but she'd tossed it to the ground, her pride almost rivaling my own. I had a feeling snow could fall from the sky, and she still wouldn't remove it from under her head. And as much as I wanted to scoff and brush it off as her own problem, my eyes refused to leave her shuddering form.

I'd been dead so long, I couldn't remember the feel of the sun on my face or the warmth of a brightly lit sky, but what I could recall was how acute the perpetual chill of the Underland had felt when I'd first arrived. Granted, my skin had been practically raw with sensitivity, but still, I knew Ace was feeling a cold my body had long ago acclimated to.

I had closed off my senses, not wanting to suffocate from the proximity of the smoke, but I opened them just enough to hear Ace's teeth vibrating against each other as she tried, and failed, to quietly control her shivering. And for the hundredth time, I wondered why the crimson she wouldn't just go home.

Why freeze to death, lying out on the hard ground with someone she hated, when she could sleep in a warm bed and return the following day? There had to be a specific reason, and I fucking hated the entire Upside for whatever it was.

Before I could close my senses off again, I caught the faintest sound of a whimper pass between her lips, grating at me until I swore I felt the sound throughout my entire body. I cursed under my breath and threw my head back, slamming it into the stone. But rather than dislodge the nagging, undesired sensation, all I succeeded at was startling her and making her violently flinch.

Goddamn it. I was going to regret this.

Reaching forward to adjust the branches one last time to make sure the fire continued going down, I shoved up and walked over to her, my spine curved low beneath the overhang.

I didn't bother being quiet, and with each step I took, the muscles in her small form tensed, uncertainty pulsing off her in waves. When I dropped down, my hip grazed her back, and she twisted, causing even more of her body to press along me as I stretched out beside her, keeping clothing between us at all points.

"What are you doing?"

"Going to sleep. What does it look like?"

Her eyes narrowed to slits, and she scooted away, adding a few inches between us. "Well, go to sleep somewhere else. There's plenty of space here. You don't need to be in mine."

Something dark and wicked within my chest sat up and grinned at her challenge, thriving at how nervous I made her. I matched her movements, closing the distance between us again and tucking my knees up behind hers, my body molding to her shape with an ease that pleased me far more than it should.

"Your full body tremors say otherwise."

She took a deep breath, like she was mentally counting down to restrain herself from twisting fully and socking me in the nose. I leaned up on my elbow, roving my gaze over her face. The dark circles under her eyes looked like they had grown just in the time she'd been lying down. The woman needed to stop arguing for once in her life and go to sleep.

"Slamming my head into the stone again would feel softer than you do. Relax, Ace. It's just body heat. Trust me, I'd rather go back to the other side of the fire."

"Then why don't you?" she snapped, her words slightly muffled behind her tightly clenched teeth.

"Because the fire is about to die out," I said, snatching my cloak and yanking it out from under her head, right as I replaced it with my right arm, her head landing on my bicep. "And I have no desire to travel tomorrow on zero sleep, which is what's going to happen if I get stuck listening to your fucking shivering until morning."

Before she could fully register what I'd done, I tossed the fabric over us and curled my left arm around her waist. My fingers bumped something hard and round as I curled them over what was likely a pocket, so I shifted them up, pressing my hand flat to her stomach and dragging her more firmly against me.

She grumbled when she failed to pull away again, calling me several names that I was sure, even decades after I'd left it, no lady Upside was supposed to say aloud. "Terek."

I positioned my head on my shoulder as comfortably as I could, trying not to choke on the intoxicating hint of vanilla clinging to her hair. "Stop overthinking it, Ace. It's just body heat, and it's only one night."

She worried her lip but didn't argue the point, and for a long moment, we just laid there, each silently waiting for the other to submit. I almost smiled. If Ace thought she could outwait me, she was going to be painfully mistaken.

There were few things I was more skilled at than waiting. The same was true of everyone in the Underland. Lizbeth had made sure of it.

"Fine," she finally said, resting her head down so her cheek lay flat against my arm, "but don't get any ideas."

"I can promise you, little rabbit, that will never happen." The words felt like ash on my tongue, the memory of our kiss slamming into the back of my eyelids, as if daring me to repeat the words while reliving the moment.

She mumbled something about stupid nicknames, but then sighed and slowly—like she was forcibly releasing each of her muscles, one by one—relaxed in my hold.

I held still, letting my warmth seep into her body until her diaphragm began to rise and fall steadily beneath my arm as she lost the battle to unconsciousness.

And it wasn't until I'd allowed my own eyes to shut and take in just how perfectly she fit against me, that I realized the level of shit I was in. Ace shifted in her sleep, causing her ass to press firmly against my cock, and I bit my tongue hard enough to taste blood.

So much for not making any more stupid decisions.

ADELAIS

CHAPTER TWENTY-EIGHT

R azor-sharp teeth. Wide, unseeing, yellow eyes. The stench of death in the air, and the sound of screams. *My* screams. My blood raced in my veins, and I felt my heart beat wildly in my chest as I ran through the Wood, a woman's laughter trailing behind me.

My breaths came faster and heavier as I felt her draw nearer, no matter how hard I pumped my legs. A hand curled over my shoulder, and I lurched forward, tripping over the body of a dead rabbit and falling down a large, black hole at the base of a tree.

Then I was lying across the ground, watching leaves dance in a canopy of branches above me. I could hear the steady rush of flowing water and the feel of a comforting warmth enveloping my body, pulling me in. In. In.

I squeezed my eyes shut, floating in semi-consciousness as I slowly drifted out of a string of strange dreams, unwilling to fully wake just yet. Though there was a mild throb in my head, and my mouth felt like an abandoned field during a drought, I felt surprisingly content as I lay there.

Light flickered behind my closed lids, like a child banging on a door and demanding I open it. I groaned, turning away from the source to bury my face deeper into my pillow and stretch my arm down, searching for the blanket to toss over my head.

But instead of finding the soft, plush duvet I'd been sleeping under for years, my hand hit something solid and rough draped across my body. I frowned, slowly dragging my fingers along the unfamiliar surface. What in the world had I fallen asleep with? It felt almost like—

My hand froze, every muscle in my body tensing to snap as the reality of what I was feeling suddenly slammed into me. The heavy weight pressing down across my abdomen. The warmth soaking into me. The graze of hair beneath my fingertips. An arm. There was an arm wrapped around me.

Frederick was in my bed.

Horror flung any sense of drowsiness from me, and I flew into full consciousness, aware of every place we touched and his sleep-heavy breaths tickling the hair along my brow. Anxiety clawed its way up my throat, quickly followed by nausea. A mere second ago, I hadn't just found the monster's hold comforting, *I'd curled into it* like a drooping flower seeking the sun.

Oh God, how had I not noticed when he'd walked in, let alone laid down? The creak of my bedroom door always woke me, no matter how slowly he opened it, my intuition sometimes waking me before he'd even touched the doorknob. But sleeping through him entering still didn't explain why the hell he would've stayed.

It was common for Frederick to slip in after a late night at Vincent's and use my body as a vessel for self-pleasure whenever he desired, but he'd never attempted to do so while I was asleep. The man had married me to fill his roster and birth him children, not to cuddle. Neither of us wanted that. So, what the hell had changed?

Shit, shit, shit.

Refusing to open my eyes so I wouldn't have the image of his face above mine ingrained in my memory, I blindly shifted back, hoping to put just enough space between us that I'd be able to slip out from under his arm. Something that, in theory, should be easy since the only logical explanation as to why he was here was that he'd stumbled in drunk on accident.

Unfortunately, the second my head raised from what I could now only assume was his other arm, a low groan whispered over my ear, and the limb wrapped over me tightened like a noose, drawing me even closer than I'd been before.

I squeaked, claustrophobia digging its claws into me when my forehead pressed into his collar and his leg slid over mine, successfully pinning my arms between us. He made another low noise and rolled his hips, causing the rough fabric of his trousers to scratch against my skin where my clothing had bunched up to bare my lower half.

Panic seized me, the fear of him having had free access to my body without my knowledge smothering all my other senses. All I could think of was Frederick's hips rolling into me and his hand sliding lower over my stomach. My sanity fractured, and I bucked, slamming the top of my head into his jaw and kicking as hard as I could, hoping to land at least one knee somewhere important.

Anything to get his hands off me.

There was a grunt, and then a sharp curse as the band over my waist finally lifted. Taking advantage of the small space that opened between us, I threw my arms up over my head, readying for the blow even as I continued to thrash.

Instead, I felt fingers wrap around my bicep, sending a spark through my skin like lightning all the way to my chest. I heard a sharp intake of breath, and then the hand disappeared, curling around my covered shoulder instead.

"Crimson hell, Ace! Stop. *Stop!*"

I froze.

That voice. I knew that voice.

The scent of wood and rain drifted into my lungs with each measured breath I took, and the events of the previous day came rushing back to me like a slap to the face, jarring my mind and flinging my eyes open.

Running away, Chesie, the river, the cold. Terek.

"It's just body heat, and it's only one night."

I blinked rapidly, shoving away the remnants of the nightmare that'd bled into my waking mind. It'd been Terek wrapped around me, not Frederick. He lay there, staring down at me, his pupils blown wide in either shock at how inappropriately our bodies were intertwined, or because I'd just attacked him, and he wasn't sure what I'd do next.

Probably both.

I swallowed, trying to tamp down the fear still pumping wildly through my blood, my fight response simmering on high alert just beneath my skin, ready to leap into action again if needed. "Let me up," I said, my voice low and thick.

"Are you going to hit me again?"

I shook my head, allowing myself to exhale heavily when I felt his fingers slowly release me. He silently sat up, but I could feel him watching me intently as I shuffled back. I kept my head down and fixed my gaze on the black ash smeared across my fingers, unable to meet his probing stare.

God, I'd literally curled into Terek of all people like an affection-starved, stray animal. Could I be any more pathetic?

The man deserved a good whack to the back of the head for being a jerk all yesterday, but he'd come over to me last night with the sole intent of keeping me from freezing to death. And I'd just thanked him by trying to break his jaw and deflate his balls all before he'd even woken. Lovely.

I scrubbed my clean hand over my eyes, pressing my fingers into my lids until I saw spots. "I'm sorry."

He leaned to the left and grabbed his discarded cloak that must've slipped off us at some point in the night, shaking it out before folding it over his crossed legs, his tone speculative. "Are you?"

My face flushed, remembering how many times I'd called him an asshole to his face and glared at him like I wanted to murder him yesterday. I probably wouldn't believe me either.

"Yes, I am. I woke up and didn't remember where I was. I thought—" I clamped my mouth shut, lowering my hand and glancing toward the opening of our shelter, tempted to sprint out to avoid the intensity of his stare.

Honestly, I'd likely have tried it if I'd been with literally anyone else. Especially with how badly I suddenly realized I needed to relieve myself.

"You thought what?"

His question pulled my gaze to him, but he wasn't looking at my face—he was looking at my chest. His eyes narrowed, and I instinctively crossed my arms over myself, not liking the way he continued to stare, his head tilted ever so slightly like he was listening to something.

"Nothing. Never mind."

I needed to get ahold of myself. Terek already thought me a spoiled, naïve idiot searching for *fun*. The last thing I needed was for him to see the cracks in my armor, let alone the canyon that was Frederick. If I let Terek look too closely, I was bound to fall in, dragging him down along with me.

"Your heart is pounding."

Ugh. Of course, he could hear that. My hand subconsciously flattened over my breast, and I chewed my lip, knowing it was only going to beat faster the longer I sat under his scrutiny. I needed a few minutes alone to empty my bladder, throw some water on my face, and quiet my bustling mind.

"I'm fine," I said, pushing to stand and stepping carefully around the doused fire, absently waving my hand over my shoulder. "It was just a bad dream. I'll be right back."

Before I even sucked in my next breath, Terek was standing in front of me, his defined arms crossed over his rumpled tunic, blocking my view of the entrance. His eyes were hooded, his hair strewn across his face in chaotic, messy strands, and a faint shadow of stubble outlined his jaw.

It was truly unfair how inhumanely gorgeous this man was, even after a few measly hours of sleep on the hard ground. Somehow, I highly doubted the same could be said about me.

"You're not going anywhere without me."

"I'm not," I said. "I need to relieve myself, Terek, and no offense, but I'd rather do so in private, if you don't mind."

I rolled onto the balls of my feet, determined to look anywhere but at him. My face could've relit the fire beside us. Partaking in bodily functions may have been normal, but it wasn't a conversation I was used to having out loud, and most certainly not pertaining to doing so in the grass.

But Terek either didn't notice my discomfort or didn't care because he just reached down and began lacing up his boots. "I don't hear anything out there, but I'm going to scout the area first, just in case."

He leaned back, the muscles in his neck tensing as he stretched out his spine before sliding his hands up to palm the hilts of his knives. My brow furrowed. In case of what? Who did he expect to fight this early in the day?

If the Creatures of the Wood were as mindless as he claimed—which I still didn't believe—they would've attacked the moment they'd scented us, not waited until we stepped out to relieve ourselves. Unless…there was something else Terek was worried about.

The thought sobered me, reminding me just how much I didn't know about the man I was traveling with. There was no guarantee he hadn't been lying through his teeth this entire time with how adamant he was about not going to Ardenglass. For all I knew, I was traveling with an outlaw who was wanted for murder.

I darted a quick glance at his knives again, reminding myself how easily he'd plunged them into a child. Well, okay, not an *actual* child, but still, she'd looked like one.

With one final nod at me, he stalked away and disappeared into the trees, and I tossed the idea aside. Terek had not only saved my life when he hadn't wanted to get involved, but he'd also laid next to me all night without once attempting to take something I hadn't freely given.

Sure, he'd practically straddled me this morning and ground himself into me, the sensation of which I annoyingly hadn't been able to appreciate given my inconvenient panic attack, but he'd done so unconsciously. I couldn't exactly hold him accountable for something he hadn't been aware of.

He'd come to me to share his cloak for warmth and for warmth alone. A monster wouldn't have done that.

I stared at the place we'd been, my mind replaying how it had felt last night when his arm had wrapped around me and his fingers had splayed out across my belly, holding me close. Would he laugh at me or be disgusted if he knew he was the first man I'd ever fallen asleep next to? That it was the first time I'd ever been held, period?

I tucked my hand into my pocket to clutch my watch and was still staring at the mussed-up dirt when I heard his steps behind me. "Go ahead, but be quick and don't go far. I have no desire to still be traveling by nightfall."

Nodding, I quickly shuffled out, more than eager to put space between us until I was able to leash my depressing thoughts and shove them back into the locked chest I kept tucked in my gut.

The second my toes sank into the foliage and dirt, the wind whipped past me, caressing my cheeks and spinning my hair about my face like it was happy to see me. I smiled and tipped my head back, filling my lungs with the fresh air, and looked up at the unobstructed sky for the first time.

I'd never been able to see it in its entirety in the Wood, and although it was bright enough to be what constituted daytime here, there was no clear light source within the faded gray. No sun or moon of any kind. It was like I was viewing the sky through a thick film of clouds that were impervious to the push of the wind.

Gooseflesh rose on my arms at the chill lingering on the morning breeze, but it was nothing compared to the bite of the cold against my wet skin last night. And with how hot my blood had been pumping since the moment I'd awoken, I appreciated the slight chill.

Finding the first convenient spot that wasn't too far but was out of Terek's eyesight, I bunched my dress at my waist and took care of my business, feeling crasser than I had the previous day when I'd reeked of it. For some reason, knowing Terek could hear every sound I made was somehow worse than him just smelling it.

Oh, if only my parents could see me now. The thought almost made me laugh until it was quickly followed by thoughts of Frederick. He would have woken from his drunk stupor, noticed I was missing, and be raging through the house by now.

After having the staff search the property around Vincent's for me, Ellington Estate would be the next place he'd check. I wondered if he'd admit to my parents that he'd lost me, and if they'd bother to pretend to care, if he did.

Why do you care? My brain demanded. If I knew Frederick, he'd show up to the estate fuming, accusing my parents of harboring his property to wiggle out of their deal. And if I knew *them*, they'd adamantly deny it and assist in his search, if only to keep him from slandering their name.

Carefully stepping back until I could safely drop my dress to the ground, I made my way out of the trees and to the river, muscles tensed as I waited for Terek to magically appear to stop me. But he didn't. Whether because he wasn't aware of how far my steps had taken me, or because he'd rather I wash up than smell of smoke and sweat all day, I didn't know. And as I splashed water over my face, I decided I didn't much care.

By the time I got back to our campsite, most of my skin was damp, and I felt marginally better. The nicks and bruises on my feet and my overall sore body prevented me from feeling completely back to normal, but I ignored it all, knowing it was likely to worsen during our travel today.

I stood at the entrance, watching Terek meticulously kick dirt over the remnants of the fire, the ashes already spread out, and any remaining branches long gone.

"If anyone shows up after we're gone, it'll be obvious someone stayed here, but I'd rather not waste what time we have covering our tracks more than this. We overslept as it is."

I arched my neck back to look at the overcast sky again. How the heck could he even tell what time it was without the position of a sun to go by?

"Why do we need to hide that we've been here? Is this private land or something?" I hadn't seen any homes or signs of life nearby when we'd arrived, but it'd been dark out, and my senses hadn't exactly been running at their best.

Rather than answer, Terek just brushed his hands on his trousers and tossed his travel pack at me, not even bothering to check that I'd successfully caught it. I didn't.

"Eat quickly, but only one piece since I have few left. I didn't exactly anticipate being stuck feeding more mouths than my own. I'll return shortly."

I gave a vulgar gesture to his retreating back and knelt to grab the bag, snooping through the contents with no shame—which included some coin, a glass vial of some kind of ointment, a tinder box, and two more small blades—until my fingers grasped another wrapped chunk of meat.

I eagerly ripped into it, the notion of consuming the animal far less disgusting to me now that I was even hungrier than before and, so far, hadn't died from the first piece. But that didn't mean it didn't still weird me out.

Chewing slowly so I wouldn't lose a tooth to the hard texture, I stared after Terek, imagining he was likely doing the same as I had. The thought, crude as it was, brought up several follow-up questions I dearly wished I had the nerve to ask. He'd said their bodies worked similar to how they always had Upside, but did he mean they worked the same in…all ways? I shook my head, throwing that thought very, very far away.

I'd ask someone else once we made it to Tover. Preferably someone with a womb and a far kinder smile that didn't make me question every emotion I'd ever felt.

ADELAIS

CHAPTER TWENTY-NINE

When Terek finally returned, he was no longer the ruffled man I'd woken up next to, but the shadow walker I'd come to know all my life. His dark cloak was secured at his neck, hiding most of his body from view, and his trousers were tucked back into his boots, laces knotted.

His hair was damp and slicked back from his face, accentuating his heavy brows and smooth-shaven jawline. I gaped, my mind reeling at the thought of him taking a sharp blade to his skin without a mirror. He hadn't even nicked himself once.

"See something you like?"

My eyes snapped to his, a flush highlighting my cheeks at getting caught staring. "Nope. I was just trying to decide the nicest way to tell you you'd missed a spot," I said, covering my embarrassment and smiling sweetly.

His lips flattened, and I had to hold back a snort when I turned away, still watching him in my peripheral as he reached up and brushed his fingers over his jaw. I hoped he wondered all day whether or not I was lying. It'd serve him right.

He quickly dropped his arm when he saw me stealing a peek and snapped, "Let's get moving," before striding out and through the trees, heading in the opposite way of the river.

I followed, biting my lip to keep from spoiling the quiet air with curses when I stepped on all manner of sticks, unable to avoid them at Terek's barreling speed. There was no way he expected us to walk at this pace the entire way. I grumbled; who was I kidding? Of course he would, if he thought it'd make me give up.

"The main road would take us three times as long and send us through a less-than-ideal town before making it to Tover, so we'll have to use the smaller, less-traveled paths for a while," he said over his shoulder when I'd finally caught up. "They're a little overgrown, but they should get us there before nightfall."

He pointed ahead, and I squinted, making out the barely visible dirt path. Only a few feet wide, it was large enough for Terek and me to walk side by side, but not wide enough for a coach. I pursed my lips in thought. Did the Underland even have such things, or did everyone have to walk to get to wherever they were going?

Normal Upside animals obviously existed here, so it made sense to assume horses did as well. But by the size of the road and the lack of wheel grooves, if coaches existed, they weren't used this far out. Which I supposed made sense given that animals didn't stay here long.

Terek glanced down at my feet as we finally stepped onto the path and began making our way northeast, which he'd explained he knew by the direction of the river. It flowed north past Ardenglass and another town called Gissan before it curved, heading northeast near Tover. Our apparent destination.

"Mind telling me why you opted not to wear shoes if you came with no intention of going home?" *Mind telling me why you decided to be an idiot?* Although he didn't add on that last part, his derisive tone implied it enough.

I side-eyed him, now more determined than ever to keep pace with his long strides. "I didn't own any shoes that I could have walked outside in. It seemed like the better idea at the time."

He twisted toward me, his expression mocking. "I wasn't aware fashion these days involved specific indoor and outdoor foot attire. What happens if you wear the wrong ones? Are you shunned from the spring ball?"

I bristled, wanting to poke back and make a comment about how long he'd been dead, for if he could make fun of me, it only seemed right I could do the same to him. But I didn't. Even irritated, I had enough manners not to joke about a death I knew nothing about.

"That's not what I meant." I kicked at a stone, watching it bounce into the overgrown grass along the side. "I could've worn any shoes I owned, but I was only allowed to wear heels, and they didn't seem practical for the Wood. I'd rather scratch up my feet than break my ankle trying to hike in the mud in improper shoes."

"Allowed?" Terek huffed a breath and turned away from me, tucking his hands into his pockets. "You're a grown woman, Ace, as you've so adamantly pointed out. You don't need your mother choosing your outfits for you anymore."

I didn't correct him, even though my pride desired to. Let him think I still lived at home, for I'd spent years wishing and praying that I did and would rather pretend those wishes came true than be reminded of the reality that they hadn't.

When I failed to reply, he glanced down at me again, and even without looking at him, I could practically hear the cogs of his mind working as he analyzed my expression and posture. Damn him and his heightened senses.

Not wanting him to see through me anymore than he already could, I took a deep breath and smiled wide, clapping my hands together. "So, do you wash out of habit, or do you actually sweat here?"

He blinked, and his steps faltered. "What?"

"You said your bodies work about the same as before. I was just curious how much."

The wind whipped at me, shoving long, black tendrils in my face, and I absently batted them away, hoping the color of my cheeks wasn't giving away my discomfort at my own question. "It seems so strange to me that our bodies cease working only to wake up here as if nothing happened. And then to be able to die a second time?" I shook my head.

What kind of afterlife made you suffer through death only to possibly suffer through it again? What was the point? I must have mumbled my musings aloud because a moment later, Terek had a blade in his hand, spinning it through his fingers like a magician twirled a coin. As if even the mention of death brought it whispering from its sheath.

"I'd imagine dying here is the punishment for overstaying our welcome. The Underland isn't meant to be a forever home. It was only meant to be a middle ground for souls to rest before making their last journey."

He cleared his throat, something dark flashing across his eyes before he blinked it away. "Or so the story goes."

"That doesn't quite seem fair." Who was to say how long a soul could stay here? Would the Underland punish me and try to kill me off if I overstayed my welcome as well? I had so many questions, most of which I didn't think even Terek could answer.

"Life isn't fair anywhere, Ace."

Didn't I know it. "If people aren't supposed to stay here forever, why do they?" *Choice doesn't exist here.* Terek's words from last night came back to me. *Those of us who wander here for eternity only do so because of her.*

"I'll tell you why they stay, if you tell me why *you* are."

I shot him a glare from behind my messy curtain of hair and sped up my steps to walk ahead of him, blocking out the sound of his resounding chuckle.

We walked in silence for over an hour, each lost in our own heads, and with every minute that passed, my shoulders loosened until the tension between us lapsed into something almost comfortable.

The land around us was mostly flat, apart from a few gentle hills that rose and fell to the left and what appeared to be farmland far to the right. I almost asked Terek about it but thought better of it, not wanting to ruin the easy silence.

The cloudy barrier over the sky seemed to thicken as we walked, muting the colors around us until it truly felt like walking in an alternate reality. I thought of the lush lawn of Ellington Estate and the deep, wild shades of green of the Upside woods. Even the house I'd shared with

Frederick seemed vibrant compared to the world around me.

I again found myself wondering what he was doing right now, imagining how much of the house he had trashed in his bid to find me. How many more sketches had he burned while drowning himself in drink, thinking of all the ways he'd punish me when I was found?

But I never would be. Frederick could spend his last penny and send every constable, and he'd never find a trace of me. I'd never have to see him again.

A lightness bloomed in my chest, a small flower opening its petals for the first time in years, hesitant it'd get smashed. Energy pulsed through my veins, and I breathed so deeply, I thought I'd lift off the ground.

This was what freedom felt like. I was sore, scratched, hungry, and tired, but I'd chosen this fate. I could do whatever I wanted. Live how I wanted. It was a power I'd never been granted before. Terek claimed choice didn't exist here, but he couldn't have been more wrong.

"You're driving me insane."

I blinked, darting my gaze up to see Terek staring down at me, an annoyed expression painted across his features. Lord, I hadn't said any of that out loud, had I? Maybe he meant that I was breathing too loudly or something.

I swallowed, inhaling slowly through my nose in the hopes of calming my lungs, which were definitely working overtime with how unused to exercise I'd become. "What have I done now?"

"Annoyed me. Tie your hair back before I chop it all off. I'm tired of it slapping me in the arm. No wonder you have no common sense. You wouldn't be able to see it even if it stood in front of you."

I rolled my eyes, making sure to add a little extra flare to my hand when I shoved the next face-full of locks out of my eyes. "Ha. Ha."

Coming to a stop in the middle of the path, Terek reached into his pack only to pull his hand out a second later, a piece of the twine he'd used for his travel fare dangling from his fingers.

"What are you doing?"

"Shut up and be still," he said, coming to stand directly behind me.

The roughened tips of his fingers brushed against my nape, and I bit my tongue, hoping he wouldn't catch the responding gooseflesh that shot down my neck. The last thing I needed was to give him any more ammunition to tease me with.

He froze, his fingers gripping the strands of my hair a little too tightly for several long seconds. And then they were moving, separating chunks and pulling this way and that as he secured my hair behind me, his touch surprisingly gentle around the snares and knots littered throughout it.

After a few minutes, he stepped back, dropping my hair to let it thump against my back. "Better."

My mind emptied of all words as I reached a hand over my shoulder and ran my fingers along the perfectly snug braid that now lay flush against my spine. I ran my eyes down the corded muscles of his arms to land on his fingers. Never in a million years had I expected Terek to know how to braid. I barely knew how to braid my own hair. Who the hell *was* this man?

"How do you know how to do that?"

Terek shrugged, looking completely unbothered as he turned and started walking again. "I know how to do a lot of things, Ace."

That, I believed. "It must be nice to have the time to learn all that," I said absently, tipping my head up to stare at the sky. Was it just me, or did it look even grayer than it had when we'd left?

Terek turned so abruptly, I smacked into him, bouncing my forehead off an extremely hard and unforgiving chest. I straightened my arms to free my face, feeling his muscles tense beneath my hands as I looked up.

But that was a mistake.

His dark eyes glittered beneath lowered brows, pulling me in until I thought I'd get lost in their depths. I had no idea eyes could display such emotion, especially ones so good at appearing devoid of it.

"Eternity is as much a plague as it is a privilege, Ace. Being trapped in the same place, decade after decade is not something to be fucking admired, no matter how convenient you seem to believe it is. We are not meant to exist forever."

I licked my lips, my mouth feeling suddenly parched even in the cool day's air. I didn't know what to say to that. I hadn't been trying to glorify his fate. Hell, I didn't even understand it. I'd just been trying to compliment him without sounding like a little girl with a crush. "Okay."

His soul-searching gaze dropped to my lips and paused before continuing down to the hands I still had pressed to his abdomen. I quickly dropped them, my face flushing as I retreated too quickly to pretend it was anything but a reaction to the heat of his stare.

Traitor, I thought furiously as I smoothed down the front of my dress, hoping he couldn't hear how my heart raced but knowing he could. My mind may have known Terek wasn't someone I had any desire to be attracted to, but my body clearly hadn't gotten the memo yet.

He sighed, like he'd just lost whatever internal battle he'd been waging in his own head and motioned for me to start walking again. "I didn't learn it here. I've simply always been good with my hands. Hat maker, remember?"

I stumbled after him, my jaw likely appearing similar to Chesie's with how far it hung open as I gaped. Partly at the fact that he'd answered my question, but mostly because I couldn't believe I'd forgotten that tidbit of his past. Then again, his demeanor was so dark and foreboding, it was hard to ever picture him having wanted to work with something as delicate as hats.

A flicker of memory tickled at the back of my mind of a day when I'd felt like breaking under the weight of my parents' expectations and hatred, and Terek had told me a story about his own father. About his desire to work with his hands and his apprenticeship.

He shifted his weight, clearly uncomfortable with my blatant staring, and stuck one hand in his pocket, pointing the other to the sky. "Come on. We're still a ways out, and it looks like rain."

Of course, it rained here. I chuckled, earning myself a raised brow. I just shook my head, imagining the horrified face our local priest would give me if I went back and told him everything I'd learned about the

Underland.

He'd have me locked away for blasphemy before I ever got around to mentioning the weather.

⚸—⚹

WE DIDN'T EVEN make it another hour before the mist began. It was light at first, similar to what I'd imagine walking through a puffy cloud would feel like. But by the two-hour mark, it'd turned into a solid drizzle that refused to abate. The kind that didn't seem all that bad until I'd been walking barefoot in it, on a now-muddy path, for nearly a full day.

I glared at my feet, caked with mud and aching profusely, and rubbed vigorously at my arms, trying in vain to keep my shivers at bay. Terek had frowned at me several times already, and although he hadn't said a word, I could hear every consonant and vowel of his displeasure in his silence.

I still didn't regret my decision to come here, perpetual cold weather and all, but there was a good chance I'd punch him in the nose if he complained about my chattering teeth again. There was an even bigger chance I'd burst into angry tears if there wasn't some form of a warm bath when we arrived in Tover.

Squinting through the fog for any beginning sign of civilization, I stared bleakly ahead at the flat, empty horizon. *This is better than what you would've been doing.* I just needed to repeat that to myself a few hundred times until we arrived.

"It looks like it's about to get worse."

Of course, it was. Even the familiar rumble of his voice couldn't dull the misery I felt at that sentence. "How much longer?"

"We should see the beginning of Tover within the hour."

I groaned, unable to keep it in. If my bruised, cut-up feet didn't give out before then, my rain-saturated dress would drag me to the ground all on its own. I pulled the sodden, clinging fabric away from my body and scowled, wishing I could remove my watch and rip the entire thing off me. I swore I'd walk the entire rest of the way naked if

I could.

Go figure, the first time I'd ever been stranded in bad weather was also the first time I'd ever left the shelter of the Wood. Seriously, wherever we were, there wasn't a tree or rock formation in sight. The contrariety wasn't lost on me.

Terek made a strangled sound, and my head shot up in worry only to find his eyes pinned to my chest, my nipples visible through the wet garment since I wore no brassiere as a second barrier. But when I blinked, his eyes were still on the road ahead of us, his expression as flat as ever.

Great, now I was seeing things.

Dropping my dress, I crossed my arms over my chest and rolled my neck to stretch out the stiff tendons. "Tell me something to distract me."

He turned, an annoyed expression on his face. "Like what?"

"Anything that will make the next hour go by faster. Tell me something no one knows."

"No."

I threw my hands up, an exasperated sigh leaving me. "Okay, tell me something very few people know, then. What do you do when you're not throwing knives at children or staring at trees and being broody?"

Terek came to a stop, eyes narrowed. I could see the word 'no' hovering on his lips again, but he pressed them tightly together, regarding me. Without even uttering a word, I could already tell he was weighing his odds, debating if indulging me was worth it and what he'd get out of the game.

It didn't surprise me. I'd yet to meet a man who didn't view every interaction with a woman as transactional.

"All right. I'll humor you, *if*...you tell me why you came here."

The rain fell harder, fat droplets falling with tiny thumps on our heads, creating even more rivulets down our faces. My heart ached to spill itself to him. To sit down and tell him everything the way I once had. To have that comfortable trust of a quiet ear and know he'd give me harsh advice, but true advice all the same.

For a moment, I was that little girl again, ready to open my mouth and spill all the stories of my life. But I didn't, as much as my soul begged me to share the burden with someone. Anyone. Terek had lost the right to my secrets when he'd turned his back on me like all the others.

He might've listened once upon a time, but he'd also forced me to go home time after time, even when he would find me crying in the dirt. He'd pushed me away when I'd offered him my heart and destroyed the courage and support I'd so desperately needed to save myself.

No, Terek no longer possessed my trust in that way, and I also didn't really believe he cared. He just didn't like being in the dark on anything and likely only wanted to know so that he could work to change my mind. Sadly for him, he hadn't worded his request well, and nothing said I had to tell him the entire reason. Just enough to appease him.

"Fine," I said, holding my hand out. "A secret for a secret. You first."

He hesitated, and my shoulders drooped, assuming he'd already changed his mind. But to my surprise, he slowly began walking again and spoke so low, I had to lean closer to hear him.

"I was thirty-three when I fell into a river."

I stumbled over a hole, my ankle twisting sharply, but I bit the insides of my cheeks and kept pace, too terrified he'd stop talking if I made a sound. He tipped his head, eyes faraway.

"It was a foolish death, one that happened quickly but felt like a lifetime to me. I'd been walking over a short, wooden bridge in our town, distracted by an ugly fight I'd had with my father that morning. I didn't hear the man behind me yelling to get out of the way. Not until it was too late, of course."

He rubbed at the back of his neck, jaw spasming, and I knew I should tell him he could stop, but I selfishly wanted to hear the rest. Desperate and eager for any door into this man he would open for me.

"Something had spooked his horse, and when I turned to see what the fuss was about, the beast was already on me, knocking me off the bridge and into the river. I drowned before anyone could pull me out."

He shrugged, casting me a quick look as if to say, *and that was that.*

"You couldn't swim to the side?" Maybe he'd hit his head on a rock, or his clothing had gotten caught on something below the surface.

He raised a single brow. "I came from money, Ace. What use did I have to learn a skill such as swimming?" He barked a harsh laugh devoid of any humor. "Fate always did like irony."

I hadn't thought of that, but now that he'd said it, I felt silly for having asked, because the same was true even for society now. The only reason I'd learned how to swim was because Vincent's had used it as a way for us to exercise without leaving the grounds.

Even so, that was it? Drowning?

"What?"

"I don't know," I said, pointlessly rubbing my hand over my wet forehead. "I guess I just imagined you'd died doing something like fighting a group of brigands or something."

"Sorry to disappoint."

I flushed, realizing how rude that'd sounded. I hadn't meant it that way, but my apology slipped from my grasp when I caught the barest hint of a smirk on his face. One which fell as soon as I returned it.

"And what happened then? When you got here?"

He didn't answer at first, his keen gaze tracking our surroundings like he wanted to be absolutely sure no one else could hear. "When I realized I was dead, I was angry. Furious, to be exact. I'd had so much left to live for, and I felt robbed. But I'd hoped I could make the same life for myself here."

He shook his head, water coursing down his face and plastering his hair to his forehead. "I'd been wrong, of course. Blinded by a future of what-ifs and lost opportunities."

Thunder rumbled distantly, the rain now a solid blanket that turned our clothes into a second skin and littered the path with small puddles. Something about being drenched to the bone made Terek look softer, or maybe it was what he'd just admitted to me that took away the harsh lines of his face.

He grimaced and brushed at his trousers, which clung to him in a way that accentuated each defined muscle of his lower half. Not that I'd been staring at the backside of his trousers while he walked or anything.

"Your turn, Ace."

I blinked up at him, suddenly aware that we'd both stopped walking. We stood so close, I could feel the heat from his body seeping into my own, teasing me with images of last night. I blocked it out, shoving at each glimpse with both hands until all I could see were the pair of midnight eyes staring down at me.

"I'm here because I can't breathe anywhere else," I admitted, voice a mere whisper against the current of rain. "I come back because every time I step foot here, it feels like stretching my wings after being trapped in a cage. It feels like coming home."

Terek's eyes scanned my face, from my brows down to my lips, before coming back up. Like he was trying to decipher the honesty of my words by taking in every inch of my expression.

His head cocked to the side ever so slightly, and for a moment, I thought he was going to close the gap between our faces. I froze, my heart beating so hard, I feared it'd leap from my chest. I didn't know what he wanted. I didn't know what *I* wanted.

But before I could match his movement, or push away on my own, Terek looked over my head and straightened, simultaneously throwing up his walls. Whatever emotion had been swimming in his eyes disappeared faster than I could blink, and I wondered if I had seen it at all.

"Game's over," he said, brushing past me and walking away so fast, I nearly tipped forward onto my face.

I sighed. Every time I thought I had him figured out, he showed me just how wrong I was. Because whatever he'd been thinking or about to do a second ago, it apparently hadn't been even remotely what I'd thought.

Rubbing my hand over my face and mentally berating myself for letting my body overrule my brain again, I wrangled my sodden skirt and trudged after him. "Fine. What now?"

His body tensed, and he kept his back to me as he pointed toward the dark streak highlighting the horizon. "That's Tover, but we're never going to make it before you fall ill and die if we keep stopping. Can't have you dying your second night home."

Even though he'd meant it as a dig to make fun of me for what I'd admitted, I couldn't keep the responding smile from tugging at my lips anyway.

Home.

ADELAIS

CHAPTER THIRTY

Whatever I might have expected out of a town full of dead people, Tover wasn't it. The logical side of my brain hadn't exactly expected it to be a bunch of gravestones lined up or people sleeping in caskets, but my imagination couldn't claim the same.

We passed the first houses, neat wooden constructions with small patches of well-maintained yards, while the rain continued to wage a full-out war over our heads. I ran both hands over my face, wiping as much water away as possible and looked on with awe, my eyes unable to take in every sight as fast as I'd like. Because even with the gray sheet obscuring the details, it was amazing.

The road turned to cobblestone, and we walked along it as the homes grew closer and taller, eventually merging into a long line of row houses bordering the street on either side, painted in more vibrant shades than I'd ever seen in my life.

Movement caught my attention, and I looked up in time to see an older woman leaning out of an upper window, holding a bucket. A surprised gasp flew from my lips as Terek yanked me out of the way, just as what I dearly hoped was water cascaded over the street beside us.

He released me not a second later, leaving me teetering to catch my balance while he wiped his palm over his soaked tunic like I was covered in excrement.

He bared his teeth, muttering a string of curses up at the woman, but she just responded with a wave of her hand and an uncaring, "Shove off, you're already wet," before slamming her shutters closed.

I couldn't help but chuckle at how completely unfazed she'd been at the terrifying man glaring up at her. "I think I love it here already."

Terek dropped that hard gaze on me next, his hair so plastered to his face it looked like it was close to merging with his skin. "Say that again when you get robbed in an alleyway."

I crossed my arms and watched him walk ahead, irritated that he was determined to ruin my excitement. Apparently, I was going to have to carry a sense of humor for the both of us because he was thoroughly lacking in that department.

We traveled deeper into the town, walking past more shops and buildings than I'd ever known could exist all in one place. Markets, inns, taverns, dressmakers, shoemakers, and even a smithy.

The Underlanders—or was it Toverians?—who braved the weather, scuttled from shop to shop, hooded cloaks pulled far over their faces as they pushed carts and carried boxes, going about their business like it was any other day for them. Like they had no idea how much freedom they had in their death.

Guilt immediately swarmed me at the thought, snuffing it out like a candle. Who knew what any of these people had gone through to get here or even how long they'd been here. For all I knew, every person in Tover could've been brutally murdered.

I straightened my spine, determined to stop throwing myself a pity party. If growing up with my mother had taught me anything, it's that pity and misery only gave one a permanent pout and extra wrinkles.

As we passed a modiste, I slowed to a stop, watching a young woman with fair skin, a plain brown dress, and white-blonde hair cropped close to her scalp slouch down in a chair, legs propped up in the most unladylike way I'd ever seen.

She gave a radiant smile and a thumbs up to someone I couldn't see across the room, but who I assumed was likely in the process of getting pinned for a dress. I shuddered, remembering how much I hated getting fitted. The man who'd serviced my family had never failed to prick my skin no matter how still I'd stood.

The woman sighed and rolled her head against the back of the chair to look out the window, inadvertently meeting my stare. My face flushed red at getting caught, and I tensed, expecting her to sneer like the girls Upside would've done. Instead, she only took in my haggard appearance and flashed me a sympathetic smile, holding a hand up to give a vulgar gesture to the sky, which had blessedly started to subside.

I smiled back and took a step toward the door, wanting to go in and ask her about Tover. Maybe have a conversation and get detailed answers from someone who wouldn't ignore or insult me every five seconds.

But a hand around my elbow stopped me, pulling me back to the road and ushering me forward. "Now isn't the time to go shopping, Ace. I understand your hurry to find dry clothes, but there will be some where we're headed. Hopefully."

"And where is that again?" I asked, only half-listening as I twisted around to watch a few citizens bicker in front of what smelled like a bakery. God, I was hungry.

"Are you listening to me?"

"What?"

A finger jabbing into the side of my face had my head snapping forward again just before I would've walked straight into a potted plant. I side-stepped it, grimacing when the motion had my chafed thighs bumping together. "Sorry, what were you saying?"

Terek frowned down at me, dropping his hand. "Why do you seem more fascinated by selfish people arguing in the rain than you did by a Creature threatening to rip out your throat?"

I ducked my head, feeling my cheeks heat. After a lifetime of being ridiculed for everything I did, there were few things that still got to me, but appearing naïve in front of Terek, who probably had enough life experiences for ten people, was one of them. It was hard to claim independence and strength when you knew so little about the world.

Any world.

"I've never seen one before," I admitted.

He led us around a corner, tipping his head back to the bickering people who were now out of sight. "What? People bartering?"

"A town."

"You've never walked through a town? You're what? Twenty-two, now? Twenty-three?"

I narrowed my eyes. "Twenty-seven, and no, I haven't."

He lurched to a stop, whipping around to look at me. "Are you seriously trying to tell me you've never stepped foot in any town in twenty-seven years?"

I shrugged, chewing the inside of my lip. There was no honest answer I could give that wouldn't humiliate me. What would I say? That I'd always been locked up somewhere? That I'd gone from the prison of my home to Vincent's, then to Frederick? That I'd seen my fair share of walls, but they'd all had the same locks?

Thanks, but no thanks. The thought of Terek looking at me with pity, or worse, believing I'd deserved any of it, was far worse than him simply believing me to be inexperienced by choice.

I tipped my head to the sky, giving it a silent thank you that it finally seemed to be slowing its incessant downpour. "I didn't get out much. Spoiled, rich girl and all."

He continued to stare at me, his eyes roving over my face, like he heard every word that had flittered across my mind and could tell I was full of shit. And I suddenly wished he'd left my hair down so I could hide behind the dark layers.

"Okay, so I got out a little bit. I just didn't wander off our property," I said, wording my answer carefully. He may sense I was leaving something out, but he didn't know what. All I needed to do was slip into a new conversation until he inevitably got sick of me talking. Luckily for me, that wasn't exactly difficult to do.

"I liked the woods behind my parents' estate, though." As if the word 'like' could ever describe the comfort and peace those trees had given me. The touchless hug each step within them had been. I cleared my throat. "Then again, I'm sure you already knew that."

Whether my rambling had worked to distract him, or he'd decided he didn't care enough to press, Terek released me from his damn-near hypnotic stare and turned on his heel. "All right. I'll bite. What had you been expecting to find here?"

He asked it just as we stepped past a man who appeared to be relieving himself in an alleyway. I swallowed back a gag and jogged after Terek, wincing with each step. "I don't know. Chaos, I guess. Everything here is colorful and busy, but it also just seems so *normal*, like what I imagine the towns Upside are like."

"Normal isn't always what you think it is, little rabbit. Normal for you is misery to someone else."

That was true. "I just..." I gestured to a couple running hand-in-hand, laughing as they held a cloak over their heads. "The shops, the people, even the look of this place. I feel like if I died in my sleep and appeared here, I wouldn't even know I was dead. I'd just be somewhere...different."

We came to a square bordered on every side with more shops and buildings. A raised, wooden stage stood to the far left, with only a large, iron chair sitting in the center and a single wooden beam a few feet away. I squinted, thinking I saw ropes dangling from different spots of the wood. Weird.

I couldn't imagine what kind of performance required such things and was about to ask Terek about it when a pack of children sprinted past us, hoods pushed back to reveal tangled wet hair of different shades.

I jumped back when they began screaming and laughing, having some kind of race to the edge of the stage and back, their voices bright and happy. They were so *young*. "Are all these children dead or..." I paused, rolling in my lips as I tried to figure out the most appropriate way to word my question. The last thing I wanted to talk to Terek about was sex, but I was incredibly curious.

"If you're asking if any were born here, the answer is no. Death sees no age. Children arrive the same way as everyone else." He slashed a judgmental gaze my way. "Minus you."

I ignored his dig, my breath catching as I continued to watch them play. "Children aren't born, at all?"

"The dead cannot create life, Ace. No matter how our hearts pretend to beat, everyone here is but a walking corpse. We could fuck until our bodies disintegrated into dust, and still nothing would come from it."

I flushed crimson, which, by the twitch of his lips, was his intention. I knew he hadn't meant me and him specifically, but the way he'd worded it had my insides clenching all the same. I desperately brushed it off, trying to focus on the point of his answer.

People of all ages died every day, but until meeting Chesie, it'd never dawned on me that children awoke in the Underland without parents. The thought was incredibly depressing, especially since Terek's unchanged appearance over the years meant they'd never grow up.

"Who looks after them?" I asked, assuming there had to be some version of an orphanage here or something.

He spared me a quick glance, directing us to continue through the square. "Family and blood can exist without the other. People fall in love here just like anywhere else, and when they do, they often form temporary families, giving younger ones what they need in order to pass on."

"Temporary?"

"Children don't fear the afterlife the same way adults do. As long as nothing hinders their ability, they tend to move on quickly once they feel safe. Much like animals."

I choked out a laugh. "Did you just compare children to animals?" I'd noticed he'd, yet again, let slip that something was preventing people from moving on, but though the urge to ask was on the tip of my tongue, I refrained. If he wouldn't tell me in the privacy of our camp, he definitely wouldn't out in the open like this.

And now that he'd mentioned animals, I realized I'd yet to see a single one since leaving the Wood. There'd been plenty of cultivated farmland, but no cattle, and no stray cats or dogs within Tover that I'd spotted.

"Although I'm sure they share many other qualities, I was referring to the fact that animals do not fear death either. They move on even quicker, having no mental turmoil or religious trauma to reconcile with first."

I hummed, contemplating that. The only non-Creatures I'd had contact with here were Cotton and the random school cat. Neither time had I stuck around long enough to see what became of them. For all I knew, they'd disappeared from the Underland the second they'd run out of sight.

"That sounds dreadfully inconvenient when you want a deer to dry out for dinner."

I'd meant it as a joke, the image of Terek leaping on a deer, only to plummet to the ground when it disappeared beneath him, making me snort. But he didn't seem to notice, his attention fixed on something ahead of us.

"Hundreds of thousands of animals die every day. If you're a good hunter, you eat well. If you're a bad one, you buy from the good ones. And luckily for us, one of the good ones just happens to be right over there."

He pointed at a large, stone building on the far corner of the square with thickly filled flower boxes beneath each window and a prominent sign above the door that read, *Tweeds.*

"That's where we're going."

My heart soared clear out of my chest. After an entire day of destroying my feet and feeling my belly consume itself, our destination was only a span of steps away. Food, water, dry clothes, shoes. God, did I want a comfortable pair of shoes.

My face split into a grin. I shot forward, fully prepared to run there if it meant sitting down for a real meal, but all I succeeded at was slamming into the muscular arm stretched out in front of me.

Following the obnoxiously attractive limb back to the man attached to it, I frowned. Surely, we were headed there now. I mean…he'd said *we,* right? Because if he was about to ask me to wait outside, I was going to find the first hard object I could and smack him with it. Okay, I wasn't brave enough to do that, but I'd most definitely imagine it while I glared at the back of his head.

Unaware of the violence swirling in my mind, Terek's usual flat expression didn't waver, but as he stepped closer—far too close—I could've sworn a flicker of what looked almost like fear shot across his eyes, dampening my ire.

Darting a quick look around us, he leaned down until his lips hovered just above my ear. "I know ignoring me is your favorite pastime, little rabbit, but it's imperative that you listen to me right now. You cannot, under any circumstances, tell anyone that you are—"

"Less dead than they are?" I suggested, hoping beyond hope he hadn't noticed the way his whispered breath spread gooseflesh across my neck and arms.

"Something like that. Tweeds is the safest place here, but that doesn't make it safe. Understand? I do not wish to draw attention to ourselves. Duma will send me to the dark abyss if I start a fight in his establishment."

The last part was said more to himself than me, but his clear warning settled between us. I sensed he was waiting for me to verbally agree before he'd allow us to move, but I was struggling to wrap my head around it.

Why would someone like Terek be so worried about safety? The man could literally hear someone sneeze from a mile away if he wanted. If there was anything that would make me feel like the world couldn't touch me, it'd be that. But between how he'd scouted the area of our camp and how quickly he'd hidden any sign of our fire, Terek was definitely nervous about someone taking an interest in us. Specifically, me.

What I didn't understand, was *why*.

Knowing I wouldn't get anything out of him if I didn't appease his demand, I took a healthy step away and nodded. "Pretend I'm dead. Got it."

Terek's mouth flattened, but he finally lowered his arm, gesturing for me to continue. "Come on, then. I'm starving."

ADELAIS

CHAPTER THIRTY-ONE

When Terek opted to mention that Tweeds was a tavern, right as I was stepping over the threshold, I felt every muscle in my body lock up, anticipating the worst. I'd never stepped into a shop before, let alone a place Mother used to say horrid people went when they tired of their spouses.

But to my shock, it wasn't like that at all. Yes, there were people sitting around tables in varying degrees of soaked, their hoods up and their faces lowered over frothing mugs. And yes, there was a tangy scent in the air that made my nose curl, but I'd smelled far worse on Frederick's breath.

The main floor was a large, square room, the front of which was filled with tables varying in size to fit either two or four chairs, and a crackling hearth that gave the entire area a cozy glow. I rubbed my palms together, wanting to snuggle up in front of it, but my growling stomach quickly rejected the idea.

Sconces lined each wall, and in the far back was a narrow hallway and a long bar with a row of backless seats, positioned in front of a set of wooden, half-doors.

Terek, obviously used to the layout, stalked straight to the bar in the back, ignoring the curious gazes of the few patrons who glanced up. The second their eyes landed on him, they filled with an instantaneous hesitancy that had my hackles rising and my defenses building back up around myself.

It was possible their natural instincts could simply sense the darkness Terek seemed to be imbued with, but I had a feeling it was more than that. They recognized him, and they didn't trust him.

In the far back, standing behind the bar and towering over the well-worn surface, was a man who looked to be in his mid-thirties and was at least double my size. My eyes widened despite myself, and I unabashedly stared, my neck craning back to see the entirety of him. He wore a navy tunic and beige trousers, his dark brown skin shifting over the corded muscles of his arms as he swirled a white rag inside a mug before setting it to the side in a line of clean ones.

Where Terek was beautiful in a sharp, almost inhuman way, this man was the kind of handsome that would've had whispers exploding around a ballroom, fans whipping open to cover blushing faces. He had a strong, wide-set nose, a squared chin with the slightest divot, and a head shaved as smooth and shiny as the water he was now pouring.

"Is this what you call hard work?"

Terek's question pulled me out of my rude staring, and I snapped my jaw closed, glancing up at him. But rather than facing the man he was clearly talking to, he was watching me, his jaw tight and his lips pressed flat like something had just royally pissed him off.

Before I could form a silent, "What?", the man's head lifted from the mug he was drying, and his brows shot up, his brown eyes lighting with surprise when they landed on Terek.

"Look who the Wood dragged in! Why didn't you say you were headed this way? Actually, scratch that. I know better than to believe a recluse like you would willingly travel with anyone." He laughed, a great booming sound that both startled me and drew a smile to my face. I couldn't remember the last time I'd heard someone laugh that freely.

"Oh, I'm not opposed to travel companions, just as long as they're not you, Duma," Terek said.

I tensed, about to demand why the hell he was insulting the one person who could give us what we needed, but his lips were quirked up in the corner, softening his words. I looked back and forth between them, realizing they were…friends? Leave it to Terek not to mention that part.

The man—Duma—smiled wide, flashing two rows of straight teeth. "So I see," he said, flicking those soft, brown eyes on me before turning them back to Terek and grabbing a new mug. "You here on…business?"

"Not this time," Terek said, shifting to sit on a stool and gesturing for me to do the same. What business was he talking about? Why would guarding the Wood bring him all the way to Tover? I couldn't imagine a Creature would make it past him this far.

"Good. Otherwise, I might've had to take you out back for a calm, friendly discussion," Duma said, pouring a pale, yellow liquid into the mug and sliding it toward me with a wink. "First drink is always on the house for new faces."

How did he already know I was new here? I mean, I knew I'd gaped a little when we'd walked in, but damn, I didn't think I stood out *that* much compared to everyone else. Everyone in here looked like wet, stray dogs wandering in for scraps.

Duma must've seen the hesitation in my posture because he reached across the bar to inch the foaming mug a little closer. "I may be old, but I'd have remembered a face like yours."

I gave him a small smile and relaxed, wrapping my fingers around the handle when he eased back. I had no idea what he'd poured me, but honestly, I was too thirsty to care. Whatever weird, dead fruit he'd squeezed for it was fine by me, just as long as it wasn't dried leaves that'd been left to wilt in water long enough to be called tea.

Suddenly worried that's exactly what it was and not wanting to be rude when I'd have to plug my nose to drink it, I raised it and took a small sniff. The sticky tang of it hit me like a slap to the face, singeing my nose hairs and nearly making me gag. Frederick's angry, reddened face embedded itself behind my eyes, and I squeezed them closed, heaving in a sharp breath.

"Now look what you did, Duma. Offering the poor thing that bottom barrel shit," a deep voice said from over my head, "when she's clearly been through something. Have you no decorum?"

My eyes flung open, and I twisted around to find Terek staring at me with far-too-seeing eyes and Duma standing directly behind me. Wait.

Second-guessing my sanity, I turned back around to see…Duma still standing behind the bar, glancing at the cut on my forehead before arching a thick black brow at the man behind me. "You don't call it shit when you're sneaking down here to steal some of it away to your room."

The man behind me, who was apparently *not* Duma, threw a hand over his chest and gasped in offense as he walked to the far side of the bar and rounded it. "I do not. Well, not the ale, at least."

He snagged the mug from in front of me, sloshing ale over the sides as he shoved it in front of Terek, who hadn't spared a single glance to the identical newcomer. "Your companion's taste in drink is about as poor as his taste in clothing, so he can have that. I'll get you some wine made from the grapes in Abgrove that is far better."

I looked between them, trying not to blatantly stare. I'd known that twins existed and had read about twin sisters once in a storybook, but I'd never actually seen two people in real life who looked exactly the same. And I wasn't sure what it said about me that I found identical humans more magical than Terek's ability to hear my heart beating.

"You have wine here?" I asked before I could think better of it. In my peripheral, Terek shot me a warning look, his hand instantly sliding up his thigh to rest closer to his sheath. Oops.

But Duma thankfully misunderstood my question. "Well, we're certainly not going to serve river water to our customers. Though, to be fair, my brother's right. The ale tastes about the same. I'm Duma, by the way. That's Dex."

"You can tell us apart by how attractive we are. He's got the bigger ears," Dex added, chuckling when Duma's wide palm smacked him in the back of his matching bald head.

I smiled, the tension from the smell of the ale already dissipating at their honest expressions and friendly demeanor. "I'm Adel—"

"This is Ace," Terek said over me, his eyes pinning me to my stool with a silent warning. "She arrived just yesterday, and I happened to stumble upon her."

I wasn't sure what about Terek's sentence caught their attention, but the brothers stared at him for a solid three seconds before their eyes dragged over to me.

"And yet you brought her here, instead of Ardenglass." Although voiced as a statement, there was a clear question in Duma's eyes. One Terek could apparently read because he shrugged and sat back, tapping his fingertips along the mug.

"She got dropped in the Wood and survived a run-in with a Creature. It caught my attention. Besides, I was headed this way, anyway."

He took a drink, and although I knew his story was a quickly concocted lie to hide my non-dead status, his disinterested tone when he referred to me didn't sting any less. The man wouldn't know tact if it sat on his face.

Duma twisted back to me, looking me up and down again, as if to check for a missing limb he might've overlooked before. "Dropped in the Wood?" He ran a hand over his jaw. "I've never heard of an arrival appearing within the Wood before."

"Not that survive long enough to tell us about it, at least," Dex added. "Does she have an ability—"

"No."

The brothers silently studied me, and I squirmed under their gazes, feeling like I was sitting naked before them. Why were they looking at me like Terek just announced to the world I was alive?

"Well," Dex finally said, shaking himself out of it and elbowing Duma to draw his attention away from me. "Although I'm sure there's a story to tell here, I promised the lady a fine wine, so if you'll excuse me…"

"Actually," I said, raising my hand, only to flush and tuck it back in my lap when all three pairs of eyes came to rest on me. "Could I just get some water, please?"

Terek's insistence that their bodies worked the same here led me to believe that also meant they could get drunk, and no matter how nice they seemed, lowering my defenses around drunk strangers was a definite no for me.

"With all due respect, Ace dear, considering the state of your feet I saw when I walked up, I can only imagine the rest of you. Not that I'm picturing you naked or anything," Dex quickly added, hands raised in Terek's direction. "But you'll fall asleep far faster with a warm, liquid hug."

When he put it that way, the thought was tempting—incredibly so—but there was no way I'd be able to down any form of alcohol without thinking of Frederick and vomiting. "I really appreciate it, but I don't drink alcohol at all. Water is fine."

He shrugged, offering me a smile in direct opposition to the all-too-seeing glower of the overly tense man sitting on the stool beside me.

"I'll get her taken care of," Duma said, grabbing another mug and nodding at his brother. "I need you to go have a chat with those nice lads over at table six who appear to be walking out without payment."

Dex whipped his head around and smiled wide, stretching his arms out straight and cracking his knuckles. "My favorite."

ADELAIS

CHAPTER THIRTY-TWO

Two full mugs of water and a plate of cheese and apples later, I was beginning to feel a little more alive, as ironic of a notion as it was. My contracting stomach could still use a little more food, and I was in definite need of some clean clothes and a long night of uninterrupted rest, but by morning, I was confident I'd be ready to take any necessary steps needed to begin my new life.

Step one being to find work and start earning whatever currency they used here so I didn't go hungry or freeze out on the streets. I'd never worked outside the home before, and I wasn't sure what skills I possessed that might actually be helpful, but I'd figure out something. Even scrubbing chamber pots would be better than a lifetime with Frederick.

I leaned back and sighed, smiling to myself and only half-listening to Duma and Terek discuss something about the correlation between the lack of resources and crime in Gissan.

Dex caught my eye and walked over from a customer he'd just finished handing a drink to, his soft expression at odds with the way he'd stalked across the room earlier and successfully put three men in a headlock all at once.

"So, you and Duma own this place?" I asked once he'd come close enough to hear me over the noise of the quickly filling tavern.

"Own it. Renovated it. Work it."

"All by yourselves?" It wasn't the stealthiest way of asking if they ever hired anyone to help them serve drinks and clean, but I was desperate and had no idea where else to go that wouldn't take advantage of me or turn me away.

From what I could tell, Terek trusted literally no one, but he at least trusted these men not to mistreat me, so I felt assured this was the best place to start.

Granted, the thought of smelling ale every day had my stomach turning, but I'd rather suffer through that than starve. Because unlike the people surrounding me, starving would most definitely kill me. Probably.

"We have a small staff that should actually be in shortly to assist with the busy hours, but yeah, it's mostly just us. Day in and day out, for all eternity."

"Bless her royal fucking Majesty," Duma tossed out, turning from his conversation with Terek to grab a few coins from another customer before waving him off and walking closer.

"The queen? As in, the Crimson Queen?"

"The one and only," Dex said. "Though I'm surprised Terek told you—"

"Whenever you two are done flirting and wasting our time, I'd like to wrap this night up," Terek snapped, knuckles whitening around the handle of his empty mug.

Dex's smile fell, and he crossed his arms, the muscles in his chest flexing beneath his tunic. "Years certainly haven't changed you at all." He slanted a look at his brother. "When you said you'd run into him outside of Ardenglass, you failed to mention he was still a fucking dick. Excuse my language, Ace."

Although my muscles still stiffened at the fear of being kicked out due to Terek's ungratefulness and general unappealing personality, I was beginning to understand this was just how they spoke to one another. Insulting but in a…friendly way? It was incredibly confusing, and I still couldn't quite decide if they were actually friends or not.

Sure enough, Duma just rolled his eyes and leaned over, resting his thick forearms across the bar. "I'd already figured you were here to rest and not for our company, so no need to get your trousers in a twist. I assume by the grumbling I can hear from poor Ace's belly that you'll also be wanting a full meal brought up to you. We're sold out of Dex's bread, but we got meat pies and boiled vegetables available."

I sucked in my cheeks to curb the saliva that immediately gathered at the mention of food. "That sounds amazing, thank you."

But as Duma leaned over to drop the coins the customer had given him into a box he quickly relocked with a key, I was reminded that I had no way to pay. A free apple and some cheese was one thing, but a full meal was another.

I knew Terek had money from when I'd gone through his pack, but my pride had no desire to be indebted to him for anything. "I can't. I mean, I don't have any money yet. But I'm willing to work—"

"Meals, clothes, and board," Terek said, cutting off my offer. His eyes dipped down to my feet, which I'd kept tucked beneath my stool and hidden from the second Dex had mentioned them. "And a pair of outdoor shoes."

Dex snorted. "What the fuck are outdoor shoes? Like, boots?"

I blinked at Terek, who was no longer looking at me, unsure if he was sharing an inside joke only I would understand, or if he was trying to make fun of me again. His stoic expression made it impossible to tell.

"I'm not picky," I told them. "Just nothing with heels, preferably. Please."

"You'll find fashion such as that is only found at the White Castle, my dear. Boots, stockings, and a dress, we can do," Dex said. "Will you be needing a cloak?"

I opened my mouth to say 'no', since I already had no idea how I was going to pay for any of this, but Terek nodded and held up his pointer and middle fingers. "And two rooms."

Duma raised a brow, a challenge in his eyes. "Not sure we have two. We seem to be busy tonight." He glanced around the tavern, raising his hand to a teenage boy running past us with an apron tied around his waist.

Terek smiled, but it was more a flash of teeth than anything. "If memory serves me, you owe me several favors, *friend*. I'm sure you can scrounge up a vacancy."

"I don't owe you that many favors. I can get you food, clothes, and two rooms, but you'll be paying full price for the lot of it, same as everyone else."

Terek's nostrils flared, but he reached into his pack and tossed a fistful of coin onto the bar. "Fine."

"Perfect," Duma said, clapping his hands together and scooping the coin into a pile before dropping it into the same lockbox as before. "Follow me, then."

Terek stood, tucking his pack back at his waist. I twisted, preparing to scoot off and follow them, but Duma shook his head, gesturing for me to stay put. "You rest. You look seconds from tumbling onto the floor as it is. I'm sure Terek can figure out what you need."

Terek's body tensed, and we shared a long look, his jaw clenching as he considered whether he wanted to let me out of his sight. I bristled. What the hell did he think I was going to do? Run away *before* he'd gotten me clean clothes and food? I may not have wanted to be indebted to him, but I wasn't as stupid as he liked to claim.

"I'll be fine, Terek. I'm not going to move. I promise."

"It's not you I'm worried about," he growled, eyeing the man who stood across from me, arms spread and hands resting on the bar.

Dex's hands gripped the edge, seeming genuinely insulted that Terek didn't trust him alone with me. "I may have the smile of a gentleman, but in case you forgot, she's not exactly my type. No offense, Ace. I'm sure your body is lovely," he added, winking at me. "And I'm also more than capable of making sure no one takes a step over here in the three minutes you'll be gone."

Terek didn't reply. He just gave Dex one last warning look, hands resting on the handles at his waist, before stalking toward Duma, who was leaned against the end of the bar, waiting for him with an amused smirk on his face.

I released a sigh once he'd stepped out of view, my lungs expanding and my body seeming to relax with the weight of his attention no longer on me. Dex chuckled, reaching out to tug on a chunk of hair that'd come loose from my braid.

"Possessive, isn't he?"

I snorted. Terek? Possessive of me? I could agree with Dex that he had a breathtaking smile, but reading people wasn't something he should be adding to his list of talents anytime soon.

I rested my elbows on the bar, plopping my chin in my palms and yawning. "You mispronounced pigheaded."

Dex choked, spitting ale back into the mug he'd started chugging the second his brother left the main room. I laughed, my eyes and limbs heavy, but my heart so beautifully, blissfully goddamn free.

He joined me, smiling and pulling his apron up to wipe at his chin. "All right, so tell me about yourself, Ace. I know you just arrived and had a rough start in the Wood, which I still can't believe, but what exactly are your plans? Are you staying in Tover, or just passing through?"

That had me sitting back up, blinking back the fog of sleep that had begun to creep in. I glanced to the hallway Terek and Duma had disappeared to, wondering if he was listening to us right now, ready to come whack me upside the head if I answered wrong.

"I'm staying in Tover. For now, at least. But I'm not really sure what to do yet. I'm still very new to...everything," I admitted, widening my hands in front of me.

He nodded, his eyes far away as if he was thinking about how he'd come to be in Tover. How he'd died. I wondered how long he'd had to live here, waiting for his brother to join him, or if maybe it'd been the other way around, or if they'd died together.

With how inseparable they seemed, I couldn't imagine what being separated by death must've been like. Not when I had no experience of that kind of love, myself.

He leaned forward, but his eyes moved about the room, keeping an eye on things. "The Underland can be a shock for sure, especially with the shit they spout Upside about their version of the afterlife, but you'll find it's not so different than what you were used to. What all has Terek told you?"

I huffed a laugh. The list of things that man *hadn't* told me was far longer than the list of things he had. "Not much. Terek claimed the Underland is a middle ground where souls wait to move on, but he acts more like it's hell. He made it seem as though everyone is miserable here."

Dex shook his head, his eyes soft and understanding as he met mine again. "Terek's not the only one to feel that way, but he is of the minority. Even those who want to move on aren't miserable. Look at Duma and me," he said, stretching his arms out to gesture at Tweeds. "Sure, we'd like control over our souls so we can make our own choices, but we have a life here. A good one."

There it was again, a reference to lack of choices and their souls. I pushed forward, lowering my voice and speaking quickly, hoping I could finally get some real answers about whatever was going on here. "What do you mean by control?"

"Let's go."

I lurched back at the clipped tone, not realizing just how close Dex's and my head had been until I met Terek's harsh gaze beside me, his arms ladened with a stack of folded clothes.

I raised my brows, silently asking him what the hell he was glaring at. If he was so worried about me spilling my guts and telling Dex about my ability, maybe he shouldn't have brought me here in the first place.

"Aren't we going to eat?" I asked, aware of how hypocritical my question was, given I hadn't wanted him to spend money on me. But I was hungry, and he was irritating me.

"They'll bring it up in a little bit after we've had a chance to clean up. Unless you don't want to use the bath that's currently being prepared for you?"

He hadn't even finished his sentence before my ass was off the stool, motioning for him to lead the way. Instead, he tossed half the stack of clothes at me, not looking the least bit remorseful when I had to jolt forward to catch them before they landed on the ground.

"Follow me."

Duma and Dex chuckled beside us, both bald heads shining in the orange glow of the room as they bent their heads down to keep from making eye contact with me. Assholes, the lot of them.

In my arms was a simple blue and white dress, though short-sleeved to my dismay, a white cotton chemise, a pair of stockings, and a thick wool cloak. As I re-stacked everything and counted to ten to keep myself from cursing Terek's entire family line, he set a pair of brown boots on top of the pile and held out a key with a large number six on it.

Holding my head high, I snatched it and followed him to the same hallway he'd disappeared down just a few minutes ago to find a single door at the end I assumed was a supply closet. Beside it was the mouth of a steep staircase, which I painfully climbed, my exhausted feet and thighs screaming at me with every step.

We'd just topped the stairs, and I'd begun squinting at the doors to try to make out numbers in the dim corridor lighting when Terek spoke behind me, his body far closer than I'd anticipated.

"That one is yours."

I jumped when his hand appeared beside my head, pointing at the door to my right. I happily darted toward it, needing to put some space between us. My mind was near its breaking point as it was, I didn't need the feel of his chest brushing against me in the dark, making it even harder to concentrate. All I wanted was a hot bath and a soft bed.

I unlocked my door, sparing a look over my shoulder to bid him goodnight, only to freeze when he stood at the door across from mine. My knuckles whitened around the doorknob, and my heart skipped a few beats when he inserted his key and twisted the lock.

Of course, out of two floors filled with rooms, he'd wind up directly across the hall from me. I exhaled heavily, trying to calm my nerves. Terek might be onto something that fate had a cruel sense of humor, but at least he'd be on the other side of two closed doors. There'd be no chance of accidentally waking up with my nose buried into his chest again. It'd be fine.

For a long moment, neither of us said anything. We just stood like silent sentries at our doors, watching one another. Terek's hair was mostly dry now, the thick strands sticking up in every direction and giving him a mussed-up look that softened his face. Or maybe it was the shadow of the corridor that hid the sharp edges that usually feathered and strained along his jawline whenever he was around me.

His eyes swirled, and he worked his jaw, as though deciding whether or not to say something. I gripped my doorknob even tighter and twisted it, unsure if whatever he was about to say would be a kind goodnight or a cruel whip. The truth was, as much as I didn't want him to be cruel, I didn't want him to be kind either.

With the way my heart raced as we each stood at our doors, about to disrobe and bathe our naked skin, mere feet from the other, it was best if he were nothing to me at all.

He opened his mouth, but I beat him to it, cutting him off for once as I muttered a quick, "Goodnight," before shoving into my room.

ADELAIS

CHAPTER THIRTY-THREE

M y room was smaller than the one I'd had at Frederick's, but the stark difference made me love it even more. The bed was narrow, not quite as much as the one I'd had at Vincent's, but enough so that I doubted two bodies would fit unless they snuggled. Which was perfect, considering I didn't plan on waking up with anyone other than myself tomorrow.

On one side of the bed was a square side table, it's top slightly misshapen but smooth, with an already-lit lantern flickering shadows against the wall. On the other side of the room, directly across from the foot of the bed, sat a single table and chair and a wooden dresser with a spare lantern, some kind of leatherbound book, and a stack of folded blankets on its top. And just next to it, tucked into the corner, was a chamber pot, a wash basin with a fresh bar of soap, and a copper tub already filled with water.

Forcing myself not to sprint across the room and leap into the tub fully clothed, I walked across the room to the back wall, throwing open the lone window and resting my hands on the sill to lean out. I smiled, pushing farther up onto my toes to peer down when I realized I had a perfect view of the square.

The best part was, that for the first time in my life, I finally felt completely and utterly alone. Yes, I'd often been left alone at the estate and at Frederick's house, but that sense of alone was different. It'd been an abandoned solitude, not a safe one.

But this? What I had right now? It felt like fucking freedom. Like my lungs had been frozen for years and had only now begun to contract and pull in air.

Finally allowing myself to walk to the tub, I dipped my hand in the water, a flare of disappointment shooting through my cold, brittle bones when it was a few degrees below lukewarm. I'd known a place like this might not have the same access to hot water I'd had at my disposal growing up, but it still sank my heart a little when I'd so hoped to all but boil my skin.

However, the fresh bar of soap gave off a mild scent of vanilla and quickly rose my spirits back up. That, and the knowledge that, hot or not, I'd be able to slip beneath the surface of the water and submerge my senses without a lick of fear that Frederick would come home early and catch me undressed. Hell, the latter didn't just lift my spirits, it made them *soar*.

Even with only Terek's sour mood to keep me company and the incident with Chesie, the past twenty-four, Frederick-free hours had been the most freeing of my life. I'd endure it all again, just to feel the elation I did by that fact. A shudder worked its way through me, reminding me of my sodden clothing. Okay, maybe I would've changed *one* thing.

My face scrunched as I peeled my dress and underclothes from my body, the cool air pebbling my still slightly damp skin. I cringed at the layer of dirt covering me and dropped the clothing, immediately wincing again when my watch slipped from the pocket and thudded to the floor.

Picking it up and gently setting it on the side table with a silent apology, I climbed into the tub, groaning loudly despite the temperature as I submerged my weary body in the water.

For a long while I just sat there, holding the soap but doing nothing with it as I slouched as deep as I could without my nose going under. The only sound was the occasional footsteps of people passing down the hall and faint laughter from downstairs.

When had I last felt so good? The only thing that would've made it better would be if I had my drawing supplies with me. To be able to crawl out of this tub and curl up in bed with a fresh sheet of parchment and a new stick of charcoal. Lord knew I wouldn't be able to get the image of Chesie lunging at me with those inhuman eyes and sharp teeth out of my head until I was able to give life to her likeness.

Maybe I could ask Duma if they had any, or where I could go to buy some. For surely in a place that had alcohol, shoemakers, and smithies, they were bound to have some form of charcoal or painting supplies. Or at least ink and a sketchpad.

If so, I could have everything I wanted here. Everything. I couldn't believe I'd wasted so many years of my life, too scared to make the jump and stay here.

I was never going back, no matter what Terek said or threatened me with. I'd die before I willingly set foot in the Upside again.

Feeling my face pull with the force of my smile, I finally sat up and scrubbed myself with the rough, vanilla-scented soap until there wasn't a single part of me I hadn't rubbed raw.

My fingers were miniature prunes by the time I got out, and I was sure my hair was now more matted than straight, but at least I smelled and felt clean. Though I was going to have to ask about a comb the next time I saw Duma or Dex. I chuckled, the idea of asking bald men for a comb feeling a little absurd.

Hanging my sodden clothes to dry, I picked up the chemise Terek had thrown at me. It wasn't the high-quality material I was accustomed to, and it smelled more like a musty closet than fresh laundry, but it was soft, and most importantly, dry.

I'd just laid it across the bed and was slipping my hands beneath the hem to pull it over my head when a quick, hard rap came against the hallway door. I jolted, the sound loud compared to the silence of my room. But just as I was about to call out to whoever it was to wait, the door flung open.

I shrieked and spun, smashing the thin garment to my torso in a desperate attempt to cover all the important bits that were currently hanging out in the open for anyone to see.

Terek stood in the doorway, holding a tray ladened with a thick mug, a rounded loaf—the meat pie, I assumed—and a bowl of multicolored root vegetables. He wore a fresh set of clothes, and his hair was soaked again, his skin pink from the bath he'd clearly already taken.

I clutched my clothing to my chest, all too aware of the inches of bare skin exposed to him from where the fabric wasn't long enough to hide it. "I…"

His dark eyes traveled down my body before slowly working their way back up, pausing to take in every part of me I couldn't cover. My calves, the sides of my hips, the top curves of my breasts.

And like a puppet attached to his strings, my body responded to that gaze as if it were his fingers gliding over me rather than his unwavering attention. Gooseflesh erupted across my skin and heat speared through me like lightning, pooling between my legs and making me feel like my insides had caught on fire.

I squeezed my thighs together, and Terek's nostrils flared, his body lurching forward before he stopped himself. His throat worked over a swallow as he finally met my wide eyes. "It's been over an hour. I thought you'd already be done."

He cleared his throat, sliding the tray onto the table by the door before tucking his fisted hands into his pockets. "I assumed you'd have washed quickly since I'd told you food would be brought up. Incorrectly, it would seem."

Was he seriously trying to turn this around on me as if I'd done something wrong? The man had literally just barged into my damn bedroom with only a two-second knock as a warning.

"If that's your version of an apology, I don't accept," I snapped, a little irritated, a lot embarrassed, and even more of an emotion I refused to touch with a mile-long rod.

I tightened my fists around my chemise, smashing it to my chest as hard as I could. Why the hell was he still standing there? Was he waiting for me to say thank you? Because if so, he'd be there all night.

His eyes dropped again, almost instinctively, and his mouth

worked on whatever rude reply he'd no doubt provide, but just as he'd finally parted his lips, he suddenly froze. And like the flip of a coin, his eyes leached of all color, deepening to a black so acute, I swore they drew in the very air around us.

He almost seemed to grow, his spine straightening and his shoulders and legs widening as he bared his teeth. "What. *The fuck*. Is that."

It wasn't a question, so much as a demand, and I stumbled over my response, thinking he meant my chemise. That is, until I realized where, exactly, his death glare was latched onto. He was staring at my chest. Specifically, the scar at the center of it.

I yanked the garment up, sacrificing more of my thighs in order to cover my chest up to my collar bone. "Leave," I said, trying to keep my voice as steady as I could while my heart and stomach all seemed to be sitting in the wrong places. "Barging in here and ogling me is pushing it a little far, even for you."

Terek took a single step in, kicking the door shut behind him. "You have no idea how far I'll fucking go. I'll shove you to the goddamn edge of the world and hold you over the abyss until I get what I want. So, I'll ask again. What the fuck is that?"

His fingers wrapped around the lock behind him, and I fought the urge to curl in on myself when he twisted it, instead forcing my shoulders back. I refused to look weak in front of a man anymore, though my trembling spine apparently hadn't gotten the same message.

"It's nothing, Terek."

"Like hell it's not."

"You're right," I said, eyeing his steady approach and taking a small step back. He only lengthened his stride, cutting across the room faster. "What I meant by nothing was that it's none of your business."

He was so close now, I had to crane my neck back to see the entirety of his face, and his eyes were murderous. I slapped a hand to his chest, locking my elbow in a futile attempt to keep him from removing the last foot between us.

His corded muscles tensing beneath my palm was my only warning before his hand shot up and wrapped around my wrist, yanking my arm down and pinning it behind my back. I shot out a curse, wishing I was brave enough to release the chemise and slap him.

As if he could sense my thoughts, Terek's eyes dropped from my furious ones to the hand over my chest. I watched, almost in slow motion, as his free hand came up to cover my fist. His nostrils flared, and a deep rumbling vibrated through him as he pushed the garment down just enough to reveal my deepest humiliation.

Although it was barely more than raised pink lines now, feeling Terek's rough fingers gently trace over it made it burn as raw as it had the day Frederick had done it. Tears sprang to my eyes, and I hissed in a breath, making his fingers still over the small 'FT' burned between my breasts.

"Who did this to you, little rabbit?" His voice was barely more than a whisper, the guttural threads of it making it sound more like a growl than a question.

I debated lying, or not answering at all. But the way his eyes refused to leave it, and the featherlight caress of his breath along my abused skin, had the truth breaking through my teeth like a curse.

"My husband."

Terek's chest stopped moving, the world around us stopping right along with it, as his entire body went dangerously, preternaturally still. Only his eyes moved as they left my chest and shifted to the hand still gripping the chemise over my breasts. My *left* hand.

His chest rattled when he finally sucked in a breath, the hand around my wrist tightening until I swore I could feel the bones grinding together.

"And who, exactly, are you married to?" he asked, his voice now devoid of all emotion, his anger dying out to a lethal calm that had my veins turning to ice.

In all the years I'd known him, I wasn't sure I'd ever seen Terek's nice side, but as his eyes sliced up to mine, pinning me in place more than his grip did, I knew without a doubt that I'd never seen this one. And I wasn't sure if the thrill burning to life in my core was fear or excitement at the sight.

I shifted, trying to twist my wrist from his hold. "You're hurting me, Terek."

His grip immediately loosened, but he didn't release me as he repeated his question.

I sighed, not wanting to think about the horrid man, let alone talk about him. But I'd already admitted the truth, and I likely wasn't going to see Terek again for a long time once he left Tover, so who cared if he found out he'd cuddled a married woman all night? He'd live.

"The school I told you about? The one my parents sent me to. They left me there until I aged out and was no longer allowed to stay. The day I came home, they informed me I'd already been bargained off to its dean and would be leaving with him the next day." I laughed, trying to cover just how much it hurt to admit out loud how much my parents hated me.

"Your hands."

My brow furrowed, and I glanced down at the one hand I could see, still holding the fabric for dear life. Was he asking why I wasn't wearing a ring? "What?"

"The day you arrived with the cat. You'd come from that school, and your hands had been gashed and welted. Was that him?"

He remembered that? A shiver shot through me, both at the way his black eyes were taking me in and at the memory of that day. The soul-deep pain that had consumed me. That girl had thought it was the worst day of her life.

She was a naïve, stupid little thing.

I swallowed, watching his eyes track the movement down the column of my throat. "Everyone was punished there."

In an instant, he'd pulled me flush against him, both our hands pinned between our torsos. "I don't give a fuck about everyone else. Was. It. *Him.*"

The burning in my eyes spiked as I felt his fingertips press into my chest, like he could erase the mark by will alone if he only tried hard enough. I closed my eyes, feeling a single tear drip down my cheek.

"Yes."

"Do you," he sucked in a breath. "Do you have children?"

I shook my head. It was the only blessing life had ever given me. Not because Frederick hadn't tried every month, but because I was almost certain he couldn't. Though that hadn't kept him from blaming my womb for its emptiness over the years.

There was a heavy pause, one so silent, I feared I'd lost all ability to hear until his breath coasted over the shell of my ear. "His name, little rabbit. Give me his name."

Another tear leaked out, traveling along the length of my nose and dripping off the end. We both knew the letters burned into my body were his initials, but saying it out loud, telling someone for the first time since it'd happened, felt like breaking off a piece of my heart and handing it to Terek to stomp on.

"Frederick Turner."

"When?"

He didn't elaborate, but I knew what he was asking, just as he knew my answer before I spoke the broken words into existence. "The last time I saw you. That's why I…" I stopped. *That's why I'd wanted so badly to choose you. Why I'd winced when you'd pulled me close.*

He made a choked noise, a mixture between a roar and a cry getting trapped in his throat, and then cold air swirled around me, sending a new wave of shivers over my skin and hardening my already-pebbled nipples.

My eyes flew open at the sudden absence of his heat, just in time to see the door to my room slam shut, quickly followed by a series of crashes echoing through the hall and vibrating the thin walls. I dropped my hands to my sides and stared numbly at the cold, untouched food sitting near the door, confused, and appetite gone.

I didn't understand Terek's anger, nor his interest in my story. Not when he'd been so cruel and heartless the day he'd pushed me away. More than anything, I didn't understand how, even knowing all of that, my heart had felt so compelled to remove its armor for him anyway.

TEREK

CHAPTER THIRTY-FOUR

The doorframe shuddered, the poorly crafted hinges bending past their limits and ripping out of the wood as I slammed the door to my room. My hands shook, and I buried them into my hair, clawing at the strands while my lungs failed to work, and my mind splintered in half.

There was now me, and the devil I'd become.

He'd fucking branded her.

She'd been sold off like cattle, to a man who'd abused her, by the very people who were supposed to love her unconditionally.

My mother hadn't been overly affectionate, and my father and I had a lot of anger built up near the end, but I'd never doubted that my family wanted what they believed was best for me. I'd never had to question my safety at home or been locked inside like some prized possession.

He'd fucking branded her.

Red filled my vision, and I grabbed a chair and flung it across the room, reveling in each splinter and crack of the wood when it smashed into the dresser. But it wasn't enough. I could still see the tears that dripped down her face, her cheeks tinted red from her bath, hear the rapid beat of her heart as it pounded just before she said the name of that piece of shit.

Her fucking husband.

God, I could still taste her humiliation and defeat in the air, as if she had anything to be fucking embarrassed about. She hadn't chosen that life. Hell, she'd tried to escape it more than once.

I unsheathed a dagger and let it fly, embedding it into the door. Then the second one. Ace had kept coming to the Underland, time and time again, even after I'd been so fucking cruel, not to prove a point to me and drive me insane, but because her goddamn husband hurt her.

Because he'd continued to hurt her.

And instead of taking notice of something I never should have missed, instead of growing a pair and doing something when I'd seen her wither inside of herself over the years, I'd shoved salt in her wounds and told her she wasn't welcome here.

No wonder she'd refused to tell me each time I'd asked why she was here over the last few days. Why would she ever believe I'd fucking care? I'd made fun of her for having no experience in the world, not even considering that maybe it hadn't been because she'd yet to mature, but because she'd been forced to mature too young and had her entire life and body stripped from her.

He'd fucking branded her.

I'd failed her so thoroughly, I could never take it back. Never fix it. She'd wanted to stay here, with me, and now she'd have another man's initials on her body for the rest of her life.

My hands clenched and unclenched at my sides, my jaw grinding and cracking with the effort of holding everything back. How she could even stomach looking at me after I'd ignored her obvious pain and sent her away was beyond me, and it spoke volumes of her strength.

The last time we'd met, when we'd fought so horribly, I'd sensed something was wrong. But I'd been so caught up in my self-disgust for seeing a woman where there'd once been a girl, so twisted in my corrupted sense of right and wrong, I'd refused to consider that there might be a real, raw reason for everything she'd been doing. For her obsession with courting death.

I hadn't been able to fathom it when I'd spent so long wishing on every breath I took, to be anywhere but here. To be Upside.

And that had been seven goddamn years ago. She'd lived with a man who'd burned his initials into her skin, claiming ownership of her body, for seven goddamn fucking years. He'd had her. Touched her. *Tasted her*.

My stomach heaved, and I flung the table out of my way and raced toward the window, flinging it open to suck in desperate gulps of air. The memory of her waking up in my arms and the smell of her fear as she'd tried to attack me, seared the backs of my eyelids like a thousand needles.

My nails curled into the wooden frame until splinters dug into the pads of my fingers. In all the decades I'd been in the Underland, never had I wished to be Upside as much as I did in that moment. I wanted to track down Frederick fucking Turner and repay him for every touch he'd laid on my little rabbit.

I wanted to carve her initials into his skin and gift her the sound of his screams as he begged me for mercy. And when his entire body was covered in her name, I'd peel every inch of skin from him so there would be no chance of him entering the afterlife with any blessed trace of her—only the memory of *me*.

But I couldn't. I was stranded here. A soulless demon.

I could rid the Underland of every human, animal, and Creature, and still Turner would live his life, unbothered for decades to come. Shoving off the ledge, I dug my hands through my hair, trying to calm my senses down before the sounds and smells of the entire town smashed through my hold and tore my sanity to pieces.

The question I couldn't wipe from my mind was whether I hated Frederick Turner more for hurting her, or if I hated him because he'd been given the chance to have the woman my blood and body sang for, and he'd wasted such a gift.

"*Fuck!*"

I headed for the door and ripped my daggers out, sheathing them back at my sides before snatching my cloak off the bed. I couldn't stay in this room a moment longer. Not when I couldn't shut out every sound Ace was making across the hall.

I could hear the shifting of her chair as she took a seat to eat, hear the beat of her heart, calming but still unsteady. Smell the hint of her arousal that'd assaulted my senses as I'd stared at the glimpses of skin I hadn't meant to see.

I'd been trying for two days to shut her out, to eradicate her voice from my mind and her smell from my nose, only to fail each damn time. Even when I'd locked away every single one of my senses until it felt like I was standing alone in the middle of a black void, there was still her.

There was only her.

She'd already been forbidden to me, a glimpse of living bliss I was too tainted by death to possess. But now, even if she was dead, even if she'd come here the way she was supposed to, I'd never deserve her.

Staying here—*staying with me*—might not be as safe as Ace believed, but at least I'd have the control to protect her here and the ability to exact vengeance when necessary. But that didn't mean it was without its own dangers, especially when she didn't know the truth about anything.

I couldn't stay in Tover forever when I was still bound to Lizbeth, nor could I take her back to Ardenglass, but I could protect her for a while. And once I needed to depart, I would make sure she was taken care of, safe, and far from the claws of the White Castle.

Lizbeth's face flashed across my mind. The way her emerald eyes would alight if she got her hands on Ace, and the way her blood-red lips would form a wide, exuberant smile if she ever found out about my connection to her.

I needed to tell Ace about the bounty and my role in telling Lizbeth about her. She deserved to know, but fuck, if the idea of her flinching away from me with distrust didn't make me want to reach into my own chest and rip out the cold, dead heart residing there.

A knock came at my door. "What?" I growled. *Please don't be Ace.* I couldn't face her again so soon. Not before I'd had a chance to pick a fight at another tavern and release this goddamn bleeding rock sitting inside my chest.

I wasn't sure what I'd do if I opened my door and saw her standing on the threshold in that thin ass chemise. Other than throw myself at her feet and worship her body until she screamed her forgiveness and clawed it into my skin.

"It's just me. Cover the goods; I'm coming in," Duma said, voice gruff.

The door latch clicked, and he grunted, shoving against it. "Seems to be stuck—Crimson fucking hell!" The door whipped open as he slammed himself against it and bounced off the turned table, coming back to pop him in the face.

He rubbed at his nose and then froze, his brown eyes going wide as saucers as he took in the room. Or what was left of it.

Remnants of food painted the floor, the bowl and plate shattered. The dresser drawers were cracked down the front, along with the chair I'd thrown at it, while the table lay before the door. I could feel blood dripping from my knuckles, and I fisted my hand, not even remembering when I'd punched something.

"What?" I growled, tightening my grip on my cloak. I needed to get out of here.

"What do you mean, *what*? What the hell happened in here? Because unless you're about to tell me you just had the best sex of your life, I'm going to be selling your body parts to pay for this shit, Terek."

Duma folded his arms, his eyes still darting about the room in disbelief. I might've trusted him and Dex not to stab me in the back or sell Ace to the skin trade in Gissan, but not enough to pour my damn heart out to him like a couple of clucking hens.

"I'll replace everything, Duma. You know I'm good for it." I paused, steeling my spine and biting out my next words. "I'm sorry."

"Sorry? What the hell is going on, Terek? And don't you lie to me again unless you've a craving to sleep on the street. You turn up with a woman in tow for the first time in all the decades I've known you, and coincidentally, you also happen to be losing your ever-loving mind at the same time."

He bent to pick up the shards of the bowl, stacking them in a pile in his hand. A flash of guilt tickled at the base of my spine. Tweeds was his home, and he'd never turned me away, no matter how much of a prick I was. He hadn't deserved my rage.

"It was a lapse in judgment. It won't happen again, I promise."

"The woman, or my poor bowl?" he asked, lips quirking up for the first time since entering the room. Why he was so set on the idea that Ace and I had been fucking in here was beyond me, but I really didn't need the image of her legs wrapped around my neck in my mind right now.

I stared at him for a long moment, but he just stared back, waiting. I sighed, feeling my shoulders deflate as I lost the battle, and rubbed a hand over the back of my neck. "Both. Neither."

"Company's not a bad thing, Terek," he said, dropping the jagged pieces into the pocket of his apron and brushing his hands off. "If it weren't for having Dex with me, I'd have gone mad a long time ago."

"I know full well what company can do to you," I snapped, my body immediately tensing again. Duma didn't know everything that had happened to me before the war, but he knew enough.

"Yeah, but you don't know what it can do *for* you is what I'm saying. I'm not blind, Terek. I saw the way you two—"

"She was married, Duma. So, the only thing you saw tonight was your own big ass nose when you decided to shove it into my business." The words came out vicious and biting, but fuck if giving them voice didn't make me feel like I was spiraling all over again. I wasn't sure what made me tell him when Ace clearly hadn't wanted anyone to know, but I just needed this conversation to be over.

I didn't need Duma trying to play matchmaker. I just needed *out*. Whether he realized my rage wasn't for him, or whether he simply realized I was about to destroy his entire establishment if I didn't leave immediately, he sighed and stepped to the side, sliding his eyes to Ace's door.

"I know that look. Go do your thing. I'll stick around to make sure she doesn't need anything."

I nodded my thanks, purposefully not looking anywhere near her room as I stepped out into the hall. The steady beat of her heart told me she was finally asleep, and the last thing either of us needed was for me to lose control and barge in a second time. Who knew when she'd last slept an entire night alone.

I threw my cloak over myself, pulling the hood down low, and sent one last glance over my shoulder to the man filling the doorframe. "If you do anything to her, I will demand your life as payment for the debt you owe me, Duma."

I was well aware the words showed my hand, proving there was something, at least on my part, going on between Ace and me, but I meant every word. She may not have been mine, but she was mine to protect, and I'd be damned if I let another man touch a hair on her head without her explicit permission.

But rather than smirk at me or threaten me back, Duma just smacked my shoulder, knocking me off center. "I'm not going to do shit, and that includes this here room. So, I suggest you grab the kitchen broom on your way back up, because if you leave my inn looking like this, it'll be *your* life taken as payment."

I nodded again and headed out without a second glance. Because what he didn't know was just how close I was to giving in and letting him take it anyway.

ADELAIS

CHAPTER THIRTY-FIVE

"Wait. So, he just…left?"

Dex popped up from beneath the bar, and I wasn't sure what my face was telling him, but he elbowed Duma, who'd just informed me that Terek had apparently left Tweeds last night not long after he'd stormed out of my room.

I'd been awake for a while, teeth brushed, hair braided over my shoulder, dressed in my clean clothes and slightly too-large boots. I'd been pacing a hole in the floor, fingers caressing over the face of my watch as I waited for Terek to come and get me.

When more than an hour had passed, and I could hear other patrons coming and going, I'd finally left, sticking my tongue out at his closed door and making my way downstairs in the hopes of helping Duma and Dex in the kitchen. Or whatever would earn me a hot breakfast.

But Duma hadn't even let me get my entire question out before he'd turned me down and informed me that Terek owed him money anyway, so he'd just add my meal onto his tab. I'd happily agreed, too hungry to care this time, and asked if they'd seen my surly guide yet, only to discover he wasn't here at all.

Duma, either ignoring his brother or unaware of the reason for the elbow, nodded at me, handing a stack of dirty dishes to a young girl just inside the kitchen door.

"Well, he must've been up at the crack of dawn, or whatever dawn is here, because I didn't hear him leave his room this morning," I said, consciously keeping my voice level and uncaring.

It stung a little that he'd left without even checking to see if I was all right, or if I wanted to go with him, but I brushed it off. We were both adults, ones who didn't even get along all that well. He didn't have to invite me to go grab supplies or whatever it was he was doing.

"He's been gone all night, actually."

"Oh." I bit my lip, staring holes into the wooden surface of the bar. There was no brushing off the second sting. It came quick and hard, jabbing into my chest. There were very few things I could think of that would've kept Terek gone all night, and not a single one of them was a reason I wanted to contemplate.

"Eh, don't worry yourself, Ace. He's probably still wandering town in search of a new table set," Dex said, making his brother grunt in agreement.

"Don't forget the dresser."

"Right, and a dresser."

I looked up and smiled, appreciating their attempt to change the subject, and took a seat at the bar, eyeing the plates of bread and fruit set off to the side.

I wasn't a hundred percent sure what they were talking about, but I vaguely remembered hearing crashing right after Terek had stormed out last night. At the time, I'd ignored it, assuming it to be a drunk patron. I couldn't handle drunks on my best days, and I'd been too exhausted and overwhelmed by Terek's abrupt entrance and exit from my room to go investigate.

But the fact that they'd made Terek go shopping for the replacements brought me a simple kind of joy. It would serve the man right if he'd started a fight with a drunk man in their tavern right after they'd been kind enough to give us board, just because he'd been angry at me.

"Are we expecting him back anytime soon?"

Duma shrugged, grabbing a clean plate from below the bar and loading it up with food before setting it in front of me. "Knowing Terek, there's just as good a chance that he won't come back at all."

Something twisted in my chest, making the mouthwatering bite of freshly baked bread clog my throat. Dex elbowed Duma again, harder this time, and he winced, giving me an apologetic smile. I waved them off, taking the proffered water Dex handed me and pushing the food down.

"It's fine. I was just curious is all."

They shared a look, but thankfully, neither said anything more on the subject while I finished my food. In all honesty, I wasn't sure why I'd expected anything different. Terek hadn't wanted to bring me to Tover in the first place, and he'd been anything but happy with me last night.

"We're going into town soon, before the lunch rush, to speak to someone about an empty building across town. You want to join?" Dex asked.

"Yes!" I said, louder than I'd meant. My cheeks flushed, and I lowered my voice when several people around me turned my way. "Please. I didn't get to see a whole lot when we came in. We were kind of in a rush."

The quiet voice in my head that had guided me and kept me alive the last seven years whispered that I shouldn't be going anywhere with two men I didn't know. They'd been nothing but kind, but I'd learned long ago that kindness could just as easily be a weapon. One that men often enjoyed using to build a film over women's eyes so they wouldn't see the manipulation concocted behind it.

Duma and Dex hadn't yet proven to me they weren't like that. Still, despite that, for reasons I didn't know, I wanted to trust them with every fiber of my being.

Dex laughed, his smile as warm as I imagined his hugs would be. "I figured you would."

I licked the melon juice from my fingers, wiping them on my dress in a way that would've killed my mother where she stood. "What are you looking at an empty building for? Are you thinking of moving Tweeds?"

Granted, I hadn't seen the new building they were talking about, but I couldn't believe anywhere was better than their square-front location.

"Expanding," Dex corrected, puffing his chest out and drawing a grin from me. "When you have eternity ahead of you, my dear, you might as well think big. And who knows, maybe with a second Tweeds, Duma might actually hire you on."

"Not if she's not ready by the time I drop these off," Duma called out over his shoulder, bustling past the bar with plates stacked up both arms.

I'd never eaten so fast in my life.

WE LEFT SOON after I'd washed the last bite down, Duma saying something about wanting to leave early enough to swing by the bakery before their meeting. And then after the lunch rush, they'd agreed to wander around with me again, showing me the parts of Tover I hadn't yet seen.

To say I was giddy was an understatement. Just the thought of going to the bakery alone was enough to bring me a ridiculous amount of joy. Even with a full stomach, I'd practically drooled remembering the delicious scents that'd come from it when Terek and I had arrived.

Sadly for my sweet tooth, Duma informed me the trip there would be quick and wasn't to purchase treats but to discuss supply runs with the owner, Tomas. He was hoping to convince the baker to start making larger flour and sugar orders together so they could each save money by splitting the delivery cost.

Dex, however, said little, grumbling to himself every time his brother mentioned Tomas. When Duma spotted the baker in question, a shorter man with curly brown hair, amber skin, and a thick, dark mustache over a wide smile, Dex visibly slowed, pretending to read the headline on a newspaper he'd already shown me earlier.

Duma must have already anticipated that Dex wouldn't join him, because he didn't give his brother a second glance before stalking over to Tomas and clapping him on the shoulder.

Part of me wanted to join him in the hopes of both convincing Tomas to let me try a sticky bun and asking him for work, but the other part of me recognized the look of longing in Dex's eyes and couldn't leave him to stand alone.

Walking over to where he stood, I took the newspaper from his hands and set it back, nudging his arm with my shoulder. "Why am I getting the feeling you really don't like Mr. Tomas all that much?"

"What?" he asked, snapping his head over to look at me. "Why would you think that?"

I gestured to the paper. "Maybe because you're standing way over here, rereading an article on the current availability of produce and the next town meeting instead of talking business with your brother?"

He sighed, not denying it, and nudged me back, making me stumble forward into the rack. I righted myself and laughed, attempting to shove him to the side, only to fail epically when he didn't budge an inch.

We started walking again, and he dared a quick look to where his brother and Tomas stood in front of the bakery. "I don't dislike Tomas," he finally said. "He's a gorgeous man with a kind heart and a good sense of humor. And he truly has a gift. His lemon cakes could make the toughest man shoot his loa—"

His eyes widened, and he snapped his lips closed, looking almost sheepish as he cleared his throat. I rolled my eyes and chuckled. "I'm twenty-seven, Dex, not a virginal child. I like orgasmic lemon cakes just as much as the next person."

He blinked at me and then threw his head back, releasing a booming laugh and causing several people, including Tomas, to turn and look. I blushed at the attention, which didn't exactly help my case, but Dex just flicked the tip of my nose.

"Noted," he said, his smile dimming. He raised up, waving at an older woman who passed by with an armload of what looked to be potatoes. "Anyway, like I said, Tomas is fine, if not slightly my competition. He just reminds me of someone I used to know, and some days, I find it hard to look at him."

His tone stayed light, and his posture relaxed, but there was something bitter and sharp in his eyes that gave me pause. "Someone Upside?" I asked, not sure if bringing up his previous life would be considered disrespectful.

He nodded, his throat working. "Yeah. It's unfair to Tomas, and it shouldn't bother me anymore, given how long it's been since I've seen Jack, but..." He shrugged, attempting to cover his pain with a forced laugh.

As someone who didn't have a single person Upside that I missed, it was easy to forget that not everyone felt that way. I couldn't imagine what it must've been like for Dex to be in love with a happy life ahead of him, only to wake up one day, never knowing it'd be the last time he ever saw them.

"I'm sorry."

He shook his head, brushing his haggard expression away with a cheeky grin. "Nah, don't be. Death is a bitter bitch who comes for us all, eventually. And who knows, maybe one day I'll see Jack again, or maybe I'll get the nerve to say more than two words to Tomas."

I hoped, for his sake, that it was the second. Not because I didn't want him to see his long-lost love again, but because the idea of Dex waiting an eternity for someone, only for it to never happen, made my heart feel like it was being crushed.

Seeing Duma still deep in conversation, I twisted around and looked at the shops around me, sensing Dex needed a moment to himself. I'd just taken a step toward the bakery when my eyes landed on a small, hole-in-the-wall shop catacorner to it, and I stopped dead in my tracks.

I'd been so focused on the smell of food when Terek and I had passed through, I'd somehow completely missed it. But right there, with a giant window and a bright red sign that read *The Painted Table*, was a shop filled with every possible thing I could ever want. Charcoal, parchment, paints, blackboards, frames, and more.

My feet moved without conscious thought, squeezing between people and crossing the street until I stood a foot away from the window, my eyes shooting to each corner of the store to take in every possible detail.

A minute later, I felt Dex's arm graze my back as he came to stand beside me. "Do you draw?"

I nodded, placing both hands on my chest to keep from plastering myself to the window. I felt like I couldn't breathe. Tears burned behind my eyes, and my lungs heaved in air, trying not to have a full-fledged emotional breakdown in the middle of the street.

They had art here.

They had food, and warmth, and safety, and *art*.

"I love it more than anything."

I swallowed, watching a little girl accidentally break a piece of charcoal and tuck it under another, glancing around to see if anyone had noticed.

"I haven't done it in a long time. Frederick...my husband, didn't allow me to draw." Neither did my parents, but I didn't feel like getting into my whole pathetic backstory.

"Because you didn't have the money for it, or..." Dex frowned down at me, his eyes roving over whatever expressions my face was making without my permission.

"Because he didn't like what I chose to draw." Because he hadn't liked the number of times I'd drawn Terek, perfecting his likeness until his eyes had seemed capable of watching me from the parchment. Because he, and the other teachers who'd seen them, had either believed Terek was an unhealthy figment of my imagination, or a man who'd tried to groom me as a child.

Neither could have been more wrong.

"You know," Dex said, looking across the way to where Duma was now shaking Tomas's hand. "Men like your husband, whom I feel like you can call your ex now that the *'until death do you part'* has occurred and all, make me consider giving women a try."

I snorted and pushed away from the shop. He winked at me, and his hands unfurled, like he was considering whether or not to pull me in for a hug. I waited with bated breath, desperately wanting him to, but he just shifted back and tucked them into his pockets.

Disappointment washed through me, but I pushed it away, knowing I had no right to expect that. Just because Dex had showed me kindness and told me part of his history didn't mean we were suddenly into the hugging territory of our friendship.

But it *did* mean I could drag him into this art shop and convince him to let me work off a basic set of materials. Maybe he'd let me pay him by drawing his portrait.

"We need to go. Right now."

Dex and I both spun at the sudden, hushed words to see Duma standing directly behind us, his face drawn low and his chest moving rapidly. His hands were fisted at his sides, and when I glanced around him, Tomas was urging nearby people to run into the bakery.

"Why? What's up— Crimson hell." Dex's eyes flared, and he straightened to his full height in front of me, blocking my view of the street. "Come on, we can go this way."

He pointed back the way we'd come, but I hesitated to go. I could hear shouts beginning to build and the roar of a crowd running in our direction, desperately trying to either get somewhere quickly, or get *away* from something.

"What's going on?" I asked. I stepped around him to try to see what had everyone so frantic, but my voice came out more of a squeak than actual words when Dex's hands wrapped around my waist and yanked me back. He picked me up just enough to spin me until I was facing the way we'd come.

"Nothing, Ace. We just need to go this way, and with haste."

I craned my neck up to see their two bald heads towering above my own. "Nothing, my butt. Why? What's everyone running from?"

"The White Guard," Duma said, as loud as he dared over the growing noise. His brows were low as he scanned the crowd of people scurrying to go in the direction Dex had faced me. "We'll never make it to the meeting on time if we go the long way, Dex."

I twisted to peer through the small gap between their shoulders. "It looks like most people are going this way. If we just go the way we originally were, we could probably get there on time just fine."

Duma shook his head, firmly taking my arm and pulling me to keep pace with the rushing bodies so we wouldn't get trampled. "They're going the other way for a reason, Ace. The White Guard only arrive when they have a list of names to take to Ardenglass."

I scrunched my nose, trying not to trip at the pace they were setting. "That doesn't sound so bad." Unless the people they called were being taken in for not paying taxes or something, but even that didn't seem like something every person on the street would be running from.

"It's bad."

"Couldn't we just take a quick peek? Maybe it's something else."

Duma suddenly darted to the side, dragging me along with him until the three of us were tucked into an alcove. "Listen to me, Ace. If there is anything you learn about the Underland before all else, it's to stay far away from anyone who works for the queen."

"Well," Dex started, raising his brows at his brother, "I mean, except for—" He cut off at Duma's pointed glare.

"Very few people go to Ardenglass willingly when their name is called, Ace. They are forced, and that's not something you want to see."

I pressed my lips together, taking in their unmoving faces. Dex's eyes kept glancing over my head, but Duma was staring only at me. He wasn't going to budge on the matter.

Luckily for me, I may have possessed very few skills, but telling men what they wanted to hear when I didn't actually mean it was one of my best ones.

"Fine," I said, pouting and relaxing my arm so that it hung limply in his hold. As expected, both men relaxed, and Duma released me, clearly assuming he'd won the argument.

I didn't want to lie to them. I genuinely liked these giant men who were taking the time to talk to me even though they could physically force me to do whatever they wanted. But I also wanted to learn about this world and about Ardenglass, and I was so very tired of people refusing to tell me. This was *my* home now, too.

"All right, let's go," he said, glaring at a man who'd stumbled a little too close to him. "We'll have to run to get there on time, but it's far enough away that we should be safe to go. It'll take the guards a few hours to reach that side of town."

Dex nodded in agreement and looked down at me again, a mischievous grin on his face despite the worry hiding behind his eyes. "Your little legs are going to struggle. Need me to toss you over my shoulder?"

I shook my head, smiling. "No, that's okay. I actually think I'm going to head back. You two go ahead."

Dex's grin fell into a frown, and Duma's face snapped to mine from where he'd been staring out over my head, suspicion painting every corner of his face. Okay, so maybe it wouldn't be quite as easy as the self-absorbed men Upside.

I raised my hands, knowing if either of them voiced their disbelief, my resolve would crumble.

"Dex is right. I can't keep up, and I have no desire to be carried like a sack of flour through the streets. Tweeds is right over there. I'll be fine, I promise."

Dex wanted to argue. I could see it in the way his jaw flexed and his hands twitched at his sides. But although Duma narrowed his eyes, he surprised me by being the one to agree first.

"You'll go straight there?"

"Straight there." God, what was I? A child? *Yes*, a voice whispered, reminding me I was lying through my teeth like I was twelve all over again.

"Fine, but I want you to wait in the tavern with the staff until we get back. They know what to do if guards enter the building."

I bristled, feeling like he was patronizing me, but when I met his brown eyes, I saw only the lingering hint of suspicion and a touch of worry. "My butt will be planted in front of the hearth when you return."

That part wasn't a lie. I did plan on getting back to Tweeds before they did. Right after I got a quick look at the White Guard and figured out what they were collecting names for.

ADELAIS

CHAPTER THIRTY-SIX

R egret and a healthy dose of self-loathing filled my chest as I twisted away and ran in the other direction the second the brothers stepped out of sight. But I shoved both feelings down to the pit of my stomach to overthink and hate myself for later.

I'd spent my entire life putting men's feelings first, making sure they were content and satisfied, even while my own plate remained permanently empty. Now that I was finally free, I had no desire to continuing living like that, even for men as kind as Duma and Dex.

And it wasn't that I didn't believe the warning Duma gave me about the queen's guards being dangerous. If a man like him was nervous around them, I knew there'd be a legitimate reason. I just also knew their list, whatever it was for, posed no threat to *me*, since there was zero chance of my undead self being on it.

Never having seen a guard of any kind before, I wasn't exactly sure what I was looking for as I turned the corner to where I'd seen everybody hurrying away from, but it didn't take me long to figure it out.

Though I assumed their name came from the fact that the queen resided at the White Castle, it appeared the White Guard also got their name from the fact that they literally bore no other color. From their shoulders down to their feet, they were solid white, apart from a single red rose on their chest plates and the deep, blood-red handles of knives far larger than Terek's.

No, not knives. Swords. Literal, giant swords.

There were several dozen, each with short hair that was shaved on the sides and clean-shaven jaws. They were scattered throughout the street, which appeared to have only homes built up and down it, and they held rolls of parchment. I watched in confusion as they casually knocked on doors, their armor sharp and loud against the wood.

I frowned. Besides the fact that they were all armed with frighteningly large swords, none of them looked dangerous. The people who'd chosen to stick around didn't even look worried. If anything, they appeared not to care about the guards at all. They just went about their lives, heads bowed and steps slow.

Sure, some of the guards wore expressions like they were eagerly waiting for someone to piss them off and give them a reason to retaliate, but even those select few weren't actively hurting anyone. They were just…holding up their rolls and talking to people.

I stepped out of the alcove I'd tucked myself into, daring to walk a little closer to the nearest guard to hear what they were asking or telling everyone. He'd just caught a young man who'd been attempting to scurry past and slip into a pale blue house, shooting a hand out and blocking the door.

"Why in such a hurry?"

The boy said nothing, his eyes darting around from person to person, clearly searching for someone to step in. No one did. Besides me, I wasn't sure anyone had even noticed or cared that he'd been stopped.

"This your house, boy?"

He nodded.

The guard dropped his hand and turned his body so that the boy was backed against his door, parchment held in his face. "Take a look at these names and tell me where they live, and you can go back to your sad excuse of an existence."

The boy's entire body trembled, and he stared down at the parchment, his eyes unseeing as he stuttered out a barely audible, "I d-don't know. I don't know anyone here. I'm n-new."

Rather than step back and move to the next house as I'd expected, the guard seemed to grow bigger, his eyes looking like a kid who'd just spotted a table of sweets in an abandoned room. "Is that so? And what did the Underland gift you in death?"

"N-n-nothing."

The man stepped closer, lowering the roll of parchment to his side as his other hand casually rested on the blood-red handle of his sword. The boy visibly balked, his back pressing as far back into his door as he could get, trying to put space between them.

"You're lying, boy."

"No, I'm—I'm not."

"Want to know how I know?" the guard asked, baring his teeth like a predator who'd just spotted the perfect prey. "Because *that* is what the Underland gifted *me*. I can smell the lie on your tongue."

That had my curiosity popping like a soap bubble, but it was the hand now wrapped around the boy's throat and hefting him off the ground that had me retreating, nausea coiling in the pit of my stomach.

I didn't know what to do. If I should run out and yell something to get the guard to stop, or if that would make it even worse. Anytime Frederick had gotten angry, saying anything to him that wasn't agreeing or apologizing had only made him react harsher, and I didn't want to do that to the young man. He looked barely sixteen.

"Don't make me ask you again, boy. What ability do you possess?"

"It's nothing!" the boy choked out, his face growing almost purple while his legs dangled and his hands clawed at the guard's wrist. "J-just a useless…"

His words turned into a heaving gasp as the guard released his throat and dropped him to the ground, allowing the boy a split second to push up onto his shaking hands before replying, "The queen will be the one to decide that," and kneeing him in the face.

His body fell with a thud, his forehead cracking against the cobblestone in a way that had my flight mode rearing up and screaming at me to *move* and get to Tweeds with haste. I'd assumed the guards' lists meant those were the only names they were searching for, but that boy hadn't been on the list at all.

I'd had no idea the guards would have abilities. The possibility was obvious now, but since Terek was the only person I'd ever seen use his, I'd stupidly forgotten he wasn't the only one to have one. God, I didn't even know if Duma and Dex did.

But if that guard could truly sense when someone was lying to him, I needed to get as far away from him as possible before he thought me another new soul and questioned me.

I wasn't sure what the queen needed the boy's unknown ability for, but his unconscious body being dragged across the ground was enough for me to know I didn't care anymore.

Forgoing my slow retreat, I twisted, intent on sprinting back as fast as my legs could take me, when my gaze locked onto a pair of blue eyes staring straight at me from across the street. Eyes that belonged to a man clothed in shining, blinding white.

The red emblem on his chest glared at me almost as harshly as he did, its vibrant shade reminding me of the blood I'd once seen painted all over a poor rabbit's body when I was eight. A warning.

He took a step closer, almost as if in a trance. Then another, and another. His brow pinched, and his eyes pinned on my face with such intensity, I felt like he was trying to peel my skin off with his gaze alone.

Instinct had me shuffling backward, already not liking the way he was looking at me through the crowd of people who hadn't left the street. Something akin to recognition lit across his face, and his lips parted, his hand falling away from his sword. He glanced around, as if to see if anyone else had noticed me, and then, with zero warning, shot forward, sprinting toward me and barreling through any person unlucky enough to be in his way.

Panic surged, and for a moment I couldn't move as I watched his bulk of a body grow closer. But then I was running, adrenaline pumping through my veins as I made a mad dash down the street, my shoulders slamming into signs and people in my desperation.

My heart beat so fast within my ribs, I feared I'd drop dead right in the middle of the street before he'd even caught up to me. I had no idea what he wanted or why he was chasing me, but there was something about the way he'd looked at me that had my hackles rising.

It was like he knew who I was, and that, combined with the image of the boy falling to the ground, was enough to keep my legs moving even when it felt like daggers were stabbing my lungs.

"Stop right there!"

The nearness of his voice had a whimper slipping through my lips, but I didn't turn, knowing if I slowed for even a second, he'd be on me. I just needed to get to Tweeds. I wasn't sure if the twins would be there, but I held onto the hope that they'd meant what they said when they'd told me their staff knew what to do. Because I had no idea.

If today had taught me anything, it was that Terek was right, and I was really fucking bad at making smart choices.

I muttered a slew of apologies as I elbowed my way faster down the street. Several people whipped around to see what the new commotion was about, but the second their eyes landed on the man behind me, they spun back around like they'd hadn't seen a thing.

"I order you to stop!"

I flung myself around the next corner, hoping and praying with every fiber of my being that I'd recognize the next street. *Oh God, oh God*, I never should've left Duma and Dex. I should've stayed with them and waited until we got back to demand answers.

Go figure, the one time I decided to ignore a man's orders and give in to what I wanted, it backfired stupendously.

Rather than a street I knew or even a busy one, when I rounded the corner, I was met with three towering walls closing me in. I slammed to a stop, bending my ankle at an odd angle when I spun, attempting to slip back out of the blocked alley before my pursuer caught up.

But it was too late. I crashed face first into a hard chest, the metal breastplate covering his torso ramming into my nose and causing instant tears to well. I shoved back and gripped my nose, wanting to scream at the sheer size of him as he used his body to create a fourth wall, successfully caging me in.

Acid crawled up my throat, and I swallowed, trying not to vomit when his hand gripped the handle of his sword. I instinctively raised my hands, showing him I was unarmed, but he either didn't trust that I had no hidden knife, or didn't care, because he removed his sword anyway, pointing the tip a few inches from my chest.

"There's nowhere left to run. Calm down. I'm not going to hurt you, and neither will anyone else. Guard's honor. Well," he paused, looking me up and down, "as long as you behave, that is."

I blinked, devoid of words for several seconds. Did this man seriously expect me to walk off with him after he'd just chased me into an alley and looked at me that way? With a weapon?

Honestly, he was lucky I didn't possess the skill to turn his sword around and cut off his balls, though I was certainly tempted to draw myself doing so if I ever got my hands on some charcoal.

"The sharp object pointed at me," I breathed, nodding at his sword and sucking in a deep breath to steady my racing heart, "makes me believe otherwise."

He smiled, and the emotion behind it had every warning in my body going off simultaneously. He wasn't leering like I'd expect of a man who'd just cornered a woman. No, he was looking at me like he'd just found the greatest treasure known to mankind.

He wiggled the blade, attempting to soften his smile to something less creepy but failing. "This is just for insurance purposes to make sure you don't try to do your little disappearing thing on me. Because if you choose not to behave, sweetheart, I promise I can slide this through you faster than you can magic yourself home."

I completely froze, dread lancing through me like a sheet of pure ice. *He knew.* How the hell did this man know what I could do? I shook my head and shuffled backward, moving my feet faster when he matched my steps. It wasn't possible. Neither Terek, nor I, had said a word about my ability since arriving in Tover. There was no way this man could know.

Unless, of course, Terek had said something when he'd disappeared today. I brushed the thought away as quickly as it'd come. He'd never tell anyone about me. It was the only truth I believed about him with my entire being.

The man had to have meant something else.

Slipping my hand into my pocket, I wrapped my fingers around my watch to calm myself and took a deep breath. I could do this. He was just another man who thought himself above me. I just had to convince him I wasn't whoever he thought I was.

"I think you've mistaken me for someone else, sir. I only ran because you frightened me."

His smile widened into something greasy and vile, all pretense falling to dust at our feet. "Oh, I think not, sweetheart," he said, taking a step closer. "I've known every plane of your face for over half a decade. Age may change curves and texture, but it doesn't change everything."

He lowered his sword, just enough to reach out and brush his hand over my cheek, snagging a few strands of hair and sliding them through his fingers. "The Underland gifted me with the ability to remember every person, every place, and every occurrence. A perfect, unfailing memory, if you will. I *never* forget a face, especially one that's worth so much."

What? My brow furrowed, confusion clearing the haze of my fear just enough to consider what he was saying. I wasn't worth anything here. I hadn't even arrived with shoes, for God's sake. "Sir, I'm sorry I ran, but I swear we've never met. I don't know who you are."

He grinned, running the pad of his thumb over my lips to stop my rambling. "Oh, but I know who you are, World Jumper."

Shock shot through me at the term, no longer able to deny he knew what I could do, but it was nothing like the terror that filled my veins when his hand fell from my face to wrap around my throat. He didn't squeeze, but his eyes told me he would if I so much as breathed wrong.

"Personally, I don't give a shit about my soul. The queen can keep it for the rest of my eternal life for all I care, but I know many who'll pay a fortune to exchange you for theirs." He lowered his sword and stepped closer, brushing his lips over my cheek and making my spine stiffen. "You're going to set me up for li—"

A loud whack echoed off the alley walls, and I startled, terrified another guard had joined us when the large hand at my throat contracted. But rather than turn to see whatever had caused the sound, his blue eyes stared unseeing at me before rolling up into the back of his head. He dropped like a sack of potatoes, his sword clattering to the cobblestones as his head bounced vulgarly off a nearby crate and his body hit the ground.

I watched it all happen in slow motion, my mind attempting to keep up with what my eyes were seeing. I blinked, and then blinked again. Sure enough, the man who'd sounded like he was hoping to sell me, or something just as awful, was sprawled out at my feet.

Blood trickled from the back of his head onto the stones, and I had the sudden disturbing desire to grin at the sight. I didn't know much about head trauma, but I hoped that if he woke up, he had one hell of a headache.

Movement on the other side of his body caught my attention, and I scrambled back, scared another White Guard had knocked him out to claim whatever reward they believed they'd get for me. But instead of another towering, muscled man staring at me with a sword, my mouth fell open as the complete opposite met my eyes.

Because although there was definitely a person standing a few feet away from me, with a heaving chest and the handle of a dagger she'd apparently just smashed into the back of the man's head, it was a...girl.

Well, sort of. At first glance, I'd have guessed her to be no older than eighteen, but her hollow cheeks and the heavy, deep-set shadows beneath her pale blue eyes seemed to eat away at her youth, making her somehow appear both child-like and ancient at the same time.

She had chin-length, stringy blonde hair contrasting against tan skin, and her nose and chin were both slightly pointed, giving her a unique elegance that would've been beautiful had she not looked like she'd gone an entire week without sleeping. She wore a weathered and beaten pair of trousers, a long-sleeved tunic with a leather corset, and a pair of brown boots not too different from the used pair on my own feet.

I may not have known all that much about the Underland, or cities and towns in general, but even I could tell the afterlife had not been gentle to this girl. Yet, unlike all the people I'd run past, she'd been the only one willing to risk helping me.

She straightened up, fist gripping the handle of her weapon tightly like even though she'd saved me, she still wasn't sure I wouldn't try to hurt her in return.

I raised both hands to show her I was very much still unarmed and attempted a small, reassuring smile. "Thank you."

She sniffed and looked away, flipping the small dagger in her hand so the blade faced up. "No problem."

I eyed the sharp tip of it and then the one I could see peeking out at her waist, wondering what in the world a teenager needed so many weapons for here. Surely things like this didn't happen *that* often. Right?

Terek and Duma had both claimed the Underland was similar to the Upside, but the sheer number of people carrying sharp objects was beginning to make me think they were full of shit.

My young savior crossed her arms and leaned back against the wall, tucking one foot up under her butt. "Why was he chasing you, anyway? White Guards are assholes, for sure, but they don't usually mess with anyone not already on their list. You steal his coin purse or something?"

My jaw dropped, my heart and lungs still working overtime in my chest from the man's touch and my desperate sprint through the streets. "What? No! I'm not a thief. I have no idea why he was chasing me. He was just being…"

"A man?"

I snorted, liking her more and more by the second. "I was going to say asshole, but that about sums it up. How'd you know?"

Her lips tipped in a hint of a smile but quickly fell again as she nudged the guard's unconscious body with her scuffed boot. "Men are always after something to own. Even death can't save us from their greed."

She rubbed her free hand over the base of her neck, almost

subconsciously, and something about her expression made my heart sink. Frederick had been cruel, but my gut told me this girl had been through worse.

"I'm Ace, by the way," I said, trying to make my face as friendly as possible. "What's your name?"

Her blue eyes flashed with something I couldn't quite catch, but before she could respond, a shuffling came from behind her. She flung herself away from the wall so fast, her knife clattered to the ground, and she cursed, her eyes darting around like she'd only just realized we were in an alley with only one exit.

I took a hesitant step toward her, reaching out a hand. "Are you okay?"

"Ace! What the crimson hell are you doing back here with—Oh God, tell me that isn't a White Guard at your feet."

I twisted at the familiar, deep voice, every muscle in my body relaxing at the comfort of Duma and Dex's gruff faces filling my line of sight. Dex, who'd been the one to shout at me, was staring down at the body, his eyes comically wide, while his brother outright glared at my savior.

It was he who spoke next. "What the fuck happened?"

"Honestly, I'm not entirely sure."

"Did he step foot into Tweeds?" he asked.

I shook my head, glad for the shadows of the walls when my face flushed with shame. "No. I didn't go to Tweeds. I think he thought I was someone else," I added, though I didn't really believe that anymore. But I couldn't exactly tell them that when they didn't know the truth about me.

"He spotted me through the crowd and started chasing me. I got lost." I swallowed, letting them fill in the blanks on how that ended up with me cornered in an alley.

"She saved me, but she didn't hurt him. Well, not any more than to knock him out so he'd let go of me," I said, turning to introduce them to the girl, but when I looked behind me to where she'd just been standing, there was nothing but open air and stacks of crates.

I gaped, spinning to see if she'd hidden behind one or something, but she was nowhere to be seen. I craned my neck back, wondering if she'd somehow started climbing the brick wall, but no small body hovered above us. She'd disappeared just as suddenly and silently as she'd arrived.

Stepping forward, I knelt and picked up the knife she'd left, the only proof I had that she'd existed at all. It was simple enough, but heavier than it looked, and I couldn't help but wonder how much easier my life might've been if I'd have known how to defend myself like she did.

I twisted back around, smiling at the realization that I had all the time in the world to learn now, only to trip over the guard's sprawled foot and stumble backward, nearly cutting the tip of my nose off.

Dex stared up at me in horror from where he'd been checking the guard on the ground. "Crimson take me, Terek's going to kill us."

Tucking the knife into my boot like I'd seen the girl do and hoping I wouldn't slice my ankle when I started walking, I stepped over the offending limb that'd tripped me. "Terek's not my keeper. Besides, if he was that worried about me, he wouldn't have left in the first place."

Duma stood silent for a moment, eyes pinned to the empty alley behind me like he expected my savior to reappear from the shadows. But then he sighed and dropped his gaze to the guard, rubbing a large hand over his scalp.

"He's not your keeper, Ace, but I made a promise to a friend to keep you safe, and you made me almost break it by lying to us. We were worried sick. This," he said, waving his hand over the unconscious man, "is exactly what we were warning you about. Curiosity kills the cat for a reason."

"I know. I'm sorry," I said, feeling like a child all over again. He was right, what I'd done had been risky and immature.

"No, you don't know. That's the thing." He looked down at me, eyes roving quickly over my body to check for wounds. "The White Guards work for the Crimson Queen. They live and breathe by her rule. They don't track down random women who aren't on her list, and they certainly don't abandon their post and give chase. That's what her Soul Seekers are for."

"Soul Seekers?"

He frowned, glancing behind me again and then sharing a look with his brother. "I don't have time to get into all of that right now. We need to get you into Tweeds and out of sight before our friend here wakes up."

Dex nodded and stood, brushing his hands over his trousers to dust the lingering dirt off his knees. He held his arm out, stepping to the side to let me pass out of the alley first. "If you're lucky, he won't remember what you look like by the time he wakes."

I shuddered. That definitely wasn't going to happen after what the guard admitted to me. I walked past them, feeling Duma's hand gently caress my arm just above a set of scratches I'd been too scared to notice before but were now stinging. His eyes hardened. "I should've already asked this, but are you okay?"

I nodded, swallowing down a lump in my throat at the way these two men were looking at me like they actually fucking cared about my answer. "Yeah, I'm all right. I'm sorry I made you miss your meeting."

"You didn't. The long way made us late. He wasn't there. We got back to Tweeds, and when we didn't find you, I had a hunch you'd lied."

My cheeks heated even further, but Duma had already turned away from me, sharing another look with his brother that communicated something I wasn't privy to.

He sighed, his entire chest deflating like he'd lost a few years in the last five minutes. "Fine, Dex, you win. We'll keep this little incident between us for now. But if any guards come to Tweeds, I'm fucking telling Terek, and I'm blaming *you*."

Dex flipped him off, but I just nodded again, not worried in the least. I doubted Terek would come back at all now that he was free of me, but even if he did, what I chose to do, no matter how childish or dangerous, was my own business. I'd already admitted my deepest secret to him. I owed the man nothing else.

"Are you keeping it between us because you forgive me for lying, or because you don't feel like listening to Terek rant like a crotchety old man?" I asked, trying to lighten the mood.

Duma darted one last look at the guard and then ushered me back out onto the street, smooshing my body between himself and Dex like he feared another guard might pop out and attack at any moment.

"Because I don't feel like burying a corpse today."

ADELAIS

CHAPTER THIRTY-SEVEN

"**W**here the hell have you been?" The words slammed into me before my foot had even touched the floor of Tweeds. The handful of straggling patrons who'd stayed through lunch and the lone worker meandering between tables all shot their heads up and stared back and forth between us, as if waiting for a dramatic marital dispute to unfurl.

Luckily for them, I supposed, I was tapped out for the day, sick of people in general, and ready for a fight.

"Hello to you, too," I said, watching Terek prowl forward from where he'd been standing before the hearth, having clearly been waiting for us to return.

A fact I definitely wasn't going to look too far into, despite the weird flip his unwavering gaze made my heart do. The rogue organ had a mind of its own and, based on how things had gone the last time I'd listened to it, not a very good one.

Terek's jaw ticced beneath a thin layer of rough stubble he'd yet to shave, and his hair was an absolute mess, the longer strands on top sticking in a few different directions like he'd spent the last hour digging his hands through them. His body fared no better. His cloak was nowhere in sight, and his tunic was rumpled and untucked, the sleeves rolled up in a way that was positively indecent.

He looked like he'd just climbed out of someone's bed. My heart sped up at the thought, and something that felt a whole lot like betrayal roiled in the pit of my stomach. Is that what he'd run from my room to do? And why was I surprised? He had no interest in me that way. The man couldn't have made it any clearer.

I side-stepped to put Duma, who was currently standing statue-still, between us, his brown eyes wary as he watched his friend. I didn't know him well enough to read his exact expression, but he looked like he either didn't trust Terek not to hurt someone or knew what Terek had been off doing and didn't approve.

Holding my chin high and pretending I was completely unbothered by the furious man quickly approaching me, I headed toward the bar, purposefully keeping a line of tables between us. I trusted my head to stay away from someone who'd clearly been with another woman, but I didn't trust my stupid heart to do the same.

Especially when it was currently giving me away to the man who could hear how easily it reacted to just the sight of him. Honestly, his heightened senses were incredibly inconvenient.

He growled, rounding the last table in less than a breath and blocking my path in two long strides. "Do you have any idea how risky it was to go sightseeing today? Or who is prowling through Tover as we speak?" he demanded.

His words should've been for all three of us since we'd walked in together, but his eyes never strayed from me. I bristled, not appreciating his attitude when he'd been the one refusing to tell me anything about the Underland no matter how many times I'd asked.

Nor did I appreciate the fact that he was currently standing between me and the delicious-smelling stew I could see the young worker dishing out into several bowls on the bar behind him.

"No, but I have a feeling you're about to tell me," I said sweetly, plastering on my happy wife smile. His chest rumbled in answer, and someone, likely Dex, sounded like he'd choked on his tongue.

Did I know better than to antagonize someone who could snap my neck in two seconds? Probably. Should I definitely not have been around the guards? Absolutely. But if Terek thought he could disappear without a word to go sleep around all night, only to come back and lecture me about guards *he omitted telling me about*, he could go right to hell.

Or the dark abyss, or wherever it was that existed after this.

His midnight eyes seared into my face, making it impossible to look away, even though my body screamed at me to flee. To put space between myself and the predator prowling closer to me. Because the man who'd kept me warm and shared the story of his death with me? There was no hint of him now.

When he was only a few steps away, his nostrils suddenly flared, and I swore the planes of his face grew even sharper as he inhaled deeply. "What happened?"

I crossed my arms, as if that might prevent him from sensing the way my blood pumped faster at his question. How did anyone hide anything from this man? I shuffled backward, but he only matched each step.

"Nothing, Terek. I ate a breakfast you'll have to pay for, Duma told me about the White Guard and the queen's list that you opted not to mention, and then we left for a meeting with Tomas, who owns the nearby bakery. I didn't really get to see all that much."

I shrugged, like it'd been a normal day and not one where a dead man tried to kidnap and sell me before a teenage girl hit him upside the head. Technically, it wasn't a lie. Considering the size of Tover, I saw very little.

However, when I attempted to step around him again to head to the bar, where Dex now stood watching us, Terek's hand curled around my bicep. The contact of his skin on mine instantly shot a spark down my arm, but other than a feathering in his jaw, he didn't seem to notice. He just stepped closer until his chest pressed against me as he lowered his face to my ear, his nose sinking into my unbound hair.

"I can sense the fear lingering on your body, little rabbit," he whispered, his voice dangerously calm. Gooseflesh erupted down my neck, his breath hitting somewhere much deeper than the shell of my ear and coiling tight.

"I can smell the blood on your arm and the musk of another man hovering over your skin. So, tell me what happened before I assume the answer and track down the motherfucker matching that goddamn stench."

His grip tightened, making his knuckles curl against the side of my breast, and my traitorous body immediately responded. My core heated at that single touch, and I sucked in a breath, somehow wishing he'd both release me and press closer.

The uncontrollable feeling was confusing and infuriating. I had no right to be attracted to a man who'd just spent the night with someone else. The same man I'd once tried to give myself to, only to be told to my face that I'd simply been *convenient*.

I knew he could sense the way my body reacted to his touch, and it only pissed me off more. It wasn't fair that he could hide a thousand secrets, but I couldn't even hide my own emotions from him.

I stepped away as much as I could with his hold of my arm and arched my neck back, glaring up at him. The weighted stares of our audience made me want to curl up and die, but I ignored the desire to run away and hide, refusing to back down from Terek's silent demand.

No matter what shit he'd spouted to Chesie to save my life, he didn't own me.

"It's really none of your business what I did today, Terek," I said, watching his eyes flash. "You don't see me asking who you spent your night with, so I'm in no position to tell you who I spend my personal time with either."

"You left Duma's side."

It wasn't so much a question as a sharp blade slicing through the air to cut into the large man still standing somewhere behind me. I didn't answer, not wanting to throw Duma under a coach when he'd done nothing wrong.

But that didn't stop the corner of my lips from curling ever so slightly, knowing it would infuriate Terek to not know where I'd been.

Good.

Nails dug into my skin, and the air seemed to charge around us, thickening until I could practically taste the fury radiating off him. "You have approximately ten seconds to tell me who you've been with before I—"

"Throw a fit, I know," I finished for him, mentally adding that there was nothing for him *to* do since there was already a chance the guard in question had met his final resting place in that alley. Though, I doubted it. Thank God my savior had been the only one to see Duma and Dex arrive.

"Ace—"

"I came here to get away from the monster who'd controlled everything about my life," I said, interrupting him again and giving him a pointed look so he'd understand I wasn't referring to Tover. "I have no intentions of sitting in a corner and letting you do the same."

If he'd have asked rather than demanded, or if he'd simply not disappeared in the first place, I would've told him about the guard so that we could figure it out together. But commanding me to heel like I was a misbehaving dog? I sure as hell wouldn't tell him anything now.

Letting my hurt, confusion, and fear from the day mix with my anger until I felt ready to explode, I twisted my head and leaned up onto my toes until our noses nearly touched. Terek didn't move to add space between us, but I could've sworn his chest rumbled ever so slightly.

"I belong to no one, so if I want to go out and talk to people, or if I want to open my legs for a handsome man, I will. At least I'm not a hypocritical asshole who slips from one woman's room to another's in the same night."

His pupils blew wide, and for a moment, I thought he'd either throw me across the room or drag me away somewhere to yell at me in private. But just as quickly as he'd reacted, his expression flattened out, and I blinked, wondering if I'd imagined it.

Straightening to his full height, he released me and stepped back, tucking his hands in his pockets like he didn't trust himself not to change his mind and throttle me. Then he tilted his head and inhaled deeply, a cruel smile tainting his mouth as his eyes trailed down my body.

"Is that so?"

"Yes," I snapped, recrossing my arms and wishing he'd go ahead and throw an insult or something so I could scurry off and pretend I hadn't just brought up my sex life in public. Especially when I hadn't even been lucky enough for it to be true. Hell, I hadn't even had a single orgasm in my entire life that hadn't been provided by myself, let alone a handsome man.

"Well, what a disappointing fuck it must have been," he said, each word as uncaring as the last. "For I'm well acquainted with the scent of your arousal, little rabbit, and there's not a hint of it on you."

He didn't raise his voice, but he might as well have screamed with how my body reacted. My cheeks didn't flush—they *flamed*, catching my entire face and neck on fire until I swore I'd be nothing but a boiling puddle at his feet any moment.

"Crimson hell, Terek," Duma said, coming up to stand beside me and gently placing a hand on my arm in silent solidarity. "Calm down. She left with us and is fine. She saw a boy get taken against his will, and it rattled her."

My hands tightened around my body, the reminder of the boy crumpling to the ground as horrifying as it'd been when it'd happened. I'd told the twins about it as we'd made our way back to Tweeds, and if I wasn't so humiliated right now, I might've hugged Duma for his impressive ability to skirt around the truth without actually lying.

Terek's eyes shot to the wide hand resting against my bare skin and then flicked up, searching Duma's face like he expected my touch to burn the man or something. When nothing happened, his brows dropped low again, and his voice hardened.

"That's the exact fucking reason she shouldn't have been out in the first place. What if she'd been seen?"

Duma widened his stance, straightening his spine to stand several inches above Terek. Behind him, I could see Dex's eyes flare dramatically, as if to say *I told you so*, while he began setting glasses out next to the bowls.

"We had a meeting and took her, as is both her right and ours. Since I didn't exactly know when you'd stumble back, I felt no need to leave word," Duma said, lifting his brows in challenge. "And unless Ace has an ability you two failed to mention when you asked for our assistance," he added in a lowered voice, "it wouldn't matter if she'd been seen. Regardless, Dex and I aren't exactly useless, and you well know that."

Terek's jaw worked, but he didn't argue. "Who was she with?"

He didn't even bother looking at me this time, and I saw red. "Don't talk like I'm not standing right here."

"You've proven to be untrustworthy with the answer. Who do I smell on her, Duma?"

Duma opened his mouth, but I stepped between them, letting his hand fall from my arm. If Terek wanted to humiliate me, he'd succeeded. I could still feel a few pairs of eyes on us from those who hadn't gone back to their food yet. But I wasn't going to put Duma in a position to lie for me if I could help it. Not after he and Dex had gone looking for me when I hadn't deserved it.

"I talked to a man who turned out to be just another asshole, is that what you wanted to know? That I attract them even here? Why did you bother coming back if you're just going to be an even bigger one than he was? You said you'd get me to Tover, and you did. I appreciate your help, but I'm not your concern anymore."

I thought I'd be doing him a favor and giving him the out he'd made clear he wanted since the moment he led me from the Wood, but it was the wrong thing to say. Terek's entire body went still, and his eyes flashed black, my only warning before venom spewed from his lips.

"Bored of me already? Tell me, did you make a habit of sneaking around to meet random men Upside too? Or was that none of your husband's concern either?"

My arms fell, and I flinched back like he'd slapped me, the ease with which he mentioned Frederick hurting worse than any strike he could have landed to my face. Regret immediately filled his eyes, but it didn't stop the memories of the night I'd left the Upside from flashing behind my own.

Of Frederick sitting across the table, eyes already glassy as he berated me for my *worthless womb*. Of me finally losing my temper and blaming it on his drinking and failing body, not mine. The threat he'd made as he'd watched me over his next glass. The one that had spurred me to risk everything to run to the Underland when I'd survived everything else he'd thrown at me.

I could practically feel my chest shredding to pieces with each image that slammed into me. Terek may not know what Frederick had planned to do, but he'd learned enough last night. I'd opened my heart yet again and shared part of my deepest shame because I'd trusted him, and he'd tossed it back at me like it didn't matter. Like *I* didn't matter.

Terek stepped forward, an apology in his eyes, but I shook my head, holding my hands out in front of me and swallowing the lump quickly rising up my throat. I was going to cry, and I refused to do it outside the privacy of my room. Instead, I bottled the coming storm as tightly as I could and glared at him with all the anger I possessed.

"Goodnight, Terek." Then I shoved past him and bolted for the stairs, keeping my head down to avoid making eye contact with anyone and praying to God he didn't follow me.

He didn't.

Something crashed downstairs as I wiped at the hot tears already dripping down my cheeks and dug around my pocket for my key, jamming it into the lock of my room.

I heard a curse and a grunt, and then, "Terek, if you even think about touching a thing in this building, I will drag your ass to the Wood myself and feed you to Huka. The whole point of last night was to get this shit out of your system before you came back, you temperamental—"

Not caring to hear the details of what Terek did last night, I slammed the door shut behind me, making sure to lock it this time so he couldn't use food as an excuse to burst in uninvited. I was still starving, my mouth watering at the thought of Dex's warm stew, but I'd rather fall sleep with a screaming stomach than let Terek see me cry over him.

The man was nothing but a beautiful, raging asshole, a fact he was all too happy to remind me of every time my heart convinced me to forget. I knew he cared about my safety in his own dark, twisted way, but it was too overshadowed by how much he clearly loathed himself for it.

There was no way I could tell him about the guard now, even though part of me was terrified to leave Tweeds again until every single one of them left Tover. I had a feeling Terek would lock me in this room until I gave up and went Upside if he found out someone knew the truth about me.

A voice whispered in the back of my mind that he had to have known, and that was why he was so angry about the thought of me talking to anyone. He knew my ability would make people want to…sell me, or whatever the guard's plan had been. Because Terek was the only person who could have told anyone.

I shook my head and squashed the thought as quickly as it'd come. I was almost a hundred percent certain Terek wasn't exactly a good person, but he wouldn't have made me lie to Duma and Dex if he was willing to tell random strangers about me. It had to have just been that one guard's ability, and I had no desire to fight with Terek over a singular man knowing.

More tears escaped, and I wiped my shoulders across my cheeks before reaching down to unlace my boots and remove the blade I'd tucked into one. The second we'd put distance between us and the unconscious guard, Dex had hauled me to the side and made me remove the weapon—which he'd informed me was called a dagger, not a knife—so he could wrap it in cloth.

Apparently, he hadn't trusted me not to cut my ankle off. I hadn't argued. I hadn't trusted myself not to either.

But as excited as I was to finally have the means to defend myself, I didn't have it in me to admire the weapon right now. Not when I had more and more tears blurring my vision. Leaving it wrapped, I laid it on the table beside the bed, where I could easily grab for it if that guard somehow showed up. Then I pulled Mrs. Gayle's watch from my pocket, fingering the familiar, worn metal before placing it beside it.

I had no idea if Mrs. Gayle was wandering the Underland

somewhere, or if she'd gone straight to the afterlife without the need for a middle ground, but if she was, I hoped with all my heart that she was faring far better than I was.

Not caring to change out of my dress, I fell back onto the bed and curled into a ball, allowing myself only five minutes to drown in all the emotions I'd been pushing away since that young boy fell and I'd done nothing. I still didn't understand why they were hunting down people and asking about abilities, or what their queen had to do with it, but I'd talk to the twins and worry about that tomorrow.

Along with finding work and a permanent place to stay.

Steps sounded outside my door, and I curled tighter, wondering if Terek had finally come up to apologize or yell at me some more, but they continued past our rooms, and a door farther down the hall slammed shut.

More tears fell, leaving salty raindrops across my pillow as I tried to convince myself it wasn't disappointment I felt. I didn't want to see him or hear what he had to say. The best thing for both of us was for him to leave. He could go back to patrolling the Wood without a random girl popping up to distract him, and I could make a life without a man attempting to control me.

No matter how much the organ in my chest seemed to riot at the idea.

ADELAÏS

CHAPTER THIRTY-EIGHT

F rederick's face loomed closer and closer, the flash of something bright and orange just out of sight. Oh God, no. Please. He smiled, and teeth that had once been yellowed and dull were now sharp and black, the tips drawing dots of blood along his bottom lip.

I twisted left and right, trying to scream, but he slapped a hand over my mouth so only a choked sob escaped. He raised his other hand, and the tip of the orange glow entered my line of sight. But rather than the letters F.T. at the end of it, a single rose glared back at me.

"Shh," he soothed, his eyes now a piercing blue and his chest covered in white armor as he lowered it to just below my jaw, the heat searing into my skin. "You'll never escape, no matter where you run, Adelaïs."

I thrashed, grabbing onto the hand holding the scalding iron to my neck and gouging my nails in. It made the heat bite deeper into my skin, but I only kicked and tore harder, tears pouring down my face.

Off. I needed it off me.

"*Adelaïs.*"

A sharp flash of pain in my cheek violently flung me into consciousness, and my eyes flew open, relief that it was only a dream hitting me almost as strongly as the pain still lingering across my neck and face. But instead of the outline of my room at Tweeds against the dull glow of the lantern I'd left lit, I saw the dark outline of a form hovering over my bed.

My eyes bulged, and I lurched to the side, panic overriding any other sense as I opened my mouth to scream, but only a muffled sound slipped through as the hand over my mouth squeezed tighter. The intruder leaned in closer, their features hidden beneath a wrapped scarf.

"Stop, Adelais. I'm not going to hurt you."

Hearing my name only made me panic more, and I flared my nostrils, desperately pulling in quick bursts of air through my nose as I fought to open my mouth wider. If I could just bite them and release my face, I could scream for Terek.

I expected them to squeeze harder, but they just shifted, and the pain at my neck suddenly increased, making me hiss in a breath and halt my movements. A dagger. There was a dagger cutting into my neck.

"Crimson hell, Adelais, you're going to get us both killed if you don't stop."

I blinked rapidly, trying to make out more of the intruder's profile while processing their threat. No...*her* threat. That was definitely a female voice, and now that I wasn't blind with panic, the hand around my mouth felt far too small to be any of the guards I'd seen.

With the dim light behind her casting dark shadows around her form, all I could make out were two thin arms stretched toward me, and a pair of pale eyes staring down with nervous fear, not hostility.

"I'm not going to hurt you. I swear. Now, can I move my hands, or are you going to try to scream again?"

I gave the barest shake of my head, not wanting to slice my throat open, but the intruder must have caught it because she immediately pulled back. Her eyes, however, stayed pinned on me, as if ready to leap on me again, if needed.

"Who are you?" I croaked, my voice thick and hoarse.

"Someone who's trying to help you," she repeated, her voice barely audible, even with her close proximity to me. When I made no move to scream or attack her, she tucked her blade into her boot and yanked down the scarf covering her face.

My fear left as shock replaced it, and my mouth fell open. "You!" I said, scrambling to push myself up into a sitting position.

My young alley savior jolted forward to slap her hand over my mouth again, holding her other to her lips and darting a nervous look toward my door. "Unless you feel like entering the final afterlife tonight, lower your damn voice."

I blinked, the urgency in her tone chasing away the last strings of grogginess from my mind. I nodded, and she pulled away again, keeping her attention on the door like she expected someone to barrel through any minute.

"How do you know my name?" I asked, making sure to whisper this time so she wouldn't slap me again.

"What?" she asked, turning back to me.

"My name. How do you know it?"

Something flashed across her face, but I couldn't make it out in the dark before she'd replaced it with a frown. "You told me after I rescued you. Remember?"

"No, I didn't. I said it was—" I paused, suddenly second-guessing myself. I could've sworn I'd introduced myself as Ace, but apparently, I hadn't. Then again, my mind had been a mess of fear and adrenaline when we'd met, so it wasn't all that surprising. I cringed. Great—yet another thing Terek would admonish me for.

"I'd prefer it if you called me Ace," I whispered.

"Fine," she said, darting another look at the door before gesturing to my neck. "I'm sorry about your throat. I wasn't sure if I could trust you, and I had to make sure you wouldn't scream."

I slid off the bed and pressed my fingers to the small cut across my neck, hissing at the sting and trying for the life of me to figure out how she'd thought waking me with a weapon was going to make me *not* want to scream.

"Do you always break into someone's room and wake them with a dagger to the throat?" I asked, feeling something rough brush the side of my foot. I looked down to see the discarded cloth Dex had wrapped around the dagger before noticing the empty table, and my stomach fell.

That's why she was here. She'd risked her life to help me, and I'd thanked her by stealing her weapon. I'd been so blinded by my desire to have protection, I hadn't stopped to consider if it meant something to her.

I was about to apologize, but she'd already stepped away, and I had to crane to hear her hushed whisper from across the room.

"I tried to shake you awake, but you started shouting and thrashing around like a dying fish. I want to help you, but not if it costs me my life," she said, shrugging like that was the most normal explanation in the world.

My instincts screamed at me that something was wrong when she glanced at the door yet again, her own nerves growing stronger by the second. She was scared of something coming in. Or some*one*.

"What do you mean by help? What do you want?"

If she'd only wanted her dagger, she could've broken in, grabbed it, and run. But she hadn't. And she may have saved me once, but I had no idea who this girl really was. Hell, she still hadn't even given me a name, even though she now knew both of mine.

She whipped her head toward me and again held a finger over her lips for me to lower my voice while her other twitched like she was considering pulling that dagger back out. I sighed, tired of this charade already. I was exhausted, wearing dirty clothes, and needed food. Besides, I'd already been whispering. Who on Earth did she think was going to hear—and then it hit me.

Terek.

I narrowed my eyes, suddenly even more cautious about the stranger in my room, but she didn't seem to notice as she stepped right up to me, determination visible in every line of her face. "I'm sorry I scared you, but we need to leave right now."

"I'm not going anywhere with you. I appreciate you saving me before, and I'm sorry I took your dagger, but I'm not—"

"The White Guard are on their way here."

My jaw snapped shut, and I frowned. The White Guard were on their way to Tweeds? Like all of them? According to the twins, Tweeds was the nicest inn in Tover, but a warning crawled up my spine regardless. It was the middle of the night. Why would they just now be coming when rooms were filled, and the tavern was closed?

"They're staying here?"

She shook her head, the chopped edges of her blonde hair shifting along the scarf bunched around her neck. "No, Ace. They're coming here for you."

I lurched away from her, fear rising to the surface again as I desperately searched my room for anything I could use as a weapon—a lit lantern to the face or a book to the back of the head. *Something.* The guard had mentioned some kind of reward for me, and this girl must've heard and come here to make sure I didn't leave before they arrived.

Fuck, if I thought Terek had been angry last night, he was about to lose his mind.

My eyes latched onto my door, and I contemplated my chances of making it to his before she caught me. Yelling wouldn't do me any favors if the guards were already downstairs, but she was smaller than me, so there was a chance I could get there if I caught her by surprise.

I clenched my fists, readying to make a run for it, but she shot forward and blocked me, horror etched into her features. "I know what you're thinking, Ace, and if you ever trusted anyone in your entire life, trust me on this. If you wake him, we are as good as dead. I came to get you out of here, and I mean it, but I won't if you're intent on seeing the afterlife."

I froze, apprehension trickling into my limbs as that voice from last night began to whisper in the back of my mind again. "Terek wouldn't hurt me, nor you, if I asked," I said, though I wasn't all that sure about the last part.

She released an irritated breath and crossed the room to grab the boots and socks I'd abandoned at the door. "Crimson hell, you don't know anything, do you? I knew you were new, but I didn't realize you were a damn infant here."

I bristled, but she continued, dropping everything at my feet and motioning for me to put them on. "You must have an ability if they're after you, so surely you know about the magic here, yes?"

I nodded, following her silent order. I had a feeling I'd need them anyway if the White Guard was truly headed this way. Even if this girl was wrong about them coming for me, Terek would never let us stay with them here. Not with how viscerally he'd reacted to them simply being in Tover.

"Every member of the guard has an ability," she whispered.

"I'm aware." Horrifyingly so.

"Well, let's just say a few of them have ways of tracking their targets," she added, throwing my cloak at me next. "And after what happened in the alley, you are target number one. So, unless you want to be woken again by your very angry admirer, we need to go. Right now."

My fear turned to terror as I snatched the cloak and threw it over my shoulders, wincing when the clasp hit the cut on my neck. I was such an idiot. Why hadn't I thought of that? The guards were literally hunting for names on a list, of course they had a way to track people down.

"All right," I whispered, twisting my tangled hair back and stuffing it under the cloak so I could throw the hood up over my head. I still needed to relieve myself, and my breath was probably horrid, but I'd deal with all that later.

Right now, I needed to suck up my pride, get Terek, and hope he'd let me explain everything before he strangled me and the twins. "Let me go wake—"

"You're not listening to me," she snapped, her voice finally rising above the faintest whisper. "If you wake him, you are fucked, Ace. Royally fucked, and I will leave you here. Are you so blinded by his pretty face that you can't see he's working with them?"

I shook my head, but that damn voice grew stronger. *He was the only one who knew what you can do.* "You're wrong; Terek wouldn't do that."

Her face dropped, a deep-seated hatred I'd only ever felt for one person igniting her pale eyes as her jaw spasmed. "You have no idea what that man is capable of. How do you think the guard knew who you were in the first place?"

My head whipped side to side until I felt like it would fall right off my shoulders. "You're wrong. He didn't even want me here to begin with." But the words no longer had any strength behind them as doubt crept in about the man I didn't really know at all.

Her face contorted, disgust making her eyes appear even more hollow. "Yeah, well, I'm guessing things changed when he saw the reward for you. Tell me, where was he last night?"

I opened my mouth only to close it again, betrayal lashing through me like a whip. Terek had never been kind, but he'd been acting testier than usual ever since we got here. Was that why? My eyes stung as uncertainty coiled inside me. Was Duma in on it too? Dex?

The girl's eyes softened, and she reached out and took my hand, squeezing it. "If you don't believe me, you can come back tomorrow after the guards have left and do whatever you want, but I'm leaving, Ace. You can either come with me or put your trust in a man who's turned in many others before you."

I nodded. I'd think over everything she'd said later when I wasn't half asleep and terrified. For now, I was going to put myself first and make sure I was safe.

She smiled and grabbed the lantern from the table, holding it in front of her while she used her other hand to yank her scarf back over her mouth and nose. "Great. Now seal your lips up tight and let's go."

"Wait," I said, suddenly realizing I was about to trust a complete stranger with my life. "What's your name?"

She looked over her shoulder at me, doubt clouding her expression before she sighed and turned back, unlocking the door. "I'm Hara."

EVERY STEP WE took down the silent hall had my heart sitting so high in my throat, I thought I'd choke on it. Though Hara seemed to possess the same skill as Terek to magically avoid making noise, I did not. With each creak of the floor beneath my boots, I tensed, waiting for Terek to slam open his door and demand where I was going, daggers gripped in his palms.

But he didn't. Even as we made it to the stairs with only the lantern Hara held and the flickering sconces sporadically placed along the walls, he didn't show. And it suddenly hit me that he might not even be here anymore after I'd all but ordered him to leave.

When we finally made it to the main floor, I automatically turned left to head into the tavern toward the front door, but I only made it a step before Hara fisted my cloak and wrenched me back. It caused my cloak to dig into my cut, and I cursed, nearly stumbling into her.

I rubbed at my neck as I righted myself, shooting her a glare. She could've just tapped my shoulder. The girl had absolutely zero social skills. But Hara didn't react to my irritation other than to silently jab her finger to the door at the end of the hall. The one I'd originally assumed was a supply closet.

Pulling my hood down lower, I obeyed and hurried after her, prepared to make a run for it when she opened the door. But rather than a back alley and a blast of cold, night wind, only a square room and musty air greeted us.

Shelves lined the walls, each ladened with crates, clothes, blankets, candles, and numerous other necessities. And besides a few brooms tucked into the corner, the only other things in there were two huge barrels that reeked of ale sitting below a lone, square window.

All right, so not a back door after all then. Wonderful.

Slicing Hara a look, I whispered, "If there's a back door, it's likely through the kitchen. We're better off just going through the front. If there are any night workers, I doubt they'll think twice about people leaving an inn."

Hara ignored me and closed the door behind us, waving her hand at the window which appeared to already be open as far as the pane would allow. Which wasn't much. "We can't risk it. The guards have almost everyone in their pockets. We're going to have to leave the same way I came in."

"You want me to fit through that?" I asked, my voice rising in pitch on the last word. I may not have been the curviest woman to ever exist, but I definitely had a larger frame than my slender companion did and was not convinced I could twist my lower half through the gap.

Although I couldn't make out her expression behind her scarf, I could definitely hear the huff of laughter that slipped out at whatever she saw in mine. "I can always cut a few inches off your hips, if you think it'd help."

I bit both my cheeks to keep from laughing at her offer, my sanity clearly at its breaking point. "You may have to if I get stuck."

Testing the barrels to make sure I wouldn't fall into a vat of ale, I laid my hands down flat over the tops and attempted to push up onto them, my feet scrambling against the sides to hoist myself up. Upper arm strength wasn't something I'd ever had need of before, but the round edges weren't exactly helping either. As my face heated with embarrassment, it was the latter excuse I was going to stick to.

I was just about to let go and use the shelf to help me up when a hand smacked into my ass and shoved, practically tossing me over and through the window. I flung my hands out to grab the ledge and glared daggers over my shoulder, my heart a steady beat in my ears. "That wasn't necessary."

"Yes, it was. Now get the fuck out of the window before even this way is blocked."

I cursed under my breath and stretched my arms through, carefully twisting and working my lower half over the well-worn frame one uncomfortable, bruising inch at a time. I'd barely landed face first onto the filthy cobblestones and pushed up to my feet when Hara dropped down next to me like a damn rabbit, looking around and dusting off her clothes.

"I don't hear them yet, so we should be fine."

I nodded to show I'd heard her and looked up at the line of dark windows along the back of Terek's and my floor. I had no idea if he'd truly tried to collect a reward for me, or if he was even in his room tonight, but I couldn't help but look for him anyway, imagining him standing in the window, watching me. The way his jaw would tighten as he clenched it, and how the black would overrun the blue of his eyes when he realized I was leaving.

My heart squeezed painfully, and I subconsciously pressed my fingertips against it, feeling like there was a sudden pressure sitting on my chest, urging me to go back inside. But it was probably just a combination of nerves and hunger. I certainly had more than enough of both to go around.

"Okay, now what?" I asked, glancing around the corner to make sure no guards were coming up the street yet. "Do you live nearby?"

I shivered, praying she said yes. If we could get to wherever she lived or was staying at, I could just hunker down for the night and wait the guards out. Though, now that I thought about it, I supposed once they found me missing from Tweeds, they'd just start tracking me again to wherever I'd gone. I frowned. Come to think of it, how *did* Hara plan to keep them from finding us?

"I'm sorry, you know. It's nothing personal."

"Sorry about what?" I asked, glancing at the windows one last time before dropping my gaze. "Waking me with a dagger or shoving me out a window?"

"Lying. And for this."

I turned to look over my shoulder just in time to see a torn expression cloud her features a split second before something slammed into the side of my head. There was a moment of sharp pain, and then blackness crashed through me like a wave.

TEREK

CHAPTER THIRTY-NINE

E ven in sleep, her heartbeat spoke to me. A steady rhythm I couldn't shut out. With each thrum against my ears, my body begged me to respond to her call. To answer it with my own, matching each chaotic beat with the slam of my hips until her screams drowned out everything else.

I ground my teeth together and locked my senses as tightly as I could, but it only got louder, vibrating through me until I thought I'd lose my mind. I was seconds from grabbing the blades from beneath my pillow and driving them into my eardrums to shut her out when I heard the telltale click of a latch, followed by soft footsteps padding across the hall.

My broken door creaked as it opened, and I shot up, a hand shooting to my daggers as my gaze sliced through the darkness, only to see Ace standing on the threshold. She wore nothing but the chemise I'd seen her clutching the night before, her curved form and nipples clearly visible beneath it as the pebbled tips pushed at both the thin cotton and my fucking sanity.

What in the fiery pits of hell was she doing in here?

I waited for her to speak, half expecting her to rip into me the way I deserved after what I'd said downstairs and demand I leave again. Which I wasn't going to fucking do, even though every working part of my brain knew I should.

But she didn't. She said nothing as she silently closed the door behind her and stepped deeper into my room. My brow furrowed as I took in her face, searching it for whatever had sent her in here when I was certain I was the last person she wanted to see.

Then her scent hit me, effectively shoving every conscious thought out of my head except for the thick, heady smell of her arousal. It crashed into me like a sledgehammer, catching me off guard and drawing an instinctual rumble from my chest.

Crimson take me, she smelled *fucking divine*.

I watched her cross the room, my body practically convulsing as I attempted to block out her scent, knowing I should tell her to run back to her room while she still could. Demand it. But no matter how I tried to force my mouth to work, I couldn't get the words past my clenched teeth.

Not as her legs hit the edge of my bed, igniting a burning ember in the center of my chest, and not as she climbed up onto the mattress on all fours and crawled over my body, detonating that ember into an uncontrollable inferno that set every inch of me on fire.

I couldn't peel my eyes away from hers, even as her chemise dipped to show the swells of her breasts and her hair fell in dark curtains around her face, begging to be wrapped around my fists. I was utterly enraptured by the glow of life staring back at me in those hazel depths.

Yet, even as her hands landed on my chest and her soft center settled over my painfully hard one, I still didn't speak. Because I knew if I did, I'd taste her arousal on the air, and I wouldn't be able to stop myself from launching her over my face and sinking my tongue into the source itself, smothering this cursed desire with the taste of her own.

Then again, maybe if I did, I'd finally be able to claw this constant awareness of her out of my chest.

Taking advantage of my silence, Ace crawled higher and slid her hands up my body until she reached the top of the blanket strewn over me. The one hiding my very naked body from view. She bit her lip in a way that immediately made me want to do the same and curled her fingers in, pulling the blanket down to where her hem bunched at her hips and her center pressed into me.

My nostrils flared.

Her bare fucking center.

I swallowed hard, thanking God when her eyes dropped and freed me from their trance, only for the demon inside me to rise to attention when she stared down at my body with pure hunger in her gaze. And when her pale fingers traced along my muscles and up over my nipples, my demon threw itself against the walls of its cage.

My eyelids fluttered shut at her tentative touch, and I shuddered, using every bit of my strength to keep that part of me contained while it smashed into its splintering cage again and again, snarling and fighting to escape. To take over my body and mind and destroy her. To permanently mark her as *mine*.

I sucked in another lungful of air saturated with her scent, focusing on closing my senses and getting her out of the room before I lost control completely, when her nails suddenly dug in, and she rolled her hips down into me.

My eyes flew open, and a growl ripped from my chest at her quiet moan as she ground along the length of me. I fisted my hands to keep myself from grabbing at her. It would be so damn easy to slide the blanket out from between us and thrust myself into her wet heat.

"Crimson fuck," I murmured, unable to hold it in any longer as I tried and failed to remind myself of all the reasons I couldn't get close to this woman. Each thought flickered to life, only to immediately disappear with each flare of her arousal as she continued to move, the blanket slipping lower with each roll.

She needed to leave. This couldn't fucking happen. She shouldn't feel so good, shouldn't look like a goddamn goddess above me, shouldn't taste and feel and smell like she was made for me.

She belonged with the living, with fresh air and a warm sun, and I belonged here, eternally tied to the red-haired devil who sought to destroy the utterly perfect soul of the stunning creature above me. But even that painful truth died the second the blanket finally slipped beneath my waist.

"Ace, you need to—*fuck*."

She sighed at the contact and fell against me, her hands sliding up to grasp onto my shoulders as she brushed her mouth over mine. "Please, Terek."

The cage disintegrated before the last syllable of my name left her lips, and I smashed my mouth to hers, sinking both hands into her hair and fisting it at the roots in a way that made my cock throb painfully between us. I pulled the strands taut, trapping her in place and forcing her mouth wider so my tongue could dive in, taking everything I needed, whether she wanted to give it or not.

Her taste swirled in my mouth with each demanding sweep of my tongue, reminding me of that first kiss that had destroyed me and poisoned the way I'd seen her. The one I'd spent years trying and failing to forget.

Another moan slipped past her lips, and I kissed her harder, dropping my hands to her waist and sliding them beneath her chemise to press into the soft skin of her stomach. Then I launched up, nearly blacking out as my tip pressed against her clit, and twisted us to the side, needing her beneath me.

But I underestimated the strength coursing through my muscles as my abilities roared to life unchecked, and we shot off the bed.

The back of my head audibly cracked against the floor, and I cursed, reaching out to catch Ace, only to grasp at empty air. My eyes flew open at her absence, and I heaved in air, my body stunned and my senses making me lightheaded and nauseated, like I'd just woken from drowning all over again.

Lurching upright, I held my head in my hands and sprinted through my mind, slamming every door to my abilities shut before I inevitably signed my death warrant with Duma by vomiting on the floor.

"What the actual fuck," I muttered, finally gaining a firm hold on my control and resting a hand over the back of my head where I'd nearly dented it into the floor. In all my years Upside and Under, I'd never had a dream like that. Sure, I'd dreamt of fucking a woman before, that woman being Ace more times than I wanted to admit, but crimson hell, this one had felt so undeniably real.

I ran the tip of my tongue over my lip, almost expecting them to be swollen and taste of her, but I was left with nothing but a throbbing head, an excruciatingly hard erection, and my growing self-hatred.

Goddamn it, I'd just sworn to protect her from all men who might hurt her, and that included me. *Especially me.* Hell, I'd lost my shit downstairs just a few hours ago when she'd walked in carrying someone else's scent, because I'd thought I'd already failed.

Dreaming about fucking her so hard she wouldn't be able to walk around town for days wasn't part of that plan, no matter how much the lower half of me disagreed.

Cursing my inability to control myself around her, even in my dreams, I snatched up my clothes and threw them on, resolved to sleep fully dressed from now on. The fabric grated against my sensitive skin, and I winced as I walked to the basin and splashed cold water on my face. It did nothing to shut her out, the lingering sensation of her lips on mine still as vivid as it'd been in the dream. I cursed, slamming my hands down onto the counter.

Kissing Ace all those years ago had changed everything, but I knew, now more than ever, that I could never let it happen again. I'd never recover, and I'd never let her leave. I'd become even worse than Lizbeth herself, because I wouldn't just take Ace's soul, I'd consume it entirely, letting my darkness smother out her light until there was nothing left for her except me.

I'd ruin her just as she'd so easily ruined me.

I bared my teeth at the thought and picked up the basin, dumping the entire thing over my head and focusing on each freezing rivulet as they coursed down my body.

She was not mine.

TWENTY MINUTES LATER, fully dressed, and with every barrier of my mind firmly in place, I walked across the hall and knocked on her door, both needing and dreading to see her.

"Ace."

She didn't answer, and I frowned, having expected her to already be awake and waiting. According to Dex, she'd been up bright and early the previous morning, not wanting to waste a second of the day. I raised my hand to knock again but hesitated, the idea of waking her when she was finally getting decent rest irking me.

We'd traveled hard to get here, and she'd had another long day yesterday with whatever she'd been out doing with Duma and Dex. Something I planned to weed out of one of them today. Still, as much as I'd rather let her sleep, she needed to wake up so we could discuss our next steps. Especially when I knew how much she was going to fight me on it.

Ace was slowly coming back to life again, and not just because she was finally free from the shackles she'd worn for so long, though I was sure that was a large reason. She liked it here. I could see it in the way she'd let her guard down around Duma and Dex, and in the way her hazel eyes had begun to light up again.

When we'd left the Wood, I'd had every plan to leave her ass at Tweeds until she inevitably worked out her personal issues and went home, but that was before she'd trusted me with the truth of why she'd stayed. As much as she didn't belong here, I couldn't find it in myself to push her back Upside. Not yet.

But with the White Guard now actively searching for souls when that had once been a job left to Soul Seekers, she wasn't as safe in Tover as I'd originally hoped. Not with how many were here and how quickly they could have her dragged to Ardenglass.

There were a handful of other towns within a few days' travel, but none of them felt safe enough if the White Guard continued on as they were. Canden wouldn't be much safer, given the amount of trading the city regularly did with Ardenglass, and Abgrove, a rural town just east of Canden, may have been small enough not to attract Lizbeth's attention, but they lacked both defenses and supplies.

Wenham, however, was a different story. Far north and located miles within the Wood itself, the secluded settlement was not only significantly newer, but it had been built by a group of people who hadn't feared Lizbeth's response.

Having thought them fools for making a home surrounded by Creatures, I'd never once visited the town, but I'd yet to hear any stories regarding attacks on Wenham, nor had Lizbeth expressed any intent on sending her guards through to punish them.

Though that was likely due to the fact that the Creatures tended to viciously attack her guards anytime they stepped foot within the trees, rather than a lack of interest on her part.

It was the latter that had circled my head as I lay in bed last night, staring at my door and the woman asleep just across from it, that sealed it for me. Traveling to Wenham was going to be miserable and dangerous, but once there, she'd be safe from Lizbeth and her damn hunters.

She could get an apprenticeship wherever she wanted, draw until her fingers went numb, and live out her days for as long as the Underland allowed her to. And I'd go back to Ardenglass to live out the rest of mine, killing at Lizbeth's command until the darkness finally took me. Just like Ace had wanted yesterday.

As it was, I was already toeing the line of how long I could be gone from the Wood without drawing both Lizbeth's attention and the Creatures'. They may not have attempted an organized attack yet, but my gut told me they weren't far from it. And if something happened even remotely close to the city, and I wasn't there to stop it, Lizbeth's wrath would hit anyone I'd ever been associated with.

Duma and Dex were skilled at pissing me off and sticking their noses into my business, but I'd never risk their eternities over my inability to stop involving myself with the wrong women.

Shaking my head and tucking those thoughts away for another day, I reached up and knocked on Ace's door again, louder this time. "Come on, Ace, wake up. I know you're mad, but we need to talk. Plus, if you don't hurry up, there'll be nothing left downstairs but tea."

There was still no response, not even a grumble about dirty plant water or the rustling of her sheets. My frown deepened. It was one thing to avoid me last night after I'd unfairly lashed out at her in my fear and panic, but it wasn't like her to ignore me. She was more likely to swing the door open and tell me to piss off.

It wasn't until I knocked a third time, and she still hadn't made a sound, that the hair on the back of my neck suddenly stood on end, my instincts telling me something was wrong. Wrapping a hand around her doorknob, I cracked open the barrier to my hearing and zeroed it in on the inside of her room, my body freezing when I realized what felt off.

It wasn't just the lack of movement, but the lack of life.

I couldn't hear her heartbeat.

I'd been so fucked up after that damn dream that I'd thrown myself into the day's plans, desperate for any kind of distraction that would help me keep my head where it needed to be. I'd been making lists, plotting which roads to take, and figuring out what all I'd need to buy that I hadn't noticed just how silent my mind was outside of my own thoughts.

And now that I had, the silence was deafening.

"I'm coming in," I said, giving her one more chance in case she'd somehow been indisposed. Then I twisted the knob sharply, intending to break the lock and incur even more of Duma's wrath, only for it to nearly break off in my hand when it twisted with ease.

I glared down at it, a curse already building in my throat. What was she thinking going to sleep with the goddamn door unlocked? Did she have any idea the kind of people who occupied the other rooms? The sheer number of drunken idiots who stayed downstairs until they were kicked out and could waltz right in while she slept?

Fuming with irritation at a woman who seemed incapable of making a single good decision when it came to her safety, I slammed my shoulder into the door and flung it open. Both daggers were in my palms a second later when my eyes took in the half-made bed and empty room.

"Ace."

Silence. I stared at her abandoned bed, the covers hastily thrown aside as if she'd left in a hurry. Then I slowly took in the rest. Nothing was amiss, no broken furniture or ripped clothing, but there was something about the space I couldn't quite put my finger on. It just felt *off.*

I walked farther into the room, noticing the soiled clothing from her trip to Tover, tossed in a corner like she would've rather burned it, and the thin chemise that'd haunted me still folded over the back of a chair. There was no other hint of her, apart from the lingering scent of vanilla, and another female scent I recognized but couldn't place. A maid, maybe?

"Where the fuck are you?" I mumbled.

I strained my hearing, but I couldn't make out her heartbeat from downstairs either. I tucked my daggers back into their sheaths, considering the possibility that she'd left the Underland. Not on purpose, no matter how angry I'd made her, but maybe there was a limit to how long her body could withstand being here. But I quickly tossed the idea out.

She was still here somewhere. I could feel her. It was more like an awareness within my chest than a pull, but I knew it was her. I just needed to take a deep breath and calm down. She likely raced downstairs to eat after skipping dinner last night while I'd still been in bed, fantasizing about feasting between her legs.

I'd just twisted away from her bed, ready to sprint down there and bite into Duma for whatever errand he'd apparently sent her out on, when a glint of something caught my eye from just underneath it. Curious what Ace would hide beneath her bed, I crouched down and slid my hand under to find a small, chainless pocket watch. My brow furrowed as I straightened up, turning it in my hand.

The lace design was unique, if not old and chipped, but there wasn't a remarkable thing about it, save for the deep blue of its face as I popped it open. Even the intricate hands no longer appeared to work. I would've tossed it right back onto the floor, assuming it to have been there awhile, had it not been for the strength of Ace's scent all over it.

I could practically see the path her fingers had worked over its worn lid, caressing the discolored metal over and over for reasons I could only begin to imagine. How long had she had it? I'd never seen it before, which told me she had to usually keep it close to her. So why would she have suddenly left it?

She could've forgotten it, since it seemed to have fallen off her side table, but given the infuriating woman had arrived to the Underland not even wearing shoes, if she'd brought this, it had to be more than just a broken watch to her.

Everything about this was wrong. Ace may hate me right now, but she wouldn't have left in such a hurry that she forgot her only belonging.

Nostrils flaring, I blew open my other senses, letting the world slam in, and I smelled it. A faint, metallic tang emanating from her bed that had my hand gripping her watch so tightly, the laced design embedded itself into my palm.

That roiling darkness raised its head inside me and inhaled deeply as I dropped the watch into my pocket and flung Ace's blanket off the bed. Sure enough, right in the center of her pillow was a constellation of blood.

The walls were a blur as my hold disintegrated, and I flew down the hall at a speed that burned my eyes, barely avoiding cracking a hole in the wall as I launched myself around the corner and down the stairs.

I slammed my hands onto the bar, and every eye in the packed tavern shot to me in unison. "Where the fuck is she?"

TEREK

CHAPTER FORTY

Dex gaped at me over the jug of freshly squeezed juice in his fist, the cup beneath it tipped and pouring across the surface. He wore a hunter green tunic today, and both it and his arms were covered in a light dusting of flour.

"Come again?"

"Ace," I growled, forcing her name out through clenched teeth and trying to rein in my strength so I wouldn't unintentionally crack their bar in half. "Where is she?"

There were pounding steps, and then the door behind him whipped open, revealing a matching bald head and a scowling face. "What the crimson is going on out here?"

Dex twisted to grab a towel from the hook on the wall behind him and began mopping up the spilled juice. "The deranged man from last night is back."

Duma leaned farther out of the cracked door, and his eyes met mine before nearly rolling up into the back of his head. He heaved a sigh. "Give me a minute. I'll be right out."

The door shut, and I snapped my gaze back to Dex, fuming and gripping the edge of the bar to keep myself from pointing a very real weapon at him instead. Friend or not, if he sent Ace off into Tover alone, he was going to be covered in a lot more than flour.

"Answer the question. Have you seen Ace?"

Dex's humored expression fell when he finally seemed to pick up on the urgency behind my demand. As if the death staring out at him from my eyes wasn't enough.

"No," he said, hanging the towel back up and leaning his forearms on the bar. "Not since last night when you showed your ass, and she gave you what for."

Duma pushed into the main room, the scent of seared meat wafting from the kitchen as he wiped his hands over his apron. He looked from Dex to me and crossed his arms, more than ready to go toe-to-toe with me if I made a single move against his brother.

"What's going on?"

"Ace isn't here, and there's blood on her pillow. Just tell me if you've seen her." I pressed my lips together, realizing I'd begun yelling again, and inhaled slowly, forcing myself to release the wood one finger at a time. "Please."

They both stiffened, sharing a loaded look I didn't like, but it was the way their hearts began beating just a little too fast that immediately set me on edge. "What is it? What do you know?"

Duma cleared his throat and widened his stance, his brown eyes darting around me to take in all the customers, as if calculating just how many were about to become casualties if I lost my shit.

"Something may have happened yesterday."

I swallowed down a curse, already knowing by his careful tone what he was about to say. I fucking knew it.

"What?" I demanded, my voice sounding like I'd choked on a pile of rocks as it took everything in me not to slap my hand over his mouth to prevent him from giving life to the words.

"Nah, that's not how this works," he said, shaking his head. He shifted his weight, leaning forward to rest a hand suspiciously close to the fruit and paring knife. "I'll tell you, but no matter how pissed you get, you're not to touch a single thing in my business. I know you can't always control it, but I fucking mean it, Terek. Lose your shit outside my walls, or I'll pin your hands to this bar."

"What. Happened."

"Your word. Not a single thing."

My nostrils flared, and it took everything in me to remind myself that I trusted both of them and didn't actually want to press my daggers to their throats. Exhaling sharply, I bit out a gruff, "Fine."

Duma eyed me for one more weighted moment before nodding. He was right, I couldn't always control my heightened senses and emotions. Hell, my entire history with Ace proved that. But he knew better than most that I didn't go back on my word, even when I wanted to.

"We all left together, as she told you, but she didn't stay with us the entire time. Don't give me that look," he said, stabbing a finger at me. "The White Guard showed up, and the crowd responded as expected. She'd agreed to come back here while we went ahead with our meeting."

And she'd lied. Of course, she had. Ace had never had freedom and had always been too curious about the Underland for her own good. There was no way she would've locked herself back up inside, and honestly, I should've known better than to expect her to.

But I knew there was something else Duma still wasn't telling me, something I hadn't stopped thinking about since I'd caught the scent on her yesterday. The hesitancy in his gaze was all I needed to confirm what I'd already known but hadn't wanted to accept.

"The man I smelled on her. It was a White Guard, wasn't it?"

He dipped his chin, and fury exploded inside me, licking at the walls of my control as unfiltered panic built up them like rotting ivy. I was going to find whoever had laid a hand on her and cut off each of his fucking fingers.

Right after I broke Duma's nose.

"Let me get this straight," I said, tilting my head and listening to his heartbeat. "You let a White Guard approach her and didn't think that was pertinent information to tell me?"

"I didn't *let* him do anything, so take your hands off your damn daggers. I would've handled the bastard if it'd come to that, but he was already incapacitated when we arrived. Ace wasn't harmed—"

"Yes, she was," I snapped, remembering the dried blood on her arm.

It hadn't been more than a scratch, but it'd been enough.

Duma slanted me a look, silently telling me to calm down, but he didn't waste his breath arguing. "Ace is a grown ass woman and didn't want you to know, Terek. Besides, since when did you start caring so much about new arrivals? Last we spoke, you made it clear she wasn't yours."

My lip curled, hating that he was right. I didn't have a claim on her, apart from the thread that connected us, tugging me toward the door of Tweeds even now. That tug didn't make her mine, nor could I follow it until I completely understood what I'd be walking into, and something Duma said about the guard being incapacitated didn't add up.

Ace had a fire in her, even if she didn't see it yet. I knew she'd go down kicking and screaming before she rolled over for anyone again, but passion and determination didn't make her a match for a trained guard.

I speared his brother with a look. People always thought Duma was the more terrifying of the two because of his quiet nature and uncanny aim with an axe, but it was Dex they needed to be cautious of. Duma might have a temper, but Dex would take someone down with a smile on his face.

"Did you kill him?"

Dex's jaw rolled, but he didn't answer. Glancing behind me, he raised an arm and gestured for one of the workers to take over before tipping his head for me to follow them into the kitchen. The moment the door shut, he sighed heavily.

"You're thinking Ace was taken last night?" he asked.

"Yes."

Between the blood, the watch weighing heavy in my pocket, and now the guard, there was zero doubt in my mind. My hatred for the utter uselessness of my abilities when I slept rose, and the worst part was, Ace had no idea. Did she think I'd heard her be taken but hadn't cared? Did she fight to get to my room before being silenced?

The possibilities had me wanting to hunt down every guard in

Tover, but no matter how much I craved to smell their blood, there was no way to kill an entire host without warranting Lizbeth's attention. Our history may have granted me more liberty than most, but even my leash was only so long. She wouldn't bat an eye to shorten it if I pushed her too far.

Duma reached behind his back to untie his apron, folding it in half and laying it beside a deep sink that reeked of soap and stale food. "Ace has an ability, doesn't she?"

I worked my jaw and glared. Not because his question had pissed me off—they already suspected the answer—but because I was pissed at myself. If I'd just told them from the beginning, none of this would've happened. They never would've let a new soul with an ability go off alone, and Ace's life was worth more than her secrets.

"Yes."

"A strong one?"

I nodded. "One Lizbeth would sacrifice almost anything for."

Dex seemed to pale, and Duma cursed. "Well, that explains your involvement, I guess." He rubbed a hand over the back of his neck and grimaced. "And I think I'm about to make it a whole lot worse."

The demon inside me raised its head and growled, hackles rising within its cage. What the hell could be worse than Lizbeth's men dragging Ace to Ardenglass, unless the bitch herself was here?

"Just spit it out already. I don't have time for this."

"You asked if I killed him," Dex said, removing his apron as well to wipe away the flour along his forearms. "I didn't. I didn't even touch the bastard. He was already unconscious when we found her, Terek."

Duma cursed again and turned to grab a small pack from the corner shelf, quickly stuffing it with meat, cheese, rags, and a flask. "He'd cornered her in an alley. We only found her because someone pointed us in their direction when we'd asked after her likeness."

I saw fucking red. The woman had run away from someone who'd branded her like a damn animal and had finally made it here, only to be cornered like one all over again. And I'd had no idea.

She'd been upset about the way I'd run from her room, thinking I'd ditched her to sleep with a random woman rather than fighting drunkards in the streets as I'd done. She'd made a dig about sleeping with someone as well to try to hide the fact that I'd hurt her, and I'd lost all sense, practically gutting her in punishment. Crimson fucking hell, no wonder she hadn't told me what'd happened.

"—knocked him out."

"What?" I snapped, focusing back in on Dex and realizing I hadn't been paying attention to whatever he was rambling about. "What did you just say?"

"I said, Hara was the one to knock him out. She did her little disappearing act the second she saw us, but I don't know how long they were together, or what Ace might've told her before we arrived."

Everything went silent in my head. Hara. Hara had found Ace. Not a random guard who only hoped she had an ability worth something, but Hara. The person who was conniving and selfish, who knew what Ace could do, and who hated me with a passion.

The coincidence of Hara not only being in Tover but stumbling upon Ace out of the thousands of souls here was incomprehensible. If I ever laid eyes on whatever deity controlled fate, I'd pluck theirs from their sockets and shove them down their throat.

"Hara is a Soul Seeker," I gritted out, my head beginning to pound from all the noises and smells I was failing to block out. "What the fuck else did you think she was there for?"

"Don't even think about blaming us for this. You asked me to keep an eye on her, but you didn't say shit about her having an ability. You of all people know how fucking stupid that was. *Especially* when you also obviously failed to tell Ace anything that might've kept her from wandering off in the first place," Duma said, moving to tower over me and shoving the full pack into my chest.

I gripped it, thankful Duma knew me well enough to know my intention to follow her without me having to say it out loud. I had no argument to his accusation. I *did* know how stupid it'd been to keep the truth from Ace. It'd been an oversight I'd already planned on rectifying today, and now, it was too late.

God, it was no wonder I hadn't heard anything last night, even with normal senses. Hara would've used her ability to get into the room and then manipulated Ace's ignorance against her. It was her specialty and the reason she was one of Lizbeth's favorites.

And depending on if Ace was in a position to fight back, who knew how far Hara would be able to transport the two of them? From what I could remember, there was a limit to how many times Hara could use her ability before she grew too tired, but when she could move miles in the span of a blink, a few times was all she'd need to get far ahead of us.

"*Fuck!*"

"I know it's not ideal, Terek, but she'll be okay," Dex said, raising his hands and wincing when my eyes sliced to his. "We've all been through it. It sucks, but it's just life here. She'll be dropped in Ardenglass after it's done, and you'll be able to—"

"No, she won't."

Lizbeth wouldn't let Ace go until she'd experimented and learned to control whatever ability Ace's soul gave her. And if it was anything like mine, the process could take years.

I wasn't convinced Lizbeth could go Upside with Ace's soul, not when her own body had desecrated centuries ago, but it was the unknown of what ability it *would* give her that had ice blanketing my fury. Anger and destruction weren't going to help, no matter how my muscles sought an outlet. I needed to think through my next steps carefully.

"Did you ever hear word of the bounty Lizbeth put out that promised a soul as reward?" I asked, keeping my voice low and listening for their physical reactions to my words. It was dangerous to tell them, to tell anyone who'd suffered from the queen's greed, but they had none. Only open curiosity on their faces.

"Vaguely," Duma said, his brow furrowing as he grappled for the memory. "I remember laughing about it and thinking she'd finally lost her mind. Wasn't it supposedly about…oh, fuck."

Yeah. That about summed it up.

"WAIT," DUMA SAID, after I'd quickly given them a rundown of how Ace was alive and how Lizbeth had come to know about her existence. I barely turned toward him, already tucking the pack beneath my cloak and checking my daggers. I needed to leave.

"What?"

He hesitated. "Have you considered…"

"Considered *what?*"

He sighed, as if I was purposefully not seeing an obvious possibility, and he didn't want to be the one to tell me. "If she can leave at will, have you considered that maybe she went home? No offense, Terek, but you haven't exactly treated her well. Maybe she realized this wasn't where she was meant to be."

The thing was, she *wasn't* meant to be here. That had never been a question, just a cold hard fact that neither of us fully wanted to admit for very different reasons. But as much as I wished Duma could be right, and that Hara hadn't clearly held a blade to her throat, I knew without a shadow of a doubt Ace was still here.

"She didn't. She'd have never gone back to her life Upside. Trust me."

It was Dex who spoke next. "I agree with Terek. You should've seen the fire that blazed behind her eyes when she saw the art shop. I swear she fucking glowed at the sight. It doesn't sit right with me that she'd leave so suddenly."

My heart squeezed at that, jealousy slinking in like a serpent that he'd been the one to take her there and see her soul flare to life. Duma, however, still didn't look convinced. "Be that as it may, I'm not abandoning my business to search for a woman who got tired of you treating her like an unwanted burden."

"I can feel her," I ground out, hatred burning through me at his words. Not at him, but at myself. Because I *had* been treating her that way, trying to keep distance between us. Thinking that even if she hated me, she'd at least be safe.

They both straightened, glancing around the room as if Ace was hiding in a corner somewhere. "If you can sense her, she must be close," Dex started, but I cut him off with a shake of my head.

Fuck, I didn't want to be here. I should have left the second I'd noticed her missing.

"I didn't mean with my abilities." I slipped a hand into my pocket, fisting Ace's watch as I rubbed absently at my chest with my other. "I can feel her, no matter where I am. It's why I knew when she would appear in the Wood. I can't shut her out. Trust me, I've tried."

"All right."

"All right?" All right, I was insane? That I was fucked in the head for losing my damn mind over a woman who shouldn't even be here? For feeling like my entire body would turn inside out if I didn't hear her heartbeat soon?

"All right, as in, that's enough for me. Dex, pack two more bags. I'll be right back," Duma said, nodding to his brother and moving around me to slip back through the door to the main room.

My hand whipped out and snagged his arm, halting him. "Why?" I needed to know, to hear his reason while I was attuned to his heart so I could discern his motives. I trusted him with my life, but I no longer trusted anyone with Ace's.

"Because I owe you a life debt, and I would love nothing more than to repay it by pissing off that motherfucking crimson bitch," he said, a sad smile curling at the corners of his lips. "And because even though I know you'll deny it, we both know what that connection means, my friend."

My hold slackened, and he stepped out, his deep voice booming across the room for his workers to join him at the bar. I'd thought the same once upon a time, but we were both wrong. We had to be. I would accept no other alternative.

"And you?" I asked, watching Dex as he grabbed more supplies and shoved them into the bags, his eyes glinting with determination. "You owe me no such debt. Why risk your soul for a woman you don't know?"

Because that's exactly what we were about to do. By the time we got out of here and to Ardenglass, Ace would already be within the walls of the White Castle, and we'd have to break her out. I knew it as well as they did.

If we failed, Lizbeth would punish me, but she'd destroy them. And though the selfish, wicked part of me would let him help no matter what his reason was, if it meant getting to Ace, I needed to know what I was dealing with.

Dex didn't look up or stop what he was doing, but his knuckles whitened around the bag. "Because I've felt what you have—a bond that exists no matter how you wish to snap it. And because somehow, I know that woman would do the same for me."

An hour later, I stood on the outskirts of Tover between the twins, each of us packed and armed. Me, with a few extra daggers I'd picked up on our way, Dex with his long sword strapped to his back, and Duma with two axes hanging from his waist.

I raised a brow, silently asking them if they were ready and if they were sure. My plan to get her back was already clicking together in my mind, and once it was set in motion, there'd be no stopping it.

Duma just snorted and smacked me on the back before adjusting his pack and staring down the road that would take us to Ardenglass. "Fuck the Crimson Queen."

A wicked grin spread across my face. "Right to the bowels of Hell."

ADELAIS

CHAPTER FORTY-ONE

A nauseating concoction of sweat, dirt, and urine swirled around me, threatening to make me heave again as I stared back at the pale blue eyes watching me through the iron bars. I hadn't heard her arrive. Then again, my face had just been buried in a chamber pot, my ears preoccupied with the sound of my own misery while my eyes stung and my muscles seized.

When the last wave had subsided, I'd sat back, half-tempted to let myself pass out, only to catch her small form in my peripheral. Smiling at me from the other side of the tiny, square cell she'd been the one to throw me into.

"I was wondering when you'd wake up. The sedative tends to work differently for everyone. A dose that size would knock me out for a solid day, though I think I'd take that over whatever it's done to you." Her nose crinkled as she darted a disgusted look to the corner, where my vomit-filled chamber pot sat.

"What the hell do you want?" I snapped. "To gloat?"

Hara raised her hand and began picking at her nails, like my anger meant absolutely nothing to her. Like this entire situation was one she'd long grown accustomed to, and she was just going through the motions.

"Hardly. Gloating is typically left for marks who were difficult to bring in," she said, huffing out a laugh that made me want to scrape my nails down her face. "You were quite easy."

I felt like snarling at her, wondering if this was the kind of hatred Terek felt every time he fought a Creature. He viewed them as beasts who only sought to harm innocent Underlanders, but at least they mostly killed for food. The kind of monster Hara was, was far worse. She'd played me, using my pathetic insecurities about men to make me doubt Terek and believe I could trust her.

I shook my head, feeling the motion sting the shallow cut on my neck, and gave her my back as much as my tight bindings allowed. The last time I'd seen her, we'd been in the alley, and she'd been ramming the hilt of her dagger into the side of my head. The next thing I knew, I woke up chained to a cold, stone floor. I'd sat up, only for the world to spin, and had immediately begun heaving.

The passage of time was hard to tell with only my thoughts and distress to keep me company, but I was positive I'd been here for at least an hour. Well, an hour that I'd been conscious for, at least. I had no idea how long I'd laid here prior to that. The stiffness in my muscles said awhile.

Humiliated and angry, I'd sucked up my pride and tried to go Upside once I'd seen the shackles around my wrists, planning to turn right back around and hopefully appear in the Wood, but I was still too out of it from whatever sedative Hara had apparently given me. I'd tried until my head pounded, but I couldn't concentrate long enough to feel even an ember of heat that came with traveling.

"I'm here because the queen has put me in charge of making sure you don't go anywhere until she finishes her business and can see to you," Hara said from behind me, her terse voice giving away how she felt about babysitting me. "We're in the castle dungeon at the moment."

I blinked at the wall, letting that information seep in through the lingering dizziness that licked at the edges of my mind. The castle? Wait...we were in *Ardenglass*?

I spun, forgetting I was supposed to be ignoring her until she went away. "How are we in Ardenglass?" More importantly, how long did that mean I'd been out? I pressed a hand to my stomach, wincing as it roiled again. "And what the hell did you give me?"

With the nausea and headache, I wasn't surprised to hear she'd drugged me, but I had no idea how her bony limbs had dragged my dead weight all the way here. Had she had help? I mentally slapped myself. Of course, she had. She'd probably been working with that guard all along. God, I was so stupid.

Hara raised an eyebrow, like I'd somehow disappointed her with my question, and then her entire body disappeared. My eyes widened, but before I could move a muscle, she was suddenly standing in front of me again, on *my side* of the bars.

I lurched back, whacking my head against the wall while the too-tight, iron bands cut into my wrists. I gaped up at her, shock rendering me near useless as she held a chunk of bread and a vial of clear liquid in my face.

"Take this. It's a smaller dose. You'll still feel lightheaded, but as long as you eat something, you shouldn't pass out."

The way she said "shouldn't", like she wasn't entirely sure, snapped me to my senses, and I twisted my face away, wishing my mouth wasn't so parched so I could spit on her. "I'm not taking anything you give me."

She rolled her eyes. "I'm not going to kill you. That would kind of defeat everything I went through to get you here, don't you think?" she asked, setting the bread on the floor and waving the vial closer. "It's just a mild sedative to keep you from disappearing."

"You hope."

She huffed through her nose. "You're still here, and your ability is similar to mine at its core, so let's call it a well-educated hunch."

"Pass."

"Suit yourself," she said, shrugging. "It's either this, or a hit to the head again. Your choice. If I were you, I'd rather have my eyes open around the White Guards who work these cells."

I hated her, almost as much as I hated my parents and Frederick, but the threat of being unconscious around anyone was enough to have me snatching it from her hand and downing it in one gulp. I gagged, pressing my hand to my mouth to keep it from pouring right back out. It tasted like I imagined ink might.

The vial disappeared from my hand a second later, and then Hara was back on the other side of the bars, tucking it into her pocket and looking at me with something akin to pity. As if she possessed such a thing.

"So, that's your ability?" I asked, my voice thick as I struggled not to vomit all over again. I could feel my body revolting against the contents, but I fought it back. If she believed it dulled my ability, it was safe to assume she'd just make me drink another if this one came back up.

"About time you caught on. Yes, I can send my body anywhere I want, within reason."

The pieces began clicking together. How she'd gotten us all the way to Ardenglass, and how she'd disappeared from the alley. She could do what I could, but on a different scale. God, no wonder everyone I met was armed. You never knew what the people around you could do. The idea sent a shudder through me.

Adjusting my weight, I crossed my legs beneath my dress and picked up the bread. It was softer than I'd expected, and as much as I didn't want to accept anything from her, I didn't have the luxury of making any more stupid choices. Starving myself would hurt no one but me.

"And we're in the White Castle?" I asked after a few bites.

"Kind of beneath it, but yeah."

"If you could bring us here, why make up the story about the guards showing up and shove me through a window?" I asked, trying to twist my wrists within the binds and wincing when it only further angered the raw skin. *Why did you make me doubt Terek, and why did I so easily believe you?*

Hara leaned against the wall across from my cell and slid to the ground, tucking her hair behind her ears only for the short, greasy strands to immediately fall forward again.

"I didn't bring us straight here. I can only go so far, especially when I'm taking another person. Plus, it's draining as hell. It took me hours to get you here, and I almost couldn't make the last stretch. Using it to get you out of Tweeds when I knew I could convince you with a few little lies would've been a waste."

"You can't do it as much as you want?" That was good to know. If she tried to take us anywhere else, I could fight and make it harder on her until she wore herself out, maybe? Though the chance of winning a fight against someone with a weapon was slim.

She didn't seem bothered by my question, going back to picking at her nails. "Every ability has a weakness."

Finished eating, I stared down at my own hands, taking in my dirt-crusted nails and scratched palms, thinking about my own. The pain of going back and forth was agonizing, but it only lasted a few seconds so I wouldn't count it as a weakness. But being unable to use my ability without a dead body for years, definitely had been.

"Are you trying to figure out your precious Terek's?"

"No." But now that she'd brought him up, I was. He used his all the time and so easily. I'd never noticed anything that could've been a weakness, though he'd likely have been careful to hide that from anyone, including me.

"Liar," she laughed, bouncing a loose stone into my cell that rolled to a stop at my feet. "I can tell you if you want, but if you think hard enough, I'm sure you could figure it out."

Grabbing the stone, I lifted my hand as high as my bonds allowed and threw it back at her, seething when my blurred vision and renewed nausea caused me to miss by a full foot. I couldn't tell if this was just another lie, but I didn't like the thought of her knowing something so personal about him.

"Just leave me alone, Hara. You won. Go get your stupid reward or whatever it is you want to gain from me." I still didn't understand what it was, or how she knew anything about me, but there was no point in asking, since I doubted she'd be honest. She certainly hadn't been before.

"Sadly, I don't get my reward until the queen confirms your identity." She tilted her head. "Nice try for a distraction, though. Why are you so protective of him? That asshole would've brought you in eventually, once he was done enjoying you."

She wiggled her eyebrows, and my lip curled at her insinuation, bitterness taking root in my stomach. Terek had said and felt many things about me, but enjoyment wasn't one of them.

"Why are *you* so determined to talk about him? You obviously hate him."

She leaned her head back so that she was staring at the ceiling and snorted. "That's putting it mildly. I guess I'm just curious how he got you to be so devoted to him, because it certainly wasn't his glowing personality. Then again," she said, glancing down at me, "you've known him your entire life, haven't you?"

I heard someone cough from farther down the hall, and I stiffened, but no footsteps approached. Another prisoner rather than a guard then. I focused back on Hara, trying to find her tells to figure out her lies from her truth.

"How do you know that?" Was there a guard who'd read my mind and flipped through my memories while I'd been drugged? The thought was terrifying.

Hara pushed forward so that her elbows were resting on her knees. She looked genuinely sorry for me, like I was a puppy that'd been locked in a cage all its life, headed to my death without ever knowing freedom.

"The better question is how I knew your name, *Adelais*."

I froze, the memory of her using my name and my confusion rushing back with a vengeance and making my head pound even harder. I *knew* I hadn't given her that name. God, I should've followed my initial instincts and known something was wrong.

"If you're trying to convince me that Terek hired you to bring me in or something, you can save your breath." She'd already lied about him working with the guards. I wasn't about to believe her again.

Her neck arched as she straight up laughed at me, the dark circles under her eyes in sharp contrast to the soft tenor of her laughter. "No, he'd never allow himself to rely on anyone, but he *is* the reason I know your name. Believe me or don't. It won't change the truth."

She was lying. She had to have somehow overheard Terek talking to me, even though I knew that wasn't possible. He'd only ever said my real name once, and that was years ago. He hadn't even let me tell Duma and Dex. Hara was just trying to confuse me like she'd done in my room.

I fought the urge to dig my fingers into my temples and scream at her to leave while I curled into a ball on the floor. I swore I could see two of her now, the drug already kicking in and messing with my head. Instead, I sucked in a shaky breath and blinked to clear my vision, another memory coming to me.

"I don't believe you. The guard you knocked out knew who I was by my face, not my name."

She slid her eyes to me, and I realized just how exhausted she looked. Bringing me here had taken everything out of her, and she looked like she was barely staying conscious herself. "That's because the queen sent your portrait to nearly everyone in the Underland years ago. Be thankful I didn't let that guard take you. Whatever bounty hunter he'd planned to sell you to would've gotten his fair share of coin from you in other ways before finally bringing you here."

I shuddered, not wanting to give that nauseating possibility any space in my mind. "Nice try, but I never left the Wood before now, and if you say Terek drew a picture of me, you might as well save your breath."

"He didn't need to."

I only raised a brow in question, earning me a smirk.

"How can I move miles at a time? How can you travel to the land of the dead?" she asked, gesturing toward my body. "The queen likes to…find people with valuable abilities and use them at her convenience. One of those people just so happens to be a woman who can see recent thoughts."

I stiffened. "She can read minds?" That would explain Hara knowing my name then. Why on Earth would the queen want someone like that around her? It was convenient, sure, but also risky for someone in power.

"I said she can see recent thoughts, not read minds. She just needed to touch someone who'd seen you, and then draw up your likeness. The queen had it sent to every town and city within her reach so we could find you. She didn't anticipate it taking so long."

Hara shrugged, like we were talking about the queen sharing apples with her citizens, not sending out a worldwide notice of my existence.

"So that's what you do, then? You bring people to her, and if they refuse, they get added to a list for the guards to hunt down?" I asked, hoping she could feel my disgust through the bars.

"I'm a Soul Seeker. It's my job. Not all of us have choices, Adelais. I bring in those with abilities because to have one and not report it to the queen is considered treason. I'm not going to risk my eternal soul for someone else's."

I ran my fingers over my shackles. Yeah, no shit. I'd already figured that much out. "So, you're saying I'm here because the queen believes I've committed an act of treason I didn't even know existed?"

She sucked on her front teeth. "No. You're here because the queen has wanted your ability since the moment she found out about you."

And Terek had known. That's why he hadn't wanted me to leave the Wood and had been hiding our tracks. He'd known there were people who knew what I looked like. God, no wonder he'd been so angry when he'd seen the White Guards in Tover and couldn't find me. The man was so infuriating. Why hadn't he just *communicated* and told me?

"Anyway," Hara continued, wrapping her hand around her head to crack her neck. "You can thank Terek for all that."

"You're lying. He wouldn't have told anyone about me." Not when he'd been trying so hard to protect me. *Unless he was trying to make up for a mistake he'd already made*, a voice whispered in the back of my mind.

Hara's lips quirked, like she could hear that voice as well. She reached into a pack at her side and removed a flask, tossing it through the bars at me.

"Yet, he did. Sorry to destroy the happy cloud you live on, but while you've known him your entire life, he's only known you for a blink of his. Which is nothing compared to the decades he's known his lover."

My heart skidded to a halt, and my lungs began contracting faster, sure I'd heard her wrong. "What are you talking about?"

"Drink that, and I'll tell you. You look like you're about to pass out, and I have no desire to drag your ass to the throne room."

I took the flask, not even comprehending my own actions as her words circled my head, and I took a long drink. And then another. When I'd drained the water, I tossed it back, wiping the back of my hand over my lips.

"I'm not dumb. I know Terek's been here a long time and has had lovers." He'd all but shoved that fact in my face when he'd snuck away the other night. Something that still made me want to find the random woman and rip her hair out of her head for reasons I wasn't going to touch right now.

She eyed me, not moving to grab the flask. "I'm talking about the fact that he's Queen Lizbeth's lover, Adelais. He pledged himself to her willingly and gives her whatever she wants, no questions asked. And right now, what she wants…is you."

I fisted my hands in my lap, something acidic and bitter swirling in the pit of my stomach that wasn't from the vial of liquid. There was no arrogance or smirk in her expression, just hard facts. But just because she believed it, didn't make it true. People believed incorrect things all the time. Upsiders having no knowledge of the Underland was a perfect example.

Terek had a hundred opportunities to take me to the queen if she'd truly been a lover he wanted to please. He'd known me as a child, for God's sake. But he'd done the opposite, refusing to let me leave the Wood.

I knew better than to believe he'd always been honest and upfront with me, but the vicious hatred in his tone and on his face anytime he'd mentioned the queen couldn't have been faked.

"Somehow I don't think he would be enjoying me, as you so crassly put it, if he wanted to turn me in to his lover."

Hara shrugged, taking a coin from her pack and spinning it over the stones, lazily watching it until it clattered to the side. "I assume he's a bit torn up about it, with the queen having repaid his love by stabbing him in the back and forcing him into an eternity of servitude."

My heart bottomed out, falling somewhere on the cold floor.

"It's pretty fucking hard for your soul to move on when you're no longer in control of it. Those of us who wander for eternity only do so because of her."

It suddenly hit me, like the ceiling had crashed down around me, piece after piece smacking me in the head.

"Let's just say, she would be very interested in your ability, and she is not known for her kindness."

"What is she known for?"

"For taking things that don't belong to her."

Oh, my God. The queen had control of Terek's soul, and likely Hara's as well. I wasn't sure how—if it was because she was the ruler, and therefore a sort of god over the Underland, or if it was something else—but I was almost sure of it.

And now, she wanted control of mine as well. Was that why she'd been searching for me for so long? Because she didn't like that she couldn't control me and how I used my ability? I stared at Hara through the bars, watching as she spun the coin again, her eyelids heavy.

"Why are you doing this, Hara? What does the queen have on you?" *How does she control your soul?*

Her hand snaked out and grabbed the coin, clutching it in her fist. "Because the reward for you is worth more to me than your life. You can hate me all you want, but when you've been here as long as I have, you'll understand."

What the hell was the reward? Hara didn't seem like the kind of person who cared all that much about money, but I could be wrong. What I couldn't wrap my head around was, why me? Why did the queen care that much about one person out of thousands?

Her wanting skilled people in her corner to help maintain her position and take what she wanted made sense. I imagined all people in power would do the same, but my ability wouldn't help her with that. I couldn't do anything but bring news of the Upside, and what good would that do? I had nothing of value.

I must have said at least part of my thoughts out loud because

Hara's face darkened, and she glared at me, her pale gaze sharp as she practically snarled, "You have no fucking idea what it's like to have nothing. Nothing to own, nothing to do, nothing to live for. You have the most valuable thing of all, and you don't even appreciate it."

Exasperated, I flung my hands out, the bite of the cuffs blending into the unending throb I couldn't ease. "Are you talking about the Upside? I promise you, it's no different than this right here. I simply wore a different type of shackles."

"No," she seethed, a deep pain burning in her eyes. "I'm talking about your ability to *die*. You say you have nothing while so many of us would give anything for the freedom you have."

My brow furrowed, not understanding the depth of her anger over something she'd experienced already. She was dead, and from the way she'd spoken earlier, she'd been dead for a while now. But maybe she was referring to the fact that if I could die, it meant I was still currently alive?

I bit my lip, realizing there might be more to Hara than I'd originally thought. She was a shitty person, there was no denying that. She'd played me, used me, hit and drugged me, and then sat there, shoving it all in my face. But she'd also died young and had likely been thrown into this world on her own, confused and scared.

She'd learned to put herself first and look out for herself, and hadn't I been trying to do the same? Hadn't I been willing to sacrifice Frederick's life for mine each time I'd crushed medication into his food?

"Hara," I started, keeping my voice low and as neutral as I could. "How did you d—"

She shot to her feet, the sudden movement startling me and interrupting my question. She cleared her throat and awkwardly brushed dirt off her trousers, as if they hadn't already looked crumpled and filthy before she'd even sat on the floor.

"I'm sure someone will be down any minute for you, so it's probably best if we stop talking. I'd rather not have anyone assume I share Terek's shaky conscience regarding you."

I opened my mouth to try again, but she'd already turned away from me, effectively closing the door on any further conversation. I frowned, resting my head back against the wall again. How convenient that she could push me when I didn't want to talk, but she expected me to respect when she didn't, just because she'd accidentally revealed more about herself than she'd planned.

Part of me was tempted to blurt out my question anyway, since she'd so happily tormented me about Terek, but she'd likely just appear in my cell to whack me in the head again. My headache from the first time had only just begun to lesson.

I sighed, staring down at the red, angry skin peeking out from the iron cuffs. "Fine, but can you tell me just one thing? I feel like we can agree you owe me at least that."

She was silent for a long moment, and I figured she'd just ignore me, but then she nodded, playing with the edges of her cloak. "Depends on the question."

"Is there anything I should know before you drag me up there? I don't even know what ability the queen has." Maybe if I knew that, I could figure out how to prevent her from doing to me, whatever she'd done to everyone else.

Hara scoffed and slid her gaze to me over her shoulder. "Queen Lizbeth doesn't have an ability. She has *power*."

"Okay," I answered, not understanding the difference. "But what can she do with it?" For her to be capable of controlling so many others—control someone like Terek—whatever she could do had to be awful.

A slamming door echoed from my right, and both our heads snapped toward the sound, my muscles tensing while Hara's body almost seemed to vibrate, like she was fighting the instinctual urge to disappear. She watched whoever it was continue down the hall and dipped her head before she glanced back over her shoulder to me.

Her eyes dropped to my chest for a split second before returning to mine, right as the white armor of a guard came into view. "You'll see."

ADELAIS

CHAPTER FORTY-TWO

All six guards were watching me. I fidgeted before the large, ornate doors leading to the throne room while Hara handed her weapons to them, wishing my hands were free to pull my hair forward to hide my face. I figured they knew who I was, but did they have to stare so blatantly?

I'd pointlessly tried to convince the guard escorting us to remove my shackles, since it wasn't like the bindings did anything to keep me from using my ability, but he'd only nudged at my back, silently demanding I follow Hara up the stairs and out.

My path through the castle passed by in a blur of white. It was breathtaking and more pristine than anything I'd ever seen, even compared to the wealth I'd grown up in, but I found myself unable to focus on any of it. Between the sedative and my out-of-control nerves, I was lucky I could get my feet to walk at all.

After everything Terek had hinted at regarding the queen, and the ominous warning Hara had given about her power, I was utterly terrified of who I was about to meet. Was she going to have me shoved to my knees while she threatened to cut off my head or something if I didn't do whatever she required of me?

Before I could let my imagination convince me to turn and sprint back through the halls, the guards stepped forward to open the doors, and I was pushed through.

"Give away nothing you do not want her to use against you," Hara said under her breath, wrapping her hand around my arm and nodding at the guard behind me to step back. "And whatever you do, don't threaten to disappear unless you want another dose shoved down your throat."

No worries there. I had no desire to speak at all, let alone issue threats. I just wanted to get this over with and be let go. I had no idea how long it'd take me to get back to Tover, but I didn't imagine the main roads would be too hard to figure out. Even another random town would be better than Ardenglass. After waking in a cell, my childhood dream of seeing the queen's city didn't seem all that enticing anymore.

Hopefully, as long as I could figure out a way to get a basic pack and food, I'd be able to make it back to Tweeds in one piece. The key word being *hopefully*.

The doors clanged shut behind us, and I blinked rapidly, trying to decide if what I was seeing was real or if the sedative was still messing with my vision. The room was three times the size I'd expected with dozens of lit candelabras and sconces all around, making the white walls and floor so ridiculously bright, I was sure I'd see it even after I closed my eyes.

Ahead of us, raised several feet above the floor, was a large platform with a massive white throne in the center of it. It was a thing of beauty, something my fingers itched to be able to sketch out in detail, from the irregular feet it stood on to the thorned wings stretching out on either side of it. They were crafted with individual pieces rather than large, sculpted slabs, and I found myself leaning forward as we passed rows of benches, trying to make them out.

"Do you like my throne, Adelais?"

My gaze whipped off the intricate structure to land on the woman standing just off to the side of it, a delicate hand curled around one of the thorns. Between her ivory skin and the iridescent, pearl gown she wore, she could've easily been part of the winged display behind her. The gown slipped over the curves of her body like a second skin and cut deeply between her breasts, two matching slits up each leg revealing more thigh than I was used to seeing in public.

Her auburn hair was pinned high on her head in an elegant updo, accentuating her long neck and heart-shaped jawline, and nestled within the curls was an ascending peak of straight, white spikes, each connected to the next by a thin web of lace. But even if she'd bore no crown, there'd be no doubt who this woman was. Every part of her expression and mannerisms exuded grace and power.

Hara dropped into a low bow, yanking on my arm to pull me down into a clumsy excuse of a curtsey when I continued to gape up at the woman now descending the steps toward us.

Ever since Terek had let slip that the queen had been the ruler for longer than he'd been dead, I'd pictured her as an aged, cranky monarch. A woman with more silver hairs than she could keep hidden anymore and distinct wrinkles around her eyes and mouth. I should've known better with Hara's jabs about her relationship with Terek, but never would I have pictured her as the young woman before me.

With bright green eyes, smooth skin, and the barest touch of color on her full lips, she was the most beautiful woman I'd ever seen. I'd known Terek had remained the same age, physically, for decades, but I was struggling to wrap my mind around the fact that the ruler of the entire Underland appeared to be around twenty-three-years-old. And that she'd probably looked this way for at least a century.

If ever I needed a reminder that I was no longer Upside, this would do it.

"It's so lovely to finally meet you, my dear Adelais. How was your trip in? I certainly hope you're not feeling too sick."

I could've sworn Hara snorted beside me, but I could only stare blankly at the queen, who was smiling softly at me like she was genuinely curious how her sedatives had made me feel. As if asking me about being kidnapped was no different than asking me about the weather.

"No, Your Majesty," I finally said, forcing the words out when one perfectly shaped brow arched high on her face, clearly expecting an answer. "I can't honestly say I enjoyed any of the experience."

I tensed, unsure if the question had been a test, and if so, whether I'd passed or failed. Was the proper etiquette to be honest or lie? But the queen just waved a slender hand, dismissing my answer like she'd already known and hadn't actually cared.

"It was a necessary inconvenience," she said, dropping her hand to rest on her collar as she gave a breathy chuckle. "I was quite impatient to meet you, as I'm sure you can imagine. I couldn't have you leaving before we even had a chance to chat. I mean, it isn't every day we receive a visitor from the Upside."

I swallowed, trying not to fidget as she trailed her emerald gaze down my body and back up, her lips pressing together like whatever she saw disappointed her. I wasn't sure if it was because she'd wanted me to be *more* or *less* than what I was.

"Forgive me if I'm wrong, Your Majesty, but apart from the Creatures of the Wood, isn't…everyone a visitor from the Upside?" I asked, not yet wanting to confirm the truth outright until she revealed more of what she suspected.

Hara's hold tightened around my arm for a split second in warning before she let go, shifting away and clasping her hands behind her back. The queen's eyes narrowed on me, and she walked closer, her heels clicking sharply across the floor. When she was only a foot away, she pointed one long nail back toward the platform.

"I do not have many rules, Adelais, but consider this one of them. Unless you are complimenting the beauty of my throne, do not speak of those monstrosities in my presence."

I bit the inside of my cheek and glanced to where she pointed, my muddled brain trying to keep up with what she was talking about. Complimenting her throne? What did—oh, my God. My mouth fell open, and my hands instinctively shot up to press over it.

The Crimson Queen's throne wasn't created with broken shards of marble or stone as I'd believed, but with fucking bones. *Creature* bones. I ripped my gaze away and stared at the stairs beneath it instead, my stomach cramping at the fact that I'd found such a horrible thing beautiful when I'd walked in.

How many Creatures had she murdered to make something that large with so much detail? How many other things did she have around the castle fashioned from them? Her tables? Her bed? Disgust made my lightheadedness worse, and I suddenly wanted nothing more than to sprint from the room. Only my fear of the queen's unknown ability kept me rooted in place.

Red-tipped fingers wrapped around my chin and pulled up gently, bringing my face back to hers. "Do not worry yourself, Adelais. I'm not the kind of queen who punishes someone for breaking a rule they didn't know existed," she said, her expression amused.

I merely nodded, my head bobbing in her palm.

"What I will not tolerate; however, is any attempt to deceive me. We both know what I meant by visitor, but just this once, I will give you the benefit of the doubt and clarify myself."

She released my jaw to run a finger down the column of my throat, tapping it over the cut, before stepping back. The green in her eyes was practically glowing. "It is not every day I have a visitor from the Upside with life still burning in her veins. The notion is rather peculiar, wouldn't you say?"

My instinct was to lie, Terek's warnings ringing louder than church bells in my ears, but it was too late for that. Lying would do nothing but anger a woman who'd somehow made an entire world fear her.

I pressed my palms together within my confines, wishing for the twentieth time since waking that I had my pocket watch. I'd been so confused and scared when Hara had arrived at Tweeds, I hadn't thought to grab it, and my side felt depressingly empty without its comforting weight.

"So, you just brought me here to…meet me, Your Majesty?" I asked, hoping she couldn't hear the tremor in my voice. Given she had passed my likeness around and offered a reward, I already knew the answer, but I wanted her to get to the point and send me on my way.

Her lips twitched, like she easily saw through my attempt and found me thoroughly amusing. The expression reminded me of my mother, and a burrow of hatred flared in my belly. If there was anything that would power over my fear, it was someone making me feel like a stupid little girl again.

"I think it best if we speak plainly to each other, Adelais. It'll make this all go far smoother, yes?"

I agreed, not exactly having much of a choice. I had no desire to see what the queen's version of things going *rough* would be. Hara said nothing beside me, but her pale eyes bounced between us.

"Perfect," the queen said, clapping her hands together. "Now, ask me the question I can see burning on your tongue. Oh, and please, call me Lizbeth."

The allowance surprised me, but I recovered quickly. It was now or never, I supposed. "What do you want from me?"

Lizbeth's smile widened into a flash of straight, white teeth, and I immediately shuffled back a step, my weariness growing.

"Several things, dear Adelais, but right now, let's start small. Tell me how your ability works. Do you have to kill yourself each time? Is there a limit on your time here? Can you go Upside at will, or are you stuck here until your physical body heals? I find everything about your ability absolutely fascinating."

I visibly balked, revolted by the idea of killing myself over and over again. I'd certainly been unhappy Upside, but I wasn't sure I could go through something that horrendous each time I wanted freedom. The mind could only handle so much.

"No, I don't kill myself," I said, suddenly acutely aware of the absolute silence in the room, as if even Hara and the guards were holding their breath, straining to hear my answer. I shifted my weight, my cheeks flushing under the attention.

"My entire body comes with me. It doesn't...stay Upside when I travel." Thank God. Who knew what Frederick would've done with free access to my body. "And I have no idea how long I can stay here. This is the longest I've ever tried."

Lizbeth slowly leaned closer while I spoke, her eyes so bright, I feared she might be feverish. "So, you don't have to have a physical body Upside waiting for you? You just appear as you are?"

I nodded, unable to speak as pressure built within my chest, almost like someone had wrapped a string around my heart and had begun to pull, wanting me to follow.

"How do you use this ability then?" she asked, her eyes darting down to my hands that I'd subconsciously raised to press against that tugging pressure.

Warning bells sounded in every corner of my mind at the hungry look in her eyes, like she'd lay me out and carve me open to understand my ability if she could. For all I knew, maybe she would.

"I'm not entirely sure. It hurts to travel back and forth though, like someone tossing me into a raging fire." Maybe if she knew that, she wouldn't be so interested in it.

Lizbeth stared at me for a moment, like she could sense the hesitancy in my answers, and I stiffened, wondering if she'd accuse me of deceiving her again. Technically, I wasn't lying about anything.

Her face hardened for a moment, something harsh filling it before she schooled her expression and straightened. She pulled at something around her neck, and my gaze caught on a thin chain I hadn't noticed before. Whatever was at the end was tucked safely into her bodice, but it appeared to be a necklace.

Lizbeth tilted her head to the side. "Hara, leave us."

Hara nearly jumped out of her skin at being addressed so suddenly. She bit her lip, looking like she might cry. "My Queen?"

Lizbeth rolled her eyes and flicked a hand, waving her off like an irritating child. "Go stand by the door until I'm ready for you."

Relief washed over Hara's face, and she bowed low again before scurrying off, her boots far softer against the floor than Lizbeth's sharp heels. Once she was far enough away, Lizbeth slid her gaze back to me, all signs of frustration falling.

"I understand your hesitancy to confide in me, Adelais. There is something within you that reminds me so much of myself, and I know how hard it is to open up to someone you do not yet trust. But I promise on my crown and throne that the secrets of your ability are safe with me. I shall not tell a soul."

The pointlessness of her promise wasn't lost on me. If there was anyone I didn't want to tell my secrets to, it was the woman who'd ordered me to be chained in a cell, not a random person on the street. It also didn't help that no matter how long she'd been here, I felt like I was being patronized by someone younger than me. Still, I knew she wouldn't let up until I gave her at least something.

"I'm telling you the truth, Your—Lizbeth. I don't know how it works. Most of the time, it's on accident when I'm emotional. Usually when," I paused, feeling the heat of her stare, "I'm hurt or upset."

She gifted me a small smile and reached forward, cupping my cheek in such a tender way that I almost found myself closing my eyes and leaning into it, my body instinctually seeking any form of affection. I didn't think someone had held my face with such tenderness since Mrs. Gayle, and the thought made me want to burst into tears.

"I can feel the hurt in your soul, Adelais," she whispered, placing her other hand over my heart. "The pain, the loneliness, the feeling to belong. It is so heavy, my dear. Let me help you lift that burden."

That warning tug suddenly became a harsh, demanding yank as Lizbeth's hand grew hot over my breast. I lurched back out of her reach, my eyes wide and heart thumping. That hurt. What the hell had she been trying to do?

Irritation flickered over her face, but she brushed it away quickly and smirked at me, her hands dropping to her sides. "I have a theory about our abilities, Adelais. One I think many here agree with."

"Okay," I said, still feeling the residual warmth from her touch. She jumped from topic to topic so quickly, it was hard to keep up with.

Lizbeth walked toward one of the walls, gesturing for me to follow. "There are some who believe our abilities are random, that they are given out with no underlying reason, but I don't believe that."

Nodding, more to myself than her, I hurried to follow. Terek hadn't believed that either. Hara's taunt trickled into my mind again, and I wondered if they'd come to that conclusion together, but Lizbeth continued, clipping that line of thought.

"You see, I believe those of us with abilities have them because we earned them. They were gifted to us because we were angry enough in death to demand *more*."

My feet stumbled, and I frowned as she led me slowly around the benches, walking along the right wall. "Like some people are more worthy than others?"

I didn't agree with Terek that we were cursed, but I didn't agree with Lizbeth either. Even if she was right, how would she explain me? I hadn't exactly died angry when I was eight years old.

She waved her hand, chuckling softly. "Of course not. I simply meant that there are those who arrive with small desires in their hearts, and then there are those of us who came with fire burning in our souls. A fire that turned our desires into something *more*."

She stopped near a window and pursed her lips as if in thought. "You've met my Terek, yes?"

Her Terek? I bit my tongue hard enough to taste blood, hating the way the words sounded from her lips and the infuriating, knowing glint in her eyes. Like she knew just how badly I'd once wanted him. It made me want to claw off her face. She had no right to claim him after stabbing him in the back. I may not have been told exactly what she'd done, but given the depth of Terek's hatred, she had no right to call him her anything.

Her smirk reappeared as she twisted that verbal dagger a little deeper. "I realize you don't know him as well as I, but if you had to guess, what would you say he desires more than anything?"

"I don't know," I bit out, trying to keep my knee-jerk, jealous anger under control. Letting her know how much her comments bothered me would only reveal another weakness for her to exploit. I wasn't sure what all she already knew, and Hara had warned me to tread carefully.

"Humor me."

Something dark and oily curled in my chest. Lizbeth spoke so nonchalantly, like discussing Terek's death and desires was some kind of game to her. Jesus, how had he ever seen anything worthwhile in such a vindictive, selfish woman?

Hoping to make her as uncomfortable as she was trying to do to me, I looked her in the eyes and said, "Freedom."

She made a clicking noise with her tongue and shook a slender finger at me, completely unbothered by my accusation. "Yes, but that plays into a much larger desire. Think harder."

I bristled. "I don't know. The power to make his own choices, I guess. Like you said, I don't know him well." The truth of the words tasted bitter.

Lizbeth's smile fell slightly, and she reached out, twirling a lock of hair that hung over my shoulder a little harder than necessary. "Terek seeks pure, unquestionable control in all things. He desired it before death, and even more so after."

"And his abilities give him that?" I asked, unable to keep the doubt from my voice when I thought of my last interaction with him. Control was not something I'd connect with Terek's name. Unless, of course, it involved shoving me away and ignoring me for seven years. Then his control was iron tight.

Lizbeth winked at me. "He seems to think so."

I stared out the window at the lush courtyard beneath us, walls of roses that would've made my mother green with envy, and pushed down another surge of anger. Maybe it was the sedative messing with my emotions, but I couldn't seem to stop it every time she mentioned him. It was like she wanted me to know just how close they'd once been and how much I didn't know him at all.

Whether that was her goal or not, she was right, and I hated her for it.

"And what about you?" I dared to ask, sliding my gaze back to her bright, emerald one. "What did you want so badly in death?" *What is your ability?* I regretted the careless words as soon as I'd said them, but rather than a flare of irritation, a wicked grin spread across her face.

"Revenge, Adelais. I wanted revenge."

"Against who?"

"The who and why is a story for another day, I'm afraid. The point stays the same."

Did it? If she'd wanted revenge at death, that meant whoever had wronged her so horribly likely hadn't even been here when she'd started putting herself into a position of power through fear. She'd simply decided to take her hatred and pain out on everyone else.

As much as I'd been hurt Upside, as much as I'd wanted to murder Frederick in his sleep—and still did—the kind of baseless revenge Lizbeth referred to wasn't something I believed in. It was no different than how my parents had treated me when my mother couldn't bear a son, even though her pregnancy complications hadn't been my fault.

"What exactly do you want from me?" I asked.

"The same thing I ask of all my subjects," she said, waving a hand in dismissal. "I want you to swear over your soul."

ADELAIS

CHAPTER FORTY-THREE

I'd known—had already anticipated it to be the reason she'd sought me out—but hearing it still sent a trail of gooseflesh along my neck and arms. Lizbeth wanted to control me the same way she controlled everyone else in the Underland. Everyone with abilities, at least.

She traced a finger over my pebbled skin, her gaze hooded and dark. "I'll take good care of it," she crooned, an almost sensual lilt to her voice. "And you'll get what you want most."

"What is that?" I asked, shoving away the image of midnight eyes that flashed in my mind. Somehow, I doubted Terek was going to be her answer.

She gave me a knowing look. "I will grant you permission to stay in the Underland for the rest of your life and provide you with whatever you need to get settled, just like I do with all my other citizens."

My heart beat faster. Her offer was everything I'd wanted from the moment I made the choice to stay here, a fact Lizbeth appeared to be painfully aware of. She didn't know my story, but she didn't need to. My presence here alone, when I had a life Upside with living people, was enough. It didn't take a genius to deduce I preferred it here.

I glanced back at Hara, who was still watching us closely, her eyes squinted like she was desperately trying to read our lips. No matter how tempting Lizbeth's offer was, there was more to this than simply promising her my soul. Hara was utterly terrified of what the queen might do to her if she didn't follow her orders.

"What does swearing over my soul involve?" I asked, tensing when she lowered her face even closer to mine. Her proximity was making my skin clammy. "Do I sign an oath in blood or something?"

"You do give me something, but I promise it won't involve you bleeding for me. I'll even allow you to stay within my castle if you wish." She winked, and the hairs on the back of my neck stood on end.

This woman was insane if she thought I'd willingly stay anywhere near her after she'd locked me in a cell. There was dried blood all over my wrists, and it was taking every ounce of my concentration not to curl up into a ball and sleep off the lingering effects of the sedative.

"We don't have all day, my dear, and it's really quite simple." Impatience bled into her voice when I didn't immediately agree, but I ignored it, needing more. For someone so against being deceived, she'd yet to say a single thing to me that wasn't misleading.

"The people here can't move on to the afterlife once they promise their souls to you, can they? They're stuck here whether they want to be or not."

Her nostrils flared, and I shuffled back a step, suddenly aware I was standing precariously close to a high window as I accused a woman who was beginning to look like she might throw me out of it.

"That's your ability, isn't it?" I pushed, more sure of it with each word I spoke. "I swear my soul to you, and you'd be able to control when I leave." Terek had once told me the Underland had only continued to grow when it was supposed to fluctuate both ways, and I was willing to bet Lizbeth was the cause of it. No one was moving on anymore—not enough of them, at least.

Her gaze narrowed. "You sure are opinionated for someone who knows absolutely nothing. I make the hard choices every ruler must, to do what's best for my people. I keep them safe from the monsters that'd happily rip them apart, and all I ask for is loyalty. Sacrificing a little control in exchange for order and safety is the least they can do."

Being unable to move on to an afterlife that'd been promised since before death wasn't giving up a *little control*. It was all their control, their freedom to make their own choices. The Underland was supposed to be a middle ground to help people feel secure and content before their final death, not an eternal purgatory.

"But how does keeping so many people here help maintain control? What benefit does that give—"

"My patience with this conversation has expired, Adelais," she snapped, wrapping a hand around my binds and yanking. I cried out, feeling like my wrists might slice clean off, but she continued stalking back toward the center of the room, forcing me to follow.

"You will swear your soul to me, and, in return, I will swear to give you board and continue holding the border to keep you, and everyone else, safe. It's *simple*."

Her last word came out more like a growl, and I stumbled after her, biting my lip to keep the tears at bay when fresh blood dripped over my palms. Bitch. *She* wasn't doing anything. It was Terek who guarded and protected the border, which he did against his will, while she sat on her throne of stolen bones.

"Now, Adelais. I have more important things to attend to. Swear your soul, and I will let you rest."

I shook my head, even while every part of me screamed to give in and do it, if only to get out of there. To say yes and roll over like I always had Upside, and allow her to walk all over me so I could survive another day.

Her brows rose, and something dangerous flashed across her eyes. "You think being alive makes you better than everyone else? That you don't have to abide by the same rules just because you have the ability to leave?"

I swallowed, the bread I'd eaten feeling like lead in my stomach as every instinct in my body screamed at me to run at the way Lizbeth's tone dropped from angry to lethally calm. Frederick's voice had always done the same before his worst punishments.

"I don't think I'm better than anyone, Your Majesty, but if the cost of staying is my soul, I would rather leave."

Her jaw worked. "Are you threatening me?"

I blinked, taken aback. "What? No, of course not."

Her lips twisted, and she tightened her grip on my chain like she imagined it was my throat instead. "Just so I understand, you're refusing to willingly swear loyalty to me?"

I fumbled for a response, not liking her pointed use of the word 'willingly' and unsure why she was acting like I'd held a weapon to her throat. None of this had anything to do with loyalty, and we both knew it. The way she'd carefully avoided explaining how her ability worked or how she was able to control people's souls told me enough.

"I meant no disrespect, Your Majesty. Just let me—"

"*Hara!*"

I jumped at her shouted order and turned toward the main doors to see Hara hastening across the room, her feet moving at nearly a jog as a mixture of trepidation and naked hope warred on her face.

She bowed low once she was a few feet away, her thin chest moving quickly with each labored breath. "Yes, Your Majesty?"

Lifting her hand from my binds, Lizbeth snapped two fingers, and a guard who'd been standing flush with the wall stalked forward. He wore the same white armor as the rest, but he was far larger than any others I'd seen, his size reminding me of Duma and Dex. My nerves went wild as he grew closer, unsure what Lizbeth had called him over to do.

I chewed my lip, both hoping and dreading that he was about to drag me back to my cell, until I noticed the way Hara's body had begun to shake. I glanced at her uneasily, then back at the man in time to see him raise one hand before his breastplate, a small, white box gripped firmly within it. I narrowed my eyes, trying to see it better. Was that supposed to be Hara's reward?

It seemed too small to be holding something worth kidnapping for—certainly not large enough for an abundance of wealth—but by the way Hara's eyes latched onto it like it was the only raft on a sinking ship, it had to be whatever she'd been promised.

I moved toward her, genuinely worried her legs might give out before she even received it. Hara may not have been my favorite person, but she was higher on the list than Lizbeth, and I didn't want to see her crack her head open on the floor.

When I was confident she wasn't about to pass out, I glanced back at the guard, expecting him to hand the box to her. Instead, he only held it out in the center of his palm, his brown eyes trained on me from within his helmet in a way that immediately made me squirm. Like he was a starving man, and I had the ability to feed him for eternity.

It reminded me far too much of the way the guard in the alley had looked at me, but Lizbeth didn't seem to notice or care. She just curled her fingers around the lid and tipped it up, silently watching Hara with almost the same intensity as the guard watched me.

From how tall the guard was and where I stood, I couldn't see what was inside the box, but the moment she lifted the lid, a soft, blue light lit the inside, turning the white interior a calming, ocean hue.

Hara violently lurched forward, like someone had reached into her ribcage and yanked, but one sharp look from Lizbeth had her slamming to a halt. Her eyes glistened, and she let out a low whimper, wrapping her arms tightly around her body. I darted my attention between the three of them, trying to piece together what was happening. What the hell was in that box?

Confirming Hara wasn't going to move again, Lizbeth slowly reached her fingers in and plucked out whatever was inside, the pulsing blue light visible between her closed fingers as she removed her hand. It fit perfectly within her palm, no larger than an apricot.

She turned to hold her closed hand closer to Hara, and a buzzing filled my ears as the blue color seemed to flare. I waited for something else to happen, or for Lizbeth to do something with it, but she just held still and silently tipped her head at the guard.

The man immediately clicked the box shut and tucked it into a bag tied at his side, but rather than retreating to his original place, he circled Lizbeth to stand just behind us, closer to me than to her. I shuffled to the side a little, not liking him so close to me when I couldn't see what he was doing.

"How long has it been?" Lizbeth asked, gifting Hara a genuine smile.

Hara swallowed, her hands twitching at her sides as tears pooled in her eyes, and her voice came out ragged. "Three decades, Your Majesty."

My mouth popped open. I'd noticed how worn and exhausted Hara looked and had assumed she'd been here awhile, but *thirty years?* God, that would put her around twenty years older than me and closer to my mother's age.

She certainly hadn't acted that much older than me. Then again, Lizbeth and Terek didn't seem like they were as old as they were either. Maybe one's maturity always stayed the same as the age they died? I shoved the thoughts away to ponder later—much later—and focused back in on their conversation.

"You've earned this twice over, my dearest Hara, and I've kept it as safe as I've kept you, as promised." Her carefully chosen words felt more for me than Hara, and sudden understanding hit me like a strike of lightning, horror shooting through me. My eyes widened and landed on what Lizbeth held in her hand.

"Personally, I don't give a shit about my soul. The queen can keep it for the rest of my eternal life for all I care." That's what the guard in the alley had said. I'd thought he meant figuratively because he'd sworn an oath or something, not that Lizbeth physically had his soul in her possession.

It seemed so obvious now as I stared at that blue glow, but never in a hundred years would I have known, or even guessed, it was possible for someone to keep people's souls in boxes like trinkets.

I'd thought Lizbeth's ability allowed her to somehow control them, but no, the reward for bringing me in was Hara's literal fucking soul. Holy shit.

The poor girl was practically convulsing next to me, clearly fighting to keep still and not grab for Lizbeth's outstretched hand. She'd been working for the queen for thirty years, not because she was a monster who didn't care, but because, like Terek, she'd had her choices stripped.

Everything she'd done to me had been to earn her soul back. *That's* what she'd meant by my ability to die. She hadn't been jealous I was still alive; she'd been referring to being trapped here, unable to move on even if she wanted.

With a nod from Lizbeth, Hara stepped forward and bowed low, thick tears dripping onto the floor as she lost her battle to withhold them. "Thank you, My Queen."

Lizbeth's smile softened, and she caressed the back of her free hand along Hara's cheek, wiping her tears away. The sight was so at odds with the anger still simmering in her eyes, it immediately put me on edge. But Hara must've been used to the mercurial queen because she didn't seem to notice.

"You have always been indispensable, Hara. Your ability has brought more souls under my protection than most of my other Seekers combined. And it has certainly come in handy for my own use, which I will miss."

Although barely perceptible, Hara flinched, and I had to bite down on the inside of my cheek to rein in my anger. Lizbeth truly saw nothing wrong with anything she'd done, all but throwing it in Hara's face like her years of misery didn't matter.

I clasped my hands tighter, feeling my cuffs dig deeper as I snapped my daggered gaze to the queen, only to see her already staring at me. Instead of looking irritated by my anger or frustrated with losing Hara's soul, she looked triumphant, like whatever silent battle she and I were fighting, she'd somehow already won.

Keeping her green eyes locked with mine, she leaned down until her lips hovered over Hara's ear and said, "I promised the return of your soul, and I always keep my promises."

More tears tracked down Hara's face.

"But I never said in what condition I would return it. And let's be honest, moving a few miles is no longer indispensable when I'll possess the ability to move to an entirely different world."

Hara's head snapped back, and her eyes grew inhumanly large as every trace of color drained from her face. "My Queen?"

"Oh, don't look so horrified. It's nothing personal, my dear,"

Lizbeth said, palming her damp cheek. "I'd considered giving it back to remind everyone of my benevolence, but it has been made clear to me that a different lesson must be learned today."

I couldn't tear my eyes from Hara's horrified ones as she turned to gape at me, trying to grasp what they were talking about. It was clear Lizbeth was referring to me, but I wasn't sure what lesson I needed to learn that involved Hara, other than the confirmation that Lizbeth was a both a bitch and a liar.

"Something you need to accept sooner than later, Adelais," Lizbeth said, closing her hand tighter until the glowing blue was barely visible through the cracks between her fingers, "is that power and control are the only things worth living for, and you have neither here."

Then she squeezed her fist, and the sound that erupted from Hara was like nothing I'd ever heard before. Pure, unadulterated terror filled her blue eyes as she crumpled to the floor. Her body convulsed as she screamed, her agony echoing through the room and reverberating in my skull until I feared I'd never get it out.

I tried to lunge for her, but the guard who'd brought the box snatched my arms and ripped me back, smacking the back of my head against his armor so hard, I bit my tongue.

"Hara!" I yelled, ignoring the way my shoulder popped and throbbed as I fought to get out of his grasp. It was like the boy in Tover all over again, but I couldn't hide away and do nothing this time. Not when the punishment was because of me.

I stared at Lizbeth's clenched hand to see the blue light flickering frantically, like she was squeezing the life right out of it. I had no idea what would happen to Hara if her soul was crushed entirely, but from the blood-curdling screams tearing from her throat, I feared she wouldn't survive it.

"What's happening to her?" I yelled, no longer caring to speak with care. Lizbeth was torturing a defenseless woman for no reason. "Stop! She hasn't done anything."

Lizbeth didn't even deign to look at me, too enthralled with the thrashing girl on the floor, as if Hara's pain fed her in a way food could not. "No, she hasn't, but *you* have."

"Then punish me!" I yelled, feeling my binds cut deeper as I fought to free myself from the guard. "Please, Lizbeth. Stop! It has nothing to do with her. She did exactly what you asked."

"How long we do this is entirely up to you, Adelais. Give me your soul and swear to help me master it, or this continues, and I'll bring in children next." Her knuckles whitened as she squeezed tighter, and Hara's screams became screeching pleas, each word shattering another piece of my resolve.

"*Please! Oh God, I'm sorry! I'm sorry, please, please—*"

Hot tears poured down my cheeks as her begging turned to incoherent prayers, wishing I could slap my hands over my ears to block it out. Hara's skin had gone ashen the moment Lizbeth whispered in her ear, but she was now practically gray, her convulsing slowing as the blue light dimmed.

I cried harder, wanting to give in, to swear my soul to Lizbeth and prevent this from happening to anyone else, but I couldn't force my lips to form the words. I could feel the shadow of Terek's hand around my jaw and his voice in my mind, as if he were the one restraining me, refusing to let me speak. Demanding I be smarter and put myself first so I could survive as long as possible until I could escape. But God help me, I didn't want to.

I couldn't watch Hara wither away in agony over something she hadn't done. I couldn't watch children scream and thrash on the floor, their skin graying as their mothers beat at the castle doors. After so many years of abuse, I couldn't sit back and watch it happen to someone else.

I fucking refused.

"Leave her alone, Lizbeth. I'm begging you."

"No. Swear to me."

Terek's voice yelled louder, and something burned hot in my chest. "You don't even know if my soul will do anything for you. For all you know, I'll drop dead the moment you pull it out, and both my soul and ability will cease to exist."

She clicked her tongue. "Have it your way."

Lifting one pointed heel, she kicked Hara in the chest, sending the now unconscious girl onto her back, and my body stiffened, a memory I'd long since buried rising to the surface. Of the first time Frederick had laid a hand on me after our wedding.

I'd spent all evening trying to cook dinner, even though I'd never made a single meal in my life, and it'd turned out nearly inedible. He'd accused me of burning the food on purpose and struck me so hard, I'd fallen. When I hadn't immediately apologized, he'd started kicking me.

My shackled hands flew to my chest as that heat built hotter under my skin, flowing through my limbs and into my fingers. It seared my flesh, but it was different than the heat of my ability. It was like my anger was a tangible, vicious thing, and from it, something dark snapped inside me, wanting out.

"No!"

It erupted from me with such force, I swore my body went numb until all I could feel was that growing fury. Like it wasn't just mine, but everyone Lizbeth had ever hurt. The windows along the walls shattered, and I stumbled forward, my cry breaking off when the floor beneath us began to shake.

Benches vibrated and candelabras crashed around us, sending candles and splattered wax across the floor in all directions. Lizbeth's head snapped to me, and her fingers slackened over the now dull orb.

"Gag her!" she shrieked, something akin to panic flashing through her eyes as she stared at me like she'd never seen me before. *"Gag her right now, you imbeciles!"*

The hands around me tightened, and he twisted us away from her as another guard gripped my jaw, forcing something stiff and putrid into my mouth. I bucked harder and screamed around the gag, ramming the back of my head up into the man behind me. The edge of his helmet snagged my hair and cut into my scalp, but I caught the underside of his jaw, and he cursed.

"You stupid fucking bitch," the new guard spit, pulling his arm back and slapping me across the face so hard my head rang, and I swore

I felt my cheekbone shatter.

The quaking came to a halt, and I sagged, my arms falling uselessly in front of me while the man cut a thick strip from the bottom of my dress and wrapped it over my mouth, securing the gag in place.

I flared my nostrils and pulled in deep breaths, wincing from the pain and desperately trying not to go into a full panic attack at how helpless I was. I'd never known someone could hit harder than Frederick had, but I'd just add that to the growing list of things I was wrong about.

Hara still hadn't moved, her eyes open and unseeing, while her body lay sprawled across the floor at the queen's feet. Once I was successfully gagged and fighting to stay conscious, Lizbeth stepped over her and walked toward us, her fingers opening to reveal the flickering orb still within her palm.

She glared at me with all the rage of a storm, and for a moment, I thought she'd drop it to the floor as well, but instead, she sent a shockwave through my veins as she inhaled sharply and slammed Hara's soul directly into her chest.

What. The. Fuck.

I gaped, watching the blue disappear beneath Lizbeth's freckled skin and trying to comprehend what I'd just witnessed when she suddenly blinked out of sight, reappearing a second later a foot away from me. I flinched back in surprise, but the guard held me firm, digging his fingers into my biceps so hard it felt like he was trying to break bone.

Lizbeth's lip curled, and she stared down at me, nothing remotely sane remaining in her eyes. "You little bitch. I should've known it'd be *you*. Here I was, thinking Huka had lied to me all this time."

I stopped fighting, my swelling face throbbing in pain as confusion furrowed my brow. That name sounded so familiar, but I didn't have a chance to contemplate what she meant before she sneered and splayed her fingers over my breast.

My whole chest ignited, but unlike with my anger before, it didn't spread through my limbs and warm me, nor did it come with the tingling that always accompanied my traveling. Instead, it stayed centered over my heart and blazed like she'd turned her hand into a white-hot brand.

"The hard way it is, Adelais."

A muffled scream pushed against my gag as I realized what she was doing. What she was *taking*. Tension lined her face, and her arm trembled as she slowly began to remove her hand. A light flared in the inch of space between us—but rather than a cold blue like Hara's, it was blindingly bright and golden.

A triumphant smile lit her face when she saw it, and she widened her stance, posture straining as she fought to pull away another inch. I leaned back into the body behind me, wanting to kick out at her, but a wave of ice prickled at my extremities and flowed up, leaving them suddenly heavy and boneless.

My body slumped forward, and my head lolled against the guard, my neck unable to hold it up any longer. The cold hit my thighs and shoulders next, and I groaned, the world blurring around me. Her smile fell, and she strained harder, sweat beading along her brow. But just as the cold hit my ribs and darkness licked at the edges of my vision, the doors to the throne room flew open.

"Your Majesty!"

Lizbeth lurched away at the bellowed call and spun, her hand dropping from my chest. My spine arched as the golden light disappeared back beneath my skin and warmth flowed through me, but rather than return my energy, it only seemed to drain me more.

The six guards who'd been at the doors when Hara and I arrived were now standing just within the room, each with a hand gripping their weapons. A seventh guard, the one who'd spoken, stood before them and bowed low at the waist, her helmet tucked under her arm.

"Your Majesty," she repeated, her brown hair damp with sweat, face red, and chest visibly heaving. "Please forgive me, but it's urgent that I speak with you."

Lizbeth teetered slightly, and then she was stalking toward the woman, her spiked crown askew and poised mask disintegrating as she screamed at the top of her lungs, "How *dare* you barge in here and interrupt me!"

All seven guards shifted, the woman in front going so far as to take a small step back before catching herself and planting her feet. "Forgive me, Your Majesty, but it's…it's the Creatures. They're headed this way. I don't know how many."

Lizbeth stopped so abruptly, I had to squeeze my eyes shut several times, wondering if I'd finally lost my mind and time had frozen around me.

"They're at the wall?"

The guard shook her head. "Not that I know of. I couldn't see anything yet from the upper castle floors, but the Watch at the wall lit the torch for aid, so it cannot only be a couple."

Lizbeth's shoulders tensed, and she wiped at her forehead as she drew herself up. "Terek?"

"I haven't seen him, Your Majesty. I came straight here to inform you and request permission to send a group to the wall to confirm."

"That's not good enough," Lizbeth snapped, brushing her hands down her skirt and taking a deep breath. "Confirmation isn't going to keep them from my fucking wall. I don't care how many there are, I want them killed immediately. Take every guard readily available and take care of it. *Now!*"

The doors hadn't even shut behind them when Lizbeth blinked out of existence and appeared in front of me again, her fingers wrapping around my chin before my mind could process her movement. Her face was flushed and her hand clammy as she lifted my head, seemingly unsurprised by my inability to pull it from her grasp, though I glared at her with every bit of hostility I possessed. God, I was so tired.

"Consider yourself lucky that I no longer have the time to deal with you today, but let this be another lesson, Adelais. No matter how lenient and forgiving you are, there will always be those who seek more than they are given and who must be crushed."

Was she referring to the Creatures? Because being banished to the Wood didn't seem very lenient or forgiving at all. I continued to glare, unable to speak my thoughts past the gag bruising my tongue.

She patted my injured cheek and flicked her gaze to the man behind me. "Give her another dose and put her back in her cell, but make sure to remove her gag once she passes out. I don't want her choking on her own vomit. And for Underland's sake, someone get Hara out of here. The sight of her is beginning to irk me."

The guard turned me toward him, and I felt his hands circle my waist before he lifted me and tossed me over his shoulder. I wanted to fight and kick, to strike at him with everything I had until he dropped me, but my body was no longer responding. I could do nothing but hang over his back uselessly as he carried me toward the doors.

My eyelids grew heavy, and the last thing I saw, before the darkness finally closed in, was Lizbeth standing in the middle of the white room, watching me with a look of such unveiled envy, I swore I could taste it on my tongue.

TEREK

CHAPTER FORTY-FOUR

"Just get her past the gate," I said, going over the plan I'd begun devising from the moment the twins and I had stepped out of Tweeds. We'd discussed it during our mad dash here, but it was vital no one made a single mistake, or it'd all go to shit.

"What the crimson had you been planning to do if we hadn't come?" Duma asked, amusement in his voice. "Force your way into the castle and kill anyone who happened to see you?"

Set the city aflame until the guards were drawn out by the screams and chaos, follow her pull until I found her, and then *kill whoever saw me.*

I glared at him. "More or less."

He chuckled and ran a hand over his jaw, the crackle of the coarse, unshaved hairs scraping through my ears. "If the innate desire to murder everyone you see in order to protect one person isn't your clear sign that she's your—"

"I'll keep my senses wide open," I said over him, in no mood to hear the man lecture me about his stupid beliefs again. "If something goes wrong, I'll get you out. If all goes right, I'll meet you at the gate, and you can leave and make haste back to Tover."

My head was already pounding at just the idea of keeping my senses open in a city of thousands. Picking out familiar voices wasn't hard—not after decades of practice, at least—but that didn't mean I wouldn't want to rip my ears off every second they were in there.

I fucking hated that I couldn't be the one to storm into the White Castle and get her, knowing it'd take the twins twice as long to do it. But being seen anywhere near the castle with Ace there, after I'd convinced Lizbeth she'd been a random fling, would do far more damage than good.

The best I could do was to be ready to make a mad sprint through the city the second she was in my arms and pray Lizbeth's deranged belief that I still secretly loved her would keep her from suspecting I was involved.

Risking Duma and Dex's souls wasn't something I wanted to do either, but there was no way to get Ace out without someone going in. Since Duma had just purchased supplies here, they had the only alibi with any chance of working. Such a shame his entire load was overtaken by thieves on his way back to Tover, and they were returning for necessary replacements.

Or so their story would go.

"Where do you plan to take her?" Duma asked. I knew he and Dex wanted me to bring her back to Tweeds, but I'd declined each time one of them had brought it up. They believed Lizbeth would've already taken Ace's soul by now and wouldn't need her anymore, but I didn't share that belief.

"I'm going to take her to the outskirts of Gissan. It's risky, but it's the best choice of action. Lizbeth will expect her to be in Ardenglass, and when she's not found, the next place she'll have checked is Tover. If we're lucky, she'll assume Ace went Upside and isn't here, but I doubt it. At most, we should have at least a few days' head start."

Duma didn't look convinced. "And you're absolutely sure Ace hasn't already done that?"

I nodded. The tug toward her had steadily grown stronger the closer we got to Ardenglass. "Positive."

It was *why* she hadn't gone Upside yet that was the main reason for my continually darkening mood. Was it because she was so impressively, infuriatingly stubborn—which wouldn't surprise me one bit—or because she was no longer capable of doing so?

The twins shared a look, communicating in that silent way of theirs whenever they thought I'd said something unhinged or stupid.

"Spit it out," I said, cutting my eyes away from them to stare at the white wall in the distance, the last barrier separating us from the city that had taken so much from me. That apparently would never *stop* taking from me.

"We don't like the idea of you two going to a place like Gissan alone," Duma said. "We know you can handle your own, but what if Ace is hurt more than…well, you know."

Yeah, I did fucking know.

He rubbed a hand over the back of his neck, following my line of sight. "We have Tweeds taken care of, Terek. Our staff are good people, and they were already trained to take over when we began looking into buying another property to start up. Tweeds will be all right for as long as you need us."

My jaw popped, his words about Ace's condition cutting into me and making me want to murder someone. "Her life will pay your debt, Duma. You have no obligation to help once she's returned to me. We'll be even."

"It has nothing to do with being even, Terek. What's the goddamn point of eternity if we spend it not giving a shit about the people around us?" Duma said, irritation flashing across his usually stoic face.

Dex, who had the riskiest part in all of this, scoffed and sheathed his sword behind him again, returning the whetstone he'd been using to his pack. "Did you consider that she might need me? Just because we hope she's only soulless doesn't mean that's all that has happened. I may not be able to do much, but I can do more than you, and we all know the guards in the castle are the worst of them."

He smacked a large hand over my shoulder, unfazed by the daggered look I gave him in reply. "Besides, I still owe her a stew, and who else would cook it for her? You—"

The rest of his sentence fell away as I whipped around and dropped my hands to my daggers, my eyes connecting with the line of trees just on the other side of the river. To where a dull humming had suddenly begun. Although I could sense their unease, both Duma and Dex stayed deathly silent behind me, giving me time to focus my attention and listen.

"Balance your weight," I yelled over my shoulder, feeling the beginning of tremors beneath my feet before either of them could. They obeyed without question, planting their legs wide just in time for the ground beneath us to quake, and not just a little. It was as if God, himself, had wrapped his hands around the Underland and started shaking.

"What the crimson hell is happening?" Dex shouted.

"I have no idea," I said, keeping my eyes on the trees. I'd never before experienced a quake of any kind here, but the ground shaking was the least of my concerns as the steady hum emanating from the Wood got louder. It sounded almost like... My eyes flared, and I spun back to my companions, my teeth practically vibrating together even as the trembles slowed.

I checked my weapons, making sure they were secure enough not to fly off as I ran and met Duma's questioning look. "Creatures are coming. A lot of them."

"*What?*" Dex said, looking past me with a frown, only for his brows to shoot up as his eyes blew wide. "Oh, fuck."

I didn't turn around, already knowing what they could now see. The horde sprinting from between the trees. "Can you get her to the outskirts of Ardenglass if I'm not back in time?"

Duma white-knuckled his axes but nodded. "Yeah. Last I knew, toward the west of Gissan's road are some new homes no one's in yet. We could probably take her to one for a bit."

"Perfect. I'll meet up with you as soon as I can."

His stare locked over my shoulder onto the fast-moving forms. "You're sure you want to head toward that? Even you have limits, Terek."

"I don't have a fucking choice," I growled, my gut roiling as the torch at the wall was lit, signaling a call for help. Lizbeth's rage if I didn't stop them from reaching the wall was something we couldn't risk having right now. But this fight also meant she was going to be very distracted, which the twins could use to their advantage.

And as I pushed additional strength into my muscles and took off toward the Wood, I found myself thankful for the goddamn Creatures for the first time in my undead life.

ADELAIS

CHAPTER FORTY-FIVE

My senses returned to me slowly, each new one making me wish they hadn't. The chill of the floor, the putrid scent of stale vomit, a harsh yank at my stinging wrists, and then the sound of heavy boots disappearing before the slam of a door.

My muscles ached, but it was the deep exhaustion penetrating every inch of my body that kept me pinned to the unforgiving floor. I felt like I'd been washed up to shore after somehow surviving at sea for hours during a violent storm. A fate that would've been far less traumatizing than the reality of what had happened in that throne room.

I was used to pain, had acclimated to differing levels and built up my tolerance, compacting my reactions into a little corner of my mind until I was safe enough to process them. But this was different. Everything I'd been through Upside had never been my fault. I hadn't chosen Frederick, and I hadn't deserved my father's disdain.

But this? Wandering Tover after I'd promised not to, believing Hara without thinking my actions through, angering Lizbeth? I had no one to blame but myself, those immature mistakes nearly costing me my soul.

Tears streamed down my face, dripping steadily into my ears at the memory of the golden light that'd flared from my chest under Lizbeth's hand. I had a soul. Terek, Duma, Dex, Hara, they'd all had them at one point. It wasn't just a flimsy religious belief to hold onto at night, hoping that if we lived up to someone else's standards of purity, we could enter a perfect afterlife.

No, they were tangible. Beautiful. *Real.*

More tears flowed until they were pooling from my ears to the tangled mess of my hair. The next time I was dragged from here, Lizbeth was going to try to take my soul again, and there was nothing I could do about it, nothing I could offer her that she wanted more. And unlike everyone else here who were already dead, I had no idea what losing my soul would do to me.

I begged my body to move, wanting to curl up tight and hide away like I used to after I'd stumble from my father's study. For the first time, I wished I'd listened to Terek and had never left the protective cover of the Wood.

Living with Frederick, I'd bottled myself up tight, using my anger and hatred as a shield until I could escape to the trees for a few precious hours. The Wood had been a safety net I could fall into anytime I needed, but here, drugged and chained, I had nothing. No net. No backup. I'd simply traded one prison for another, and it turned out the chains here were far tighter.

"How did you do it?"

I startled at the voice, instinct urging me to push up from my helpless position on the floor, but I only succeeded at feeling even more vulnerable, my body refusing to listen. Instead, I had to make do with sucking in a breath that sent lashes of pain through my chest and force my head to flop to the side where the cell bars were.

A frown pulled at my brows, causing my swollen eye to throb in protest as I stared hard at my visitor. A visitor who'd sought to sell my soul in exchange for her own, and whom I hadn't expected to ever see again. A visitor I shouldn't feel so relieved to see standing whole and alive.

I closed my eyes, convinced the third dose of sedatives had sent me straight past nausea to full hallucinations, but when I opened them again, Hara still stood just on the other side of the bars. Her skin was a sickly hue, and she was chewing on a nail, her eyes and body fidgeting like she was terrified to be here.

My lip curled at the thought of her crawling across the floor, trying to stand, as Lizbeth demanded she fetch me again after just torturing her in front of an audience. Hara had done exactly what she'd been asked, and Lizbeth had nearly wiped her from existence for it, just to make a point to me that she could.

Sympathy for this girl, who'd been molded by the cruelest side of the Underland into the only version she could become to survive, flared hot in my belly. It mixed with the anger, misery, and hatred already there until I thought it'd surge up, and I'd choke on it all.

"How did you do it?" she repeated, dropping her hand to curl around the edges of her untucked tunic.

I licked my lips, my tongue peeling off the roof of my mouth with a sticky pop. How long had it been since Hara had shared her flask with me? Hell, how long had it been since I'd *eaten?*

"Do what?" I asked, my voice hoarse and brittle like I'd been screaming for hours on end.

Instead of answering, Hara's brows furrowed deeper, whether at my answer or my pathetic condition, I wasn't sure. Nor did I comprehend how she was moving after what she'd just been through. I couldn't even lift a hand to brush the stray hairs from my face. Then again, she hadn't been drugged numerous times in one day.

She shot a quick look down the hall before squatting to be more eye level with me. Her gaze darted over my face with purpose, like she was trying to decipher if I was lying or not. But it'd be hard to lie to someone when I didn't know what we were talking about, or if this conversation was even real.

"Interesting."

"What is?" I asked, pressing my palms against the floor and trying to roll to my side to face her. The wasted effort only shot a wave of nausea through me, and I had to hold my breath until the dizziness subsided.

"Stop trying to move. You're going to ache for a few days, and you'll feel like you haven't slept in a year, trust me. The sickness is from the sedative. They gave you a full dose, but it'll wear off soon. I'm supposed to give you more to keep you unconscious, but I'm not going to."

Did she want me to thank her? I could barely blink. A lack of more sedatives wasn't going to make a difference with using my ability. Why the hell was she here and talking to me like we were on the same side anyway? *How* was she here?

"I saw…" I swallowed, trying to wet my mouth and center my thoughts. My right eye was blurry and throbbing, and it was making it hard to focus.

"I thought she…I thought she killed you." It sounded stupid, given we were in the Underland, but I knew Hara would understand my meaning. "You looked *dead*, dead."

Hara's face darkened, mixing with her pallid skin and sharp features until she looked almost skeletal. "I have a lifetime of experience playing dead and waiting for monsters to finish with me."

I blinked up at her, my chest hollowing out, unsure what to say. From the moment I met her, it was clear she hadn't lived an easy life, but the pain in her eyes, the lingering, deep-seated kind I knew all too well, made me think it started long before she entered the Underland.

"I know you want your soul back," I said, forcing the words out even as each one felt like running a race, "but you deserve better than what she's forcing you to do, Hara."

But even as I said it, we both knew she didn't have a choice when Lizbeth had shown just how easily—and how willingly—she could crush her soul in a matter of seconds if Hara ever ran. Still, I wanted her to know that someone cared, and that as much as I resented what her choices had led to, I didn't resent *her* for making them.

She looked away, her blue eyes going out of focus as she ran her fingertips over the base of her throat. "Lizbeth wasn't wrong, you know."

I frowned, wondering if I'd somehow missed something she'd said. "About what?"

"Our abilities. That they're gifted to us based on what the Underland believes we want or need more than anything else, even if we don't know it." She huffed a laugh devoid of all life. "As a way to make our journey to the afterlife as fulfilling as possible."

I considered that, remembering how devoutly Terek believed everyone with an ability was cursed rather than gifted. "How do you know that?"

She shrugged, shifting her weight and wincing. "I don't. It's not like there's an ancient book on the creation of the Underland or anything. It's just what many of us believe. You'll learn soon enough that time will give you all kinds of reasons to overthink life."

That was true, I supposed, though I hoped I'd learn that without having to be trapped here until I became as mad and selfish as everyone else.

"So, your ability was based on your need to…" Go places she wasn't supposed to? Help her steal things? Sneak into rooms and kidnap people?

"Run away."

My heart squeezed when silver pooled in her eyes, and I dropped my gaze to where she was still subconsciously running fingers across her neck as she stared, unseeing, at the ground.

"I have only ever wanted one thing my entire life."

"And the Underland gave it to you?" I asked.

It felt odd discussing this world like it was sentient, but in a way, I knew what she meant. I'd often felt a presence brush against me whenever I'd arrive, as if in welcome, and thought it was just in my head, but maybe it hadn't been.

Blinking back her tears, she caught me staring and immediately dropped her hand, a wall slamming down over her face. She cleared her throat. "It just makes one wonder what the Underland thought you needed so badly that it was determined to bring you here early."

I nodded that I was listening, or at least I thought I did. My head was beginning to feel heavy again, and I was suddenly struggling to keep my eyes open.

"Anyway," she continued, "I just wanted to tell you that I'm sorry. I won't lie and say I wouldn't do it again if I thought it'd go differently, but I won't push to make anything worse for you."

"Worse?" I was chained to a floor until an insane queen came to rip my soul from my chest so she could shove it into her own and test it like a new toy. How on Earth could Hara make it worse?

"You and Terek," she clarified, drawing circles on the ground with the toe of her boot. "I can't exactly lie when Lizbeth has the ability to detect it with one of her souls, but I won't go out of my way to tell her about you two."

A laugh bubbled up my throat, but it came out sounding more like a ragged cough. "There is no *us*."

Her brows shot to her hairline, like she'd truly thought there was something going on between us, but she didn't push. "Regardless, I won't tell her he's been with you. Right now, she just thinks I found you staying in Tover. I'll try to keep it that way if I can."

She chewed her nail again, darting more looks down the hall, and I had a feeling she was getting ready to disappear. "If you think you've seen Lizbeth mad, that's nothing compared to what she'll do if she discovers Terek found you first and didn't bring you in right away."

I bit the inside of my cheek to keep myself awake, trying to push the fog of confusion at bay long enough to focus on what Hara was saying.

"Why are you suddenly helping me?" She'd made it obvious she had no problem screwing over Terek. I wanted to ask what he'd done to make her hate him so much anyway, but knowing Terek, he'd probably just been his usual asshole self too many times.

"Because I owe you a life debt, and because I saw the queen's face when you shook—when you screamed. She was utterly terrified of you," Hara said, a pained flinch crossing her face as she took a few steps away from my cell.

Wait, what? Lizbeth terrified of *me*? Now I definitely knew I was starting to hallucinate.

She looked down at me again, misery painting her features. "I'd do anything to get my soul back, Adelais. Anything. I don't want to live forever, but I'm also terrified to move on without my soul and go to whatever black void of hell there is for the soulless."

She sighed, rubbing her fingers beneath her eyes. "I just want to experience the peace that death was supposed to grant me, and Lizbeth is never going to let me have it."

No, she wouldn't. If there was anything stronger than Lizbeth's obsession with being loved and feared, it was the way she thrived on being cruel. I could almost guarantee she expected Hara to continue bringing in new souls as if nothing had happened.

"I'm sorry," I said, meaning it.

"Anyway, if there's anyone who even has a chance at ripping the throne out from under that crimson bitch, my bet's on you two." She sucked on her front teeth, making a soft whistling sound. "Feel free to tell him I refused to drug you again and am keeping his secret. I have no desire to be on his list when he takes in your state."

What list? I wanted to ask, but my eyes had already fallen shut, and then she was gone, leaving me in silence until my exhaustion pulled me under.

⚷

THE NEXT TIME I awoke, it was to large hands wrapping around my body. One slipped beneath my neck while the other curled under my knees, lifting me from the floor to press into a firm chest.

I bucked in the guard's hold, instantly wide awake as my eyes struggled to take in the shadowed head above me in my darkened cell. He didn't hit me to make me submit or shove anything into my mouth like the guard in the throne room had, but neither did he release his firm hold on me.

I was well aware fighting back was pointless and would only further exhaust me, but I also knew where he intended to take me and, regardless of the inevitable outcome, I wouldn't return to that throne room willingly. Lizbeth said we'd do things the hard way, so that's what she'd get from me.

At least, that's what rushed through my mind at the feel of those hands. My sore, sluggish body, however, apparently didn't feel the same rage. Because rather than slap and kick at my attacker, my hands merely flopped out, patting uselessly over his.

I seethed, feeling my eyes sting with angry tears as I glared up at the hovering form, but I didn't let them fall. None of these bastards deserved to see me break any more than they already had. They could do whatever they wanted to my body and hit me until they felt better about themselves, but my emotions were *mine*. Not even Lizbeth could take them away from me. The only one she'd get was my hatred.

"I got you, sweetheart. It's just me. I'm going to get you out of here."

The hand beneath my knees retreated, and a soft yellow glow appeared above me as he raised an ornate, white lantern near his head. It illuminated his face, and a choked sob burst from my throat at the sight of a shaved head and a familiar, kind smile.

"Duma."

"It's me, Ace." He held the lantern closer to me, and his wide brown eyes roved over me, his smile quickly falling. "Crimson hell, I need to get you to Dex. Do you know if anything's broken?"

I shook my head, thankful when it listened. "Nothing broken," I got out, my tongue still feeling far too thick for my mouth. "But I can't walk. Lizbeth—"

His lips pressed flat. "I know, sweetheart, and I'm so sorry. Don't worry about that right now. Let's just get you out of here. There's a bed and stew waiting for you, okay?"

"Okay."

He gave me another smile, but this one didn't quite reach his eyes. "Good. Keep leaning against me. I'm going to set the lantern down so I can look at your bindings. Why are they so fucking tight?"

The last part seemed more for himself than me, so I didn't answer, instead absorbing his warmth and straining my ears for anyone approaching. He had to have passed numerous guards to get through the castle and down here. The man was a giant, surely, someone had seen him.

"How are you here, Duma? How did you even find me?"

He grunted. "A diversion, and it wasn't me who found you."

I wanted to ask what the hell kind of diversion would occupy every guard in the castle, but the last part had another thought hitting me first. "Terek's here?"

A heady emotion I didn't want to name flickered to life in my ribcage at the thought of him coming for me after our fight, but I tamped it back down, remembering what Hara had said. If Lizbeth saw Terek here and thought he was betraying her for me, she may very well kill me on the spot.

Thankfully, Duma shook his head, concentrating on my bound wrists as he analyzed the iron cuffs and crusted blood. "No, Terek isn't capable of being in public at the moment. Dex is working his charm on the few guards who know we're here."

I watched his fingers as he carefully turned my wrists this way and that, unsure what he meant but glad Terek hadn't been reckless enough to barge into the White Castle. Yet.

"That's nothing new. Terek's never been public friendly," I mumbled, readjusting myself over Duma's legs as best I could and resting my face against his collar. After the freezing floor, he felt like wrapping up in a blanket by a hearth.

Duma chuckled. "Trust me, Terek had been a damn puppy before compared to how he's been since you've been gone. I honestly don't know how you'll put up with the bastard. I'm as dead as they come, yet I swear the trip with him fucking aged me."

I tried to return his smile but couldn't. The thought of him and Dex taking such a risk when they'd only just met me weighed me down more than any sedative. No matter how much Terek had likely threatened them to help, my life wasn't worth the risk to their souls, especially when we'd all be sitting safely at Tweeds if I'd only listened.

He carefully released my wrists and grimaced. "I can't get these off without hurting you, Ace. They're too imbedded into your skin. I'm going to break the chains, but the cuffs will have to stay until we can get you somewhere safe enough for Dex to help with the pain."

"I'll be fine. Just do it." I didn't care if I wore the cuffs for the rest of my life, as long as it was as far from Lizbeth as possible.

Duma curled me tighter into his body so that my head was supported by his shoulder and wrapped both his hands around the chains leading to the floor. Then he closed his eyes and exhaled deeply, his face straining as his shoulders tensed behind me. I twisted my head toward the floor, trying to see what was causing his look of pain, when I saw what was happening.

What he was doing.

He hissed, and smoke began curling from the sides of his fists, sending a burning, metallic scent to my nose. My eyes widened when the barest hint of orange peeked out from his palms, and then a *thunk* echoed out as his hands opened and the molten links dropped to the floor.

I lifted my wrists over my lap, the now short chains dangling from each cuff. "Holy shit, Duma."

A groan sounded from down the hall, and Duma's head snapped up, a hand going to his waist where a weapon likely sat. "You can swoon over my ability later, Ace. We need to get out of here before we're both locked up."

I stared at the chains on the floor, the edges of the last links deformed. "Somehow, I doubt you could be locked in any cell."

He slanted me a look. "Everything has limits, Ace."

Shooting to a standing position and making me yelp in surprise, he tossed me over his shoulder like I weighed no more than a feather pillow and removed an axe from his side. Then he snatched up the lantern and stalked out into the dark hall, each sconce purposefully extinguished so that his light was all there was.

From my upside-down position, I noticed a key sticking out of the door rather than a broken lock and had a strong feeling the groan we'd heard belonged to whoever had originally held that key.

"Sorry about the potato sack hold, but I need my hands," Duma whispered, sprinting down the hall. "We got lucky that most of the guards were sent to the Wood to fight, but there's bound to be some wandering back in from the city, and definitely a few at the castle gate."

I gripped the back of his tunic, my stomach jostling uncomfortably over his shoulder. "Oh, my God, I'd forgotten about the Creatures. Please tell me that's not where Terek is," I said, already knowing the answer.

Duma awkwardly patted my leg with the flat side of his axe and began ascending the stairs two at a time, pausing only long enough to knee a slumped guard in the head to knock him unconscious again.

"Terek will be fine and will meet up with us as soon as he can. In theory, at least. Fate may be on our side right now, but that doesn't mean it'll stay that way."

Didn't I know it. I raised my head and tried to keep the blood from rushing to it as unease thickened in my gut at the idea of Terek fighting a horde of Creatures. He was fast, but I'd seen him injured by one before, and who knew what abilities some of them might have.

Though, it was also possible the earthquake was what had lured them out, and they were only spurred by fear rather than an organized attack. For all we knew, the shaking could've been far worse in the Wood than here. Not that it mattered much now since Terek was already gone, but still.

I crossed my fingers, hoping the Creatures would see him and the approaching army of White Guards and choose to flee rather than fight.

Reaching the top of the winding stairs, Duma tucked the lantern next to a matching one on a window ledge and peeked around the corner before taking off down the silent corridor. Then another and another until I worried I might vomit all down his back. At the end of each one, we listened for any sign of life—footsteps, shuffling, a throat clearing, *something*—but we appeared to be the only people anywhere on this side of the castle.

"This feels too easy," I whispered, my spine screaming at me from my valiant attempt to raise my head.

Sensing my struggle, Duma stepped into the next arched doorway and sheathed his axe, carefully setting my feet on the floor. I nearly groaned when the blood started rushing back to where it was supposed to be, making me lightheaded.

"You underestimate how much the queen fears the Creatures of the Wood. Considering the number of guards Dex and I saw making haste toward the west wall, I'd bet Tweeds there's no more than a couple dozen left within this castle. Like I said, fate is suspiciously on our side right now."

I leaned against the wall and stared up at him, finally able to see him clearly for the first time now that we were in a well-lit corridor, and I wasn't headbutting his rear end. The hard line of his jaw was covered in short, coarse hair, and there were lines around his eyes showing his clear fatigue, but otherwise, he appeared as at ease as he had in Tweeds.

As if sneaking through a deranged woman's castle was something he did all the time before brewing ale and kneading bread.

"So, if everyone's gone, where is Dex?" I asked.

"At the side gate the merchants use, which we've just about reached." Duma glanced down at me and pointed to a line of windows at the end of the hall, showing a courtyard I desperately hoped was where we were headed.

"I'll admit, though, I did expect *you* to be guarded more heavily," he added, giving me a loaded look that told me Terek had informed him of what I could do and why Lizbeth wanted me so badly. Shame coiled in my belly.

I stared at my shoes and adjusted my weight against the wall, struggling to stay standing but not wanting to admit it out loud. I was so damn tired of appearing weak in front of everyone.

"It's probably because Lizbeth assumed I'd be asleep for a while." At Duma's questioning look, I lifted a shoulder. "Hara was ordered to sedate me again, but she didn't."

His eyes immediately narrowed, and he opened his mouth to say something, but a door far closer than I'd like suddenly slammed, and several voices began speaking at once. I stiffened and held my breath, hoping they'd go the other direction, but they grew steadily louder, accompanied by the thunderous metal footfalls of a handful of armored bodies.

Duma cursed under his breath and gripped my waist, whispering a gritted apology before pushing me deeper into the doorway. My back smacked against the wood, but I'd barely registered the discomfort before he was pressing his body flush to mine. One hand braced his weight beside my head, and the other lowered to rest loosely on my hip, the heat of his body enveloping me.

He dropped his lips to my ear just as the voices and clang of armor rounded the corner and said, scarcely above a whisper, "Whatever you hear me or them say, keep your face down."

My hands were tucked awkwardly between us, my wrists screaming at how hard he pressed into them, but I didn't dare shift them as I obeyed a split second before the group came into view.

Adrenaline pumped through my veins, and my nerves fired in all directions with each shadow that crossed the doorway. I dug my hands into Duma's tunic and prayed, to any and every god, that they wouldn't notice us. And for one blessed moment, I thought he might be right about fate being on our side.

Until the last guard in the group passed by, stretching his neck to the side and laughing at something another said, just in time for his eyes to land directly on us. I yanked my gaze away from where I'd been peeking around Duma's arm and tucked closer to his chest, genuinely worried I might pass out when the guard lurched to a stop.

"And what do we have here?" he asked, his voice nasally and drawn out, like stumbling upon us was the high point of his day, and he'd be all too happy to stick around and watch what we were up to.

I heard several other steps backtracking to see what had caught his attention, and I braced for them to instantly know who we were and to tear Duma off me before dragging me to Lizbeth. I squeezed my eyes shut and bit my tongue hard enough to bleed, wishing with all my might that my ability worked like Hara's and I could transport us both somewhere safe.

But rather than shouts and the sound of weapons being removed, a few of them laughed, and a deep, older voice spoke over them, humor clear in his tone. "Oh, leave 'em be, Ridek. If we're about to be called in to fight those crimson fucking monsters, you better believe I'll be finding my own quick pussy somewhere around here, too. The man's got the right fucking idea."

"Ain't that the truth," another said, coming closer like he wanted to see me and decide for himself if I was worth waiting for his turn instead of searching for someone else.

Every muscle in my body locked up, and my eyes snapped to Duma's in horror, bile filling my throat. No. This couldn't be happening after everything I'd done to stay in the Underland and escape that exact future with Frederick. I'd rather die than let these men rip away even that from me.

Duma's brown eyes held mine, an apology filling them even while his jaw ticced and his nails scraped against the door. "Can you blame me?" he said over his shoulder, forcing an arrogant laugh that didn't match his expression. "I'm stuck traveling with all that shit going on. I could use a little enjoyment first, so, if you'll excuse us…"

He slid his hand to my thigh and hiked it up as high as it could go, forcing me onto my toes. I sucked in a surprised breath and dropped my gaze to where my leg clamped around his, understanding dawning when I realized how close the move had conveniently placed his hand to his axe.

His fingers twitched over my dress, readying to release me and snatch his weapon if needed, and his unwavering gaze never left mine, letting me know that whatever happened, I'd be safe. He'd push no further to fake the act, and he wouldn't let them touch me.

I stared back, trying to convey my own message. Duma was strong, but he was only one man, and there were at least five behind him, all with abilities we had no knowledge of. With everything he and his brother had put on the line for me, I'd rather admit to the guards who I was than stand by and watch them hurt him.

But the older-sounding guard only smacked the wall and turned away, crass laughter following him as he instructed them to continue on, their boisterous conversation now on which of the servants they'd search out if the Creatures, indeed, breached the wall.

Once silence had settled back over us and my heart had calmed to a more normal beat, Duma shoved away from me and glanced down the hall after them. Confirming they were gone, his nostrils flared, and he ran a hand over his scalp, his mannerisms radiating fury.

"Crimson hell, I fucking hate it here. I'm sorry—"

I reached up and smacked my hand over his mouth, stopping him and enjoying his flinch of surprise. "Do not apologize that there are horrible people. They exist in every world. You have my permission to do whatever is necessary to get us the hell out of here. Now, pick me up, I think my legs are about to give out."

He chuckled and scooped me up, carrying me in front of his chest this time, rather than over his shoulder. Though he didn't state it, I had a feeling the observant man had noticed the fresh blood around my shackles and didn't want to risk hurting me more.

"Would you feel the same if you'd have had to kiss me to convince them?" he asked, a mischievous tilt to his lips as he ran down the hall and turned the corner, all but sprinting down the next and barreling through a small, wooden door.

A comforting breeze hit my clammy skin, and I sighed, the suffocating pressure that'd been on me since I'd first woken in the cell finally beginning to lift. I patted his chest. "I'd feel the same even if I'd had to climb you like a tree."

His deep laugh vibrated against my cheek, and I smiled, swallowing back my own.

"Just do me a favor and don't let Terek hear you say that. I'm quite attached to my balls."

ADELAIS

CHAPTER FORTY-SIX

"What the hell is he doing?" I asked, staring wide-eyed and horror-struck, as Dex stood in the center of a group of guards, his brown head glistening with sweat and a long sword clasped in his hands.

"Distracting," Duma said far too calmly while he shook his arms out, like it was the most obvious answer, and his brother fighting an entire group of guards was a normal, everyday occurrence.

"Shouldn't we be helping him?" I asked, frustrated at Duma's lack of reaction. I couldn't even walk without falling to the ground, but I was willing to try in order to help him. No one could take on that many guards at once. Well, except for maybe Terek, but I didn't always believe he was fully human, so he didn't really count.

"They're sparring, not fighting, Ace. Trust me, he's fine."

I glanced around the corner again, supporting my weight against the outer wall of the castle as best as I could with my legs shaking. After sprinting across the empty courtyard and along a path, we were now only a few yards away from the gate…and freedom.

Duma had reluctantly set me down to stretch out his arms before our next mad dash into Ardenglass, while we waited for whatever scene Dex planned to distract the guards. I'd assumed, incorrectly it would seem, that he'd accuse people of causing issues at the front gate to make the guards run off, or he'd enrapture them with some ridiculously inappropriate story or something. What I hadn't expected was the sound of metal clashing together.

Now, as I watched Dex spin the blade in his hand, I was questioning both of their sanity.

"He could have done literally anything else as a distraction. He's going to get hurt," I hissed. I couldn't claim to be the best decision maker, but surely this would only cause negative attention and make them remember Dex had been here.

Duma's chest pressed into my arm as he leaned around me to watch his brother. But rather than nerves or fear, pride shimmered in his eyes. "My brother is one hell of a fighter. He doesn't come here as often as I do, but he challenges the guards every time he visits. It's the only way he gets practice in. They don't always agree, but after so many years, they're used to him asking."

I chewed on my lip as Dex flashed a wide grin and reared back, avoiding a blade to his ear. The guard barely had time to regain his balance before Dex had him retreating, curses flying as their blades met again and again. It was almost like a dance and might've been beautiful if every move didn't look like someone was about to lose their head.

"Where did he even learn to do that?" I asked, resting my hands on Duma's shoulders as he scooped me up again. The brothers ran an inn and tavern; why would either of them need to know how to spar with a sword? Unless, of course, Dex had learned prior to his death.

"Terek," was all Duma said before Dex's amused voice caught both of our attention, and I tucked that tidbit away to question later.

"Come on, is that all you've got? Make it hard!" Dex shouted, his familiar, booming laugh drawing a reluctant smile to my face. Leave it to Dex to get away with insulting the White Guard.

A second guard came forward and removed his weapon, the red hilt making my smile fall and stomach churn. Duma's arms tightened around me as Dex inched to the side, still talking shit and drawing everyone's attention away from where we hid.

The second the last guard gave us his back, Duma was sprinting for the gate faster than I'd ever known a man his size could move. I clung to his tunic and buried my face in his neck, my heart in my throat as I waited for one of them to notice us and yell out. But all I heard as we shot through the gate and down the cobbled street into Ardenglass, was Duma's heavy breaths, Dex's laughter, and the harsh clang of swords resuming.

⚷

WE'D ONLY MADE it about a mile before Duma maneuvered us into an alley, beside what smelled like a bakery, and unceremoniously plopped my ass onto a crate. I groaned and gripped the edges, trying not to sway as he began to mutter and rifle through a pack I hadn't noticed before. Between it, me, and his weapons, I might've questioned if the giant man had Terek's strength and steel will, had the rapid movements of his chest not given him away.

"Here," he said, pulling out a leather flask and a small, wrapped bundle from the bag.

I crossed my legs beneath my dress and greedily took them, uncaring what it was. It could've been ale and moldy cheese, and I'd have consumed it with just as much gusto. Besides the bread Hara had given me, I had no idea how long it'd been since I'd eaten, and my stomach was practically caving in on itself.

Thankfully, it was a few strips of tender, dried meat with far more spice than the hard, flavorless pieces Terek had shared with me. The moan that left me as I ate it would've made every person at one of my mother's parties gasp in horror.

Duma, however, didn't bat an eye as he practically shoved some into his own mouth and clasped the food wrappings in his palms. He flinched, so slight I'd have missed it if I hadn't been staring so closely, before the smell of smoke hit my nose, and he opened his hands to drop a small pile of ash onto the ground.

I sat up a little straighter and leaned my head against the wall, hugging my knees and pointedly pretending like I didn't know how filthy the bricks behind me were. "It hurts you, doesn't it? Using your ability."

Duma brushed his hands over his trousers and cleared his throat, clearly uncomfortable with either discussing himself in general or discussing what could be considered a weakness. "Yes. I may produce heat, but I'm not wholly immune to it. It doesn't blister my skin, if that's what you're worried about, but that doesn't keep it from fucking feeling like it is."

I chewed my lip and tucked my hands back in my lap, my shackles suddenly feeling extra tight. Melting them enough to break them off me wouldn't be as quick as burning a wrapper, and I didn't like the idea of causing him pain.

Maybe we could just wait until Terek met up with us, and then he could try to break them off without Duma's help. Or we could wait until we got back to Tover and ask a local smithy to configure a key or something.

Duma's hand landed on the top of my head with a thud. "I know what you're thinking. Stop. I use my ability every day to light the kindling in the hearth at Tweeds. I'm used to it, Ace. I promise."

Still unconvinced, I was about to voice some of the alternatives when a shadow darkened the entrance of the alley behind him. I immediately stiffened, and Duma whirled around, one arm outstretched to block me while the other held his axe aloft.

"You should've thrown that, brother. If I had one of the nastier abilities some of these fuckers around here have, you'd already be dancing your way to the dark void."

The hand in front of me formed a vulgar gesture. "Took you fucking long enough. You were supposed to distract, not make a day of it."

Dex raised a brow and ran his tongue over a split in his lip. The sword I'd seen him holding was strapped to his back, and there were shadows of sweat beneath his arms and around his neckline, while rivulets ran down his head.

"If that's your version of a thank you, it could use some work. I couldn't exactly sprint off the second I spotted you without looking suspicious. Now, where is—" His mouth dropped open when I leaned around Duma, and Dex shoved past him, his hands coming up to cup my face. "Oh, crimson hell, Ace."

"We don't have time for you to do anything right now," Duma said, his stress finally starting to seep through his stoic resolve the longer we dallied near the castle. "We should've been halfway across the city by now, and you'll need your strength just in case we're stopped."

Dex glared up at his brother before he sighed and dropped his hands, offering to help me off the crate instead. "Fine, you ass, but I'm helping her the moment we get there."

I wasn't a hundred percent sure what they were talking about, but with how my face still throbbed, I assumed it likely had to do with cleaning and bandages.

Smacking away his brother's proffered hands, Duma removed his cloak and draped it over me, covering the entirety of my body and securing the latch at my neck. Then he yanked the oversized hood over my head and hauled me off the crate and into his arms in one smooth movement.

"I can probably walk for a while," I started, guilt and a thread of embarrassment creeping in at the idea of him carrying me all through the city. But even as I said it, I knew I couldn't back up the words, and by the way his brown eyes landed on me and softened, he knew it, too.

"You're fine, Ace. You won't be the first drained person these people have seen carried or dragged out of the White Castle, nor will you be the last."

I blanched, the truth in his statement sinking low in my belly and making it clench with disgust. I'd like to think I wasn't someone prone to irrational hatred, but if I ever saw Lizbeth again, I'd happily bury a knife in her chest.

Dex leaned in close and tapped the side of my leg. "Come on, let's get you out of here."

He didn't have to tell his brother twice. Duma didn't even wait to make sure Dex was behind us before he darted out onto the street, walking faster than my short legs ever could've kept up with.

EVEN IN THE dark, with a hood pulled low over my eyes and my face tucked into a chest, there was no hiding the overwhelming magnitude of Ardenglass. The size and number of buildings alone made what I'd seen of Tover look like a children's dollhouse in comparison, but it was the noise and the chaotic bustle of thousands of people that had my curiosity flaring to life.

As Duma quickly led us around corners and buildings, somehow knowing his way down each identical street, I couldn't help but stare in wonder at everyone we passed.

No one seemed miserable or depressed. In fact, most looked content as they went about their lives, bartering with shops, ambling about, and laughing over tavern tables. It wasn't at all what I'd expected people this close to the castle to behave like, for them to live happily and untroubled in the same city as the woman who had so readily taken their freedom from them.

How many here still had their souls? Had every citizen been stripped of that choice the moment they arrived, or was it only those who possessed abilities Lizbeth deemed worthy of taking who were assaulted that way? Watching a pair of women usher a group of rambunctious children into a building, I had a feeling the answer might not be so black and white.

The queen may not actively have her guard searching for *unworthy* people, but she kept all her citizens in line by keeping the fear of it around their throats like a noose. Pain didn't always have to be used to keep people in line. Often all they needed was the fear of it to keep them curled in a corner and prevent them from believing they could ever fight back.

"Where exactly are we headed?" I asked, after we'd traveled far enough outside the heart of the city that I felt safe to finally speak. Not knowing who walked around us or what abilities they possessed to hear or hinder us—especially the few guards we'd seen along the way—was terrifying.

Back in my cell, Duma had said a bed and stew awaited me, and at the time, I'd assumed he meant once we got back to Tover. Now that I knew we weren't leaving until after Terek met up with us, I was curious where Duma planned to take us. An inn with a hot bath and meal sounded to die for, but I also knew places like that would be the first Lizbeth would check once she noticed my absence. If she hadn't already.

Duma adjusted me in his arms and tipped his head forward. "The city outskirts. There's a section of homes there that were built to house new arrivals while they found occupations and got settled. They're usually well-furnished and decently sized, since multiple people would have to stay in them at once, so we should all be able to have a room."

"Won't they be occupied then? I'm not going to kick anyone out or threaten them just so we can stay there. These people have been tormented enough."

Dex clicked his tongue. "Nah, they've been empty for a while. Not a whole lot of new souls these days, even in Tover."

I frowned and pulled my gaze from the starless night sky to squint at our surroundings. That didn't make any sense. Thousands of people died every day, and with Lizbeth preventing them from leaving the Underland at will, it should mean the Underland had more of a population problem in general. Right?

But maybe there was more than one Underland, or maybe this one was simply a whole lot larger past the Wood than even Lizbeth knew.

"Do you think it's because more people are being warned to stay away from Ardenglass?" I asked.

"It's possible," Dex agreed, "but since Tover hasn't been seeing new souls either, if people are trying to keep away from the city, they're all traveling west through Gissan. We certainly haven't seen them."

"Well, anything's better than here," I said, noticing we'd moved onto a narrower street bordered by rows of identical gray and brown homes. "I can't imagine why anyone would want to stay so close to the White Castle."

Dex pointed to something I couldn't see from Duma's arms, and his brother nodded and cut across the street. "Once you've lost your soul, there's not much else to fear from the queen unless you're going out of your way to cause trouble," he said, keeping pace with us. "And not many here care enough to."

"Ardenglass citizens are all just making it from one day to the next like the rest of us," Duma agreed. "But if you ask me, the lack of souls isn't so simple."

I arched my neck back to look up at him from beneath the large hood. "What do you mean?"

"I'm just saying, I wouldn't be surprised if the Crimson Queen's attempt to play God is messing with more than just those of us already here. I think it's plausible to assume more souls are being unrightfully punished than we know."

Gooseflesh covered my arms. "As in, you don't think souls are coming here at all?" I asked, bracing my hand on Duma's shoulder as he lowered me to my feet in front of a brown, two-story home.

He tested the knob—which didn't budge—and then placed two fingers over the lock. I watched in fascination as his brown skin darkened to a reddish hue before sinking into the metal. Smirking at my fish-like stare, he turned the knob again, and I nearly wept when it opened with ease.

Now that we were this close to safety and rest, I could feel my exhaustion weighing in on my very bones, warning me my body wasn't going to last much longer. God, did I hope Duma was right about this place being furnished.

He didn't pick me up again, but he did place a firm hand on my back in support as I shuffled inside the dark house. There was a scraping noise behind us, and then Dex squeezed past into the entryway, a tinder box and lit candle in hand.

"Hello?"

I jumped, Dex's voice practically a shout with how silent the home was.

"Is anyone here?"

When still no one answered, Duma shut the door behind us and dragged a worn entry table over to shove against it. The thin wood wouldn't exactly keep anyone out now that the lock was useless, but it'd at least give us a two-second head start if anyone attempted to open the door.

With Dex lighting the way the best he could with a single burning flame, he led us through an arched doorway to the right and into a sitting room. Or what had once been a sitting room before occupants stopped coming and thin, cotton sheets had been thrown over everything. Two wingback chairs and a large couch sat in the center of the room with small, circular end tables between them, and an unlit hearth built into the adjacent wall.

Since I had no desire to cram my sore body into a chair, I shuffled over and flopped onto the couch, the protective sheet puffing up a thin layer of dust beneath my weight. Any other day, and I might've wrinkled my nose, but today, I wouldn't have cared if mice crawled out of it.

Confirming I was settled, Duma took the candle from Dex and began making his way through the main floor, lighting whatever other candles or lanterns he could find. I laid out straight and rested the back of my head on the armrest as Dex sat beside me, his hip bumping my ribs.

"Hey, sweetheart."

"Hey," I said, smiling up at the man who was apparently as skilled at fighting as he was at being kind and ornery.

"Think you can stay awake for a few more minutes?"

I nodded, though I wasn't sure just how long I could keep that promise. Fatigue had hit me like a sledgehammer the moment my butt hit the couch.

He smiled back, but it was a sad one as he gently brushed his fingertips over my wrists. "I know you want these horrible things off, but I'll need my brother's help with that, and although he won't admit it, he's too tired right now. But I can at least start on your face so you can hopefully rest a little easier."

I pulled my hands away from his touch on instinct, apprehension flaring to life. "Start what? Is something broken?"

When I'd been fourteen, I'd seen a physician at Vincent's set a poor girl's nose after she'd tripped and fallen down the stairs. Her scream mixed with the nauseating crunch had haunted me for days.

I ran my fingertips over my nose, trying to stay calm. My entire body ached, but I hadn't been in enough pain to believe I'd broken anything. Thankfully, Dex kept his expression soft and shook his head.

"No, Ace, I don't think anything's broken, but I can relieve your swelling and heal the cuts on your neck and beneath your eye," he said, raising his hand to gently press it to my cheek.

I gawked at him, understanding hitting me slower than it should have. "Your ability is to heal?"

He nodded.

"Oh, my God, Dex. That's amazing," I said, biting back the desire to ask him a hundred questions about him, about Duma, and about their life Upside.

I wondered—given if what Hara said was true—what they had to have been through for the Underland to grant them the abilities it had. But I successfully shoved it away. Their history wasn't my business unless they wanted it to be.

Dex poked his tongue at his split lip and chuckled at my obvious amazement. "My ability is limited. I can't do much about the bruising or the ache in your muscles, but I can mend your skin and hopefully prevent infection. It'll take me a few times, though. My ability is far weaker than the healers Lizbeth keeps on hand."

That weakness, if being able to mend skin could ever be called that, was likely the only thing that had kept her from forcing him to work here as a healer. I glanced to Duma, who was still moving about the home, lighting rooms and pulling covers off furniture. His ability was extremely useful, too, but his weakness of feeling pain would've definitely been a turn off for Lizbeth.

I thought of Hara, wondering where she was and what she was doing. If Lizbeth had noticed me missing yet and punished her. She hadn't been quite as lucky as the twins with the attraction of her ability.

Dex waggled his fingers, bringing my attention back. "I should be able to do both your face and neck, and then after you've rested, my brother and I will work on these cuffs."

I stared at his hand and then down to mine, my skin angry and red around the bands. "That's why Duma said he couldn't take these off in my cell without you, isn't it? Because he can't do so without burning me."

Fury filled his brown eyes for a moment, but he blinked it back, sucking his bottom lip in. "He'll make it as quick as he can, and I'll be right there to heal you up, I promise. For now, let's fix your pretty little face, because I have to tell you, you look downright horrifying."

I laughed and nudged him with my shoulder. "I may or may not have headbutted a guard in the face and tried to kick another one."

He flashed me a wide smile and spread his fingers over my eye and cheekbone. "That's my girl. Now, relax those shoulders and sit still. You look like you're about to go into battle. This won't hurt."

I nodded and tried my best to relax as Dex took a deep breath and pursed his lips, his brow creasing in concentration. At first, I thought maybe I'd feel nothing at all, but then a light tickle ghosted over my skin like the tip of a feather. Then came a rush of prickles, reminding me of when I was young and I'd sit on my foot wrong, causing the extremity to sting like a dozen needles when the blood returned.

When only a light numbness lingered around my eye, he clicked his tongue in disappointment, as if he'd hoped to do more than he had, and dropped his hand to my chin. Clasping it, he turned my face to the side and focused on my neck, nostrils flaring.

"This cut looks older. Hara did it when she took you from Tweeds, didn't she?"

I blinked. "How did you know that?"

"I didn't. Just an educated guess. Terek knew something had happened because he smelled your blood."

Of course, he had. "Well, I don't think Hara meant to actually cut me. She'd just wanted to frighten me enough to keep me quiet. She was terrified of Terek hearing her."

He grunted, clearly not believing me, but he didn't argue, and I was thankful. I didn't have it in me to hash out all my confusing thoughts when it came to Hara without divulging everything that had happened in the throne room. And although I trusted Dex and Duma, I wanted to talk to Terek before anyone else.

Once Dex had finished with my neck, he sighed and slumped forward over his lap, pinching the bridge of his nose. He looked about as drained as I felt, and I couldn't stop myself from reaching over and squeezing his hand, emotion clogging my throat.

"Thank you," I said, meeting his eyes and then Duma's, who stood near the archway into the kitchen. The words weren't enough, but I hoped they knew how much I meant them. "And I'm sorry."

Dex frowned but twisted his hand to squeeze mine back. "Sorry for what?"

"Everything," I said, forcing a laugh to cover how much I suddenly wanted to cry, but it only came out as a choked huff. "Lying, risking your souls, trying to exist in a place I don't belong." Taking them away from their business, making them hide away like criminals. The list was endless.

Instead of laughing it off with me or disagreeing, Dex wordlessly released my hand and pulled me into a soul-crushing hug. "I don't know who made you feel like you aren't worth being saved, Ace, but you are. Not because of your ability or because we promised Terek, but because you matter, and that's enough."

I stared up at the ceiling and blinked faster, desperately trying to hold back my tears as his words curled around the cracks I'd been carrying all these years. But when he cupped the back of my head and tightened his hold rather than let go, my restraint crumbled to dust, and for the first time in my life, I wept.

Not from fear, or pain, or anger, but for me, and for everything I'd never had. For the little girl my father had beat and my mother had despised, for the woman Frederick had stripped every last piece of confidence and self-worth from, and for the beautiful, golden soul I'd almost lost. Dex said nothing as he held me through it all and brushed his palm over my hair until my sobs finally slowed to wearied hiccups.

"I'm sorry," I said. "I—"

"Don't be," Duma said. He pushed off the wall and came to squat beside the couch. "You're allowed to be upset, Ace. Your feelings are not a burden to the people around you. It's okay to need help, just as it's okay to make mistakes. Anyone who says they haven't is a liar."

He reached up to wipe his thumbs over my puffy cheeks. "Dex and I have lived full lives twice over. You've barely started yours. Do we hope to keep working at Tweeds until we have our souls and are ready to move on? Sure, but if we start sacrificing each other to achieve that, we're no better than that crimson bitch."

Another choked sob broke through, and I sniffed, pulling back and awkwardly wiping at my face. "My real name is Adelais." I wasn't sure why I'd said it, but something about them being so genuine and understanding while still not knowing made me feel undeserving of their friendship.

Duma handed me a handkerchief and stood. "You think we're using ours? Everyone changes when they arrive to the Underland. Some for the better, some for worse. Most find it easier to accept the hand they've been dealt here if they're not constantly comparing it to the lives they can never go back to."

That was true, I supposed, and I found myself wondering if Terek had done the same the day he'd let the creative, young man he'd once been die. When he'd become the man who hunted from the shadows and lashed out at anyone who got too close.

"Would you prefer we use that name? Or perhaps 'little rabbit'?" Dex asked, a mischievous smile teasing his lips. "Or is that last one more of a pet name you two use in the bedroom?"

Duma snorted, and I flushed, a laugh bubbling out of me as I smacked Dex's arm. I felt emotionally depleted, but in a way that was more freeing than I'd ever experienced before. As if, even though I'd said goodbye to my life Upside the moment I'd left Frederick at that table, I hadn't fully put it behind me until now.

But Duma was right. Coming to the Underland had fundamentally changed me, and I'd never be the same. I may still possess my soul, but the naïve, quiet Adelais was dead and buried, and I had no intention of ever digging her back up.

"You can call me Ace."

ADELAIS

CHAPTER FORTY-SEVEN

After a few more pieces of travel fare and an hour of rest, in which I slept so hard I didn't even dream, I was finally beginning to feel more like myself again. Enough so, that Duma and Dex had come back from where they'd been prepping rooms upstairs to see if I was ready to get the shackles off my wrists. I'd nearly tangled myself in the blanket they'd given me and fallen off the couch in my hurry to sit up.

Retaking the spot he'd been in when I'd fallen asleep, Dex settled beside me with an encouraging smile while Duma knelt on the floor beside us, his large hands so very gentle as he picked up mine. His face was expressionless, but not unkind, as he met my eyes.

"I'm going to focus on the locks and put as little heat into them as possible, but I won't lie to you and say it won't hurt. It will. It'll feel like a cattle brand, but it'll be quick, and Dex will immediately heal you."

I took a deep breath. "Okay."

"Would you like something to bite down on? Because I mean it, Ace, it's going to hurt."

"I've been burned by one before. I know very well how much they hurt." The words came out harsher than I'd intended, but it was hard to keep my guard down when the memory of Frederick dragging me to the fireplace was trying to claw its way to the forefront of my mind.

Duma blinked at me, shock visible in his expression, either from my admittance or my tone, I wasn't sure. Dex nudged me with his elbow. "Would you like to wait until Terek arrives?"

The tenderness in his tone nearly brought me to tears all over again, my nerves fraying at the seams at the thought of being burned again. I *did* want Terek to be there. I wanted him to glare at me and remind me how strong I was, remind me that Frederick wasn't here. But I shook my head and shoved it down. I'd never needed anyone to hold my hand through my struggles, and I didn't now.

"Just get these off me, please."

To my relief, Duma didn't push or ask me again if I was sure. He just laid my wrists in his brother's waiting palms and pressed his thumbs over the locks. My skin instantly grew warm, and within seconds, it was like a white-hot agony searing into me.

I squeezed my eyes shut and sucked in a breath, throwing myself into the darkest corner of my mind while I counted the seconds. Only seven passed before Duma grunted and yanked the bindings from my wrists, Dex's hands immediately wrapping around to replace them. A tingling swirled over my skin, an almost comforting numbness washing away the pain as quickly as it'd come.

"You know, Ace," Dex said, once he'd finished and applied a thin layer of salve. "I may not know what you've experienced in your life that made you want to be here instead, but I like to think everything happens for a reason. Even pain."

I opened my eyes to frown up at him, seeing the strain in his face. He needed rest as much as I had. They both did. "And what do you believe the reason is?"

Dex winked at me as he grabbed the long strip of fabric he'd washed and torn and began wrapping it around one wrist. I still had two angry red marks that circled them, but there were no longer cuts or burns.

"Terek. I think fate molded you to be exactly who you are so you could deal with his mean ass."

Duma chuckled in agreement, and I couldn't help but join. I didn't think Dex meant it in the same way my heart wanted him to, but I appreciated his intention, nonetheless.

"He's not *that* mean," I said, laughing harder at the look they both gave me. "How long have you been friends with Terek, anyway? Duma said he was the one who taught you to fight."

Dex nodded. "He did. A few decades ago, not long after we'd opened Tweeds, we had a group of guards come in and start shit. I'd tried to kick them out, but I'd never fought a day in my life, so it didn't turn out so well for me."

I watched him pick up a second strip and move to my other wrist to repeat the process. Duma stayed knelt beside to us, a smirk on his face as he remembered whatever trouble his brother had gotten into.

"What happened?"

"Terek had been brooding in a corner, as he often does, and watched it all play out. He'd had them all unconscious out on the street within seconds of approaching them, but not before they'd made me a bloody mess. The asshole."

I smiled, wishing said asshole was here with us to tell his side of the story. "And he took pity on your poor defensive skills?"

"Something like that. Honestly, I think the bastard was just lonely and desperate for something to focus on. Not that he'd ever admit it."

No, he definitely wouldn't, but I didn't think that was why he'd helped. Terek hid behind his asshole mask and pretended not to care about anyone, but I was starting to realize just how deeply he did.

Dex tied the bandage off and tucked my hands beneath the blanket, saying something to Duma about travel supplies when a thunderous crack split the air. Our heads all shot up in time to see the table Duma had placed in front of the door fly past the archway as the door slammed open.

Duma shot to his feet, his fist tightening over the broken shackles in his hand while his other went to an axe. His muscles tensed, readying for a fight, only to go lax a second later when he realized who had arrived.

Terek looked an absolute mess as he stood frozen just inside the door, a wild darkness pouring off him in waves. His cloak was torn and his tunic and trousers speckled with dried blood. He leaned slightly to the left as if he didn't want to put weight on his right leg, and there was foliage in his hair.

His forehead was damp with sweat, and the beginnings of a beard graced his jaw, but more than anything, it was his eyes that captivated me. They sliced straight past Duma and appeared almost feverish as they locked onto me.

The naked emotion and relief that blanketed his expression lasted only a second, almost too brief to see, but it was enough to make something flutter to life in my chest. He looked at me like he didn't truly believe I was there, like he'd been half-convinced he'd never see me again.

Dex, who'd snaked an arm around my shoulders as if to snatch me up and run if necessary, immediately pulled away and stood like I was on fire. I gave him a questioning look, but he just winked and went to stand beside Duma, smacking him on the back.

"You know, brother, I feel like now is an exceptionally good time for us to head out to get some ingredients for a stew."

Duma's eyebrow arched high, but after glancing back at me and then Terek, his shoulders sagged in understanding, and he nodded. With firm smacks on Terek's shoulder, they both slipped past him without another word. I stared after them, the suddenness of their departure leaving behind an awkward silence.

Just the thought of stew had saliva building in my mouth, but I found it odd they hadn't said a word to Terek before running out. What had been the hurry? The man in question, however, clearly wasn't as curious as I was because he hadn't so much as moved a muscle or looked away from me.

I bit my lip, feeling like I needed to say something, but I wasn't sure what. *Hello? Thank you? Sorry I trusted a stranger and ran off? You're right, I'm an idiot?* Whatever it might've been, the words died on my tongue when I returned my gaze to him, and his eyes took in the side of my face, where a dark purple bruise still circled my eye and cheekbone.

His eyes widened as he stared at me, and I swore all the air in the room turned to ice, chilling me beneath the blanket. His chest began to heave as his knuckles whitened around the hilts of his daggers, like it was taking everything in him not to lose his shit and tear the entire house to the ground.

"Terek?"

When he ignored me and continued staring at my cheek, I pushed to sit up more, keeping the blanket over me like a shield. My muscles listened, but the action still took far more effort than my pride wanted to admit. "Terek? Are you okay?"

The question got his attention, but it was the wrong thing to say.

The blue in his eyes melted into the black, and in an instant, he was across the room and standing at my feet. I flinched back, his speed startling me, but he didn't seem to notice as he all but snarled at me.

"Am I okay? You're lying there reeking of the dungeon with a sluggish heartbeat, looking like someone punched you in the goddamn fucking face, and you're worried if *I'm* okay?"

I resisted the urge to raise a hand to my ratted hair, suddenly self-conscious about how I looked and smelled. Duma had found a dust-free cloth and had left it on an end table next to a basin of water, but I hadn't had enough energy to use it yet.

"And *you're* standing there covered in blood and sweat, looking like you're about to either fall asleep while standing or murder me," I said, watching the muscles beneath his scruff clench.

He grunted but tempered his voice, running a hand through his hair and glaring when a few leaves fluttered to the floor. "No, Ace. I'm not remotely okay."

I watched the strands slide through his fingers, hating how even now, after everything, my own itched to follow the same path. To push it back from his face and curl into him, pulling his lips to mine. I hadn't realized just how badly I'd missed him. How much I still wanted him, no matter how hard I tried not to. I'd gone years without seeing him, yet the last few days away from him had felt like a lifetime.

"What's wrong?" I asked, hoping my thoughts weren't written

across my face, and leaned forward, looking for any sign of injury. I assumed the blood on his clothes wasn't his since he was moving just fine, but then again, Terek had always been quite skilled at hiding his feelings from me.

A dark chuckle rumbled out of him, but it was devoid of all emotion. "What's wrong with me?"

"I just meant that if you're hurt, Dex can probably help when he gets back. He might need a few hours to recover, but if—"

"I'm not the one hurt," Terek snapped, each word angrier and louder than the last. "What's wrong is you were *taken* from me. I have more abilities than any other person here, yet they were fucking worthless when I needed them most. Hara came in and stole you away, and I had no idea because I am utterly useless while I sleep."

Wait...what? I gaped up at him, speechless. That was Terek's weakness. His abilities didn't work unless he was conscious. No wonder Hara and I had been able to get past him unnoticed.

"What's wrong is I could feel exactly where you were, yet I couldn't step foot in that goddamn castle to get you without risking her hurting you further." He closed another foot between us until his legs hit the couch, and he was towering over me.

"What's fucking wrong is I had to fight an entire horde of Creatures, all the while unable to stop thinking about *you* and whether or not you were safe. It's all I've done since you arrived, and I'm going insane. Is that what you want to hear?"

His chest heaved in and out, and I swallowed, feeling his anger wash over me like a wave. For once, it didn't bother me, not when I knew it was his crutch to hide his fear and what he cared about. When I now knew the reason behind every horrible thing he'd ever said to me, and why he'd always protected me, yet never welcomed me here.

He didn't trust himself to keep me safe from Lizbeth, and that gave me hope that he might feel more for me than he wished to. That maybe he felt this same pull every time he was near me, like something was pushing us together.

I gripped that kindle of hope with both hands and took a deep breath, lifting my chin and meeting his anger head on. "It's exactly what I wanted to hear, but I must admit, I'd imagined you saying it in a slightly lower octave."

His eyes flashed, but I didn't fail to notice his hands relax at his sides. "I have every right to yell at you. You omitted telling me about a guard recognizing you."

True. "And *you* omitted telling me about the bounty and your history with the woman who created it. So, I believe, if one of us has a reason to yell about lying and a lack of mature communication, it's me."

"You're right."

"If you'd have just told me, I never would've—wait, what did you say?"

He huffed an irritated breath, but there was no heat behind it, and I caught the faintest twitch of his lips. "You're right. I should have told you."

Whoa. I fumbled over my reply, not having expected those words to ever leave his mouth. Hell, he'd only just arrived. When I'd imagined this moment, I'd figured he'd still be yelling at me, not admitting to having made a mistake.

"So, why didn't you?" *Why didn't you trust me?* I knew he'd wanted to keep me safe, but why would he have thought keeping those kinds of secrets would help him achieve that?

He sucked on his front teeth and looked away from me, his eyes landing on the basin and cloth. "It didn't feel necessary at the time. I was hoping to get rid of you before you could ever find out."

The words stung, but not as much as they might've before when I'd thought he was pushing me away because he couldn't stand me. I watched him walk over and pick up the cloth, dunking it into the water. "Did you tell Lizbeth and Hara about me?"

Terek's head snapped to me, and the basin creaked beneath his hand. "I have never claimed to be a good man, Ace, but do you truly believe I would ever betray you to someone who wished to harm you?"

"No," I admitted, trying not to look guilty for asking when I'd never fully believed Hara. "But you were the only person who's ever seen me,

Terek, and you've acted differently ever since I came back. When Hara told me they'd learned about me from you," I shrugged and looked down at the blanket, "I was confused and hurt."

His expression softened. Releasing the basin, he squeezed out the excess water from the cloth and walked back over.

"Scoot over."

"Why?"

"Must you make everything complicated? Just move over, Ace. Unless you're hoping to sit in my lap instead?" he said, a challenge flashing through his gaze I immediately wanted to encourage.

My face heated, but it wasn't embarrassment that warmed me as my mind pictured what it'd be like to curl up in his lap and feel his arms wrap around me. When he silently raised a brow, I had to bite the inside of my cheek to keep from telling him I'd prefer his lap, just to see what he'd do.

Instead, I made do with rolling my eyes and turning my body so my legs hung off the couch. I'd expected him to sit on the other side where my feet had been, but Terek sat directly beside me, his thigh pressing into mine and making every nerve along it hum. We might as well have been naked with how painfully aware I was of every place we touched.

I stared down at that connection, unable to meet his gaze, half-convinced I was imagining all of this. Him being here, the worry in his voice, and the way he'd yet to call me out for being an idiot, which was one of his favorite things to do. That feeling only grew when he gripped my chin between his thumb and forefinger and forced my face up, demanding my undivided attention.

I obeyed without comment, transfixed by the way he was looking at me like I was the most precious thing in the entire Underland. My heart nearly exploded into a million pieces when he began rubbing the cold cloth over my face. His motions were firm but gentle, cooling my heated skin while avoiding the area that was still sore and bruised.

"You don't have to do that," I whispered, a mixture of nerves and something much headier swirling inside me at his ministrations and the way the hand holding my chin was sending lightning straight into my chest.

"The sight of you claims otherwise."

I huffed out a laugh, and his eyes darkened as he tilted my head to the side and began gently washing my neck. Dex had fully healed the cut, but somehow, I had a feeling Terek could still sense exactly where it'd been. He was quiet for several moments, and I could do nothing but sit there like a frozen fawn, terrified any sudden move would break the spell and he'd return to the aloof, unfeeling man he'd previously been.

Never in my life had someone treated me with such reverence, and I was so caught up in trying not to let my heart see too far into it that I startled when his fingers spread over my jaw. Gooseflesh erupted across my entire body, and I swallowed, imagining that hand sliding lower to grip my throat the way he'd done in the Wood. To squeeze as he pulled me in and demanded my lips.

His nostrils flared, and when he spoke, his voice was low and guttural. "What's wrong is I want to raze all of Ardenglass to the ground for hurting you. If I'd had any other choice, I'd have stood by and let the Creatures do it for me, and I would not have felt a single second of remorse."

That lightning sparked and simmered lower at the dark truth in his eyes, and my throat went bone dry as I suddenly forgot how to breathe. "You can't murder an entire city just because one man decided to slap me, Terek."

"I would do far worse things if it meant keeping you safe, little rabbit."

His gaze flicked to my lips and lingered, and with that one look, something hummed to life between us. I leaned toward him instinctively, feeling like my body was connected to his by some thread I couldn't see. Like I was drowning in an unending ocean, and he was the only thing that might keep my head above the water.

His eyes fell to my chest, and for a moment, I thought he felt that consuming connection, too, but then he fisted the cloth and cleared his throat, releasing me. "I'll let you rest until Duma and Dex return."

I pressed my lips together, feeling that connection dampen as Terek attempted to slam a wall between us, and I knew if I let him, he'd build it stronger this time and never tear it down again. His worry for me had unintentionally knocked a few bricks off, and I wanted nothing more than to keep him from replacing them.

The urge to reach out and touch him was nearly overwhelming. I hated how guarded he was, not because I wanted to change him, or because I didn't want him exactly as he was, but because I now knew what had caused it. Or, more specifically, *who* had caused it.

Deciding to give in to that urge, I tossed the blanket off my lap and grasped Terek's hands, my pounding heart giving away my nerves.

"I know what Lizbeth did to you, and I'm so—" A small yelp escaped me when his hands twisted to grip me back, and he yanked, all but pulling me into his lap.

"God," I muttered, unsure if the heart attack I was having was because of his speed, his familiar smell, or because of the sudden proximity of my hands to his crotch.

"God doesn't live here," was all he said as his fingers deftly undid the bandages Dex had just put on.

I gave him a flat look, but his focus was only on my bare wrists. He flipped them over carefully, his touch oddly gentle compared to the fury lining his features.

"This is after Dex healed them." It wasn't a question so much as a confirmation. We both knew Dex was too kind to leave anyone untreated when he had the ability to help.

"Yes," I said, my breath catching when I realized how close his face was to mine. "Lizbeth had me chained to the floor of a cell, though I don't know why. It's not like I could've fought back with all the sedatives she kept shoving down my throat," I said, purposefully not mentioning Hara's part in it.

He worked his jaw and ran a thumb just beneath the reddened circle of skin. "Do you know what Lizbeth's ability is?"

"Yes," I whispered, memories of Hara's screams and the icy chill of my soul leaving my body making me wish I'd kept the blanket wrapped around me.

He watched me closely. "Then I can assure you, Lizbeth didn't have you restrained because she feared you'd fight back, Ace. She's never without a powerful soul in her possession. Even if you'd been at your best, you'd have never stood a chance."

I frowned, something he said about her possessing a soul not sitting right with me. Something wasn't adding up, but I couldn't quite put my finger on what it was.

Misunderstanding my confusion, he carefully began rewrapping my wrists over his lap. "Lizbeth trusts no one, Ace."

"Not even you?" I dared to ask, knowing two things were possible. Terek would either add a layer to his wall and shut me out completely, or he'd finally drop it and let me through. It took everything in me not to sag with relief when he didn't hesitate to choose the latter.

"Especially not me."

TEREK

CHAPTER FORTY-EIGHT

"Will you tell me why?" Her question was hesitant, and she avoided my eyes, instead staring down at her hands, still clasped within mine.

I had zero reason to still be touching her, yet I couldn't seem to tear myself away. I'd come so close to losing her. Exhaustion still plagued her, though she was doing a good job at pretending otherwise, and I could hear the consistent rumbles of her hunger. But it was the abuse that bore far deeper that gutted me.

Her soul, that beautiful, soft glow that had slowly begun to strengthen with each day she'd been away from the Upside, from *him*, was now barely discernible again. I'd still been able to sense her, but when I'd run into the house and seen her listless on the couch, her hair a nested halo and her skin dull, for a moment I'd thought Lizbeth had succeeded.

Even now, though I knew she hadn't, it was killing me not to pull Ace into my arms and demand she tell me what had happened. It was taking everything in me to fight the innate urge to whisk her away and protect her from anything and everything. I'd never be able to take her to the small place I called a home here, not under Lizbeth's watchful eye, but that didn't stop me from wishing I could hide her away there for as long as necessary.

I'd tried ignoring Ace. I'd tried hating her and pushing her to hate me back, but none of it had severed how I felt. If anything, the more I fought it, the more my body seemed to act of its own accord. Kind of like right now, as I continued to find any way to touch her skin and reassure myself that she was with me. She was safe.

There was no denying the connection between us anymore, not to myself, at least. Adelais Ellington was mine in every possible way. She always had been. Even when she'd been married off and claimed by another, she'd been mine. And it was because of just how badly I'd protected her so far that I refused to allow that connection to flourish.

I was too selfish of a man to push her away completely anymore, but she deserved better than a life tied to a soulless demon. One day, Ace might very well decide to go back and make a new life for herself under a real sun and sky, and if we solidified what was between us, I'd never fucking let her. I'd steal her choice and be no better than any other person in her life.

"Terek?"

I glanced over at her hesitant tone, realizing I hadn't spoken in several minutes. I'd forgotten she'd asked a question, and the hope in her eyes was so potent, I found my lips moving even before I'd fully decided to answer.

I didn't want any more secrets between us about Lizbeth. They sure hadn't fucking helped either of us so far, and she deserved the truth.

"I don't make a habit of talking about her, Ace. It's not exactly a part of my existence that I particularly like returning to." That was an understatement. Any and all memories of Lizbeth, of how I'd once felt or what I'd done for her, made me want to crack my skull open and dig them out.

"I know," she said, and for a moment, I genuinely wondered if my heart might finally cease to beat when she laid her head on my shoulder. I instinctively tensed, her casual show of affection far outside my comfort zone, but I didn't move. Nor did I dislike her nearness. Apparently, even when she was filthy, I craved her.

"I know what she did to you…to all of you. I want to tell you how sorry I am, but I also know how worthless of a sentiment it'd be. I can't even begin to understand what it must've been like, especially for you."

The feeling of ice crawling through me like snaking vines, freezing every cell in my body until I couldn't breathe, couldn't move, couldn't think past the agony of it. And then an overwhelming numbness as my heart slowed and my knees hit the floor. The sight of Liz's worried eyes as she knelt before me and asked me if I was okay. The shaking of my hand when I'd pulled her face to mine and kissed her softly, assuring her I was fine.

I cleared my throat and took a deep breath, coating my senses in everything that was her. "You'll never have to understand it, Ace. She won't come anywhere near you again, I swear it."

She shifted closer but didn't lift her head. I could practically hear the thoughts swirling in her mind and knew exactly what she was going to ask before the words left her mouth. "Is it true? That you and Lizbeth were...together?"

I didn't reply at first, my jaw working so hard to keep the answer in that I thought my teeth would shatter. My defenses rose, and I wanted to lash out and leave, avoiding ever admitting the truth out loud, to her of all people. I didn't want to see the hesitation in her eyes when I unleashed all the shadows I'd so desperately tried to keep away from her. The mistakes I'd made and the damage I'd caused to more than just myself because of it.

But I didn't.

"Yes. Though it was a very long time ago."

She sucked in a breath, and something sharp stabbed into my chest when she tilted her head back and stared up at me, her lips mere inches from mine. "I'm trying really hard not to judge you for that right now."

A dark chuckle escaped me, a weight I hadn't even realized had been crushing me lifting when she didn't move away at my admittance. "Trust me, little rabbit, the only thing I feel for Lizbeth now is the overwhelming desire to bleed her out all over her white throne room."

Her teeth bit into her bottom lip as her eyes darted down to my mouth, and I shifted, that single look making my trousers suddenly feel like they were suffocatingly tight. How easy it would be to close the distance between us and lay her back, replacing this conversation with one that involved only the sound of my name as she chanted it.

"With all your abilities, how come you haven't been able to…you know."

"Tear her head from her body?"

Her nose crinkled at the image, but she nodded against me.

I sighed, reaching over to twirl a few strands of her hair. "Because Lizbeth is the one who taught me how to use them. She found me while I was at my lowest, unable to function or shut out the world around me unless I was drowning in drink. She, of course, lied to me about who she was, but she spent months helping me crawl my way out of the hole I'd been trapped in."

At that, Ace finally sat up, several emotions warring across her face, and I grumbled, immediately missing her warmth. "Wow, I wouldn't have ever thought that."

"Don't misunderstand me, Ace. It wasn't out of kindness. Lizbeth does nothing that isn't ultimately for her gain. By helping me control them, she helped herself to do so as well. Once she possessed them, it didn't take her long to become lethal. She didn't admit to who she was until she started the war, and it was only after we'd won it for her that she'd stopped pretending with me."

"Pretending what?"

"To love anyone but herself."

I watched Ace closely, trying to decipher her heartrate and the flush of blood in her cheeks, wishing this connection came with the ability to read her mind.

"She lied to you the entire time you were together?" she asked, voice soft.

"The majority of it, yes. Lizbeth is as patient as she is determined. Once she decides on something, she won't stop until she succeeds, and she is exceptionally persuasive."

Ace seemed contemplative at that, comparing it to whatever memories she had with the Crimson Queen. "I'm not sure I'd call it determination, so much as an obsession with maintaining control of everything," she mused. "Especially the Creatures."

"Indeed."

"Why do you think they ran from the Wood, anyway? The Creatures, I mean. Do you think it was the quake that scared them?"

My mind had been racing with so many thoughts—most of a rather violent nature—since she'd been gone, I hadn't really given it much thought, but I appreciated the change of topic.

"I've never experienced something like that here before, but even so, I doubt it. They were far too determined to have simply been running from fear."

What I didn't add was how much the encounter had unnerved me. I'd fought overly hostile Creatures before, but these had been different. They'd had no interest in attacking me or the approaching guards, even after I'd begun actively taking them out. They'd only turned their attention to me after I'd blocked their path to Ardenglass. As if their only focus had been getting into the city.

She pulled her knees up under her dress and wrapped her arms around them, resting her chin on top. "Well, whatever the reason, they saved me."

"Duma and Dex saved you," I snapped. My tone was brittle and accusatory, and I could see the clear flash of guilt in her eyes as she straightened. "I know that, Terek, and I'll never stop being grateful to them both. I meant when Lizbeth—"

Her mouth pressed shut at the hell fire I was sure she could see blazing from my eyes at what I knew was about to come out of her mouth. "When she *what*, Ace?"

She chewed her lip again and rubbed at her chest, just over where scarred initials sat. I followed the movement, willing myself to stay focused and not get distracted by my immediate anger or the full shape of her breasts.

"She didn't take your soul." It wasn't a question, but Ace answered like it was anyway.

"No. Lizbeth wanted me to give it willingly, and when I didn't, she started torturing Hara and threatened to start bringing in children."

I held back my scoff. Barely. I couldn't have cared less about Hara.

She'd probably deserved it, but I did care about Ace having been forced to watch it happen.

"Then the quake started, and she got so angry, Terek." She met my eyes, and her face seemed to pale, her hazel eyes distant with memory. "She started saying things that didn't make any sense, and then I just remember a golden light and an icy cold."

"You were right to deny her, Ace. Lizbeth feeds off manipulation. Giving your soul over to her willingly wouldn't have hurt any less. It simply would've fed her a full-course meal rather than a travel ration."

She shivered and looked away, picking at a dried patch of dirt on her dress. "Anyway, guards came running in to announce the Creatures, and it seemed to break whatever concentration her ability requires. When they left, she looked too drained to try again."

Footsteps sounded near the road, but recognizing Dex's long-winded chatter, I ignored it. "You're saying *Lizbeth* looked drained?"

She nodded, and I immediately stood to think, running a hand through my hair. That couldn't be right. I'd seen Lizbeth take dozens of souls back-to-back, none willingly, and she'd never so much as had a hitch in her breath. Her ability came as easy as breathing for her.

Then again, Ace wasn't like anyone else, and maybe it was the one thing that kept her from belonging that had protected her. I wouldn't bet Ace's safety on the hope that Lizbeth couldn't remove her soul, but she at least couldn't do it easily. That alone was enough to slightly calm my nerves.

"Terek?"

I tipped my head to show I was listening but stared at the hearth, considering my options. I was more sure now, than ever, of my plan to take her to Wenham.

"Can Lizbeth use more than one soul at a time?"

I twisted back to her, arching a brow. "No. Her ability might be powerful, but even hers has its limits. Why?"

"I don't know, something you mentioned earlier has just had me thinking. You said Lizbeth would've likely only met me with a soul already in her possession to use if necessary."

"There's no 'likely' about it. She definitely had one hiding within her chest like a coward. I told you, she trusts no one."

Ace pursed her lips and leaned back into the couch. "It's just, she used Hara's ability after the quake to cut across the room to me. How could she have done that if she already held one?"

I walked over to the basin to toss the washcloth. "She probably just used a similar one. Hara's ability is unique in how far she can go and that she can take someone with her, but Lizbeth has others that would allow her to cross a room." Hell, knowing her, she was likely using mine and just moving fast.

"No, I *saw* her absorb Hara's soul, Terek."

"You're sure?"

She lifted her chin, as if annoyed I'd ask. "Yes."

"Interesting." I supposed there was a chance she hadn't gone into the throne room with a stolen soul, but my history with her wasn't buying that. Lizbeth was never without one at her disposal, but to absorb more than one at a time?

Either Lizbeth's ability had grown more than I could've imagined, or she was somehow removing her own soul to allow her to use two foreign ones, rather than only one. I prayed it was the latter, because Lizbeth's soul being left somewhere within the castle, out of her reach, could change everything.

I unlatched my cloak and laid it over the back of one of the chairs. I was going to need another one. Again. "I suppose that answers my question as to whether Hara got her soul back. Can't say she didn't deserve it for believing she would."

I'd been talking mostly to myself and didn't expect the venom that laced Ace's tone, each word clipped and angry.

"I don't know why you two hate each other, but no one deserves what she went through. Lizbeth tortured her to *teach me a lesson,* and yet Hara still helped me in the only way she could. She deserves to move on just as much as you do."

I would never agree, and I told Ace as much, reveling in the flare of anger that lit up her eyes for the first time since I'd walked in. It made me want to push her further just so I could see how bright they might get. She was always beautiful, even when she was sad, but when she was angry, she was fucking radiant.

Instead, I positioned the chair between us as a barrier and rested my forearms over my cloak, clasping my hands. "The worst of humankind are those who believe their one, meager life is worth more than hundreds of others. Hara would sacrifice thousands. That is why I hate her."

"Says the man who just threatened to destroy an entire city for my *meager* life."

I flashed her a wicked grin. "I never said I was any better."

The vixen shot me a glare that did nothing to lessen the way my blood ran south, especially when a delicious flush crept up her cheeks.

But then she snatched up the blanket and settled back down, telling me everything Hara had said before and after the throne room. How Hara had seemed to know I'd come for her and had refused to sedate her again because of it, as if my knowing any of that would change my mind.

Was I thankful Ace hadn't been drugged when Duma arrived? Of course, I was. Would I take Hara off the list of people I planned to disembowel slowly? Fuck no. She'd still been the one to alert Lizbeth, take Ace from me, and leave my little rabbit chained to the floor of a cold cell. Nothing she did would ever earn my forgiveness.

Irritated voices, now whispering just outside the house, snagged my attention again.

"*Crimson hell, Dex, open the fucking door already. My feet hurt, and I can hear a bed calling out my name from here.*"

"*I'm surprised you remember what that sounds like, Duma. Ain't no one called out your name for a while—ow, fuck.*"

"*I know you can hear me, Terek. Open this damn door before I murder my brother.*"

I chuckled, earning me a curious look from Ace that caused a little furrow to appear between her brows. Rather than walk over and press my lips to it like I wanted, I forced my legs out of the room and tossed the door open, startling both men.

"If you murder Dex before he satisfies the growling stomach in the other room, you'll be quick to join him."

Duma snorted, and I stepped to the side to let them through, darting out a look to make sure I could sense no one else. When I returned to the room, Ace's face was lit up with equal parts delight and relief as she smiled at them.

I crossed my arms, unable to completely tamp down the flare of jealousy that struck me like a blade. I wasn't sure if she'd ever smiled at me like that, not that I'd ever done anything to earn one. Hell, I couldn't even convince myself to part with her pocket watch, even though I knew she'd want it. I was far too selfish when it came to possessing even a piece of her.

However, when her gaze came back to rest on me and she subconsciously rubbed at her chest, her eyes unable to resist taking me in the way I was doing to her, my demon settled inside his cage. I'd share all her smiles, even her brightest ones, as long as I was the only person she ever looked at with such naked desire.

"Well, I don't know about you all, but I'm starving," Dex said, sauntering toward the archway to the kitchen. "It shouldn't take me long, and then we can figure out our next steps over steaming bowls, right before we all pass out for a solid ten hours."

Ace shot up, and I growled, instantly beside her and gripping her elbow when she tripped over the blanket that'd fallen to her feet.

"Can I help?"

"Dex doesn't need help, and you need to rest."

"That's all I've been doing," she said, slanting me an aggravated look. And crimson take me if I didn't want to fuck the look right off her face.

She turned back to Dex with a much softer expression. "Please? I had to teach myself to cook when I got married, and I was never very good at it. I'd love to learn."

Dex winked, pointedly ignoring my disapproving glower. "Absolutely, sweetheart, just as soon as you take that bar of soap Duma bought and wash the ever-loving shit out of your hands."

I LEANED OVER a map of the Underland—or at least, the section of the Underland that fell within a week's or so travel north of Ardenglass. I'd discovered it tucked behind a few abandoned books on a shelf upstairs after I'd left Duma to snore in an armchair and Ace and Dex to play with vegetables. It was faded and a little outdated, but the main information was still accurate enough to use.

Now that everyone had finished eating—Ace having consumed more stew than I even knew was physically possible—I'd rolled the map out across the dusty table, using our empty bowls to pin the corners.

"So, what's our next step?" Dex asked, rubbing his stomach and crossing one leg over the other, his other hand resting over his knee.

Duma grunted, not even bothering to open his eyes as his head rested against the back of his chair. "Sleep."

"I'm good with that," Dex agreed, a well-timed yawn emphasizing his words. "Give me three days, and I'll be good as new."

I shook my head, even though I didn't disagree. My enhanced strength was the only thing keeping my muscles moving at this point. "Ace can't stay here. This entire city will be full of guards within hours. The only reason it isn't already is because Lizbeth was distracted. We got fucking lucky, but testing that luck a second time would be foolhardy."

Dex's face grew serious. "She can't stay here forever, no, but we also can't afford to make mistakes, Terek. We need rest."

"It's too risky."

He threw his hand up, gesturing to where Ace stood silently beside me. "Going anywhere with her is going to be risky. Her face is about to be plastered in every city and town from here to Abgrove. We *all* need to have the strength to travel, and she still looks like a feather could knock her over. No offense, Ace. It's just as risky to have guards on our tail when we're not at our best than to wait a day or two to recover and restock our supplies."

I glared at him, grinding my teeth because I knew he was right.

Every instinct I had was screaming at me to get Ace out of Ardenglass as soon as possible, but my leg was still aching from a hit that'd nearly dislocated my knee, and Ace's skin was still just a little too pale.

"Fine. It's nearly dawn as it is. We can use the rest of the day to recover and leave once night has fallen."

He rolled his eyes but wisely chose not to push the subject when he realized I wouldn't budge. One day was all I'd give. If they wanted to stay longer, they could, but Ace and I would be leaving.

"Guess I should be glad you're even semi-reasonable, given what she is to you," he muttered. When he noticed Ace's furrowed brow and the threat of violence seeping from me, he sat up and clapped his hands together, startling Duma. "Anyway, if we only get a day, let's get this over with so we can all piss off."

"I'd already been thinking on this since before I noticed Ace had been taken," I said, tracing a finger over the main roads from Ardenglass to Canden until the last road disappeared into the Wood at the northwest edge.

I already knew Duma and Dex were going to hate this plan even more than my plan to leave immediately, but my gut knew it was the best option Ace had. Twisting my head, I caught her gaze. "If you're going to stay in the Underland long term, the town of Wenham will be the safest place for you."

As expected, both men stiffened, Dex's face one of horror while Duma sat up straight, his brown eyes narrowed. I pushed on, already aware of every warning they were about to throw at me.

"Wenham isn't on this map, nor any you'll find within this city, because Lizbeth does her best to pretend it doesn't exist at all. She won't go looking there, and I doubt she'll guess you'd even know about it, let alone be willing to go."

"Why? What's in Wenham?" Ace asked, leaning farther over the table to squint at where my finger lay.

The motion caused her arm to press against mine, and a shudder ran through me. It'd barely been an hour since I'd last touched her, yet my body was acting like it'd been weeks. I kept my attention on the map with far more effort than it should've taken and tapped where the edge of the Wood began.

"Because of this. Wenham is rarely shown on any map that isn't made by a merchant because you have to travel several miles through the Wood to get there."

"That doesn't sound so bad."

"It'll be nothing like the Wood you're used to, Ace. You always appeared in an area near Ardenglass, where very few Creatures dare to be. Wenham is through one of the most heavily populated areas of the Wood."

Ace's eyes slid up to mine, and crimson take me if the way they narrowed on me in disagreement didn't make my blood heat. The stubborn woman still refused to believe the Creatures were as dangerous as we claimed, even less than a day after they'd tried to attack a city.

"If it's such an unsafe area, how does Wenham even exist? If you want to go, I'm assuming there are people surviving there."

"Wenham doesn't exist within the Wood the way you're imagining, Ace. I haven't been there, but I've spoken to merchants who've dared the trip. The town wasn't built within the trees, but within a large clearing several miles in. They fend for themselves and live a far simpler life because of it, but they're as free from Lizbeth as anyone could be. Hence, why I'm taking you there."

She dragged her teeth over her bottom lip, and I had to look back at the map to keep myself focused on the task at hand. I needed to get ahold of myself. I'd gone this long ignoring that goddamn pull, I could keep fucking doing it.

"Okay, but if they're surrounded—"

"I know what you're going to ask," I interrupted, busying myself with rolling up the parchment. "And the truth is, I don't know how they've survived being surrounded by the Wood, but from who I've spoken to in the past, it's never been a war zone."

Dex scoffed and leaned back in his chair, crossing his arms over his chest. "Wenham gets by because they're small, defenseless farmers. We all know the Creatures prefer the hunt. There's nothing in it for them to kill humans asleep in their beds. Even merchants slip by because they're no threat."

He shook his head. "You, however, scream threat with every fiber of your being. The look you're giving me only proves my point. The second they see our group passing through and sense *you*, we'll be as good as dead."

I shrugged and tucked the map into my pack, feeling Ace's attention on me like a hot iron. "You and Duma are not obligated to continue forward. I can get her through safely."

Dex's expression tightened before he sighed, arching his neck back and rubbing his eyes. "Brother, talk some sense into your friend."

"*My* friend?" Duma asked, huffing out a breath. "You're the one with a soft spot for him."

Dex rolled his eyes. "I have a soft spot for *Ace*, who wants him around for some reason. There's a difference."

ADELAIS

CHAPTER FORTY-NINE

"Wenham is the only option," Terek repeated, widening his stance like he was preparing for battle. "Ace disappearing right out from under Lizbeth's nose is not something she anticipated, and she will take it as a direct act against her. She will retaliate, and it will be ugly."

"We understand that, but Wenham, Terek?" Duma asked, shaking his head. "My brother's right, it will not be the same for us to pass through the Wood as it would a lone merchant. We should head back to Tover. Ace can stay at Tweeds as long as she needs."

He met my eyes, as if to confirm that was what I'd like, and I nodded enthusiastically, my heart already swelling at the idea of making a home in Tover. I wanted to work in Tweeds and earn my own living, help the men who'd been so willing to help me, and venture into The Painted Table for new charcoals whenever I desired. It sounded like a dream come true.

Unfortunately for my dreams, Terek sighed heavily, his next words dousing my excitement with a fresh wave of guilt and making the three bowls of stew I'd consumed roil in my stomach.

"No matter how careful you were, Duma, eventually word will get out that you were present the same time Ace escaped. All it will take is Hara mentioning exactly which inn she found her in, and Lizbeth will have guards banging on your door. Ace cannot stay there without putting you both in deeper shit than you're already in."

Duma's face tightened, and I didn't miss the light nudge Dex gave him with his elbow, silently agreeing with Terek. It made the churning of guilt turn to nausea, and I laid my palms flat on the table, blinking back tears. I hated it. It felt like all I did anymore was cry.

"Ace?" Dex asked, his worried tone earning me the unflinching attention of the man beside me. "Hey, are you okay?"

"You should've left me there," I whispered, feeling the truth of each word hammer into me as I spoke. If I'd stayed Upside, none of this would've happened. They'd all be living their lives as normal. Chained, soulless lives maybe, but at least they wouldn't be sitting around a dirty table, exhaustion weighing heavy on their shoulders while they discussed where best to hide.

Calloused fingers wrapped around my chin, shooting sparks along my jaw as my face was tilted to meet a pair of searing midnight eyes. He didn't assure me I was wrong, nor did he seek to hurt me by telling me I was right, as he might've once done.

Instead, Terek seemed to sense the anguish writhing within me, and I could've sworn I felt the pad of his thumb stroke ever so softly over my skin. "Why? Because you're worried about Lizbeth?"

A single tear fell, quickly flicked away before I'd even processed his fingers had moved. "Because they're risking everything for me. Their souls, their freedom, Tweeds."

Apart from the few sentences I'd squeezed out of Dex about Jack, the man he'd loved Upside, I didn't know either of their stories yet. Who they'd been before death, what they'd done, or how they'd died. But what I did know, without a shadow of a doubt, was how much Tweeds meant to them.

I sniffed, my eyes and throat burning. "I should have stayed Upside, where I belong. If Lizbeth does something to them or to Tweeds, it'll be my fault. I have no right to—"

"Stop," he said, his voice low and his eyes sparking with so many emotions, I couldn't pin down a single one. "You do not belong there anymore than we do, little rabbit."

I blinked up at him, feeling that swirling nausea lessen as a blanket of warmth curled around my heart, both soothing me and causing my heart to flutter all at once. "Yes, I do. You said it yourself."

His thumb pressed over my lips, silencing me, and I couldn't help but suck in a breath, my body responding like I'd never been touched before in my life.

"You. Do not. Belong there."

You belong with me.

My lips parted, and that flutter tripled as my heart attempted to leave the confines of my ribs entirely. I wanted him to utter those words so badly, it physically hurt. I wanted him to pull me into his arms, uncaring of our audience, and press his lips to mine, telling me I was exactly where I needed to be.

But though his gaze flicked down to where he still held my face in his palm, he didn't close the distance or say anything else.

"None of this is on you," Duma said after several painfully silent seconds. Terek's hold loosened, and I reluctantly twisted my face out of his grasp to look at Duma, thankful when both men acted as if nothing had happened.

"I mean it, Ace. Lizbeth's actions are her own fault and no one else's, just as ours are. In the end, no matter what she does to us or our business, we both agree that it was worth it."

I blanched. How could he say that? I could be the most valuable person in the entire Underland, and I still wouldn't be more important than their goddamn souls. Their *home.*

My thoughts must've been clear on my face because Duma's mouth curved into a soft smile. "We wanted to help Terek, but we got involved for more reasons than just to rescue you, Ace." He shrugged. "We believe in fate."

Terek scoffed, plopping back down into his seat and crossing his arms. "Fate is a pretentious bitch who likes to stick her fingers in places they don't belong."

Dex's eyes widened, as if fate were a person who would smite us down for talking ill. Duma, however, continued speaking to me, unfazed by his friend's disbelief. "Even if you'd been a murderous wench we didn't care for, we still would've done it."

"To keep Lizbeth from my ability?" I asked, sitting as well and tucking my hands in my lap to pick at the ends of my wrappings.

"Because sitting back and doing nothing is never going to amount to anything. Eventually someone must fight back, or nothing will change. Why not start with us?"

He pushed to stand, grabbing up our bowls. "Nothing we do from here on out is about you, Ace. You were merely the first log to start the fire. No matter what you believe, fate wants you here." His eyes cut to Terek, and though the recipient didn't meet them, his body tensed. "For several reasons."

I glanced between them, feeling like I was missing out on an important conversation, but neither expanded on what reasons Duma meant. I chewed my lip, shifting my weight in the uncomfortable chair.

His words quieted my guilt until it was more of a whisper than a head-pounding shout, but it didn't stop me from wishing there was still something we could do to keep Lizbeth from sending her White Guard anywhere near Tover.

"Do you truly think Lizbeth will go to all those efforts to find me? Just on the hope she can use my ability? I mean…she's dead." Uttering the last part was pointless, since literally everyone here was dead, but the idea just seemed so preposterous.

Lizbeth wouldn't have a body Upside—not a usable one, at least—but then again, my entire body left when I traveled, so maybe if she had my soul, hers would, too. If my ability worked both Upside and Under, then who's to say it wouldn't do the same for Lizbeth?

I shuddered. The thought of someone so unaffected by the idea of murdering and torturing others for her own gain, having access to the souls of two worlds, was utterly terrifying.

"I'll let my brother answer that one," Duma said, stretching his arms above his head and groaning. "I'm going to pour us all a little something to help us sleep."

I cringed, knowing he likely meant some kind of ale or liquor.

Though I didn't want to partake, I considered forcing myself in the hope that it'd knock me out hard enough not to dream. I had no desire to have either Frederick or Lizbeth haunting me tonight.

Dex leaned back in his chair, pushing off the table to balance it on two legs. "I think Lizbeth being dead is exactly the point, Ace. The most dangerous side effect of living forever is boredom. There are those of us who work through it by throwing ourselves into our jobs and newfound families, and then there are those who do none of those things, their boredom festering into resentment and cruelty."

He ran a hand over his jaw, his palm scraping against his scruff. "So yes, I believe Lizbeth will go to insane efforts to find you. Hell, she'd probably wage a war against the Underland for far less because she has nothing else to live for."

"Does that mean she used to *not* be like this?" I asked, daring to steal a look at Terek, who was watching me intently. She'd obviously already been cruel when Terek had arrived, but just how long had Lizbeth been here? Surely anyone would go insane after so long.

Terek rolled his jaw, clearly disliking the conversation. "That's hard to say, since most of the people that'd been here long enough to know have conveniently either moved on or been sent to the void, but supposedly," he said, derision leaking from his tone, "she started out fair."

I tucked my knees up to my chest, listening to Duma move about the kitchen. "Lizbeth told me the Underland gifted her ability because it believed she deserved revenge, although she wouldn't tell me more than that."

But if she'd supposedly started out fair, then that couldn't be the entire story. There had to be more, and maybe if we discovered what had caused Lizbeth to start stealing souls to begin with, we could figure out a way to convince her to give them back.

"You're looking more into it than there is," Terek said, stretching out his legs. "Lizbeth doesn't care about whether people move on. She happily sends innocent people to the void every day. All she cares about is power because she believes that with it, she can force people to love her."

His expression darkened, and I had a feeling he'd been referring to himself. But before I could decide whether or not to reach out and grasp his hand, which was fisted over the table, Duma stalked back in with four cups balanced in his palms.

The scent of ale instantly hit my nose as he set them down, and I held my breath, trying not to let the smell dissuade me. Whatever he slid in front of me didn't look like any ale I'd ever seen. Curious, I picked up the thin wooden cup and took a hesitant sniff, smelling something that reminded me of the Wood.

Duma retook his seat, flicking his brother in the ear when Dex started chugging his. "I remembered you don't drink alcohol, so I steeped you some tea, Ace. It's not hot, since we put out the hearth, but there's an herb in there that should help you relax."

It took everything in me not to gag at the murky water and slide the cup far away from me. "Thank you, Duma. That was very thoughtful," I said, careful to keep my face neutral when I was all too aware of the wicked smirk spreading across the face beside me.

I waited until Duma's attention was back on his brother to slice a look at Terek, who only raised his brows and took a sip of ale, a challenge in his gaze. Damn him, the asshole knew how much I despised tea.

Refusing to let him win and admit to the considerate man across from me that people enjoying plant water made me question all of humanity, I stared Terek down and raised the cup to my lips.

It tasted exactly like it smelled, like Duma had taken a handful of leaves outside and sprinkled them in the water. My eye twitched. It was by far one of the worst things I'd ever tasted, but by the way Terek was hiding a shit-eating grin behind his cup, I would've rather cut off my tongue than show it.

So I took another sip, and then another, swallowing as loudly as possible just to spite him, and thanked both fate and the Underland when I succeeded at not only keeping it down, but also smiling at Duma who'd glanced back over.

"So, it's settled then?" he asked. "We're going to Wenham?"

Terek nodded and took a long pull from his cup. His expression was suspiciously blank, and I had a sudden urge to reach over and pinch him. "Yes. I'll take her through Gissan to rest for a night and restock, and then we'll head straight to Canden."

I frowned at the names, trying to remember where those towns had been and wishing Terek had left the map on the table. "Gissan is closer to the Wood, right?"

Dex set his empty cup down harder than necessary as irritation flared to life in his brown eyes. "Yes, and it also happens to be full of bounty hunters who will be searching for you soon. Are you secretly hoping to meet the void, Terek, or have you just lost your mind completely?"

"I'm not worried about the void, nor did I ask you to join us. You and Duma are welcome to go home," Terek replied, his voice calm and matter of fact. They didn't need to continue with us when they clearly didn't agree with his choice of Wenham to begin with.

I couldn't say I agreed all that much either—not because of its proximity to the Wood, but because I'd liked Tover, and I *really* didn't want to travel for days on end. Regardless, my desire to be as far from Lizbeth as possible was far stronger.

Duma narrowed his eyes. "Stop being so goddamn stubborn. We're not going home until we know it's safe for our staff. We'll swing by to check on them and grab what we need, but then we'll be continuing to Canden right along with you. Don't go through Gissan, Terek. I didn't like it the first time you mentioned it, and I don't like it now."

Terek huffed an irritated breath, but I didn't miss the flare of relief that hit his eyes, and by the way the strain left Duma's face, he didn't miss it either.

"Good. It's settled. Can we go the fuck to bed now?" Dex asked, already pushing back his chair and hopping up. His brother stood as well, but they both lingered when Terek turned to me.

"I'm sorry if it feels like I'm deciding your life for you, Ace. I know that's what everyone else has done, and that's not my intention. I'm just trying—" He ran a frustrated hand through his hair, as if for the first time in his life, he had no idea what he was doing.

Well, that certainly made two of us.

Swallowing back my nerves before I could chicken out, I reached out and placed a hand on his arm, feeling the muscle tense beneath his tunic. "I know. I didn't take it that way, Terek."

He nodded and stared down at my hand, clearing his throat. If he'd been anyone else, I'd have said he almost seemed embarrassed, but knowing Terek, he was likely just uncomfortable with having witnesses to his apology.

Duma and Dex shared a silent look I didn't quite understand, and then Dex muttered something about fate under his breath and grabbed his cup, heading into the kitchen for a refill. Duma followed after him but paused at the threshold, glancing back at me.

"Would you like me to top you off before you head upstairs, Ace? It only takes a few minutes to steep."

I shot to my feet, wincing when my chair scraped across the floor behind me like nails on a blackboard. "No, that's okay, Duma. I'm fine. I think I'm going to go ahead and head up. I need to wash before bed," I said, unable to stop my rambling. My face heated.

"Are you sure? I can bring it up on my way—" he started, but I was already scurrying from the room, the sound of Terek's laughter, loud and carefree, following after me all the way upstairs.

And though I muttered the word, "Asshole," just loud enough for his heightened hearing to catch, I couldn't stop the soft, answering chuckle that slipped past my lips.

ADELAIS

CHAPTER FIFTY

Folding the washcloth I'd been using to squeeze excess water from my hair, I set it next to the comb and rough bar of soap Duma had given me and picked up the toothbrush. The taste of the minty paste after the thick film the sedative and stew had left in my mouth was nearly orgasmic. Bless those men, they'd literally thought of everything.

The only necessity they hadn't been able to pick up for me while they'd run out was clean clothes, and I was secretly thankful for that. They'd spent enough already.

After he'd had some sleep and was hopefully a little more relaxed, I planned to ask Terek if he could find something else for me to wear, preferably something warmer, and for some sanitary cloths for my menstrual cycle. I still had a week or so before I had to deal with that inconvenience, but if Terek stayed firm on his desire to take me to Wenham, we'd be traveling for a while, and it'd be unavoidable.

I stared down at my chemise, the thin fabric sticking to my damp skin. I hadn't been able to soak in a warm tub—a luxury I was beginning to think I'd left Upside—but I'd spent the last twenty minutes scrubbing every inch of my body and hair until my skin was pink and my scalp sore.

Once my hair had been combed out and I was sure I no longer smelled wretched, I'd slipped my chemise back on, not bothering with anything else. The thought of wearing dirty undergarments made me shudder, and although my dress had fared better than I'd assumed, I had no desire to sleep in it.

It'd started raining while we'd eaten, and the small drops hitting my window were the only sounds in the entire house. I listened for footsteps or quiet conversation from the men, but they'd apparently all dispersed to their own rooms not long after I had.

After their sleepless trip from Tover, at Terek's speed no less, and then sneaking in and out of the castle, I wasn't sure how they'd made it as long as they had before passing out. The thought of how exhausted they must be planted a fresh seed of guilt in my mind, but unlike before, this time I immediately dug it out, refusing to let it sprout into a garden of self-hatred.

Dex said I was worth being saved, and I was going to allow myself the grace to believe him. However, I also didn't want to ever be in a position to need them to again. I wanted to become strong and brave enough that these men would never have to risk their lives for me. Not because I wouldn't deserve it, but because I would be capable of saving myself.

Growing up, I'd fantasized about someone coming to rescue me more times than I could count. I'd kneeled at the side of my bed and begged and prayed for a long-lost uncle to show up, or for Mrs. Gayle to whisk me away, but those fantasies didn't work for me anymore. I didn't want to be the damsel waiting to be saved.

I wanted to fight back and not just be told that I mattered and was worthy of a happy life, but to *feel* it as well. No matter what anyone said or believed, I belonged in the Underland, and I'd do whatever it took to stay.

Letting that resolve settle into my bones, I'd just taken a step toward the bed when I heard three firm knocks on my door. It snapped me out of my thoughts, and I flung my arms over my chest, darting a quick glance to the dress I'd laid across the end of the bed.

It was likely just Dex coming by to check on me before he went to sleep, but though I trusted both him and his brother wholeheartedly, I'd prefer if that trust occurred while I was fully dressed.

"Ace."

My heart skipped a beat. Terek. He'd actually...*knocked?*

"Are you still awake?"

His voice was low, but it still somehow slithered through the door and curled around my spine, causing that weird pressure in my chest to increase. I pressed a palm flat to my breast, wondering if all the stress and adrenaline was finally catching up with me.

"Ace," he repeated.

I smiled, imagining the annoyed look on his face as he stood on the other side, trying to be patient and not barge in when we both knew he could hear me moving around. I highly doubted his resolve would last for much longer.

"I'm awake, just give me a second," I said.

Hurrying to the bed, I snatched my dress up and quickly stepped into it, not bothering with the entire line of buttons. I just secured the top one at my neck to keep it from falling off my shoulders and brushed out the worst of the wrinkles. Good enough. It's not like he'd see the back anyway. He was probably only here to confirm whatever he and the twins had continued discussing after I'd left.

"Come in."

I'd barely said the words before Terek pushed the door open, his eyes immediately finding me, and I swallowed. Why was I suddenly so nervous? And why did just the sight of him in my room make me feel like I was having a heart attack?

His hair was damp and strewn across his forehead as if he'd scrubbed it in a rush, and his tunic was wrinkled and untucked. A shadow still lined his jaw, like he hadn't wanted to waste the time it'd have taken to shave. The dark stubble made him look even more dangerous than he was, if such a thing was possible.

Though the irrational part of me couldn't help but imagine what it'd be like to feel it scrape against my skin, I preferred when I could clearly see the lines of his face. The small twitches in his jaw were the only signs of emotion I could squeeze out of him sometimes.

Honestly, I was surprised he'd had the energy to wash up at all.

Traveling without stopping all the way from Tover was strenuous enough as it was, but also being forced to fight who knew how many Creatures? And then he'd somehow still had the strength to make it back here to find us. To find *me*.

I stared at him, waiting for him to state whatever it was he needed, but he just shut the door behind him and twisted the lock. The sound of it clicking sent gooseflesh over my skin like he'd caressed his fingers along the back of my neck rather than the door.

"What are you doing?" I asked, clearing my throat when my voice sounded breathier than I'd intended. "I was just getting ready to go to bed. Is there something you needed?"

I rubbed my palms over my dress, suddenly regretting my choice to ignore the buttons, and acutely aware that I wore nothing but my chemise beneath the undone garment.

Terek took another step in, laying folded clothing I hadn't noticed over the back of a chair. "I'm going to sleep. What does it look like?"

Um, come again? "You're not sleeping in here," I said, the words coming out more like a stuttered question that a firm statement.

"Yes, I am."

I crossed my arms, wishing he was sitting so I didn't feel so short. It was annoyingly difficult to appear like a strong and capable woman when I had to crane my neck back to maintain eye contact.

"I'm not going to sneak away with anyone, Terek. Shockingly enough, I learned my lesson."

His eyes dropped to where my arms rested over my breasts. My wrists were still wrapped to keep a layer of salve on them and help heal anything Dex's ability might've missed, and I fidgeted under Terek's pointed stare.

"Well, *shockingly*," he said, over-emphasizing the word, "I'm tired and not in the mood to risk waking up to you missing again."

I narrowed my eyes, even as my heart did an idiotic flip my brain was going to promptly ignore. "I said I won't leave. I thought we were going to finally start trusting each other?"

After what had happened, if there was anything he could trust, it was that my ass wasn't wandering off anywhere in this city without him or Duma and Dex.

"It's not you I don't trust, Ace," he said, his voice softer than I'd expected as he unlatched his belted sheaths and set the contraption and weapons on the seat of the chair.

Was he referring to not trusting whether Hara would show up and snatch me away, or not trusting himself because he couldn't sense me while asleep? Likely a little of both, but I was going to focus on the first, since I wasn't sure what to do about the second yet. I was still struggling to imagine this man with any type of weakness.

"I'll be fine. If Hara shows up, which she won't, I promise to scream loud enough to wake all three of you."

He ignored me, bending over to work his boots and socks off and set them beside the rest of his things. I slid my eyes to the covered window, his naked feet on the bedroom floor feeling too intimate.

"I know you'll be fine because I'm going to be sleeping beside you to make sure of it."

That yanked my attention right back, and my mouth opened and closed twice before I managed to say, "We're not sharing a bed, Terek. If you're going to be a stubborn ass, you can sleep on the floor."

His eyes flashed, and the corner of his mouth twitched like he was fighting back a smile, but my desire to see it bloom across his face died when he said, "I seem to recall you quite liked the last time we slept together. Or do you not remember the way you curled into me?"

Remember? I'd have to have my mind scrubbed with a wire brush to forget the way it'd felt to have Terek's body pressed to mine. The memory alone had heat coiling up everywhere it shouldn't, which only further proved why I should absolutely not, under any circumstance, be sharing a bed with him.

"No, I don't, actually. Must not have meant as much to me as it did to you."

His smirk grew as he reached an arm back over his shoulder. "Your racing heart tells me otherwise, little rabbit."

God damnit. The traitorous organ beat even faster at the way he all but purred the nickname I'd once hated. "Yeah, well, it tends to go a little crazy when I want to punch someone in the—" My breath caught in my throat, and I sputtered, suddenly forgetting how to form words.

Terek had gripped the back of his tunic while I'd talked and yanked it over his head in one smooth movement, tossing it to the side to stand before me in nothing but a pair of trousers.

Holy fucking hell.

I'd felt how firm his chest was, had seen the definition in his shoulders and arms, but never in my life had I imagined a man could look like that. Muscles I didn't even know existed tensed and shifted as he sauntered across the room, and my mouth went dry.

I pressed my lips closed and fought to look unaffected, but when he slid his hands into his pockets, my eyes betrayed me by instinctively following them, dipping to where his torso disappeared into top of his trousers. He was perfection personified, and I desperately wanted to touch him everywhere, to trace the numerous small scars I could see and taste his skin as he told me about each one.

Walking past me with a suspiciously satisfied expression, he moved to the opposite side of the bed and sat down, stretching his long legs and placing his hands above his head in a way that almost felt like foreplay with how overheated I suddenly was.

"You're more than welcome to punch me as many times as you'd like, Ace. I'll even pretend it hurts. But your ass will be in this bed with me once you're done."

I swallowed, wishing I could submerge my entire being into an icy river, and reminded myself Terek didn't mean those words the way my body clearly wanted him to. His smirk grew, and I knew without a shadow of a doubt the arrogant asshole had undressed on purpose to fluster me out of arguing.

Well, it'd certainly worked, but I wasn't the doe-eyed, innocent woman he thought I was anymore, and two could play his little game. If I was going to have to lay there all night, feeling uncomfortable and ready to explode, so was he.

"Fine," I said, reaching up to undo the lone button I'd secured at my neck. "Have it your way then."

His dark eyes flashed, and his arms came down, pushing himself up onto his elbows. "What are you doing?"

"I'm going to sleep. What does it look like?" I said sweetly, raising an eyebrow and taking a steadying breath to calm my racing heart.

His eyes traced over my shoulders where I gripped the collar of my dress, and the air between us charged with an energy so heavy, I could practically taste it.

Terek fisted the blanket, every inch of his body radiating a warning that made my nipples harden and my breath catch. The darkest part of me reveled in how easily I affected him, and I ached to push him farther, to see just what he might do if I nudged him to the same edge I was balancing on.

Because he could erect the white wall of Ardenglass itself between us, but he could no longer hide that he felt something for me. He could lash out and verbally strike me all he wanted, but we both knew he wanted me as much as I did him.

No man who only saw me as *convenient* would've been willing to take on an entire regiment of guards to get me back, nor would he have gently washed my face or be looking at me the way Terek was now. Like I was the very poison my mother had always claimed me to be, but one he desperately wanted to consume anyway.

I let the smallest smile shape my lips, and then I let my dress fall, pooling around my feet and leaving me in only a thin, sheer barrier. His body went preternaturally still, and his midnight eyes seared into me like he wasn't sure whether he wanted to sprint out of the room or tear it from my body.

I waited for the embarrassment to hit, for my cheeks to flush and betray my nervousness, but as I walked toward the bed—toward him—I felt nothing but that demanding pull and an overwhelming throb between my legs.

Terek watched me approach with an almost unnerving focus. He'd yet to move a muscle, but his gaze was molten hot as it slid down my neck, pausing to rest on my peaked nipples, before trailing lower to where the fabric shifted between my thighs.

When I reached the edge of the mattress, I tore my attention away from him and busied myself with pulling back the covers, internally praying I didn't lose my mind and orgasm right there without him even touching me.

Sure, it'd been a while since I'd given myself a release—a very long while—but holy hell, I'd never been so turned on in my life by just the sight of a man. I hadn't even known it was possible.

Trying to breathe through it, I lifted my leg to climb onto the bed, only to freeze when a choked curse escaped him. The sound pulled my gaze to him, but though his eyes were on me, they weren't on my face. They were pinned to the apex of my thighs, where my chemise had risen to several healthy inches above my knee.

Terek seemed to convulse, his nostrils flaring wide, and then the next thing I knew, he'd yanked the blanket up from under him and thrown it over his waist, his hands clenched over his lap as he glared at me. "You appear to have forgotten your undergarments," he bit out.

"Not at all," I said, curling up onto my side with my back facing him. I didn't bother pulling the blanket up, far too hot in my own skin. "I wasn't aware I'd have company, and I prefer to sleep without them."

Although not exactly the truth, it wasn't a complete lie either. I *hadn't* wanted to sleep with them tonight. It wasn't my fault Terek had decided to stay in here.

Silence settled between us, but if anything, it only heightened the desire roaring to life in my veins. I didn't feel in control of my own body anymore, like something was coming to life within my chest and pushing me toward the man behind me. *Demanding* it.

He groaned and shifted behind me. That warmth coiled tighter, knowing he could scent my arousal and wondering if he felt this sudden uncontrollable need, too, and if I'd be able to feel just how much if I reached back and slid my hand along his trousers.

God, what the hell was wrong with me?

"Ace," he warned, his voice a low growl, even as I felt the heat of his chest along my back as he rolled toward me.

My heart smashed against my ribcage, and I sucked in a breath as I pressed my thighs together. Wetness pooled between them, the combination of his smell and his nearness making me feel inebriated. I inched my fingers below my belly and pressed them over my chemise to where that throbbing heat built.

What would it even feel like to have him touch me? To have his long fingers learn my body and push me over the edge rather than simply use me and leave me empty? I closed my eyes and instinctively arched my hips back into him, circling my fingers ever so slowly.

Not even a second later, he threw his arm over me and seized my hand, impeding its motion. When he spoke, his voice was pure gravel, each word forced as if he was in pain. "Crimson hell, Ace. What are you doing?"

My lungs worked so hard, I felt dizzy. "I don't know."

I felt thoroughly out of control, and I wasn't sure what was happening or why I was doing it. All I knew was that the second he'd removed his shirt, that tugging pressure in my chest had tripled until I swore I could roll over and straddle him, and it still wouldn't bring us close enough.

"I'm on fire, and I feel like my chest is going to burst," I whispered.

Terek's grip tightened, squeezing my wrist. "I know, I'm sorry. Just go to sleep. Please."

What? My thighs were practically drenched at that point, his fingers only an inch away from feeling it, and he wanted me to go to sleep? I tried to twist, wanting to meet his eyes, but I only succeeded at pushing my ass more firmly against him. Something hard pressed into me, and he cursed, releasing my wrist and instantly shifting back.

"Go the fuck to sleep, Adelais," he growled, his breath coasting over my ear just before he shoved away, rolling to the far side of the bed. The sudden absence of him left me cold, but it was the sound of my real name on his lips that froze me in place.

I'd told Duma I wanted to be called Ace, but as I dragged up the covers and fought to control my heart, I was fairly certain I just might sacrifice my soul if it meant hearing Terek say my name again.

TEREK

CHAPTER FIFTY-ONE

She was naked. Completely and utterly naked beneath that flimsy gown. I couldn't move, couldn't fucking breathe. Not when the smallest inhale would flood my senses with the overpowering scent of her desire, guttural and raw and only for me.

My jaw screamed from how hard I ground my teeth, but I didn't relent, knowing if I relaxed even the slightest, I'd roll back toward her and caress my hand down her soft stomach, burying my nose in her hair while I discovered what would make that wicked mouth beg me for mercy. And I'd never be able to stop there.

One crack in my resolve, and the entire wall would come crumbling down until I'd eaten her alive and damned us both, and I wouldn't feel a single dose of remorse for it.

Crimson fucking *fuck*.

ADELAIS

CHAPTER FIFTY-TWO

The Wood loomed before us, its thick expanse of trees an unending wall as far as the eye could see, apart from a solitary split where a wide path cut through. But even that did little to break up the overcast of shadows that decorated the dirt road from the towering trees. Though their roots ended several feet from the road, their trunks were taller and wider here, bowing toward each other while their branches intertwined, as if seeking to block out the sky entirely.

I squinted, trying to see if they thinned out along the way to allow in more light, but although the merchants Duma and Dex had questioned in Canden had confirmed Wenham to be a straight shot through the Wood, I could see no light or end in sight.

Traveling with Terek over the last week had been stressful enough beneath the open gray sky, but spending the next several hours doing so in the dark? I may have felt a kinship to the Wood after all the years it'd helped me hide, but I wasn't sure how much more tension Terek and I could hold between us.

I winced and shifted my weight, listening to said man continue arguing with the two others behind me. My feet had new blisters, not counting the first ones Dex had healed on day two, my shins ached, and my general sense of time was completely shot.

I'd walked more over the last few days than I had in my entire life Upside, and my body had been quick to let me know it wasn't a fan. It felt like we'd been traveling for weeks rather than days. I'd eaten so much flavorless, dried fare, I was convinced I might've finally died and entered some version of hell.

But as exhausted as my body was, and as much as I wished we could've stayed an extra night in Canden to rest, my mind was acutely, painfully awake. It had been ever since our night in Ardenglass, my every waking thought accompanied by a buzzing awareness of Terek so heady I could practically taste it.

He'd disappeared by the time I'd climbed out of bed the following morning. I'd woken from a dream that'd done nothing to abate the growing need suffocating my sanity to find the bed cold and the room empty. Every hint of him gone, albeit for the faint smell that clung to his pillow.

I'd considered staying in the room for the rest of my life to avoid the crushing humiliation of seeing him after my display the previous night, but when I'd sucked it up and entered the kitchen where he'd been speaking to Duma, he'd said nothing about it. He'd only stared at me with unnerving intensity, his eyes trailing down my body before he'd bit out something about getting me clean clothes and stalked out of the house.

Every day since had felt like we were walking on eggshells, each night beside him pure torture. The tavern stories Duma told while he'd start our campfires, and Dex's infectious laughter as he'd taught me random card games, had been the only reprieves I'd had to distract me from the string pulling ever taut between us.

It felt like one wrong move would sever it, and neither of us knew how to act around the other anymore. I'd practically thrown myself at him twice now, only to be rejected, and Terek apparently feared that even talking to me might encourage feelings he didn't wish to reciprocate, though I knew he did.

However, he'd stayed true to his word about not allowing me to be alone at night when his senses were dulled. He was always close by when we made camp with the twins, and he'd demanded to stay in my room in both Tover and Canden, though there'd been no lack of vacancy in either. Even so, unless we were laid out on the ground beside a fire with our friends a few feet away, he rarely spoke to me.

Both nights we'd had a room, we'd slept on the far edges of the bed, fully clothed, in tense, awkward silence. It'd been less restful than the nights I'd curled up on the cold, hard ground, because no matter how much space Terek kept between us, the moment his body laid next to mine, I'd felt the heat of him scorch through my core as surely as if his hand slid between my legs.

It'd flare instantly and unbidden, that tug toward his body practically screaming at me to touch him, made worse by the fact that I could never hide it. The grinding of his teeth told me enough about what he scented on me, and both mornings, he'd slipped out before I'd risen, stopping only long enough to leave food and a flask on my end table.

Dex had tried covering for him when we'd met downstairs, claiming Terek was just restocking supplies and eager to leave, but neither of us believed him. The man was determined to keep me at a distance, but no matter how tall he built his wall during the day, it couldn't hide the fact that this morning, I'd woken before dawn to find his body wrapped tightly around mine, his hand splayed below my breasts and a very hard—very notable—length pressed firmly against me.

His chest had risen and fallen steadily against my back, his breath over my ear sending gooseflesh down my neck. I'd shamefully laid there, careful not to move a muscle as I'd allowed myself, for a single moment, to pretend. Pretend we weren't on the run, and he wouldn't rip away from me the moment his eyes opened. Pretend instead, that he'd crawl over me and do whatever it was he was dreaming about to make him so hard and ready.

Pretended that, for once, I could give myself to a man of my own volition. To allow him into my body not because *he* wanted it, but because *I* did, and to come apart beneath his touch, rather than my own. Eventually, I'd drifted off again, waking an hour later to an empty bed.

Now, staring up at where the Wood met the gray sky, I brushed the thoughts of us away, knowing they'd do me no good. I sighed, hearing the voices behind me pick up again as they continued bickering about the best course of action. Terek wanted to go through as a group, while Duma thought it best to go in pairs.

"I'm telling you, we'll look more threatening as a group, Terek. You heard what the Canden merchants said. If we look the part—"

"And I told you, I cannot help you if you get attacked on your own, and—"

"—we may get all the way through without them making themselves known to us at all."

"—I'll be forced to listen to you and your brother die while getting Ace the rest of the way through."

Positive we'd all kill each other if we didn't get a break from traveling soon, I twisted around and stomped up to them. Dex was currently cross-legged on the ground, running some kind of stone along the edge of his sword, but he glanced up at my approach, winking at me.

"Can we just go already?" I asked, placing my hands on my hips. "I'm tired, my feet hurt, and I want a goddamn bath. I agree with Duma that going in pairs would draw less attention, but I think we can all agree that Terek could never pass as a merchant, even if he tried."

Duma grumbled but didn't argue. There wasn't a soul in the Underland, including him, who could claim Terek appeared anything less than the walking threat he was. "Though since I don't believe we'll have an issue either way, I don't see the point in you continuing to argue like a bunch of angry chickens."

Dex began chuckling, and I pressed my lips together to keep away the smile his infectious laughter always pulled from me. "You're not exactly helping either, you know."

"Oh, I know," he said, pushing to stand and sheathing his sword. He stretched his arms above his head and groaned. "I can't help it. I quite like it when Terek gets all hissy. It reminds me of a stray that used to bite the shit out of Jack's legs whenever he'd…"

Pain rippled across Dex's face, and he quickly cleared his throat, covering the tight expression with a smile that didn't quite meet his eyes. "What I mean is, irritation adds a little flare to Terek's otherwise beautifully stony features, wouldn't you say, Ace?"

I moved to touch his arm, but he was already sauntering toward a group of smaller trees, avoiding his brother's gaze and shouting something about needing to take a piss.

"Is he okay?" I asked, knowing Dex had already gone to that exact spot to relieve himself fifteen minutes ago and was likely just needing a little bit of space for a moment.

Duma said nothing at first, his mouth a tight line as he stared after his brother. "Are you asking for my answer or his?"

"Yours. I already know what he'd tell me." Dex would flash me a wide smile, make some offhand joke, and pretend like nothing bothered him, even if no life lived behind his brown eyes while he did.

Duma sighed, rubbing a hand over his scalp. "Is anyone okay when the person they love is ripped away from them? Dex may have been the one to lose his life, but Jack still died for him, in a way."

I chewed my lip, feeling Terek's eyes on me. If Duma had asked me that a few years ago, I wouldn't have understood that kind of devotion, but now? I knew exactly how I'd feel, and it made my heart rupture into a hundred pieces for Dex.

"Do you think Jack is here somewhere, and they just haven't found each other yet?" I asked, knowing that's what Dex was hoping for, that it was what kept him from pursuing the baker in Tover.

Duma shook his head and turned back, giving me a look that seemed to hold a hidden meaning I didn't understand. "No, Ace, I don't. If there's anything I know for certain, it's that my brother and Jack were fated souls who were lucky enough to find one another in their first life. If Jack had ever entered the Underland, even for a day, Dex would've immediately felt the pull—"

"As beautiful as that is," Terek snapped, interrupting Duma with a stare that could cut ice, "in case you've all forgotten, we're about to spend the next several hours within the Wood. So, if we could keep to the task at hand and get going, that'd be great. I have no desire to still be within those godforsaken trees when we lose what little natural light we'll have."

I blinked up at him, surprised by the clipped anger in his tone, but Duma just stared back, like he wasn't at all surprised by Terek's reaction. Something silent passed between them before Duma shook his head again and spun away, presumably to fetch his brother.

"That was rude. Just because we're about to do something *you* think is dangerous doesn't mean we all become unfeeling statues, Terek." The words came out harsher than I'd intended, but I was struggling to match this cold version of him with the soft one who'd washed my face and promised me truths.

He seemed to consider me, subconsciously running a hand over something held within his pocket. "Feelings only get you killed or get the person you care about killed. Either way, they're not going to help us through the Wood."

I crossed my arms and rolled my eyes. Go figure, this was the longest conversation we'd had alone since Ardenglass, and we were fighting. "You're impossible."

"I'm also the person trying to protect you in there, so for once, listen to me and just…behave," he said, adjusting his cloak and running a hand through his hair. "This won't be the time for you to wander off the path and play with some poisonous Creature you think looks sweet."

"Maybe if you didn't kill them just for breathing, they'd be sweeter to you, too."

"Crimson hell, I mean it, Ace. I need you to behave in there. As long as we are within those trees, I need you to do whatever I say."

"I don't—"

The words died in my throat when Terek's fingers suddenly pressed over my lips, the first hint of warmth flickering within the dark blue of his eyes. "If you feel inclined to argue, little rabbit, I encourage you not to."

I sighed and waited for him to remove his hand, while my heart raced from his simple touch like I was an affection-starved idiot. "I wasn't going to argue. Just because I see the Creatures differently than you do doesn't mean I don't want to get through the Wood quickly. I'll behave."

A loud snort came from behind me, and I turned to see the twins already returning, Dex's normal, ornery smile stretching his brown cheeks. "Yeah, I'll believe that when I see it," he said.

"That means you, too," Terek said, leveling Dex an exasperated look of a parent with a wayward child. He stared down at me again. "Stay between us at all times."

"Can I carry one of your daggers?"

"No. You won't need to."

"You're the one who said the Creatures here were dangerous. Are you saying you were mistaken?" I asked, tilting my head and pressing my lips together to keep from laughing when Duma and Dex made faces behind Terek's head.

He crossed the remaining foot of space between us, his cloak brushing up against my arms as I was forced to tip my head back to maintain eye contact. "I'm saying you won't need to because if anything, Creature or man, is bold enough to attack, they'll have to get through me first."

"And if you fail and you're sent to the black void?"

Terek's lips curled up at the corners. "Then you'll have your pick of whichever dagger you desire off my corpse, little rabbit."

⚷

THE DAYS WE'D spent traveling between towns hadn't exactly been bustling with noise, but until we finally crossed within the cover of the large, arching trees, I'd almost forgotten how quiet the Wood was. I hadn't realized just how much I'd missed its comforting stillness, or the way the darkness enveloped me, and the breeze gently swirled loose hairs from my braid.

Pressure I hadn't even realized had built around my chest evaporated, and I tipped my head back, smiling up at the crisscrossing branches above me. I suddenly couldn't remember why I'd dreaded coming through here.

A soft nudge to my arm pulled my face back down. Although it was too dark to make out the fine details in Dex's typically expressive face, the intrigue in his hushed voice was clear.

"Why do you look like you just came home after a long day at work rather than entered Hell's gate?"

I glanced around us as I mulled over his question, noting the way the slits of sky gave some of the top leaves an almost silvery edge. The desire to step off the path and brush my hand along the trees gnawed at me, but I refrained, reminding myself I'd promised Terek to behave less than an hour ago.

"I don't know, maybe because it *is*, in a way," I finally admitted, making sure to keep my voice low. "I've been coming to the Wood most of my life, and for a long time, it was the only home I had. The only safe one, at least. Anytime my father or Frederick hurt me, I could come here and enjoy knowing they didn't exist at all."

I shrugged, realizing Duma was also listening in. The thought of having an audience to my pain would've humiliated me once upon a time, but I found no weight pulling me down with the admission. I didn't feel guilty for speaking it. It was just a fact, a past I'd grown from and become stronger because of.

"Well, if you could share some of that calm, it'd be appreciated. This place always makes me tense up like there's a stick shoved up my ass." Dex shuddered, his eyes darting over my head as a branch cracked far away.

I huffed a laugh, pushing any thoughts of him and sticks far from my mind. "When I was younger, I used to believe the Wood was magical. I remember thinking the trees would move and press against me in greeting when I'd sit at their bases to draw in the dirt," I said, my heart squeezing at how long it'd been since I'd had the chance to draw anything at all. "I'd thought coming here meant I was magical, too."

"Can't imagine who ruined that idea," Dex said, dramatically tipping his head in Terek's direction ahead of us. "When did you first run into that asshole anyway? I can't imagine having only him to talk to and still choosing to come back."

I snorted, aware Terek could hear our whispered conversation and thoroughly enjoying the way his shoulders tensed. Good. Served him right for making me feel so awkward these past several days.

"We met during my first trip here. I was eight, and it'd been an accident. I had no idea where I was. He found me almost instantly."

"Did he now?" Dex asked, though he didn't sound surprised at all. Duma grunted beside him. "And how'd that go?"

"She threatened to stab my eye out," Terek said, not even bothering to turn around.

I genuinely feared Dex's eyes might pop out of his head. "You threatened to stab his eye out when you were *eight?*"

"That explains a lot," Duma muttered, his focus back on our surroundings.

"Explains what?" I asked, unsure if he meant it as a good thing or a bad thing, but neither of them answered before Terek twisted back to glare at us.

"By all means, keep talking. I'd love to alert even more Creatures to our presence."

I glared right back, my breaths coming faster as I attempted to keep up with his long strides. Clearly, being in the Wood gave someone else the feeling of a stick up his ass, too. But the three of us listened and walked quietly, and before I knew it, Terek was holding up two fingers.

Two hours. We were already two hours through, and we hadn't spotted a single Creature. Between the steady cracks of sticks, the rustling of dried foliage, and Terek's hands regularly twitching over his sheaths, I knew some were definitely nearby, but none came close enough for me to see.

It wasn't until we'd taken a short break and pushed through hour three, which, according to the merchants, was over halfway, that I had the sudden distinct sensation of being watched. Not like the curious gazes of a few small Creatures hiding within the trees, but of something else. Something that had the hairs rising on the back of my neck.

I glanced up at Terek to gauge his reaction, but he seemed

completely oblivious to whatever it was I could feel, his gaze pinned to the path ahead. I darted a look behind me at the twins, but they didn't seem to be worried either, their eyes wary but steps casual as they surveyed the thick trees around us.

I turned back around and tried to brush it off, reminding myself it was literally impossible for me to sense something Terek could not, and that I was letting his distrust of the Wood get to me. But within minutes, I felt it again, like a cold sweat along my skin, warning me something was wrong.

I squinted into the darkness to the right, just to prove to myself there was nothing there, only for my heart to stop beating entirely when a small figure peeked out at me from behind a tree. The hem of her white dress blew up against the side of the trunk, and when I met her piercing yellow gaze, she smiled and raised a long, clawed finger over her mouth.

My feet slammed to a stop, causing Dex to curse just before he crashed into me and sent me flying forward. I squeaked as my arms flailed, but instead of face planting into the dirt, I smacked into Terek's firm chest, the clasp of his cloak bumping my forehead.

He steadied me with two hands on my upper arms, and I vaguely heard him ask me what was wrong, but all I could do was stare at where I'd seen Chesie standing. No matter how hard I squinted, she never reappeared, but given she could make herself invisible as easily as Terek could hear my heartbeat, I wasn't sure if her absence made me feel better or worse.

"Ace," Terek said again, more forcefully this time. "What is it? What happened?"

I shook my head, not wanting to tell him and look ridiculous when I'd been the one claiming there was nothing to be scared of, especially when it made zero sense for me to have seen her so close. Even invisible, Terek would've been able to hear her steps, or at least her heartbeat. Right? Did she even have a heartbeat?

Realizing the men were still watching me with worry, including the midnight eyes that could somehow always read the thoughts on my face before I was ready to share them, I forced a laugh.

"Nothing. I just thought I saw something, and then I tripped," I said, urging my heart to steady and not give away the strength of my unease. I'd only imagined her. "I'm fine."

Terek's eyes narrowed, but he thankfully didn't press. "You probably did. There are no less than a dozen Creatures following us at the moment," he said, gesturing toward the trees on either side of us.

When I didn't immediately answer, he leaned closer, and I could've sworn I felt his thumb brush ever so gently along the inside of my wrist. "Don't worry, I've been keeping close tabs on them. We've piqued their interest, but I don't think they're brave enough to leave the shadows."

"I'm not worried about them," I said, even as I found myself searching one last time for the flicker of a white dress. Creatures following us, I could handle. I was well acquainted with their curious nature. But Chesie? Chesie scared the shit out of me.

Terek watched me for another moment, brow drawn, but it was Duma who spoke, his attention on a large shadow shifting between the branches above us. "Terek, I really think we should start moving again, and fast."

Terek's face hardened, and I could tell by the way his jaw tightened and he stared down at my legs that he was considering whether to toss me onto his back and run. He'd only just unclipped his cloak, confirming my suspicions, when a sound echoed out around us, making my heart drop and each one of us freeze. The soft, childlike humming of a song I'd tried so desperately to forget.

The chest is made with twenty-four ribs. Snap, snap, snap. It houses your heart but only so well. Snap, snap, snap.

Terek dropped his cloak to the ground, his eyes wild and hands flying to his daggers as the Wood exploded around us.

ADELAIS

CHAPTER FIFTY-THREE

M y eyes didn't know where to land as something shrieked and dropped from the sky, raining sticks and leaves on us as it snatched Terek's shoulders and launched him several yards down the road. I threw my arms up to protect my head, barely ducking in time to avoid a second Creature that leapt over me as Terek's body slammed into the ground and snarls filled the air.

Scratches marred my arms, and my blood pounded in my ears as I caught sight of more fur and scales sprinting from the trees, seconds before Dex's body barreled into me.

One muscular arm wrapped around my waist and flung me behind him, knocking me onto my ass, while his other hand reached back and wrapped around the pommel of his sword, unsheathing it in one smooth motion. I scrambled to my feet, Duma appearing in my peripheral a second later, twin axes gripped in his hands as we watched the scene play out before us in horror.

Because although there were currently six enormous Creatures on the path, varying in every possible way, they weren't trying to attack. At least...not us. They didn't even seem aware of our existence as each of them simultaneously launched themselves at one thing.

Terek.

A scream left my throat as one of the Creatures, a cat twice my size with bright plumes of feathers at its neck, spit a sizzling poison at his head. Terek easily dodged, his body moving at speeds I'd never witnessed as he dove for the one who'd crashed in from above, cleaving its wings from its back in one fell swoop before immediately unleashing himself at another.

I lurched past Dex, not sure what the hell I'd do with no weapon, but knowing I couldn't just leave him to fight alone. There were still five uninjured against his one. Dex snagged my arm at the last second, yanking me back. He shouted something I couldn't make out in my ear as even more Creatures began edging out of the trees to our right, muscles tensed and teeth bared.

Terek didn't spare them a glance, and I wasn't sure if he was aware of them. He hadn't slowed for even half a second, slashing and weaving in and out of the original six that'd attacked him, and a cold fear enveloped me.

I knew he'd fought this many Creatures numerous times before, but we'd been traveling for days on end with little rest, and he'd warned me that the Creatures here would possess stronger abilities than those residing near Ardenglass. I wanted to trust that he'd be fine, but something in my gut, an instinct that sliced and cut at me, screamed that he would not.

The blood that suddenly gushed from his nose as a Creature with pulsing green eyes and black feathers roared at him only made that instinct cut deeper, forcing panic to rise like bile in my throat. Terek staggered and coughed, but he still managed to slice open another's neck just before spitting a mouthful of blood onto the ground.

His shoulders shook from the effort of fighting whatever the green-eyed Creature's ability was, but he dropped to one knee, retrieving the small blade from his left boot, even while fresh blood dripped down his face. With a snap of his wrist, he flung it faster than my eyes could track, directly down its throat. It slumped to the ground, its roaring cut off, but Terek only had a second of reprieve before others were upon him, teeth, claws, and blades meeting in a flurry of chaos.

I twisted to face Duma and Dex, who stood like stone sentries beside me. Their weapons were drawn and their eyes fixed on Terek's fast-moving form, but they made no move to join the fight. I stepped closer, shouting to be heard over the horrific sounds of snapping jaws and keening wails.

"Why are you just standing there? We need to help him!"

"Don't you think we fucking want to?" Duma shouted back, not bothering to look down at me. "We leave you, and you'll be dead within seconds. Terek stands a far better chance than you."

I shook my head so hard my neck popped. "If I die, I have the chance of staying here. If he dies, he's *gone*. Please. Help him," I begged, my voice breaking as I watched a scaled tail pin Terek to a tree.

When still neither of them moved, I gripped Duma's tunic and yanked his face down to mine, finally earning me his frantic, brown eyes and praying he could see the soul-crushing truth in mine. "I cannot lose him, Duma. Please. I swear to you, I'll be fine."

I knew it as well as I knew my name or how to breathe. The Creatures of the Wood had every chance over the last two decades to take my life, and they never had. Whatever their reason was, whatever kinship or comfort they felt with me, it would protect me even now.

Duma yanked away from me with a curse and stared out at his friend, raising both axes. "Crimson fucking take me, I told Terek this was a bad idea. If we survive this, I'm going to kill your fated."

I didn't know what that meant, and I didn't fucking care. All I cared about was all of us making it out of the Wood alive. But I didn't have the chance to say any of that before Dex was standing in front of me, sword raised. His muscles flexed and shifted in his arms as he stared at a two-headed Creature that'd begun creeping out from the trees toward the fray.

Flames curled at the corners of both its mouths, and though it was hunched low, ready to lunge, it was twice the size of the men and moving silently. I swallowed and widened my stance, ready to bolt to the side if it leapt at the twins, but it continued to stare straight past us like we weren't even there. Its focus, like the others, was only on Terek.

"I'm too old for this shit," Duma said, moving to stand side-by-side with his brother.

Dex nudged him and shifted his weight, eyes pinned to the flames pouring from the Creature's mouths. "What's eternity without a little adventure, right?"

Duma grunted, the sound forced and strained, but whatever he said back I didn't hear as a roar of pain had me whipping around to Terek. His tunic was torn, and my heart lodged in my throat at the sight of the three bloody claw marks down the length of his back.

He kicked the Creature hard enough for its neck to break with a grotesque snap and then spun, avoiding the teeth of another. It growled in warning, readying to strike again, but Terek just snarled right back, flinging his arm and sinking a dagger between its eyes faster than lightning.

It was like a dance only he knew, each move precise and deadly, but with every Creature Terek felled, another came slinking out of the Wood to take its place. I slapped my hands over my ears, wanting to scream at the twins to hurry up and help him, but they were already locked in their own battle with the two-headed Creature.

Dex was doing his best to distract both of its heads while Duma circled behind it, his teeth clenched and axes glowing as he shot heat into them. His legs widened as he prepared to lunge, but before he could bury the lethal weapons into the Creature's thick skin, one of its heads suddenly twisted, nostrils smoking as it spotted him.

My eyes and nose stung, the realization that these men were not going to make it out of the Wood hitting me like a punch to the gut. All three were about to enter the void while I stood there in the midst of it all, doing fucking *nothing*, just like I'd always done.

I'd carry on to Wenham, untouched by a single Creature, to live out my weak and worthless life alone, while their minds deteriorated in a vast sea of nothingness for all of eternity. The image had panic building, and I pressed a hand to my chest as something dark yawned open inside me.

Duma and Dex were the first real family I'd ever had, the first people in my life to see me and accept me exactly as I was. And the thought of losing that, losing *them*, made me want to scream until my throat bled.

But it was the thought of losing Terek that had that darkness curling up my spine as an uncontrollable fury consumed me. My body began to vibrate with the intensity, and I clenched my teeth, watching Terek's sharp features contort in pain as he took a hit to his injured back.

Though he'd finally begun to slow, the man still refused to concede, throwing himself onto the nearest Creature and severing its spine with his remaining blade. And it was as it dropped to the ground, and another immediately slunk out from between the trees, that it truly hit me that this was not a random attack by starving Creatures.

They knew who Terek was, or at least what he could do, and they were saving their strength, wearing him down one at a time. They were never going to stop coming, and if I didn't do something, they were going to succeed.

That infuriating man had never once stopped protecting me, even when he'd hated me for it, and now, it was my turn. I had no idea what it was that was roiling inside of me, but I gave into it, letting that darkness leach into every last cell.

My muscles tightened and my vision tunneled as random images flashed before me, an ancient, unending fury filling my mind. The world seemed to shake around me, and for a moment, all I could see and feel were the trees of the Wood, their branches swaying and their leaves decaying as the blood of their children drowned their roots.

A wave of such despair and hopelessness poured over me, it ripped a guttural wail from my throat. The blood painted higher up the trees, and I tried to move, to run, to do *something*, desperate to save someone, though I didn't know who. My legs refused to obey, and when I looked down, it was to find my own feet buried in the bloodied ground, my skin hard as bark.

But I felt no panic or fear at the sight, only white-hot rage as the agony of a thousand deaths scorched through me. The ground quaked harder, the earth groaning and cracking around me, and then I was suddenly crashing to my knees, my sight and feelings mine again.

The pain and river of blood were gone, but the lingering burn of that unyielding anger remained, and I clutched at my heart, trying to swallow it down as hot tears tracked down my cheeks. Before I could settle my pounding heart or even attempt to grasp what I'd just experienced, several things happened at once.

The ground ceased its shaking as if it'd never happened, and every Creature surrounding us dropped to the ground in unison, their gazes pinned on me. Terek stumbled, sweat and blood pouring off him, and his head whipped to the left, sensing something off the path we could not.

He let out a sharp curse and tightened his grip on his dagger, the other still inside a fallen body somewhere. He shouted at Duma to take me back the way we'd come, but I was too busy gaping in horror to so much as glance at the twins, let alone move. Because what shot from the dark shadows between the trees and across the path in a flurry of leaves and upturned dirt was the largest fucking snake I'd ever seen.

Its vibrant, purple scales seemed almost blinding compared to the dull colors of the Wood, the colors shifting from a sweet wine to nearly black as its tail coiled up behind it. But it was the flared hood shadowing its triangular head and a pair of fangs the length of my arms that had me scrambling to my feet.

Despite being thicker than all three men put together, it'd crossed the path and blocked us nearly as fast as I'd seen Terek move, its body writhing and shifting as if to strike. There was no doubt in my mind it could swallow a body whole with little to no effort, and with the way its milky-white eyes zeroed in on Terek, I had a feeling it was contemplating doing just that with the man before me.

In turn, instead of running like he'd just demanded us to do, Terek's legs widened, and he spun his dagger, readying to launch himself at it before the others attacked again. The second Terek shifted his weight though, the snake let out a long hiss, and my heart dropped as dozens more Creatures stepped out from the trees, snarling in answer.

For a split second, so brief I wouldn't have noticed if I hadn't been so attuned to him, Terek's shoulders sagged forward an inch. As if he knew, as well as I did, that there was no way he was going to survive this. Yet, he still didn't back down, didn't turn to run, desperate to give us what he believed was our only chance.

I didn't need that chance. These Creatures were never going to hurt me, just the same as they hadn't moved to hurt Duma or Dex. They didn't seek to hurt anyone who hadn't hurt them first, and Terek, whether by his command or Lizbeth's, had only ever sought to hurt them.

The thought broke my heart, and before I knew what I was doing, I was sprinting forward as fast as my shaking legs could carry me, determination steeling my spine to not only save Terek, but *them*.

I heard Duma's panicked shout behind me, but I didn't stop, letting that desire center me and pull me the rest of the way from that consuming darkness as I flung myself at Terek. He twisted before I could slam into his injured back, just like I knew he would, and pressed me into his chest.

One arm curled around my back in a fierce hold, while his other kept his dagger out in front of us. "What the crimson fuck are you doing? *Get back to Duma.*"

His heart raced beneath my ear, but I didn't need to feel it or hear the strain in his voice to sense the magnitude of his fear. It was the naked honesty of that fear and the sticky warmth of the blood coating my hands from his ruined tunic that gave me the strength to shove against his hold rather than sink into it.

He released me immediately, his eyes flicking away from the Creatures just long enough to rove over me, checking me for injury. The depth of his emotions called to me louder than his words ever could, silently begging me to run, to leave with Duma and Dex and not look back.

But I just shook my head and whispered, "Not without you," before spinning to glare out at the very Creatures I'd defended to him my entire life. "They won't hurt me, and I won't let them hurt you."

Whether it was because they knew I'd never meant them harm or because they could sense the life within me, I had no idea, and as long as it kept these men safe, I didn't fucking care. All I could do was hope that if I staked a claim on this family that I'd made, the Creatures wouldn't hurt them either.

None moved toward us, but each one remained tensed, their defenses rising in whatever form they took. Claws dug into the dirt, venom pooled at hissing mouths, and barbed tails rose, like children who'd just been denied their favorite toy.

"Ace."

Terek's arm curled around me again, pressing his palm to my stomach and pinning my back to his chest. His nails dug into my dress, like he feared I'd sprint forward at any second and try to hug them or fight them with my bare hands. "I need you to get back to Duma. Now."

"No," I said, staring straight into the slitted, milky eyes of the snake that I was beginning to think was a leader or elder of some kind, since the second it'd stopped moving, they all had, too.

"This is not a fucking game, Ace. I cannot watch—"

"No," I repeated, more for the snake, than Terek. I had no idea how many Creatures were surrounding us now. I only knew that I was tired of being saved and protected, and I refused to watch anyone else die, man or Creature.

"Adelais, *please.*"

The crack in his usually controlled voice killed me, but I stood my ground, raising my arms out beside me and feeling his grip on my dress tighten. If any of them even twitched toward me, he'd toss me like a pillow and launch himself at them all over again.

"We only wanted to pass through," I said, pushing every ounce of strength I possessed into my voice to hide how it shook. "I'm sorry if we did or said something to frighten you or make you think we meant you harm. That wasn't our intention. We're just trying to get to Wenham."

For a moment, nothing happened other than Terek's hold on my waist becoming iron tight, but then the snake rose higher, its tail rattling. Two forked tongues darted out, and it almost seemed to be considering me before it let out a long hiss.

"We fear no mortal man. We protect and defend what is ours."

The smooth, syrupy voice slid through my mind as gently as if it'd leaned in close and whispered in my ear, and I startled, eyes wide. Holy shit. I'd always believed they could understand more than Terek gave them credit for, but I hadn't expected any of them to actually talk back.

Straightening my spine as best I could with Terek practically melding into me, I said, "It's not defense when you attacked first."

I felt Terek stiffen behind me and wondered if he could hear it, too, or if he just thought I was talking to myself. Before I could ask, the voice came again, and its words sent a blanket of gooseflesh across the entirety of my body. *"The passage of time means nothing here, and his wrongs are great. The black-eyed soulless will not leave the Wood."*

I leaned back into Terek's hold for a moment, letting his warmth calm the pounding of my heart as I realized I'd been right. Terek hadn't attacked first...today, but he had numerous times before now. I'd lost count of how many Creatures he'd killed over the years just for venturing too close to me while I'd visited. I'd hated it each time, but there was nothing I could do about the past, and I wouldn't let them kill him.

I couldn't, not without cutting out part of my chest and leaving it here right alongside him.

"I'm sorry for what he's done," I said, meaning every word, "but you cannot have him."

The snake hissed again, its tail rattling faster, and the Creatures around it drew closer. *"He abuses his gifts and kills us without cause. He holds us here and cares not if we starve. Why should we grant him a mercy he would not give in return?"*

I didn't have an answer to that, not when this Creature, whose intelligence far surpassed any I'd met apart from Chesie, clearly knew what Terek had been doing in the southern border of the Wood all these years. It may have been by order of Lizbeth, but it'd still been by his hand. And the Creature was right, even now, Terek wouldn't bat an eye at killing every last one of them if it meant getting us out.

However, I also knew he hadn't been that way before Lizbeth had betrayed and twisted his heart. He'd been a man who'd loved creating and who'd wanted nothing more than to have both his dreams and the respect of his family. I may not have ever met that Terek, but I'd seen glimpses of him over my life, and he was beautiful.

"I won't claim that what he's done hasn't been wrong, but it was the queen's decree that banished you here, and I can assure you, we hate her as much as you do."

Its tail slammed into the ground, shaking the trees and sending dirt flying in all directions. The Creatures around it snarled and snapped, each one almost seeming to be yelling at me.

"You know nothing of hate. The collector of souls is no queen and has no claim on the land she's painted with our blood."

I flinched back, the image of blood rising up my legs alongside the pain and anger it'd caused, still fresh in my mind. The slits of its nose flared in anger, as if it could see my thoughts, too.

Swallowing down the sudden lump in my throat, I tried to raise my hands in a placating way, but Terek was quick to pin them down. His chest rumbled in barely contained violence as he leaned down over my ear. "I don't like this. What is it saying to you?"

Well, that answered my question of whether everyone could hear what it was saying. "It's probably in your best interest not to speak right now," I whispered back, glancing over to where Duma and Dex now stood beside us, weapons still drawn, but lowered.

Duma nodded once, but Dex's brow only furrowed as he met my eyes, and he was quick to look away. It gave me a weird feeling of being judged, but I brushed it away. This entire situation was fucking weird.

Meeting the lead Creature's slitted gaze again, I decided on a different route. "Do you have a name?"

Its hood retracted into its head slightly, and it gave me such an odd look, I could've sworn it'd have blinked in surprise had it possessed eyelids.

"Absekesh."

"Hello, Absekesh. My name is—"

"I know full well what you are called, Adelais," it said, drawing out my name like a caress.

Now, it was my turn to be caught off guard. "How do you know my name?" Terek stiffened behind me.

Absekesh slithered several feet closer, but Terek matched it, pulling me back while Duma and Dex raised their weapons again. But Absekesh didn't move to attack, nor did any of the others that seemed to be protecting its sides.

"We know much more than your living name, Adelais Ellington. The trees whisper of you, but they also whisper of him, and they seek retribution. As do we." Its tongues flicked out again, like it was tasting my frustration and confusion on the air, and liked it. *"You three may pass, but he may not."*

Ice filled my veins as words Chesie had spoken flashed through my mind, something about the trees waiting to consume us. I'd thought she'd simply been mad, not that she'd meant literally. I glanced around at the trees, but not a single one moved, apart from the quiet shifting of their leaves.

I fisted my hands and glared up at Absekesh, realizing it was just doing the same thing Chesie had done and was spewing nonsense in an attempt to frighten me. Likely in the hopes I'd flee and abandon Terek. And it pissed me off.

"Well, I'm sorry to disappoint you, but Terek is leaving with us. Your retribution will have to wait." I was too angry to be sure, but I could've sworn I heard Duma snort beside me.

Absekesh's hood flared wide again, and it hissed. *"Even you can only demand so much of us, Adelais Ellington. The Wood does not give without take, and the soulless is not worth the bargain it will demand of you."*

"Stop calling him that," I seethed, nearly cracking my teeth with how hard I clenched them. "His name is Terek, and he is more than worthy."

"His soul belongs to the collector—"

"She has no claim on his soul, no matter how tightly she clings to it."

"—and his life belongs to the Wood."

"He belongs to *me!*" I screamed, feeling the ground rumble anew as that ancient fury ate at the edges of my mind again. "You cannot have him, and neither can the fucking trees."

Terek sucked in a sharp breath, and the hand pinned to my waist contracted until I swore I'd have finger-shaped bruises over my ribs. The wind licked at our faces, and something warm flared to life in my chest, grounding me and keeping me from delving back into that darkness.

Then the wind picked up, whipping at us with renewed fervor, washing waves of foliage across the path, between the four of us and the line of Creatures. Every one of their heads snapped toward the trees, but while the others bowed and immediately began to back away, Absekesh hissed, its fury evident in the way it coiled before its voice reentered my head.

"Your bargain has been accepted, Adelais Ellington. Your fated will not be touched by anything born of this Wood, but nothing comes for free. The trees whisper your name, and eventually, they will demand you answer. When the time comes, step into the Wood and speak the name Huka."

Huka. I knew that name. It was the same one I'd heard Terek mention to Chesie, and who Lizbeth had spoken of after the first quake. But before I could ask who the hell this person or Creature was, or why everyone seemed to know them, Absekesh was shooting back into the trees, followed by every other Creature, until there was nothing left but our heavy breathing, Dex's murmured curses, and the distant sound of their retreat.

Terek didn't ask me what had happened or pause to go searching for his missing dagger. He just snatched up his cloak from the ground, caged my hand in his, and uttered one word.

"Run."

TEREK

CHAPTER FIFTY-FOUR

Shoulders hunched forward, I rested my hands on my sheaths, one infuriatingly empty, and scanned our surrounding area. My lungs contracted just a little too fast, evidence of how long we'd been running, and a coppery film coated the inside of my mouth with each inhale.

Whatever that feathered Creature's ability had been, it'd filled my head with an agonizing pressure, making me nearly black out with the effort it'd taken to throw my blade at its throat. Thankfully, most of the others had possessed far lesser abilities, such as strength or venom. Though lesser probably wasn't the best word to describe them considering the open gashes down my back.

I winced, the memory of Ace's chest bumping into them threatening to make nausea surge again. I'd nearly vomited all over myself as I'd all but thrown her onto my back and shot down the road, Duma and Dex on my heels. Now, an hour later and safely out of the cover of those cursed trees, I fought to push my pain down to a controllable level as I stared at Ace.

I'd already confirmed by scent that she hadn't been hurt, apart from a few scratches, but though her body was lax and uninjured, her feverish eyes and unsteady heartbeat told me a different story.

She'd stayed suspiciously silent the entire time we'd run, and she'd been a little too quick to move away from me when we'd burst from the

Wood and I'd set her down. My fingers flexed, the feeling of gripping her thighs as they clamped around my waist still seared into my brain, regardless of my discomfort.

Duma and Dex stood off to my right, both bent in half while their lungs heaved in dry, rattling breaths, but I didn't even have it in me to ask if they were all right yet. Not when it was taking everything in me not to throttle the woman before me. Something had happened between her and that Creature, and I needed to know what.

The image of her sprinting toward me, face flushed and determination in her eyes, before she'd thrown herself into my arms, played on repeat. Along with the sound of her voice cracking as she'd screamed at a line of Creatures. For me. All while I'd stood there with no fucking idea what was happening or what to do.

Closing my eyes, I inhaled deeply in a futile attempt at tamping down the desire to curl my fingers around her pretty little neck and shake her for doing something so goddamn stupid after swearing she'd behave. Instead, I made do with tightening my hand over the pommel of my dagger and glared at the side of her face.

As if she could feel the shadow of my thoughts, her hand fluttered over the column of her throat, and her hazel eyes, which had been pinned on the Wood, finally locked with mine. Several emotions crossed them at once as she took in my scowl and the blood staining my face. Fear, relief, horror, worry—each one for *me*.

She chewed her lip, her nerves clear as she wiped her sweaty palms down the pale blue dress she wore. The one I'd purchased for her in Ardenglass, even though it'd cost twice as much as the others, simply because I'd wanted her to have something soft and forgiving after the stiff, filthy one she'd worn in the cell.

"Terek? Are you okay?"

With that single, genuine question, I snapped. After everything we'd just experienced, the infuriating woman still felt zero fear for herself, and because no, I wasn't fucking okay. I was beginning to realize that as long as Ace was in the Underland, I never would be.

"What the fuck was that?" I demanded, my words coming out

guttural and harsh as a whip. Duma's spine straightened, and he swiveled his head my way, eyes wary. Dex, however, cut his gaze to Ace, his brow pinched in an almost apprehensive look I didn't much like. Like she was a Creature who'd suddenly decided to follow us out, rather than the woman we'd been traveling with for days.

She blinked up at me and shuffled back a step, as if she truly hadn't expected my vitriol. She rolled her lips in and paused, like she was contemplating her answer. "You're referring to why they attacked you?"

My knuckles popped from how hard I gripped my dagger. "They were Creatures of the Wood; they don't need a reason to attack. That's not what I'm talking about, and you know it."

Ace frowned. "Surely, you don't truly believe that? They definitely had a reason, Terek. They only went after you because they recognized you."

She was right, of course. I didn't believe that anymore, not with how controlled and strategic their attack had been. "It doesn't matter what I believe. What I *know* is that you risked your life on a goddamn gamble that they wouldn't touch you. What the fuck were you thinking?"

Her frown flattened as she began building a wall up over her emotions. Or at least, trying to. There was little she could hide from me when her heartbeat told me the secrets her lips did not. "What I was thinking was that I wanted us all to make it through."

"And you thought starting up a conversation with a giant fucking snake was the answer?"

Beside me, Duma cleared his throat. "Considering we're all standing here, Terek, I'd say it was a pretty good answer." I sliced him a glare I hoped he felt all the way to his core.

"Absekesh believed they were owed your life because of how many of theirs you've taken," Ace said, pursing her lips in a way that told me at least part of her agreed with it.

Hearing her speak the fucker's name immediately sent fury and a deep-burrowing satisfaction through my veins. Fury that it had dared to speak to her, and satisfaction that Ace had claimed me to it without abandon. Even now, my cock stirred at the memory, at the way my fucking heart had felt ready to explode as it'd attempted to flee my body and into hers.

Dex's brow furrowed even deeper. "So, it was truly talking to you? In your head?"

Ace gave a single nod.

"That's insane," he said, glancing back toward the Wood. "I mean, I knew some of them could communicate, but I never thought I'd meet one that could, let alone survive it."

Duma was quick to agree, pointing out how it had seemed to be a leader of some kind, the others quick to obey and follow, but I didn't give a shit what any of them were capable of. I only cared what the snake had said, because no Creature, not even an intelligent one, would release its prey simply because a beautiful woman told it to.

"What exactly did you promise it?"

Her expression shuttered, and she threw up that wall again, trying to block me out like we weren't connected by the very strings of fate. "What makes you think I promised it anything?"

I growled, and before I even knew I was moving, I'd taken two steps toward her. "Playing dumb is not a good look for you, little rabbit. Nothing comes free in this world, especially not from a Creature of the Wood. What did it demand of you?"

"Nothing, Terek. You heard everything I said about you," she said, her heart picking up as a deep flush filled her cheeks. "I was the one who demanded something of them, not the other way around."

"You're lying."

"No, I'm not," she snapped, her hands balling into fists. "I swear to you on my soul that neither Absekesh, nor any of the other Creatures, demanded anything from me. You're blinded by your hatred of them."

My nostrils flared, and blood flowed south, my body reacting the way it always did when her anger called to mine. "And you're blinded by the few who crawled into your lap."

She groaned, running both hands over her face and shoving the loose hairs back. "You're impossible, you know that? I saved your life, and you're acting like I did something horrible."

"My *life?* Crimson hell, I am *dead*, Ace. I've been dead long before your parents were even alive, and I will continue to be dead. There's no saving my life; there's only making it fucking worse."

She flinched back as if I'd struck her, and I wasn't sure which of us I hated more in that moment. "As long as your heart beats within this world, you have a life, Terek. You can yell at me all you want, but I won't feel guilty for caring about you moving on without your soul."

I crossed the distance between us in three long strides until I was only a few feet away, the gashes down my back screaming as my chest heaved. "And what, Ace? You thought watching you die and having to live with that image for literal fucking eternity was a kinder outcome? How generous of you."

Her heartbeat pounded like a drum in my ears, a siren's song pulling me in no matter how I thrashed and fought against it. It caused bitterness to coat my words as I tightened my hold on my abilities, trying to retain control amidst my crumbling shields.

She raised her chin, hiding her shaking hands within the folds of her dress. "That's not fair. You can't compare us when our versions of death are so vastly different. I would've just ended up right back in the Underland with you, the correct way for once, while you would have been gone *forever.*"

Her voice cracked on the word, and the urge to wrap her in my arms and steal that wicked mouth while telling her how stupid she was, overwhelmed me. But the innate desire to comfort her did little to lessen the wild emotions powering through me.

"I know very well where I would've ended up because I've been thinking about going ever since the last woman I cared about decided what was best for me."

Her face blanched, pain that I knew was for me embedding itself into every flutter of her expression. "Terek—"

Not wanting to hear whatever sympathy those full lips sought to curse me with, I closed the remaining feet between us and finally allowed myself to wrap a hand around her throat, arching her neck back.

My body was practically vibrating with the force of my fear and my need for her to understand, with absolute certainty, where I stood and that I would not yield on this. Not when it came to her safety and her future.

"I would rather spend the rest of my eternity in the pits of Hell itself than spend one single, fucking day here knowing you were dead. I would rather be leashed to that bitch for three-hundred years than ever see the light leave your eyes. You can hate me for it all you want, but I will not apologize for it."

The hazel in her eyes brightened as a drop of silver slid from her dark lashes, and she reached up, curling her hands around my wrist. "I will die one day, Terek, whether by a Creature, Lizbeth, or natural causes. You can't change that. I'm not scared of death."

Her words, though meant to assuage me as if I were simply being unreasonable, mixed with the scent of salt on her skin and made the demon inside me slam harder against his cage, eyes black as night. Whatever Ace thought she knew about how I felt, was wrong. I wasn't unreasonable when it came to her. I wasn't unfair or even insane.

I was absolutely fucking unhinged.

"You're right, little rabbit," I seethed, watching her eyes flick down to my lip as it curled. "I can't change it. I can only hope that when that day comes, you will be far away from me and too old and content to require a middle ground."

Her brow pinched ever so slightly, and then her entire face fell as realization of my meaning sank in. In every town and city she'd been through, she would've only seen a handful of people over the physical age of sixty. Not because they avoided walking the streets and stayed inside, but because most weren't here, period.

The Underland was created to help those who died suddenly and weren't ready to move on yet, or who feared death. Children tended to leave quickly, and the elderly—people who'd already lived full lives— rarely needed to come at all.

What she didn't know was just how much I was lying through my damn teeth. The minuscule, decent part of me may have wanted the best life for her, one away from all the danger I would inevitably bring, but that tug in my chest? The one that kept trying to unlock the cage—not to let me out, but to drag her in and keep her forever? It didn't want that at all, and that fueled my rage more than anything else Ace had done or said.

I was a hypocrite and an asshole, and it only further proved why fate was a petty, manipulative bitch for deigning to leash someone as caring and resilient as her to someone as selfish and soulless as me.

Ace shoved against me and ripped my hand away, her cheeks darkening even more when she glanced at the twins to see their rapt attention. She wiped angrily at her eyes, not saying a word, and twisted toward the direction of the Wood.

"Where do you think you're going?" I asked.

She didn't slow or turn around, but her thick, scratchy voice told me enough about what expression I'd see on her face if she did. "To find Absekesh and tell it that it can have you."

At my warning growl, she threw up a vulgar gesture she'd definitely learned from Dex and stopped at the tree line, glaring over her shoulder when she saw me slowly stalking after her.

"I'm taking a piss, so unless you want to lecture me about that, too, I don't need your damn assistance. I think I've proven my point that the Creatures won't touch me, so I'd prefer it if you kept your hearing to yourself while I do."

Every basic instinct bristled at the idea of her stepping foot within the Wood, even though I hadn't heard a single Creature within the surrounding mile of us since we'd exited.

"You have ten minutes," I said, opting not to confirm the last part of her tirade. I had no intention of listening to her relieve herself, but I was too angry to let her know that. Especially when that gesture made me want to drag her deep within the trees she so desperately loved and fuck her until she begged and pleaded for a mercy I would not give.

A throat cleared beside me once her form had disappeared, and I clenched my teeth, sensing Dex's irritation before he even spoke.

"You know...I liked you better before you were bonded. At least then, you were only an asshole sometimes," he said, fiddling with the sheath strap over his chest.

"Funny, I only like you when you're several drinks in and minding your own business."

I didn't wish to take my anger out on him, but I was too on edge for his brand of blunt sarcasm. But rather than scoff and walk off like he usually did when I was a dick, Dex crossed his arms and straightened his spine, putting his head several inches above my own.

"So, you're fine with us getting involved when it puts our lives on the line, but when I point out that you're being a fucking asshole to a woman who didn't even hesitate to save your life, suddenly I need to mind my own business?" He sucked on his front teeth, pointing back at Duma, who stood a few feet behind him, jaw tight.

"I'm not expendable at your convenience, and neither is my brother. I know you have issues trusting people, and I get it. I would too if Jack had done to me what Lizbeth did to you, but we're not her, and neither is Ace. I may tell you shit you don't want to hear because I'm your friend, but I'm not going to fuck you over, Terek."

I rolled my jaw. I knew they wouldn't, but fuck if it didn't kill me inside to admit it. I trusted no one. It was better that way. I'd already respected him and Duma—it's why I'd taken Ace to Tweeds to begin with—but I hadn't truly trusted them until they'd gone into the White Castle and brought my little rabbit out.

I didn't just trust them now, I owed them fucking everything.

"I know, I didn't mean it that way. I'm just…" I exhaled heavily and ran a hand through my hair. "I feel like I'm losing my mind."

His lips twitched. "That's because you are, my friend. Now get naked so I can close those damn gashes, and settle in, because I got a lot more to say."

I sighed and reached back to yank my tunic off over my head, cursing colorfully when parts of it stuck to sections of torn skin.

"Crimson hell, how were you even moving, let alone carrying her? These must hurt like a bitch," he said, walking behind me and gently prodding the edges.

They did. "I've had worse. Just do what you can without exhausting yourself before we've made camp. I don't care about scars just as long as they stop bleeding."

I needed to follow Ace soon anyway. Pulling in a steadying breath, I threw my senses out toward her just long enough to confirm her safety, and when I still heard no Creatures, I quickly reined them back in. Even those few seconds had been enough to have pain slamming full force into every nerve ending on my body. My muscles stiffened. Fucking hell.

I expected Dex to jump right up my ass again while he worked, telling me how much of a dick I was, but it was Duma who chimed in. He settled onto the ground before me, digging through his pack for his flask. "You're losing your mind because you're trying to fight something that can't be beaten. You and she are inevitable."

Leave it to Duma not to beat around the bush about it. "She doesn't even know soul bonds exist, let alone that she might have one," I countered.

He raised a dark brow at me, as if my weak defense only proved his point. "Whether she knows the details or not is irrelevant—though you know our opinions on that. Ace feels it regardless, same as you. Crimson hell, Terek, the woman didn't even hesitate to save you."

Dex's hands pressed over my back, and I cursed, fisting my tunic to avoid ramming an elbow into his face on instinct when he pinched the edges of a gash together. "She wanted to save everyone, including the same Creature that attempted to rip my spine out. She's a fool who wears her heart on her sleeve."

"Call her whatever you want," Dex said as my skin prickled and burned beneath his touch, "but that *fool* is your other half. Your souls and futures are bound together, whether you want to admit it or not."

I opened my mouth to deny it out of habit but snapped it shut again. There was no point lying to the two people who'd seen it for what it was before I'd even accepted it myself.

"It's better for both of us if I keep her at a distance. We'll be going our separate ways soon enough once she's settled in Wenham. I'm risking all of us by being gone this long as it is. Who knows how many guards Lizbeth has sent looking for me after what happened with the horde."

Duma scoffed into his flask as Dex sealed the last wound. "Soul bonds can't be ignored, no matter how far apart you are. That's literally the opposite of how they work, and you know it. Your bond will only pull harder at you the farther you go."

"I don't know anything, and neither do you," I said, muttering a thanks to Dex and pulling my torn tunic back over my head. "Every bonded pair I've ever run into have still possessed their souls, and in case you've forgotten, Ace isn't dead, and I don't have one."

Duma tossed the flask at me, gesturing for me to clean up my face. "That's probably the only reason you've been able to fight it this long. That, and being a prideful idiot."

Catching it, I gladly poured it over my nose and jaw, scrubbing the dried bits of blood off before tossing it back at him. I shouldn't have let them start this conversation. I didn't need the reminders of what I so desperately wanted and could never have. My mind tortured me enough about it on its own.

"All I've ever wanted is to protect her, and if that means forcing her to hate me so Lizbeth never catches wind of our connection, then so be it. She doesn't belong with me, Duma."

"Fate says otherwise."

"Fuck fate," I growled, staring out to where Ace had disappeared, to where that tug was all but tearing at my chest to get me to obey it.

Duma laid back and closed his eyes, resting his arms behind his head as if he hadn't just shoved a hot poker into my self-control. "All I'm saying is you need to figure out your shit soon, because stringing her along when you know exactly what she's feeling is fucked, even for you."

I didn't have a reply. I wanted Ace more than I'd ever wanted anything in my life, not just because she was tied to me, but because I knew her heart better than I knew my own. My restraint was balancing on a fraying line that got thinner with each day I spent with her. The ambush in the Wood had nearly shoved me over already.

All it'd take was one small push, and I wouldn't just fall toward her,

I'd fucking throw myself at her like a starving man.

Snatching up my cloak from where I'd dropped it near my pack, I brushed it out and clasped it around my neck, covering the cuts of my tunic. We needed to get going. The faster I dragged Ace back, the faster we could continue and set up camp, and the faster we would arrive at Wenham.

I only made it a few paces toward the line of trees when a hand wrapped around my arm, pulling me to a halt. I stared down at it and then up at its owner, raising an eyebrow.

"Whatever you need, Dex, make it quick. I need to go find Ace so we can put some distance between us and the Wood. It's already darker than I'd like."

"It's about Ace," he said. He winced on her name, and my senses immediately sharpened, zeroing in on the way his heart thrummed and his lungs moved faster. Whatever was on his mind, it made him nervous.

"What about her?"

"I saw something happen while Duma and I were fighting."

My mind began racing, anger quick to resurface at the idea that something had happened, and I hadn't known. My gaze whipped toward the trees again, and my muscles pulsed with the need to sprint after her. I needed her next to me and to know she was safe, no matter how mad at me she was.

"Did something hurt her?"

Dex shook his head, his voice hesitant as if he wasn't actually sure he should be telling me. "No, it was more like something she *did*. I wouldn't have even noticed if I hadn't been tossed onto my ass a few feet away from her, but it was like...I don't know, like she started glowing."

"Ace has always had a light to her. It brightens depending on her emotions," I said, though I'd only ever seen it happen when she was happy, not scared.

"This was different, Terek. It wasn't a soft flare. I'm telling you, she was fucking glowing golden."

He rubbed a hand over his scalp, looking as unsettled by his claim as I felt. "I don't know what happened or why I saw what I did. All I know is that the ground only started shaking when that glow appeared, and the second she stopped, so did the quake."

My head snapped to his, unease swirling as my need to have her beside me flared so strong I thought I'd tear the skin from my body. "What are you implying?"

He met my gaze, his eyes holding zero doubt in what he believed he saw. "There's more to Ace than simply having the ability to travel here. I don't know what, but whatever it is, I think the Creatures can sense it. With the way they reacted to her today, I wouldn't be surprised if they tried to take her the second you're no longer around."

Before he could take his next breath, I was already gone. Pushing strength into my muscles, I shot into the Wood, barely seeing the trees as they blurred by. Dex's words pounded in my ears like a scream I couldn't shut out as questions and memories I'd been mulling over for years finally began to fit together.

Why the Creatures had become more active in the last two decades and had always seemed to be searching for something. Why they'd never once hurt Ace, no matter how starved or miserable they appeared. Why the horde I'd fought near Ardenglass had left the Wood with no warning after all this time, not to fight the men attacking them, but to get to the city.

Where Ace just happened to be.

I didn't have proof, but I knew in my gut that Dex was on to something. The Creatures could sense something about her that even I couldn't, and the thought that anyone, or any*thing*, felt a connection to her had something dark and oily slicing through me like knives. She was not theirs to sense or theirs to have. She was *mine*.

I pressed my hand over my pocket, feeling the shape of the small, round watch tucked within it as I spotted her in the distance and slowed. She was sitting pressed up against a tree, eyes on the ground and knees tucked into her chest, while she dragged her fingers through the dirt.

Whether he'd meant to or not, Dex's words had shoved me far over that line, shattering my restraint and sending me careening down to a depth of Hell I'd never crawl back from. The idea of leaving Ace I could handle. The idea of never having her or tasting her tore my mind apart, but I could survive it.

But the idea of her being *taken* from me? Of someone or something else wanting her? It made the jealousy inside me ignite so hot, I feared I'd burn the entire Underland to the ground.

A good man would keep fighting this bond like I'd just sworn I would do, and let her decide what happened to her. A good man would ignore the way everything about her made my blood soar and my cock throb. But as I pulled my hood down over my face and stalked up behind her, dragging her scent deep into my lungs, one thing became abundantly clear to me.

I would never be a good man. Though I knew I couldn't keep her, neither would I let anyone else have her—queen or Creature—and I was going to make sure my fated knew it.

ADELAÏS

CHAPTER FIFTY-FIVE

I was being watched again. But unlike before, when the Wood had gone eerily silent and the hairs had raised along the back of my neck, I knew who watched me now. Knew it in the way his silent, brooding stare practically bore into me.

I continued dragging my fingers through the dirt, weathering his anger and refusing to turn around. I could barely see what I was doing, but I kept going, each stroke of my fingers soothing the bitter claws that'd begun to dig into my soul.

Claws *he'd* put there, sharper than any that'd touched his back. No matter how hard he glared at me from the shadows, Terek couldn't take back what he'd said. Any of it. He felt something for me, something as real and visceral as I did for him, and he hated himself for it. If it were up to him, he'd send me Upside and wash away every memory until I no longer existed for him at all.

I'd already known it, of course, had survived his brand of rejection enough times to know the taste of its sting. But this time was different, because instead of nursing my wounded pride as I'd done before, I felt only anger now, curling up inside me to rest behind that constant pressure in my chest.

It was almost as if the darkness I'd found in the Wood had nestled in to stay, seeking to protect me and waiting to see when I'd need it again.

I knew I should fear it, fear what had happened in the Wood. The blood I'd seen splashing against the trees and the agony that'd obliterated my mind. To say I felt none would be a lie, but more than anything, I found myself welcoming that seed of shadows.

It was the only thing keeping me angry, rather than crying over the asshole behind me.

"I'm assuming if you're out here, either my ten minutes are up, or you're ready for round two. If it's the first, I'm coming. I lost track of time. If the second, you can save it. I'm not in the mood to fight with you anymore."

Lies. I knew exactly how long it'd been, and there was nothing I wanted more than to fight with him. To dip into that anger and wound him as much as he kept wounding me.

He said nothing. I made a few more sweeping lines in the weighted silence, completing my rendition of Absekesh's face—or as close to it as I could in the loose dirt. "There's no point in ignoring me. I know you're there."

He still said nothing, and if it wasn't for that annoying awareness in my chest, I might've questioned my blind assurance that it was him watching me rather than something else. It made me bristle, his silence irritating me more than his yelling did.

I tried again, wanting to push him for reasons I didn't quite understand. To see the blue leach from his eyes and feel his hand wrap around my throat while he yelled at me. I wanted a reason to hate him.

"I said I'm coming, Terek. I just wanted a few minutes to be alone. The least you can do is respect that."

There was a beat of continued silence, and then his boots crunched over the leaves as he stopped hiding his movements and stepped closer. His voice was low and drawn out, a huskiness to it that ran over me like the brush of silk.

"I have respected it. You said those exact words to me once before, and I listened."

I squeezed my eyes shut, trying to block out both what his voice did to me and the memory he stirred. When I'd been fifteen and my husband, still Dean Turner to me then, had locked me in his office.

"Good," I said, keeping my eyes shut and hoping he couldn't hear the tremor in my voice as I leaned away from the tree and rested my head in my hands. "Then you'll have no trouble remembering how to walk away."

More leaves crunched, directly behind me now. "I've been trying to walk away from you from the moment you came back, and my continued failure to do so has taught me something," he said. His voice was lower, sinking into me and burrowing everywhere I wished it wouldn't.

"And what's that? That you make just as many bad decisions as I do?"

"That I shouldn't have listened back then. I should have stayed and forced you to tell me everything."

My heart skipped a beat, but I didn't open my eyes or turn, afraid of what I'd see in his face if I did. "*Dean Turner* punished everyone. My experience had been no different than anyone else's. That day had simply been the first time he'd told me to get on my knees."

I scoffed, remembering how stupid I'd been when I'd thought that was the worst day of my life. "I'd refused. That's why he'd whipped my hands."

Bark snapped above my head, making me flinch as bits of wood rained down over my shoulders. "I should have stayed."

"It wouldn't have made a difference. My future had been set in stone from the moment I stepped foot in that school," I said, not sure why I was trying to comfort him. He'd just told me less than an hour ago that he hoped I left and never came back.

He lowered himself to the ground, situating between me and the tree until all I could feel was his heat and the organ attempting to flee my ribcage. "Why did you come here, Ace? After all those years, everything he did, what made you stay this time?"

With every fiber of my being, I wanted to turn around and look up into those eyes, to let him read my answer so I wouldn't have to give life to it and taint the air. But I kept my body forward, knowing the second

I looked at him, I'd break apart.

And though I trusted Terek to pick up my pieces, I knew better than to think he'd put them back together.

"Producing an heir was all I was good for, like most of the other daughters I'd met over the years. It was part of the deal Frederick made with my father. He would provide large donations to the school, and, in return, Frederick would give him our second son. But year after year, I never got pregnant."

Terek went so still I didn't think he was even breathing. I shrugged, trying to silently convey that it didn't bother me. Not anymore. I wasn't even sure how we'd gotten to talking about this when I'd been daydreaming of throwing all manner of items at his head. The man was annoyingly good at slipping past my highest defenses.

"Anyway, I made the mistake of verbalizing what we and the physician had known for years. That it was the fault of his body, not mine. I'd expected him to hit me or yell, but instead, he'd gotten this horrible smirk on his face, like he'd just been waiting for me to say it. The night I left, he'd gotten drunker than usual and informed me he'd contacted some of his more…discreet colleagues to *solve the problem.*"

I stared out at the trees, watching their branches gently sway in the breeze, and pressed my fingers over my scar. "I wasn't an idiot, no matter what you always believed. I knew I couldn't hide indefinitely in the Wood, so I dealt with the hand I was given and married him. But being impregnated like cattle would have stolen something vital from me I would've never gotten back. I refused to give that to him."

Terek's chest grazed against me as he pressed his nose into my hair and inhaled deeply. "And what if I want it?"

"Want what?" I asked, trying to keep my voice calm when I felt anything but, as his calloused fingertips tucked loose strands behind my ear, baring my neck to him.

"Everything. Your freedom. Your choices." His hand disappeared only for his mouth to replace it, his lips gliding down my neck in a way that had gooseflesh erupting and my thighs squeezing together. "Your body."

I swallowed, trying to remember how to breathe when all I could feel or think about was his lips on me and the coiling, surging heat screaming for release in my core.

My eyelids fluttered closed again, hoping if I shut out one of my senses, maybe I could gain control over the others. This should not be happening. He was a damn asshole, and I was supposed to be mad at him. I *was* mad at him.

"Then you'd be just as bad as he was."

Terek's laugh rumbled through me as he took my right hand and laced his fingers with mine, forcing me to release the ironclad grip I'd had on my dress.

"Oh, little rabbit, I am so much worse," he said, sliding our joined hands to where my thighs pressed together in front of my chest. "The only difference between him and I is that when I break you, you'll beg me to do it again."

"I highly doubt it," I said, trying to yank my hand away, furious that he was right. Terek could do a hundred horrible things, paint my soul in a hundred purple bruises, and I'd crawl right back to him, bathing myself in his darkness, eager for more.

He chuckled again, laying my hand flat over my thigh, and rested his on top of it. His chest was now flush against my back. "Shall we find out?"

"Fuck you," I seethed, but it came out sounding far huskier than I'd intended when his scent grew stronger with his proximity, invading my space and causing that heat to boil over. Every inch of my skin felt flushed and over-sensitized.

Two long fingers traced along the seam of my thighs, and my legs instinctively parted beneath my dress, betraying me and all but pleading for him to call my bluff.

I needed him to touch me, to sink inside and cure this unending ache I had for him. To break me open like he promised and tear out the constant awareness that hummed every time he was near and hurt whenever he wasn't.

But instead of answering my silent request, Terek leaned closer and scraped his teeth over my ear. "Tell me, do you hate me?"

"Yes," I lied, because oh God, how I wished I did.

"Good, because right now, I fucking hate you, too. Now pull up this dress and show me how wet you are for me."

My eyes flew open, but before I could so much as contemplate an answer, his other hand snaked around my throat. He pinned me back against the roll of his shoulder, his words barely more than a growl in my ear.

My desire was a wild, tangible thing. I wanted to taste his skin, feel him move against me, and memorize just how he sounded when he truly lost control. I wanted to be what *made* him lose control. And so, I stopped. I stopped trying to fight it, stopped trying to hate him, stopped trying to deny the fact that I wanted Terek in any way I could have him, more than anything else in my life.

My fingers curled into my skirt, fisting the soft, blue fabric and pulling, inch by inch, until it fell back over my knees to pool at my waist and bare me to the air. I wore no stockings and only a thin layer of cotton over my center, but I might as well have been utterly naked for the sound that left Terek's throat.

His chest expanded as he inhaled deeply, and he cursed, gripping my hand and roughly positioning it between my legs, right where the top of my underclothes met skin.

"That's it, Adelais. Show me what hating me looks like."

Every muscle in my body went taut at the way he purred my real name, drawing each syllable out like he enjoyed the taste of it. The sound made me wetter, and I greedily sucked in air, wondering if it was possible to die from pent-up desire.

Knowing what he wanted, I inched my hand beneath that final layer, nearly combusting at the knowledge that Terek's hand was so close to touching me. So close to feeling exactly what he did to me every time he was this close, even when he pissed me off.

His coarse fingertips pressed almost painfully into the tops of my own as I reached that throbbing bundle of nerves. He shuddered violently, like it was taking everything in him not to move that extra inch and glide them through the arousal I knew he could scent.

I groaned at the image and arched into him, burying my face in his neck and letting my knees fall wider, mentally begging him to give in. To sink inside me and erase every horrible thing he'd ever said or done. To erase my past and my pain.

To break me into a million pieces all so that he could wrap them in his shadows and help forge me into something stronger.

But no matter how I wished for it or rolled my hips, those fingers didn't move. They just laid over mine, feeling the way I touched myself, like he was memorizing what pressure and speed made my heart beat the fastest. And something about knowing those midnight eyes were zeroed in on how our hands shifted beneath my underclothes had me climbing up that hill faster than I ever had.

"Tell me, do you think of me when you spread these thighs at night and touch yourself?"

"No," I breathed.

"No?" he asked, and my mind splintered as his fingers suddenly began moving, rendering my own useless as he pressed in with the exact firmness and speed I needed. My hand went limp, allowing him to use it in whatever way he wished, circling that throbbing spot again and again.

"You've never imagined me sliding in and out of you, my name on your lips as you came apart? You've never once wondered what might've happened the day you kissed me if I'd laid you out on the ground and buried myself between your thighs?"

I tried to lie again, to tell him I'd never gotten off to the thought of him and never would. But as if sensing it before my lips could form the words, Terek dropped his head and sank his teeth into my shoulder, sending a flash of pain and pleasure to every corner of my mind. It wasn't hard enough to break skin, but enough to make sure I'd still feel it tomorrow. A warning.

"Do not lie to me, Adelais."

Oh, my fucking God. He flicked his tongue over the tender spot, moving his fingers at an almost punishing pace, and I lost control of my mouth, practically screaming my shameful truth. "Yes! I thought of you every time, even when I didn't want to, and it made me wish I'd never met you."

"Why?" he demanded, his voice a growl as his fingers continued torturing me, yanking me higher and higher up that hill even though he'd yet to touch anything other than my hand and throat.

My breathing became embarrassingly labored, and I reached back, searching for his thigh and digging my nails into his trousers when I found it. "Because I hated you for making him be my first when I'd wanted it to be you."

Terek's hand froze. His heart, his lungs, the very air around us, stopping along with it. His muscles tensed, and a deep, agonized sound vibrated over my ear as the hand around my throat squeezed, just enough to have my back reflexively arching.

"Do you feel it?" he whispered, his anger a palpable thing in his tone and the way he left sharp nips along my shoulder. "The deep pull in your chest whenever I walk away? Like something is reaching in and trying to remove your heart?"

Oh God. I practically whined, lifting my hips and trying to urge him to move again as he abandoned me at the cliff's edge, my release only a touch away. But he just tightened his hold on my neck, causing tears to pool as I sucked in air.

"Do. You. Feel it?"

"Yes," I wheezed. I'd never known what it was, but I'd felt it for longer than I could remember. In the back of my mind, I knew I should wonder how he could possibly know, but I was too overwhelmed, too close to that edge to think about anything other than falling off it.

His chest rumbled behind me, and his fingers convulsed over mine, like he was fighting the desire to toss my hand aside with every fiber of his being.

"That pull means your heart is mine, little rabbit. It doesn't matter who had you first. You belong to me."

"I belong to no one," I said, eyes fluttering closed again as I tried to move my fingers beneath his frozen ones, seeking any friction I could get. "I will give my heart to whomever I wish."

"Wrong. You are *mine*, and I will rip the heart from your chest and hold it for eternity before I let you give it to someone else."

A cry left my lips as his fingers began moving again, faster and harder than before, and I dug my nails in deeper, trying to center myself and form a semblance of coherent thoughts.

"That's not fair," I said, stars dancing behind my eyelids. "You don't...want me."

He growled and pushed his thumb against my jaw, twisting my head until his lips hovered a hairsbreadth over my own, the edges of his hood tickling my cheeks. "You have no idea what I fucking want. No idea that just the thought of sinking into you makes me feel like my sanity is crumbling into dust. But I *can't* have you."

"Then why are you here?" I breathed, his words hitting me so deep, I'd never get them out.

"Because I'm a selfish son-of-a-bitch. Now, open that wicked mouth and curse my name when you come for me."

And like he truly did own me, he circled our fingers one last time, and I broke, crying out his name as I erupted into a million pieces I'd never get back. Waves of pleasure racked my body, and I held onto his thigh for dear life, letting my head loll against his shoulder as I came down.

Terek said nothing else. He just continued his steady movements until the last wave shuddered out of me and I went lax in his arms. I murmured his name, content for the first time in days. But instead of chuckling at my display or hinting at me to touch him back, which I desperately wanted to do, he was suddenly ripping his hand away like I'd burned him.

Then, as if he hadn't just given me the best orgasm of my life and staked claim on my body and heart for all the Wood to hear, he released my throat and shifted back, immediately putting space between us.

I felt that inch of space like a chasm, and I could practically hear his mind catching up with what he'd just done. How he'd let his guard down and crossed a line he'd never meant to cross. Probably because my own was doing the same.

With painful, blistering certainty, I knew Terek was about to get up and walk away, leaving me here to recover my shattered pieces alone while he built up his walls again and pretended this never happened. And the worst of it was that I had no right to be angry with him, not when he'd been honest the entire time and warned me what would happen. I'd chosen to open my legs, even knowing the outcome.

Yet, I found tears pricking my eyes anyway, anger and humiliation forming a knot in the pit of my stomach while my heart continued to beat a little too fast from what we'd done.

His cloak brushed against my arm as he stood, and a humorless laugh passed through my lips. "Well, congratulations, I guess. You proved your point. I didn't hate you."

He didn't answer, but neither did he leave.

"I don't think I've ever hated you, even when I wanted to," I continued, staring up at the dark slits of sky and wishing we were already in Wenham so I could find a room to lock myself away in.

"Even when you disappeared for seven years, when you made me believe I was all alone in both worlds, I still never hated you." I sucked in a shaky breath. "But I'd give anything to right now."

For several heartbeats, he still didn't speak, and I allowed myself one solitary second to hope he might actually stay. But like the inevitability of death, Terek backed away from the tree, taking my hope and every lingering flutter of warmth with him.

"That's okay, little rabbit. Hate me if you must, I'll love the taste of that, too."

Just like when he'd arrived, I didn't hear him leave, but I felt it in the way my body sought to follow like an abused puppy. Cold air swirled around my shoulders, and I swallowed back a scream as I yanked my dress down. What the hell was wrong with me?

It was like I lost all sense and dignity every time he touched me, and no matter how clearly I understood that, I couldn't seem to stop doing it. It was like I secretly wanted to be used and discarded on the ground, my years of abuse conditioning me to seek it out like the broken woman I was.

I cursed and rubbed my hands over my face, wishing I could dig a hole right there at the base of the tree and bury myself inside of it.

Anything would be better than going back and facing, not only the flat, unfeeling mask Terek would have erected, but also Duma and Dex, who were too smart *not* to know what we'd been doing. There'd certainly be no denying it once they saw me return, flushed and ruffled.

I wasn't sure how long I sat there, letting the breeze cool my cheeks and my mood before I finally pushed to stand. I'd just smoothed out my dress and was giving myself a mental lecture about acting unfazed in front of Terek long enough to make it to Wenham when something rustled above me.

Retreating a step, I tipped my head back, expecting a little Creature to be staring down at me now that I was alone. But rather than a curious face, two large, yellow eyes met mine as Chesie dangled upside down from a branch high above my head. She was swinging back and forth and smiling at me, the hem of her white dress tucked under her bent legs.

Panic surged, and I lurched away, slamming the back of my head against the tree. Before I could let out the scream rising up my throat, she'd already landed and was leaning into my face, pressing a finger to my lips. When I made no move to run or shout—due more to my absolute terror of the clawed hand inches from my neck rather than her request—she pulled away and smiled at me.

I plastered my back against the tree and felt the bark dig into my arms, waiting for her to say something, or for Terek to come racing back, dagger in hand. When neither happened, I swallowed, swearing that once I was settled in Wenham, I was going to buy myself a goddamn weapon.

"Are you...following me?" I asked, voice shaking.

Had she been hanging up there watching us the entire time?

Common sense said there was no way he wouldn't have noticed her, but then again, he hadn't noticed her in the Wood either. The thought made my stomach turn.

Her smile fell, and she smacked a finger over my lips again, her cat-like, yellow eyes sliding past me toward where he'd disappeared. I followed her gaze and nodded that I understood, the hair along the back of my neck standing on end that he didn't seem to be aware of her yet. Had he shut his abilities off?

Her eyes met mine again, and she cocked her head to the side in a sharp, stilted manner before leaning into my space. I fought the urge to squeeze my eyes shut, instead keeping them trained on her for any sign her jaw was about to tear open. Once had been enough to last me a lifetime. I'd rather yell for Terek and risk a quick death than see it happen this close to my face.

Chesie just smiled wide and pointed her clawed finger at the tree that was currently keeping my quaking body upright. Assuming she was trying to show me something behind it, I dared a quick glance around the trunk, keeping her in my peripheral, but I saw nothing out of the ordinary.

I silently lifted my brow in question, and Chesie inched closer, her eyes seeming to enlarge in her pale face. Then she stretched her thin arm up to tap her nails against the bark beside my head, and my stomach dropped as a cold sweat broke out across my skin.

She smiled wider at my fear, and the scent of carrion filled my nose. "I told you to be wary, silly heart," she whispered, barely loud enough for me to hear over the blood roaring in my ears. "Tell me, have you noticed yet, that which the Wood has taken as your payment?"

She pressed something hard and cold into my hand, and then, in the next breath, she was gone. I blinked at her sudden absence and glanced down in surprise to find the pommel of Terek's dagger laying within my palm. I curled my fingers around it and stumbled away from the tree, half expecting her to leap out at me. But no matter how many times I spun around, eyes searching, I neither saw nor heard anything.

Not sure what she meant by my payment or why she'd want to return a dagger that'd just been used to kill other Creatures, I didn't wait another second to sprint back toward the road, hoping and praying she didn't follow me.

Explaining what just happened to a man who had no idea of the bargain I'd made for him and who already believed the Wood to be evil, was going to be bad enough without Chesie coming to sing a demented lullaby to us while we slept.

I burst through the tree line and gripped the pommel tighter as all three men twisted toward me. This was going to go over swell.

ADELAIS

CHAPTER FIFTY-SIX

Wenham wasn't at all what I'd expected. Surrounded by a Wood everyone in the Underland seemed to be frightened of, and cut off from any other form of civilization, I'd prepared myself to step into a town almost as dark and eerie as what lay within the trees bordering it.

Rundown homes, haggard citizens barely scraping by, and the scent of fear tingeing the air as they went about their day on high alert, afraid each one might be their last. But what we arrived at was as far from that assumption as it could possibly be.

Once I'd burst out of the Wood last night after *that which shall not be discussed* happened with Terek, he'd pushed us to travel another hour before finally deciding we were safe enough to make a fireless camp. We'd been able to see the beginning of the town in the distance, the buildings a dark line of shadows breaking up where the sky met the land. But by the equal looks of shock currently on Duma's and Dex's faces, I wasn't the only one who'd had incorrect assumptions about how Wenham would be fairing.

Even Terek, who hadn't shown a flicker of emotion other than the steady ticcing of his jaw when I'd told him about Chesie bringing me his dagger, appeared genuinely surprised by the lush, open haven hidden within the trees. For before us, bordering the single road in, wasn't bare, cracked earth like what I so often saw beneath the Wood's foliage, but colorful gardens tilled in perfect, straight rows. There was even a small orchard to the far left of the last field, its weighted trees drooping with an abundance of unripe fruit that had not yet been thinned off.

If this had been the first place I'd ever seen of the Underland as a child, Terek never would've been able to convince me I was in the land of the dead. Even now, I felt like pinching myself to make sure I wasn't imagining it.

We continued through the fields toward the town center, my eyes flicking from my surroundings to my feet, trying to avoid twisting an ankle on the wheel groves of whatever farming equipment they used. Eventually, the rows of vegetables thinned out to become raised wooden beds filled with all manner of flowers and herbs.

Duma's eyes brightened in surprise, and he stepped off the path to carefully pluck a few leaves from the closest plant and place one on his tongue, humming in pleasure before holding one out to me.

"I can't remember the last time I was able to get my hands on some of this. Here, taste it."

I scrunched my nose but took it, not quite trusting his herb preferences ever since he'd given me the god-awful tea in Ardenglass. Hesitantly laying it on my tongue, I sighed in relief when a normal, not gag-inducing, peppery taste filled my mouth. It made me think of thick stews and fresh bread. I hadn't tasted anything with flavor since we'd left Canden, and the thought of having a hot meal tonight immediately perked up my mood.

Unlike the bright gardens, the homes weren't all that different from those I'd seen in the outskirts of Tover. But where those homes had been mostly browns and grays all tucked in tightly to fit the large population, these were painted various shades and separated out far enough to allow for small yards. One of which, contained a clothing line and a soft-statured woman who immediately stopped what she was doing when we neared.

Her skin was a warm tan and her hair straight and black, the ends brushing past her laundry-filled arms to sway at her waist. I gave a small wave when her brown eyes met mine, noticing the two tiny faces that peeked out from behind her skirts as I did. But instead of waving back, she spun away from the road, shifting the laundry to one arm and ushering the children toward their door with the other.

My hand fell limply at my side as she slammed the door behind them. Her reaction had been odd, but I tried my best to brush it off. Not everyone was going to be overly friendly to strangers, but when the next two people we passed also avoided us, my frown deepened. Did we look that horrible? Surely everyone who traveled through the Wood arrived as dirty and worn as we did. It wasn't like I'd expected them to cheer, but they were scurrying away like we'd brought a disease with us.

"I didn't realize everyone would be so friendly," I muttered, stepping back to walk between Duma and Dex when yet another citizen quickly moved to the opposite side of the road.

Duma gave me a small smile. "Don't take it personally. I doubt they get many visitors. It's also safe to assume any who risked the Wood to reside here likely don't trust easily to begin with."

That was true, I supposed.

Dex nudged me in the side with his elbow, eliciting a hissed-out curse as I smacked him. "Can you really blame them when that's the first one of us they see?" he asked, gesturing to the cloaked man stalking a few spans ahead of us.

That was *definitely* true.

Terek hadn't spoken a single word to me since I'd told him about Chesie—well, about her giving me the dagger, at least. I still hadn't figured out what she'd meant by my payment, and Terek was already on edge, so it seemed unwise to admit the bargain I'd made for him. He'd simply accepted the dagger from me, taking care not to touch my hand, and sheathed it before walking away to ask the twins if they were ready.

His sudden, cold absence after everything he'd done last night stung no matter how many walls I erected or how hard I tried to ignore it. But I was determined not to linger on it, choosing, instead, to use my hurt as kindling for the heated glare I bore into his back.

His shoulders stiffened, and he twitched his head to the side ever so slightly, like he could feel my stare burning into him. Yet he didn't slow his gait or turn to meet my challenge. He just led us deeper into Wenham until the road turned, opening up to what appeared to be the town square.

It wasn't busy and packed with stalls as Tover and Canden had been, catering to selling wares and food to all the travelers passing through. Instead, Wenham's center was small and simple, appearing to be more for entertainment and socializing than bartering.

A worn-looking stage stood off to the left with several wooden benches lined up before it, and on the other side was a plain, circular fountain with a dozen chatting people sitting on the ground before it. They all held small, wrapped food and appeared to be on some kind of break. By the time we'd reached the center of the square, their conversations had ceased entirely, apart from a few hushed whispers, their shocked eyes glued to us.

Terek's head tipped their way, his expression blank and hands loose as he listened, reassuring me that whatever our sudden audience whispered, it wasn't threats or plans to chase us out of town. Not that it made their staring any less uncomfortable. How long had it been since they'd received a visitor who wasn't a merchant?

I smiled down at a group of children who'd been tossing a rock and hopping over hastily drawn squares just a moment before. Although none gave me giant smiles in return, two of the girls grinned, clearly not seeing us as the potential threat the adults behind them did.

"You guys spot anything that looks like an inn?" Duma asked, squinting into the distance at a line of buildings across the way. They definitely looked like businesses rather than houses, but they lacked any form of signs above their doors and didn't scream 'inn' or 'tavern' to me.

If Wenham never received visitors, it was possible they didn't have an obvious one, but their merchants had to have somewhere to stay, right? I groaned under my breath and shoved some hair out of my face. If I had to continue sleeping on the ground while arrangements were made to stay long term, I was going to scream.

Then again, given Terek's previous, non-negotiable requirement to share a room whenever we stopped somewhere, the ground might actually be preferable. I'd rather dig a rock out of my back than suffer the awkwardness of sleeping next to a man who was determined to pretend I didn't exist.

I turned toward the man in question to give him another well-deserved glare, only to nearly leap out of my skin when he suddenly twisted toward me at unnatural speed. I swallowed, my heart skipping a beat thinking I'd accidentally voiced my thoughts out loud, only to find he wasn't looking at me. He was staring over my head to where a tall, reedy man with short-cropped, brown hair and a thick beard over pink, flushed skin had appeared.

He wore a plain tunic tucked into trousers, and he was covered in a thin layer of dirt from his beard down to his boots. One of their farmers, if I had to take a guess. His chest rose rapidly, indicating he'd run from wherever he'd been, but he kept his voice surprisingly steady as his gaze stopped on me.

"I'm John of Wenham. Is there something I can help you with?"

Terek's muscles tensed, his eyes dropping to where the man's hands were tucked into pockets, before he yanked his hood back and walked forward, immediately positioning himself between John and me. His dark hair fell over his forehead in a chaotic mess, and I bit my lip, mentally reiterating all the reasons I was supposed to hate him as he widened his stance and rested his hands over his sheaths.

"I'm Terek of Ardenglass. This is Duma, Dex, and Ace of Tover. For the time being, we seek only a place to eat and rest. The rest can come later."

John's lips pressed thin, and he untucked his hands to cross his arms over his chest, chin lifting as his look of apprehension turned into a seething glare. "Were you sent here to deliver us a message, Terek of *Ardenglass*?"

My eyes widened at his tone. It was abundantly clear exactly where Wenham's stance was in regard to anything to do with Lizbeth. Which, as unwelcoming as it sounded, would hopefully work in our favor.

Terek's eye twitched, his irritation evident, but Duma quickly shifted forward before Terek's asshole personality could rear its head.

The last thing we needed was for him to say something he couldn't take back.

"We're here on no one's business but our own and have no intentions of starting trouble," Duma said, raising his hands in a placating gesture. "We request no accommodations that we are not willing, and able, to pay for."

Silence met his statement, long enough that I began to shift nervously, wondering what the hell we'd do if we were turned away. Absekesh had sworn no Creatures of the Wood would attack us again, but I had no desire to test the flexibility of that promise so quickly after Terek barely survived the first trip.

After a few seconds, John seemed to come to some silent conclusion, and he nodded at Duma, accepting his answer. He turned and pointed at a blonde-haired boy perched on the edge of the fountain eating a meat pie.

"Cal, go fetch the Speaker. You're not supposed to still be out on break anyway."

The boy, who looked no older than eight, jumped up at being addressed and shoved the rest of the pie into his mouth before sprinting off with bulging cheeks. Terek watched him go, noting which buildings Cal disappeared between before twisting his head toward Duma.

"I don't like this," he said under his breath, eyes darting over the people still sitting around the fountain, his hands tightening over his pommels as each person continued to watch us with unveiled caution.

"No offense, Terek, but you don't like anything," Dex said, raising a brow in challenge when Terek sliced his angry gaze on him instead.

"Just be ready."

"Ready for what, exactly?" Dex asked, lowering his voice even more when a few people frowned at him. "What do you think a bunch of farmers are going to do?"

"He has a point, Terek," I said, sliding my hand over my side and wishing, for the hundredth time, that I hadn't lost my watch. "The worst they'll do is turn us away. I admit, it's not ideal, but—"

"Nothing about bringing you here has been ideal," Terek snapped, the muscles in his jaw rolling as he pointedly refused to look my way.

My nose and throat instantly burned, but I wrapped both hands around the rising hurt and shoved it back down, replacing it with the anger that was becoming my closest companion. Taking a deep breath and ignoring the gentle nudge Dex gave me, I fought the desire to whack Terek in the head with my boot and instead, walked off toward the children who'd stopped their game to watch us.

I may not have known a whole lot about children, or ever wanted any, but I'd rather figure it out and sit with them while we waited for the *Speaker* than stand next to Terek.

The adults eyed me carefully, their postures tense, but no one stopped me as I plopped onto the ground beside a young girl. She had thick, yellow hair that reminded me of my mother, pale skin, and looked to be around six or seven, holding a piece of chalk in one hand and a stone in the other.

"What are you playing?" I asked.

She hesitated for a moment, a bewildered expression on her round, pale face. "You've never played Skips and Stones?"

I shook my head. "No, but I didn't play much of anything when I was your age, so there's probably a lot of games I don't know."

Her little brows shot up, and several other children scooted closer, their eyes taking in everything from my dark hair to my dirty travel clothes. The young girl tilted her head to the side and quirked her lips in thought. "Is that how you died?"

I pulled away and blinked down at her. "What?"

"Because you didn't get to play. Sasha told me she died of boredom because her parents never let her do anything fun. Is that what happened to you?"

"No, definitely not," I said, unable to hold back a laugh.

She smiled back, wide enough for me to notice that her front top teeth were missing. "If you didn't play games, what did you do?"

I pretended to think, picking up her chalk and sketching out a simple flower on a stone. "I mostly sat around drinking tea and learning how to be a good wife," I said, earning me a sea of scrunched noses. "I also always liked to draw, which was far more fun."

A second girl, this one looking to be closer to ten, with twin auburn braids over her shoulders, scooched closer. She tentatively reached out to run her fingers around my quick drawing, smudging the lines a little. "And were you?"

"Was I what? Bored?"

She tried and failed to hide her grin. "No. A good wife."

Her question was an innocent one, yet I froze as if she'd slapped me. I'd never been a good wife according to Frederick's or society's standards, and if I considered the manhunt that would've gone into trying to find me when I went missing, maybe not according to my own standards either.

I cleared my throat and handed the chalk back, trying to pretend I hadn't noticed just how silent the square had become and wishing the so-called Speaker would hurry up.

"Not really, but then again," I said, leaning in to whisper between the girls, "I find men to be quite atrocious and have never been very good at following any rules at all."

They both burst into giggles, and I couldn't fight the genuine smile that lit up my face. But it quickly fell when the unavoidable truth of the moment hit me, reminding me that no matter how happy these young girls seemed, they were still dead. The thought was sobering.

"All right, children," a smooth voice called out, snagging their attention as they all leapt up like they'd just been caught skipping lessons rather than playing with chalk in the square.

I followed their line of sight to a woman, who hadn't been there before, standing a few feet away. More than just a little surprised, I blinked, trying to confirm I wasn't imagining her. Compared to the sea of young faces around her, she stood out like a white rose in a field of marigolds.

She had tight, graying-white spirals atop her head and brown skin, accentuated only by deep wrinkles and pink lip stain. She wore a shapeless, lavender dress over her soft frame and leaned heavily on a curved cane, making her appear far shorter than everyone around her.

Her brown eyes lacked no warmth as she took in the three men behind me, and then me, but neither were they soft. She had an edge of command about her, and I found myself pushing up to stand right along with the children.

"Why don't you all run home for a little while so I can converse with our visitors?" she said, keeping her eyes on me even while she lifted a hand to wave them off in a shooing manner.

If it hadn't already been clear that she was the Speaker simply by the way everyone around her had shifted to give her space, I'd have known it by the way each child immediately abandoned their game and took off without a single complaint. Whoever the Speaker was to the people of Wenham, it was clear she was either highly feared or respected.

Maybe both.

Once the last child had run off, she turned to John, who hadn't moved a muscle the entire time. "Is it only these four? Or are there more Cal was unaware of?"

John's mouth opened, but it was Terek who answered. "There are no others."

She raised a brow at his interruption, taking a moment to look over his threatening posture and visible weapons before she lifted a single finger and gestured us to follow.

"Then come with me."

⚷

THE INSIDE OF the building she led us to reminded me of a church. A much smaller one than Mother made me attend growing up, but I couldn't imagine what else the tall windows and lines of wooden pews could possibly be for.

At the back of the room, where the Speaker was slowly making her way down the center aisle to, was a stage, smaller than the one outside, but it still took up the majority of the width of the room. Though it held no sermon podium or alter.

As if sensing my interest, the Speaker waved a hand dismissively toward the stage as she rounded one side of it. "We had this built, oh, maybe ten years ago when the Underland wouldn't stop its insufferable rain. Entertainment is popular out here, and we got tired of canceling our shows."

I nodded even though she couldn't see me and ran my eyes over the paintings I could now make out between the windows. Most were abstract colors splashed over parchment, but just the sight of them lifted my spirits. After days on end of traveling, the thought of curling up in bed and painting sounded like a dream.

A large hand prodded at my shoulder as Dex ushered me to keep walking. I tore my gaze away from the bright colors on the walls to see the Speaker patiently waiting at a door beside the stage I hadn't noticed.

"Don't worry, it's not a holding cell, nor does it have a lock of any kind," she said, giving a pointed look at Terek, who'd still yet to remove his hands from his daggers.

"While we have any necessary town meetings in here or outside, this particular room is what I use for any private matters that arise." She shoved it open, revealing a small room with a long table and eight roughhewn chairs. "Call it an old woman's intuition, but I have a feeling you would prefer a stronger semblance of privacy than the open room gives."

She led us inside and made her way around, opening up a few curtains to allow in more light. "Don't worry, these windows look out on my own personal garden, so no one will wander by," she said, leaning her cane against the table and lowering herself into an end chair.

Duma pulled out a seat beside her, but she stopped him mid-squat, snapping her fingers at him. "You there, go grab that pitcher in the corner before you get settled. I filled it this morning when I met with someone to discuss the coming harvest, so it should still be full."

Duma's eyes widened, and his brows shot up to an invisible hairline. The Speaker just raised hers right back and rested her elbows on the table, unhurried and unfazed. "There should be some cups in the cupboard."

Dex's deep laugh rumbled out of him as he plopped into the seat next to Duma's and crossed an ankle over his knee, resting his leg against the table as he watched his brother cross the room without a word. "Would you like him to make you a snack while he's at it?"

The Speaker's brown eyes fell to Dex as she stared at him, steepling her hands in front of her. I watched their stare-down as I quickly took my own seat, trying to pretend I didn't notice when Terek passed two open chairs to sit directly beside me.

Her pink lips pursed in disapproval. "I'm assuming by your tone that you are insinuating I should've been the one to serve you all since I'm your host. But I'll tell you right now, young man, I am neither your spouse, nor your mother. If you all want something to drink, especially in a room and with a cup that belongs to me, you can get up and get it with your own hands. It'll taste no different served from my feeble ones. Now sit up straight and get that filthy boot off my table."

A pin hitting the floor could've been heard as Dex lowered his leg and sat forward, his lips working as he tried and failed to come up with anything to say. It wasn't often my loud, ornery friend was rendered speechless, and I found myself immediately liking the woman for putting him in his place.

Duma returned, a shit-eating grin on his face as he placed the pitcher and five cups on the table and sat down. "Something tells me there's not a single feeble thing about you, Madame Speaker."

She winked, the wrinkles in her face deepening with her smile. "Indeed. Now then, let's get started. As you are aware, I am the Speaker for Wenham, but you may call me Diana."

ADELAIS

CHAPTER FIFTY-SEVEN

"I can practically see the questions swirling in your heads, so, as your host," Diana said, over-enunciating the last word for Dex's sake, "I will give you the floor to ask, as long as you accept that I have some of my own."

Terek leaned back, his elbow grazing the side of my arm. "You can ask as many questions as you'd like, but that doesn't mean we'll answer them. We're visitors, not guards sent to spy on you."

"Says the man who's yet to remove his hands from his weapons."

Terek's expression darkened, his grip tightening over the handles before he slowly pressed his palms flat on the table. "You should know better than to judge danger based only on the weapons you can see. I promise you, my daggers are the least of your worries."

The temptation to reach over and pinch him was overwhelming. Coming here had been his idea. Why was he being such an ass now that we'd made it? And to the one person who apparently held the power to allow or refuse us.

"I can assure you, I am well-versed in many aspects of danger, Terek of Ardenglass."

Before Terek could reply and further incite her clear dislike of him, Duma sat forward and began filling cups for everyone. "We understand your caution, Diana, and we promise we mean no harm, in any way."

He darted a stern look at Terek as he added the last part before sliding a full cup to her. "As for questions, I have to admit, I'm dying to know how you all have made such a thriving settlement out here. Your gardens alone are," he hummed, kissing his pinched fingertips, "astounding."

The change of subject was obvious, but she thankfully accepted his olive branch and sipped the water, her lips leaving pink smudges on the rim.

"Thank you, Dex. It has certainly required some trial and error, but the soil here is closer to the Upside than I've found anywhere else."

"Duma," he corrected, hiking a thumb toward his brother. "Dex is my brother. He's the easiest of us to pick out because he's the one always running his mouth."

She smirked, and I had to take a drink to hide my smile when Dex seemed to sink a little farther into his seat, grumbling.

"Well, as I was saying, it took trial and error, but you will find that things are far different here than what you've been spoon-fed down south."

I sat up at that, curling my fingers around my cup. "What do you mean? Different how?"

Her brown eyes moved about my face, and something in the way they brightened had me fighting not to fidget under their scrutiny. I didn't know her well enough to know if she looked at every new face that way, or if she could somehow tell there was something *off* about me.

"What I mean, my dear, is that things between us and the Wood are not as those on the other side believe, and we like it that way. We have no issues with the Creatures here."

I sat up straighter. "Really?"

Diana nodded and took another sip of water. "In truth, we cross through their land to hunt far more than they've ever crossed through ours."

"You travel through the Wood whenever you want, and they just let you?" Terek asked, skepticism clear in his voice.

"Let isn't the word I'd use. We have an understanding, one I can see would go straight over your head," she said, shooting him an unimpressed look.

"All who come to the Wood are after the same thing. Safety. Much like humans, the Creatures do not enjoy being slaughtered in their home. As long as we stick to the road and do not venture into the Deep Wood, they leave us alone."

"Tell that to the ones we ran into," Dex muttered, rubbing at the back of his neck.

"I said *we* have an understanding with them. That doesn't include new scents and faces they don't recognize."

I released a breath, baffled. With how everyone else acted toward them, I'd begun to think I was the only person in the Underland who believed the Creatures weren't mindless, vicious monsters. I wasn't sure why the thought brought me joy, but it made the kernel of darkness hiding away in my chest almost seem to purr.

Dex tipped his head and ran the backs of his fingers over his jaw. "They've never once attacked your settlement?"

"Is that not what I just said?" Diana countered, looking down her nose at him. "We wish to live without fear of having our souls ripped from our bodies, and they wish to live without fear of being cut down for the crime of existing."

There was a beat of silence in my mind as what Diana said sank in. The people of Wenham, or at least the majority of them, still had possession of their souls. It made sense, since there wouldn't be much point in hiding if they'd already been taken, but it still shocked me. Did Lizbeth know that?

Terek, however, didn't seem nearly as surprised, his mood no better than it'd been the last time he'd opened his mouth. "Crime of existing? How poetic. Did they tell you that while you sat down together at a town meeting, or did they send you an official letter?"

This time, I did reach over to pinch him. What the hell was his problem all of a sudden? He'd been broody since last night, but now it was like he was purposefully trying to be an ass so she wouldn't allow us to stay.

My fingers had just made contact with the underside of his arm when he yanked it away from me, not even trying to hide the fact that he didn't want me to touch him. A flicker of hurt beat within my chest, and I found myself thankful when Diana's clipped tone rang out, keeping me from lingering on it.

"I've been alive far longer than Wenham has existed and know who you are, Terek of Ardenglass. Your reputation isn't a pretty one, nor is it laced with intelligence. You see only the worst part of the Creatures because it was *you* who forced that behavior upon them. Tell me, do you cower or bite when cornered?"

Terek growled and opened his mouth, but she only pushed on, speaking over him. "In all my years in the Underland, I've only met one type of being who hunts for vengeance and sport, and it doesn't live within the trees."

She wrapped a hand around the knot at the top of her cane, running her fingers over it. "Now that that's settled, if you don't mind, I believe it's my turn to ask a few questions." She slid her gaze from Terek to me. "Why have you come to Wenham?"

Her question hung in the air a beat too long as I opened and shut my mouth, unsure exactly how to answer. The woman may have shared my beliefs when it came to the Wood, but that didn't automatically mean I could trust her with the truth. Seeking safety for my soul was one thing, admitting I'd escaped a White Castle cell and was on the run, was another.

Duma, thankfully, spoke for me, his expression soft and understanding as he looked at me and then her. "We are seeking asylum for Ace here."

"Just her?"

He nodded. "The three of us are already lost causes, but she's still got something worth protecting."

"That she does," Diana said, unease threading through me as her eyes practically sparkled. "We are always willing to accept another soul in Wenham, but we do have rules. As long as you swear to abide by them and agree to work and pull your weight, you would be welcome to stay."

My shoulders loosened, that trickle of unease falling away in my relief. "Thank y—"

"However, I must ask," she said, her fingers still running methodically back and forth over her cane. "I couldn't help but notice the use of the word *protecting* versus *hiding*. One indicates that you do not wish for the queen to be aware of your soul, while the other indicates she is already aware, and you are on the run. Which is it?"

Fuck. I blinked back at her, unable to answer as a betraying flush filled my cheeks. Were all older people this perceptive, or did she have some form of lie-detecting ability like the guard I'd met? Or were we truly just that transparent?

"Is that going to be a problem?" Terek asked, casually laying a dagger on the table and spinning it. I hadn't even seen him remove it.

Diana didn't so much as blink, locking eyes with his midnight ones as her hand finally stilled over her cane. "On the surface? Not at all. Many here arrived on the run from the queen, myself included. I hold no fear of her tantrums."

Well, that answered my question on whether Lizbeth knew that the people here still had their souls.

"Then again, your soul is quite different from anyone else's, isn't it, Miss Ace?" Diana asked, sliding that knowing gaze to me as she took another long drink of water. "It's quite...lively."

The blood drained from my face just as Terek's hand flattened over his dagger, freezing its movements. "You want to explain what you mean by that?"

"Oh, I don't think that's necessary," she said, calmly sliding her empty cup toward Duma for a refill, completely unbothered by the violence in Terek's tone. "I'm fairly confident all five of us know what I mean."

"That number's about to be one less," he snarled.

Fucking hell, this was about to end badly.

"You're either brave or incredibly stupid to threaten me in my own town."

Terek flashed his teeth, the sight sending a cold sweat down my spine. "Your town?" he repeated, his blade spinning again over the smooth wood. "Interesting. I was under the impression you were only the Speaker for the people of Wenham, not their ruler."

Diana's temples pulsed, the first hint of true anger she'd shown. She honestly looked ready to launch her cup at his face at any moment. "I founded this town, bled for it, and have worked to provide for its people every day since, so *yes*, that makes it mine."

She inclined her head, anger, but no fear, in her eyes of the sharp man sitting a few feet away, nor the edge of his blade. And I couldn't help but wonder again what her ability might be, because if there was anything I'd bet my life on, it was that this woman had one.

I ran my hands over my face and met Dex's gaze from across the room. Where Duma looked ready to leap over the table to stop Terek from doing something impulsive, Dex looked like he was enjoying the best show in town.

Since apparently neither of them was going to step in, I reached over, wrapping my hand around Terek's wrist and digging my nails in before he could pull away again. He didn't so much as flinch. "He didn't mean anything by it. Wenham is—"

"Oh, I meant something by it," he snapped, the blue in his eyes fading out as they fell to my skin resting against his. "I brought her here seeking protection from a power-hungry bitch, not to throw her beneath a different one."

The air around us turned chilly.

Diana's nostrils flared, and she straightened, looking every bit her physical age as her hands shook and the wrinkles in her face deepened.

"I didn't make myself the head of this town by painting myself in the blood of its people. I'm not sitting at this table with you, deciding whether you stay or go, because I'm entitled to do so. I was *elected* because I *earned* it. Compare me to her again, and I will remove my offer."

Terek's jaw tightened, the muscles twitching, and then he twisted, meeting my eyes for the first time all day. My hand was still wrapped around his wrist, and the feel of his skin mixed with the heat of his gaze had me almost forgetting what he'd done. Forgetting how badly I'd opened myself up to him, in more ways than one, and he hadn't stayed.

But instead of sliding my hand down and lacing my fingers with his as I wanted, I removed my hand and placed it in my lap. "How did you know? About me."

She considered me for several long seconds before she deigned to answer. "I am very good at reading souls, Miss Ace. One might say *gifted.*"

I nodded slowly, not sure what to make of her expression. It felt almost…calculating, like she was sizing me up or waiting for me to lie. Not wanting to risk the latter, in case she did indeed have the ability to sense it, I chose honesty.

"You're right. Lizbeth does know about me. She's probably already sent guards searching for me, but I'm asking to be allowed to stay anyway. Please. I have nowhere else to go." Not in the Underland, at least.

Dex opened his mouth to argue, likely to remind me that they were more than happy to take me in at Tweeds, but I just smiled and shook my head. I wouldn't risk staying with them, not until Lizbeth gave up looking for me.

Diana leaned back in her chair, laying her hands over her breast and taking me in, her expression already back to the calm look she'd been wearing when she first led us into the room.

"I will grant you asylum, my dear. But only you, and only if that one keeps his mouth closed. Do you have any specific skills?"

I chewed my lip, half relieved she'd said yes, even after Terek's ridiculous behavior, and half nervous because no, I didn't. Not really. "Um…I can clean or help out in a kitchen, maybe?"

"She can draw."

My head whipped toward Terek, surprise and something I didn't want to acknowledge lighting up at his words. Apart from the simple doodles I'd sometimes made in the dirt when we'd sat in the Wood together over the years, he'd never seen anything I'd drawn. He didn't know how many times I'd traced the lines of his face with charcoal until it was burned into my memory. He had no idea if I was actually any good at all.

He simply knew that I loved and missed it, and that had my heart feeling like it was ready to burst. Only Terek could make me simultaneously want to punch him in the face and kiss him at the same time.

Diana narrowed her eyes, apparently serious about not wanting to hear him speak again. "Are you willing to teach?"

"I'm willing to try."

She nodded her head, as if already contemplating where she'd set me up. "That will be perfect. Like I said before, all forms of entertainment are popular here. Meet me back here in the morning, and we'll get you everything you need."

Duma sat forward, his voice tentative, like he was afraid anything he said might start an argument again. "Do you have an inn we might stay at for the night? Just to rest and recover while Ace gets settled?"

"A few nights, preferably," Dex added, putting on his wide, stunning smile that could make even the hardest shell crack.

Oh, so *now* they remembered how to talk. I narrowed my eyes at both of them.

Diana smiled, as if she hadn't just been ready to pummel Terek with her cup, and reached out to pat Duma's hand. "No, but we do have a small house our regular merchants use. It's only a two bedroom, I'm afraid, but I can see if one of the young ladies here would be willing to house Miss Ace with her for a while."

"That won't be necessary. She'll stay in the house with—" One second, Terek was growling across the table, and the next, he was shoving away from it, his chair flying behind him to slam against the wall with a resounding crack.

I shot to my feet, along with Duma and Dex. My eyes widened as I watched Terek stumble forward, one hand on his chest while the other curled around the edge of the table as he closed his eyes and let out a sharp hiss of pain.

"Terek?"

He didn't answer. He only bared his teeth and gripped the table harder, the wood cracking and groaning beneath his hands.

"Terek," I tried again, fear coursing through me as I stepped closer and touched his arm. He let out a choked breath and yanked away from me, his eyes solid black pools as he snatched up his dagger from the table. And then before I even had time to register what was happening, he was running past me and out the door.

I could only stand there, my hair flying back from the speed with which he'd moved, and stare at the empty spot he'd just been standing in, having absolutely no idea what had just happened.

TEREK

CHAPTER FIFTY-EIGHT

*F*evered green eyes filled my vision, not quite matching the look of concern etched into her forehead and mouth.

"Are you okay? Did I hurt you?"

"No. No, I'm fine," I said, trying to get up off the floor, but giving up and raising my arms when my legs failed to obey. I clasped her freckled face and kissed her softly before my shaking limbs flopped back down and didn't rise again.

"I'll be fine. Just…tired." In truth, I was so drained, I could barely even feel my abilities, but I kept that detail to myself, not wanting to worry her.

Liz smiled, and even through the residual pain and the growing exhaustion, it lit up my heart, just as it always did.

"Well, go on, take a look," she said, holding up her hands so I could see it from my prostate form. A pulsing blue color lay nestled in her cupped palms.

"That tiny thing?"

She nodded, her smile taking on an almost wicked glint. I could practically see the wheels of her mind turning. "Isn't it beautiful?"

I tried to shake my head, but it'd stopped obeying now, too. "Not compared to the woman holding it."

I'd wanted to see her smile again, but she didn't seem to hear me, her gaze riveted to the blue light she'd pulled from my chest. "It's amazing, isn't it? That something so delicate can cause so much trouble."

"Much like you?" I teased, her stunning face beginning to swim in my *vision as my eyelids grew heavier by the second.*

"Yes, my love," she said, curling her fingers around it. "Just like me."

She squeezed, and then there was only pain.

For the sixth time in as many hours, the pain had me stumbling into a tree, stealing my breath and causing me to clench my teeth so hard I thought they'd crack. It only lasted a handful of seconds, but each time felt like an eternity while it was happening. Like a damn clock I couldn't escape, ticking down the hours Lizbeth waited for me.

I slid my hand into my pocket and wrapped it around Ace's watch, trying to center myself to the present. Something Lizbeth was determined to make it impossible to do. I wasn't scared of pain, oftentimes welcoming it as a way to clear my mind. But this? This was excruciating, and not just because of the feeling of my chest shredding apart, but because of the memory of her betrayal that always came along with it.

When I'd felt the first flicker of pain in Diana's meeting room, I'd hoped I'd imagined it. Hoped that instead, I'd simply been poisoned somehow and would finally have a not-so-unhinged reason to say "fuck it" to Wenham and cart Ace away. But then my instincts had flared to life just as it became white-hot, and my responding anger had been deep and feral. I'd have thrown the entire fucking table through the wall if Duma and Dex hadn't been sitting on the other side.

That goddamn crimson bitch.

Growling, I shoved off the tree and ripped my daggers free of its trunk, launching them too fast to track into the bark of another. But it did nothing to lessen the suffocating hold on my chest. Nor the other two-hundred times I'd thrown them since sprinting to the Wood to get as far away from anyone as possible.

It wasn't enough. I needed to feel something beneath my hands, lose myself to my instincts, and let my abilities run loose. I needed...Ace.

My head whipped back toward the town from where I hid just within the eastern edge of the Wood, eyes searching for her. I'd caught sight of her and the twins a few hours ago, following a woman I didn't recognize. Ace's head had swiveled side-to-side, like a visitor seeing a new town for the first time, but the way she chewed the shit out of her lip told me otherwise. She was looking for me.

And then she'd passed out of sight, and it'd killed me not to go to her and find out where she was headed. To make sure she wasn't going to some random woman's home in a futile attempt to sleep under a different roof than me. But at the time, I'd barely made it out of Wenham before I'd started launching weapons, let alone tried to be around a woman who lit me on fire just by existing.

I closed my eyes and felt for that tug in my chest, blocking everything else out and listening to her heart's steady rhythm. But like Lizbeth knew what I was doing, another squeeze echoed through me. It was softer this time, a gentle caress rather than a punishment, and I nearly vomited all over the ground.

"You fucking bitch," I seethed, desperately grappling for the feeling of Ace again to keep me from sprinting all the way back to Ardenglass and removing the Crimson Queen's head from her body. Right after I ripped out every single one of her fingernails and forced them down her throat.

Lizbeth didn't seek me out often, but when she did, she always sent a guard to find me, even though she didn't need to. Her lying, poisonous lips claimed she didn't want to cause me pain, but we both knew it was her way of putting eyes on me and making sure I was where I was supposed to be.

The furious claws that'd dug into me repeatedly since coming out here told me she'd already sent the guard, maybe several, and they'd each returned without me. And now, she was *pissed*.

In my growing obsession with Ace over the past week, I'd foolishly forgotten just how far Lizbeth's power reached. How quickly she could remind me what little power I had, and how easily she could push past my boundaries and force her touch on me against my will.

And the longer I ignored it, the worse it was going to get.

Ripping my daggers out again, I finally sheathed them and turned back toward Wenham, my chest practically caving in on itself with the need to be closer to Ace. The steady beat of her heart was the only thing keeping me tethered as a second caress quickly followed the first. As if Lizbeth was telling me goodnight.

I gritted my teeth and shoved my hands in my pockets, finally leaving the shadows of the Wood. Even though I'd demanded she stay in the same house, I hadn't actually planned to share her room, knowing the proximity would only hurt her and drive me crazy. But right now, I didn't fucking care. The thought of curling up next to her and filling my lungs with her scent was so enticing, it felt like an addiction. Like I'd be just fine, if I only touched her for a moment.

I repeated my reasoning a dozen times as I followed that tug to a small, two-story house set slightly apart from the others. Like it'd been an add-on they hadn't originally planned for once merchants became more regular. I pushed in, immediately noticing two things: that the house clearly wasn't used often with its dusty surfaces and drab furniture, and that there were two men occupying said furniture with giant glasses of ale.

Both glanced up and quieted their discussion, but neither bothered to greet me or ask if I was okay. Which I appreciated more than I could express. We all knew the answer anyway.

Duma set down his glass and met my eyes, his brown ones crinkled with sympathy. "This entire time?" He didn't specify, but I knew what he meant. Had Lizbeth been fucking with my soul ever since I ran out of the room. They both would've known the second I'd grabbed at my chest.

"Yes."

He closed his eyes, and Dex cursed, throwing his head back and chugging the rest of his drink. "Do you think Lizbeth knows you helped Ace?"

I shook my head, positive in at least that. If Lizbeth knew I'd aided in the escape of a soul she'd been waiting years to possess, she wouldn't be giving me hourly warnings. She'd have me on the ground, screaming.

"No."

Neither pushed me to elaborate, yet another reason these men had earned my undying respect, even if I wasn't always so great at showing it.

"Diana tried to get Ace to stay elsewhere, but she was adamant she stay with us, in case you came back. You planning to stay in her room?" Dex asked, leaning back in his chair and crossing his arms over his chest like a disapproving father. I only blinked at him, and he huffed, sucking on his front teeth.

"You sure that's a good idea?"

No. It was probably going to be the worst, but here I was, doing it anyway.

"Is she asleep?" I asked, heading toward the small staircase in the corner since I saw no door to a bathing room on the main floor.

"I doubt it. Diana had someone come by earlier with a few things, including toothbrushes and soap for all of us and some art supplies and clothes for her. She hasn't come back downstairs since," Duma said.

He eyed me closely, like he was trying to decide the quality of my current mental state. "Try not to be an ass when you finally go in there. I didn't feel it was my place to tell her what had happened, and she about ripped me a new one when I wouldn't let her go looking for you to make sure you were okay. She thinks you left."

My nostrils flared, and I moved a little faster, not liking the thought of her worrying for me. I'd just gotten to the door of the bathing room, planning to take the fastest wash of my life, when I heard Dex mutter downstairs.

"Something tells me we should probably make ourselves scarce for the next few hours, brother. There are some things in this world I was not made to hear."

I didn't listen for Duma's reply before I flung open the door and began undressing.

AS DUMA HAD suspected, Ace wasn't asleep when I finally cracked open the door and slipped in after my wash, and I wasn't sure whether or not the knowledge disappointed me.

She sat in the center of the bed, drawing by the light of a lantern at her bedside table. Her hair was undone and a little damp, hanging down her back in a dark, wavy curtain. She wore only her chemise, and it bunched over her crossed legs, baring her knees as her sketchbook rested over them, fingers hard at work.

And fuck me if every resolve I'd ever had, every wall, every pathetic barrier, didn't nearly collapse around me at the sight. Ace had never looked more fucking beautiful, and all I wanted was to wrap myself around her and watch her sketch. To taste her skin and see that perfect pink flush fill her cheeks as she tried to stay focused.

I wanted to utterly drown in her, deeper and more thoroughly than I had in that cold, murky river. I wanted to sense nothing but her. *Needed to.*

Engrossed in her work, she hadn't heard me come in, but her head shot up when I locked the door behind me, surprise and relief fighting for dominance in her expression.

I quickly looked away, knowing if I met her stare, I'd crumble the rest of the way beneath it and give in to those thrashing urges. Crimson hell, I shouldn't be in here. I'd walked into the house with only the intention of folding her sleeping form into my arms and being gone before she awoke, but seeing those hazel eyes fix on me and smelling the fresh soap wafting from her skin? Fuck, if it didn't make my cock immediately throb.

The room was already thick with tension, her heartbeat screaming in my ears exactly how I'd needed it to. And all I could think about was the last time we'd been alone together—the way she'd spread her thighs so perfectly, bucking and writhing as she came for me. My chest rattled at the memory, one so much better than those that had plagued me earlier.

Walking toward a small, padded chair, I laid my cloak over the back and dropped my boots beside it even while I mentally held my demon at bay with both hands, cursing at myself to leave. I couldn't do this. Couldn't be this damn close to her, *alone*, and not touch her.

"I wasn't expecting to see you tonight."

It was clear by her tone that she wanted to know where I'd been, and when I glanced back at her, it was to see that she'd raised her pad to hide her breasts, barely concealed behind the thin fabric. The rattling increased. I hated her for trying to hide her body from me, and I hated myself even more for hating her for it.

"Are you seriously never going to talk to me again?"

Leave. This will only end badly. Just fucking leave.

I cursed and ran a hand through my damp hair. "What do you want me to say?" My voice was sharp and clipped, anger not meant toward her lacing each syllable.

Her fingers tightened over the pad, charcoal staining one hand, and the flush I loved so much rose up her neck. God, she was so fucking stunning when she was mad.

"I don't know. Maybe why you were such an asshole today when coming here had been your idea? Or why you broke Diana's furniture and then disappeared for hours? Or why you're in here when you clearly don't want to be? Take your pick."

"You have no idea what I want," I said, spending longer than necessary to set the rest of my belongings down. Anything to keep myself from admitting the truth out loud. That I was a selfish bastard and had been an ass because now that we were here, the thought of leaving her with people I didn't trust made all sense leave my mind.

"Fine," she snapped, lowering her pad again and twisting away from me, her hand slashing over the parchment in sharp, angry strokes. Even still, I couldn't help but notice she didn't ask me to leave. She wanted me here, even if she wouldn't admit it, and that pleased me far more than it should.

Unable to help myself, I walked closer, peeking over her stiff shoulders to see what she was working on. Duma's profile stared back at me, as detailed and exact as if she possessed the ability to pull his likeness from her mind. There wasn't even a question that it was him and not Dex, not with how perfectly she'd captured his harsh brows and the slight press of his lips.

I'd known she loved art. She'd told me a thousand times over the years, but I'd never known she possessed a skill like this. It was extraordinary, and I couldn't keep a smile from pulling at my lips at how goddamn amazing she was.

"Dex is going to be quite jealous, you know."

If possible, her shoulders tensed even more, and she huffed through her nose. "I'm doing one for each of them. It's a goodbye present for when they leave."

Before I knew what I was doing, I reached forward and brushed my thumb over a dark smear of black on her wrist. "What about me? Do I get a goodbye gift?"

Gooseflesh exploded down her arm, and she shuffled back, exhaling heavily in an attempt to hide her responding shudder. She placed the drawing and charcoal down on the side table a little harder than necessary. "No."

Oh, how I wanted to kiss that word right out of her mouth, especially when I could now clearly see the peaks of her nipples beneath her chemise. I shifted, my trousers becoming increasingly more uncomfortable. "And why's that?"

"Like I said, I didn't expect to see you again."

"You thought I just decided to run out and leave? Without a word?" I stepped closer to the bed, my nostrils flaring as hurt flickered over her gaze before she could hide it.

"That's what you do. You run away."

I gripped her wrist and had her off the bed and stumbling into me in an instant, her chemise bunching between us as her hands flattened over my chest to steady herself, eyes wide.

"You thought that's what I was doing today?" I asked, the words ghosting over her lips as the feeling of her breasts against me had my cock hard as steel and straining against my trousers. "Running away from you like a fucking coward?"

Her head barely dipped as the slim column of her throat worked on a swallow. I allowed my eyes to linger at her lips before flicking them back to her face.

"If you're going to accuse me of something, have the spine to say it with your words, little rabbit."

"Yes," she said, her voice carrying a hint of a rasp as the first hints of her arousal invaded my senses. "You've been avoiding me for days now. Ever since Ardenglass. And today, you ran out, and no one saw you for hours. I'm not naïve enough to think you owe me a—"

"I can feel her," I said, my voice sounding broken even to my own ears as I cut her off and fought not to tighten my hold on her arm.

Her brow furrowed in confusion. "What?"

I brought her hand to my chest and splayed her fingers over the empty, gaping hole inside me. The one that, until today, Ace had begun to help me forget existed with each day I'd spent with her.

"Lizbeth. I can feel her. She's ordering me back. I don't know why or what exactly she knows, but she's demanding my presence."

Her frown deepened, a cute little divot appearing between her dark brows. "How do you—" Her eyes widened. "Oh God, your soul. She's…she's hurting you. That's what happened earlier with Diana?"

"And in all the hours since, yes," I said, unable to resist tucking a strand of hair behind her ear and reveling in the way her pulse thrummed beneath her skin as my knuckles grazed her ear.

Ace's eyes roved over my face, as if to check for a visible wound, and she curled her fingers into my tunic, fisting it with a possessiveness that nearly made me combust. Gone was her anger, and in its place sat a fierce determination that sank into my very bones.

"Ignore it, Terek. She won't do more than threaten you with it. Not when she wants your ability so badly. Don't let her win."

"There's no ignoring red-tipped nails digging into your soul, Ace. If I do not answer her demand, especially after your disappearance, there will be consequences."

She gripped my tunic harder and pressed closer until I was sure she could feel exactly what her proximity was doing to me. "Then I will help you shut her out. We can get drunk or something, or maybe I can bribe Dex to pick a fight with you. Just tell me what you need, Terek, and I will do it."

She had no idea how dangerous that promise was. I hadn't lied to her in the Wood—I wanted everything from her. Her thoughts, her smiles, her heart, her body. And I was just enough of a bastard to take it right now.

Sliding my hand from her ear to the nape of her neck, I fisted her hair at the roots and arched her head back, giving me unfettered access to those perfect, full lips.

"You, little rabbit. May I rot in an eternity of darkness for it, but I need *you*."

Whatever her reply might've been was lost between us as I stole her mouth for the first time in years. I'd dreamt and fantasized about it, dragging my hand along my cock more times than I could count, imagining what it would be like to have her mouth on mine again. Her body soft and supple as she melded into my hold.

But it wasn't until my tongue swept into her mouth and I felt her own slide against mine with a groan, that I realized just how inadequate those dreams and memories had been.

Because this? This was fucking everything.

Tightening my hold on her hair to keep her neck arched the way I wanted, I slid my other hand up to her jaw, squeezing just enough to force her to open even more for me. More sounds escaped her as I swept my tongue into her mouth again, tasting and claiming every inch in harsh, demanding strokes.

I needed more. Needed to hear those groans turn to desperate pleas, needed to feel her clamp around me as tightly as I knew she would've done around my fingers in the Wood. I needed to drown in her until I forgot every reason this was destined to fail. Every reason I should walk away and follow that torturous order.

Only when her body shook with the need to breathe did I break away, sucking in each of her gasping breaths and pulling them into my own lungs. "If I don't leave right now, Ace, I won't be able to stop. I will ruin you."

She said nothing as she stared up at me with the same fierce intensity I knew was visible on my own face. Wrapping her fingers around my wrist, she pulled my hand away from her jaw, never taking her eyes off mine as she dragged it over the swell of her breasts and down her torso. She didn't stop until my hand rested between her legs, and my control began to shatter as her thighs parted for me.

"Tell me to stop," I begged, even as I greedily pressed my fingers against her clit through her clothing. "Please."

Her eyelashes fluttered, and her heart beat a faster rhythm against me, speaking to me in the way it always had. I began to trace small circles, remembering the speed and pressure that had ruptured her in the Wood, and she arched in my hold, wrapping her hands around my shoulders to keep herself steady. "Ace."

"If you try to walk out of here right now," she breathed, nails biting into me, "I will send you to the void myself."

And with those words, my control shattered completely.

Gripping the top of her chemise, I ripped it straight down the front, not pausing to admire the absolute masterpiece before me until I'd done the same to her underclothes, baring her entirely. Her lips parted, shock painting her features as I dragged the destroyed items off her body and shoved her back.

Her legs hit the bed, and she toppled backward with a squeak, her hair splaying around her head in a dark halo as I let my eyes finally feast on her nakedness. Her full breasts and peaked nipples, the soft planes and divots of her stomach, the flare of her hips, and the thighs that were seconds away from being around my neck.

Even with the raised scar that still made me rage, she was the most beautiful thing I'd ever seen in my entire life, both Upside and Under. She was utter and complete perfection, and it made my chest feel like it was going to explode. Not in pain, but in a warm buzzing that took off in every direction, all but screaming in my ears that she was *mine*.

"Crimson hell, you are magnificent," I murmured.

A deep flush poured over her features, and the courage she had a moment ago when she'd shoved my hand between her legs vanished as she attempted to nonchalantly cover her breasts, specifically the scar between them.

Her fingers had only just brushed over her nipples before I was yanking them off and replacing them with my own. "Absolutely the fuck not," I growled, pinching them in reprimand and causing her back to arch beautifully. "You don't get to accuse me of running away and then turn around and try to hide from me."

Moving too fast for her to react, I dipped my head and flicked the tip of my tongue over one of her nipples, circling it once before biting down just hard enough to draw a hiss from her. She cursed and wrapped her arms around me, her nails raking down the back of my tunic as I repeated it with her other nipple.

"Oh God," she whispered, bucking her hips against me as she blindly searched for friction.

"A god may have brought you here," I said, giving her breast another flick of my tongue as I lowered my hand down and finally— fucking finally—slid my fingers through her wet heat, "but it's me you're drenched for."

"Terek."

"You want to know what I need?" I asked, sliding my fingers back up to circle her arousal over her clit as I sucked hard on her nipple again. "I need you to beg me to fuck you, little rabbit."

I expected her to argue, or her eyes to flash with irritation, but she only groaned, diving both hands into my hair and tugging. The sting sent even more blood rushing south, but not nearly as much as her next words did. "I want you to fuck me, Terek. Please."

I *tsk*ed, pulling my hands away from her body and earning me a whine of frustration as I placed them on the bed and lowered myself down her torso.

"I said please!"

"That you did," I agreed, making my way down her stomach with small nips and kisses. "But you didn't specify with *what*."

I wanted to continue kissing every inch of her body, teasing her and drawing out her desire until she was cursing and screaming at me to satisfy it. But goddamnit, I couldn't, not when I'd been dreaming of her taste ever since I'd first scented it.

Crawling down even farther, I ran my nose along the delicious crease where her thigh met her body. First one side, and then the other. God, she smelled fucking divine.

But rather than spread wider for me, she stiffened and shot her head up, eyes wide. "Wh—what are you doing?"

"I'm going to taste what's mine," I said, watching her teeth sink into her bottom lip as I slid a single finger into her. "Why? Would you like a taste first?"

If possible, her eyes flared even wider, but I just continued pumping my finger again and again before adding a second.

"It's just," she paused, a low grown halting her words when I added a third and began to pump them faster while she clenched around me. "I've never—he never..."

Fury flamed to life in the pit of my stomach. How many times had that bastard forced her to sink to her knees but had never once done the same for her? I may not have been her first, but I'd be damned if I wasn't going to be the first one to show her what it should've always been like.

"Good, because my tongue is the only one that belongs between these thighs anyway."

Pulling my fingers from her and reveling in the way she instantly demanded I put them back, I placed them into my mouth and sucked them off, nearly coming in my trousers. Her smell was intoxicating, but it was absolutely nothing compared to the way she coated my tongue.

She licked her lips as she watched me, and my chest rumbled with satisfaction. Spreading her thighs wider to accommodate my shoulders, I stared down at what waited for me, and for the first time since this morning, my nightmares were gone and my head blessedly silent.

Tomorrow, I would hate myself more than the crimson bitch herself, but tonight, I was going to *feast*.

ADELAIS

CHAPTER FIFTY-NINE

W ords had never failed me before, but tonight, they ran from me in a spectacular fashion the moment Terek's mouth disappeared between my legs.

The first swipe of his tongue had me tensing like a thread about to snap. But it was the following ones, the ones that ended with several firm flicks against my clit, that had my spine bowing beneath him.

His hands, which had been gripping my thighs hard enough to bruise, lowered to join his tongue, his thumbs spreading me open until I was completely bared to him. Then, he began again, lapping at me in smooth strokes and gently sucking at my clit, swirling over those nerves again and again until I wanted to scream.

I fisted the sheets, desperately trying to gain control over my instincts. Because right now, they were begging me to grind my hips up into his face and wrap my thighs around his neck to keep him in place. The effort of not doing that had me panting like an animal in heat, my entire body shaking.

Terek was taking me up that hill, the same one he'd shoved me over that night in the Wood, but this time, he was doing it slowly. Like he was determined to savor every second of it. The problem was, I didn't want to savor it. I didn't want him to slowly walk me up that hill. I wanted him to fucking *run*.

He suddenly froze, his mouth pulling away from me so abruptly I gasped, and my eyes flew open. He was…stopping?

"Why," I swallowed, trying to remember what a sentence was and how to form one. "Why did you stop?" My voice was hoarse, each word rough and grated, sounding perilously close to begging.

I was. If the asshole demanded I beg in order to keep going, I just might. Anything to get his mouth back on me and his tongue doing whatever magic it was conducting against that glorious bundle of nerves.

He lifted his head a few inches, just enough to meet my gaze over the curved plane of my body. In the dim light, his eyes were liquid pools of black, not a speck of blue to be found. Demanding, unrelenting, and if I didn't know any better…possessive.

He glanced down at my center again, nostrils flaring as he slid his thumb up to press against my clit—not moving, just adding the slightest hint of pressure. He pressed a kiss to my skin, barely an inch above where I wanted him, his voice pure gravel as he said, "I want you to do something for me, Ace."

I swallowed again, the action harder this time. "Okay."

Yes. Whatever you want. It's yours. I'm yours.

Instead of answering, he released me, pulling up until he knelt between my legs. He stared down at me with feral lust but made no move to touch me.

"What are you doing?" I asked, wondering if he'd suddenly changed his mind.

Had I done something wrong? Or worse, had he simply realized doing this with me wasn't worth it? *You'll never be enough*, the voice in my head whispered, causing my muscles to tense beneath him. Ready for yet another one of his rejections.

As if sensing all of that and more, Terek's eyes hardened. "If you think, for even a second, that I'm done with you," he said, lowering one of my legs to the mattress so he could move over it, "you haven't been fucking paying attention."

He made his way to the head of the bed, his eyes never once leaving mine. His breathing was quiet, but the too-quick inhales within his sternum gave him away as he laid his head on the pillow beside me.

"You want my mouth on you?" he asked, tucking his hands behind his head in a manner that screamed arrogance.

I nodded, even though the smirk on his face made me want to punch him. There was no use in lying when he could smell my arousal and knew its taste.

"Give me that voice, little rabbit."

"Yes," I breathed.

"Then get up here and ride me."

I shoved up to my elbows and twisted my head toward him, eyes wide. "What?"

"You heard me," he said, raising his brow in a silent challenge.

I pushed the rest of the way up, chewing the inside of my lip as my eyes fell to his trousers and the hard bulge there. I'd never been on top before. Giving me that kind of control wasn't something Frederick would've ever demanded, but it couldn't be that hard to figure out.

Hesitating for only half a second, I leaned over him and tugged at the waistband of his trousers. His erection was straining against the fabric, and as much as I'd wanted him to touch me, I'd be lying if I said I wasn't dying to touch him back.

His long fingers closed over mine, pulling my hands off his clothing and resting them over his stomach.

"No, Ace," he said, shaking his head at me. "As much as I'd love to see you ride my cock, I meant I want you to ride me here." He tapped his lips before wrapping his hands around my waist and squeezing, his thumbs dipping into the deep creases where my hips met my thighs.

I barely had time to squeak out a surprised yelp and catch my balance before he hauled me up his body. A pink flush shot across my face and down my neck, quickly flowing to every other inch of my skin as my nakedness straddled his torso.

"I don't know how," I admitted, tightening my thighs around him as if scared he might launch me up over his face without notice. I wouldn't put it past him. "I mean...wouldn't that be uncomfortable for you?"

"What's uncomfortable is how hard my cock is while I sit here waiting to taste you again. Stop stalling, and sit that pretty little pussy on my face."

Innocent or inexperienced were never descriptions I'd have used regarding my history with sex. Frederick had made sure of that. There were several things with my mouth I knew for a fact I was damn good at, but when it all boiled down to it, everything I'd done had centered around how to please an undeserving man.

Everything else was new.

And like always, Terek read every word of that on my face. He always did.

His grip on my thighs tightened, and anger flashed across those midnight eyes. "You second-guess this because you've only experienced the touch of a man who *takes*. And while there are many things I want to take from you, little rabbit, your power isn't one of them."

Those gripping fingers traveled, his calluses caressing my heated skin until they reached my bare ass, cupping and squeezing the soft flesh. Then he yanked, thrusting me up off his body until I was kneeling on either side of his head, my hands flying to the headboard to support myself.

A deep rumble moved through his chest, and his next words were laced with a growl, his breath coasting along my sensitive skin. "I want you to know what that kind of power feels like, and I want to taste every drop of it while you do."

I gasped, my knuckles whitening around the headboard as a burning sting shot across my ass. "Did you just *spank* me?" I asked.

He only did it again, harder this time. "Sit on my fucking face and take your goddamn pleasure, Adelais. And don't you dare think of me as you do unless it's to scream about how good my tongue feels inside of you."

His words, mixed with my real name on his lips, and the way he saw straight to my stripped and battered soul—and didn't run—was enough to have me almost climaxing right then and there. As such, it was enough to have me shoving his head back down to the pillow.

His eyes flashed in pure delight as I slowly began to lower myself down. I hesitated for only a split second, unsure if I was supposed to hover or settle the entirety of my weight on him.

"Do you want me to—"

Terek didn't even allow me to finish before he wrapped his hands around my hips and slammed me down on his face. I groaned and let my head fall back the instant his tongue slid through me.

His motions were fast and aggressive, and I vaguely wondered if he was using just a touch of his abilities to move his tongue faster—harder—like he was desperate to saturate himself with me. As if anything less wouldn't be enough.

And when he finally thrust that gloriously talented muscle up into me, I no longer cared about anything—my weight, his comfort, his pleasure. Hell, our two worlds could've collided, and I wouldn't have given a shit. I only cared about making him do it again. Deeper.

I rolled my hips, demanding more. Taking more.

Terek obliged with glee, thrusting inside me, along my slit all the way to my ass, then back up to my clit. Again and again. He gripped my hips almost to the point of pain, urging me on.

My eyes fluttered shut as I sprinted up that hill, my rolling turning to desperate bucking as the edge appeared above me. I felt brittle, like a broken tree branch dangling over the abyss, ready to snap at just the lightest breeze and tumble down. I was so close. So fucking close.

"Terek," I whispered, squeezing the headboard so hard it creaked beneath my hands. He only groaned, the vibration doing wicked things to me right as he slid a hand between us and plunged two fingers inside me.

I chanted his name, this time on a scream, as he took my clit and sucked, nipping me with his teeth, right as his fingers curled up and caressed that damn perfect spot.

I combusted, breaking against him like an avalanche barreling down a mountain, uncaring who or what I took out on my way. It was mind-blowing and utterly consuming.

My lungs heaved to drag in air, and it wasn't until the stars stopped dancing across my vision and my heart didn't feel ready to burst out of my chest that I realized I'd released the headboard.

I scrambled back, flames shooting up my neck at the fact that I'd literally just collapsed against the man's face, taking my sweet time to steady my own lungs while he'd likely been half-suffocated beneath me.

"Oh God, I'm so sorry," I said, attempting to slide off his torso with thighs that were still trembling from the aftershocks of my orgasm.

A firm grip stopped me in my tracks. One hand wrapped around my hip to keep me on top of him while the other wrapped around my throat, pulling my face down to his.

"What the hell are you apologizing for?" he asked, his hold gentle but unyielding.

"For being too rough. I know you're strong, but your nose can still break, and what a way to break your nose than smothered in—"

Terek's lips split into a breathtaking smile just before he pressed them to mine, halting my humiliating rambling. His kiss was slow and thorough, like he wanted not only for me to taste myself upon him, but to claim me at the same time. The pulsing of his fingers around my throat his own silent command.

You're mine. You're mine. You're mine.

When he finally broke away and smirked up at me, my breath caught for an entirely different reason. He claimed not to have his soul, but with the way he was looking at me, I swore I could see it pouring out of his eyes and sinking into my chest to wrap around my own.

"Terek?"

"I have spent every day of my afterlife cursing whatever god deigned to force these abilities on me," he said, running his thumb along the length of my jaw. "Cursed and despised them with every crevice of my cold, dead heart."

I opened my mouth, immediately wanting to rebuke those last words, but he slid his thumb over my lips and continued.

"But tasting you so thoroughly? Knowing I'll get to feel you come apart with every goddamn nerve ending on my body? I want to fall to my knees and fucking pray."

His admission had heat coiling in my belly all over again, snapping and thrashing, already wanting more of him. *All* of him. "Pray for what?"

"Absolution. Because sinking inside you will be my damnation, Adelais. A glimpse of heaven I'll never be allowed to keep."

My heartbeat quickened, knocking against my ribs in earnest. What did that mean? Was he afraid I'd go back to the Upside? Disappear and pretend none of this happened? He was ingrained into my heart, carved on my bones, and flowing through my veins. I couldn't leave him even if I tried.

"Terek," I whispered, reaching up to cup his face and tell him the three little words that hovered on my lips. But before I could utter a single sound, his eyes darkened, and he shot up, causing me to fall backward onto his lap.

He stared down at me and reached back with one hand to yank his shirt over his head, launching it at the wall. My eyes ate up the sight. I'd seen him shirtless before, but never when I'd been allowed to look, to touch.

I sat forward again, rising until my nipples brushed his chest. I reveled in the way he shuddered at the contact and continued my perusal, caressing my fingertips along his shoulders and down his arms, memorizing every scar and imperfection. They were perfect to me, and I wanted to prove it by kissing every last one of them.

"Take my trousers off."

My eyes flicked up to his at those four guttural words, and my hands froze. Could he hear how hard my heart pounded at that command? Sense how fast my blood rushed, flushing my skin and warming me at even the thought of him moving in and out of me?

"Now, Adelais."

My eyes narrowed at that damn smirk; aware he was only using my full name because he knew the visceral reaction it had on my body. The wetness that immediately pooled between my legs. Asshole.

His eyes flared, daring me to ignore him, and hell, I was tempted. But we both knew that'd punish me, too, and goddamn it, I wanted this just as badly as he did.

Fingers shaking, I slowly unlaced his trousers and popped them open. He lifted himself off the bed, the toned muscles along his abdomen tensing, so I could work his trousers down over his ass and legs. I flung them behind me, barely noticing when they thudded to the floor.

When his hard length finally sprang free, he groaned, the sound practically dripping in relief. A bead of white leaked from his thick tip, and I licked my lips, wondering what he'd taste like. And for once, I wanted to find out. For the first time in my life, I wanted to wrap my lips around a man and watch him fall apart.

He was larger than I'd expected, even after feeling him through his clothing, and he watched me stare at him, his jaw clenched so hard I worried it'd break.

"Fucking hell," he bit out, wrapping his fist around his shaft and working himself in sharp, punishing strokes. Each crest over his tip coated his hand, making his rough movements sound wet and vulgar.

Still on my knees, I crawled closer, assuming he wanted me to take over. I'd just reached my hand toward him when he stopped his jerks and snatched both my wrists in his hold.

"No. Tonight is about you."

"But I want to taste you, too."

His nostrils flared, and for a moment, he looked like he was in physical pain. But he surprised me by shaking his head and maneuvering me back over his body. Straddling my legs around himself, he positioned me so that his length rested along my center, the heat of him clashing with my own.

"I told you not to think about what I want. Tonight is about *you*," he said, slipping his hand between us to angle himself up and press his glistening tip to my entrance. "If you want to stop and go no further, we can stop. I'll lay you down and eat a hundred orgasms out of you if that's what you'd prefer."

I believed him. Even with him pressing against me, his jaw rolling and body tensing under me, begging to push up, he didn't move a muscle. The image of him feasting all night between my legs had my inner muscles clenching painfully. The thought was exquisite, but his tongue wasn't what I wanted.

Stealing my spine, I shook my head and lowered myself until he pushed in an inch, my wetness giving him no resistance. We both groaned, and I felt his hips twitch up like it was taking everything in him to hold himself back.

But unlike him, I had no such desire. Leaning over his face so that my hair fanned down like a curtain around us, I murmured, "What I want is for you to stop calling me powerful and then treating me like I'm fragile. Either fuck me like you mean it, or get out so I can finish the job myself."

Something within him snapped at that, and whatever control he'd had fluttered uselessly to the ground. He bared his teeth, and quicker than I could comprehend, Terek slammed me down, burying himself to the hilt.

"*Oh God,*" I yelled, falling forward and planting my hands on his chest to steady myself. The intrusion of his size burned, my muscles seizing and squeezing around him, working to accommodate the sudden wide stretch.

He didn't ask me if I was all right or if I wanted him to wait. Not after the challenge I'd just laid out. He just lifted me and repeated the action, again and again. Pleasure began to build, mixing with the pain until the two created something so intoxicating, I had to blink back tears.

His gaze stayed pinned to me the entire time, watching every emotion play out across my face. "Now you know what I feel every time I look at you."

My eyes snapped to his, his features stark even while the world around us seemed hazy and insignificant. I wasn't sure if he meant the pleasure or the pain, but by the way he looked at me, I had a feeling it was both.

"Never have I been so incapable of restraining myself as I am around you, and part of me hates you for it." Another slam of his hips, emphasized by several upward thrusts against that blessed spot.

My eyes nearly rolled into the back of my head as I crested that hill again with far more force than before. If his hatred felt like this, I'd gladly live with his scorn.

A small noise escaped me as I struggled to withstand the storm of sensations barreling me toward an end I was sure would kill me. Terek saw it and only moved faster, punishing me. Punishing us both.

"I tried so hard to resist you," he growled, "but just like that night in the Wood, I am but a moth throwing myself at your flame, seeking that blinding oblivion, yet knowing I'll only burn."

My eyes shot open, and I dug my nails into his chest, something that felt a whole lot like a kaleidoscope of butterflies taking flight in my ribs. "Then stop resisting."

In a flash of movement that was anything but human, Terek flung himself up and shifted onto his knees, spinning me so that my spine was flush to his chest. With me straddled over his lap backward, he reached between us and plunged back inside with no remorse, his other hand finding my clit. Each hard circle of his fingertips was mind-numbing, punctuated only by the vicious hammering of his hips.

Tears pricked at my eyes as I gripped his thighs to steady myself. He was everywhere, his scent coating me, his warmth enveloping me, his touch, his taste, overtaking me until I knew nothing but him.

"That's it, Adelais. Give me that glimpse. Come for me."

Every muscle in my body tightened, fighting it off. Not yet. "Not unless you do, too—*oh God.*"

He rammed up so hard, I swore I could see the stars from the Upside spanned out across my vision. Then he did it again with enough force that the pooling tears poured down my cheeks.

"I'm going to fill you until you can't take a step tomorrow without me dripping down your thighs," he growled, the hand on my clit moving faster while his other flew to my throat and squeezed, pinning the back of my head to his shoulder.

"But not until you give me another. So do what I fucking said, and come on my cock."

I didn't break at his command. I *shattered.*

Screaming out his name, I fell apart across Terek's lap so thoroughly, I knew I'd never be the same. And as he whispered out a plea and pushed me facedown onto the mattress, I didn't want to. There was no point in picking up pieces that had always belonged to him anyway.

My cheek had barely grazed the sheets before he was plowing into me at a frenzied rate, like a man chasing his future with pure, unfiltered desperation. When he finally followed after me, spilling himself as deep as he could go, I could've sworn I felt a burst of heat spark within the center of my chest.

Neither of us spoke as we heaved in air. He just rolled us to our sides, careful to keep himself seated inside me, and wrapped his arms around me, pulling my back to his chest.

The feeling of being in Terek's hold, of being wanted by not just anyone, but *him*, was everything I'd been seeking for years. But while I expected him to be as relaxed and spent as I was, he felt even more tense than before. He buried his nose in my hair and inhaled deeply, like he was memorizing a scent he'd never have again.

Panic surged as my happiness instantly sputtered out, leaving no sign it'd ever been there in the first place. I knew what every one of Terek's silences meant. And this one? It was the same as the weighted silence he'd had in the Wood just before he'd walked away from me.

"Stay," I whispered. The word was quiet, hesitant, but within it, I held out my heart to the man behind me, blindly hoping he would finally take it and give me his in return.

Although his chosen position prevented me from seeing his face, I felt his chest halt its movements, and his next words came out low and choked. "I can't do that."

I nodded, swallowing back the lump in my throat as fresh tears burned my eyes. I'd already known from the way he'd spoken of

Lizbeth's warnings that he intended to leave. That he felt like he had no choice but to go back to her. But when he'd said he needed me, when he'd smashed his lips to mine and chosen me, I'd stupidly thought that it'd meant he'd found a reason to fight it. That I was enough of one.

I should've known better by now.

Unable to prevent a hot tear from leaking out and soaking the pillow beneath me, I tried to slide away from him to distance both our bodies and my cracking heart. But his hand whipped up and snagged my own, lacing our fingers and twisting me toward him so he could rest his forehead against my temple.

"I can't stay," he said, the words blistering my skin, "because if I do, I will keep you for my own, little rabbit, and we will both pay dearly for it."

"Because of *her*?" I didn't try to check the bitterness leaking into my voice. I already knew the answer, and I hated it.

He sighed against my cheek. "I won't tell you to leave because I know you won't listen, so I'm simply making the choice for you. Lizbeth is furious enough about losing you. If she realizes what you mean—" He cleared his throat, lifting his head from mine and releasing my hand.

"If she realizes how involved I am, she'll never give up the chase. She won't just take your soul and set you free like everyone else." He sneered, his expression darkening. "She will do despicable things to you, Ace. Just to spite me."

"She won't take my soul, Terek." *How could she when I've already given it to you?*

"Well, excuse me if I don't feel like betting my eternity and your life on hope-filled words."

Anger flared in my chest, and I twisted, glaring up at him until he had no choice but to meet my gaze. "And what about what I want, Terek? Does that not matter?"

"No."

I flinched, the quickness with which he answered feeling like a slap to the face.

He winced and ran a hand through his hair, but he didn't apologize. "No one's wants matter here, Ace. No one's but hers. And as much as she wants your soul, she wants to control the Wood and Creatures more, and she needs me for that."

When I didn't respond, he pulled away from me, his release slickening my thighs as he finally slipped free of my body. I steeled my heart, fully expecting him to get dressed, but he didn't. He just snagged the duvet from the bottom of the bed and laid it over us, settling back down and pulling me against his chest again.

Surprise flickered through me, but it was overshadowed by everything else he'd said and the things he hadn't. He'd said so many times that Lizbeth would never release his soul, and although he'd hinted at how she'd come to have it, I had to know.

"Is she in love with you?" I asked, soaking up the humming warmth in my chest to keep me stitched together until morning.

"No."

"Did you love her?"

A pause. One so long I accepted that he wasn't going to answer. And then he spoke the one word that could destroy me.

"Yes."

An immediate stab of pain twisted in my heart, unbidden. *Stupid Adelais, what did you expect? That he'd spent decades alone waiting for you when you hadn't even existed yet? When you were a fucking child?*

But even knowing he'd just been inside me, that he'd said so much tonight and filled more than just my body, I couldn't quite swallow down my jealousy. He'd loved not just anyone, but *her*, while he'd only ever tried to get rid of me.

A second later, two fingers gripped my chin, twisting me back until my gaze again met his. He didn't even bother trying to conceal the self-loathing painted across his face.

"Understand, I didn't know her as the Crimson Queen. She was just Liz to me, and I thought she was my future. She didn't take my soul, Ace. I gave it to her willingly because I wanted her to know I loved and trusted her." His lip curled, and he swallowed, forcing out his next words. "Turned out, she'd never been after something so worthless as that."

"She was after your abilities," I whispered, realizing what he meant. Even when he hadn't been in control of them, Terek had always been too strong for her to be able to take them by force. Helping him learn his abilities had, in turn, helped her, and all the while, she'd worn him down with false promises.

"Yes."

My heart physically hurt for the undamaged man Terek had once been. The young man who'd loved to create with his hands and had died suddenly, finding love after death and trusting it with his entire soul. Only to be betrayed. I didn't even want to imagine the look in his eyes when he'd found out the truth.

And I couldn't help but wonder how much longer Terek would last before he began to lose his mind and his cruelty grew to rival hers. It was something I hoped never came to pass.

Not wanting to think about such things so soon after what we'd shared, I tried to pull my chin from his grasp. I just wanted to go to sleep and wake up to a better day, one where Terek might still change his mind. But he refused to let go, only digging his fingers harder into my jaw.

"Please, Terek, I don't want to talk about her anymore."

"Nor do I," he said, and it was only then that I realized I could feel his shaft, hard and ready again, press into the crease of my ass.

Heat pooled in my core, responding to his desire like he held the key to my body. His gaze roved over the side of my face, and I knew he'd pull away and go to sleep if I asked.

I didn't.

"I can't give you what you want, Ace."

"I know, and I hate you for it."

A mixture of regret and pain flashed across his face, and then he was rolling me onto my back and climbing over me. "That's okay, little rabbit. I hate you, too."

The head of his erection nudged at my entrance, and my thighs instinctively opened, my gluttonous body accepting every inch of him inside me like he belonged there.

Maybe it was wrong to want him after everything he'd done and said. To allow his lips to coast over my scar and breasts, and his fingers on my clit as he pushed me over that edge again. Maybe it made me utterly sick in the head to want to be filled by a man who'd just said he would inevitably leave me.

But I did. I wanted whatever he was willing to give me.

ADELAIS

CHAPTER SIXTY

I awoke to birdsong. It was soft, like even they were hesitant to break the calm of the morning's silence. Still half-asleep and groggy, I smiled at the sound. I couldn't remember the last time I'd woken so content and rested. The sensation of feeling such peace, maybe for the first time in my life, was intoxicating.

Not ready to break that feeling and wake Terek to start a day that was sure to be full of work, I kept my eyes shut and gently rolled over to face his side.

The act made me exceedingly aware of just how sore I was. Not only between my legs, but all along my inner thighs and breasts, as well. Terek hadn't been gentle with his hands nor his teeth the second time he'd taken me.

I welcomed the discomfort like a soothing balm. The memory of how much rougher Terek had gotten by the third time he'd climbed over me, like he'd lost all control completely, already had me aching for more.

I squeezed my thighs together, reveling in the way my skin and core throbbed in tandem. Surely Diana wouldn't burst into the house to find me if I was only a little late to meet her. I just needed a few more minutes of peace, and possibly two more orgasms.

That, or maybe I'd wake Terek up slowly with my mouth, showing him just what he'd be missing out on if he left. He claimed Lizbeth was the queen of getting her way, but waking up next to him made me determined to prove him wrong.

Slowly, so I wouldn't wake him, I stretched my arm and leg out, aiming to slide over his body before he'd have a chance to turn the tables. He'd said last night was only about me, but he'd never set any such rules for today.

When my stretched-out limbs met nothing but sheets, I cracked my eyes open, wondering just how far he had to have rolled in his sleep. Confusion swept through me, and I frowned, sitting up and yanking the blanket over my naked chest as I stared at the empty place beside me.

"Terek?"

His spot was still warm, so wherever he was, he'd only recently left. He was probably just using the washroom down the hall or chatting with Duma and Dex. Knowing them, they were likely already wide awake and figuring out breakfast by now.

I was just readying to lie back down and wait for him to return when something about the room niggled at the back of my mind. Something that wasn't quite right.

My heart fell to my stomach when I realized it wasn't the room that was wrong, but all the things that should've been there and *weren't*.

While my dress and shoes were still perfectly stacked where I'd left them and my ripped chemise sprawled across the floor, Terek's belongings were missing. Not just his clothing and boots, but his cloak, sheath, and pack. They were all gone.

If it weren't for the ache between my legs and the scent of wood and rain lingering on the pillow beside me, I might've thought I'd officially lost my mind and imagined last night. He'd successfully made it appear as if he'd never entered my room at all.

I snatched his pillow up and brought it to my face, inhaling his scent deep into my lungs as hot, furious tears lined my eyes, burning and stinging until they trailed down my cheeks in a rush. After everything we'd done, everything he'd admitted, he'd left without even bothering to say goodbye.

The bliss I'd woken to drained out of me, and I suddenly had the desire to shatter the window with my bare hands and tear the birds from the sky, screaming to cover the sound of their song. They had no right to flutter so close to my room, shoving their innocent joy in my face while a chasm opened in my chest.

He'd actually left.

I collapsed back to the bed and curled my body around the still-warm pillow as I allowed myself to finally fall apart and use the few minutes I'd wanted to spend exploring his body to cry until I feared I'd vomit. And when those precious minutes were up, and my eyes were swollen and my muscles weary, I sucked in a shuddering breath and forced my spine to straighten.

My hands gripped his pillow so fiercely, my knuckles spotted white, and it took everything within me to release them, one by one, and drop it to the mattress.

Terek had made his choice, and it hadn't been me. And as much as that knowledge dug the chasm deeper and made me want to shrivel in regret over what I'd freely given him last night, I refused to give him anything else of me. Including my tears.

I'd be damned if I cried over another man who treated me like forgettable garbage. Terek may have warned me he wouldn't stay, but only a fucking coward would fall asleep still impaled inside my body and then leave without saying goodbye.

Fuck him.

Wrapping the blanket around myself, I grabbed my sketchbook from where I'd placed it on the side table, and flopped back against the headboard, hearing it whack the wall behind me with a dull thud.

It'd done more than thud last night when Terek had pushed me facedown and hammered into me.

I growled, shoving out the memory, and snatched up my charcoal, nearly snapping it in half. I knew Diana would be waiting for me this morning to explain the drawing class she wanted me to teach, but right now, I didn't care.

The unfinished portrait of Duma stared up at me, begging me to finish it, but as much as I wanted to, my friend didn't deserve any less than my best. My mood was far too foul to do him justice.

Instead, I flipped to a new page and let my heart take over, slashing and shading in violent, sharp angles as the darkness inside me lifted its head. If I concentrated on the details of this one singular thing, I could almost pretend I didn't have to think about the mess that was my life no matter where I went.

I wouldn't have to think about how betrayed I felt that the only man I'd allowed into my heart had slipped from my body and room to run back to his first lover. Whether he hated her or not, it didn't really matter. Once upon a time, he'd seen her as worthy of his love, while I hadn't even been worth a goodbye.

But with each piece of me I poured onto the page, my walls grew taller and the darkness lifted to cover them, the pain lessening just a little bit more. By the time I was almost done, there was an iron fortress inside of me, and I blissfully felt nothing at all.

I wasn't sure how much time had passed, but when three firm knocks came on the door, I jumped, my fingers dropping the small remaining nub of charcoal to the floor. The rest of me froze, my eyes boring twin holes into the door.

Hope fluttered at the barricade I'd painstakingly built, seeking entrance at those three sharp raps, but I'd finally learned my lesson. There was no room left for hope, just as I knew it wasn't Terek at my door.

"Yes?" I asked, clearing my throat when the word came out scratchy and broken, rather than uninterested like I'd intended.

"It's me. Can I come in?" Dex asked.

"Go ahead."

I didn't bother looking up as the door creaked open, instead setting my sketchbook on the table to lean down and wrap my smudged fingers around the charcoal I'd dropped.

"Crimson fucking take me," Dex cursed, and I shot up, whacking the back of my head on the edge of the table.

"What's wrong?"

His eyes were closed, head lifted to the ceiling. "You could've said you were naked, Ace. I'd have waited for you to dress."

Blinking in confusion, I looked down at myself to see the full swell of my breasts visible over the blanket wrapped around me that smelled like *him* and regret. I'd been so caught up in my drawing, it hadn't even crossed my mind.

I shrugged, tightening the fabric around me for Dex's sake. "They're just breasts, Dex, but they're covered now. What do you need?"

His brown eyes snapped to mine, worry lines spidering out across his skin as they softened. I wasn't sure what he saw, but he didn't poke at me like I'd expected him to, especially since I knew he and Duma likely heard us last night. Probably because he could see Terek was gone and could add two and two together. The thought sent a flush to my cheeks, proof that I could feel at least *something* still.

He stepped farther into the room, gesturing at the sketch on the table in front of me. "New piece?"

I nodded and reached out, flipping Duma's unfinished portrait over to cover it, hiding the jagged trees I'd drawn, ripped open to reveal bleeding hearts gushing onto a bone-littered ground. Dex witnessing my humiliation mapped out so fucking clearly made me feel more naked than my bare skin did.

He took the hint and forced out a chuckle, pointing at the portrait. "Duma is going to love that. If you give it to him, he'll probably plaster it above the hearth in Tweeds."

That image had a smile trying to pull at my flattened lips. Almost. "How do you know it's him and not you?" I asked, pushing to stand and shuffling toward the water basin, careful to keep myself covered.

He snorted. "You're skilled, Ace, but not that skilled. You couldn't possibly capture all this."

I peeked at him over my shoulder as I washed the black smudges from my hands, seeing him smirk and gesture to his face. I gave an indulgent smile I didn't quite feel, knowing it was what he wanted. "Did Diana send you to fetch me?"

"No, but I'm sure it's only a matter of time," he said, poking around the folded clothes the woman in question had given me for today. He grabbed a soft green dress from the pile and threw it at me, smacking me in the face.

"I trust you can find your undergarments on your own. If not, you can continue the day naked. I doubt many will complain."

I yanked it down and glared at him, earning me a wink before he strutted back to my door and flung it wide open. I smashed the wadded garment over the top of my chest, throwing several not-so-friendly phrases his way.

He just laughed and stepped out, yelling over his shoulder, "There's a few biscuits downstairs if you hurry." Then he was gone, the click of the door radiating out in the silence.

Still clutching the dress, I let the blanket fall, feeling a sudden swell of guilt as it pooled at my feet. Here I'd been marinating in self-pity for something I'd been told to my face would happen, all while my friends had prepared breakfast and patiently waited on me to leave my room.

Stop being a shitty friend. You have things to do today, I mentally lectured myself as I located my undergarments and shoes and quickly got dressed. I dragged my comb through my knotted sex hair, threw open the door, and marched down the stairs.

Screw this room and screw Terek. I was going to spend the day being nice to the two men who'd stayed, earn my place in Wenham, and prove to both of us that I could be happy without him, no matter what that pressure hiding behind my fortress claimed.

Walking under the archway separating the sitting area from the kitchen, my eyes snagged on Dex standing by the front door, holding a flask in one hand and a biscuit in the other. Although he smiled at me, his easygoing manner seemed dampened, and his eyes lacked their usual sparkle. I could see what he wasn't voicing out loud as he looked at me. Pity.

I kept my own gaze firm. I didn't need him or anyone else to feel sorry for me. I'd jumped into the raging water with hands bound and eyes wide open, knowing I'd never come back up. The only thing I deserved pity for was my pathetic desperation to be wanted.

"Ready for the first day of your new life?" he asked quietly, placing a hand on my back and handing me the still-warm bread.

I took it and nodded, letting him gently usher me out of the house to where Duma was waiting for us. He hadn't meant anything by it, but the words sank into my gut, reminding me that they wouldn't be here forever either. They'd stay long enough to rest and help me get settled, and then they'd start the return journey to Tover, jumping back into their lives and growing their business.

It was everything they deserved, and yet the selfish, shameful part of my soul hated it all the same, wishing they would stay.

We'd almost made it to the last road, one remaining corner separating us from Wenham's square, when Dex's arm shot out across my chest. Lost in my miserable thoughts, I slammed into it, knocking the air from my lungs and nearly catapulting myself backward.

"What the hell was that for—"

Duma cut me off with a harsh curse, stepping in front of both of us and dropping his hand to the axe at his side. "Crimson hell, I hope that isn't what I think it is."

"Hope what isn't what?" I asked, shoving Dex's arm down so I could peek around his brother's bulk of a body. Nothing but buildings and an empty road stood before us. *What were they talking about?*

Then I heard it. The distant shouting of what sounded like a growing crowd mixed with the low rumbling movements of said crowd...or horses. But considering animals didn't stick around the Underland long enough to ride, I could only assume the first.

Which meant there were likely new arrivals in the square. I couldn't imagine what else would bring people out of their homes all at once unless there was some morning announcement we hadn't been made aware of. Whatever it was, it wasn't making the townspeople very happy by the sound of it.

My gut twisted. Diana had said they rarely got visitors. What were the chances of innocent, fellow travelers risking the threat of the Wood and traveling to Wenham so soon after we'd arrived?

"Slim," Duma said, making me realize I'd voiced the errant thought out loud. "Stay here with Dex, Ace. Let me see what's going on."

Surprising both him and myself, I listened, my body tense as he jogged to the corner of the last building. Axe now gripped in his large hand, he pressed his back flush to the building and peered around it.

In the span of a few seconds, his expression went from serious, to confused, to exasperated, and then he tipped his head back, muttering under his breath, "Crimson hell."

The words had me jolting forward, shrugging off Dex's warning grip on my elbow, and jogging toward the corner. All I could think about was the queen's guard having somehow tracked us here and putting everyone at risk.

"What's wrong? What is it?"

He peered around the corner and swore again, sheathing his weapon. Then he twisted back and eyed me as I approached, his brown eyes full of warning. Whether to behave myself, or for what I was about to see, I wasn't sure. At least, until the next word left his lips, shooting across the space between us and tearing through me like a dagger to my chest.

"Terek."

My jog turned into a panicked run, and I sprinted straight past him, rounding the corner and ignoring his shout to stop. I couldn't have stopped if a stone wall erupted in front of me. Not at the thought that Terek might be in trouble. Asshole or not, the thought of him hurt made me want to sprout fucking claws.

What I saw as my eyes finally took in the commotion across the square had my stomach dropping and my heart racing like a damn idiot. Because Terek was still here. And although he didn't appear to be hurt, he also wasn't okay.

He was fucking furious.

Even from several spans away, I recognized the dark look of death carved into his features. He stood in the center of the square, clothed in his usual black, gripping the collar of a man I didn't recognize. His chest heaved rapidly like he was seconds from losing control, every inch of him promising violence.

I sprinted across the square, shoving bodies out of my way and hearing the twins behind me as I tried to make out who, exactly, Terek held. The man appeared to be in his late forties, with a thick amber beard and long hair tied at his nape. One eye was widened in terror while the other was puffy and squinted, a bruise already blossoming the pale skin around it.

Off to the side of them, the crowd was growing larger, people running from their homes and businesses to see what was happening. The faces of the ones within hearing distance of Terek wore a mixture of anger and fear. It was honestly a marvel they hadn't turned into a mob and swarmed him for attacking one of their own. What had he gotten himself into?

Seeing him caused a storm to rage within my ribcage because even angry, he was so painfully beautiful. The sight of him felt like a heavy rain chasing away the black cloud around my heart, only to immediately strike me like lightning, reminding me of just how much he also burned.

He shook the man, saying something under his breath I couldn't quite hear but that made the poor man buck in his hold. I ran faster, unable to resist watching the way Terek's muscles flexed along his arms. They'd moved much the same when—*no, Adelais. Stop it.*

He didn't deserve my memories, nor my thoughts. I would not mindlessly revolve around a sun that'd been so content to leave me frozen. Terek could go fuck himself. Digging my nails into my palms, I elbowed my way through the last of the crowd, refusing to let the asshole lose his shit and get me kicked out of Wenham. He might've had no desire to stay, but I didn't have that choice.

I made it within a few feet of him before Duma shoved past me, gripping Terek by the arm and stealing his attention. Dex came to a stop next to me, hand at his side, ready to intervene as well, if necessary.

"What the hell are you doing?" Duma snapped, eyes darting to the murmuring crowd growing larger by the minute. "I thought you'd be gone by now."

"I tried," Terek said, flashing his teeth. "But on my way out, I ran into this piece of shit showing people *this*." He released a hand from the man just long enough to slip it into his pocket and thrust a crumpled piece of paper at Duma's chest.

Duma frowned down at it before cautiously unfolding it, and his eyes widened. He swallowed, gaze flicking up to meet my furrowed one.

Wordlessly, he handed his brother the paper, who held it low enough for me to read along with him. I froze, not only at the uncanny sketched likeness of me staring up from the page, but at the words scrawled above it.

WANTED FOR TREASON.
DELIVER THE TRAITOR TO THE WHITE CASTLE TO
RECEIVE THE REWARD OF ONE SOUL.

In smaller print, just beneath my face, it continued:

Any citizens found harboring, aiding, or abetting this traitor will be punished with the severity befitting such acts of sedition. You have been warned.

I stumbled back, only staying upright by the hand Dex slapped to my spine to steady me. Each letter landed like stones on my lungs until I was sure I'd suffocate right there in front of everyone. Black spots swam across my vision, and I squeezed my eyes shut, blocking out the parchment.

So this was what Lizbeth had been doing while we'd been running north. Throwing these up to entice people who, either never knew of the first bounty, or had forgotten, and threatening anyone who might have seen me.

The sudden, utter silence had my eyes shooting back open to find every eye in the square on me. Fuck. I swallowed, letting Dex pull me into his side, his hands clenching and unclenching as if seeking the handle of a sword he didn't have on him. Had everyone here seen this already? Had their murmuring when we'd arrived been them plotting to drag me back to Lizbeth?

The terrifying thought had Hara's face flashing to the front of my mind, of the devastation she'd worn like a second skin as she'd tried and failed to find peace here. I couldn't blame a single one of them for wanting to turn me in.

"Continue what you were telling me," Terek said, the words barely audible over the dark growl in his voice. Despite the man having made no move to attack or even scratch his head, Terek still held him by the collar of his tunic.

"I didn't—didn't know she was here. I swear, I'm not going to do anything. I only wanted to warn—"

Before the man even knew what was happening, Terek had a blade out and pinned to his throat, cutting off his panicked babbling. "*I said continue.*"

Terek had yet to so much as look at me, but I still flinched at his tone. I'd seen him lose control more times than I'd seen him smile, but I hadn't seen him this undone since he'd found me after I'd escaped the White Castle. Whatever the man was about to tell us, it was bad.

"She—she's coming. The Crimson Queen," he stuttered, his tongue sounding sticky and thick. "She's making her way north with her entire guard."

His eyes darted back to me, beseeching me for help, as if I might save him from Terek's wrath. "They're searching Tover for you."

Terek snarled, sounding more Creature than man, and pressed his dagger in until a single drop of blood beaded over the edge. "You don't speak to her."

The terrified man slammed his lips shut, letting out a whimper, and I fumed, anger flushing out some of the fear I'd felt when I'd seen the parchment. How dare he speak for me when he didn't even have the balls to fucking look at me.

I was about to step forward and say as much, but Dex caught my eye, shaking his head. Swallowing back my retort, I listened, but only because Terek was already speaking again.

"What are they doing in Tover?"

The man didn't dare take his eyes off Terek this time as he answered. "I didn't see it myself, but people in Canden said they're dragging people from their b–beds and destroying homes. Questioning everyone, even ch–children."

Duma's eyes widened, and he took a step away, meeting Terek's gaze when his whipped up, and something passed between them. Unable to decipher whatever silent conversation they were having, I looked to Dex to see the same horror on his face.

The man dared a quick look at me while Terek's attention was off him, fear *of me* filling his expression, like I was an omen sent to destroy them all. And the meaning behind that one look made my blood turn to ice in my veins.

The residents of Wenham hadn't crowded around to see the spectacle Terek had been making, nor had it necessarily been because of the parchment the man had brought. They were afraid of the *news* he'd brought along with it.

Pushing past Dex, I went to stand on Terek's other side, ignoring the way his jaw ticced and he studiously ignored my presence. It hurt more than it should, but I shoved it down, letting it and every other hurt he'd caused form a boulder in my stomach.

"What is Lizbeth doing to the people her guards are dragging out?" I asked.

"Duma," Terek snapped, *still not looking at me*, "take Ace away from here and find Diana."

My nostrils flared, and before I could think better of it, I reached up and smacked the back of Terek's head as hard as I could. What I really wanted to do was punch him, but the dagger he was holding to the sobbing man's throat made that impossible.

His head whipped toward me at a speed that would've broken any other person's neck, his eyes depthless black pools as they finally— finally—landed on me. I took it all in, letting his hate and anger pour over me, only to warp it with my own and throw it right the fuck back.

"Duma isn't your goddamn servant, and I speak for myself, thank you."

His lip curled. "Little rabbit—"

"*Don't* call me that," I snapped, the words like a steel blade drawn between us and pressing into his chest. "Never again."

Something I refused to acknowledge flashed across his eyes, but I didn't let it so much as knock at the barrier around my heart. Instead, I turned to the messenger watching us with owl-like eyes and repeated my question.

"What is the queen doing to the people she's questioning?"

To his credit, he answered, even though I could tell he didn't want to, his lips forming the words Terek hadn't wanted me to hear. "They said she's taking souls. Everyone's. Even those with no abilities. She accused Tover of harboring you and..." He broke off, taking a shuddering breath that only succeeded at nicking his skin again.

Grunting in irritation, Terek finally released him and shoved him back, his dagger instantly disappearing.

"Tover," I whispered, bile shoving up my throat. Duma tensed and sucked in a sharp breath, preparing himself for an answer we all knew would be bad. How bad, was the question.

"What did she do?" I demanded.

The man's tear-streaked face met mine. "They said she's burning it to the ground."

ADELAIS

CHAPTER SIXTY-ONE

I flinched back, slapping my hand over my mouth to keep the quickly surging vomit from spewing out. In my peripheral, I saw Dex leave my side to stand beside his brother, his clenched hands shaking.

I stared at the ground, unable to look at their horrified faces as the news settled inside me like a poison. The painful, unescapable truth that whatever was happening, whatever Lizbeth was doing, it was because of me. I hadn't just taken Duma and Dex from their home and the business they'd been trying to expand and grow…I'd probably destroyed it, along with who knew how many others.

Just by setting foot there.

What would Lizbeth do if she found out Wenham hadn't just housed me for a night but accepted me in and offered full sanctuary? I pressed my hand harder over my lips, unsure how much longer I'd make it before I vomited. The buttery biscuit I'd greedily inhaled now felt like a rock in my stomach.

"Did they say anything about survivors?" Dex asked, tone harsher than I'd ever heard it. "Where they're headed?"

I stared harder at the ground, wishing it'd suck me in and suffocate me as my mother's voice crawled through my mind. Choking down dirt until it filled my lungs sounded a whole lot better than standing out in the open.

You're a poison, Adelais. You ruin everything you touch. Her soft, caressing laugh played in my head over and over until I almost didn't hear the messenger's answer.

"From wh–what I know, the few hundred who survived fled to Gissan, but I was in Canden when word came with those…those posters, so I don't know."

A few hundred. The responding silence throughout the entire square was deafening.

"What the hell do you mean, *the few hundred?*" Duma bit out, face scrunched and morphed into something unrecognizable through his anguish. "There are fucking *thousands* of citizens in Tover. No fire moves so fast that only a few hundred can escape it."

Terek was the one who answered, and the sound of his voice, low and sharp, had my face finally snapping up, taking in the way his hands fisted over his daggers like he wanted to rip into someone's throat. "A natural fire, no, but a purposeful, controlled fire can."

Duma's face lost all its warmth, and he slumped forward, hand pressed to his chest while the other gripped his brother's shoulder. Dex didn't move, his body frozen in shock. The crowd, however, broke their silence at Terek's comment and began shouting and screaming, panic turning them into cornered animals fearing the lash of a whip.

Lizbeth hadn't just invaded Tover and interrogated people. She'd filled it with guards possessing the ability to control flames, blockading anyone in who tried to flee before answering to her. People who knew nothing about me and held no threat. Children. Innocents. All being violently removed from this world with no tether.

Lizbeth was ripping away their chances at an afterlife, all to send a message to me, just like she'd tried to do with Hara. To show me the consequences of defying her.

I twisted away from them, spewing my meager breakfast over the cobblestones as I felt a deep pit open within me. I heaved again, sucking in gulping breaths of air as I started to spiral, fury like I've never known filling every inch of me until I thought my skin would peel off from the searing heat of it.

Terek was wrong. Lizbeth wasn't going to forget about me no matter how long I hid or how quickly he returned to her. Whatever she thought she'd gain from me, she was willing to sacrifice this entire world to get it. She'd warned me I could either give up my soul the easy way or the hard way, and like the selfish bitch I was, I'd chosen the hard way.

"That can't be us!"

"The queen will burn us all while we sleep!"

"Give her the girl!"

"Yeah! She's the traitor!"

The manic shouts of the crowd pulsed in around me like a weight, pushing on my curled spine and threatening to smash me into the ground. Warmth bled into my sides, and I raised up just enough to see Terek, Duma, and Dex standing around me, facing the crowd.

Rage still rolled and boiled in my gut, but with it also came fear. Not at the crowd's shouted threats, but that these men—specifically, the one holding daggers and ready for blood—would start a fight these terrified people could never win.

I forced my body to move and shoved up, ready to leap onto his back and steal his weapons if I had to. But sensing my thoughts like he always could, Terek whipped his face back to glare at me. Those midnight eyes had just met mine, sending a whirlwind of other emotions through me, when a voice sliced through the tension, parting the crowd like a thundering wave.

"Enough!"

The four of us turned in tandem to see Diana rushing through the open gap. Her hunched body moved surprisingly fast as she came to stand at the front of the crowd, cane whacking the stones in a loud, unsteady beat.

Although she bore no weapon, it was impossible to miss the way she placed her body between us and her people. And I couldn't help but wonder again what ability she possessed that she'd be willing to wield against anything she saw as a threat. Even if it was us.

Where her face was a mask of calm, her eyes were anything but. There was a sprinkle of fear in them, but far stronger was the same anger

I knew she could see reflected in ours, aimed at a selfish, power-hungry demon inflicting pain on a world that didn't deserve it.

Diana beckoned for the bruised messenger, who still stood off to the side, too terrified of Terek to move. Darting a nervous glance our way, he approached her, releasing a heavy breath of relief when she placed a comforting hand on his shoulder.

"I'm glad to see you safely through the Wood, Augustus."

He dipped his head in respect, and she gifted him a small smile in return, patting his arm. "Go home. You've had a long journey. I'll send someone to check on you after you've rested."

The man—Augustus—nearly sagged to the ground before mumbling a rushed thank you and taking off through the crowd. Diana watched him until he disappeared, and then she turned to Terek, voice sharper than the knife he still held aloft.

"You are willing to protect your own at any cost, and I respect that. It's the only reason I allowed you to stay, knowing your history." She took a single step toward him, gripping her cane so hard I feared it'd crack. "But the problem with allowing your heart to walk outside your body is that it becomes visible to everyone."

His eyes flared in warning as her own gaze pointedly landed on me before flicking back to him. "Is that a threat, *Speaker*?"

"No. It's a promise. If you touch one of my people again without fair cause, I will retaliate with equal violence."

Terek snarled, but whether he knew something about her I didn't, or had simply decided to pick his battles, he slammed his daggers back into their sheaths, eyes two black voids as he stared at her. She merely raised a brow like one would at a hissing kitten, then shuffled forward to pluck the parchment from Dex's hands.

I tensed as she read it, waiting for her to kick me out of Wenham, or worse. But rather than turn on me, or yell in fear like the rest of the crowd had, she faced her people and held it out, pointing the top of her cane toward the words at the bottom.

"The Crimson Queen does not speak for Wenham," she said, voice ringing out across the square though she did not raise it. She didn't need to when she held the respect of every person there. Several nodded in agreement, but most didn't respond, their fear still thick and potent as she continued.

"We have granted this woman asylum, and once asylum is given, it is not revoked. Especially not to please a queen who only shines because she's filled her pockets with *our* souls."

A symphony of cheers broke out as people screamed their hate for the Crimson Queen, but among them were several people who did not, including a young man with wavy, dirty-blonde hair and piercing blue eyes. He stepped forward, bowing his head to Diana.

"Yes, Tobias?"

"With all due respect, Madame Speaker," he said, his voice surprisingly deep, "one soul is not worth more than all of Wenham. The Crimson Queen may not speak for us, but she will not hesitate to crush us either. She's burning Tover, and they aren't even the ones hiding the traitor."

In a blink, Terek had both daggers back out and spinning in his palms. Tobias swallowed nervously but stood his ground, and I found I immediately liked him for it. "I mean no disrespect," he said, tipping his head my way. "I'm only stating the truth."

I nodded, agreeing with him. For all I knew, he had an entire family he'd found and created here. Who was I to take offense and claim I mattered more?

There was a brush of air across my neck, and then a rumble vibrated through my body as a firm chest pressed into my spine. My muscles went rigid at that single touch, fighting the instinct to collapse into the false comfort of his warmth.

Checking my fortress for any cracks he might slip through and finding none, I grit my teeth and shot my elbow back into Terek's stomach, enjoying his grunt of surprised pain far more than I should.

"Mean no disrespect? There was literally no other way for that to be taken—" Dex started, but Diana cut him off, holding her hand out and walking over to the young man.

"Tell me something, Tobias. Do you truly believe the Crimson

Queen will spare us if we turn this young lady's soul over? Do you believe with your entire chest that she has forgotten how many of us fled here after refusing to turn over our own?"

She clicked her tongue at him like a mother scolding a misbehaving child. "She's left us alone because, thus far, we have not been worth the effort, *not* because she has forgotten or forgiven."

Doubt flickered in Tobias's eyes, but he lifted his chin. "Exactly. If we give her no further reason to risk the Wood, she'll leave us be. It's worth the chance."

Diana hummed, shifting her weight to her other foot and wincing slightly. "Do you know what that chance sounds like to me?"

"A fair cause," Terek interjected, not touching me but still standing far too close for my liking. Both Duma and Dex nodded, giving Tobias matching smirks that would've terrified me had I not known how kind they actually were.

"Naïveté," Diana answered instead, ignoring him. "The queen's fear of the Creatures of the Wood has kept her chained, yes, but the stronger her need for power grows, the more those chains will weaken. It will not protect us forever, and only a fool would trust his life to a smattering of trees."

Tobias opened his mouth to argue again but quickly shut it when she pointed a stern finger at him. "My decision is final. Now run off, all of you," she yelled, speaking to the rest of the onlookers. "I expect every single one of you to be at your assignments within the next ten minutes."

Tobias paused, his hard blue eyes roving over me like he was memorizing every detail and cataloging them for future use. Unimpressed with whatever he saw, he spun and stalked off, disappearing into the crowd of people who'd already begun to amble away.

Diana watched them go with an expression I couldn't quite place. Before I could examine it closer, she wiped it away with a shake of her head and turned to the four of us, my companions still huddled close to me. Her brows rose, but she didn't comment on their stance.

"I meant what I said, Adelais. I will not revoke my promise of sanctuary. You are free to stay in Wenham, your willingness to work still standing."

"Yeah? Tell that to pretty boy over there," Dex said, jutting his chin toward where Tobias had gone. His brother grunted in agreement and crossed his arms over his chest, lips pressed thin as he scanned the remaining people.

Diana waved her hand, brushing off their worries. "The boy's headstrong, but he's a good apple. He won't do anything as long as I'm offering you my protection."

"Why are you?" I asked, unable to stop myself from blurting out the question every person in Wenham was now wondering. "Don't get me wrong, I'm grateful, but I wouldn't blame you if you didn't. You don't know me."

As much as I wanted to believe Diana was like Mrs. Gayle—a kind, old woman who didn't want to see me suffer—I wasn't stupid, and neither was she. She either wanted something from me, or she had something to gain from me being here. I just wasn't sure which it was yet.

She didn't answer right away, considering me for so long I began to fidget beneath her gaze.

"Because something tells me you're the key, my dear, and I don't throw away keys to doors I want to unlock."

I frowned. "The key to what?" I asked, keeping my voice low. Wenham may not have refused to protect me, but neither had they agreed. I didn't trust them enough to not be lingering in the shadows, eager to soak up anything they could use against me. The last thing I needed was someone like Tobias to realize I wasn't dead.

Diana, however, didn't seem to share that same fear and kept her voice steady and strong as she said, "The Underland."

Terek shifted to stand closer to me, as if considering whether or not he needed to snatch me up and run, but I matched his step, keeping several inches of space between us, even though that pressure in my chest begged and yearned for his touch.

When he growled and shifted toward me again, I took a larger step away, leaning into Duma and letting him wrap a comforting arm around my shoulders instead. Terek's black stare embedded itself into the side of my face. Good. I hoped he drowned on my dismissal. It was nothing compared to the ocean of hurt he'd poured inside me.

"You say that as if the Underland itself is locked," I said, keeping my attention on Diana.

"Isn't it?" she asked, smiling at me in a way I didn't quite like. "Souls are no longer arriving at the speed with which they used to. That they *need* to. They've been shut out because the ones here aren't leaving. They're locked in, and new souls are locked out. Yet, you can open and shut the door as you please."

We all froze, staring at her as the truth of her statement sank in. I wasn't sure how Diana could prove anything, but I didn't doubt her claim. It made sense. With Lizbeth holding so many hostage here for decades, the Underland would've been overrun with people by now.

Terek had once said the world changed and grew to best suit its inhabitants, but surely there was a limit to how many souls God, or whatever higher power there was, allowed to linger in limbo.

I chewed my lip, worry biting at me at what else that might mean. "So, if souls aren't being allowed in, are they going straight to the afterlife, or..."

"That's the question, isn't it, my dear," Diana said, eyeing me closely. "What happens when mortals interfere with the balance of nature? In my experience, nature tends to fight back."

She shrugged, but that calculating look remained. Like I was a blade she was checking for nicks, testing me to see how sharp of an edge I had. Duma must've sensed it too because his arm tightened around me, pulling me flush to his side.

Terek scoffed, dragging her attention away from me. "Her ability notwithstanding, Ace isn't whatever magical key you believe her to be. If anything, your logic would claim the opposite, painting her as only another interference with the *balance of nature*."

Diana smirked. "What makes you so sure she's not the very weapon nature created for its fight?"

"What makes you so sure she is?" he snapped back.

Diana only hummed and turned from us, leaving Terek's question unanswered as she walked away and left us standing alone in the square.

The men immediately began arguing over what we should do, their voices low but harsh. Terek was practically frothing at the mouth, demanding we all grab our stuff and leave, while they shook their heads, arguing that I should stay while the three of them left.

It all went in one ear and out the other, my feet feeling glued to the ground as Diana's words had me spiraling even further into the darkness that had been brewing since the news Augustus had brought of Tover.

If a woman hidden far from civilization, who'd only just met me, had already considered what effect my ability might have on the future of the Underland, someone as intelligent and calculating as Lizbeth definitely had.

Lizbeth was never going to let me go. Even if I went Upside, she'd never stop looking for me, burning towns and carving into the very heart of the Underland until all of it was drowning in red.

That darkness, the one that had flickered into existence in her throne room and had only grown stronger in the Wood, was now a raging inferno, made brighter with every soul I imagined Lizbeth ripping from this world. Dipping into it, I bathed myself in its heat, letting it scald away every fear and insecurity I had.

I no longer cared whether I belonged here. I didn't care if I was some key or just another random person with a strange ability. All I felt was that dark, pulsing fury. Lizbeth could paint my entire home in red until even the roses bled, and I'd gladly cut out her heart with their fucking thorns.

The Crimson Queen wanted a fight? She had one. The hunt was on, but there was no rule that said I had to be the prey.

So go ahead, Lizbeth. I dare you.
Paint the fucking roses red.

ACKNOWLEDGEMENTS

As always, first and foremost, I want to thank everyone on my team who had eyes on this story before it published. My beta readers, editors, sensitivity reader, and all my ARC readers. You helped make this story everything it could be, and I cannot thank you enough.

Second, I must thank my daughter's ridiculously long car-rider line at her elementary school for giving me far too much time to ponder different plots. If it weren't for the hours I spent sitting in my vehicle, day after day, the first outline of *Into the Wonder Dark* never would have existed.

Honestly, I lost count of how many voice memos I left myself of every idea I had while staring out of my windshield, long before I ever had the chance to write this book. How Adelais's and Terek's story changed from a woman with a strange ability helping a serial killer to what it is now, is still beyond me.

Third, I want to thank my mother for always being my first reader and my biggest cheerleader, even when my stories aren't fleshed out yet and I have embarrassing typos. I know my morally grey men make you question my sanity. They make me question it most days, too. I love you more than mimosas and pie.

Next, I must thank my husband and three children for dealing with months of me working well into the evening and powering through the days when I was too stressed out over my deadlines to function at my best. I could not love, or appreciate, any of you more than I already do.

And lastly, I want to thank all of my readers for being so patient and understanding when I bounce between writing my different series. I know it can be frustrating, and I cannot thank you enough for sticking with me anyway. I am so incredibly lucky to have you all.

Want More Romantasy and Fated Mates?

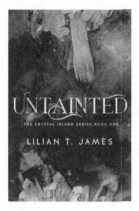

There were several things Vera was quite skilled at. Wielding a blade and pretending to be human were two of them. Following the rules and controlling her anger, were not.

Raised in the heart of the Matherin Empire, Vera spent most of her life forced to hide what she was and what she could do. Until one day, she foolishly confronts a strange male she spies tailing the Crown Prince.

Not only does the altercation not go as planned, but the male claims she possesses a power his people vitally need. He's desperate to return home and refuses to leave without her.

Staying would give her a life she never thought she'd have but leaving could provide her with the only chance to learn more about her past.

The more answers she uncovers about herself, the more questions arise, and nothing is adding up. Vera must decide what to do, not only with her life, but with the ancient power inside her.

ABOUT THE AUTHOR

Lilian T. James was born and raised in a small town in Kansas until she finished high school. Enrolling at a University on the East Coast, she moved there with her son and obtained degrees in Criminal Justice, Social Work, Psychology, and Sociology. After graduating, she met her husband and moved to the West Coast for a few years before settling back in Kansas in 2022. She has three kids, two dogs, and has been an avid romance reader her entire life. Lilian writes all things romance, including contemporary, fantasy, and paranormal.